Suddenly, as if in answer to a prayer, Gaia heard voices behind her. She stopped and fumbled through her backpack as if she were looking for something. Jeez, what a girl had to do to get mugged in this city.

The voices turned into whispers, and then she heard footsteps, slow. Oh, *yes*. Finally. She turned toward the noise, pasting what she hoped looked like a terrified expression on her face. Inside, her heart was leaping with anticipation.

There were three of them, and they looked young— around sixteen or seventeen. Two of them had shaved heads. The smallest brandished a razor blade.

The little thug was up front, covering the ground between them with a menacing lurch. The other two were hanging back, present to witness this feat of loyalty. It was becoming obvious to Gaia what was up here, and it pissed her off.

Come on, boys, she silently encouraged them. *Come and get me.*

Don't miss any books in this thrilling new series
from Pocket Books:

FEARLESS™

#1 Fearless
#2 Sam
#3 Run
#4 Twisted
#5 Kiss
#6 Payback
#7 Rebel
#8 Heat
#9 Blood
#10 Liar
#11 Trust
#12 Killer

All Pocket Book titles are available by post from:
**Simon & Schuster Cash Sales, P.O. Box 29,
Douglas, Isle of Man IM99 1BQ**
Credit cards accepted. Please telephone 01624 836000,
Fax 01624 670923, Internet http://www.bookpost.co.uk
or email: bookshop@enterprise.net for details

FEARLESS™

FRANCINE PASCAL

. . . a girl born without the fear gene

POCKET
BOOKS

An imprint of Simon & Schuster UK Ltd
A Viacom Company
Africa House, 64-78 Kingsway, London WC2B 6AH

Produced by 17th Street Productions, Inc.
A division of Daniel Weiss Associates, Inc.
33 West 17th Street, New York, NY 10011

A CIP catalogue record for this book is
available from the British Library

ISBN 0671 03745 5

3 5 7 9 10 8 6 4

Printed by Cox & Wyman Ltd, Reading, Berkshire

Losers with no imagination say that if you start a new school, there has to be a first day. How come they haven't figured out how to beat that? Just think existentially. All you do is take what's supposed to be the first day and bury it someplace in the next month. By the time you get around to it a month later, who cares?

When I first heard the word *existential,* I didn't know what it meant, so I never used it. But then I found out that no one knows what it means, so now I use it all the time.

Since I just moved to New York last week, tomorrow would have been my first day at the new school, but I existentialized it, and now I've got a good thirty days before I have to deal with it. So, like, it'll be just a regular day, and I'll just grab my usual school stuff, jeans and a T-shirt, and throw them on. Then just like I always do, I'll take them off and throw on about eighteen different T-shirts and four different pairs of jeans before I find the right ones that hide my diesel arms and thunder thighs. Not good things on a girl, but no one else seems to see them like I do.

I won't bother to clean up when I'm done. I don't want to trick my new cohabitants, George and Ella, into thinking that I'm neat or considerate or anything. Why set them up for disappointment? I made that mistake with my old cohabitants and . . . well, I'm not living with them anymore, am I?

George Niven was my dad's mentor in the CIA. He's old. Like fifty or something. His wife, Ella, is much younger. Maybe thirty, I don't know. And you certainly can't tell from the way she dresses. Middle of winter she finds a way to show her belly button. And she's got four hundred of these little elastic bands that can only pass for a

skirt if you never move your
legs. Top that with this unbelievable iridescent red hair and
you've got one hot seventeen-
year-old. At least that's what
she thinks. We all live cozy together in Greenwich Village in a
brownstone—that's what they call
row houses in New York City.
Don't ask me why, because it
isn't brown, but we'll let that
go for now.

I'm not sure how this transfer
of me and my pathetic possessions
was arranged. Not by my dad. He is
Out of the Picture. No letters. No
birthday cards. He didn't even
contact me in the hospital last
year when I almost fractured my
skull. (And no, I didn't almost
fracture my skull to test my dad,
as a certain asshole suggested.) I
haven't seen him since I was
twelve, since . . . since—I guess
it's time to back up a little. My
name is Gaia. Guy. Uh. Yes, it's a
weird name. No, I don't feel like
explaining it right now.

I am seventeen. The good thing about seventeen is that you're not sixteen. Sixteen goes with the word *sweet,* and I am so far from sweet. I've got a black belt in kung fu and I'm trained in karate, judo, jujitsu, and *muay thai*—which is basically kick boxing. I've got a reflex speed that's off the charts. I'm a near perfect shot. I can climb mountains, box, wrestle, break codes in four languages. I can throw a 175-pound man over my shoulders, which accounts for my disgusting shoulders. I can kick just about anybody's ass. I'm not bragging. I wish I were. I wish my dad hadn't made me into the . . . thing I am.

I have blond hair. Not yellow, fairy-tale blond. But blond enough to stick me in the category. You know, so guys expect you to expect them to hit on you. So teachers set your default grade at B-minus. C-plus if you happen to have big breasts, which I don't particularly. My friend from before, Ivy, had this equation between grades and cup size, but I'll spare you that.

Back in ninth grade I dyed my way right out of the blond category, but after a while it got annoying. The dye stung and turned my hands orange. To be honest, though (and I am not a liar), there's another reason I let my hair grow back. Being blond makes people think they can pick on you, and I like when people think they can pick on me.

You see, I have this handicap. Uh, that's the wrong word. I am hormonally challenged. I am never afraid. I just don't have the gene or whatever it is that makes you scared.

It's not like I'll jump off a cliff or anything. I'm not an idiot. My rationality is not defective. In fact, it's extra good. They say nothing clouds your reason like fear. But then, I wouldn't know. I don't know what it feels like to be scared.

It's like if you don't have hope, how can you imagine it? Or being born blind, how do you know what colors are?

I guess you'd say I'm fearless. Whatever fear is.

If I see some big guy beating up on a little guy, I just dive in and finish him off. And I can. Because that's the way I've been trained. I'm so strong, you wouldn't believe. But I hate it.

Since I'm never afraid of anything, my dad figured he'd better make sure I can hold my own when I rush into things. What he did really worked, too. Better than he expected. See, my dad didn't consider nature.

Nature compensates for its mistakes. If it forgot to give me a fear gene, it gave me some other fantastic abilities that definitely work in my favor. When I need it, I have this awesome speed, enormous energy, and amazing strength all quadrupled because there's no fear to hold me back.

It's even hard for me to figure out. People talk about danger
and being careful. In my head I
totally understand, but in my gut
I just don't feel it. So if I see
somebody in trouble, I just jump
in and use everything I've got.
And that's big stuff, and it's
intense.

I mean, you ever hear that
story about the mother who lifted
the car off her little boy?
That's like the kind of strength
regular people can get from
adrenaline. Except I don't need
extra adrenaline because without
fear, there's nothing to stop you
from using every bit of power you
have.

And a human body, especially a
highly trained one like mine, has
a lot of concentrated power.

But there's a price. I remember once reading about the
Spartans. They were these fantastic Greek warriors about four
hundred something B.C. They beat
everybody. Nobody could touch

them. But after a battle they'd
get so drained, they'd shake all
over and practically slide to the
ground. That's what happens to
me. It's like I use up everything
and my body gets really weak and
I almost black out. But it only
lasts a couple of minutes.
Eventually I'm okay again.

And there is one other thing
that works in my favor. I can do
whatever I want 'cause I've got
nothing to lose.

See, my mother is . . . not
here anymore. I don't really care
that my dad is gone because I hate
his guts. I don't have any brothers or sisters. I don't even have
any grandparents. Well, actually,
I think I do have one, but she
lives in some end-of-the-world
place in Russia and I get the
feeling she's a few beans short of
a burrito. But this is a tangent.

Tangent is a heinous word for
two reasons:

1. It appears in my trigonome-
try book.

2. Ella, the woman-with-whom-I-now-live-never-to-be-confused-with-a-mother, accuses me of "going off on them."

Where was I? Right. I was telling you my secrets. It probably all boils down to three magic words: I don't care. I have no family, pets, or friends. I don't even have a lamp or a pair of pants I give a shit about.

I Don't Care.

And nobody can make me.

Ella says I'm looking for trouble. For a dummy she hit it right this time.

I *am* looking for trouble.

He lay
sprawled in
a half-
conscious
pile, and
she was **walking**
tempted to
demand his **trap**
wallet or
his watch or
something.

a

DON'T GO INTO THE PARK AFTER *sunset.* The warning rolled around Gaia Moore's head as she crossed the street that bordered Washington Square Park to the east. She savored the words as she would a forkful of chocolate cheesecake.

There was a stand of trees directly in front of her and a park entrance a couple hundred feet to the left. She hooked through the trees, feeling the familiar fizz in her limbs. It wasn't fear, of course. It was energy, maybe even excitement—the things that came when fear should have. She passed slowly through a grassy stretch, staying off the lighted paths that snaked inefficiently through the park.

As the crow flies. That's how she liked to walk. So what if she had nowhere to go? So what if no one on earth knew or probably cared where she was or when she'd get home? That wasn't the point. It didn't mean she had to take the long way. She was starting a new school in the morning, and she meant to put as much distance between herself and tomorrow as she could. Walking fast didn't stop the earth's slow roll, but sometimes it felt like it could.

She'd passed the midway point, marked by the miniature Arc de Triomph, before she caught the flutter of a shadow out of the corner of her eye. She didn't turn her head. She hunched her shoulders so her tall frame looked smaller. The shadow froze. She could feel eyes on her back. Bingo.

The mayor liked to brag how far the New York City crime rate had fallen, but Washington Square at night didn't disappoint. In her short time here she'd learned it was full of junkies who couldn't resist a blond girl with a full wallet, especially under the cover of night.

Gaia didn't alter the rhythm of her steps. An attacker proceeded differently when he sensed your awareness. Any deception was her advantage.

The energy was building in her veins. Come on, she urged silently. Her mind was beautifully blank. Her concentration was perfect. Her ears were pricked to decipher the subtlest motion.

Yet she could have sensed the clumsy attacker thundering from the brush if she'd been deaf and blind. A heavy arm was thrown over her shoulders and tightened around her neck.

"Oh, please," she muttered, burying an elbow in his solar plexus.

As he staggered backward and sucked for air, she turned on him indignantly. Yes, it was a big, clumsy, stupid him—a little taller than average and young, probably not even twenty years old. She felt a tiny spark of hope as she let her eyes wander through the bushes. Maybe there were more . . . ? The really incompetent dopes usually traveled in packs. But she heard nothing more than his noisy, X-rated complaints.

She let him come at her again. Might as well get a shred of a workout. She even let him earn a little speed as he barreled toward her. She loved turning a man's own strength against him. That was the essence of it. She reversed his momentum with a fast knee strike and finished him off with a front kick.

He lay sprawled in a half-conscious pile, and she was tempted to demand his wallet or his watch or something. A smile flickered over her face. It would be amusing, but that wasn't the point, was it?

Just as she was turning away, she detected a faint glitter on the ground near his left arm. She came closer and leaned down. It was a razor blade, shiny but not perfectly clean. In the dark she couldn't tell if the crud on the blade was rust or blood. She glanced quickly at her hands. No, he'd done her no harm. But it lodged in her mind as a strange choice of weapon.

She walked away without bothering to look further. She knew he'd be fine. Her specialty was subduing without causing any real damage. He'd lie there for a few minutes. He'd be sore, maybe bruised tomorrow. He'd brush the cobwebs off his imagination to invent a story for his buddies about how three seven-foot, three-hundred-pound male karate black belts attacked him in the park.

But she would bet her life on the fact that he would never sneak up on another fragile-looking woman without remembering this night. And that was the point. That was what Gaia lived for.

An Easy Crowd

"WHO CAN COME TO THE BOARD AND write out the quadratic formula?" Silence.

"A volunteer, please? I need a volunteer."

No. Gaia sent the teacher telepathic missiles. *Do not call on me.*

"Come on, kids. This is basic stuff. You are supposed to be the advanced class. Am I in the wrong room?"

The teacher's voice—what was the woman's name again?—was reedy and awful sounding. Gaia really should have remembered the name, considering this *was not* the first day.

No. No. No. The teacher's eyes swept over the second-to-back row twice before they rested on Gaia. *Shit.*

"You, in the . . . brown, is it? What's your name?"

"Gaia."

"Gay what?"

15

Every member of the class snickered.

The beautiful thing about Gaia was that she didn't hate them for laughing. In fact, she loved them for being so predictable. It made them so manageable. There was nothing those buttheads could give that Gaia couldn't take.

"Guy. (Pause) Uh."

The teacher cocked her head as if the name were some kind of insult. "Right, then. Come on up to the board. Guy (pause) uh."

The class snickered again.

God, she hated school. Gaia dragged herself out of her chair. Why was she here, anyway? She didn't want to be a doctor or a lawyer. She didn't want to be a CIA agent or Green Beret or superoperative *X-Files* type, like her dad had obviously hoped.

What did she want to be when she grew up? (She loved that question.) A waitress. She wanted to serve food at some piece-of-crap greasy spoon and wait for a customer to bitch her out, or stiff her on the tip, or PINCH HER BUTT. She'd travel across the country from one bad restaurant to the next and scare people who thought it was okay to be mean to waitresses. And there were a lot of people like that. Nobody got more shit than a waitress did. (Well, maybe telemarketers, but they sort of deserved it.)

"Gaia? Any day now."

Snicker. Snicker. This was an easy crowd. Ms.

What's-her-face must have been thrilled with her success.

Gaia hesitated at the board for a moment.

"You don't know it, do you?" The teacher's tone was possibly the most patronizing thing she had ever heard.

Gaia didn't answer. She just wrote the formula out very slowly, appreciating the horrible grinding screech of the chalk as she drew the equals sign. It sounded a lot like the teacher's voice, actually.

$$x = \frac{-b \pm \sqrt{b^2 - 4ac}}{2a}$$

At the last second she changed the final plus to a minus sign. Of course she knew the formula. What was she, stupid? Her dad had raced her through basic algebra by third grade. She'd (begrudgingly) mastered multivariable calculus and linear algebra before she started high school. She might hate math, but she was good at it.

"I'm sorry, Gaia. That's incorrect. You may sit down."

Gaia tried to look disappointed as she shuffled to her chair.

"Talk to me after class about placement, please." The teacher said that in a slightly lower voice, as if the rest of the students wouldn't hear she found Gaia unfit for the class. "Yes, ma'am," Gaia said brightly. It was the first ray of light all day. She'd demote herself to memorizing times tables if it meant getting a different teacher.

Times tables actually came in pretty handy for a waitress. What with figuring out tips and all.

HE SAW HER RIGHT AFTER THE

seventh-period bell rang. She seemed dressed for the sole purpose of blending in with the lockers, but

Not Cloying

she stood out, anyway. It didn't matter that her wide blue eyes were narrowed or that her pretty mouth was twisted into a near snarl—she was blatantly beautiful. It was kind of sick the way Ed was preoccupied with beautiful girls these days.

There weren't many people left in the hall at this point. He, of course, had permission to take his own sweet time getting to class. And she was probably lost. She cast him a quick glance as she strode down the hall. The kind of glance where she saw him without actually seeing him. He was used to that.

He felt a little sorry for her. (He was also preoccupied

18

with finding ways of feeling sorry for people.) She was new and trying hard not to look it. She was confused and trying to look tough. It was endearing is what it was.

"Hey, can I help you find a classroom or anything?"

She swiveled around and glared at him like he'd made a lewd remark. (Was she some kind of mind reader?)

"Excuse me?" she demanded. She wasn't afraid to give him a good once-over.

"You look lost," he explained.

Now she was angry. "This is not what lost looks like. This is what annoyed looks like. And no, I don't need any help. Thanks."

It was the spikiest, least gracious "thanks" he'd ever heard. "Anytime," he said, trying not to smile. "So, what's your name?"

"Does it matter?" She couldn't believe he was prolonging the conversation.

"Mine's Ed, by the way."

"I'm so happy for you." She gave him an extra snarl before she bolted down the hall to the science wing.

He smiled all the way to physics class. He almost laughed out loud when he passed through the door and saw her shadowy, hunched-over form casting around for a seat in the back.

She was in his class; this was excellent. Maybe she'd call him a name if he struck up another conversation.

Even curse him out. That might be fun. God, he'd probably earn himself a restraining order if he tried to sit next to her.

He was so tired of saccharine smiles and cloying tones of voice. People always plastered their eyes to his face for fear of looking anywhere else. He was fed up with everybody being so goddamned nice.

That's why he'd already fallen in love with this weird, maladjusted, beautiful girl who carried a chip the size of Ohio on her shoulder. Because nobody was ever mean to the guy in the wheelchair.

September 23

My Dearest Gaia,

I saw a mouse race across the floor of my apartment today, and it made me think of you. (What doesn't make me think of you?) It reminded me of the winter of Jonathan and your secret efforts to save his little life. I never imagined I'd think longingly upon an oversized gray field mouse whose contribution to our lives was a thousand turds on the kitchen counter, but I grew to love him almost as much as you did.

Oh, Gaia. It feels as if it's been so long. Do you still love rodents and other despised creatures? Do you still carry a pocket full of pennies for luck? Do you still eat your cereal without milk? Do you ever think about me anymore?

I write it and think it so often, it's a mantra, but

Gaia, how desperately I hope you'll forgive me someday. You'll understand why I did what I did, and you'll know it was because I love you. I have so many doubts and fears, my darling, and they seem to grow as the days between us pass. But I know I love you. I'd give my life for you. Again.

Tom Moore lifted his pen at the sound of the beeper. God, he hated that sound. He didn't need to look at the readout to know who was summoning him. It wasn't as if he had friends and family swarming about—it was his self-inflicted punishment that if he couldn't be with his daughter, he would be alone.

He snatched the wretched little device from his desk and threw it across the room, mildly amazed at his own rare show of temper as the beeper bounced off the windowsill and skittered across the wood floor. It was always the same people. It was always an emergency. By tomorrow he'd be in a different time zone.

Before he picked up the phone, he walked to the ancient aluminum filing cabinet and opened it. He thumbed through the files without needing to look. Locating the thick pile of papers, he placed the letter at the front, just as he always did with all the others, unsent and locked in the drawer.

MacDougal and LaGuardia—*bzzzt*—slashing victim, female African American in her thirties—*bzzzt*— young male perpetrator—*bzzzz . . .*

a stupid hobby

"HELLO, CEEENDY."

"Hi, Zolov. What's shaking?"

"Shakeeeng?"

Gaia laughed. "How are you playing?"

Zolov worked his mouth. He drew his wrinkly brown hand over his lips, thinking about the question seriously. "I beat everyone."

Her Favorite Place

"Of course you did," Gaia said loudly. "You're the best."

He nodded absently. "Tank you. You are a good geerl."

In spite of the fact she was practically shouting at him, Gaia could tell he was reading her lips and that it was tiring for him. He sat back in the sunshine, ready for his next opponent, who would very likely not show. His favorite chessboard was set. As always, it was presided over by one of the Mighty Morphin Power Rangers, a red, helmeted action figure he'd probably picked up in somebody's garbage. He never played without him.

Gaia would have sat down across from him if she'd had more than twenty cents in her pocket. Instead she lay back on the bench and closed her eyes.

This park, these chess tables, was Gaia's favorite place. It was her home in New York more than George and Ella's house ever

24

would be. Zolov was at least ninety years old and thought her name was Cindy, but even so, he was her favorite person.

Who says I have no life? she mused as she stretched her arms behind her head, feeling the fabric of her gray T-shirt creeping over her belly button. She inhaled the scent of sugary nuts roasting in a pushcart nearby. This was her favorite place, and that was her favorite smell. It was so sweet and strong, she could practically taste it. One of these days she was going to buy a big bag of those nuts and scarf them down without even pausing to breathe.

She felt a shadow come over her face and squinted one eye open. "Hey, Renny," she said. "You ready for 'dimes of demonstration'?"

Renny was a thirteen-year-old Puerto Rican boy— Gaia's second-favorite person. He was a self-proclaimed poet and such a whiz at chess he hustled great sums of money out of almost anybody who was dumb enough to sit down across from him. Today his face didn't light up with its usual bravado.

Gaia sat up and put a hand over her eyes to block the sun. "You're scared I'm going to steal your money and make you cry?" she taunted. She scanned the tables for a free board.

As she did, her eye snagged on a new piece of graffiti splayed on the asphalt just to the left of Zolov's usual table. A swastika. It was at least a foot across, and the white paint was as fresh and bright as a new pair of sneakers. Gaia's stomach was filled with lead. Could it be for her benefit? she wondered. Could somebody possibly know how the Holocaust had decimated her mother's family and made her grandparents into heroes? No. Not likely. She was being paranoid. How would anyone know about her Jewish background? In fact, when she told some people, they acted all surprised—like if you had fair hair and blue eyes, it wasn't possible. That really annoyed her.

Her eyes flicked over the ugly shape again. Had Renny seen it? Had Zolov? Did they think anything of it?

For some reason Renny wasn't jumping in with his usual rhyming insults and eager put-downs.

"Gaia, you oughtta go home," Renny said almost inaudibly in the direction of his sneakers.

This was odd. "What's up, Renny?"

"It's gonna get dark," he noted.

"Thanks, Ren. It usually does." He was wearing a stiff new jacket that advertised its brand name from three different spots. He licked his lips. "You oughtta, you know, be watching out," he continued.

"For what?" she asked.

He considered this question a moment. "The park is real dangerous after dark."

Gaia stood, impatient. She swept a strand of hair behind her ear. "Renny, cut the bullshit. What's the matter? What are you talking about?"

"Did you hear about Lacy's sister?" His face was slightly pink, and he wasn't meeting her gaze.

"No, why?"

"It was on the news and everything. All the kids are talking about it. She got slashed in the park last night," Renny explained. "She had to get sewn up from her eyebrow to her ear."

"God, that's awful," Gaia said. "What kind of blade?"

"What?"

"What kind of blade?"

Renny gave her a strange look.

"Was it a razor blade?" Gaia persisted.

"I guess. I don't know." He looked up at her a little defiantly. "How am I supposed to know?"

"Just asking, Renny." She softened her tone. "Thanks for warning me. I do appreciate it."

He nodded, his face growing pinker. "I was just . . . you know, concerned about you." He tried to look very tall as he shuffled away.

Gaia swung her beat-up messenger bag over her shoulder as she watched him. She had a bad feeling about this. She sensed that Renny was no longer satisfied with the insular world of chess misfits. He was starting to care what the big boys thought—those stupid boys who hung around the fountain, trying to look tough. Renny was smarter and funnier and more original than they'd ever be, but he was thirteen. He was at that brutal age when many kids would sell all the uniqueness in their character for the right pair of shoes. She longed to tell him not to spend so much time in the park, to go home to his mother, but who was she to talk?

Yes, Renny might be concerned about her. But not as concerned as she was about him.

She herself loved this misfit world, Gaia mused as she surveyed the tables. Curtis, a fifteen-year-old black kid, was sitting across from Mr. Haq, a Pakistani taxi-cab driver who appeared to like nothing more than parking his yellow cab on Washington Square South and killing an afternoon over a chessboard.

She loved that people who couldn't begin to pronounce each other's names played and talked for hours. She loved that a forty-something-year-old cab-driver and a fifteen-year-old from the Manhattan Valley youth program had so much in common. She loved getting a break from the stupid hierarchy of high school.

She loved that there weren't people like . . . well, people like . . . him.

The him was walking by slowly, looking confi-dently over the boards in play. His hair was light in color—a tousled mixture of blond and brown and even a little red. His chinos were cuffed, and his preppy gray jacket flapped in the autumn breeze. Gaia felt her stomach do a quick pitch and roll. She felt queasy and strangely alert at the same time.

You didn't find people who looked like that . . . as in, stunningly, astonishingly good. People like him sipped coffee at Dean & Deluca or swing danced on Gap commercials or spouted Woody Allen–style dialogue on *Dawson's Creek,* where they belonged.

So what *the hell* was he doing lingering over chessboards with the freaks and geeks? She had half a mind to walk right over and tell him to get lost.

This was her favorite place, and he had no business here, reminding her of things she would never be.

Don't Be Afraid

"Thank you, Marco, you're a sweetheart."

Marco nodded at the woman, making sure to tilt his chin so she had a good look at his left side, the side where his broken nose hardly showed at all. "No problem." He kept his voice deep and smooth. She probably thought he was like twenty-five or something.

She took a long sip from the bottle of Coke he'd brought her, exposing her pale neck. She lifted one leg to rest on the low wall of the fountain, revealing several more inches of thigh under her stretchy aqua miniskirt. He tried not to stare. Or did she want him to stare?

He stopped breathing completely as she slowly, slowly brushed her fingers over his upper arm. "What happened here?" she asked.

He glanced at the purplish bruise. He paused before answering and cleared his throat, trying to make certain his voice didn't come out squeaky. "Nothing much. I got jumped last night. These three big guys thought they were real tough. Probably black belts in karate or something."

Her eyes widened in just the way he'd hoped. "You're okay? Did you call the police?"

"Uh-uh. That's not how we—how I—do things." Marco ran a hand through his dark hair. It had come out perfectly today. "I've got some friends who will back me up if those guys ever come back here." Marco loved the way she watched him when he talked. So he kept talking. He wasn't even listening to what he was saying.

Man, she was gorgeous. She was older than he, twenty-something at least, but sexy as hell. Like some kind of goddess with her straight red hair and green eyes. And the legs on her. He couldn't look away.

He'd first noticed her at the beginning of the summer. All the guys noticed her—it was hard not to. She lived around here, he guessed, because she walked by this fountain almost every afternoon. He wasn't the only one who magically turned up each day around four o'clock to watch the show.

Lately he'd noticed she'd started returning his looks. Just a glance at first, but then her eyes stayed longer. Last week she'd said hello to him, and he'd practically peed in his pants. Today she'd been late, so most of the guys had wandered away, but some kind of crazy instinct made him stay.

He took his eyes off her breasts for a moment to see if he spotted anybody he knew. He would love for any one of his buddies to see him right now.

Just then she reached toward his collarbone and rested her index finger on the pendant that lay there. The electricity from her touch surged through his chest and seemed to throw his heart off rhythm. "What is this?" Her voice was almost a whisper. "I've seen this before."

He studied her face before he answered. He wasn't sure how much to tell—how much she really wanted to know. "It's, uh, it's called a hieroglyph—you know, like ancient Egyptian writing? It's the symbol for . . . uh, power."

"Where have I seen it before?" Her green eyes fixed on his.

His glance darted around the fountain. "I don't know. Maybe you saw one of the other guys wearing it. Maybe a tattoo on somebody's arm. It's kind of a . . . I don't know . . . kind of a . . ."

His voice trailed off awkwardly. He didn't want her thinking he was some kind of thug. He sure didn't want anybody to overhear him telling her secret stuff.

"A mark?" she supplied. "Some sort of identification?" She didn't appear wary the way most girls he knew would. Her eyes were wide and intense, fascinated.

"Yeah, like that."

"Ah. I see. Are you part of—"

Marco sucked in his breath. Suddenly this didn't seem so cool. What if she was an undercover cop or some kind of informer? He'd heard of stuff like this. He backed up, putting a few feet between them. "I gotta be going. It's, like, after six, and I—"

With two steps she closed the distance. "Marco. Don't be afraid of me." Her fingers fluttered over his cheek. "Don't tell me anything you don't want to. I'm just . . . interested, that's all. I'm interested in everything about you."

All the blood in his body seemed to pool in his

head. He felt dizzy. "You're not, like, a cop or anything?" He was pretty sure she'd have to say so if she were.

She laughed. "No. Most definitely not." She gave him a look. It was a mischievous, sexy kind of look. "*Definitely* not."

GAIA SMACKED THE SHORTWAVE RADIO

Rapunzel Monkey

that sat on the table next to the bed. Her bed. She had trouble thinking of anything in this house as hers.

"Piece of crap," she murmured. She'd picked up the radio at a junk shop on Canal Street. She'd gotten it to tune in to the local police frequency, but the damn thing emitted almost nothing but static. She rearranged the antenna she'd rigged until she heard a break in the fuzz. She rolled off the bed and walked to the window. Ah, that was good. She could decipher various bleeps that sounded almost like words. She stood by the door. Oh, it liked that. Now she could actually understand the words.

Bzzzzt—MacDougal and LaGuardia—*bzzzt*—slashing

victim, female African American in her thirties—
bzzzt—young male perpetrator—*bzzzz* . . .

Dammit. She tried jumping up and down.

—lost him in the park—*bzzzzzzzzz* . . .

Shit. Gaia grabbed the radio and threw it off the table. What a stupid hobby. Why couldn't she just watch *Roswell* like a normal girl?

Well, for one thing, because the television was in the so-called family room. It would mean walking past, possibly even fraternizing with, George and his bimbo bride. It wasn't that she didn't like George. She did. He was trying really hard to make her feel comfortable. He tried so hard, in fact, that she found it awkward to be around him. He put on this peppy voice and asked her about her classes or her friends. What was she going to say, "I see my math teacher through crosshairs"? "My best friend has Alzheimer's"? George wanted something within the universe of normal, and she simply couldn't give him that.

Ella was another story. Stupid, vain Ella she genuinely disliked. There were Ella's fingernails, her passion for Victoria's Secret catalogs, her love of Mariah Carey. That was about it for Ella. How in the world had a sensible man like George fallen prey to a tarty thing like her? And God, he had fallen.

Gaia really needed some air. She strode to the door

34

of the room and listened for signs of life. What sucked was that her room was on the fourth floor of the four-story house. She hid up there during the little time she spent in the house because she hated walking past every other room on her way in and out. She was like a latter-day Rapunzel except her hair was only a few inches below her shoulders, slightly fried, not all that blond, and furthermore, who the hell was ever going to climb up to give her a hand? The guy in the wheel-chair from school?

What she—and Rapunzel, frankly—needed was a decent ladder.

Gaia opened the door slowly. Hopefully George was still at work and Ella was—who ever knew where Ella was? By profession Ella considered herself a pho-tographer, but Gaia had a hard time taking her seri-ously. It gave Ella an excuse to saunter through hip downtown neighborhoods with a camera slung over her shoulder. Apparently she got the odd commission to photograph somebody's dog or living room or something. Her "work," as George called it in his pious way, was displayed over most of the wall space in the house—mostly arty black-and-white pictures of dolls' heads and high-heeled shoes.

Thank God for the automatic camera that makes it all possible, Gaia thought sarcastically as she crept through the hallway and down the stairs.

At the second landing she was faced once again

by "the photograph." Most days she averted her eyes. Although Ella hadn't taken it, it was by far the most upsetting in the house. It was a picture of an eleven-year-old Gaia with her parents, snapped by George the week he visited them at their country house in the Berkshires. Once Gaia looked at the photo, she found it hard to look away and, after that, hard to get her mind to cooperate with her.

The Gaia in the picture made her think of a little monkey, clinging to her dad with long skinny arms, her wrists circled by several filthy friendship bracelets, her narrow shoulders lost in the beloved brown fisherman's sweater he'd bought for her on a trip to Ireland. Gaia's smile was big and exuberant, so pitifully unaware of what the next year would bring.

Now Gaia moved her gaze to her mother, even as she willed herself not to. If Gaia's face in the picture was all embarrassing openness, her mother's was pure mystery. No matter how many times Gaia searched it, no matter how clearly she saw those features, she felt she couldn't tell what her mother really looked like. She *needed* something from that face that it never gave. The same miserable questions started their spiraling march through Gaia's brain: *Why am I holding Daddy and not you? Why aren't I beautiful like you? Did you love me, anyway? Did you ever know how much I loved you?*

And then, as always, the thoughts got so unfathomably sad, they didn't even come in words. Her throat started to ache, and her vision swam. She couldn't pull enough air into her lungs. Without exactly realizing what she was doing, her hands shot out and yanked the framed photograph off the wall.

"What are you doing?"

Gaia spun around. Her heart was bouncing in her chest, and it took her a moment to focus her eyes on Ella. She cleared her throat. She took a deep breath. She tried to rearrange her posture into something less rigid.

"I am removing this picture from the wall."

"Can I ask why?"

"Sure."

Ella waited impatiently. "Okay, why?"

Gaia placed the picture facedown on the bookcase. She glanced at her watch. "I didn't say I'd answer."

Ella got that eye-rolling martyred look. "Gaia, you know George loves that picture. He put it up for you."

Gaia cleared her throat again. She tried shrugging, but it didn't come off with the indifference she was aiming for. "If George put it up for my benefit, he won't mind if I take it down."

Ella's hands found their way to her hips as they mostly did within a few minutes of starting a conversation with Gaia. "I swear, Gaia, George does so much for you. I would think you could at least—"

Gaia tuned out the shrill voice as she made her way

down the rest of the steps and out the front door. She knew every word of the speech. There wouldn't be any vocabulary words or clever turns of phrase. Ella wasn't going to surprise her.

Gaia took the sidewalk at a near run. She felt like she might explode. The sky was darkening as she turned left on West 4th Street, leaving bustling outdoor cafes, overpriced little restaurants, all-night delis, her favorite subterranean record shop behind her in a blur.

She headed straight for the park. No one was going to scare her out of her shortcut. And certainly not tonight, not in the mood she was in. And in fact, she hoped they'd try. Let them find her instead of some kid or some old guy who wouldn't know how to handle it. Maybe if she did this enough, those creeps would learn that everyone who looked vulnerable wasn't necessarily so. What a gorgeous lesson to teach them. After all, wasn't that what her gifts were all about? Power to the little people!

She spun
around,
instantly
accosted by
strange
blurred
images.
A flash of
chrome. Two
large
wheels.

mr.

valiant

THREE MORE STEPS. OKAY, FIVE MORE

steps. Okay, ten more. Just to
the maple tree. Okay, not that
one, the one behind it.

She was a little nuts. She knew
it. Skulking around Washington
Square Park for three hours and
twenty-three minutes, counting

A Force for Good

steps (and okay, seconds), looking for trouble. It could be
called entrapment. That's exactly what she wanted to do,
entrap those lowlifes.

Gaia lingered under the tree, feeling drops of sweat
sliding down her spine. Wasn't New York City supposed to be getting cool in September? The smell of
late season pollen was so thick, it felt like paste in her
nostrils. Please, somebody. Anybody. She'd come here
with the secret hope that one of the notorious slashers
would have a go at her, but now she'd grown desperate. She would take absolutely any criminal, from
petty shoplifter to ax murderer; she
really wasn't choosy. Hey, who even needed a criminal? She was ready to pounce on the strength of a big
mouth or a bad attitude.

But she wouldn't. Gaia would never attack anybody unprovoked. She would never do more harm
than necessary. That was the code, and as much
as she hated her father, she was still bound to honor it.
It was bred into her, just like her blue eyes that seemed

40

to change shade with her mood, the weather, the color of her shirt. Just like her love of sweets. She had to use her Miraculous Gift (that's what her father always called it) as a force for good. Her mission was to draw out violent behavior and squash it, not to produce more violence.

But sometimes carrying out her mission felt more self-indulgent than honorable. Did it count as a good deed if you enjoyed yourself? She liked to think she thrived on self-defense. But there were times, really upsetting times, when she saw the line between defense and offense as clear as day and barreled toward it. Hey, she had an extraordinary talent, and she wanted to use it.

What if one day she crossed that line that separated good guys from bad guys? It would be easy. There was only a hair's width between them. Why hadn't anyone warned her that inside the crucible of real anger, good and bad were so nearly the same?

Worse yet, what if one day she'd stop being able to see the line at all? She wouldn't know anymore if she was good or bad or crazy or sane. Maybe Gaia didn't know the meaning of scary, but that sounded an awful lot like it.

Gaia made a slow loop around the maple tree. She had to get out of this park, but she really didn't feel like going back to George and Ella's. God forbid

George would put on that earnest face and try to talk about "her loss" as he often did after Ella complained about her.

She didn't feel like walking on Broadway—the street was mobbed with NYU students, tourists, and shoppers at every hour of the day. Instead she turned south on Mercer Street. She loved the deserted, `canyonlike feel` of the narrow street and the sound her steps made on the cobblestones. She'd walk straight down to Houston Street and see what was playing at the Angelika.

Suddenly, as if in answer to a prayer, Gaia heard voices behind her. She stopped and fumbled through her backpack as if she were looking for something. Jeez, what a girl had to do to get mugged in this city.

The voices turned into whispers, and then she heard footsteps, slow. Oh, *yes.* Finally. She turned toward the noise, pasting what she hoped looked like a terrified expression on her face. Inside, her heart was leaping with anticipation.

There were three of them, and they looked young—around sixteen or seventeen. Two of them had shaved heads. The smallest brandished a razor blade. `Gaia detected more than a hint of nervousness under his swagger.` She backed up (fearfully, she hoped), wanting the situation to escalate. She hated herself, but there it was.

The little thug was up front, covering the ground

between them with a menacing lurch. The other two were hanging back, present to witness this `feat of loyalty`. It was becoming obvious to Gaia what was up here, and it pissed her off.

Come on, boys, she silently encouraged them. *Come and get me.* Her mind hovered on the swastika she'd seen painted on the ground in the park. That coupled with the shaved heads and the leather jackets gave her the strong suspicion that these assholes were some kind of neo-Nazi white supremacist outfit.

Her concentration was so keen, she had to remind herself to keep breathing. She couldn't let her anger get the best of her. She had to play this just right. If she struck back too quickly, she might scare them away. The kid was trying hard to look tough, but `his toughness went about as deep as the sheen of sweat on his upper lip.`

Now. He was right on her, razor blade lifted. She screamed helplessly as she drew back her arm for a sharp blow to his wrist. And just as she balanced her weight to deliver the strike she heard a thunderous shout and a commotion behind her.

Suddenly noise was coming from every direction. Her adrenaline was rising fast, but her focus was thrown. She spun around, instantly accosted by strange blurred images. A flash of chrome. `Two large wheels.` She jumped back to try to make sense of it.

"Get away from her!" a familiar voice shouted.

Gaia's razor-blade-wielding attacker fell back in confusion.

Equally confused, Gaia swiveled her head.

"It's okay, Gaia! Go! Run!"

She watched in perfect amazement as Ed, the guy in the wheelchair from school, rolled into the fray. Her very own knight in shining armor come to save the day.

"You've got to be joking," she muttered under her breath.

But no, there he was. Mr. Valiant.

Now what was she supposed to do? She couldn't just burst into action with Ed sitting on the sidelines. He'd see everything. He'd know far more than he was allowed.

It was one thing showing an attacker her tricks. Every time she did this, she made a wager that her attacker wouldn't confess to being pounded by a girl, and she'd never been wrong. But Ed was a different story. Ed would tell the nifty adventure to everybody in school. They'd probably recruit her for the judo club or something.

The adrenaline was surging through her veins, and the primary person she wanted to strangle was Ed.

The three attackers had been as surprised as she by Ed's arrival, but they were now regrouping.

Okay, fine. She'd take a couple of hits. She wouldn't

44

let the razor blade near her, but that would be easy enough to dispose of in a stealthy way. They'd hit her. She'd scream. Somebody would hear the noise and call the cops. The three losers would feel manly and dangerous and go away. The little one would earn his initiation on somebody else.

It was disappointing as hell, but she'd deal.

One Small Problem

ED FARGO PUSHED HIS WHEELS AS fast as he could. He sailed over the curb and bumped along the cobblestones. He'd often dreamed of running over somebody with his wheelchair, but he'd never actually done it before. His lungs ached for air and his arms ached with exertion as he plowed through the low bushes and into the guy with the razor blade. Thank God he'd been coming along Mercer just then. Thank God he'd heard the scream.

He heard the powerful meeting of metal and shin bone.

"Ahhhhhhh!" The attacker fell backward.

"Gaia, get out of here!" Ed shouted again. He'd never felt quite so important in his life.

She looked stunned. Why the hell wouldn't she get her ass out of there? Was she paralyzed with fear? So traumatized, she couldn't move a muscle? Thank God he'd arrived when he had. "Please go!" he commanded.

The guy with the razor blade fumbled back up to his feet, and his two accomplices came closer in for backup. Ed realized he didn't have much time. Panic was taking hold of his chest. He looked at Gaia's frozen form. He looked at the three hoods gathering for attack. Oh, man. This time their vicious eyes weren't focused on Gaia; they were aiming directly at him. Oh, oh, oh.

His brain was spinning. His heart was pounding at least five hundred times a minute. The obvious thing to do was get out of there as fast as his arms would carry him, but he couldn't. He couldn't just leave Gaia standing there. She'd be slaughtered.

"What is wrong with you?" Ed bellowed at her. "Get the hell out of here *now!*"

Three big angry thugs were closing in and that stupid girl wouldn't move. Panic was now weirdly tinged with resignation. He was dead. If they wanted to kill him, that is. Maybe they'd be satisfied just mangling him or slashing him to ribbons.

The biggest of the three took hold of the armrest of his wheelchair and gave it a powerful shove. Ed collided hard with the street and rolled from the toppled chair.

This was sad. It sure would have been handy if his legs worked right now. He looked up at the stripe of night sky between the old cast-iron buildings, waiting for the first blow. He put his arms over his face for protection.

Slam! He heard the sound of a foot connecting with hard flesh and then a deep moan. Was that him? Had he made that noise? He heard another searing blow. Jesus, was he so far gone, he couldn't even feel the pain?

He moved an arm away from his face and cracked open one eye. He heard a groan and then a barking shout. Strange. He was pretty sure his mouth was shut. He opened the other eye and sat up. Then he shut both eyes again. Had he gone into cardiac arrest and died already? God, that was quick. Weren't there supposed to be a lot of warm feelings and long tunnels and a bright light?

He simply could not have seen what he thought he saw. He was dead. Or hallucinating. Maybe that was it. His mind was dealing him some truly mind-bending hallucinations. Awesome ones, as it happened. He opened his eyes again. His mouth dropped open.

Gaia Moore, the lovely girl with the slim frame and sullen expression who haunted the back of his physics class, had suddenly transformed into Xena, Warrior Princess, only blond and even more beautiful. She crushed the jaw of Thug 1 with a roundhouse kick.

47

She struck Thug 2 in the chest with such violence, he was left gasping for breath. Thug 3 came swinging at her from behind, and she spun around and neutralized him with a stunning kick-boxing move he'd only ever seen executed by Jean Claude Van Damme.

Holy shit. Could this actually be real? Gaia's dauntless, intense, angry face looked real. The thonk of her sneakered foot in Thug 1's belly sounded real.

Unbelievable. `Gaia was a superhero.` Hair flying, limbs whirling, she was the most graceful, powerful martial artist he had ever laid eyes on. Her every move was a mesmerizing combination of ballet and kung fu. And not only was she magical, she was lethal. Thug 1 was writhing on the ground, Thug 2 was ready to flee. Although Thug 3 appeared to be rallying, Ed almost pitied him.

Suddenly Ed sucked in the moist night air. A chill began in his fingertips and crept up his wrists and arms. He saw only a flash at first, and then the image resolved itself. Thug 3 had a knife. Ed saw it clearly now glinting in the streetlight, looking awfully real.

Oh, my God.

Did Gaia see the knife? Did she realize what was coming? He certainly couldn't tell by her expression. Her eyes revealed not even the tiniest hint of fear. Jesus, she was tough. That or `paranormally stupid.`

"Gaia!" he heard his own voice bellowing. "He's got a knife!"

Her gaze didn't flicker. She stood there motionless as Thug 3 went after her. She looked as if she were in some kind of deep meditation.

Ed was hyperventilating. He didn't care how tough Gaia was; she couldn't defend herself against an eight-inch blade. Presumably her skin was made of the same stuff his was. He had to do something.

He supplied his seizing brain with some oxygen, then dragged himself toward his wheelchair. He pulled it upright and set his sights on the slouching back of Thug 3. Ed's legs might be useless, but his arm strength was formidable. He launched the chair like a missile.

Strike! The chair hit its mark, and Thug 3 staggered forward. Ed briefly registered the look of surprise on Gaia's face as Thug 3 careened into her and sent her sprawling backward. His stomach clenched. Oh, God. That hadn't been his intention at all.

Now the guy retrieved his knife and leaped on top of Gaia. Worse yet, from Thug 2's cowardly hideout behind a parked car, he saw the tide turn and was racing back to join the fight. Ed dragged himself toward Gaia as fast as he could, his eyes fixed on her vulnerable throat and the knife hovering over it. "Stop!" he roared. "You're going to kill her!" He felt tears stinging his eyes.

49

It happened so fast, Ed wasn't sure he'd actually seen it. Gaia delivered a powerful kick exactly to the groin of Thug 2 and almost simultaneously struck Thug 3 in the side of the neck with her hand. Thug 3 rolled over, unconscious. His knife skidded along the stones. Thug 2 pitched to the ground, screaming in pain.

Gaia was instantly on her feet. She scooped up the knife and stepped over the prone body of Thug 3. Suddenly Thug 1 and Thug 2 seemed to forget their pain and sprinted for safety like jackrabbits in traffic.

Ed was watching Gaia, his heart overflowing with relief and admiration, when she surprised him again.

She got to the sidewalk and collapsed. Her legs literally crumpled under her body, and without a noise she fell in a heap on the pavement.

GAIA BREATHED DEEPLY AND WAITED

for it to pass. She wouldn't struggle to move or attempt to get to her feet. She knew by now it wouldn't work. The only thing to do was wait.

That Old Kryptonite

Pretty much right on

schedule, she heard a noisy approach and felt a hand on her shoulder. Argh. She didn't need to open her eyes to see the worried, eager face.

Once he'd reached her, she heard him collapse beside her. Listening to his labored breathing, Gaia's heart was pulled forcefully by two equal and opposite desires:

1. Her desire to hug Ed for his valiant, misguided efforts on her behalf.
2. Her desire to murder him for being such an unbelievable pain in the ass.

"Are you okay?" He touched her shoulder again. She could hear the fear in his words.

She would have really liked to rouse herself right then. It was unthinkable that he should see her in this state of weakness—to see what happened to her after one of these episodes. And yet there was just no way around it short of killing him, which, though tempting, didn't seem all that sporting under the circumstances.

"Gaia? Gaia?" His voice was rising with panic.

"Mmmm," she mumbled.

"Oh, God, are you hurt? Did they hurt you?"

A yellow cab cruised past them, slowed for a stop sign, then drove on. If anyone in the car saw them, they apparently hadn't felt the need to get involved. That was New York City for you. Its inhabitants set a high standard for unusual.

With great effort she fluttered open her eyes and very slowly, by inches, shook her head. The sidewalk made a really bad pillow.

"What's the matter? Should I call for an ambulance?"

She gritted her teeth. If she'd had any energy left, she would have rolled her eyes. "Mm. Mmm." After another pause she reinforced it with another slight shake of her head.

"No? Are you sure?"

She wasn't accustomed to anyone seeing her like this, and it was irritating. She found the strength to open her eyes for real and concentrate on Ed's face. It had suddenly become a much more significant face—the face of the guy who knew her secrets.

Holy shit. How had she let this happen?

It was so ironic. So ironic and pitiful and stupid and weird, she wanted to laugh. For some reason this guy had become her self-appointed guardian angel and nearly gotten her killed in the process. How typical that her guardian angel would be a slightly scruffy ex-skate rat in a wheelchair who caused so much more trouble than good. How strange it was that he suddenly knew more about her than anyone else on planet Earth. (Except her father, of course.)

Gaia had been so careful over the years to keep

everything secret. It was another of her father's curses: *I'll make you into a freak and not let you tell anyone.* Not like she was going to tell, anyway. She had no confidant and meant to keep it that way. Besides, the strange facts of her life were all connected. Telling a little would ultimately mean telling a lot.

"Gaia? Please tell me you're okay?"

It always seemed that when her body sank into this state of paralytic exhaustion, her mind zoomed into overdrive. She summoned the energy to move her lips. "I'm fine," she whispered.

"You don't look so fine."

Patience, Ed, she asked of him silently. She felt the energy returning to her muscles. It was tingly at first, as if her whole body had fallen asleep. She groaned a little as she sat up. She studied Ed. Worried, terrified, astonished, concerned Ed. She couldn't help but smile a little.

"I'm fine," she said. She paused for breath. "Except for the fact that I may have to kill you."

To: L

From: ELJ

Date: September 25

File: 776244

Subject: Gaia Moore

Last Seen: Mercer Street, New York City, 10:53 P.M.

Update: Subject observed in fight with 3 suspected gang members, one armed with knife. Attack complicated by appearance of young man in wheelchair. Motive unclear. Confirmed subject's mastery of jujitsu. Subject displayed other martial skills previously documented. All 3 attackers subdued.

Subject appeared injured but later observed to walk from incident unharmed.

To: ELJ
From: L
Date: September 26
File: 776244
Subject: Gaia Moore

Directives: Identify and create file on young
man in wheelchair.

Issue immediate instruction: Subject not to
be injured under any circumstances.
Repercussions will be severe.

There is this other really freakish thing about me. I've never told anyone. I'd be way too humiliated.

Humiliation, by the way, is a truly terrible emotion. It's at the bottom of the pile. Much worse than fear, I bet. Since I don't have to have fear, why do I have to have humiliation? If only I could toss it wherever fear went. And while I was at it, I'd get rid of anger, hurt, compassion, betrayal. And self-ishness. Oh, and guilt. Definitely guilt. It's out of there. Without all of those things, I think I could imagine maybe being happy someday.

Hey, that's it. I, Gaia Moore, have discovered the secret to happiness. People have been searching for it since the beginning of time, but it took me, a seventeen-year-old with no philo-sophical, medical, or psychologi-cal training, to discover the truth:

Lobotomy. You don't have to feel anything at all.

You heard it here first, folks. And a full frontal lobotomy probably costs no more than the average nose job.

Okay, where was I? Oh, yeah. No wonder I'm digressing—I don't feel like putting this into words.

I'm a virgin.

No, no. It's way worse than that. I wish it were only that.

I've never had a boyfriend.

True, but nope. That doesn't convey the depth of this particular humiliation.

I've never kissed anybody.

Okay, there you have it. Can you say "loser"?

Let me try to soften this information with an excuse or two. When I was twelve, I had something approaching a boyfriend, in a preboyfriend kind of way. His name was Stephen, and he lived around the corner. He was the one with the right kind of hair (light brown, straight, no cowlicks), the right kind of bike (specialized, like you care), the right kind of jeans (Gap, at the time). His parents had the right kind of car (red Jeep, good stereo) and a very large pool. For these reasons the popular girls sought him out. I liked him because he was secretly just as weird as me. We both played chess and knee football. We concocted these elaborate fantasy games set in Camelot or a mile under the sea, long after imaginary games are socially acceptable (age four, roughly). We were nerdy enough to watch Bill Nye, the Science Guy, but cool enough not to admit that to anybody but each other.

Hold on. Wait just a second. Why am I telling you all this? Am I really so desperate that I'll try to pass off a neighbor without underarm hair as some kind of romantic conquest? This represents a new low.

But it points to something

real, which is that I'm stunted.
My love life got left behind with
the rest of my life the autumn
after my twelfth birthday.
Eventually, when the moving van
came, I told Stephen I hated him,
just so as not to leave any
threads dangling.

My life ended then, but I keep
growing.

I usually pride myself on the
fact that I don't care about
being a freak or a misfit. I
don't care what people think of
me. But for some reason this
kissing business, this lack of
kissing business, bothers me, and
I can't pretend it doesn't.

That's the very worst thing
about it, really. How much it
bothers me. How much I think
about it.

I'm going to be brutally honest right now, and hopefully afterward I can snap back into some
more comfortable state of denial.

Ready? Okay.

Of all the terrible things

that have happened in my life—my
mom, my dad, the life I lost—I'm
such a vain, petty, and selfish
person that I am most ashamed of
the fact that nobody has ever
kissed me.

This thought drives me to more
than the desire for a lobotomy.
This drives me to something
worse.

Yo, Rapunzel. Forget the ladder. There's a faster way down.

Ten years from now Heather's awfulness would have caught up with her, **bitch** and she'd **queen** be a disgruntled wretch pining for the glory days.

"I STARTED THINKING/NOT DRINKING
was better for me/so it got me
to thinking/about getting a
lobotomy..."

"What did she just say?"
Gaia was sitting behind a
very large, very expensive
mug of coffee across from
Ed and squinting at the band that was playing in the
far corner. Gaia was happy to ignore them. She'd seen
plenty of unplugged garage bands in her day. But
these weird snippets of songs kept floating into her
consciousness and sticking there the way raspberry
seeds stuck in her molars.

"Huh?" Ed asked.

"That singer. Did you hear the words?" Gaia asked.

Ed strained to listen over the clink of spoons and
the hissing of the cappuccino machine. "Something
about a lobotomy."

"You're joking," Gaia declared.

Ed gave her a puzzled look. "If so, it wasn't a very
funny joke."

"No, I mean, she didn't actually say lobotomy."

"Okay, she didn't." Ed shrugged. "Why does it
matter?"

Gaia stirred her coffee. "Never mind." She studied
the singer. She looked a little like Ashley Judd before
the makeup went on. An East Village version, anyway,

with a wool stocking cap, hair so messy it was coagulating into dreads, and a tattoo of a spider that perched on her collarbone.

Gaia fidgeted in her chair. She didn't want to leave too much silence because Ed might bring up what happened last night and she really didn't want him to.

"You know what the problem is with these fancy brown sugar packets?" Gaia held one up. "The granules are too big. They don't dissolve. They just hang around in the bottom of your mug, so your coffee isn't as sweet as you want it to be until you get to the last sip, which is so sweet, you want to puke."

Ed looked both puzzled and slightly amused. "Huh. Hadn't thought of that." He gestured at the counter. "They have regular sugar up there."

Gaia nodded. Why had she gone for coffee after school with Ed?

Because he'd asked her, mainly. Because he'd tried to save her life, even though she'd ended up saving his. She should have remembered, before she'd accepted, that going for coffee with someone usually meant talking to them.

Ed was looking at her a little too meaningfully. He stretched his arms out in front of him. "Listen, Gaia, I just wanted to tell you that I—"

"I don't want to talk about it," Gaia jumped in quickly.

"Sorry?"

"I don't want to talk about it."

"What is *it?*"

Now he really was going to think she was a wacko. "It. Anything."

"You don't want to talk about anything?" Ed asked carefully.

Gaia tugged at her hair awkwardly. "I don't want to talk about last night. I don't want you to ask me any questions."

Ed nodded and digested that for a minute. "Hey, Gaia?"

"Yeah."

"I'll make you a promise."

"That sounds heavy."

Ed laughed. "Just listen, okay?"

"Okay."

"I promise that I won't ever ask you any questions, all right?"

Gaia laughed, too. "I think that was a question."

"Fine, so it was the last one."

"Fine."

Gaia was starting to sense too much friendliness in the air, so she stood up. "I'm going to, um, get that regular sugar. I'll be right back."

"Good."

"Okay."

She walked to the counter with her mug. This

was so cozy and normal seeming, she felt as if she were inhabiting somebody else's body. Absently she dumped two packets of white sugar into her coffee.

Oh, yes, she was just a happy girl in the West Village, having coffee with a friend.

A troop of familiar-looking people streamed in. They were from school, she realized. The self-designated "beautiful people." There were three girls and two guys, and they were laughing about something. Their manner and wardrobe screamed, "Put me in a Banana Republic ad right now!" One girl in particular was quite beautiful, with long, shiny dark hair, slouchy chinos, and a collared shirt that was whiter and crisper than anything Gaia had ever owned.

Much as she wanted to dismiss them as they swarmed around her at the counter, ordering various combinations of lattes, au laits, con leches, and mochas in pretentious Italian sizes, Gaia couldn't help imagining some alternate universe where she was one of them.

What if she were witty and well dressed and carefree? What if her biggest dilemma in life were whether to order a grande latte or a magnifico mocha? What if that fairly cute one, the boy in the beat-up suede jacket, called her all the time? She studied his dark hair, so pleasantly dilapidated, and his hazel eyes. She allowed herself a look at his lips. What if he'd kissed her? Not just once but hundreds of times?

She felt a weird tingling in her lower extremities as the fantasy evolved in her mind. He'd be standing next to her, studying the coffee board, as familiar to her as a brother, and he'd reach for her without really thinking about it. She'd be wearing a cute little lavender sweater set and crisp khakis instead of these oversized drawstring army pants and her faded blue football tee. He'd loop an arm around her hips and draw her a little closer and order something she knew he'd order because he always ordered it. Then he'd order for her, too. Not because he was an asinine pig, but because he knew she loved hazelnut mochaccino even though it did cost six dollars. Then he'd pay, even though she'd tell him not to. And she'd say something so funny and adorable that he'd look at her, really look at her, and remember how beautiful she was and how much he loved her. Then he'd lean toward her and kiss her on the mouth. No tongue or anything. That would be tacky in the middle of a cafe. His kiss wouldn't be long or filled with questions or expectations because he could kiss her anytime he wanted and he didn't have anything to prove. It would be soft and real and simple, yet mean a thousand

66

loving things. She would kiss him back, but not in a way that was desperate or inexperienced. And then—

Gaia suddenly realized that the boy she was kissing in her mind's eye had transformed. Gone were the dark hair and the suede jacket, replaced by ginger-colored hair that curled around his temples and a preppy gray twill jacket with a corduroy collar. And then she realized that this person who'd barged right into her fantasy was none other than him, the guy from the park—the guy who'd wandered by the chess tables. How did he get here? she demanded of herself stridently. Who invited him?

"Gaia?"

She was so startled and unnerved that she forgot she even had hands, let alone a steaming mug of coffee in one of them. In horror she watched the mug sail from her grasp and the brown sugary stuff leap out of it and land all over the front of that very white, very crisp shirt of her alternate-universe best girlfriend.

The girl screamed.

"Oh, shit," Gaia muttered.

Suddenly everybody burst into motion: The fairly cute boy was grabbing up napkins, the girls were buzzing all over their friend, the other boy was plucking pieces of mug from the mess on the floor.

Of course, Gaia knew that the right thing to do was

apologize a lot, hand the girl a few napkins, make a self-deprecating remark, and offer to get her shirt dry cleaned. But for some reason Gaia did none of those things. She just stood there, gaping like a complete moron.

The offended girl turned on her with narrowed eyes. "*Excuse* me, but you just poured boiling coffee down my shirt."

"I—," Gaia began.

"What the hell is your problem? Are you some kind of idiot? Could you at least apologize?" The girl didn't look so pretty anymore.

"I just—I—I'm really—"

"Hel-*lo?*" the girl demanded. "English? Do you speak English? *Habla español?*" This was apparently humorous to herself and to her friends.

Gaia really had been working up to a sincere and heartfelt apology, but this girl no longer deserved it. "Bitch," Gaia said under her breath. It was completely the wrong thing to do. The worst thing to do, but Gaia had a talent for that.

The ex–pretty girl stiffened. "*What?* Did you just say what I think you said? Who the hell do you think you are?"

Gaia turned away at this point. It was the only thing to do. Gaia heard the girl railing and threatening as she returned to the table and a shell-shocked-looking Ed.

"Gaia, can I ask you one question, just one, and this is really the last?" Ed didn't wait for her to respond.

"Do you get in fights *everywhere* you go?"

"MARCO! OVER HERE."

There's This Girl

Marco glanced around the Chinese restaurant casually, as if he hadn't noticed her the instant he'd walked through the door. Man, she was hot. She was wearing dark denim jeans today and a formfitting pink sweater.

"Hey, how's it going?" he said, treating her to his most charming smile and sitting down across from her.

She returned his smile and for a moment laid her hand on top of his. She was making him dizzy again.

A waiter hustled by and dropped two menus. The place was still noisy, but the after-school crowds were clearing out. Marco checked his hair quickly in the mirror that coated the restaurant's side wall. He was glad he'd refused to shave his head like the other guys. He consulted the filthy laminated menu. Was he supposed to order something? He suspected she hadn't asked him to meet her here because she was hungry.

"So, Marco, tell me how you've been." She was studying him intently and ignoring her menu. She leaned close. He felt a gentle foot on his.

Yes, dizzy. `Really dizzy.` "I've been, uh, pretty cool." He swallowed.

"What's been going on in the park?"

Shit. Was he supposed to be able to think when she was doing that with her foot?

"Not much," he said. "Couple of my buddies got beat up last night."

She looked more interested than concerned. "Who did it?"

"I'm not sure. Some real tough guys, I guess. Some guys who know how to fight." Now her foot was gone, and `he really wanted it back.`

"You'll get them," she said confidently.

He liked the way she said it and the way she looked at him. He nodded real slow, the way his buddy Martin's older brother did. "Bet your ass," he said.

"I need to ask you something," she said.

Where was her foot? Had he done something wrong? "Yeah?"

"There's this girl, a friend of mine. She likes to hang out in the park. I know there's a lot of stuff going on. You know, slashing and whatever."

"I heard about that," he said, his look just as knowing as hers.

"I want to make sure nobody touches her, okay? She's a real sweetheart, and I don't want her getting hurt."

The foot was back. Marco felt a dull buzz in his ears. "Right. Okay. You point her out to me in the park, and I'll take care of it."

The restaurant was nearly empty now. The waiters were sitting at a round table at the very back, eating their own snack. Marco felt a hand on his knee under the table. He had to stifle a groan. He leaned toward her and snaked his hand around the back of her neck. He kissed her hard, and she kissed him back. Her sweet smell combined with the heavy scents of fried wontons and cabbage. Her soft, blissful tongue explored his while the brown Formica table jammed into his stomach. God, he wanted to do it right here.

Suddenly her tongue and her hands were gone and she was standing. "Come on." She gestured at the door. "I know a place we can go."

ED SAW HER THE FOLLOWING AFTER-

noon, sitting at a chess table near the southwestern corner of the park, and his heart sped up a little. The late September breeze was blowing her blond hair out of its messy ponytail and around her face. She'd shed her rumpled jacket to reveal a sleeveless white T-shirt and lithe, sculpted shoulders. Her muscles were defined, but long and graceful. In the sunshine he noticed a few freckles along the bridge of her nose. Her eyes looked less stormy gray and more Caribbean turquoise in this light.

Her opponent at the chessboard was a man in his thirties wearing a baseball cap and a pair of expensive sneakers and appearing to concentrate about ten times harder than she was.

She was wearing an expression he hadn't seen on her before—sort of wide-eyed and distracted. She gazed around. She examined her fingernails. She even appeared to giggle while losing a pawn. Was this actually Gaia?

Ed's legs were for crap, but his eyes were excellent. It was definitely Gaia. Either that or her ditzy twin sister.

He watched in surprise as she lost two more pawns and a knight. Her opponent was looking pretty pleased with himself. He was also allowing his eyes a few breaks from the board to gawk at Gaia. *Pervert,* Ed thought irritably.

Gaia lost another pawn. She might be able to take Bruce Lee in a fight, but she sure sucked at chess. She giggled again. It was a weird sound. Like a parakeet mooing or something. What was up with her?

Gaia's opponent snatched up her rook, and suddenly her manner changed. She focused with a slight frown on the board and started making moves rapidly. The man was smiling at her when she looked up from the board again. He looked so patronizing and full of himself that Ed suspected he was about to ask her out. He hoped Gaia would break his jaw.

Instead she said, "Checkmate," in a matter-of-fact way. Ed read her lips more than actually heard her say it.

Ed watched with blossoming pleasure as the man's face fell and his mouth snapped shut. He looked confused, then a bit suspicious, and then downright sour as he pulled out his wallet and handed over a twenty. As he walked away with his *New York Times* tucked under his arm, his overly youthful baseball cap looked even more absurd. Maybe he was in his forties.

"Go, Gaia," Ed said, wheeling over.

She turned toward his voice, her eyebrows connecting over angry eyes. "What, are you spying on me?"

"No, I'm strolling through the park and stopping to say hi to a friend," he countered. "A paranoid friend." He *was* basically spying, but she didn't need to know that.

Her fierce eyes relented a bit. "Oh."

"I see you discovered how to play chess right there in the middle of the game. Wow."

She cocked her head and almost smiled. "Gee, yeah. Lucky timing, huh?"

"And you made twenty dollars to boot," Ed added.

"Poor bastard didn't know what hit him."

"So you were spying," Gaia accused, but she didn't look mad anymore.

"Maybe a little," he admitted.

She sighed. "You know, Ed, if you learn any more of my secrets, I really will have to kill you." She stood and slung her weather-beaten messenger bag over her shoulder.

He shrugged. "Okay. I guess."

She started walking toward Washington Place, and he followed her.

"But before you do," he continued, "I was wondering, will you go to a party with me tonight?"

She stopped and turned on him, her eyebrows drawing together again. "Are you joking? Of course not."

Since his accident Ed had become a near professional button pusher, but nobody's buttons gave him quite the thrill that Gaia's did. Most people pretended to be civil for far too long. Gaia got spitting mad right away.

"Come on, it's a school party. Allison Rovitz is having it—you know, Heather's friend?"

"Who's Heather?" She was walking again.

"The girl you, uh, met over coffee yesterday," Ed said, quickly catching up with her.

Gaia shook her head in disbelief. "Boy, you sure do make it sound tempting."

Ed nodded. "It might be fun. Besides, it would be

good for you to meet some people," he suggested brightly.

Gaia stopped short and glanced around her. "What is going on here? Are the cameras rolling? Are we secretly starring in an after-school special? *Wheelchair Boy Befriends Angry Orphan Girl*?"

Ed laughed genuinely. "So I'll meet you there at nine? I'll leave the address on your answering machine."

"No!" Gaia almost shouted.

"Why not?" Ed persisted. "You don't have anything else to do."

"Yes, I do," she shot back.

"Like what?" Ed demanded.

She was silent for a few seconds. "Okay, I don't." Gaia glared at him. "Rub it in."

Ed loved the way she pressed her lips together. He loved the way she stood with one hip stuck out. He tried not to be obvious when he admired the way her hair fell perfectly, framing her face and stunning eyes, no matter how hard the wind tore at it. He had heard of this mythic species, beautiful girls who were not conscious of the fact that they were beautiful. He'd seen them represented in movies and on TV—unconvincingly for the most part. He'd read about them in books. But he'd never actually met one in person until Gaia.

"I know why you won't go," Ed said suddenly.

Gaia's patience was waning. "Why?"

"Because Heather's going to be there. You're scared of Heather," Ed stated confidently.

Gaia put her hands on her hips. She looked like she really did want to kill him. "Ed. I am not *scared* of Heather. Trust me."

WHAT IN THE WORLD WAS SHE

doing? Gaia walked extra fast along Seventh Avenue, past Bleecker, past the duplex psychic shop blazing with neon, past the shop (one of many) that pierced you anyplace you could think of, past the bustling gay bars on Christopher Street.

Klutz Girl Strikes Again

As much as she despised getting railroaded into a stupid party full of people she was sure to hate, there was a small but unsquashable part of her that was happy to be out on a Saturday night with someplace to go.

She was going because she wasn't afraid of Heather and because she really didn't have anything else to do.

But she was mostly going because Ed had asked her. He was the first person in her entire high school career who'd cut through her defenses long enough to ask her to a party. He was the first person she hadn't succeeded in scaring off, in spite of her usual efforts.

The party was at 25 West Fifteenth Street. West meant west of Fifth Avenue, but not by much, so she hung a right at Fifteenth. Weeks ago, before she'd even moved here, she had committed a map of lower Manhattan to her near perfect visual memory.

She glanced down at her dark jeans and trashed sneakers. It would be impossible to tell from looking at her that she had spent over an hour getting dressed. She'd put on some mascara, then washed it off. She'd tried on three pairs of nearly identical jeans before finally closing her eyes and grabbing a pair randomly. She'd even changed her socks. Her one lasting concession to beauty was buried under shoes and (carefully chosen) socks—toenail polish in a hue called Cockroach.

As the address grew near, she spied one of the things she most disliked about New York residential life: a doorman. How much did you have to pay a guy to dress up in a butt-ugly polyester suit and embarrassing hat and open your damn door? And where were the door*women*, anyway? She hadn't seen a single one since she'd been here. Maybe she'd change her life's ambition from waitress to doorwoman. "Doorwoman." It sounded like some postmodern urban superhero.

Of course, this particular doorman wanted to know her name and whose apartment she felt privileged enough to visit. "Ed Fargo," she told him. "Visiting Allison Rovitz in apartment 12C."

The doorfellow gave her a once-over. "You don't look like an Ed."

"Tell my parents that. It's a real burden," she told him.

He shook his head, as though wishing he never had to speak to another scruffy, attitude-wielding seventeen-year-old as long as he lived.

He consulted his list, then waved a hand toward the inner lobby. "Go ahead."

"Why aren't there any doorwomen?" she nearly shouted after him as the elevator door closed.

The party in 12C could be heard throughout 12, from what Gaia could tell. She felt her muscles tense at the shrieks of laughter and loud buzz of conversation spilling into the hallway. This was kind of a momentous event. Although her capacity for nervousness was nil, her capacity for insecurity was all there. She tucked some hair behind her ear. She took a deep breath and pushed open the unlocked door.

What was she expecting exactly? Some deeply

narcissistic part of her thought everybody in the place would know that even though she was a junior, she had never been to a real high school party before. They would fall silent and turn to stare at her.

In fact, the only difference between before she had come and after was that there was one more beating heart in a very crowded apartment.

Okeydoke. Yes, here she was. Suddenly she was sure she'd been born with an extra gene for social awkwardness. Time to find the real Ed Fargo and hope he still thought she was entertaining.

She squeezed past a knot of people in the foyer who didn't care about her at all. In the living room she recognized a girl from her history class, a couple of guys who had lockers near hers. Every flat surface was covered with soda cans and beer cans in about equal number. A lot of people were smoking—mostly girls. On a table in the corner were raw carrots and dip and some unappealing chips and salsa. The meager food table was quickly being taken over by cans and cans and cans and makeshift ashtrays. Were anybody's parents here? She'd heard that New York City parents let their kids drink at parties because nobody drove anywhere afterward.

The sweet, suffocating smell of marijuana made its way over. She zeroed in on the little clutch of people passing around the joint before she turned and walked in the opposite direction. She had less than no time for that. Were those kids really so confident in their sanity, they could tempt fate?

When she finally caught sight of Ed's wheelchair in the dining room, she stifled the strong urge to sprint over to him and give him a hug. She walked toward him as slowly as she could manage, as though expecting to encounter hordes of friends and acquaintances along the way.

Gaia was shy. She'd forgotten that about herself, but she was. She was more comfortable beating the crap out of somebody than chatting about the weather. She could be sullen and obnoxious and irritable all day long, but she couldn't think of a single way to start a friendly conversation.

"Hi, Ed," she said lamely, once she was near.

"Gaia! Holy shit!" He smiled big. "You actually came."

"I never miss a party," she said wryly.

"Wow. You look great," he said.

"No, I don't."

"Okay, you don't. Hey, this is Claire." He pointed at a long-haired Asian girl he'd been talking to. "Claire, this is Gaia."

Claire waved and smiled. She was smoking a cigarette.

"And this is Mary. Mary, Gaia, et cetera."

Mary was tall, with wavy red hair. She waved in a

perfunctory way and took a swig of beer.

"You're new, right?" Claire asked.

"Yes," Gaia answered.

"Where are you from?" Claire wanted to know.

Ed shifted in his chair.

Gaia cleared her throat. "Uh. Memphis." It was a lie. She didn't want to play the "oh, really, do you know . . . ?" game about anyplace she had actually lived.

"Really? I have a cousin in Tennessee," Claire responded predictably. "In Johnson City."

"Oh?" Gaia nodded blankly.

Suddenly there was a swell of noise from the direction of the front door. All eyes turned.

"Hey, Gaia, check it out," Ed said. "It's your best friend."

Gaia gave him a mean look. It was Heather and friends—the same group from the cafe plus a couple of Hollywood extras. Heather really was beautiful when she wasn't snarling. Judging from the energy she and her crowd brought into the apartment with them, the party had only started at that moment.

Claire studied the group carefully. "I guess Heather didn't bring her boyfriend. Too bad. That guy is altogether hot."

Mary looked unimpressed. "He's a big college man. He goes to NYU. What's his name again? Carrie says

81

he doesn't like coming to high school parties."

Of course Heather would have a gorgeous, snotty boyfriend who was in college. Of course. Gaia could only imagine what kind of asshole the guy must be to choose Heather as a girlfriend.

"I guess we're blessed even to have Heather," Gaia mumbled, instantly cursing herself for being snide.

Mary glanced at Gaia appreciatively. "Yes. I mean, who better to make the rest of us feel fat and friendless?"

Gaia laughed and felt a surge of . . . something. Optimism, was it? Hope? Social acceptance? She wasn't sure exactly—it was so unfamiliar. But here she was, maladjusted freak-thing Gaia Moore, gabbing with people who could very easily have been her friends. It was utterly alien, but not in a bad way. Only now she had to try to think of something else to say.

Heather led the wave of party energy through the living room toward the dining room and, no doubt, the kitchen, where the beers were waiting. Gaia wondered a bit warily if Heather would recognize her.

As it turned out, she did.

"Oh, my God!" Heather shrieked, wheeling around to face Gaia straight on. "It's Klutz Girl! What are you doing here?"

Suddenly all eyes really were on Gaia. Her social success was evaporating quickly.

"I would watch out for this girl," Heather warned loudly. "Don't give her anything to eat or drink, or you'll end up with it on your shirt."

Heather's friends tittered loyally.

"Who let you in here?" Heather demanded.

Gaia studied the small place on the girl's neck just below her chin. `She could deliver one swift blow to that spot and put her out.`

"I invited her," Ed said, filling the awkward silence at least momentarily.

"Excuse me, *Ed*," Heather said nastily. "I didn't realize it was your party."

"I didn't realize it was yours," Ed responded.

Allison, the actual party giver, was watching the scene unfold with the rest of them. Heather turned to her.

"Al, did you realize this bitch was coming to your party?"

Poor Allison looked frightened.

"Don't worry about it, Allison. I'm going," Gaia said. She strode through the apartment without looking back.

It didn't matter so much that she was back on the outside, Gaia consoled herself as she opened the front door and passed through it. This was Heather's time. Let her have it. Ten years from now Heather's awfulness would have caught up with her, and `she'd`

be a disgruntled wretch pining for
the glory days. Let her have high school. Gaia
was holding out for something better.

Gaia stood sullenly at the elevator bank and
punched the down arrow. Mercifully the elevator
doors opened right away.

At least she was back in her comfort zone.

Some things I like:
Chess
Slurpees
Road Runner cartoons
Eye boogers
W. B. Yeats
Ed

Some things I don't like:
Heather
Ella
Skim milk
Butterflies
Baking soda toothpaste
Myself

A thing I hate:
My dad

Rain plastered thick dark cords of hair to his forehead. Now that it was no longer perfect, she could see it was beautiful.

meeting sam moon

"HI, ZOLOV."

The old man squinted at Gaia for a few seconds before he recognized her, then he smiled.

People Like Him

"Hey, Curtis," she said to Zolov's opponent. "Where's Renny?"

The fifteen-year-old chess fixture shrugged. "He hasn't been coming around anymore."

Gaia nodded and looked for a free table. She was happy to be there, even without Renny. She was glad that the bleak sky threatened rain and that the air was finally turning cold. All that warm sunshine seemed to demand perkiness and pastel-colored clothing.

She watched Curtis leaning far over the board, studying Zolov's sequence. She almost laughed to herself. She couldn't believe she was watching an ancient Jewish man in a threadbare wool overcoat teaching the Ruy Lopez opening to a black kid dressed head to toe in Tommy.

She turned her affectionate gaze to the right, and suddenly her mood went into free fall.

Him.

What the hell was *he* doing here?

God, he was good-looking. He was wearing that same gray jacket, this time with a pair of jeans and just the right shade of dark, perfectly scuffed leather shoes.

Go away, she ordered him silently. Go back to where you belong.

He didn't go away. Instead he came very close, and her mouth felt dry. Why did she all of a sudden care that she hadn't run a brush through her hair that morning? So she looked like a homeless person. What was it to him?

Oh, shit. He was looking at the board set in front of her. His eyes glanced over the empty chair across from her.

He was stopping!

He was sitting down!

He was staring right at her!

Then she felt mad. What, was he on some kind of field trip from normal-people land? Was he the Jane Goodall of the popular set, here to take notes?

It didn't help that just a few days before he'd appeared *uninvited* in her romantic fantasy and *kissed* her, for God's sake. "Do you want to play?" he asked, just like that.

He wanted to play her! What! Didn't he know that it was illegal in a cosmic sense for a guy who looked like him even to get near a board? The gods of social stratification would zap him but good.

Fine. If he insisted on turning the world upside down, what could she do? She'd play him. She'd point out to him which pieces moved which way as though she'd only recently learned herself, and then she'd hustle as much money out of him as possible. She could probably get two or three fast games out of him before the rain began to fall.

"Hello?" He scrunched down a little in his chair to try to gain eye contact.

"What?" she blurted out irritably.

"Do you want to play?"

She was so flustered, she couldn't pluck one arrow from her quiver of hustling tricks. "Fine."

"Don't feel like you have to."

Oh, wasn't he just honorable.

"No, it's fine. I only just started playing myself." God, she sounded wooden. Her acting really needed some work.

"Okay. You start, right?"

"No, I mean, I think. Well, we usually—" Dammit. She took a black pawn and a white one and mixed them up behind her back. She enclosed each in a fist and stuck them out toward him. "You pick."

He pointed to her left hand, and she produced a white pawn.

"You go first," she said.

He looked tentative. "It's kind of a custom to play for money here, isn't it?"

Custom? Yes, it is, O Great Doctor of Losers.

"Usually," was what she said.

"How much?"

90

"I dunno. Twenty?"

He blew out his breath. "Wow. Okay."

"Okay."

What was it about him that bothered her so? That he was the kind of guy who'd never look twice at a girl like her? Okay, well, there was that.

She couldn't find major fault with his wardrobe. It wasn't like he was wearing a Rolex or anything.

She didn't hate him just because he looked like . . . that. Even she wasn't quite that shallow or rabidly judgmental.

What was it, then?

He was so . . . confident. That was the big problem. Here, in her place, where he had no right to be, he was so goddamned sure of himself. He probably had no sense of humor, least of all about himself.

She couldn't wait to kick his ass.

The Fire Hose Test

SAM MOON WASN'T SURE WHAT TO make of this girl. He'd sat down at her board because she was new, and that always represented an opportunity.

Well, okay. That wasn't the only reason. Another reason

was that in spite of her somewhat disastrous personal hygiene, she was pretty. A pretty girl at a chessboard wasn't your everyday sight. He hadn't even realized just how pretty until he was within a couple of feet and had a chance to really look.

Some friends of his from high school used to rate a girl's attractiveness by what was known as the fire hose test. If the girl's looks were all about makeup and hair and clothes, she'd look like crap if you shot a fire hose directly in her face from point-blank range. A genuinely pretty girl would still look good. Now, this girl here looked as though a hose actually had blasted her, so there was no leap of imagination necessary to know that she passed the test. Passed it with an A, he decided as she bit her lip and tapped impatiently on the queen's pawn.

"Okay, here goes," he said, thumping to E4.

She predictably took E5.

Pretty as she was, though, she was annoying. She obviously thought she knew what she was doing—under her truly flimsy pretense that she didn't. Maybe she'd won some high school tournament or something. Whoop-de-do. She had no business taking over a table here.

And why was she glaring at him like that? What had he done to piss her off?

He'd give her hope for a few

minutes and then shut her down. He could really use the twenty bucks.

He flinched a little as a clap of thunder roared overhead. The air felt heavy with coming rain. He'd give her a very few minutes.

SHE WAS SURPRISED. NOT ALARMED

The Rain Starts

or anything. Just a little surprised.

She hadn't expected him to respond so adroitly to her opening. They'd progressed quickly to the midgame, and she'd achieved almost no advantage. Now the wind was blowing in soot-colored clouds and thunder rolled through the sky and she was looking at the possibility of a complicated endgame.

He wasn't the doofus she'd imagined. That much she had to admit. She hadn't thought it possible to have perfect orthodonture and a good haircut and also be great at chess, but then, she was only seventeen. There had to be a few things left to learn.

She wasn't pretending anything anymore. She was too focused on the board. All attempts at inane, gee-whiz posturing had fallen away.

His manner had changed, too. His concentration on the game was so full, he let out these `tiny, almost inaudible grunts` every so often. He had this funny tick of drumming his fingers against his bottom lip before he made each move. She couldn't exactly remember what about him had seemed so self-satisfied.

She unintentionally knocked her knee against his under the table. He glanced up.

"Sorry," she mumbled. Her face felt warm. `She prayed it wasn't actually turning pink.`

His hair had fallen over his forehead. She couldn't read the expression in his eyes.

She commanded her own eyeballs back to the board.

A fat, cold raindrop landed on her scalp. Damn. Why couldn't she just finish this up?

`TINY DROPS OF SWEAT WERE` collecting in his hairline, bleeding into the raindrops slapping on his head. Drops dribbled down his neck, and his sweater was starting to smell funky. `He was concentrating too hard to care.`

More Rain

The girl moved her king's bishop.

Ugh. He closed his eyes briefly in disgust at himself. Why hadn't he seen the pin? What was wrong with him?

He was forced to defend with a knight. That was a tempo lost.

The main thing wrong was that this girl was totally shocking. She was not good. She was very, very, very good. Where had she come from? She couldn't be from around here because he felt sure he would have met her in tournaments before. She had to be an internationally ranked player. Either that or he suddenly stunk.

He'd sacrificed material to no avail. She'd dismantled one of his most trusted combinations. But even so, it was a really exciting game. Her play was not only smart and challenging, but unorthodox. Who had taught her? Who was she?

He glanced up at her. Her light hair was soaked flat with rain. Her blue eyes darkened to mirror the sky, and they were steady with concentration. She was somewhere around sixteen or seventeen years old. He hadn't detected any accent, which would have at least helped to explain how she was so good. It seemed like foreign players always dominated in competition.

The harsh, defiant set of her face had dissolved now. Self-consciousness had fallen away as her focus intensified. Her eyes were lovely, rimmed with long, dark (wet) lashes. Her cheekbones were exceptionally prominent for a person her age. Her face was open now and almost sweet. Raindrops stood on her bare arms, and her T-shirt was . . .

She snapped her rook into the center of the action.

Okay, better not to look anymore. He was screwing up here. Lucky for him there weren't many beautiful girls who played chess, or he'd probably be bowling right now.

His heart was speeding with nervousness and excitement. He could feel warmth radiating from her legs, so close to his. His palms felt tingly.

Think about chess, you idiot, he ordered himself.

YES, ALARMING. IT WAS NOW

officially alarming. He was up a knight and coming on strong. How had she misjudged him so badly?

He was probably the best person she had ever played except for her father, maybe, and Zolov, who was nuts.

She studied his face. He was older than she, but not by much. Maybe twenty. He had to be an international master at least. She wasn't on the chess circuit, but she knew an extraordinary player from a good one.

And as he played he was becoming real to her. His

little ticks were so peculiar. The skin around his fingernails was ragged from being picked at too much. Tiny blue veins zigzagged under the surface of the transparent skin beneath his eyes. Rain plastered thick dark cords of hair to his forehead. Now that it was no longer perfect, she could see it was beautiful.

Suddenly she had this powerful urge to touch the pale skin above his wrist, where she could see his pulse thumping. She stared transfixed at that spot, feeling that her own heart was beating out the same rhythm.

Oh, Gaia. She almost groaned out loud. Get ahold of yourself, girl.

This was an inexplicable reaction she was having to him. Was she profoundly low on sleep, maybe? When had she last eaten?

Another bolt of lightning blazed through the sky. Maybe it was the plunging barometer? The electricity in the air?

When she looked back at the board, she felt dizzy and disoriented. A chess game like this one meant holding a million teetering moves and possibilities in your mind, and here all at once she'd dropped them. The crowd of pieces left on the board had gone from a thrillingly complex and significant battle in one second to a meaningless jumble the next.

Blood rushed to her face. She tried to kick-start her

memory, to patch together her lost strategy. But it was as though the whole thing had existed in someone else's mind.

Rain blanketed them. Steam rose from the surrounding pavement. Goose bumps pricked up and down her arms. Why had neither of them suggested giving up this ridiculous contest and going inside?

He was looking at her. Not silently, impatiently demanding her next move, as she would expect. Just looking. Looking for something. `Rain dotted his eyelashes with diamonds,` formed rivers down his cheeks.

His eyes had taken hers, and she couldn't look away.

Then she felt something grab hold of her chest. It wasn't fear. It couldn't be. But what was it? She had to get out of there.

With a flick of her index finger she felled her precious king. "I'm sorry," she murmured. "I have to go." She got to her feet, reaching into her bag for her wallet. He stood, too. She fumbled the wet leather and pulled out a twenty-dollar bill, then jammed it in his palm.

"No. No," he told her. The bill fluttered to the ground, but neither of them stooped to get it. She was already walking, and he was hurrying alongside her, confused, surprised, `stammering for a word.`

"W-Wait. Please," he whispered.

She was almost running. In her sneakers the water squished around her toes. The rain was so loud, it filled up all of her senses.

She hurried from him and from the strange perception that a million frozen feelings were about to thaw and the flood would certainly drown her.

HE WATCHED HER GO, FEELING A

Bottomless

terrible tightness in his throat. What had she done to him?

It had all happened in that moment, when he'd met her eyes and, like a mystic, seemed to see her past and future. Her past was haunting, marked by bottomless wounds, and the future was terrifying because it included him.

For the last
twenty-four
hours his
mind had
behaved
more like a
badly
trained
dog on a
too long
leash.

no

bad

dogs

"I WISH MY NAME WERE FARGO."

Gaia was walking so fast, Ed Fargo was having a hard time keeping up with her. Her movements were strangely jerky, and her mouth was going a mile a minute.

The Right to Ask

"Why is that?" he had to practically shout at her because she kept getting ahead.

"It's a cool name," she said.

"You could marry me if you asked really nicely," he proposed.

"Yeah, right."

"What's the matter with Moore?" he asked as they rounded the corner of Charles Street and Hudson.

"I don't know." Gaia's eyes weren't quite focused. She wasn't completely paying attention to what she was saying or where her feet were going. "Moore . . . Less," she mused absently. "Hey, Gaia Less. Guileless. I like that."

He was getting annoyed. "Gaia, would you please slow down? I'm kind of in a wheelchair here."

She glanced back at him. "Oh. Sorry," she mumbled.

In her expression Ed saw traces of impatience but no embarrassment, no pity. He loved her.

"Guileless," he continued. "What does it mean?"

"You know, without guile."

"What does guile mean?"

"Deceit, duplicity, `dishonesty`."

He slowed down a bit more. "Gaia, how do you know these things?"

She shrugged. "I'm smart."

"And modest, too."

"Modesty is a waste of time," she pronounced.

"I'll keep that in mind."

They passed Zuli's bakery and the tiny store that sold homemade ravioli. A woman passed them, pushing a toy poodle perched in a baby carriage. Gaia didn't even seem to notice.

"For somebody so smart, you sure bombed the physics quiz today," Ed pointed out.

"Yeah, well. Parabolas are so simple, they're boring."

Ed laughed. "I'll have to remember that excuse to tell my parents the next time I get a D."

Suddenly Gaia stopped and grabbed his shoulder. "What's that?"

"Ouch," he said, and she lessened her grip on his clavicle. "What?"

"That music." She yanked him around the corner. "Do you hear it? Where's it coming from?"

He pointed across the street. "That band we heard at Ozzie's. They practice in the basement of that building."

"How do you know?"

"Because I'm smart."

Gaia rolled her eyes. "What's the name of the band?"

"Huh?"

"The name of the band?"

"Fearless. They're always playing around the neighborhood. Ozzie's on Friday afternoons, Dock's on Wednesday evenings, and fully amplified at The Flood most Saturday nights. Our local OTB takes bets on when they'll actually get signed."

Gaia had completely tuned out.

"Ha-ha. That was a funny joke," Ed pointed out.

Gaia nodded dumbly. "Fearless?" she asked. "No way."

Ed shrugged. "No reason to lie." He was bored with this conversation.

Gaia paused for another moment as slow lyrics drifted up to the street.

". . . And I'm a stone/falling deeper/into your black, black ocean/let me drown . . ."

Gaia was off again like a shot.

"Where are we going now?" he asked, almost breathless in his effort to catch up.

"I don't know. We're strolling."

"Oh."

They strolled for a while in silence.

"Hey, wait a minute," he said, slowing down warily as they sailed past Sixth Avenue without a pause.

"What?"

"I have a feeling we're strolling to the park."

"So?"

"I don't want to go to the park."

Gaia looked annoyed. "Why not?"

"Because innocent people are getting slashed there practically every day. Because there are evil bald guys carving swastikas into trees. Do you watch the news?"

"Ed, it's broad daylight."

"That doesn't stop you."

"Stop *me*? Stop me from what?" she asked.

"From finding people to get into fights with," he responded.

She looked slightly abashed.

"Let's walk down Broadway toward Soho," he suggested.

Gaia was quiet, fidgeting with the threads hanging off the bottom of her jacket, but she did follow him at least.

"What's the matter?" he asked.

"I'm trying to think of a way to apologize for the other night," she explained.

"What do you mean?" he asked.

"For ruining that party you invited me to."

"You didn't ruin it," he said comfortingly. "We all had a perfectly good time after you left."

She kicked his wheel.

"Gaia, Jesus!" He regained control of his chair. "I was just kidding. I left right away. I tried to catch you, but you were too fast for me."

She slowed down a little. "Really?"

"Yeah. Anyway, it wasn't you. It was Heather who was out of control."

"You think so?"

He laughed. "For once, yeah."

"She's such a raving bitch," Gaia declared.

Ed shook his head thoughtfully. "There's actually more to her than that."

"You know her well?" Gaia asked, clearly surprised.

"Sure. I went out with her for a few months."

Gaia stopped cold in the middle of Bleecker Street. A truck honked loudly.

"Gaia, go!" Ed commanded, and she did.

"No way," she stated when they were safely on the other side of the street.

Ed looked at her peevishly. "You say that too much."

"Sorry. But I mean it. No way."

Ed held up his hands. "It's true. Heather and I went out for a while before my accident."

"Wow." Gaia was obviously struggling to absorb this. They walked for three blocks in silence.

"Hey, Gaia?" he asked finally.

"Yeah?"

"Are you ever going to ask me why I'm in a wheel-chair?"

"No," she said.

"Why not?"

"Because if I do, you would have the right to ask

where I lived before, or why I'm a black belt in karate, or what happened to my parents."

"Oh," he said. "Okay."

And they kept walking.

SAM WASN'T WALKING THROUGH THE

That Girl

park because he wanted to see that girl. He didn't want to see that girl. She was trouble.

And he had a girlfriend. That was the more important point. He had a girlfriend, and he was late to meet her, and even though it was almost dark and he knew he shouldn't be cutting through the park with all of the crap that was going on, he was doing it anyway.

But not because he wanted to see that girl.

Although he was running late, he could count on the fact that Heather would be at least twenty minutes later and that she would show up with a noisy entourage. She would be all out of breath and apologize fervently for being late, as though her lateness depended on such a rare and extenuating matrix of once-in-a-lifetime circumstances that it could never possibly happen again. And the next time she would be just as late.

107

He should just tell her it bugged him. He was basically a punctual person, and he didn't appreciate all the dramatic entrances. He didn't love the entourage, either.

But if he did tell her, she would probably listen and stop, at least for a while. And then where would he be? What could he complain about? What reason would he have for breaking up with her?

Ooh. That last bit just slipped out. He hadn't totally meant to have that thought.

Heather was gorgeous. Heather was smart. Heather was confident and funny. Heather, though only a senior in high school, was the envy of all his college friends. Heather was even capable, when she let go of her own mythology for a few minutes, of being a decent person.

But these were not good reasons for going out with a person, and he knew that in his heart. So why did he stay with her?

That was complicated. It hinged on a lot of stuff about his old life and his old self, and he didn't feel like thinking about it just now.

His thoughts wandered back to the girl. *The girl.* He'd certainly never thought so much about a person whose name he didn't know. His mind slipped back to her every time he gave it a moment's freedom. He kept picturing her eyes, infinite as the sky. His mind used to be so obedient, so precise. For the last twenty-four hours it had behaved more like a badly trained dog on a too long leash.

Did she live in the neighborhood? Where did she go to school? Would she come back to the chess tables in the park? If she did, would he try to talk to her? Would he ask her to play again?

His heart rate was rising at the very thought.

Okay, enough.

He was so distracted, he veered off the path and nearly crashed into a sign. He looked up at it.

Curb Your Dog, it said.

IF SHE SAW HIM, SHE WOULD

A Mistake

just change course. Gaia's eyesight was good. She would spot him before he spotted her, before any interaction needed to take place.

Strictly speaking, walking through the park wasn't the smartest way to avoid him. But it was the fastest way to get home after she dropped Ed off at his house. And now that it was dark, it was by far her best chance for getting jumped or slashed by one of those neo-Nazi bastards.

She wasn't going to go out of her way for this guy.

Usually the park was still busy at this hour when the weather was good, but tonight it was nearly deserted. People were spooked by the reports of slashing. Lots of kids had been talking about it in school that day.

Gaia paused to take off her jacket and tie it around her waist. Slashing was such a random, mean-spirited brand of violence and the whole Nazi mythology so profoundly hateful, she was particularly eager to draw it out. She liked to think of herself as a trap. A walking trap.

As she dawdled in the wooded area near the dog run, she heard whispers. Oh, man. Could it be this easy? She strained her ears to hear and ambled a tiny bit closer. She couldn't really make out the conversation, but she did see the flash of a knife. Not a blade this time, a real knife. Four guys were huddled together, probably plotting their next attack.

Me! Me! Choose me! she thought. Jeez, what a wacko she'd become. She made as much noise as possible while still appearing naive and oblivious. She really hoped none of them would recognize her from a previous run-in.

She walked as slowly as she could without actually stopping and yet within moments found herself on the open, brightly lit sidewalk of Washington Square West untouched. So it wasn't her lucky night. Maybe tomorrow.

She felt sulky and suddenly quite alone. It was weird, this business of having a friend, she decided, thinking of her long, aimless walk with Ed. It made being alone less fun.

Gaia looked up and saw a figure crossing the street toward her. It was a girl, and she appeared to be heading straight into the park. Gaia's mind flashed to the knife she'd just seen, and she bent her steps toward the girl. She didn't realize until she was a few feet away exactly which girl it was.

"Is that Gaia?" a not-friendly voice demanded.

It was Heather. This really wasn't Gaia's lucky night. Gaia was immediately struck by the fact that Heather was alone. Where was the famed boyfriend? Where were the adoring, fashionably dressed friends?

"Listen, Heather," she began matter-of-factly, "you probably shouldn't—"

Heather bristled and walked on. "Leave me alone, bitch."

Gaia wasn't sure what to do. Follow her? "Heather, I really don't think—"

"Get away from me," Heather snapped. "I don't care what you think."

Gaia had intended to be helpful, but now she was angry. Let the stupid girl get slashed. It wasn't Gaia's responsibility. If anybody deserved it, Heather did.

Gaia's temper smoldered as she continued across the

street. She was just about to turn onto Waverly when she spotted more familiar faces. They were all three Heather acolytes. One was named Tina, she believed. The other was a girl whose name she didn't know, and the third was the good-looking guy from the cafe.

This time she was just going to keep walking, but one of them stopped her.

"You're Gaia, right?" the non-Tina girl asked.

"Yeah."

"Have you seen Heather, by any chance?"

Gaia looked from one to the next. This didn't seem like a trick or anything. "Yeah, I just saw her about a minute ago. She was cutting through the park." Gaia gestured in the general direction.

"Thanks," they all said. They weren't oozing warmth, but they seemed perfectly friendly.

"Hey, uh . . . Tina," Gaia called over her shoulder.

They all stopped and turned.

"You really shouldn't go through the park. There's a bunch of whacked-out guys in there, and at least one of them has a knife."

Tina and her friends looked surprised and alarmed in varying degrees. "Shit. Okay. Right."

"Thanks," the guy said again.

Gaia watched with satisfaction as they skirted the park, staying on the lighted sidewalk.

See? She'd done her good deed. She wasn't a bad person. She could go home in peace.

Sometimes I dream I'm skating. Not a ramp or half pipe like one of those Mountain Dew commercials. My feet are planted on a board, and I'm steaming along straight and steady. First it's maybe a sidewalk and then a street and then it becomes a highway of at least four lanes. Then the board transforms into an airplane, and I'm in the cockpit. It's a passenger plane, I guess, but I'm not aware of having responsibility for any passengers. I have this sense of excitement and anticipation as I accelerate, gaining intense, powerful speed. Fast, fast, faster. I feel sure I've passed that speed you need to leave the ground. But I'm still on the highway. I'm still zooming past houses and fields and forests.

The highway bends slowly into a curve. It curves again. I become conscious of road signs—Deer Crossing, Boulders Falling, you know those. And I begin to pay

attention to them. I realize I've
adjusted my speed from about a
million miles an hour to just a
few above the speed limit. I peer
into the side mirror of my airplane to check for cops.

After a while it's a forgone
conclusion that I won't be taking
off. Just a plain fact, like any
of the others we learn to live
with. I'll be following signs on
the highway in my jumbo jet,
built to fly thirty-five-thousand
feet above our blue Earth.

And she
followed
them through
the exit,
distinctly
aware of
the huge
cloud of
hate
behind
her.

no peace

BEFORE HE PASSED THROUGH THE

An Angry Place

school entrance the next morning, Ed knew there was something wrong. The halls were extra crowded, but not loud enough. Kids were gathered in little clots held together by hushed voices. A lot of eyes were darting around. The air had that heightened energy, that guilty pleasure of tragedy.

"What's going on?" he asked the first person he came to, a vaguely familiar girl with a magenta crew cut.

"God, it's so scary," she said. He could tell she was trying to rein herself in to project the right amount of sobriety. "Heather Gannis got shot in Washington Square last night. She's in the ICU at St. Vincent's."

"Jesus," Ed muttered. That sick zingy feeling, as if his blood were suddenly carbonated, started under his stomach and spread through his limbs. "Do they know who did it?"

The girl was already gone, so he wheeled up to the nearest group. "What happened? Who did it? Is she going to be okay?" he burst in loudly. He didn't feel like being measured and coy.

The five faces above him were practically caricatures of gravity. "The police claim they have suspects, but there hasn't been an arrest," a black-haired girl

116

answered. "Nobody knows exactly what happened. They think it was some kind of gang activity— this white supremacist group—connected to the slashings."

"But it was a shooting," he argued.

"No, it wasn't. It was a stabbing," a guy said.

"A stabbing?" Ed asked.

At least two of them nodded.

"She's in ICU?" Ed continued, feeling impatient. He needed this information to slow his speeding heart. He actually cared about the facts and their implications, unlike most of the rumormongers.

"In a coma," another girl added.

He sighed in frustration. "We're talking about Heather?"

Black-Haired Girl's face closed in annoyance. "Obviously," she snapped.

Ed wheeled away, shaking his head. He had a feeling that if he talked to every one of the groups in the hallway, he would get a slightly different story from each.

This was surreal and terrifying. Heather wasn't the kind of girl who got shot or stabbed or stepped into a hospital for any reason but to visit her grandmother after elective surgery. He couldn't help but think of Heather's parents and sisters.

His experience on Mercer Street with Gaia came

back to him in full detail—the knife, the fear, the chaos. How had the world become so malignant? New York City was transforming from the eccentric but comfortable place where he'd grown up into the dangerous, angry place he'd always heard about.

"Attention, students." Principal Hickey's voice came blasting through the loudspeaker. "There will be an all-school assembly this morning directly after homeroom. Attendance is mandatory." Even the principal's solemnity sounded phony and exaggerated.

Ed wheeled slowly to homeroom, his mind ricocheting from big, appropriate thoughts about crime and death and police investigations to weird little inappropriate thoughts like whether Heather was wearing one of those hospital gowns that tied in the back, and, if so, who had undressed her. Then he felt guilty about having that second category of thoughts and tried not to have them, which took up a certain amount of mental energy in itself.

He was sitting in homeroom, trying not to have any thoughts at all, when he overheard Gaia's name mentioned. He didn't turn because he didn't want to disrupt the conversation.

"Gaia Moore saw what?" asked Becca Miller, a girl with long, supercurly hair who always sat behind him.

"She saw the guy with the knife in the park," responded Samantha something, a friend of Becca's, in a voice hushed but intoxicated with the thrill of conveying important information.

"What are you talking about?" Becca asked.

"Gaia was in the park just a few minutes before Heather got slashed, and she saw the guys who did it."

"Tell me you're kidding. How do you know this?" Becca demanded.

"Tina Lynch told Carrie she was with Brian and Melanie last night and they saw Gaia, right outside the park. Gaia told Tina she'd just seen Heather going into the park. But Gaia warned Tina and those other guys not to go into the park—that she'd just seen a guy with a knife."

Ed's mind was spinning with the number of names and personal pronouns, but also with the ramifications of what he was hearing. Gaia was involved. Of course she was. If trouble was magnetic north, then Gaia's head was a huge chunk of iron. In the short time Ed had known her, he'd almost gotten killed, watched three thugs get demolished, witnessed two catfights, seen one slashing victim's family crying on the news, and now learned his ex-girlfriend was in a coma.

Of course Gaia was there. How could it be otherwise?

But what had she done, exactly?

He couldn't trust these girls or really anybody but Gaia to tell him what had happened. And Gaia would give him the unvarnished truth. He and Gaia were alike in that way. They both took special satisfaction in telling you the one true thing you really, really didn't want to hear.

GAIA HADN'T PAID MUCH ATTENTION

to all the whispering at first. She had learned to be good at ignoring it. In her experience whispering either:

1. Didn't include her
   or
2. Was about her

And in neither case could she take part.

So it wasn't until the assembly that she heard the news.

"As many of you know, a tragedy befell our school community last night," Principal Hickey intoned to the enormous, totally silent all-school assembly. Gaia should have known right then that something was seriously wrong by the simple fact that people were actually listening to the guy. "Heather Gannis was slashed in Washington Square Park last night. She lost a great deal of blood before she was discovered by friends and fellow students. She is in critical condition at St. Vincent's Hospital. I know you all join me in sending Heather and her family our . . ."

He kept talking, of course, but Gaia didn't hear. An ugly, evil creature with smelly fur and sharp fangs was gnawing on her intestines, and that was hard to ignore.

Her thoughts from the previous night returned to her word for word.

Let the stupid girl get slashed. If anybody deserved it, Heather did.

But I didn't mean that, a small, panicky voice inside Gaia claimed pitifully. I meant to warn her. I was going to, but—

Shut up! Gaia screamed at her own mind. If she'd had a tire iron, she would have clubbed herself with it. She'd heard too many excuses in her life. She couldn't stomach them, especially not from herself.

The principal was droning on about safety precautions now, and the attention he'd commanded was lost. Kids were talking, whispering.

Gaia realized when she looked up that hundreds of eyes were bouncing around and landing on her again and again. What could she expect? She had known exactly what Heather was walking into, and at least three other people in this very auditorium knew that she knew. She could have saved Heather, and she didn't. She let a petty, stupid conflict, probably based more on her own jealousy than anything else, destroy another person's life.

The fanged creature devoured several more feet of intestine and moved on to the lining of her stomach.

Everybody was standing up and milling around. Gaia guessed that the assembly was over. Numbly she got to her feet and let herself be moved along by the crowd. Just beyond the doors, in the lobby of the auditorium, the puffy, tear-stained face of Tina Whats-her-name bobbed into view.

Gaia stopped.

If only shame were part of fear. If only self-loathing were part of fear.

If Gaia were a better person, she would have offered some comforting words. She didn't. She remained the person she was.

"What *happened* last night?" Tina asked her in a voice tinged with hysteria. "What was Heather *thinking* going in there alone? Did you talk to her? Did you tell her what you'd seen in the park?"

Gaia realized Tina wasn't judging her. Not yet. She was inviting Gaia to commiserate, to take part in the why-oh-why-oh-why that churned her restless mind. She wanted to think the best of Gaia.

Other people had gathered. Some were comforting,

others being comforted. Several friends clutched Tina supportively.

"I—I didn't," Gaia said stiffly. "I didn't warn her."

Tina's face took a few moments to register this. "What do you mean?"

Gaia had to remind herself to breathe. "I mean I didn't tell Heather about the guy with the knife."

"Why not? Why didn't you?" Tina's shiny doe eyes turned into slitted bat eyes.

The crowd of people readied their looks of horror but held off, waiting for an explanation.

A part of Gaia wanted to describe to all these eager sets of ears how Heather told her off, called her names, but she knew it would sound just like the lame excuse it was. She deserved the blame for this. She would take it without flinching. "I just didn't."

Tina was crying now. "God, what's the matter with you? You warned us but not her? Do you hate Heather so much that you wanted her to get killed?"

Amid the loathing, judging faces, Gaia suddenly spied blue. Dark blue uniforms, dark blue hats. The fragments resolved into two policemen.

Could you actually get arrested for failing to warn someone? Gaia wondered irrationally. The faces parted to let the police come through. The hum of voices in the lobby grew to a roar.

"Are you Gaia Moore?" one of them, a tall black man, asked.

123

"Yes," she answered. Were they going to handcuff her right here, in front of the entire student body?

"Would you please come with us to the precinct? We have some questions to ask you."

The man asked it like a real question, not a rhetorical one. He waited for her answer; he didn't slap on any handcuffs.

"Yes," she said. "Of course." And she followed them through the exit, distinctly aware of the huge cloud of hate behind her.

That was one plus about profound self-loathing. Nobody could hate you worse than you hated yourself.

Different but the Same

"AND AT APPROXIMATELY WHAT hour did you see Heather Gannis approaching the park from the west side?"

Gaia couldn't quite pull her eyes from that vague middle distance to focus them on the detective sitting across from her.

"About seven forty-five, I guess."

"You guess?"

"I wasn't wearing a watch at the time. I'd dropped off a friend at First Avenue and

Fourth Street at seven-thirty and then walked directly to the park on my way home. I figure it would take roughly fifteen minutes to walk from First and Fourth to Washington Square West," Gaia replied. She was on auto-answer. It felt to her that she'd already fielded at least a hundred thousand questions, and they hadn't even gotten to the meaty part.

"Fine. And what exactly happened when you saw Heather?" the detective asked. Detective Anderson was his name. He was in his forties probably, with thinning medium-brown hair, slightly pocked skin, and pale eyes. He looked just as tired and harassed as detectives always looked on those realistic cop shows.

Gaia let out her breath slowly. Did he really want the catty details? "I—um—sort of stopped her, and she—uh—" Gaia broke off and glanced at the detective. "See, Heather and I weren't exactly on friendly terms. A few days ago I spilled hot coffee on her, and since then—"

"Since then?" he prompted.

"We've had, uh, words, you could say," Gaia explained.

"I see." The detective nodded. "So you disliked Heather, did you?"

"I was told she is still alive."

"Excuse me. I'm sorry. Yes." Detective Anderson looked genuinely awkward. "You dislike Heather," he amended.

"That's a tough thing to say about a girl in a coma, sir," Gaia pointed out.

125

"Right. Yes. Okay." He sighed and shifted in his chair. "But as of yesterday evening, you and Heather were enemies?"

"Am I a suspect in this case?" Gaia asked, staring him dead in the eye.

He cleared his throat and shifted again. He moved his mouth a few times before any sounds came out. "Uh, no. You're not."

"Okay." She settled back in her chair. She knew she wasn't a suspect, because she knew they'd assembled a police lineup, because she'd overheard it being discussed when Detective Anderson was hunting around for cream for his coffee. She knew he was trying to pretend like she was so he could manipulate and intimidate her more easily.

"So, back to the story," she said, chilly but helpful. "Heather told me to leave her alone, and I did. Less than a minute after walking past her, I ran into her friends—Tina and two other people whose names I don't know. I think you know the story from there. After that I walked home. You have all that information already."

Detective Anderson looked even more harassed and tired. "Right. Now am I to understand that you did not warn Heather as to what you'd just seen moments before in the park?"

"No, sir."

"But you did warn the three people you saw subsequently?"

"Yes, sir."

He waited for an explanation that didn't come. After a while he stood up. "All right, Gaia, that's it for the moment. Would you come with me? I'd like you to look at a lineup."

She followed him through the precinct to the viewing room, listening to directions, warnings, assurances associated with a lineup. She felt floaty and distant as she took in the hodgepodge of beat-up office furniture, papers, files, boards, maps, clippings, notices, charts, the pathetic set of twigs on a windowsill that had probably been a live plant a decade or two ago.

It was so different in particulars, but so generally the same as the precinct where she'd spent the night as a twelve-year-old in San Rafael, California, after her mother was murdered, when they couldn't figure out anyplace else to put her.

"GAIA! GAIA! ARE YOU OKAY?"

Her Fault

It was Ed, waiting outside the police station for her, and she wasn't happy to see him. Who ever said misery loved company? Her misery did not love company. Her misery loved to be alone. Her misery threatened to bludgeon company.

"I'm fine." She hardly stopped. Another funny thing about having friends was that they expected things of you. They made you want to not be a terrible, awful, execrable person. They made you feel even worse when you were one. It was a lot easier not to have any friends.

"Gaia, wait. What's going on?" He rolled along after her.

She was tempted to find a quick set of stairs to ascend. Jesus, she really was an awful person.

"Haven't you heard from the angry hordes at school? I put Heather in the hospital. Didn't they tell you?"

"They—I—I mean—," Ed stammered.

"Come on, Ed. They did, didn't they?"

"But Gaia, you know it's not true," Ed argued, breathless from rushing to keep up with her. "You are not responsible for Heather. Even if you had warned her to stay away from the park, she would have cut through, anyway. She wouldn't have listened to you. There's nothing you could have done."

Gaia made a sharp turn onto West Fourth. Ed's tires practically left skid marks.

"Gaia, are you even listening?" Ed demanded.

She didn't bother to stop at the light on Seventh Avenue.

"Gaia! Come on!"

She practically sprinted all the way down Perry Street and pulled up short in front of George and Ella's house.

"Listen to me. What happened to Heather was scary and horrible, but it was not your fault."

Gaia walked up all fifteen steps of the front stoop before she turned around to look at him. "Ed Fargo. Thank you for trying beyond all possible reason to be my friend," she said quietly. "But it was my fault."

She turned her key in the door, went inside the house, and shut the door firmly behind her. She went up three flights of stairs with the grace of a robot. Once in her room she walked straight to the vintage turntable she'd recently hauled from the garbage and set up on the mantel. She reached behind the pile of records she kept in the nonfunctional fireplace to the LP in the very back.

She'd long ago memorized every centimeter of the faded, brittle record cover, memorized every word. She took out the record gingerly and set it on the player. She didn't need to study the grooves to know exactly where to set the needle.

The music filled the room, loud enough to destroy the speakers, to infuriate Ella, to explode her own head.

It was the second movement of the Sibelius violin concerto, the darkest, saddest piece of music on the planet. It was her mother's favorite—her weird, beautiful Eastern European mother with the embarrassing accent. Her mother knew all of Tchaikovsky, Rachmaninoff, Sibelius, and Prokofiev and nothing of Nirvana or any music Gaia held to be important at the time. She'd been so annoyed at her mother for that.

But now the soaring, wailing violin touched Gaia's cracked heart, and she did something she only allowed herself once or twice a year.

She lay down on the floor and cried.

He needed
to pull
himself
out of
this
trance,
to get a
little
distance.

the
opposite
of
love

SAM SAT IN THE WAITING ROOM OF

the intensive care unit, rhythmically whacking his heel against the foot of the couch. It was just like hospital waiting rooms were supposed to be: genuine Naugahyde couch and chairs, plastic side tables displaying magazines you wouldn't have wanted

Not Thinking of an Elephant

to read in the late eighties when they came out. A mounted television showed some wretched soap opera that might as well have been filmed and closed-captioned in that very hospital.

He hadn't seen Heather since last night, and he felt nervous. Finding her in the park eighteen hours before, white as the moon in a dark puddle of blood, was such a potent jolt to his system, he was still breathing, moving, thinking too fast.

God, she'd looked so fragile and broken. He'd thought she was dead until he detected the faintest, slowest flutter of a pulse in her wrist. After that everything exploded into sound and motion. Screaming ambulance sirens, police sirens, people hurrying every which way.

He hadn't slept since, of course, so his senses were oddly distorted—colors were too bright, noises too shrill, smells too acrid. Time was disjointed. For example, hadn't it been at least two hours since Heather's parents had disappeared with a doctor into Heather's room, telling him they would be out in ten minutes?

What little peace he had would be shattered when Heather's sisters arrived from their colleges and Heather's friends stormed the place the moment school let out. A bunch of those friends had already camped out in the waiting room through their lunch period, spewing millions and trillions of words.

But Sam would suffer them. He would deprive himself of food and drink and sleep and continue to torture himself with this ridiculous soap opera as punishment, laughably slight though it was.

What was the punishment for? For contemplating a breakup with Heather not half an hour before she nearly bled to death. For sitting here, his skin intact as a newborn's, while Heather lay slashed in a coma. For thinking nonstop of *that girl*.

Mistake. Big mistake. Better not to think of thinking about her because then suddenly he was thinking of her. No. Stop. Heel. New thought.

New thought . . . He dragged his mind back to an absorbing topic, one he could worry and fiddle with obsessively, like a bloody hangnail. What was that girl's name? The one Tina and Co. had blathered on about for a solid hour? Maia. No. What was it? Gaia? Something like that. How he hated her. Loathed and despised her. What kind of person would let an innocent girl walk straight into a situation they knew was deadly? How petty and small and cowardly this girl Gaia must be.

Of course, the knife-wielding devil who attacked Heather deserved the real blame. But he was beyond hating. He was beyond imagining. Gaia, on the other hand, was a classmate. She was one of them.

Ah. This was good. Righteous indignation got him back on course every time. If he could just keep this focus, keep railing loyally against Gaia, he wouldn't have to think for minutes at a stretch of *that girl.*

GAIA DREADED THIS WORSE THAN

she would dread a group hug with Ella and George or thirty-three simultaneous root canals or even trying out for the cheerleading squad. But she would make herself do it. She would drag herself right up to the eighth floor of this hospital, past the bevy of Heather's friends who detested her, the desperate parents who were

The Boyfriend

too broken up to care about her, the steadfast, adoring boyfriend who'd maybe take a nanosecond from his grieving to curse her name. It was the right thing for Gaia to do. The fact that she dreaded it so much only made it seem more necessary.

Gaia emerged from the elevator and hesitated in front of the nurses' station.

"You're a friend of Heather Gannis?" the orange-haired nurse asked without even looking up from her computer.

"I—"

"Waiting room on your left," the nurse said, still not looking up.

Gaia loitered another moment, feeling wrong about going to the waiting room under false pretenses. But what was she going to do, pour out her heart to the overburdened nurse? Like she'd care that Gaia dumped coffee on Heather or that Heather bitched her out at a party?

"Okay," Gaia said, as meekly as she'd ever said anything. "Thanks."

Walk. Walk. Walk, she ordered herself.

Okay, there they were, spilling out into the hallway. The Friends. When they saw her, would they make a scene right there in the waiting room? Throw stones? Burn her at the stake?

The first murderous glance came from Tina herself. Many others followed as Gaia attempted to slip past the too full room. The murmur of hushed conversation stopped.

Tina gaped at her but was apparently so appalled, she couldn't speak. Instead the good-looking boy who'd been with Tina last night, the old suede-jacketed star of Gaia's cafe fantasy, stepped in.

"Why are you here?" he demanded.

Why was she here? That was a good question.

Because it was the last place on earth she wanted to be?

Because self-flagellation was the only thing that felt right?

Gaia's real answer made her sound like a kiss-ass, so she didn't want to say it out loud: She was here because she wanted and needed to apologize to Heather, even if Heather couldn't hear. Gaia didn't want to pander to the crowd, and she wasn't looking for social resurrection. She was perfectly happy being a pariah. That was as comfortable to her as a pair of old shoes.

So, as often happened, she said nothing. She continued on her way down the hall without a particular plan in mind.

The second room on the right, through a wide-open doorway, was Heather's. Gaia drew in a sharp breath and quickly averted her eyes. She hadn't meant to go right there exactly. She hadn't imagined how Heather would look, frail as a bird, hooked up by scores of tubes to machines that dripped and machines that bleeped, shorn of the self-consciously cool clothing and the beauty that made it so much easier for Gaia to ridicule her. Gaia suddenly felt like throwing up.

There was something much, much worse than your enemy receiving praise, fame, and riches and living happily ever after with an exceptionally handsome guy: your enemy getting slashed in the park after you hoped it would happen.

Her eyes swept into the room again. There, as expected, she saw the dark head of The Boyfriend, bowed over Heather's prone, still body. Maybe he was crying.

Oh, shit. Shit. Shit. Gaia had no right to be there. What had she been thinking?

It was some selfish hope for exoneration that brought her, nothing nobler than that. Now what? She'd walk herself to the end of the hall. She'd wait a minute or two. She'd walk herself back out to the reception area, maybe find a waiting room on another floor, keep her own private vigil for a few hours—or days, if necessary—until things settled down. And then, as politely as possible, she'd apologize to Heather's parents and ask if she might have permission to apologize to Heather. They'd think she was a complete freak, but that hardly mattered, did it?

Gaia trudged to the end of the hall. On her way back she cast one last look in Heather's room. Quiet though she was, The Boyfriend chose that very moment to look up.

Gaia's eyes stuck to his, and she couldn't move them.

Her body reacted before her mind. Her head swam. The Coke she'd had for lunch climbed up her esophagus. All oxygen departed her lungs.

It was him. He was it.

It, him, he was Heather's boyfriend.

The evil, ugly monster with the matted, stinking hair and the razor-blade fangs moved up from her stomach and took a chomp at her heart.

Gaia staggered toward the elevator so he wouldn't see her when her knees gave out.

IN RETROSPECT, IT WOULD HAVE BEEN
so much better if Sam had stayed where he was.

Instead, for no good reason, he allowed his unfaithful legs to carry him from Heather's side, where he belonged, down the hall and after *the girl*.

A Salted Slug

It was impossible for him to explain why. He didn't decide to do it. His body was just suddenly up and moving. It was like when the doctor thwacked your knee. You didn't *decide* to kick your foot.

"Wait," he said as she fled from him just as she had a few days before.

Heather's sisters and a crowd of friends blocked the hallway, impeding the girl's progress. She dodged and wove like a running back facing a defensive line.

"Leaving already, Gaia?" he overheard Carrie Longman say in an unmistakably hostile voice.

The girl broke through the line and made for the elevator bank. Sam followed her there along with a lot of whispers and nasty looks. It honestly did not occur to him that *the girl* was the girl Carrie had been addressing until he was facing her, just two feet away from her, in front of the elevators.

His thoughts were covered in molasses. They moved achingly slowly with big gaps between them.

The girl Carrie had been addressing was called Gaia. . . .

This girl he was now gaping at was called Gaia. . . .

This girl was *the girl*. . . .

The girl was Gaia. . . .

Gaia was the one who had . . .

"Y-You're Gaia," he said to her.

She was silent for a long time, just staring. Her eyes were too much for him.

"You're The Boyfriend," she said slowly.

It sounded like a felony, like an atrocity, the way she said it.

"Sam. My name is Sam."

"Oh." Her face was strangely open, her eyes a whirlpool. He was scared to let himself read them this time. He was scared of getting sucked in.

"I—you—w-w-we—," he stammered. What exactly did he want to say?

He could see from the panel above the nearest elevator that it was climbing toward them. 3 . . . 4 . . . 5 . . .

"You're the Gaia who saw the guy with the knife in the park last night," he blurted out in a disorganized rush. "You're the one who didn't warn her."

The girl's face was a little too white for a person with a beating heart. Her hands trembled at her sides. She nodded.

"W-Why? I don't understand. Do you dislike her that much?"

"I—I guess I do."

Silence. 6 . . . 7 . . .

He needed to pull himself out of this trance, to get a little distance. He needed to remember who needed defending here. He looked away from her, summoning his shield of righteous indignation. "What is wrong with you? Are you some kind of monster?" He hated the way his voice sounded.

She took so long to respond, it was punishing. Those wide, boundless eyes pinned him to his spot with a look that made him feel horrible, like a salted slug.

"You're not what I thought," she said finally.

Why should *he* feel horrible? *He* hadn't done anything wrong.

The elevator arrived on eight. The doors opened with glacial slowness.

Suddenly he hated her. It was only partly rational, partly fair. She was the source of all the problems, of Heather's condition, of the shameful, disloyal thoughts that had invaded his brain. Now in her face, in her eyes, he saw none of the tenderness or the possibilities he saw before.

"I hate you," he said, amazed as the babyish words emerged from his own mouth.

She stepped into the elevator. "I hate you, too."

He watched her face until the doors closed.

Unbidden, that stupid saying entered his mind: that one about hate not being the opposite of love.

Cold Coffee

"WHO PICKED CJ OUT OF THE lineup?" the older woman asked, leaning over the table that divided them, resting her chin in her palm.

Marco could see down her lavender blouse to the tops of her breasts spilling out of a white bra with lace edges. He wanted to kiss her and touch her so bad. She always wanted to talk first. That was the way most girls were, in his experience. So his mouth went one way and his mind another.

"Nobody knows for sure. Some guys think it was that blond girl—that, uh, friend of yours. A couple of them saw her in the park last night before that other girl . . . you know." He didn't feel like going any deeper into this particular subject. He wanted to talk about how good her shiny red hair looked all loose like that and the dream of his she'd starred in last night.

She crossed her legs under the table, and her knee brushed his. "I heard on the news that the girl who was slashed—they didn't release her name—is out of a coma and expected to make a full recovery," she said.

"Yeah? That's good news for CJ. They'll stick him with assault instead of murder. He never meant to hurt her so bad."

"CJ's in custody? Nobody came up with bail?" she asked.

He pressed his shin against hers. "Nah. It was like a hundred grand or something. His mother lives in Miami. She doesn't even know about it."

"So maybe you'll need to take over in his absence?"

Marco lifted his shoulders so they looked extra big. "Yeah, that's the plan. Tarick, you know, Marty's older brother, wants me to, uh, take care of this old Jew foreigner in the park, this crazy guy who sits over by the chess tables."

She nodded and sipped her coffee.

Marco looked down at his own coffee. He'd hardly touched it. He'd only ordered it because it seemed more mature than a Coke. The coffee was cold now, and an iridescent grease slick quivered on the top. Everything in this diner was greasy, but the tables in back were private.

Why was she so fascinated by this stuff? Nothing seemed to shock her or upset her. Was she a writer for a magazine or something? Even though she was older, she was so freakin' sexy, he didn't care much as long as she changed the names and all that.

"Why the old guy?" she asked.

Marco shrugged. "'Cause he's there. He's kind of a joke in the park. This loser kid who wants to be part of things—Renny is his name—he loves this old guy. Marty and them think it would be funny."

"Are you going to do it?"

Marco smiled in a way he thought was both tough and mysterious. "I'll see."

She didn't smile back. "Do you want something else?" she asked. "A Coke?"

He couldn't wait anymore. He stood and grabbed her hand. "I want to get out of here."

She remained seated. "I want to finish my coffee."

    1 poppy-seed bagel with cream
cheese
    1 large coffee with milk and 2
sugars
    3 Wint-O-Green Life Savers

When I was twelve, my mind's
eye would sometimes flash on ex-
cruciating images from the night
I lost my mother. They destroyed
me, but I couldn't stop. The
worst thing you can do in that
situation is order your mind *not*
to think of something. You know,
the old "don't think of an elephant" problem. So I invented
these tactics for distraction.

    The first line of defense was
to think about kids at school.
Not my friends, exactly, because
I didn't have many of those, but
the people I fantasized about
being friends with. I'd weave
these scenes filled with cute
dialogue about the fun we'd all
have palling around together.

    The second line of defense was
imagining a boy to fall in love

with. What would he look like?
What kinds of things would he say
to me? Would it be love at first
sight, or would it take me a few
minutes to overwhelm him with my
charm?

If those two didn't work, I
exiled my mind to listing
European capitals, which my dad
made me memorize when I was
three.

And finally, if my mind offered absolutely no place to
hide, if thinking at all was
sheer torment, I would distract
it by cataloging what I'd eaten
the day before.

Tonight, lying on the floor of
my room, the first three attempts
led to:

1. Heather
2. Sam
3. Belgrade

I skipped directly to yesterday's breakfast.

Sam was watching the place across the park where Gaia's back had been minutes before.

the pretty one

"I don't know," he said absently. "I got distracted, I guess."

HEATHER WAS GOING TO BE OKAY.

Heather was expected to make a full recovery.

Gaia was so happy, she felt like telling the man behind the sandwich counter at Balducci's.

"Roast beef?" he asked her.

"Yes," she said. "On that." She pointed to an extravagant-looking roll.

It was all over school today, all anybody was talking about. That and the part Gaia played in the catastrophe. The way the rumor mill was spinning, Gaia expected she would be charged with the slashing herself before the end of the day.

And that was, admittedly, part of the reason why it was 11:45 A.M. and Gaia was buying a sandwich rather than listening to her imbecilic math so-called teacher botch an elementary explanation of sine and cosine.

She paid for the nine-dollar sandwich and headed down Sixth Avenue, swinging the green-and-white bag. Zolov would eat like a king today. She imagined his face when she surprised him at the unusual hour.

Cutting was a serious offense, as she'd been told a few thousand times. Ooooh. She pictured the vice principal calling George at work. Or, God forbid, Ella.

She almost skidded to a stop at a pay phone at the corner of West Eighth. She plunked in her quarter and dialed George's work number. "George Niven, please."

George's voice came on a few seconds later. "This is George Niven."

"Hi, George, it's Gaia. How's it going?"

"Just fine, Gaia. Just fine." He sounded surprised and pleased. "You sound like you're . . . uh . . ."

"I'm actually calling from a pay phone, because I left school early, because I wasn't feeling well."

"I'm sorry to hear that." His voice was filled with such genuine concern, she felt a little bad. "Did you speak to—"

"It's nothing serious. It's . . . well, you know, it's *that* time of the month, and I get these really bad cramps sometimes." Gaia knew there was no faster way to get a man off the phone than to bring up her period.

"Right, right. Of course. Understood." She'd never heard him talk so fast.

Poor George. It was hard enough having a girl in your house, let alone one who arrived fully formed at the age of seventeen.

"So, would you just give them a call and let them know what's up?" she asked.

George was clearly so traumatized, he didn't argue. "Yes. I'll give them a call at the . . . uh, office there. You, uh, just let Ella know. She'll take care of you. There's, uh, there's no better sick nurse than Ella."

Gaia almost laughed at that one. Ella's skirts were too tight to sit at a bedside, and she probably couldn't distinguish aspirin from arsenic. God help George. Love was more than blind. It was deaf and dumb, too. It was catatonic. It was vegetative.

Sixth Avenue passed her by in a stimulating buzz. The buses, the baby strollers, the three-man Peruvian band that played on the corner, the delis overflowing with fruit and flowers, the guy selling dirt-cheap tube socks, underpants, and secondhand books from a card table set up by the curb.

`The world was fresher and a lot more spacious when you were supposed to be in school.` Kind of like a public pool during adult swim.

She rounded the corner of West Fourth in eager anticipation. Maybe today she would buy a bag of those sugary roasted nuts. The exquisite smell was already reaching her nostrils. Yes, today would be the day.

She breezed into the park, `actually appreciating the sunshine` for once. It made the place seem so different from the malicious gang nest where Heather had been slashed. She saw Zolov's hunched, familiar back and almost ran for him.

Then she stopped short. She dropped the bag and watched the silver-foil-covered sandwich roll over hexagonal gray stones. She put her hand to her heart.

He was there. The Boyfriend. Sam. Whatever.

He was sitting directly across from *her* friend, concentrating on the chessboard. `How dare he?` Was he trying to hustle poor old Zolov? Couldn't he see the old man had nothing to lose besides his terrible coat and his Power Ranger? Shouldn't he be in school or something?

She hoped the old man would summon up all his skill and beat the crap out of him.

The Boyfriend, Sam, whatever, looked scruffier today. The cuffs of his flannel shirt weren't buttoned, nor were they rolled up. His hair was sticking up a little in back, and his eyes looked tired. Probably from staying up all those hours worrying about Heather.

Blah. *Blah.* The thought made her sick.

Gaia grabbed the sandwich and stuffed it back in the bag. Now what? She didn't want to see him or talk to him, but she didn't want to flee like a little mouse, either.

Of course he had to look up right then. Right then, as she clutched her pathetic green-and-white bag, paralyzed with uncertainty, eyes round and startled.

Why did he have this effect on her? Why? Had she some intuitive knowledge, the day they played chess, that he was Heather's boyfriend? Did she recognize he represented the best possible way to torment herself?

She couldn't be having these alien feelings about Heather's boyfriend. It was too cruel a coincidence. Was somebody up there having a belly laugh at her expense?

Her mind flashed back to their last encounter in the hospital, and she wanted to groan out loud. She felt her cheeks turning warm.

No doubt about it. She was a femme fatale. A romantic heroine for the ages. A heartbreaker. A female

151

James Bond. A role model for girls everywhere.

Of the two boys Gaia had ever met in her *entire life* who could have possibly ever maybe meant something important to her (and coincidentally, the only two who had ever beaten her in chess—Stephen from around the corner being the first), she'd told them both she hated them. She was two for two.

No wonder she'd never kissed anybody. "I hate you" wasn't exactly come-hither. It wasn't a big turn-on to most guys. Not ones who belonged on this side of prison, anyway.

Maybe she could sell a book touting her romantic advice. *Gaia's Rules.* Not only should you not call the sucker back; go ahead and tell him you hate him.

And as a follow-up she could publish her popularity secrets. Okay, it was time to go somewhere else. Time to let up on the mean-yet-indifferent laser beams she was directing from her eyes.

She wheeled around, sandwich bag in hand, and walked toward the fountain. It was a beautiful, warm day. Why didn't she just go to the fountain? That was a normal thing to do.

The benches were filled with mothers of babies, nannies, college students, people who didn't have jobs. There, directly in front of her, bathed in the buttery shade of a yellow umbrella, stood the pushcart filled with nuts so sugary and delicious, the smell alone could make you hallucinate.

And she was going to buy a bag. So what if her stomach felt like it had been stapled shut?

"One bag, please," she said to the cart's proprietor as he stirred the caramelized mass. She thrust two dollars in his hand, and he gave her the warm, paper pouch filled with sticky nuts. The smell was a living thing. She put one in her mouth. She chewed. She tried another.

She kept chewing as she walked herself from the fountain to the dog run near the perimeter of the park, feeling her hopes deflate as the grease from the nuts soaked through the paper to her fingers.

Sugar-roasted nuts, as it turned out, could be added to the list that included vanilla extract and bread and meeting a guy you could fall in love with—things that smelled a lot better than they tasted.

"CHECKMATE."

Six Minutes and a Pawn

Sam glanced up in surprise. Zolov wasn't looking at him with his usual winking smile of triumph. He was looking at him with pity.

He had lost? Already?

How could that be?

Of course, he always lost to Zolov. In spite of his

insanity, Zolov was a truly great player. In his day the old guy had beaten or drawn many of the greatest chess players in the world. But usually Sam and Zolov fought their way through long, dramatic battles, masterful exchanges of material. Today it was `six minutes and a pawn`.

"Vhat happened to you?" Zolov asked.

Sam was watching the place across the park where Gaia's back had been minutes before. "I don't know," he said absently. "I got distracted, I guess."

"By zat geerl?"

Sam couldn't breathe. He was choking. Was it possible to choke to death on your own saliva? "W-Who?"

"Za preetty vun. She's smart, too, you know."

"I—uh—I don't know who you mean."

Zolov was now smiling. "I teenk you do."

Sam almost bit his tongue in annoyance. After two years of listening to Zolov theorize about the young man who sold sodas by the fountain (World War I Polish spy called Tuber), the social worker from the homeless coalition (malevolent alien from a whole other solar system), the old man picked `quite a moment to be perceptive`.

"I gotta go," Sam said, standing. "Good game," he lied, handing Zolov a five. "I'll see you Thursday."

"Sam?"

Sam turned around in amazement. Zolov called

him "boy" and "keed" and "you," but he never called him "Sam."

"Yeah?"

"You go get zat geerl and tell heer I vant my sand-veech."

"No way," Sam muttered to himself. No way was he ever going anyplace near that kind of trouble again.

As a child, I was a disaster. I had a terrible stammer, which made me shy and pitifully awkward. My teeth pointed in every direction, and my hair was so thick, it lay in a stack on my head.

It started early. I was a maladjusted baby. You may think all babies are at least a little bit cute, but I wasn't. I didn't walk till after I was two. I don't think I learned to talk at all until I was four years old.

My stammer was triggered by everything but by nervousness most of all, and I was always nervous. It was your classic catch-22: My nervousness made me stammer, and the more I stammered, the more nervous I got. I even stammered in my thoughts.

I was badly isolated. I spent all my time either on the computer or playing chess. Or playing chess on the computer. I started playing in chess tournaments when I was about six. Even among chess geeks I was considered untouchable. Stop by a chess tournament sometime, and you will see how truly scary that is.

I have an older brother to remind me of all this, in case I ever forget.

When I was twelve, my parents started to worry about me in earnest. I suspect they were embarrassed to take me anyplace. I had a crash course in speech therapy. Several, to be honest. A vengeful orthodontist installed an aircraft carrier worth of metal in my mouth. My mom dragged me to a haircutter who cost about a thousand dollars. She outfitted me at the Gap.

By the time I returned to school for seventh grade, I was unrecognizable. I actually considered changing my name and just starting from scratch.

So I guess you could say life as I know it began when I was twelve. I was born that first day of junior high.

I'm fine now. Even good, according to a lot of people. I know how to dress. I know how to speak. And even so, I'm still good at chess.

I masquerade as one of the blessed. One of the normal, effortless joiners who believe, without thinking about it too deeply, that the world exists for people like us. It's a lie, of course. I come from the other side. I know what it's like over there.

There are still vestiges of dorkdom in me. (See my use of the word *vestiges*, for example.) They pop up all the time. They remind me that if I were born in another age, say, prehistory—before braces and speech therapy—I would be the dorkiest caveman who ever lived. And the person I was probably meant to be.

Her gaze swept
over Sam's
still body,
and she had an
almost **melting**
overwhelming
away
need to go
to him, to
kneel over him
and make sure he
was breathing.

SHE WASN'T *THAT* PRETTY. OKAY,

she was that pretty. But not
pretty like Heather—the kind of
pretty that everybody noticed
right away. Gaia's face, devoid of
makeup or any expression meant
to please, was unfortunately more
mesmerizing to Sam every time
he saw it. God, and those eyes.
They haunted him. He
couldn't get a fix on them—one

First and Second Punches

time they were the endless azure of a summer sky,
another time the blue-violet of early evening, and still
another the indescribable color of a typhoon.

He turned up LaGuardia. It was almost eight-thirty
in the evening, and he wanted to get to the hospital to
see Heather before visiting hours were up. He'd cut
through the park. Just a corner of it.

But it wasn't just the way Gaia looked. Was it because she was so unbelievably good at chess? Granted,
that had really thrown him. But that couldn't explain
it fully, either.

He had every reason to dislike her. He *did* dislike
her. No decent person would have treated Heather the
way Gaia had. For a while he'd tried convincing himself that he was thinking about her so much because
he disliked her, but it wasn't working anymore.

Sam was a rational person. Overly rational,

if you listened to Heather, or his mother, or most of his friends. He wasn't romantic. He wasn't poetic. He wasn't nostalgic. He wasn't obsessive—until this week, anyway. What was wrong with him? What were the chances that she, Gaia, had thought about him even a minute for each hour he'd thought of her?

He was a rational person. He would figure this out, and maybe then he could make it go away, he assured himself as he glanced toward the chess tables, squinting through the darkness to see that none of the few shadowy figures was hers.

He didn't see her, but he did see something strange. He moved closer.

He first recognized the hunched shape of Zolov swaying to get to his feet. Another figure was hovering, bearing down on the old man. He heard a groan, first quiet, then it grew loud and terrifying. Sam was running before he was able to process what was happening.

"Zolov!" he shouted.

The old man was waving his arms, trying to defend himself from the attack. He shouted hoarsely in a language Sam didn't understand.

It was a young man, Sam realized as he raced toward them, and he had a razor blade.

"Get away from him!" Sam shouted.

The young man turned his head and locked eyes with Sam for a millionth of a second. He was young, dark haired, intense, pumped up on adrenaline or

161

something else. Sam hated him. What kind of monster would attack a fragile, crazy old man? Sam watched in horror as he threw Zolov to the ground.

Zolov cried out. Sam saw blood on the old man's face, `flooding the crags and wrinkles`. His heart was seized with panic. He threw himself at the attacker and shoved him as hard as he could. Thoughts were only fragments moving through his mind at uneven speeds. The attacker lost his balance, but only for a moment. He steadied himself and came at Sam.

There was a fist, really big. Sam heard an awful-sounding crack, then saw the orange insides of his eyelids. He blinked his eyes open. He was still on his feet. His cheekbone was blazing with pain. One eye was pounding, already swelling with blood.

The fist was coming again, but `time was 0slow now`. Slow enough for Sam to dodge the fist and to remember that he had never been in a fight before, that he was out of his league. He willed his hand to clench. He trained his good eye on the guy's mouth. He swung as hard as he could.

His knuckles connected to soft flesh. The guy grunted. Sam felt a surge of energy so strong, it seemed to erase his memory, to blow out his consciousness. He swung again without thinking. He caught an ear this time, hard. The guy staggered to one side, caught his balance. He didn't come back at Sam, as Sam was expecting. Instead he stepped backward, putting several more feet between them.

"You're dead," he hissed at Sam through blubbery, swollen lips. "I'm going to kill you." And then he ran off.

Sam was almost instantly kneeling at Zolov's side. The old man was groaning softly. Sam took his shirt and gently wiped away blood so he could determine the seriousness of the wound. It appeared to be shallow and less than two inches in length but bleeding heavily. Zolov's eyes fluttered open, then shut again. His breath was short and raspy. Sam was suddenly terrified the old man's heart was going to stop. He hated to leave him, but he needed to get help.

"Zolov," he whispered, cradling his head. "You're gonna be okay, but I need to call an ambulance. I'll be back as fast as I can." He laid the gray, frizzled head on the soft ground. He stood looking at him for another moment before he took off at a sprint for the public pay phone.

AS SOON AS GAIA HEARD THE NOISE

Another Mistake

the fine, light hair on her arms prickled and her skin was covered with bumps. She had the feeling sometimes that when she sensed danger, her vision and her hearing

163

became almost supernaturally acute. She could almost feel her muscles feasting on oxygen, preparing for action. She knew the muffled cries and moans were Zolov's well before she actually saw him.

Zolov's attacker broke away as Gaia flew to the old man's side. She put her arms around the frail shoulders, examining the wound on his face. There was a certain amount of blood, but it was already thickening around the slash. That was a good sign. She clutched him gently. "You're going to be fine," she promised him, not wanting to leave him in his disoriented state.

But she had to because, amazingly, the demon who had attacked the old man was still within sight. Gaia ran like hell. In the darkness she saw nothing more than his silhouette.

The attacker sprinted toward the south edge of the park. Gaia flew after him, her rage undergoing nuclear fission as her feet pounded the pavement. What kind of monster would attack a helpless old man?

He was fast, but she was faster. She literally launched herself from the ground and tackled him from behind. He shouted in surprise. They rolled together across a grassy patch, limbs tangling. Strong arms circled her hips, pulling her down. They tumbled again before she managed to pin him under her. She secured his torso between her knees and shoved his head to the ground. Her hands were tightening around his neck before she looked him in the face.

She closed her eyes in disbelief. When she opened them again, her heart changed places with her stomach.

It was Sam.

She was so astounded, she let go of him, and in an instant he'd flipped her over. Now he was kneeling over her, pressing her shoulders into the ground with his hands.

"*Gaia,* what do you think you're *doing?*" he bellowed at her.

She saw clearly now that one of his eyes was purple and almost swollen shut. Her mind was whizzing, trying to make sense of it.

"Zolov is hurt," Sam yelled only inches from her ear. "He was slashed. I need to call for help!"

Her ears rang painfully. "Y-You," she choked out. "I thought you—"

"You thought I what? I slashed him? Are you insane?" Sam's eyes—or the one that was still open, anyway—were wild with adrenaline. Her waist was gripped too tightly between his knees. He was digging the heels of his hands into her chest.

In a lightning-quick move she managed to get one hand around each of his arms and pulled them out from under him. His weight collapsed on top of her, and she quickly flipped him over again. She drove her knee into his abdomen and held him steady with her forearms. "Then who did it?" she demanded.

He stared at her with a mixture of anger and disbelief. "Some asshole who's going to get away if you don't *get the hell off me!*" He wrapped his arms around her back in a bear hug and tried to roll her again, but this time she wasn't budging.

He was holding her so tight, her face was buried in his neck. "Fine," she said as well as she could, considering her lips were pressed against his skin. "Let me go, and I'll let you go." But neither of them moved.

"Fine. You let go first," he demanded in her hair. His voice was strained by the presence of her knee in his stomach.

Gingerly, slowly, she let up the pressure from her knee.

"Whoa!" she called out as he threw her off him, fast and surprisingly hard. Her butt landed on the pavement. "Ouch," she complained.

She was mad. She couldn't help herself. As soon as he was on his feet she sprang to hers and shoved him. He reeled backward a couple of steps, then leaped at her and shoved her right back.

Her eyes widened in disbelief. As soon as she caught her balance, she stormed at him. He was a lot taller than she, so she had to jump to jab her shoulder into his solar plexus.

"Uff!" he grunted. She was satisfied to see she'd

nearly knocked the wind out of him. She put two hands on his stomach and pushed him to the ground.

With admirable speed he rolled toward her and hugged her ankles. "Oh!" she shouted in surprise as he pulled her legs out from under her. She fell directly on top of him.

In anger and confusion she grabbed the first thing she could—his hair, as it turned out. He grabbed hers right back. She was lying on top of him, one arm around his neck. His legs were clasped around hers, his arm circling her waist.

Where had her great fighting prowess gone? She'd been baffled, confused, angered by this guy who wasn't extraordinarily skilled or trained. And now she'd been reduced to pulling hair?

"There he is!" a voice shouted.

From their tangle on the grass they both looked up, mute.

Sharp Edges

"OH, SHIT," SAM MUMBLED, STILL clutching Gaia as the guy who had attacked Zolov came near, flanked by two guys on each side. The guy's lips were grossly misshapen, and he looked mad enough to dismember, if not kill.

Suddenly Sam found himself holding Gaia even tighter, but strangely, his motive had transformed. He no longer wanted to pull her limb from limb; now he felt an urgent need to protect her.

There were five of them. Count them, five. Three of them were big. Two of them looked young—in their middle teens, maybe, and not totally filled out. For a moment he buried his eyes in Gaia's soft, pale hair.

If it weren't so surreal and horrendous, he would have laughed. In the last five minutes he'd thrown the first and second punches of his life, found himself wrestling on the ground with the object of his infatuation—not only brilliant at chess but a match for Hulk Hogan. Now he was holding her in his arms and smelling her hair as he faced imminent death at the hands of five angry gang members while his ancient friend and mentor was possibly `bleeding to death`.

"Get off your girlfriend and stand up," the slasher demanded roughly.

Somehow it didn't seem necessary to point out that Gaia was not his girlfriend. They sorted out their limbs and both stood up. They exchanged a look, filled with things he couldn't decipher. `Amazing how quickly your enemy seemed like your friend` when faced with a worse enemy.

"Jesus, it's *her*," one of the guys said.

Sam looked at Gaia again. He couldn't guess what that meant. "Leave her alone," he barked at them, stepping forward. He suddenly felt like he was playing a role in a movie, portraying a character who said and did things he never would. Best to keep pretending because reality—namely five guys (and possibly one girl) who wanted to kill him—was hard to take.

"Gaia, go," he said in a low voice. "I'll be okay." Ha! Had his character really just said that? She was standing so close, he could still feel the warmth of her body. It was intoxicating—really not what he needed at the moment.

The guy, the swollen-lipped slasher, was only a few feet away now, bouncing a little on the balls of his feet. His friends had circled Sam and Gaia. Two of them wore floppy hoods, covering their shaved heads and keeping their faces in shadow. Another had a Doo-Rag pulled low over his forehead. As he looked at them Sam was weirdly calm and disconnected. He was resigned to getting beat up. He felt more scared about what they might do to Gaia.

"Let her go," Sam said.

The guy's smile was grotesque with the swollen lip pulling in odd directions. "My bud CJ thinks she did him wrong."

One of the hooded guys came forward and grabbed Gaia by the shoulders. He dragged her several yards from Sam, pinning her arms to her sides in a bear hug.

The horror was now dawning on Sam. He felt bile rising in his throat. Anger mixed with fear to make desperation. Gaia's eyes were huge and luminous.

He went after the guy who held her. Fast, without letting himself think too much, he hauled off and punched the guy, catching his jawbone so hard, his knuckles blazed. Gaia slipped quickly out of the guy's grip.

Get away, he urged her silently. Run away and get—

He'd grabbed her waist and was about to physically shove her when a slamming blow to the back of his head shattered his mind. He spun around and got a sharp kick in the stomach. He was lying on the ground now, disoriented by the number of arms and feet and faces spinning against a sapphire sky. A kick landed on his chest and took his breath away.

He saw Gaia's face over him, glowing white like an angel's. Broken thoughts and feelings lay in pieces, with edges sharp enough to cut. He reached for her. He wanted to tell her something, but he couldn't fit the aching, full-hearted feelings into words. The last thing he saw from the corner of his eye was a Timberland coming at the side of his head. After that, thankfully, he saw and felt nothing.

GAIA WASN'T AFRAID. SHE WAS

Sleeping Beauty

never afraid. But she felt the abstract terror of a world without Sam, without the idea or the possibility of Sam, and she didn't want to live there. It felt so dark and arid that it would surely dry up all of her senses and parch her last blossom of hope.

Her rage exploded, less controlled, more intense than ever before. The five of them became an indistinguishable mass to her, without human features. She took them on as one multilimbed creature. Her adrenaline carried her, so she didn't have to think or count or predict.

She took one of them out with her fist. Clean, just like that. Another one required a combination of kicks to finish him off. In the process she took a sharp jab in the ribs and another guy's fist caught her in the forehead as she tried to duck. She could feel the blood gathering at the wound. The red drips were a nuisance in her eyes, but she was too far gone to feel pain.

Two of the guys bobbed in her peripheral vision. The third she had head-on in her sights. She planted a kick in that vulnerable place in his neck just as another one slammed her from the side. Another down, she registered as she tried to find her balance. Then came another slam from the side. The blood stung her eyes and tinctured her mouth with its coppery flavor. Head wounds bled too much. It was a shame. She might not have enough time.

Two weaving heads, eight thrashing limbs. It was an ugly but simpler creature that remained.

Her gaze swept over Sam's still body, and she had an almost overwhelming need to go to him, to kneel over him and make sure he was breathing.

Bam! A blow to her stomach sent her sprawling on the ground. *Focus, Gaia,* she urged herself. She had to focus as hard as she possibly could to get them through this. Loss of blood made her hazy and faint.

Another guy came rushing toward her at an angle she could use. She caught his momentum and threw him over her head. He rolled twice. It gave her enough time to get back to her feet. But just as she did the other one smashed her from behind and sent her back to the pavement. As she raised her head, she saw a pale, scared face peering from a stand of trees. She knew the face. He took a few steps forward.

"Renny, you little shit, get over here!" the bigger of the guys bellowed.

Renny was frozen, except for his face, which quivered like a squirrel's.

Suddenly Gaia felt her arms wrenched roughly behind her back. The two of them were holding her. She tried to jab her way free with her elbow, but she couldn't move it.

"Come on, little boy, here's your big chance!" the other guy called.

Gaia didn't feel like writhing to get out of their grip. It was a waste of time. The blood was leaving her head and making her feel tired. She wished she could just pass out and be done with it.

"Renny! Step up, man. You in or out?"

Renny took another step forward. He looked terrified at the sight of Gaia, no doubt something right out of a horror movie with all that blood on her face and shirt.

Suddenly Gaia saw the dull glint of steel. She thought she was imagining it at first. But even the idea was enough to clear her foggy head.

Yes, it was real. She could see it clearly now. The fat-lipped guy was pushing a gun, a .38-caliber pistol, into Renny's hand. Where had it come from? Why hadn't she been paying better attention? "Finish her off, Renny. Do it now!"

Gaia's adrenaline level notched up. Her body was on full alert, but her mind had entered that dreamlike state, wondering numbly, philosophically, whether this was the end of her life. There were few physical brawls she couldn't find her way out of, but a gun changed everything. It empowered the cowardly and rendered skill, bravery, and character useless.

That was why Gaia, though she was trained to be an exceptional markswoman, never used one. She'd rather lose on her terms than win on those. Now the gun was in Renny's hand. Shaky, but pointing directly at her. He wasn't looking anywhere near her eyes.

Oh, this was hard to take. Was little Renny, her favorite chess whiz, really going to sink a bullet into her? It seemed like a very bad life where that would happen. If he was going to, she hoped he would get on with it because she didn't feel like sticking around much longer to watch.

Renny looked like he was going to puke. His eyes were glazing over, and his skin was the color of iceberg lettuce. He came up so close, she could hear his breath. She was staring down the barrel of the gun. She pulled her eyes back to Renny's.

Look at me, she demanded of him silently. Look at me! *Look at me!* If he was going to do this, let him do it for real. Let him know the full meaning of popping that trigger.

Don't be a coward, Renny. Look at me!

At last he did. His eyes lighted on hers. He hesitated only a moment. Then he turned and ran like hell. Gaia heard the gun clattering on the pavement.

Good boy, Renny, she told him silently as he sprinted for the streetlights.

"Freakin' coward," one of the guys muttered.

It gave Gaia the burst she needed. She slammed her heel as hard as she could into one guy's shin. When he let her go to clutch his leg, she wrenched herself free from the other guy and followed up with a searing blow to the side of the injured guy's head. Then another rapid jab to his abdomen. He crumpled, gasping for breath.

She lunged for the gun, grabbing it from the ground. Without a pause she hauled off and threw it. It traced a high arc through the sky. She didn't have time to watch where it landed.

She faced the last one now. He was familiar to her from another time, but her head was too blurry to cobble together a memory. His lips were swollen, and his jacket was speckled with blood, probably hers. Gray spots grew and multiplied, clouding her vision. She heard the punch to her shoulder before she felt it. She stepped back and shook her head in the hope of clearing it. She came forward and cracked her fist across his nose. His fist landed hard on her cheekbone. She reeled back, losing her footing, almost falling directly onto Sam.

On your feet, girl, she begged herself. But then she heard something. It was faint but approaching fast and sounded to her more beautiful than a Mozart symphony. The guy heard it, too. He stopped. Listened. He gave her a last look before he ran.

Bless you, Renny, she thought as she fell back against Sam, listening to the siren coming near.

She turned as gingerly as she could. She put her hand on Sam's chest. He was breathing. He definitely was. She put her hand gently on his cheek, then skimmed her fingers over his battered eye. She smoothed his hair back from his beautiful forehead. She hadn't touched another human being like this in almost five years. Transfixed, she ran her trembling hand from the cool softness of his upper cheek to the masculine stubble of his chin. His perfect skin was broken in several places. What had she done to him?

And almost more disturbing, what had he done to her?

Tears spilled from her eyes and mixed with the blood drying on her face. A drop of the pink moisture landed on his forehead. And another. It blended with the beads of sweat on his brow.

She felt like she was entering a trance as she lowered her face toward his. She touched her lips against his with exquisite gentleness, slowly deepening the kiss as she surrendered her heart.

She heard voices coming near. She lifted her head. Sam's eyes fluttered open and then closed again.

She could die now. She laid her head on his chest and melted away.

To: L
From: ELJ
Date: October 2
File: 776244
Subject: Gaia Moore
Last Seen: Washington Square Park, New York
City, 8:37 P.M.

Update: Subject hospitalized after prolonged
fight with several gang members and a man identified as Sam Moon, age 20, sophomore at NYU.
Three gang members arrested at the scene, two
others fled. Old man known as Zolov was taken
to the hospital and treated for a surface wound
to the face. Subject received surface wound to
the head, resulting in considerable loss of
blood. Multiple contusions. Expected discharge
10/3.

To: ELJ
From: L
Date: October 2
File: 776244
Subject: Gaia Moore

Unacceptable. Subject was not to be injured
under any circumstances. Contact me immediately for new placement.

When he was
near her,
his own mind
betrayed
him. **dangerous**
The smartest **hope**
thing he
could do was
stay away
from her
permanently.

"IT'S SO TRENDY, ALMOST BLEEDING

to death. All the cool girls are doing it."

Gaia didn't open her eyes. Instead she considered the voice, felt the calloused hand wrapped around hers. She meant to smile, but it came out wobbly. "Hi, Ed," she said.

When she opened her eyes, she saw a small bundle of orange carnations perched in a Snapple bottle on the bedside table. "Those are such boy flowers," she noted in a weak, slightly raspy voice.

"What do you mean?"

"Only a boy would buy dyed carnations," she explained. "Girls buy less obvious stuff, like tulips and irises."

"Are you saying you don't like them?"

"No, I do like them. I accept that you are a boy. I'm happy that you are a boy."

Ed looked happy that he was a boy, too.

"So who did you beat up this time?" he asked.

"That sounded like a question," she said.

"Oh, yeah. This is like reverse *Jeopardy*. Um . . . let's see. . . . You beat up ten guys, each four times your size, and one poor bastard got in a lucky punch."

She nodded. "Pretty much. Only multiply the equation by one-half."

"Only five guys." He shook his head. "You're losing your edge."

180

Gaia studied his face thoughtfully. "I guess you could say it was six guys—only one was kind of a mistake."

"A mistake."

"I got in a fight by accident with Sam—Heather's boyfriend."

"Wow, you really do get around."

"I didn't mean to. I thought he'd slashed Zolov, the old guy who plays chess in the park. But it turned out Sam was only trying to help."

"I see. But you discovered that *after* you knocked his head off." He made an obvious effort not to let the end of his sentence bend into a question.

"Sort of," she admitted.

"Mmmm. Maybe you'll find an excuse to beat up Heather's parents next."

"Ha-ha-ha."

Gaia closed her eyes. Her right cheekbone was throbbing, the cut on her forehead stung, and her stomach muscles ached. She was suddenly too tired to think.

"Hey, Ed," she finally said.

"Yup."

"Thank you for trying to be my friend."

"Am I succeeding? Uh . . . I mean . . ." He cleared his throat. "I am succeeding." He said it in a deep, smooth voice, like a news anchor.

She laughed. "Annoyingly well."

He squeezed her hand. "I'm glad."

She moved her toes under the stiff sheets. "Is Heather still in the hospital?" she asked.

Ed nodded. "Two doors down."

"You're joking."

"No, they moved her out of the ICU. She's going home tomorrow, just like you. Maybe you two can have a joint party."

Gaia sighed. "I still need to apologize to her."

"I don't see why."

"For almost getting her killed," Gaia said.

"But that wasn't your fault."

"Yes, it was."

"It wasn't."

"Was."

"Wasn't."

"Was."

"Wasn't."

"Was."

Ed let out his breath in frustration. "Gaia."

"What?"

"You have got to get over yourself."

"What do you mean?"

"Not everything bad that happens has to be about you."

For no reason that she could understand, tears flooded Gaia's eyes. Something big grew in her throat that prevented her from swallowing. Ed was getting close to a place that hurt, and she wanted him to go away. She tipped back her head so the tears wouldn't spill over her bottom lids. Thank the Lord for water cohesion.

Ed watched her carefully. His expression was gentle but serious. "You're tough as hell, Gaia, but you're not a god. You're made of the same stuff as the rest of us."

"Ed?" she asked in a thick voice. "Would you leave now? I think I can only handle having a friend in five-minute bursts."

Remember Heather

ZOLOV WAS IN ROOM 502. HEATHER was now in room 724, and Gaia was in room 728. Sam had been released from the emergency room last night after being examined and bandaged. He had slept—or at least lain—in his own bed most of last night. Today he made his rotations like a physician. Like a disoriented, exhausted, overwrought, inept physician who hadn't actually gone to medical school.

He had no idea what happened last night. It was a complete mystery why he wasn't dead and who'd

183

fought off the gang. One of the policemen thought it was Renny, the kid who'd called 911, but that didn't make much sense. One of the paramedics jokingly suggested it was Superman.

Sam had this strange, hazy memory of Gaia . . . but no. That was obviously a fitful hallucination—a product of his own deranged fantasy life.

Zolov's slashing wound was minor, but he was so old, the doctor on call wanted to observe him for another twenty-four hours. Zolov seemed to Sam in happy spirits and was very fond of the hospital food. He'd already discovered an orderly who loved to play chess.

Heather lay in the bed only a foot away from him, almost good as new and being released the following afternoon.

Gaia, he hadn't actually spoken to. He'd only prowled around the door to her room like a cat burglar, wanting to catch a glimpse of her but feeling too weird to actually enter.

"So Carrie told me that Miles and them are all coming over tomorrow night. It was supposed to be a surprise, but . . . you know."

Sam didn't know, but he nodded, anyway. Heather had been chatting gaily at him for almost an hour. She was propped up in her bed, surrounded by at least a billion flowers, wearing her own pink linen robe. The bouquet he'd carefully chosen was hidden behind two veritable towers of greenery and a gargantuan basket of fruit. Nurses and doctors and scores and scores of visitors slipped in and out, attending to her as if she were a reigning queen. Her face was flushed and lovely.

"And you'll be there, right?"

Sam glanced up. He'd forgotten to listen to the first part of the question. He nodded again.

"Great. I mean, my mom is going to, like, shit if I'm not in bed by ten. But it will be fun, anyway."

Heather didn't know Gaia was just down the hall. She'd accepted his explanation for his swollen purple eye with a minimum of questions. She'd cooed about how brave he was and how `he'd avenged her`, which wasn't true, of course, but whatever.

". . . Don't you think?" She was looking at him expectantly after a long soliloquy on something or other.

Sam nodded, grateful Heather only asked yes or no questions and rhetorical ones at that.

"I figure we can just order more if we run out," Heather continued.

How had Heather managed to turn a hospital stay into such a social whirlwind? he wondered as two more random friends waved at her from the doorway. "We'll come back," one of them whispered loudly in a `we're-cool-to-the-fact-that-your-boyfriend-is-here` kind of way.

"Right," he said absently.

He was thinking about whether or not the door to room 728 would be fully open and what he might say if he did venture into room 728. And then he felt ashamed. What kind of asshole obsessed about a troubling near stranger when his girlfriend was in the hospital?

He was considering this when Heather's face changed distinctly. He turned to see why. He clamped his jaw down so hard, he nearly crushed his back teeth.

"Um, hello?" It was Gaia hovering at the door. Her face was tentative. He'd never seen her hair down before. It was a pale, beautiful yellow, and there was lots of it—it fell below her shoulders. Her few freckles stood out in the fluorescent light.

Heather's expression turned from surprised to pinched and angry. "What are you doing here?"

"I—I—um, actually spent the night down the hall because—"

Heather shook her head in disbelief. "I swear to God, it's like you're stalking me."

Gaia looked desperately uncomfortable as her gaze shifted from Heather to Sam and then back again. Her skin looked so pale, it was almost translucent. She tugged and fidgeted with her grayish purple hospital gown. "I don't know if you heard, but I ... there was ... this fight last night and ..."

"Do I care?" Heather's voice was so harsh, Sam winced inwardly.

"No, it's just . . ." Gaia sighed and started over. "It doesn't matter. I just wanted to tell you that I'm very sorry for not warning you about the guy with the knife in the park. It was a bad and dishonorable thing to do, and I don't need you to say it's okay or anything. I'm not looking to be friends. But what I did was wrong, and I'm very sorry for it."

Sam's heart moved up through his chest and into his throat as he watched Gaia. He saw something in her eyes (when he let himself) that was so profoundly vulnerable and scarred that her defiance only made it more moving and distressing to him. Was he the only one who saw it? Was he imagining it? He found himself hoping with unfamiliar passion that Heather would be kind to her. Gaia's speech was met with at least a minute of silence.

"Are you done?" Heather finally asked.

Sam's heart dislocated his tonsils. He couldn't swallow. He was supposed to be on Heather's side. She was his girlfriend, and furthermore, she was the one who'd been wronged. But he struggled against the impulse to put his arms around Gaia and tell Heather to go to hell.

Gaia nodded.

"Then please go away," Heather said. She was capable of causing hypothermia when she felt like it.

Gaia left just as Heather's mom arrived in the

doorway. Sam practically leaped to his feet. "Heather, your mom probably wants some time with you," he mumbled, needing to get out of that room if he was ever going to breathe again. "Hey, Mrs. Gannis," he said politely, bolting past her.

He paused for a moment or two before following Gaia into her room. Although it was only a matter of thirty feet from Heather's, it belonged to a different universe. Aside from a pitiful clump of bright orange flowers in a sticky-looking glass bottle, it was colorless, empty, quiet. Gaia was sitting with her arms around her knees on the radiator under the window, `staring out at the rain.`

"Gaia?" he said.

She turned around. She had those eyes again. "Hi."

She looked like a waif in her hospital gown. Her feet were bare, her ankles surprisingly delicate. Her toenails were mostly covered in chipped brown polish. She had such a big presence, he'd never realized how slight she could appear.

It was too quiet. He needed to say something to her, but the feelings stirring in his core weren't getting anywhere near his mouth. He found his legs taking steps that brought him close to her.

"How are you doing?" she asked softly, filling a tiny part of the silence.

"Oh, fine," he said, as if that were a surprising question. "What about you?"

"Fine. I'm going home tomorrow."

"I'm glad."

He shifted his weight from one foot to the other. "So, where are your folks?"

Her pupils seemed to dilate, but she didn't look away. "I don't have any."

Sam wanted to slit his throat. And yet somehow the information didn't completely surprise him. "I'm so sorry. I didn't mean—"

"That's okay," she said quickly. "How could you have known?"

"I—I didn't . . . I—I just . . ." His voice petered out. So much for the speech therapist.

"Sam," she said.

His name sounded different than it ever had before. "Yes?"

"I am very, very sorry for attacking you last night. I wish I had it to do over."

For some odd reason, he found himself smiling a little. That was the one thing in his life he would have left just the same. "No, no. It wasn't your fault. I'm the one who's sorry . . . for . . . for everything."

"I seem to have a lot to apologize for," she said quietly, studying her fingernails. Her hands were exceptionally graceful, although her nails were bitten down to the quick.

"Some people do, and they say nothing," he murmured. He hoped she would know what he meant.

She nodded.

"Gaia, do you have any idea what happened last night?"

She tilted her head. "What do you mean?"

"I mean, somebody beat up those guys and . . . saved my skin. Maybe yours, too. Do you have any idea who it was or how it happened?"

Her eyes didn't move from his. She was looking for something from him as intently as he was from her. "Probably no more than you," she said equivocally.

He took a deep breath. "I have these strange fragments of memories, but . . . well . . ." He found his cheeks warming at the images in his mind. "But they don't make sense."

Gaia shrugged. "Oh."

"I mean, you didn't . . ." His voice was obviously beseeching, but he couldn't supply the rest of the question.

She wasn't going to help him.

"Maybe it will come back to one of us," he said lamely.

"Maybe."

He stuck his hands in his pants pockets. "Did you see Zolov today?"

Gaia smiled. "Yeah. He's happy. He keeps asking for more pudding."

Sam smiled, too. Suddenly he wanted to stay here and smile at her for the rest of his life.

"Yeah," he repeated stupidly.

She lifted up her arm to brush a strand of hair from her face and as she did revealed a deep, prune-colored bruise on the tender underside of her arm. "Oh," he said out loud, his breath catching. Suddenly he wasn't just close to her but nearly touching her. Two of his fingers hovered around her elbow.

She lifted her arm again and glanced at the bruise, wondering at his reaction. "This?" She turned out her arm and offered it to him.

For some reason the dark, angry bruise on her soft, sweet skin pained him beyond words. It was a `helpless spot`, even on Gaia's body. She has no parents, he found himself thinking disconnectedly. She has a terrible bruise on that hidden, sad part of her arm and she has no parents.

Without thinking properly, he let his fingertips land on her skin just above the inside of her elbow. Gaia looked down at them, but she didn't flinch. Together they watched his fingers slowly graze the damaged spot so gently, he wasn't sure whether he felt her skin or simply her warmth.

The warmth radiated up into his face, now bent over her. He was hypnotized by that passage of skin. He inhaled her subtle fragrance—a faint but tantalizing mixture of chamomile and Chap Stick and caramel and faded laundry detergent.

Was he breathing? Was his heart still beating?

"It's nothing much," she said in something just above a whisper. "You should see the ones on my stomach."

Oh, God. The mere thought of her stomach was a mistake.

"And this," she said. She lifted a curtain of gold hair to show a nasty bruise on her hairline just above her ear.

Now his hand was on her hair. He'd first realized it last night, that her hair was magical stuff. It was weightless and sparkled with strangely mutable color—as if it were shot through with sunlight.

His eyes were on her wound, then suddenly his lips. It had nothing to do with thinking. If it had anything to do with thinking, he never would have done it. Because he was a cautious, rational person. Everyone said so.

His lips touched her hairline so tenderly. She breathed into him, letting her head, her body relax against him. She let out a tiny sound. A hum, not a word.

He'd found his purpose with her, in that touch of his lips, in those few seconds. Without caution or anything related to reason, he knew (he didn't know how he knew) that he had a unique power. He alone had it. Did she know? Did she care? Would she hate him for it? Or would she, could she, love him?

As his lips moved with exquisite gentleness from

the bruise in her hairline to the bandaged cut over her left eyebrow, he knew that he somehow possessed the power to kiss her and make her better. It was a puzzling, inexplicable kind of certainty that came only in dreams. It was an idea so complex and fragile that if he even blinked, he feared he would lose it.

Let me show you, he thought as his lips moved toward hers. Let me show you what I can do.

She was staring up at him in wonder. Her fingers had wrapped around his. Her breath was slow and just barely audible. Her lips were parted in a question. Her blue-violet eyes opened into a billion possible worlds.

"There you are!" The booming words cut through the spell with the force of an ax.

The pretty, plump nurse who'd spoken them was carrying only a paper cup and some pills. "There you are!" she said again, this time clearly to him. Her voice was so loud, it was disorienting. Sam wished he had a remote control to pause her or at the very least turn down the volume.

"You're *Heather's boyfriend, right?*"

Could they hear her all the way uptown? he wondered absently.

"She's *looking for you*—asking *everybody* where *you went.*"

Could they hear her in Harlem? In Connecticut? At the North Pole?

Sam had traveled deep into a netherworld, and it

was hard coming back. He looked at Gaia, but her face was turned to the window.

"Gaia?"

When she turned back to him, her face was different.

"Yeah?"

"I'll see you later?"

"Sure, maybe," she said.

Her eyes were no longer the color of the clear night sky soaring up into a universe of stars and moons and planets and galaxies. They were iced over. Shut.

"Hey, Sam," she called as he walked toward the door.

He felt something dangerous as he turned to her.

"You and Heather make a great couple," she said. Her voice was as frigid as her expression.

All hope and warmth drained away. He blinked.

"I'm not sure how to take that," he said.

She shook her head. "It doesn't matter."

Sam's sore muscles tightened. He pulled his eyes from her face and forced the fuzzy clouds in his mind apart, letting in the cold light of reason.

He was awake. He was fully awake, and the dream was gone. Now he could remember that he disliked Gaia. Even hated her. She was trouble. Within a week of meeting her he'd been beaten to a pulp and two people he really cared about were in the hospital. Gaia was angry and dangerous. When he was near her, his own mind betrayed him. The smartest thing he could do was stay away from her permanently.

The smartest and most rational thing he could do was to get himself back to Heather's room and remember why he loved her.

2 KRISPY KREME DOUGHNUTS

Distraction à la Gaia

1 Granny Smith apple
1 large coffee with milk and 3 sugars
5 roasted nuts

He refused
to look up
and pay her
face any
attention **and**
at all
until **finally . . .**
he felt the
metal barrel
against his
temple.

SHE WAS SO ANGRY, SHE'D PICKED

a fight with George. She was so angry, she was wearing her highest heels. Even her aqua miniskirt wasn't helping her mood.

Good-bye, Marco

Marco put his hands on her hips and pushed her against the wall.

The only thing the stupid, vain kid had going for him was his looks, and now he was monstrous with his swollen nose and misshapen lips.

"Come on, darling," she whispered to him. "We need some privacy." She removed his hands and used them to lead him down the narrow hall of the Gramercy Inn to room 402, their very own love nest.

Once he was in the room, she plucked the Do Not Disturb sign off the inside doorknob and hung it on the outside. She closed the door hard and locked it. She clattered the key down on the glass-topped bureau.

He was already pulling his cotton T-shirt over his head. She saw deep bruises on his ribs and shoulder. Slob that he was, he threw the shirt on the ground and came toward her with those inexhaustible hands.

"Darling," she cooed, "you know I need to talk to you. I asked you not to hurt my friend, and now I've learned she's in the hospital."

Marco, as usual, was in no mood for talking.

198

"Mmmm," he said, burying his face in her neck.

This had been fun two days ago. Today it wasn't.

"Marco, did you hear me?"

He had the unbelievable gall to throw her on the bed. She took her handbag with her. As he kissed her, she fumbled with the latch and opened it.

"Marco, I asked you a question."

His hands were gliding under her shirt. They were cold today.

He refused to look up and pay her face any attention at all until he felt the `metal barrel against his temple`. His eyes grew round, and his lips opened. He spluttered but couldn't find words.

Ella gave him another few seconds to fully appreciate her change of mood before she pulled the trigger and sent a silent bullet deep into his head.

She untangled herself from him and deposited the gun into her slim, square bag. She straightened her clothes and glanced in the mirror. Her lipstick was still perfect. She smiled wide. None on her teeth.

This interlude had done nothing to `quell her anger`. But now it was three o'clock, and Gaia, the true source of her temper, would be home from the hospital. Ella slung her bag over her shoulder, enjoying the weight of the gun, and strode to the door without a backward glance.

She was so tired of that girl.

here is a
sneak peek of
Fearless.™ #2:
SAM

Tonight, as I sat on the park bench waiting for my head to explode, I had one moment of clarity in which I learned two things.

I have to find my dad.

I just have to. As angry as I am, as much as I hate him for abandoning me on the most awful, vulnerable day of my life, I don't want to die without seeing him one more time. I don't know what I will say to him. But there is something I want to know, and I feel like if I can look in his eyes—just for a moment—I'll know what his betrayal meant and whether there is any love or trust, even the possibility of it between us.

And, two I have to have sex.

Oh, come on. Don't act so shocked. I'm seventeen years old. I know the rules about being safe. If my life weren't in very immediate jeopardy, maybe I would let it wait for the exact right time. But let's face it, I may

not be around next week, forget
about happily ever after.
Besides, I have been through a
lot of truly awful things in my
life, so why should I die without
getting to experience one of the
few great ones?

Who am I going to have sex
with?

Do you have to ask?

All right, I have an answer. In
my moment of clarity, the face I
saw belonged to Sam Moon. Granted,
he hates me. Granted, he has a
girlfriend. Granted, his girlfriend hates me even more. But
I'll find a way. 'Cause he's the
one. I can't say why, he just is.

I wish I could convince myself
that CJ wouldn't make good on his
threat. But I heard his voice. I
saw his face. I know he'll do any
crazy thing it takes. Am I
afraid? No. I'm never afraid. But
the way I see it, dying without
knowing love would be a tragedy.

She hated
that pale
blond hair,
a color
you **beauty**
rarely saw **and**
hideousness

on a person
over the age
of three.

"YOU SOUND WEIRD."

"How do you mean?" Gaia asked.

"I don't know. You just do. You're talking fast or something."

A Precious Ritual

Ed Fargo was honest with Gaia and Gaia was honest with Ed. He appreciated that about their relationship. With most girls he knew, girls like Heather, there were many mystifying levels of bullshit. With Gaia he could just tell her exactly what he was thinking.

Well, actually, not *everything* he was thinking. There was a certain category of thing he couldn't tell her about. That's why it was often easier talking with her on the phone, because when he couldn't see her, which meant he had fewer of those thoughts he couldn't tell her about.

"I almost got shot in the head a little while ago. That's probably why," Gaia suggested.

Ed made a sound somewhere between laughter and choking on a chicken bone. "What?"

That was another thing he appreciated about Gaia. She was always surprising. Though too often in an upsetting way.

Gaia let out her breath. "Oh, God. Where to start. You know that guy CJ?"

1

"The one who slashed Heather? Isn't he in jail?" Ed asked with a sick feeling in his stomach.

"I guess he got out on bail or something," Gaia said matter-of-factly. "Anyway, CJ's friend Marco is dead, and he thinks I killed him."

Ed groaned out loud. How had his life taken such a turn? Before he met Gaia, he wouldn't have believed he would have a conversation like this.

"Marco is dead, huh? Do you know who did it?"

"Uh-uh. Do you?"

"Gaia!"

"What? Just asking."

Ed clenched the portable phone between his ear and his neck and rolled his wheelchair from his room down the hallway of his family's small apartment and into the galley kitchen. His late evening phone conversations with Gaia had become as `precious a ritual` as his eleven o'clock milk shake.

"Come on," Ed prodded, hoisting himself up a few inches with his arms to reach the ice cream in the freezer. "Tell me what happened."

"Okay. I was sitting in the park minding my own business—"

"Eating doughnuts," Ed supplied.

"Yes, Ed, eating doughnuts, when that loser came up from behind and shoved a gun into my neck."

"Jesus."

2

"I didn't take it seriously at first. But it turns out this guy is half-crazed and deadly serious."

"So what happened?" Ed asked, milk shake momentarily forgotten.

Gaia sighed. "He actually pulled the trigger. I thought I was dead—a wild experience, by the way. It turned out he must have loaded the gun in a hurry, because there was no bullet in at least one of the chambers. I took that opportunity to throw him."

"Throw him?"

"You know, like flip him." She was very casual about it.

"Oh, right. Of course," Ed said.

"You're making fun of me again," Gaia said patiently.

Ed shook his head in disbelief. "I'm not, Gaia. It's just . . ." He laughed. "You blow my mind."

"Well, speaking of, I think this guy CJ is dead-set on killing me. I'm scared he's really going to do it," Gaia said.

"You're scared?" Ed asked. Gaia's voice was grave, but he couldn't help feeling it would take more than a pimply white supremacist with a borrowed gun to hurt Gaia. It would take something more on the order of a `hydrogen bomb`.

"Figure of speech. I'm scared *abstractly*," Gaia explained.

He could hear her thumping her heel against her metal desk. He resumed his milk shake making.

PrrrrrrrrRRRRR.

"Ed! I hate when you run the blender when we're talking," Gaia complained loudly.

"Sorry," he said. By the time she finished complaining, the milk shake was perfectly frothy and smooth. That was part of the ritual.

"I don't want to die," she said resolutely. "You know why?"

"Why?" he asked absently, sucking down a huge mouthful of vanilla shake.

"I haven't had sex yet."

Ed spluttered the mouthful all over his dark blue T-shirt. Cough cough cough. "What?"

"I don't want to die before I've had sex."

Cough cough.

"Right," he said.

"So I need to have sex in the next couple of days, just in case," Gaia added.

Cough cough cough cough cough cough cough cough cough cough—

"Ed? Are you okay? Ed? Is somebody around to give you the Heimlich?"

"N-No," Ed choked out. "I'm (cough cough) fine."

In fact, he had about four ounces of milk shake puddled in his lung. Could you die of that? Could you drown by breathing in a milk shake? And shit, he'd like to have sex in the next couple of days, too. (Cough cough cough.)

4

"Ed, are you sure you're okay?"

"Yesss," he answered in a weak and gravelly voice.

"So, anyway, I was thinking I better do it soon."

"It?"

"Yeah, it. You know, IT."

"Right. It." Ed felt faint. Milk shake, as it turned out, was much less handy in your veins than, say, oxygen, for instance. "So, who . . . uh . . . are you going to do IT with? Or are you just going to walk the streets soliciting people randomly?"

"Ed!" Gaia sounded geniunely insulted.

"Kidding," he said feebly.

"You don't think anybody's going to want to have sex with me, do you?" Gaia sounded hurt and petulant at the same time.

"Mmrnpha." The noise Ed made didn't resemble an English word. It sounded like it had come from the mouth of a nine-month-old baby.

"Huh?"

"I . . . um . . ." Ed couldn't answer. The truth was, although she made every effort to hide it, Gaia was possibly the most beautiful girl he had ever seen in his life—and that was including the women in the *Victoria's Secret* catalogue, the *SI* swimsuit issue, and that show about witches on the WB. Any straight guy with a live pulse and a thimbleful of testosterone would want to have sex with Gaia. But what was Ed going to say? This was *exactly* the category of conversation he couldn't have honestly with Gaia.

"Anyway, I do know who I'm going to do it with," Gaia said confidently.

"Who?" Ed felt his vision blurring.

"I can't say."

Ed definitely wasn't taking in enough oxygen. Good thing he was in a chair, because otherwise he'd be lying on the linoleum.

"Why can't you say?" he asked, trying to sound calm.

"Because it's way too awkward," Gaia said.

Awkward? Awkward. What did that imply? Could it mean . . . ? Ed's thoughts were racing. Would it be too crude to point out at this juncture that, though his legs were paralyzed, his nether regions were in excellent working condition?

He felt a tiny tendril of hope winding its way into his heart. He beat it back. "Gaia, don't you think you'll need to get past *awkwardness* if you really plan to be doing IT with this person in the next forty-eight hours?"

"Yeah, I guess." She slammed her heel against the desk. "But I still can't tell you."

"Oh, come on, Gaia. You have to."

"I gotta go."

"Gaia!"

"I really do. Cru-Ella needs to use the phone."

"Gaia! Please? Come on! Tell."

"See ya tomorrow."

"Gaia, who? Who who who?" Ed demanded.

"You," he heard her say, in a soft voice, before she hung up the phone.

But as he lay the phone on the counter he knew who'd said the word, and it wasn't Gaia. It was that wretched, misguiding, leechlike parasite called hope.

THE TIME HAD COME. HEATHER GANNIS

felt certain of that as she slammed her locker door shut and tucked the red envelope into her book bag. She waited for the deafening late afternoon crowd to clear before striking out toward the bathroom. She

Freakishly Needy

didn't feel like picking up the usual half-dozen hangers-on desperate to know what she was doing after soccer practice.

Okay, time to make her move. She caught sight of Melanie Young in her peripheral vision, but pretended she hadn't. She acted as though she didn't hear Tannie Deegan calling after her. Once in the bathroom she hid in the stall for a couple of minutes to be sure she wasn't being followed.

Heather usually liked her high visibility and enormous number of friends, but some of these girls were so freakishly *needy* some of the time. It was like if they missed one group trip to the Antique Boutique they would never recover. Their clinginess made it almost impossible for Heather to spend one private afternoon with her boyfriend.

Heather dumped her bag in the mostly dry sink and stared at her reflection. She wanted to look her best when she saw Sam. She bent her head so close to the mirror that her nose left a tiny grease mark on the glass. This close she could see the light freckles splattered across the bridge of her nose and the amber streaks in her light eyes that kept them from being the bona fide true blue of her mother and sisters.

Her pores looked big and ugly from this vantage point. Did Sam see them this way when he kissed her? She pulled away. She got busy rooting through her bag for powder to tame the oil on her forehead and nose and hopefully cover those gaping, yawning pores. She applied another coat of clear lip gloss. For somebody who was supposed to be so beautiful, she sure felt pretty plain sometimes.

She wished she hadn't eaten those potato chips at lunch. She couldn't help worrying that the difference between beauty and hideousness would come down to one bag of salt-and-vinegar chips.

As she swung her bag over her shoulder and smacked open the swinging door, she caught sight of the dingy olive-colored pants and faded black hooded sweatshirt of Gaia Moore. Heather's heart picked up pace and she felt blood pulsing in her temples.

God, she hated that girl. She hated the way she walked, the way she dressed, the way she talked. She hated that pale blond hair, a color you rarely saw on a person over the age of three. Heather wished the color were fake, but she knew it wasn't.

Heather hated Gaia for dumping scorching-hot coffee all over her shirt a couple of weeks ago and not bothering to apologize. Heather hated Gaia for being friends with Ed Fargo, her ex-boyfriend, and turning him against Heather at that awful party. Heather *really* hated Gaia for failing to warn Heather that there was a guy with a knife in the park, when Heather was obviously headed there.

All of those things were unforgivable. But none of them kept Heather up at night. The thing that kept her up at night was one small, nothing comment made by her boyfriend, Sam Moon.

It happened the day Heather got out of the hospital. Sam was there visiting, as he was throughout those five days. He had disappeared for a few minutes and when he got back to her room, Heather asked him where he'd been. He said, "I ran into Gaia in the hallway." That was all. Afterward, when Heather quizzed him, Sam instantly claimed to dislike Gaia. Like everybody else, he said it was partly Gaia's fault that Heather got slashed in the first place.

But there was something about Sam's face when he said Gaia's name that stuck in Heather's mind and would not go away.

Heather's mind flashed again on the card floating in her bag. She sorted through the bag and pulled it out. She needed to check again that the words seemed right. That the handwriting didn't look too girly and stupid. That the phrasing didn't seem too . . . desperate.

She'd find Sam in the park playing chess with that crazy old man, as he often did on Wednesday afternoons. And if not, she'd go on to his dorm and wait for him there. She'd hand him the card, watch his face while he read it, and kiss him so he'd know she meant it.

She was in love with Sam. This Saturday marked their six-month anniversary. He was the best-looking, most intelligent guy she knew. She loved the fact that he was in college.

She had made this decision with her heart. Sam was sexy. Sam was even romantic sometimes. She wanted him to be the one.

So why, then, as she wrote the card, was she thinking not of Sam, but of Gaia?

Dear Sam,

These last six months have been the best of my whole life. Sorry to be corny, but it's true. So I wanted to celebrate the occasion with a VERY special night. I'll meet you at your room at 8 on Saturday night and we'll finally do something we've been talking about doing for a long time. I know I said I wanted to wait, but I changed my mind.

You are the one and NOW is the time.

Love and kisses (all over),
Heather

Some secrets are too dangerous to know . . .

ROSWELL
HIGH

In the tiny town of Roswell, New Mexico, teenagers Liz Parker and Max Evans forged an otherworldly connection after Max recklessly threw aside his pact of secrecy and healed a life-threatening wound of Liz's with the touch of his hand. It turns out that Max, his sister Isabel, and their friend Michael are surviving descendants from beings on board an alien spacecraft which crash-landed in Roswell in 1947.

Max loves Liz. He couldn't let her die. But this is a dangerous secret he swore never to divulge - and now it's out. The trio must learn to trust Liz and her best friend Maria in order to stay one step ahead of the sheriff and the FBI who will stop at nothing in hunting out an alien...

FEARLESS™

. . . a girl born without the fear gene

Sam is gone.
No. Not just gone.
Someone's taken him.
Kidnapped him to get to me.

And I only have three hours to find him . . .

Or Sam is going to die.
All because of me.

His hand was poised on the trigger. He was going to do it. He was going to kill her right here, right now. If she moved, he would just kill her sooner.

She prayed for an intervention of some kind. A noise, a voice, even a car horn. She could turn the tiniest distraction into an opportunity. If he even flinched, she could wrench away the gun and demolish CJ with a couple of quick jabs. But the park and its surrounding streets were eerily calm.

Her mind entered into that dream state, in which you process things without quite believing them. This was it? This was the end? This was what it felt like to die?

The barrel shook as he tightened his grip on the trigger. She could see the taut, quivering muscles in his forearm.

The wind had ceased. It seemed there was no one alive on the planet. The night was so silent, she could hear the grinding of his teeth. Or was it her teeth?

His muscles strained, her heart stopped, her eyes squeezed shut. He pulled the trigger.

Don't miss any books in this thrilling new series
from Pocket Books:

FEARLESS™

#1 Fearless
#2 Sam

FEARLESS™

FRANCINE PASCAL

SAM

POCKET
BOOKS

An imprint of Simon & Schuster UK Ltd
A Viacom Company
Africa House, 64-78 Kingsway, London WC2B 6AH

Produced by 17th Street Productions,
an Alloy Online, Inc. company
33 West 17th Street, New York, NY 10011

A CIP catalogue record for this book is
available from the British Library

ISBN 0671 03747 1

3 5 7 9 10 8 6 4

Printed by Cox & Wyman Ltd, Reading, Berkshire

SAM

. . . with her back to him and his gun dug into her head, she was almost defenseless.

two things

IT REALLY WASN'T *THAT* FAR.

Gaia Moore studied the small garden
four stories below her window. Well, it
wasn't *her* window, exactly. It was one of
three back windows that belonged to the
top floor of the New York City brownstone of George
and Ella Niven, her so-called guardians.
George was a CIA friend of her dad's from way back
when. "Way back when" was typical of the vagueness
you got when living with spies and antiterrorist types.
They didn't say, "You know, George, the underground
assassin I met in Damascus?"

Jones

"Gaia?"

Gaia flinched at the voice materializing in her ear.
Ella Niven's voice didn't seem to react to air molecules in
the normal way. It was breathy and fake intimate,
yet carried to the far reaches of the house without losing
any of its volume.

"Guy-uhhhhhhh!" Ella bleated impatiently from
her dressing room one floor below.

Gaia inched open the window. The window frame
was oak, old and creaky with its lead chain and coun-
terweight.

"Gaia? The Beckwiths will be here any minute!
Come down now! George asked you to set the table
twenty minutes ago!" Now Ella sounded downright
whiny.

Gaia could smell bland, watery casserolelike odors

climbing up the stairs and mixing with Ella's strong, spicy perfume. George was a sweetheart and a terrible cook but probably a better cook than `potato-brained Ella`, who wasn't a sweetheart and never set foot in the kitchen except to whir up a fad-diet shake. The unspoken rule when they had company was that George prepared the food and Ella prepared herself.

Gaia grabbed a five-dollar bill from the top of the bureau and stuffed it in the pocket of her pants. Keys or no keys? That was the question. Mmmm. No keys, Gaia decided.

When the window was open just enough, she climbed out.

Although Ella might think otherwise, Gaia wasn't having dinner with the Beckwiths. They were old State Department people, certain to ask questions about her parents, her past, and her future, her parents, her parents. Gaia could `not deal`. Why was it that people over the age of thirty felt the need, when confronted with a "young person," to ask so freaking many questions?

Gaia had never agreed to make an appearance tonight. In fact, when Ella had demanded her presence a few hours earlier, Gaia had told Ella she would jump out the window before she'd have dinner with the Beckwiths, and she wasn't kidding.

The autumn air was scented with dry leaves and

frying garlic from the Italian restaurant on West Fourth Street. Distantly Gaia smelled chimney smoke and felt a moment's longing for a different life, when she'd had parents and a pretty house in the Berkshires with a fire in the fireplace every autumn and winter night. That life felt like it belonged to a different person.

She knelt on the narrow windowsill and gripped it with both hands before she lowered herself down. Errg. Her feet tapped blindly for her next toehold while her fingers began to tremble with the exertion of holding up the full weight of her body. Wasn't there a window top or trellis around here somewhere?

At last the toe of her sneaker found purchase in a deeply pitted slab of brownstone. She sank her weight into it, releasing her cramping fingers. And just then, the brownstone cracked under the weight and she fell.

She winced in surprise and annoyance, but she didn't scream. Her mind didn't abandon its rational sequence.

She fell several feet before her hands jammed against the windowsill of a third-floor window, and she miraculously arrested her fall, saving her skull from the slate patio below.

God, that hurt. Angry nerve endings throbbed in her palms, but her heart beat out its same steady rhythm. Air entered her lungs in the same measured breaths as always.

4

That's why Gaia Moore was different. A freak of nature. Gaia knew that any normal person would have been afraid just then. But she wasn't. She wasn't afraid now, and she wouldn't be ever. She wasn't born with whatever gene it was that made ordinary people feel fear.

It was like something was missing from her genetic tool kit. But doctors weren't sure exactly what it was. They only knew it seemed to affect her reaction to fear. Scientists know the basic setup—there's a master gene that triggers a series of minor genes that in turn control fear reactions. After extensive testing they came up with the theory that one or more of Gaia's genes in that cascade might be inactive or just plain missing.

Something moved on the other side of the window and Gaia squinted to get a better look.

Oh, crap. It was Ella.

Obviously hearing a noise, Ella swiveled her head from the mirror where she was gunking up her eyelashes with mascara and stared into the darkness outside. Ella was both dumb and otherworldly alert. She was self-obsessed but controlling at the same time. Gaia felt her blood start to boil at the mere sight of George's young, plastic wife. Whenever Ella was around, Gaia began to wonder if Mother Nature had given her extra capacity for anger and frustration when she'd left out the capacity for fear.

5

Gaia's fingers were straining so hard on the windowsill, she felt her muscles seizing up. *Go away, Ella. Go away now!*

A less annoying version of Ella would have figured the noise was just a pigeon or something and gotten on with her elaborate primping ritual. But this being the actual Ella, she came right over to the window and started to open it. Gaia glanced back over her shoulder, eyeballing the distance between her dangling feet and the patio. It had been reduced to twelve or fifteen feet.

Ella succeeded in throwing open the sash, narrowing her suspicious eyes. "What in the . . . ? Oh, Christ. Is that Gaia? Gaia!"

Gaia raised her head from her painful perch, and their eyes met for a fraction of a second.

It was weird. Ella was vapid and worthless at least nine-tenths of the time, but when she got really mad, her face became sharp and purposeful. Almost vicious. Like if Barbie were suddenly possessed by Atilla the Hun.

Ella's fingers were only inches from Gaia's. "Oh, hell," Gaia murmured, and let go.

Wump. Her feet took the brunt of the impact, then her knees, then her hands slapped down to steady her. Her knees stung, and she rubbed her hands together, doubting whether she'd ever have feeling in her palms again.

"Gaia! Get back here now!" Ella shrieked.

Gaia peered up momentarily at Ella's white face leaning out of the window. Gaia really hadn't wanted to make a scene. Poor George was never going to hear the end of it.

"Guy-uhhhhhhhhhhhhhhhh!"

Without another look behind her, Gaia ran for the back of the garden. Briefly she paused to glance at the seven fat goldfish swimming in the tiny pond before she leaped over it. She scaled the five-foot garden fence with exceptional grace.

Ella's supersonic voice followed her all the way to Bleecker Street and then dissolved amid the noisy profusion of shops, cafes, and restaurants and the crush of people that made the West Village of Manhattan unique in the world. In a single block you could buy fertility statues from Tanzania, rare Amazonian orchids, a pawned brass tuba, Krispy Kreme doughnuts, or the best, most expensive cup of coffee you ever tasted. It was the doughnuts, incidentally, that attracted Gaia.

She walked past the plastic-wrapped fruit laid out on beds of melting ice and into the deli, where the extravagant salad bar at its center emitted a strong, oily aroma. It was called a salad bar, but it was filled with the least healthful stuff Gaia could imagine (apart from doughnuts, anyway). A trough of deep-fried egg rolls, chicken blobs floating in a sea of pink grease, and some slop vaguely resembling potato salad if you quintupled the mayonnaise. Who ever ate that stuff? Gaia didn't know for sure, but she would have bet her favorite Saucony sneakers that the smelly egg rolls she saw now were exactly the same smelly egg rolls she'd been seeing for the last month.

She made a beeline for the doughnut shelf. Crullers? Cinnamon cakey ones? Powdered sugar? Glazed? Chocolate?

Oh, who was she kidding? She'd been jonesing for a sticky chocolate doughnut all evening. Why pretend any other kind came close? Her mouth was watering as she laid the crumpled five on the counter. The pretty young Korean woman took the bill and gave Gaia her change without really looking up. Somehow, in spite of the fact that they saw each other nearly every day, Gaia and this woman never made any sign of recognition. That was a New York thing— pretend anonymity—and frankly, Gaia liked it. It was perfect, what with Gaia being a not-very-friendly person with a lot of secrets and an embarrassingly large appetite for doughnuts.

Gaia said no thank you to the plastic bag and carried her box of doughnuts in her still-numb hands out of the store, along Bleecker Street toward Seventh Avenue. She figured if you weren't woman enough to carry your doughnuts with pride, you shouldn't be eating them.

Her feet went into auto-walk. They knew their way to Washington Square Park by now. That was her favorite place to eat doughnuts or do just about anything. She chose the perfect park bench, clean and quiet, and sat under a canopy of red-turning leaves that carved the glowing night sky into lace. Hungrily she tore open the box.

Yum.

This moment suddenly contained the entire universe. Hell was eating George's food, watching Ella flirt shamelessly with Mr. Beckwith, and fielding questions about her parents she couldn't imagine answering. This doughnut, this bench, and this sky, on the other hand, were heaven.

"DON'T MOVE."

No Bullet

Okay. Gaia's pupils sped to the corners of her eyes, but she didn't turn her head. Okay, it felt very much like the cold barrel of a gun pressed against her neck. Okay, if Gaia were to feel fear, now would be an obvious time.

The drying leaves were rustling sweetly overhead, the picturesque little puddles cast the glow of the streetlamps back up into the sky, but there wasn't a soul in sight besides the heavy-breathing, perspiring young man crushing the gun into her trapezius muscle.

He was standing behind the bench, but she could make out enough of him through her straining peripheral vision to recognize the nasty little hoodlum she'd seen in the park many times. His name was CJ Somethingorother. She'd not only beaten up his friends but identified him in a police lineup two weeks before as the gang member who'd stabbed Heather Gannis in the park. It didn't tax her imagination to think of why he wanted to scare her. Even hurt her. But kill her?

"Don't freakin' move an inch, bitch."

She sighed. She glanced longingly at her box of doughnuts.

"I *mean* it!"

Ouch. Jesus, he was going to puncture her flesh with the goddamned thing.

He was breathing heavily. He smelled like he'd been drinking. "I know you killed Marco, you sick bitch. And you're gonna pay."

Gaia swallowed hard. Suddenly the doughnut was a bitter clump in her mouth that she couldn't choke down. This guy's voice didn't carry the usual stupid bravado. He wasn't just trying to feel like a man.

Sweat trickled from his hand down the barrel of the gun.

He was dead serious, partly scared, maybe crazy.

Gaia had wondered what had become of Marco. He was a vain, annoying loudmouth, the most conspicuous of the thuggy neo-Nazi guys who contaminated the park. She could tell from the new graffiti she'd seen around the fountain that one of their number was dead.

Now it made sense. Marco was gone, and his boys believed Gaia killed him. That wasn't good news for her. Gaia felt sure there was any number of people who would have wanted to kill Marco.

"I didn't kill Marco," she said in a low, steady voice.

"Bullshit." CJ dragged the gun roughly from her neck to her temple. "Don't mess with me. I know what you did. That's how come you're gonna die."

She could feel her pulse beating against the dead, blunt metal.

CJ steadied the gun with both hands, breathing in deeply.

Oh, God. This was bad. Gaia eased her left hand along the thickly painted wooden slats of the bench.

"Don't move!" he bellowed.

Gaia froze, cringing with pain at the pressure of the gun against her head. A surge of anger ripped through her veins, but as badly as she wanted to break his neck, she recognized that in this position, with her

11

back to him and his gun dug into her head, she was almost defenseless.

She tried to subdue her anger before she opened her mouth.

"CJ, don't do it," she said tightly. "It's a mistake. You're wasting your time here—"

"Shut *up!*" he screamed. "Don't say *any*thing!"

His hand was poised on the trigger. He was going to do it. He was going to kill her right here, right now. If she moved, he would just kill her sooner.

She prayed for an intervention of some kind. A noise, a voice, even a car horn. She could turn the tiniest distraction into an opportunity. If he even flinched, she could wrench away the gun and demolish CJ with a couple of quick jabs. But the park and its surrounding streets were eerily calm.

Her mind entered into that dream state, in which you process things without quite believing them. This was it? This was the end? This was what it felt like to die?

The barrel shook as he tightened his grip on the trigger. She could see the taut, quivering muscles in his forearm.

The wind had ceased. It seemed there was no one alive on the planet. The night was so silent, she could hear the grinding of his teeth. Or was it her teeth?

His muscles strained, her heart stopped, her eyes squeezed shut. He pulled the trigger.

Her mind was in free fall. Perfectly blank. Then, like the burst of a firecracker, came a searing moment of understanding and regret, so complete and profound it shouldn't have been able to fit into a small fraction of a second—

Click.

What was that?

She turned her head. She realized her whole body was shaking. CJ looked just as shocked as he stared at the gun.

It hadn't fired. There was no bullet lodged in her head.

Not yet, anyway. Thank God CJ was an incompetent cave boy. Now, if she didn't get off her butt quick, she'd lose the only chance she had to save it. She shot up to her feet, grabbed CJ by the arm that held the gun, and used it to flip the bastard right over her shoulder. His body smacked hard against the pavement. The gun skidded off the path and into the brush.

She stared at his seizing body for a second. Under normal circumstances she would have stayed to pummel him like he deserved, but tonight she was too genuinely freaked out. She needed to get out of there. Her brains, thankfully, were still safely in her skull, but her emotions were splattered on the pavement.

Gaia ran. She ran as fast and gracefully as a doe. But not so fast that she didn't hear the tortured voice screaming behind her.

"I will kill you! I swear to *God* I will kill you!"

Tonight, as I sat on the
park bench waiting for my head to
explode, I had one moment of clarity in which I learned two things.

   1) I have to find my dad.

   I just have to. As angry as I
am, as much as I hate him for
abandoning me on the most awful,
vulnerable day of my life, I
don't want to die without seeing
him one more time. I don't know
what I'll say to him. But there's
something I want to know, and I
feel like if I can look in his
eyes—just for a moment—I'll know
what his betrayal meant and
whether there's any love or
trust, even the possibility of
it, between us.

   2) I have to have sex.

   Oh, come on. Don't act so
shocked. I'm seventeen years old.
I know the rules about being
safe. If my life weren't in very
immediate jeopardy, maybe I would
let it wait for the exact right
time. But let's face it—I may not
be around next week, forget about

happily ever after. Besides, I've
been through a lot of truly awful
things in my life, so why should
I die without getting to experience one of the few great ones?

Who am I going to have sex with?

Do you have to ask?

All right, I have an answer. In
that moment, when my fragile mind-
set was shattered, the face I saw
belonged to Sam Moon. Granted, he
hates me. Granted, he has a girlfriend. Granted, his girlfriend
hates me even more. But I'll find
a way. 'Cause he's the one. I
can't say why; he just is.

I wish I could convince myself
that CJ wouldn't make good on his
threat. But I heard his voice. I
saw his face. I know he'll do any
crazy thing it takes.

I won't go down easy. But I'd be
stupid not to prepare for the worst.

Am I afraid? No. I'm never
afraid. But the way I see it,
dying without knowing love would
be a tragedy.

She hated
that pale
blond hair,
a color
you **desperate**
rarely saw
on a person
over the age
of three.

"YOU SOUND WEIRD."

"How do you mean?" Gaia asked.

"I don't know. You just do. You're talking fast or something," Ed said as he clenched the portable

phone between his shoulder and his ear and eased himself from his desk chair to his wheelchair.

Ed Fargo was honest with Gaia, and Gaia was honest with Ed. He appreciated that about their relationship. With most girls he knew, girls like Heather, there were many mystifying levels of bullshit. With Gaia he could just tell her exactly what he was thinking.

Ed's mind briefly flashed on the hip-hugging green corduroys Gaia was wearing in Mr. McAuliff's class today.

Well, actually, not *everything* he was thinking. There was a certain category of thing he couldn't tell her about. That's why it was often easier talking with her on the phone, because then he couldn't see her, which meant he had fewer of those thoughts he couldn't tell her about.

"I had a bad night. That's probably why," Gaia said.

Ed wheeled himself down the shabbily carpeted hallway of his family's small apartment. Family photographs lined the walls on both sides, but Ed didn't seem to see them anymore. "A bad night how?" he asked.

18

"I almost got shot in the head."

Ed made a sound somewhere between laughter and choking on a chicken bone. "You w-what?"

That was another thing about Gaia. She was always surprising. Though too often in an upsetting way.

Gaia let out her breath. "Oh, God. Where to start. You know that guy CJ?"

Ed slowed his chair to a stop and clenched the armrests with his hands. "The one who slashed Heather? Isn't he in jail?" he asked with a sick feeling in his stomach.

"I guess he got out on bail or something," Gaia said matter-of-factly. "Anyway, CJ's friend Marco is dead, and he thinks I killed him."

Ed groaned out loud. How had his life taken such a turn? Before he'd first laid love-struck eyes on Gaia in the hallway outside physics class, he wouldn't have believed he would ever have a conversation like this.

"Marco is dead? Are you sure?"

"Only from what CJ told me."

Ed sighed. The really crazy thing was, in the brief time he'd known Gaia, so many violent and alarming things had happened, this wasn't so staggeringly out of the ordinary.

"Hey, Gaia? If trouble is a hungry great white shark, then you're a liquid cloud of chum."

Gaia's laugh was easy and comforting. "That's a beautiful image. I love it when you get poetic."

Ed resumed his roll down the hallway and into the galley kitchen. His late evening phone reports from Gaia, distressing as they sometimes were, had become as precious a ritual as his eleven o'clock milk shake.

"So tell me," Ed prodded, hoisting himself up a few inches with one arm to reach the ice cream in the freezer. "Tell me how it happened."

"Okay. I was sitting in the park, minding my own business—"

"Eating doughnuts," Ed supplied.

"Yes, Ed, eating doughnuts, when that loser came up from behind and shoved a gun into my neck."

"Jesus."

"I didn't take it seriously at first. But it turns out this guy is half crazed and deadly serious."

"So what happened?" Ed asked, milk shake momentarily forgotten.

Gaia sighed. "He actually pulled the trigger. I thought I was dead—a wild experience, by the way. It turned out he must have loaded the gun in a hurry because there was no bullet in at least one of the chambers. I took that opportunity to throw him."

Ed's mind was spinning. "Throw him?"

"You know, like flip him."

"Oh, right," he said.

"You're making fun of me again," Gaia said patiently.

Ed shook his head in disbelief. "I'm not, Gaia. It's just . . . you blow my mind."

"Well, speaking of, I think this guy CJ is dead set on killing me. I'm scared he's really going to do it," Gaia said.

"You're scared?" Ed asked a little nervously. Having seen Gaia in action, he would have imagined it would take more than a pimply white supremacist with a borrowed gun to hurt Gaia. It would take something more on the order of a hydrogen bomb. But if Gaia was scared, well, he had to take that seriously.

"Figure of speech. I'm scared *abstractly*," Gaia explained.

Ed rocked a tall glass on the counter. "Gaia, you worry me here."

"Don't worry," Gaia reassured him. "I mean, think about it. CJ is kind of a moron, and I happen to be okay at self-defense."

Ed felt reassured. That last part was an understatement to rival "Marilyn Manson is an unusual guy." He could hear Gaia thumping her heel against her metal desk. He realized the ice cream was melting and spreading along the countertop. He absently scooped some of it into the blender.

Prrrrrrrrrrrrr.

"Ed! I hate when you run the blender when we're talking," Gaia complained loudly.

"Sorry," he said. By the time she finished

complaining, the milk shake was frothy and smooth. That was part of the ritual.

"I don't want to die," she said resolutely. "You know why?"

"Why?" he asked absently, sucking down a huge mouthful of vanilla shake.

"I haven't had sex yet."

Ed spluttered the mouthful all over his dark blue T-shirt. Cough, cough, cough. "What?"

"I don't want to die before I've had sex."

Cough, cough.

"Right," he said.

"So I need to have sex in the next couple of days, just in case," Gaia added.

Cough, cough, cough, cough, cough, cough, cough, cough, cough, cough—

"Ed? Are you okay? Ed? Is somebody around to give you the Heimlich?"

"N-No," Ed choked out. "I'm (cough, cough) fine."

In fact, he had about four ounces of milk shake puddled in his lung. Could you die of that? Could you drown by breathing in a milk shake? And shit, he'd like to have sex in the next couple of days, too. (Cough, cough, cough.)

"Ed, are you sure you're okay?"

"Yesss," he answered in a weak and gravelly voice.

"So anyway, I was thinking I better do it soon."

"It?"

"Yeah, it. You know, *it*."

"Right. It." Ed felt faint. Milk shake, as it turned out, was much less handy in your veins than, say, oxygen. "So, who . . . uh . . . are you going to do *it* with? Or are you just going to walk the streets, soliciting people randomly?"

"Ed!" Gaia sounded genuinely insulted.

"Kidding," he said feebly, wishing his palms weren't suddenly sweating.

"You don't think anybody's going to want to have sex with me, do you?" Gaia sounded hurt and petulant at the same time.

"Mmrnpha." The noise Ed made didn't resemble an English word. It sounded like it had come from the mouth of a nine-month-old baby.

"Huh?"

"I . . . um . . ." Ed couldn't answer. The truth was, although she made every effort to hide it, Gaia was possibly the most beautiful girl he had ever seen in his life—and that was including the women in the Victoria's Secret catalog, the *SI* swimsuit issue, and that show about witches on the WB. Any straight guy with a live pulse and a thimble full of testosterone would want to have sex with Gaia. But what was Ed going to say? This was *exactly* the category of conversation he couldn't have honestly with her.

"Anyway, I do know who I'm going to do it with," Gaia said confidently.

"Who?" Ed felt his vision blurring.

"I can't say."

Ed definitely wasn't taking in enough oxygen. Good thing he was in a chair because otherwise he'd be lying on the linoleum.

"Why can't you say?" he asked, trying to sound calm.

"Because it's way too awkward," Gaia said.

Awkward? Awkward. What did that imply? Could it mean . . . ? Ed's thoughts were racing. Would it be too crude to point out at this juncture that although his legs were paralyzed, his nether regions were in excellent working condition?

He felt a tiny tendril of hope winding its way into his heart. He beat it back. "Gaia, don't you think you'll need to get past *awkwardness* if you really plan to be doing *it* with this person in the next forty-eight hours?"

"Yeah, I guess." He heard her slam her heel against the desk. "But I still can't tell you."

"Oh, come on, Gaia. You have to."

"I gotta go."

"Gaia!"

"I really do. Cru-Ella needs to use the phone."

"Gaia! Please? Come on! Tell."

"See ya tomorrow."

"Gaia, who? Who, who, who?" Ed demanded.

"You," he heard her say in a soft voice before she hung up the phone.

But as he laid the phone on the counter he knew who'd said the word, and it wasn't Gaia. It was that misguiding, leechlike parasite called hope.

THE TIME HAD COME. HEATHER

One Small Comment

Gannis felt certain of that as she slammed her locker door shut and tucked the red envelope into her book bag. She waited for the deafening late afternoon crowd to clear before striking out toward the bathroom. She didn't feel like picking up the usual half-dozen hangers-on, desperate to know what she was doing after soccer practice.

Okay, time to make her move. She caught sight of Melanie Young in her peripheral vision but pretended she hadn't. She acted like she didn't hear Tannie Deegan calling after her. Once in the bathroom she hid in the stall for a couple of minutes to be sure she wasn't being followed.

Heather usually liked her high visibility and enormous number of friends, but some of those girls were so freakishly *needy* some of the time. It was like if they missed one group trip to the Antique

25

Boutique, they would never recover. Their clinginess made it almost impossible for Heather to spend one private afternoon with her boyfriend.

Heather dumped her bag in the mostly dry sink and stared at her reflection. She wanted to look her best when she saw Sam. She bent her head so close to the mirror that her nose left a tiny grease mark on the glass. This close, she could see the light freckles splattered across the bridge of her nose and the amber streaks in her light eyes that kept them from being the bona fide true blue of her mother and sisters.

Her pores looked big and ugly from this vantage point. Did Sam see them this way when he kissed her? She pulled away. She got busy rooting through her bag for powder to tame the oil on her forehead and nose and hopefully cover those gaping, yawning pores. She applied another coat of clear lip gloss. For somebody who was supposed to be so beautiful, she sure felt pretty plain sometimes.

She wished she hadn't eaten those potato chips at lunch. She couldn't help worrying that the difference between beauty and hideousness would come down to one bag of salt-and-vinegar chips.

As she swung her bag over her shoulder and smacked open the swinging door, she caught sight of the dingy olive-colored pants and faded black hooded sweatshirt of Gaia Moore. Heather's heart picked up pace, and she felt blood pulsing in her temples.

God, she hated that girl. She hated the way she walked, the way she dressed, the way she talked. She hated that pale blond hair, a color you rarely saw on a person over the age of three. Heather wished the color was fake, but she knew it wasn't.

Heather hated Gaia for dumping scorching-hot coffee all over her shirt a couple of weeks ago and not bothering to apologize. Heather hated Gaia for being friends with Ed Fargo, her ex-boyfriend, and turning him against Heather at that awful party. Heather *really* hated Gaia for failing to warn Heather that there was a guy with a knife in the park, when Heather was obviously headed there.

All of those things were unforgivable. But none of them kept Heather up at night. The thing that kept her up at night was one small, nothing comment made by her boyfriend, Sam Moon.

It happened the day Heather got out of the hospital. Sam was there visiting, as he was throughout those five days. He had disappeared for a few minutes, and when he got back to her room, Heather asked him where he'd been. He said, "I ran into Gaia in the hallway." That was all. Afterward, when Heather quizzed him, Sam instantly claimed to dislike Gaia. Like everybody else, he said it was partly Gaia's fault that Heather got slashed in the first place.

27

But there was something about Sam's face when he said Gaia's name that stuck in Heather's mind and wouldn't go away.

Heather's mind returned again to the card floating in her bag. She sorted through the bag and pulled it out. She needed to check again that the words seemed right. That the handwriting didn't look too girly and stupid. That the phrasing didn't seem too ... desperate.

She'd find Sam in the park playing chess with that crazy old man, as he often did on Wednesday afternoons. And if not, she'd go on to his dorm and wait for him there. She'd hand him the card, watch his face while he read it, and kiss him so he'd know she meant it.

She was in love with Sam. This Saturday marked their six-month anniversary. He was the best-looking, most intelligent guy she knew. She loved the fact that he was in college.

She had made this decision with her heart. Sam was sexy. Sam was even romantic sometimes. He wasn't a guy you let get away.

So why, then, as she wrote the card, was she thinking not of Sam, but of Gaia?

Dear Sam,

 These last six months have been the best of my life. Sorry to be corny, but it's true. So I wanted to celebrate the occasion with a very special night. I'll meet you at your room at eight on Saturday night and we'll finally do something we've been talking about doing for a long time. I know I said I wanted to wait, but I changed my mind.

You are the one, and now is the time.

Love and kisses (all over),

Heather

He smiled at her. This time it was sweet, **lonely** open, real. **hearts**

"THAT STUPID PUNK WILL NOT KILL
Gaia!" he thundered. **Remarkable Girl**
"Do you understand?"

He strode to the far end of the loft apartment and kicked over a side table laden with coffee mugs. Most rolled; one shattered. One of the two bodyguards who hovered in the background came forward to clean them up.

He spun on Ella. He hated her face at moments like this. *"Do you understand?"*

"Of course I understand," she said sullenly. "I wasn't expecting her to climb out the window," she added in a scornful mumble.

"Learn to *expect* it!" he bellowed. "Gaia is *not* an ordinary girl! Haven't you figured that *out?*"

Ella's eyes darted with reptilian alertness, but she wisely kept her mouth shut.

"Gaia is no use to me dead. I will not let it happen. I don't care how crazy the girl is. I don't care if she throws herself in the path of a bus. I will *not* let it happen!" He was ranting now. He couldn't stop now if he wanted to. He'd always had a bad temper.

"Show me the pictures," he demanded of Ella.

Reluctantly Ella came near and put the pile in his hands.

He studied the first one for a long time. It was Gaia sitting alone on a park bench. Her face was tipped down, partly obscured by long, pale hair. Her gray sweatshirt was sagging off one shoulder. Her long legs were crossed, and a little burst of light erupted from the reflective patch on her running shoe. A box of doughnuts sat open on the bench next to her.

Her gesture and manner were so familiar to him, he felt an odd stirring in his chest. Though Gaia was undeniably beautiful with her graceful, angular face, she didn't resemble Katia. Katia had dark glossy hair, brown eyes flecked with orange, and a smaller, more voluptuous build.

In the next picture Gaia's head was raised, and in the shadow behind her was the boy pointing the gun at her head. The boy looked agitated, his eyes wild. Yet Gaia's face was impossibly calm. He brought the picture close. Remarkable. Utterly fascinating. There was no fear in those wide-set blue eyes. He would know. He had a great gift for detecting fear.

Gaia was indeed everything he had heard about her. All the more reason why he could not accept another ridiculous close call like this one.

He glanced at the next picture. The boy was leaning in closer, his face clenched as he prepared to pull the trigger.

"Keep that boy and his stupid friends away from her," he barked at Ella.

"Yes," she mumbled.

"He will not get that gun anywhere near Gaia!"

"Yes, sir."

He glared at Ella with withering eyes. "Hear me now, Ella. If *anyone* kills Gaia Moore, it will be me."

Ella's gaze was cast to the ground.

He studied the next picture in the pile. This one showed Gaia standing in all her ferocious glory, flipping that pitiful boy over her shoulder. Her face was wonderfully alert, intense. She was magnificent. More than he could have hoped for.

No, Gaia didn't resemble Katia, he decided as he studied the lovely face in the picture. Gaia resembled him.

SHE PROBABLY WOULDN'T EVEN BE there. Why would she? She'd be avoiding him if she had any sense.

Sam Moon hurried into Washington Square Park with his physics textbook tucked under his arm. Then again, if *he* had any sense, he'd be avoiding *her*. Instead he was darting around the park at all hours like some kind of timid stalker, hoping to catch a glimpse of her.

Like a Drug

He approached the shaded area where the chess tables sat, surveying them almost hungrily. No. She wasn't there. It verged on ridiculous, the physical feeling of disappointment that radiated through his abdomen.

He kept his distance, reviewing his options. He didn't want to plunge right into chess world because then all his cohorts would see him and he'd be stuck for at least a game or two. And he'd found out the hard way that when Gaia was on his mind (and when wasn't she?), he was a lot worse at chess.

Maybe she had come and gone already. Maybe she'd caught sight of him from a distance and taken off. Maybe she really did hate him—

"Moon?"

Sam practically leaped right out of his clothes. He spun around. "Jesus, Renny, you scared the crap out of me."

Renny smiled in his open, friendly way. He was a wiry-looking, barely adolescent Puerto Rican kid who was quickly becoming a lethal chess player. "You looking for Gaia?"

Sam's face fell. Was his head made of glass? Was his romantic torment, which he believed to be totally private and unique, available for public display? Was everybody who knew him talking and snickering about it? Even the chess nerds, who wouldn't ordinarily notice if you'd had one of your legs amputated?

"No," Sam lied defensively. "Why?"

"I figure you're getting tired of whipping the rest of us. Gaia could probably get a game off you, huh?"

Sam studied Renny's face for signs of cleverness or mockery. No. Renny wasn't being a wise guy. He wasn't suddenly Miss Lonely Hearts. Renny was thinking the same way he always thought, like a chess player.

Sam let out a breath. He tried to relax the crackling nerve synapses in his neck and shoulders. There was a word for this: *paranoia.*

"Yeah," Sam said in a way he hoped was nonchalant. "Maybe one or two. If she was on her game."

"Yeah," Renny said, "she's unbelievable." Renny's eyes got a little glassy, but Sam could tell he was fantasizing about Gaia's stunning end play, not about her lips or her eyes.

Unlike Sam.

"Yeah," Sam repeated awkwardly.

"See you." Renny clapped him on the back agreeably and waded into chess world. Sam watched Renny take the first open seat across from Mr. Haq, whose taxicab was predictably parked (illegally) at the nearest curb. That was the downside of playing Mr. Haq. If the cops came, he abandoned the game and put his cab back into action. And no matter how badly you were creaming him, Mr. Haq would always refer to it afterward as "an undecided match."

Sam found his way to a nearby bench with a good

view of the chess area. He opened his physics book, lame prop that it was.

What had happened to his resolution to forget about Gaia? He'd decided to put her out of his mind for good and focus all of his romantic energy on Heather, but Gaia was like a drug. She was in his blood, and he couldn't get her out. He was a junkie, an addict. He knew Gaia was bad for him. He knew she'd undermine his commitments and basically ruin his life. But he obsessed about her, anyway. Was there a twelve-step program for an addiction like this? Gaia Worshipers Anonymous?

He remembered that antidrug slogan that had scared him as a kid. *This is your brain.* He pictured the sizzling egg. *This is your brain thinking of Gaia.*

Clearly his decisions, vows, determinations, and oaths to forget Gaia weren't enough. Maybe it was time to try a different tack.

What if he attempted to relate to her as a normal person? Just talk to her about everyday things like school and extracurricular activities and stuff like that? Maybe he could demystify the whole relationship.

Maybe he and Gaia could even have a meal together. You couldn't easily idolize a girl while she was stuffing her face. She would probably order something he hated like lox or coleslaw. She would chew too loudly or maybe wear a bit of red cabbage on her front

tooth for a while. Maybe she would spit a little when she talked. Afterward she would have
bad breath or maybe a grease spot on her pants, and
voilà. Obsession over.

Yes. This was a practical idea. Demystification.

Because after all, although Gaia came off as a
pretty extraordinary person on the outside, on the inside she was just the same as anybody else.

. . . right?

SHE WAS A MESS.

She was a nightmare.

She should have her license
to be female revoked.

Gaia turned around to look
at her backside in the slightly
warped mirror that hung on the
back of the door to her room.

A Lame Come-on

Earlier that day she'd picked up a pair of capri pants
off the sale rack at the Gap in an effort to look cute and
feminine. Instead she looked like the Incredible Hulk
right after he turns green and bursts out of
his clothing.

What kind of shoes were you supposed to wear
with these things? Definitely not boots, as she could

plainly see in the mirror. Was it too late in the year to wear flip-flops?

Sam was not going to fall in love with her. He was going to take one look and run screaming in the opposite direction. Either that or laugh uncontrollably.

Why was she torturing herself this way? In her ordinary life she managed to pull off the functional style of a person who didn't care. She had no money, which occasionally resulted in the coincidental coolness of thrift shop dressing.

But now that Gaia actually cared, she had turned herself into a neurotic, insecure freak show.

Caring was to be deplored and avoided. Hadn't she learned that by now?

She stripped off the pants and pulled on her leastdescript pair of jeans. She pulled a nubbly sweater the color of oatmeal over her head.

Better ugly than a laughingstock. That was Gaia's new fashion motto.

She had to get out of the house before Ella sauntered in and recognized the beaded necklace Gaia had "borrowed." Ella was a whiny, dumb bimbo, but she had a nose for fashion trends. Gaia had every intention of returning the necklace before it was missed, so why cause a big fuss by asking?

Gaia thundered down the three flights of stairs, slammed the painted oak-and-glass door behind her, turned her key in the lock, and struck out for the park.

And to think she'd come home after school to work on her appearance.

She hurried past the picture-perfect row houses. Lurid red geraniums still exploded in the window boxes. Decorative little front fences cast long shadows in the late day sun, putting Gaia's shadow in an attenuated, demented-looking prison.

After a few blocks, Gaia suddenly paused as the sound of heavy guitar music blared through an open basement window, followed by a raspy tenor voice. "framed/you set me up, set me out and/blamed/you tore me up, tore me down and/chained/you tied me up, tied me down and . . . " It was that band again—Fearless. For a fleeting moment Gaia wanted to shout through the window and ask them where they got their bizarrely Gaia-centric name, but she had to keep moving.

She didn't have much time. CJ probably wasn't crazy enough to open fire on her in daylight, but once the sun got really low, she had to be ready for it, especially hanging around the park. How typical of her new life in the biggest city in the United States that the guy she wanted to seduce and the guy who wanted to shoot her hung out in exactly the same space.

Her stomach started to churn as she got close. What was she going to say to Sam?

"Hi, I know you have a girlfriend and don't like me at all, but do you want to have sex?"

On the one-in-ten-billion chance that he agreed to

her insane scheme, what then? They couldn't just do it on a park bench.

Suddenly the actual, three-dimensional Sam, sitting on a bench with a clunky-looking textbook open on his lap, replaced the Sam in her mind.

Oh, crap. Was it too late? Had he seen her?

"Gaia?"

That would mean yes.

`Swallow.` "Hi." She tried out a friendly smile that came off more like the expression a person might make when burning a finger on the top of the toaster.

He stood up, his smile looking equally pained. "How's it going?"

She hooked her thumbs in the front pockets of her pants. "Oh, fine. Fine." What was she? A farmer?

"Yeah?"

"Yeah."

"Great."

Oh, this was awful. This `come-hither Gaia` was a complete disaster. Why couldn't she be cute and flirty *and* have a personality?

He was clearly at a loss. "Do you, uh . . . want to play a game of chess?"

She would have agreed to `pull out her toe-nails` to escape this awkward situation.

"Yeah, sure, whatever," she said lightly. God, what a wordsmith she was.

"Or we could just, like, take a walk. Or something."

"Great. Sure," she said. Had her vocabulary shrunk to four words?

"Or we could even sit here for a couple of minutes."

"Yeah," she proclaimed.

"Fine," he countered.

"Great," she said.

They both stayed standing.

This was pathetic. How was she possibly going to have sex with him when simply sitting on the same bench involved a whole choreography of commitment?

She sat. There.

He sat, too.

Well, this was progress.

She crossed her legs and inadvertently brushed the heel of his shoe. With lightning-fast-reflex speed they both swung their respective feet to opposite sides of the bench.

Or not.

Gaia studied Sam's face in profile. It made her a little giddy to realize what a hunk he was. A classic knee weakener. He belonged on television or in a magazine ad for cologne. What was he doing sitting near *her*?

He looked up and caught her staring (slack jawed) at him. She quickly looked away. She pressed her hand, palm down, on the bench and realized her pinky was touching the outer edge of his thigh. *Uh-oh.*

Should she move it? Had he noticed? Did he think she had done it on purpose? Suddenly she had more feeling, more nerve endings (billions and billions at least) in her pinky than she ever thought possible. All of the awareness in her body was crammed into that pinky.

Now it felt clammy and weirdly twitchy. A pinky wasn't accustomed to all this attention. Did Sam feel it twitching? That would be awful. He'd think it was some kind of lame come-on. Either that or she'd lost muscle control.

Well, actually, this *was* some kind of lame come-on and she *had* lost control.

The problem was, if she took away her pinky, he would know she noticed that she was touching him, and that would be embarrassing, too.

He moved his leg. Suddenly Gaia's pinky was touching cold, lonely, uncharged air. She felt the piercing sting of rejection. Jerk. Loser. She was ready to give up on the whole project.

Then he moved it back and practically covered her entire pinky. Oh, faith! Love! Destiny! Could she propose to him right there?

He smiled at her. This time it was sweet, open, real.

Her stomach rolled. She smiled back, fervently

43

hoping it didn't look like a grimace and that her teeth didn't look yellow.

She heard a noise behind her. She jerked up her head.

She realized that the sun had dipped below the Hudson River and the streetlamps were illuminated. Oh, no. Could it be? Already?

She had to go. Fast. She wasn't going to turn into a pumpkin, but she was very likely going to get shot in the head. That could easily put a damper on this fragile, blossoming moment.

The sound resolved itself into a footstep, and a person appeared. It wasn't CJ, but just the same, it put an end to the encounter as powerfully as a bullet.

It was Heather. The girlfriend.

Her adrenaline was pumping now. Her muscles were **cold** buzzing with intensity. **blood** She was an easy target this close.

THERE WERE MOMENTS IN LIFE WHEN

words failed to convey your thoughts. There were moments when your thoughts failed to convey your feelings. Then there were moments when even your feelings failed to convey your feelings.

Cunning Intelligence

This was one of those, Heather realized as she gaped at Sam and Gaia Moore sitting on the park bench together.

They weren't kissing. They weren't touching. They weren't even talking. But Sam and Gaia could have been doing the nasty right there on the spot, and it wouldn't have carried the intimacy of this tentative, nervous, neurotic union she now witnessed between them.

Maybe she was imagining it, Heather considered. Maybe it was a figment of her own obsessive, jealous mind.

She'd almost rather believe she was crazy than that Sam, *her Sam,* was falling in love with Gaia. It was too coincidental, just too cruel to be real. Like one of those Greek tragedies she read for Mr. Hirschberg's class. Gaia was the person she most despised. Sam was the person she loved.

Had she done something to bring this on herself?

What was it the Greek guys always got smacked for? *Hubris,* that was the word—believing you were too good, too strong, invulnerable. The world had a way of teaching you that you weren't invulnerable.

Heather was paralyzed. Anger told her to get between them and make trouble, Pride told her to run away. Hurt told her to cry. Cunning told her to make Sam feel as guilty and small as possible. She waited to hear what Intelligence had to say. It never spoke first, but its advice was usually worth waiting for.

Her mind raced and sorted. Considered and rejected. Then finally, Intelligence piped up with a strategy.

"Sam," Heather stated. Good, firm, steady voice. She stepped around to the front of the bench and faced them straight on.

Sam looked up. Shock, fear, guilt, uncertainty, and regret waged war over his features.

Staring at them, Heather made no secret of her surprise and distress, but she overlaid a brave, tentative, give-them-the-benefit-of-the-doubt smile.

The effect was just as she'd intended. Sam looked like he wished to pluck out both of his eyeballs on the spot.

"Hey, Gaia," Heather said. Her expression remained one of naive, martyrlike confusion.

Gaia looked less sure of herself than Heather had ever seen her before. Gaia cleared her throat, uncrossed her legs, straightened her posture, said nothing. Heather detected a faint blush on her cheeks.

Now Heather looked back at Sam. She applied no obvious pressure, just silence, which always proved the fiercest pressure of all.

"Heather, I—we—you—" Sam looked around, desperate for her to interrupt.

She didn't.

"I was just . . . and Gaia, here . . ."

Heather wasn't going to help him out of this. Let him suffer.

"We were just . . . talking about chess." With that word, Sam regained his footing. He took a big breath. "Gaia is a big chess player, too."

Heather nodded trustingly. "Oh."

Sam looked at his watch. There wasn't a watch. A moment's discomfort. He regrouped again. "I gotta go, though." He stood up. "Physics study group." He offered his textbook as evidence.

"Right," Heather said. "Wait, I have something for you." She fished around in her bag and brought out the red sealed envelope. "Here. I was looking for you because I wanted to give you this." She smiled shyly. She shrugged. "It's kind of stupid, but . . . whatever." Her voice was soft enough to be intimate and directed solely at him.

He had to come two steps closer to take the card

from her hand. This required him to turn his back on Gaia.

Sam glanced at his name, written in flowery cursive, and the heart she'd drawn next to it. When he looked at Heather again, his eyes were pained, uncertain.

He cleared his throat. "Why don't you walk with me, and I'll open it when I get to my dorm?"

Heather nodded brightly. "Okay."

He pressed the card carefully between the pages of his physics book and anchored the book under his arm. Heather took his free hand and laced her fingers through his as she often did, and they started across the park.

Sam said nothing to Gaia. He didn't even cast a backward glance.

But Heather couldn't help herself. She threw a tiny look over her shoulder. Then, without breaking her stride, she planted one fleeting kiss on Sam's upper arm, just the place where her mouth naturally landed on his tall frame. It was a casual kiss, light, one of millions, but undoubtedly a kiss of ownership.

"See ya," Heather said to Gaia, silently thanking Intelligence for dealing her yet another effective strategy.

It was funny, thought Heather. Intelligence and Cunning so often ended up in the same place.

WHAT GOOD WAS IT BEING A TRAINED

fighting machine when you couldn't beat the hell out of a loathsome creature like **Not Yet** Heather Gannis? Gaia wondered bitterly as she stomped along the overcrowded sidewalks of SoHo.

What a catty piece of crap Heather was. No, that was too kind. Cats were fuzzy, warm-blooded, and somewhat loyal. Heather was more reptile than mammal—cold-blooded and remote with dead, hooded eyes.

Gaia was supposed to be smart. When she was six years old, her IQ tested so high, she'd been sent to the National Institutes of Health to spend a week with electrodes stuck to her forehead. And yet in Heather's presence Gaia felt like a slobbering idiot. She'd probably misspell her name if put on the spot.

"Oops. Sorry," Gaia mumbled to a man in a beige suit whose shoulder she caught as she crossed Spring Street.

Trendy stores were ablaze along the narrow cobblestoned streets. Well-dressed crowds flowed into the buzzing, overpriced restaurants that Ella always wanted to go to. Gaia strode past a cluster of depressingly hip girls who probably never considered wearing boots with capri pants.

Gaia caught her reflection in the darkened window

of a florist shop. Ick. Blah. Blech. Who let her out on the streets of New York in that sweater? Exactly how fat could her legs look? High time to get rid of the—

Suddenly she caught sight of another familiar reflection. He was behind her, weaving and dodging through the throng, staying close but trying to avoid her notice. His face was beaded with sweat. One of his hands was tucked in his jacket.

Oh, shit. Well, at least you couldn't commit fashion blunders from the grave, could you?

She walked faster. She jaywalked across the street and ducked into a boutique. She wanted to see whether CJ was just keeping tabs on her or whether he intended to kill her immediately.

Gaia blinked in the laboratory-bright shop. The decor was spare, and the clothing was inscrutable. In the midst of all the chrome shelving and halogen lighting there seemed to be about three items for sale, all of them black. It made for poor browsing.

CJ stopped outside. He knew she knew he was there.

"Excuse me, miss." An impatient voice echoed through the stark, high-ceilinged room.

Gaia spun around to see a severe-looking saleslady pinning her to the floor with a suspicious look. Salesladies in SoHo had a sixth sense for whether you could afford anything in their store. It was a superhuman power. It deserved to be investigated on *The X-Files*. This particular woman obviously knew that Gaia couldn't afford even a zipper or sleeve from the place.

"We're closed," the saleslady snapped. Her outfit was constructed of incredibly stiff-looking black material that covered her from her pointy chin to the very pointy tips of her shoes. Gaia couldn't help wondering if she ate breakfast or watched TV in that getup.

"The door was open," Gaia pointed out.

The woman cocked her head and made a sour face. "Apparently so. But we're closed."

"Fine." Gaia glanced through the glass door. CJ was pacing in an area of about two square feet. He was ready to pounce. She was pretty sure that the hand concealed in his roomy jacket held a gun.

"In the future, when you're closed," Gaia offered, trying to bide a little time, "you should consider *locking* your door. It's a common business practice. It not only alerts your customers to the fact that your store is closed but can help reduce crime as well."

"Are you done?" the woman asked, rolling her eyeballs skyward.

"Um, yeah." Gaia glanced out the door reluctantly. It opened outward. The glass was thick and well reinforced.

"Please leave."

Gaia backed up a few feet. "Okay," she said.

One . . . two . . . three . . .

Gaia slammed into the door at full strength.

Just as she'd hoped, the door flew open and caught CJ hard in the face, knocking him backward. She heard his groan of surprise and pain. It gave her the moment she needed to run.

SoHo, with its single-file sidewalks and indignant pedestrians, was not a good place for sprinting.

"Ex*cuse* me!"

"Yo, watch it!"

"What's your problem?"

Gaia left a stream of angry New Yorkers in her wake. "Sorry!" she called out in a blanket apology. It was the best she could do at the moment.

She heard CJ shouting behind her. Then pounding footsteps and the protests of more unhappy pedestrians.

Gaia hung a quick left on Greene Street. She navigated the sidewalk with the deftness of a running back.

She heard screams as CJ (presumably) crashed into a woman with a screechy voice. He was gaining on Gaia. He cared less than she did about thrashing innocent bystanders.

Gaia hooked onto Broome Street and ran west. CJ was just a few yards behind. The street was clotted with traffic, and she needed to cross to the south side,

53

where the sidewalk was clear. The crosswalk was too far. She heard more screams and then a man's voice.

"That kid's got a gun! A *gun!* Everybody down!"

"Damn it!" Gaia muttered. Her adrenaline was pumping now. Her muscles were buzzing with intensity. She was an easy target this close. Now what?

Parked cars were nose to tail at the curb without a break. Gaia pounced on the first parked car she came upon, putting both hands above the driver's side window and vaulting herself onto the roof. She was in full flee mode now, and she didn't have the luxury to care about making a spectacle. Thin metal thundered and buckled under her feet. She surveyed the traffic piled up behind the light. She jumped to the roof of the next-nearest car and picked her way across the street from car to car the way she'd use stones to traverse a river. Cars honked. Cabbies shouted. A shot rang out to her left. Oh, man.

CJ had beaten her to the other side of Broome Street. The idiot was shooting at her in front of hundreds of witnesses. God, she wanted to wring his crazy neck! It was no fair going up against someone with a gun and no sense.

The traffic light was about to change. Any second, the stones under her feet were going to start moving downstream. She hopped her way back to the north side of the street in half the time and sprinted along Broome Street to the east now. A fast left took her zigging up

Mercer. Her breath was coming fast now. The muscles in her legs were starting to ache.

This lower stretch of Mercer was nearly deserted. If she just ran north, she could cut over a couple of blocks and get to the park. She could run her way out of this. She had her Saucony sneakers on her feet. Footsteps sounded behind her, and she accelerated her pace. She knew that if CJ paused to take aim, he'd lose her. *Faster, faster,* she urged her protesting leg muscles.

"You're dead!" he shouted after her.

Not yet, she promised herself. She could see the lights of Houston Street. She was getting close.

Suddenly her escape route was obscured by a `large, silhouetted figure`. As she got closer she realized his presence wasn't coincidental. In the side wash of a streetlight she recognized the face. She didn't know his name, but she'd often seen him with CJ and Marco and the other thugs in the park. A blade winked in his hand.

Ka-ping! CJ fired a shot, which bounced off the cobblestones several feet away.

Oh, this sucked. `This really sucked.` Another wave of adrenaline flowed through her limbs and sizzled in her chest. She dragged in as much air as her lungs could take.

She juked, but he wouldn't let her pass. CJ was hard on her heels, so she couldn't think of stopping. CJ would succeed in shooting her in the back if she gave him any time at all. The space between CJ and his accomplice was closing fast.

Come on. Come on. Come on.

The guy in front of her raised the blade. Gaia didn't stop running. She lifted her arm, drew it back, and without losing a step punched him as hard as she could in the middle of his face. "Sorry," she murmured to him. Judging from the sting in her fist, she'd broken a tooth or two.

A bullet seared past her right shoulder. Another past her knee. The toe of her trusty sneaker caught in a deep groove between the cobblestones and she went down hard, scraping the skin of her forearms and shins.

Shit. Oh, shit.

Her mind was dreamlike again. She didn't feel any pain from her ragged, bleeding skin or from the impact to her wrist and knees. There wasn't anything wrong with her nervous system. It was that every cell of her body was fiercely anticipating the dreaded shot. Some atavistic impulse caused her to bring her hands over her head and curl her knees up in the fetal position.

Time slowed to an eerie, inexplicable stop. Although CJ had been within a few yards of her, the shot didn't come. She took big gulps of air. There were no footsteps. No bullets. She heard nothing.

Slowly, slowly, in disbelief she lifted her head from the street. She turned around cautiously. Her legs shook as she straightened them under the weight of her body.

She peered into the dark, desolate street.

He wasn't there. He really wasn't. CJ had disappeared, just when his duck had finally sat.

It was impossible. It made no sense to Gaia. Something told her there was no reasonable explanation for this. But she also knew it would be a mistake to hang around and try to figure out why.

Sometimes I worry there's something wrong with me. Sometimes I worry I don't actually feel things like regular people do. Often I'm watching the world rather than actually living in it. It's not just that I feel distant from the world. The thing that worries me is that a lot of times, I feel distant from myself. I watch myself like I'd watch an actor in a movie. I think, I observe, I process, but I don't *feel* anything.

Have you ever felt that way? Have you ever sat at the funeral of your great-aunt, for example, and worn a solemn expression on your face and tried to tell yourself all the ways in which it was sad, without actually feeling sad at all?

Have you ever met somebody who said, "Oh my God, that's so funny!" all the time, but never actually laughed? I'm worried that's me.

When my parents split up when

I was in fifth grade, I said all of the things a sad kid says in that circumstance. I even wrung out a few tears. When they got back together ten months later, I shared in the happiness. But for me it was abstract. I could sort of talk myself into feeling something—or at least into believing I felt something—but it didn't come naturally. The emotions certainly didn't rush over me like a wave. I was their eager host, never their victim.

Maybe that's really lucky; I don't know.

But the flip side of experiencing pain abstractly is that you experience pleasure that way, too. Sometimes Heather and I will be eating a romantic dinner together or making out in the park, and it feels really good and everything, but I find myself wondering if I'm missing out on something.

I think this is the reason I can't get over Gaia Moore. I

think it's the reason why I'm intensely attracted to her and repelled by her at the same time. When I'm with her—when I even think of her—I feel things. I feel a wave brewing just out of reach, building and swelling into a breaker of dangerous proportions.

So maybe you can see why I have mixed feelings about getting close to Gaia. I'm not sure I want to lose control. I mean, who would willingly turn himself into a victim?

Maybe that's what love is—I don't know.

Sam couldn't
help smiling.
"Yeah, I'm
getting **hazards**
lucky.
Very lucky."

GAIA IS IN DANGER.

Tom Moore looked up from his laptop computer. He'd been thinking vaguely of Gaia all evening—there was nothing unusual in that—but this was the first time a specific thought coalesced in his mind.

An Ocean Away

For most of his life he'd discounted notions of telepathy with a certain scorn, but his last five years in the CIA had opened him up to almost any possibility. Was Gaia truly in danger? He felt the familiar worry roiling his stomach.

He looked out the window of the airplane. The plane was either crossing desert or ocean because the sky was almost clear of cloud cover and beneath him was blackness. There wasn't a single light or other sign of human life. He felt terribly lonely.

He wasn't worried about danger in any ordinary sense. Gaia could get herself out of most situations. Tom, of all people, would know. He was the one who'd taught her. In the case of a mugger or purse snatcher going up against Gaia, Tom would frankly fear more for the criminal than her. Gaia was intensely strong, a master of martial arts and most commonly used weapons, and moreover she was free of the fear that compromised ordinary people. Or at least she *was*—

Was.

What did he know of her now?

He knew where she lived and where she went to school. Twice a year he received a heavily encrypted notice of her safety and general progress from the agency. He looked forward to those updates with the fervor of a man grasping for a lifeline, even though they were absurdly short, stiff, and uninformative.

That was it. He knew nothing of her friends, her habits, her pleasures, her emotional state. He had no idea how she was coping with her losses or how close the danger was.

"Sir?" An attendant offered him dinner on a tray. The smell further distressed his stomach. The food on U.S. military planes was even worse than on commercial flights.

"No. Thanks. Maybe later."

"We should be landing in Tel Aviv in approximately seventeen minutes, sir."

"Very well."

Tom looked back at his computer screen. His current briefing involved hundreds and hundreds of pages that had been downloaded via satellite during the course of the flight. One couldn't escape even for a matter of minutes anymore.

He couldn't give his mind to the intricacies of desert diplomacy right now.

There were other dangers to Gaia. More insidious ones that struck close to home. And how could he possibly protect her? Apart from his memories, that was the worst pain he faced.

In the old days, when Gaia was still a child, he'd been purely blown away by her abilities. She was a miracle. His greatest gift. Her brilliance, her beauty, her athleticism, and most of all her God-given sense of honor astonished him every single hour he spent with her. He couldn't imagine what he had done in this life to deserve such a child.

But in these strange days he found himself wishing and praying that his darling, magnificent Gaia were a meek, ordinary creature, likely to catch the attention of no one. A daughter he could trust, above all, to stay out of trouble.

A Threat

"MAN, WHAT HAPPENED TO YOUR teeth?" Tarick asked. His eyes were bugged out the way they got when he was excited about something.

Marty put his hand over his mouth. He was embarrassed. One front tooth was gone, and the smaller one to the side of it was cracked down the middle. "The girl got in a lucky punch."

CJ snorted and leaned back against the fountain in Washington Square. "The girl laid him out for like five minutes," he explained. "The girl kicked his ass." He was relieved that Gaia had busted somebody else for once.

Tarick turned cold eyes on him. He got up off the fountain wall and paced. "And you, my man. Not having a lot of luck, either?"

CJ could feel his face fall. He'd been dreading this little talk with Tarick for a good reason. "She's tough, man. She's, like, supernatural. And now she's got somebody watching her back. I had a bead on her down on Mercer Street. I had her, I'm telling you, and somebody wearing a parka and a ski mask bagged me from behind and ran off."

"Who was it?" Tarick asked. He looked doubtful.

"Somebody. I don't know. I told you—I couldn't see a face," CJ said.

"You're getting real creative about coming up with excuses," Tarick said.

CJ glared at him. It was unfair. "I am totally serious, man. Marty woulda seen 'em, too, but he was out cold."

Marty looked hurt, but he didn't say anything.

Tarick shook his head. He looked at his watch. He sighed, like he was holding back his temper.

CJ was starting to feel really uneasy. The midday sun had disappeared, and clouds were rolling in from the west. The October air was suddenly cold against CJ's bare head. He felt goose bumps rising all along his back, coursing up his neck and scalp.

"CJ, my man," Tarick started slowly. "This is not hard. You got a powerful weapon. You know where this girl lives. You gotta do what you said you were gonna do."

CJ nodded.

"And you gotta do it, like I said, by midnight Saturday. We're not fooling around here, are we?"

CJ shook his head.

Tarick sat back on the fountain wall just inches away. He put a hand on CJ's bald scalp. "I need to be able to tell the boys we avenged Marco, you know what I mean?"

CJ wished Tarick would remove his hand. It wasn't supposed to be comforting. It was a threat.

"Yeah," CJ mumbled.

"So let's make it crystal clear here, okay?" Tarick increased the pressure of his palm against CJ's shrinking scalp. "Saturday at midnight. If Gaia's not dead . . ."

Tarick paused, and CJ stared at him expectantly.

"Then you are."

SEARCH: THOMAS MOORE
No Match Found

Search: Special Agent **Search**
Moore

```
Arlington, Virginia
No Match Found

Search: Federal Agent #4466
No Match Found

Search: Michael Sage
No Match Found

Search: Robert W. Connelly
No Match Found

Search: Enigma
No Match Found

Search: My goddamned father, you
stupid morons.
No Match Found

Search:
```

Gaia threw the mouse at the monitor. She was getting frustrated. She'd hacked her way into the files of the appropriate federal agency, but the search engine refused to recognize her father's name, his old badge number, or any of his old aliases.

Was he with the agency anymore? Was he even still alive?

She'd always told herself the government would notify her if he were dead. The agency was the only place that knew her whereabouts. She'd also told herself that her dad had to have been up to some pretty covert and important stuff—like single-handedly saving the planet, for instance—to have abandoned her this way.

She told herself these things, but that didn't make them true.

Gaia heard a noise. Oh, no. If Ella was home, she'd have to jump out the window again. A moment spent with that woman was like `chewing tinfoil`. And this was not Gaia's computer to be performing illegal operations—or actually any operations—on.

She crept to the door of George's office on silent feet. The house was still. She crept back to the computer. According to the time in the right corner of the screen, she had seven minutes before Ella was due home. George wouldn't be home till after seven.

Okay. Now what? She drummed her fingers on the mouse pad. She didn't know the name her father used. She didn't know where he lived. She didn't know where he was working. He'd never, in almost five years, made any attempt to contact her. Not quite your doting father.

She felt the old anger building. Time for a little distraction. As far as Gaia was concerned, a little distraction was worth a lot of solution.

Okay. Plan 2. Sam. She had been less successful with plan 2 than plan 1, if that was possible. Could you get lower than zero? Was it appropriate to bring in negative numbers for the sake of comparison?

She aimed her fingers back at the keyboard. She called up an address-locator web site and typed in Sam's basic information.

Aha! All was not lost! Within seconds she had a definitive answer:

SamMoon3@culdesac.com

She was just one (borrowed) computer away from direct and private conversation with Sam.

Ha!

And she'd done it while leaving one full minute to hide before Ella got home.

SAM LAY IN HIS LUMPY, STEEL-

Getting Lucky

frame twin bed, considering Heather's note. He didn't need to look at the note to consider it because he had stared at it so long, he'd committed it to memory.

Heather was ready. How long had he wanted to hear those

words? How long had he fantasized about this very thing?

God, and after seeing him with Gaia, he'd expected her to be pissed or at least suspicious. But she wasn't. She was angelic and totally trusting. And he was an undeserving bastard who was about to get unbelievably lucky. Almost too lucky to be true.

So what was the problem?

Forget it. There wasn't a problem. He wasn't going to get derailed by thinking about the problem.

If there was a problem, that is. Which there wasn't.

He was really, really happy as hell, even if he didn't realize it one hundred percent yet.

Time to think about Saturday night. That was only two days away. Heather was coming here, to his dorm room, and they were going to . . .

Oh, man. He was starting to feel tingly. He stared up at the stained acoustical tile on the ceiling. It wasn't the most romantic sight. He glanced at the piles of clothes around his room. He looked at the mound of chess books, magazines, and clippings blanketing his desk. He eyed the new box of syringes he'd just bought for his diabetes treatments. He propped himself up on his elbow and studied the grayish sheet covering his mattress. Exactly when was the last time he'd washed that sheet? Had it been gray to start out with, or was it born white? The fact that he couldn't remember the answer to either question wasn't a good sign.

70

Wait a minute. Heather. Gorgeous, perfectly dressed, sweet-smelling Heather was going to come into this room? This pigpen? This landfill? Was he seriously thinking of lying her down on this filthy bed? It wasn't only unromantic; it was probably a health hazard.

He sat up with a jolt and swung his legs off the bed. He swept up a pile of clothes and threw them on the bed beside him. Lurking under the pile were dust creatures that belonged in a horror movie. Thank God his mother couldn't see this.

In his freshman year he'd kept up some semblance of hygiene (if you defined the term very loosely) because he had a roommate. But this year he had his own minuscule room, attached to a common room shared by three other guys. He pretended to get indignant when the other guys left spilled beer on the vomit-colored carpet in the common room or ground Cheetos into microscopic orange dust underfoot. But that didn't mean he'd spent even one second looking after his own room. Usually if Heather came around, they hung out in the common room and watched TV or raided the minifridge. She hadn't inspected the frightening cave where he slept.

It was high time to reacquaint himself with the laundry room in the basement. He'd sweep out whatever flora and fauna were growing under his bed. He'd get rid of the altar to Gary Kasparov—no need to subject Heather to a full-on dork fest. Besides, the knitted brow of Kasparov didn't exactly put you in the mood.

He was just consolidating his massive clothes pile when the door swung open.

"Hey, Moon."

It was Mike Suarez, one of his suite mates.

"Does the word *knock* mean anything to you, Suarez?" Sam asked.

"Does the phrase 'lock your friggin' door if you don't want company' mean anything to you?"

Sam laughed. "The lock is busted. Half the time you turn the knob, it falls off into your hand." He made a mental note to get that fixed before Saturday.

Suarez watched him clean for a minute.

"You planning on getting lucky?"

Sam paused and rubbed his nose. Dust bits were flying in his nostrils, making them itch. "What do you mean?"

"I can think of only one reason why a guy cleans his room," Suarez said suggestively.

Sam's energy sagged at the thought of being such a cliché. He tossed the ball of laundry on the ground.

"So?"

Sam couldn't help smiling. "Yeah, I'm getting lucky. Very lucky."

Can He Resist?

"SHE FOUND NOTHING, OF COURSE," Ella stated, her voice ringing shrilly through the wide-open loft space, bouncing around its few polished surfaces.

"I see. And you were there watching her for the duration of her search?"

Ella's face showed impatience. "Certainly."

He pressed his lips together to signal his own waning patience. Ella, with her sleek body, her colorfully revealing clothing, and her poorly concealed moodiness acted as much the angry teenager as his bewitching Gaia. But as potently as Ella annoyed him, she had a value far beyond the dog-loyal bodyguards who remained within fifteen feet of him at all times. "Did she display any knowledge of her father's whereabouts?"

"No. Nothing current."

He flicked a tiny piece of lint from his dark blue slacks. "I see." He sipped coffee. "And he has made no attempt to contact her?" The question was rhetorical. He didn't even know why he'd asked it.

"No," Ella confirmed.

"How can he resist?" he mused in a quiet voice, mostly to himself.

"Sir?"

"How can he resist making contact with Gaia?

73

She's all he has in the world after what happened to Katia. He adores her. He needs her. He knows she's bound to get into trouble." He was really talking only to himself.

"Yes, sir. Would you like me to continue to keep a record of her computer activity in case she makes any strides toward finding him?" Ella asked. Even when her words were perfectly dutiful, her tone was `petulant`.

He made a sharp exhale through his nose, which was the closest he came to amusement. "She won't find him. Although I despise Tom, I can't pretend he's an idiot, can I? She'll never find him, although you're welcome to leave a few red herrings that will keep her busy trying. I'm banking on the belief—no, the knowledge—that Tom will find *her*."

He picked up the impossibly slender computer from the table beside him. He'd just had a very simple and appealing idea. He sat back and crossed his legs, the computer perched on his knee. "Tom will come for her, and when he does, he's mine."

There's one thing I want more than anything else, and I know I can never have it. I don't mean Sam or finding my dad. I'm talking about something inside myself.

I want to be brave.

And I'm not brave, in case you're wondering. Maybe I could have been brave, but I guess I'll never know.

The reason is that you can't separate bravery from fear. This is something I've thought about a lot. The people with the most fear have the greatest opportunity to be brave. A woman who is terrified of the water would be braver sticking her big toe in the swimming pool than I would be surfing a thirty-foot breaker in the Pacific Ocean. She would be overcoming something. She would be challenging herself. She would experience the pleasure of expanding her world, the freedom of exercising her will. I would be surfing a wave.

My mom used to say that a poor person who gave a dime to charity was more generous than a rich one who gave hundreds of dollars. In this example, I would be Bill Gates. Only richer.

I know for a fact that my mother was claustrophobic. And most especially, she was afraid of tunnels. Deeply, seriously afraid. I think it had something to do with her childhood in Russia, which was pretty tough. Anyway, the reason I know is because when I was seven, all my friends were taking gymnastics class a few miles away and I was desperate to go. My mom didn't want to take me at first, but I begged and pleaded. I wouldn't shut up about it. Finally my mom agreed. It turned out you had to go through a tunnel to get there. So even though I wasn't a very sensitive or nice kid, I realized my mom was basically flipping out in that tunnel. Her hands were dripping wet on the steering wheel, and her skin was whitish gray. She made these weird little moaning sounds. When we finally got out of the tunnel, she pulled over on the shoulder, rested her head on the steering wheel, and just stayed like that. I was upset, but she held me and promised me everything was fine.

Every Saturday for almost two years after that, my mother drove me to gymnastics and picked me up.

When I think of that, I'm filled with horrible, wrenching, miserable guilt. I wish so much I would have dropped that stupid gymnastics class and never gone back. But I didn't. And I can't change the past.

So instead of that, I wish that for one single moment in my life, I could be brave like my mom.

Sam's long, **fragile**
beautiful
body **under—**
claimed
all of **standing**
her senses.

DEAR SAM,

I have a very strange favor to ask you. I know you don't know me that well, and what you know of me you probably don't like. I am really, truly, sincerely sorry for what happened to Heather in the park and for the part I played in it. I know she's your girlfriend, so what I'm about to ask will sound particularly insane, but

Dear Sam,

There's this guy named CJ, a friend and fellow neo-Nazi of Marco's, the guy who tried to kill us after slashing Zolov in the park. Well, would you believe Marco is dead and CJ thinks I did it? CJ has completely lost his mind and is now hell-bent on killing me. And I came to this realization that before I die, I really want to

Dear Sam,

I know I must seem like trouble to you. I know it must seem like bad luck follows me around. I know you probably wish you'd never seen my face, which I

can totally understand. And lucky for
you, after this coming weekend you'll
most likely never have to see me again.
But before then, I was wondering if you
wouldn't mind

Dear Sam,
   I am confessing to you in total confidence that in my seventeen years,
I've had very little romantic experience. Okay, none. Well, actually there
was this kid in seventh grade who kind
of liked me but—
   Anyway, I've been thinking about you
a lot recently, and I was wondering
whether—

Dear Sam,
   Will you have sex with me? Saturday
night, no questions, no commitment.

   Oh, shit. Ella was home. Gaia had to get out of
George's office right away. Ella would lose it if she
found Gaia in here and there was no way Gaia wanted
to deal with the witch in her present state of mind.
   Oh. Oh. Gaia's eyes flew over the computer monitor.
What should she do? Should she save one of these horrible letters to finish later? She had so many windows

open on the screen, she couldn't keep track of them. She heard Ella's heels clicking down the hallway. Oh, no. Um. Um.

In desperation she clicked on the Send Later icon. She clicked the X in the top-right corner to exit the on-line service. Ella was slowing down. She was right outside!

Gaia threw herself under George's desk and held her breath.

Ella paused in the open office doorway.

Don't come in here! Gaia commanded silently. *Go away* now!

Ella paid no heed to the telepathic messages. She walked right up to the computer and stared, squinting, at the screen.

Gaia knew for a fact that Ella was seriously near-sighted. But the woman was too vain to wear glasses and too stupid to put in contacts.

Ella placed her hand on the mouse.

What could she possibly want with the computer? Gaia wondered. No interface was user-friendly enough for Ella. Gaia had often snickered at the full library of "Such and Such for Dummies" titles on Ella's bookshelf.

Ella continued to stare dumbly at the screen. Her feet were a matter of inches from Gaia's shins. *Don't look down,* Gaia ordered in her head. *Do* not! Gaia tried to make her body as absolutely small as possible.

Ella clicked the mouse. Gaia heard the modem dialing up the on-line service and, within a few seconds, connecting. "Hello," the synthesized computer voice chirped.

What was going on? Gaia had never seen Ella in the same room with a computer before. Had she suddenly discovered the joy of on-line sex? Had somebody told her about the Victoria's Secret web site?

Ella squinted at the screen for another moment and clicked the mouse again.

Please don't be long, Gaia begged silently. Her knees hurt, and her back was cramping. It was so dusty under George's desk, she felt a sneeze threatening. If Ella was going shopping, it could take hours.

Then, as though obeying silent orders, Ella stood up, turned around and walked away. She walked right back down the hallway and up the creaky stairs.

Gaia's heart soared with relief. She uncrumpled her limbs and climbed out from under the desk. She was so busy congratulating herself, she didn't bother to look at the screen at first. Then the blinking box caught the corner of her eye. She came closer to read it.

"Your mail was sent."

A shiver crept down Gaia's spine. What? What mail had been sent? Probably just something of Ella's, Gaia tried to comfort herself.

She clicked on the file icon to investigate. Then she

83

clicked the Mail Sent icon. She was starting to get a very bad feeling in her stomach.

It was one of Gaia's files. Somehow, by going online, Ella had sent a Send Later file. But which one? Gaia clicked twice on the file.

It came up instantly, the letters twice as big and black as any others on the screen. She felt like someone had kicked her brutally hard in the middle of her chest.

```
Dear Sam,
   Will you have sex with me? Saturday
night, no questions, no commitment.
```

TOM MOORE WAS CROSSING ANOTHER

endless desert. For a man who traveled tens of thousands of miles every week of his life, he certainly spent a great deal of time in the same chair, studying the same screen. For a man who hadn't seen his daughter in five years, he certainly spent a great deal of time thinking about her.

Gaia Sighting

Hundreds, thousands of pages of briefings swam

before his eyes. He closed the document and looked around him. He was so accustomed to the hum of jet engines, he could hardly sleep without it. The only other passenger, his personal assistant, was asleep.

The ever present satellite connection allowed him to get on-line. He'd promised himself he wouldn't do this, but tonight, well, tonight his mind was once again `burning with worry` for Gaia, and he couldn't ignore it any longer.

His first search for her name called up nothing. That was as it should be if the U.S. government was doing what they'd promised. Then he reduced the search to just her first name and conducted it globally, typing in a series of passwords that allowed him a degree of access allowed to only a handful of people— access to virtually all e-mail posted on the web, for example. This turned up an enormous list. He allowed himself a look into one file. Just one. He'd pick it wisely, then he'd stop this nonsense and get back to his work.

He scrolled through the upper part of the list. He stopped on a note tagged by the re: field. It read:

re: supergaia

He opened the file:

To: jackboot
From: stika

> Gaia sighting at WSW. Call set for
> 2100 Sat. 2 guys and metal.

It was an unfortunately good guess. Tom's worry intensified as he read easily between the lines. He felt distressingly sure this Gaia was his Gaia. He could see that the posting had come from the New York City area and could easily assume that WSW meant Washington Square West, a very short distance from George's home and the school Gaia attended.

Now that he'd opened Pandora's box, the ghosts were all around him. He'd known this could happen. Now it didn't matter how critically his presence was needed in Beirut. He pressed the button for the intercom that connected his voice to the cockpit.

"Gentlemen," he said calmly, "I'm afraid I need to order a change in destination. Let's touch down for refueling. We'll be crossing the Atlantic tonight."

GAIA PADDED QUIETLY DOWN THE

darkened hallway. She'd never been in a college dormitory before. When she reached the room number she'd gotten from the student directory, she paused. She combed

Urgent Longing

her fingers through her hair, pushing long strands back from her face. She pulled self-consciously at the hem of her exquisitely soft red velvet tank dress. Taking a breath, she turned the heavy brass knob and swung open the door.

Her breath caught. He was there. He lay on his bed, his strong arms folded behind his head, propping his upper body against the bed frame. The rest of the room was oddly indistinct, shadowy and blurred. Sam's long, beautiful body claimed all of her senses.

He looked at her. He wasn't surprised. He wasn't upset. He wasn't happy, exactly, either. He looked . . . serious. Had he known she would come now? Had he wanted it?

His feet were bare and crossed at the ankles. His loose gray sweatpants were turned up a few times at the bottom. Keeping his eyes on her face, he swung his knees over the side of the small bed and stood. He started toward her, then stopped, leaving two feet between them. Slowly he reached his arm, making a bridge across the air, and placed two fingers on the inside of her elbow, that vulnerable place where oxygen-thirsty blood coursed closest to her surface. A chill stole up her neck and dispersed over her scalp.

She'd come prepared with a storm of explanations in her head: (1)Why. (2)Why now. (3) Why him. But in this moment, stating them felt like it would break the tentative, fragile understanding, nurtured and protected by silence.

She took a step closer. This was hard for her. She bent her elbow and wrapped her fingers around his wrist. Was he pulling her, or was she pulling him? She wasn't sure. All she knew was that she was now close enough to feel the warmth radiating from his skin. He put his arms around her. She felt his fingers on the nape of her neck. Suddenly her arms were circling his taut waist, pressing him against her, crushing her breasts against his broad chest.

God, she was dizzy. She was light-headed, giddy, tingling with excitement and disbelief. Her heart was too full to stay in her rib cage. Tears gathered under her lashes.

He bent his head down so close to hers, she could feel his soft breath on her cheek. Oh God, how she wanted this kiss. She'd waited a lifetime for it. She breathed in his subtle, masculine smell and faint mixture of clean sweat and eucalyptus-scented shaving cream. She lifted her mouth to his.

Her mind was a tumultuous sea, with thoughts listing and bobbing there. And all at once an image arrived. It was an image of her body, scarred and wounded, becoming whole and perfect under his healing lips. The picture was beautiful, and she wished she could keep it, but a wave crashed through, sending thoughts spinning and surfing in the chop.

Please, kiss me, she found herself wishing. *Please. I need you.*

And then, in a cruel trick played by fate, Sam not only failed to kiss her; he dissolved completely. He vanished into air. He was replaced by dim, grayish sunlight, a tangle of mismatched covers. The magical night in his bed was replaced by a harsh, wrenching morning in hers. No, not even in hers. In one that belonged to George and Ella. Her velvet dress was replaced by a worn-out T-shirt from Jerry's Crab House.

She turned over and buried her head in her pillow. Tears stung in her eyes. The loneliness was almost unbearable. As reality spread out before her, its stark contrast to the dream made it that much harder to take.

She wanted so much to retrieve the feelings . . . and that image.

What was that image again?

In that first moment of waking, it teased her with its closeness. It danced and sparkled on a wavelet at her feet. But then the vast ocean pulled back the tide into its dark, infinite belly, and now Gaia was faced with the terror of never finding it again. If she could only find it, she felt sure it would give her strength and maybe hope.

But she was left with nothing but the taste of Sam—her fantasy of Sam—on her lips and an urgent, painful longing in her heart.

You may have noticed my name sounds familiar. I share it with a number of people, but most importantly the great scholar, statesman, and saint Sir Thomas More, born in England in 1478.

My mother was a devout Roman Catholic, and I assumed she picked the name to remind me of piety above all else. To remind me to choose God-given principles over king or scholarship or art . . . or even family.

Since I was a child, I felt the pressure of this name. I took it seriously. That's the kind of person I am, I suppose. I wanted to serve my country. I wanted to serve God. And if sacrifices were called for, I wanted to possess the courage to make them with honor.

My namesake set forth an almost impossible record of bravery. He watched his father imprisoned by King Henry VII because of his own deeds. He wrote a brilliant critique of English

(SIR) THOMAS MORE

society in his work <u>Utopia.</u>
Ultimately he was canonized for
putting his head on the chopping
block rather than compromising
his basic beliefs for the benefit
of King Henry VIII.

I never questioned the right-
ness of More's example until
after I lost Katia and then Gaia.
Now the question haunts me every
day of my life.

In an ironic and unfortunate
twist of fate, not long after my
mother's death, I read a letter
she'd written to her father
around the time I was born. In it
I discovered she didn't name me
after Thomas More, honored saint
and statesman. She named me after
Thomas Moore, the Irish romantic
poet.

But maybe
he would be
curious. **about**
And maybe a
tiny bit **sex**
interested?
Was it
possible?

"GAIA MOORE? ARE YOU WITH US?"

Gaia snapped her head up. She glanced around at the unsympathetic faces of her classmates. Which class was this? What were they talking about? She gave her head a shake to dislodge her heavy, demanding preoccupations.

Let's see. Ummmm. Ms. Rupert. That would be history. European history. Which century were they in now? Which country? She hadn't looked at her textbook in a while.

"No, ma'am, I'm not," Gaia replied truthfully.

Ms. Rupert's eyes bulged with annoyance. "You're not, are you? Then would you be so kind as to share with me and the rest of the class what you find so much more captivating than the court of King Henry VIII?"

Gaia drummed her fingers on her desk. Did Ms. Rupert *really* want to know the answer to that question?

"Yes, Gaia? I'm waiting." Her hands were on her hips in a caricature of impatience.

Apparently she did. "I was thinking about sex, ma'am. I was thinking about having sex," Gaia stated.

The class disintegrated into laughter and whispering.

Everybody was staring at Gaia. It wasn't nice laughter. Since the incident with Heather getting slashed in the park, Gaia wasn't exactly Miss Popularity. She shrugged.

Ms. Rupert looked like she'd swallowed her tongue. She spluttered and turned deep crimson before she could get a word out. "G-Gaia Moore, get out of my class! Go to the principal's office *now!*"

"Yes, ma'am," Gaia said agreeably, striding to the door.

This was a lucky break, she thought, walking down the deserted hall with lightness in her step. The vice principal would keep her waiting outside his office for ages as a phony display of his importance and full-to-bursting schedule, and it was much easier to obsess about Sam without Ms. Rupert droning on about Henry VIII and all the various people's heads he'd chopped off.

What was Sam thinking? That was the central question nagging her. Assuming he'd received her psychotic e-mail and could tell it was from her, what must he be thinking?

That she was a nympho, for one thing. That she gave new meaning to the word *desperate,* for another. That she was an opportunistic couple wrecker, for a third.

But maybe he would be curious. And maybe a tiny bit interested? Was it possible?

She hardly dared hope.

In some ways she was happy she'd gotten the ball rolling, even if the note did make her seem like someone who deserved to be arrested and put under a restraining order. At least she'd opened up the conversation. At least it would give her the opportunity to say, Hey, Sam, I know this is weird, I know I seem like a complete sex-starved lunatic, but can I just explain?

She ascended a flight of stairs and was just passing the computer lab when she stopped. Hmmm. The room was dark, empty, and filled, not surprisingly, with computers. She needed only one, and she needed it only for a minute or two. Ms. Rupert would eat her own arm if she knew Gaia was making a detour, but so what?

Gaia crept to the back corner of the room and revived the sleeping monitor. Quickly she located the Internet server and signed on. She went to the site where she kept a mailbox and typed in her password.

Oh, God. There was mail! She held her breath and clicked on the envelope symbol. Her heart leaped. It was from Sam Moon! He had replied!

Was this good? Was this bad? At least it was something.

Now, calm down, she commanded herself. Okay. She clicked on the letter to open it.

Dear Gaia13,

Your letter was an unbelievable turn-
on. I've been hard since I read it. You
name the time and place and I am there,
honey. I am all over you. I will make
you scream, baby. I will make you beg
for more. Once you feel my—

Gaia swallowed. She couldn't read any more. Her
stomach felt queasy. This wasn't what she . . . she
couldn't quite believe he...

Her eye caught on something in the routing information at the bottom of the letter. A phrase of coded
gobbledygook in which she picked out the word
Canada. She clicked on another series of boxes to get
Sam Moon's personal profile.

Name: Sam Moon
Home: Victoria, BC
Age: 62

Gaia's body was flooded with relief. She almost had
to laugh. She had blatantly propositioned a sixty-two-
year-old Canadian man. She exited the program and
turned off the computer.

On the bright side, her beloved Sam Moon wasn't a
creepy pervert, although he shared his name with one.
On the less bright side, she was back to square one.

"SO *WHAT* IS THE PROBLEM?" DANNY Bell wanted to know. He said it so loudly, Sam had to hold the phone a few inches from his ear.

How He Feels

"Well, I guess . . . I don't know." Sam scratched the back of his scalp absently. "I'm not really sure how I feel about her."

Sam watched colorful pipes weaving three-dimensionally through the computer screen that sat on his crowded dorm-room desk. He'd set the screen saver to come on after ten minutes of idleness, but when he was talking on the phone or procrastinating, the damn pipes seemed to take over his screen every thirty seconds.

"You're not sure how you *feel* about her?" Danny didn't go far out of his way to hide the incredulity in his voice. "Let me get this straight. You have a stupendously gorgeous girlfriend who you've been with for six months. She wants to have sex, and you're suddenly not sure how you *feel?*"

Sam could picture exactly the look on Danny's face, even though he was three thousand miles away. Danny was his oldest and closest friend from the neighborhood in Maryland where he grew up. In fact, Danny was the only friend he had from the old days, before Sam had remade himself from a `stammering, buck-toothed chess nerd` into a decently dressed, mainstream guy who went out with beautiful girls and cared what other people thought.

It was funny. Sam had changed, but Danny hadn't. Danny was still an unapologetic lover of chess and Myst and Star Wars. He was an engineering student at Stanford University, which was probably what Sam would have been had he stayed the course.

"Okay, there's a little more to it than that," Sam confessed. "See, I met this other girl."

"Aha," Danny said in a know-it-all way. "I had a feeling there was something more here. So what happened? Did you go out with her behind Heather's back?"

The pipes were hypnotic. "No, not exactly."

"But you're attracted to her."

Sam let out a groan. "Yeah, you could say that."

"What's she like?"

"Well . . . she's different from any girl I've ever met," Sam began slowly. "She's an uncanny chess player, for one thing. She's probably at my level or close to it."

Danny was silent for at least thirty seconds. "No way," he said at last.

"I'm serious."

"Jesus. What's her name? Have I heard of her or read about her?"

"No. She's mysterious like that," Sam explained. "She hasn't come up through the normal chess ranks.

I don't know anybody who's played her in competition. I don't know how she learned. She's just . . . brilliant."

"Are you sure you're not just stupid when you're around her?" Danny asked.

Sam laughed. "I *am* stupid when I'm around her. But she really is good. The other guys who play chess in the park worship her—and not for her body, either. I wouldn't even play her again 'cause she'd probably beat me in a matter of seconds."

Danny was struck to the point of speechlessness. "So, what else do you know about her?" he asked finally.

"Well, I guess her parents aren't around anymore, and from what I can tell, she has very few if any friends. She just moved to New York, but I don't know from where."

"That's awful. Did you ask her where she came from?" Danny asked.

"No." The pipes were now making Sam nauseous. He moved from his desk chair and paced the three available feet of space in the room. One of the few benefits of a minuscule room was that the ancient phone cord reached every corner of it. "I can't explain why, exactly. It's like . . . I don't know. She doesn't give you the feeling that she really welcomes questions. She seems kind of . . . haunted in a way. I guess she's been through a lot in her life. I had this weird reaction to her the first time I saw her, like I knew everything about her even though I didn't know anything. I was intensely attracted to her and sort of scared off at the same time."

Sam heard Mike Suarez and one of his other suite mates, Brendon Moss, firing up the TV for a baseball game. He moved to close the door to his room.

One of the great things about Danny was that he wasn't cool. He wasn't jaded or sarcastic. He wasn't embarrassed about having a real conversation. Sam could tell Danny things he wouldn't consider telling his other friends.

"Does that make any sense?" Sam finished.

"Um. Not really," Danny answered.

Sam sat down on his bed. (Now covered with a clean, nearly white sheet.) "Yeah, I know," he said. "I guess I'm hesitant to ask her anything because I'm not all that sure I want to hear the answers."

"Huh," Danny said. "Maybe she's a spy. Or an alien. Did you ever see that movie *Species*?"

Sam laughed again.

"So what does this girl look like?" Danny asked. "She can't be as pretty as Heather."

Sam thought that one over for a minute. "In a way she's not, and in a way she's much, much more beautiful. She doesn't dress like Heather, or wear jewelry, or keep her hair nice. You don't get the feeling she's trying to be pretty. And she's got this kind of hard, angry expression on her face a lot of the time. But if you can get past that and really see her face and her eyes . . . she's by far the most amazing-looking girl I've ever met. I can't explain it."

"Wow," Danny said. "So why don't you try it out with this girl?" he suggested after considering it for a few moments. "It sounds like she's gotten under your skin."

"She has. That's exactly what it is," Sam said, rearranging his long legs as the weary dorm-room bed groaned under his weight. "But first of all, there's Heather to think of. And also, this girl is all about trouble. I can't even begin to explain to you the kind of trouble she causes. Heather is safe, and she's great. And she's . . . ready."

Danny laughed. "Yeah. God, I wish I had your problems."

Sam walked over to the window and looked out at the courtyard. In New York City they called it a courtyard even if it was `ten square feet of poured concrete, overfilled with plastic garbage cans and piles of recycling`. "It's not as fun as it sounds," Sam said.

"Well, there's one obvious thing to do," Danny pointed out.

"Yeah, what's that?"

"Take out a piece of paper. At the top put Heather's name on one side and the other girl's name on the other, and make a list."

Heather	_Gaia_
My girlfriend	_Not my girlfriend_
My parents love her	_Would frighten my parents_
Not good at chess	_Great at chess_
Belongs in a magazine	_Doesn't_
Safe	_Trouble_
Loves me	_Probably doesn't give a shit_
Ready	_?_

Sam studied his list for a moment, crumpled it in a tight ball, and tossed it in the garbage. What was he, some kind of idiot?

His heart,
his life,
his sense
of life's **ghosts**
possibilities
was shaken.

TOM MOORE KNEW HE WAS CRAZY TO BE

Remembering Katia

doing this. He walked down Waverly Place in the West Village with his head throbbing and his heart full. Just two blocks from here, in a tiny bookshop, he'd first laid eyes on Katia. It was probably the most important moment of his entire life, and yet he hadn't been back here in twenty years.

It was, without question, love at first sight. It was a freezing cold day in February, and the city was bleak and dismal. The previous night's snow was no more than a brown, muddy obstacle between sidewalk and street. He'd been looking for a rare translation of Thucydides for his graduate thesis. He was stewing about something—that his adviser hadn't credited him in a recent publication. He'd seen her as soon as he'd opened the door. The shop was a tiny square, for one thing. But Katia seemed to draw every atom in the place to her. In that moment Tom's entire life evaporated and a new one started.

She was sitting cross-legged in the corner, bent forward with a book on her lap. He remembered she wore gray woolen tights, under battered rubber boots and a red knit dress. Her hair was long, dark, and straight, falling in a shiny column on either side of her face. She was devouring a stack of books the way a starving person would devour a plate of food. He would never forget that image of her.

Up until that point, he'd had many relationships with women. Fellow college and grad students, pretty ones he'd met through friends. He'd traveled with girlfriends, even lived with one for a few months. And yet his heart had never been stirred until the time he saw Katia, a naive nineteen-year-old with cheap, old-fashioned Eastern Bloc clothing and a thick Russian accent. And then it was shaken.

His heart, his life, his sense of life's possibilities was shaken. In her eyes he became somebody he could believe in.

He paused after crossing Seventh Avenue. He shouldn't be here at all. He'd learned in the hardest possible way that a man who'd made enemies like his could not afford to have a family. His disguise was minimal. His presence was needed in Beirut. He could walk straight into Gaia if he wasn't careful. He was drowning his usually sane mind in a riptide of memories.

Still he continued on. And then stopped dead in his tracks. Of course. Of course. Virtually every single thing in New York City had changed in the last twenty years, and that bookstore remained. Katia was gone. The person he'd been with Katia was gone.

Their beautiful daughter, the greatest pleasure in their lives, was alone. And the damn bookstore winked at him smugly. The riptide threatened. It dragged on his feet. Tom walked faster.

If he had any sense, he'd get back on that plane, his home away from work, and resume his mission. It was all he could show for the terrible sacrifices he'd made.

But he couldn't. He needed to see Gaia just once. From afar, of course. He'd drink her in with his thirsty eyes, make sure she was safe, and get back to his work.

Although Thomas, sainted statesman, had boarded the plane back in Tel Aviv, it appeared that the romantic poet had disembarked here in New York.

"WAIT, SO YOU'RE NOT GOING TO Robbie's tomorrow night?" Melanie asked Heather, scrambling to keep up with her friend's long, efficient strides. "According to Shauna, it's a two kegger with zero parents."

Heather shook her head. "Nope. Other plans." She smiled in a way that was mysterious and maybe a tiny bit smug. She glanced up the crowded block of Eighth Street. There were two good shoe stores before they even got to Patricia Field, and Melanie and Cory Parkes were already loaded down with shopping bags and struggling to keep up. Heather was famous among her friends for being a very fast walker and an intensely picky shopper, but the truth was, she no longer had a duplicate of her parents' credit card, the way many of her friends did.

"Other plans?" Cory demanded, gulping up the bait as always.

"Sam and I are . . . getting together," Heather offered.

"So bring him to the party," Melanie said, falling back for a moment as she rearranged her bags between her tired hands.

"I promised him we'd be alone for once," Heather explained.

"Oooh. Does this mean you're taking things to the next level?" Cory asked.

Heather smiled ambiguously. "It's a thought."

Melanie was getting that look. Her face crumpled a little when conversation turned to Sam, partly because she was envious that Heather had a mythically desirable boyfriend but also because it got in the way of Melanie's supercontrolling go-girl solidarity. Heather had a pessimistic feeling that Melanie's allegiances would change once she found a guy she thought was worthy.

"Besides," Heather said. "You know I can't drag

him to high school parties anymore." She pulled up short at Broadway Shoes, one of their regular destinations. "Do you want to go here?" she asked.

"Let's go straight to Patricia Field," Melanie said. "They have these really cute mod dresses."

Cory strode alongside Heather eagerly. "Are you going to get the orange skirt with the thingies along the bottom you tried on last time? It looked so, so cool on you."

Heather shrugged. "Maybe. The lining was kind of itchy." The lining was only mildly itchy; the skirt cost ninety-five dollars.

They were a few yards down the block from Ozzie's Cafe when Heather's stomach dropped. It was funny. She saw Ed Fargo most days of her life. It had been over two years since they'd broken up. Yet still her physical reaction on seeing him was always the same—sometimes stronger, sometimes weaker, but always present.

He was sitting in his wheelchair at a front table by the window, seeming to scan every person who passed. His dark hair was crying out to be combed, and his awful midnineties cargo pants belonged in a Dumpster. But Ed managed to be powerfully attractive nonetheless. His jaw was a little sharp and his straight nose was a little long, but he had possibly the most beautiful mouth that had ever graced the face of a man. The parts of his face, though not flawless the way Sam's were, came together in a striking and disarming way.

As often happened, Heather had that strange, sad feeling of disconnect, knowing the ghost of the person she'd loved desperately, the one with legs that worked, was lurking within the person in the ghastly wheelchair, who needed special ramp entrances and kneeling buses.

She was shallow. She knew that. Ed was still the same person inside. He was still the same person inside. No matter how many times she said it and thought it, she couldn't make herself believe it.

She stopped abruptly and rapped on the glass. Ed looked up and smiled. It was a guarded smile. She was in a position to know the difference.

Her friends were already several steps ahead, but they had stopped now and were waiting for her. "Go ahead," she called, waving them on. "I'll meet you there in, like, five minutes." When they paused, she gestured again, less patiently. "Go. I swear I'll be there in a couple of minutes."

Once her friends started walking again, Heather stepped into Ozzie's and was embraced by the thick smell of coffee. "Hey, Ed," she said, sitting down in the empty chair across from him.

"Hey," he said back. "What's going on?"

"Nothing. Just, you know, shopping with the girlfriends."

Ed nodded.

"You're waiting for someone?" Heather asked. Before he had a chance to answer, she said, "Let me guess. Gaia Moore, right?"

He looked uncomfortable. "No, not really."

"Oh, come on."

"What?" Ed said defensively. "Sometimes she comes by here after school and we have coffee. Sometimes I have coffee by myself."

Heather put her index finger on a drop of coffee that had spilled on the table. She spread the liquid in a widening circle. "You guys have gotten to be good friends, it seems like."

"Yeah."

Heather laughed at a memory, pretending it was impulsive. "Did you hear about her classic line in Rupert's class today?"

Though still guarded, Ed now looked interested in spite of himself. "No. What?"

"Rupert asked her why she wasn't paying attention, and Gaia said, and this is an exact quote, 'I was thinking about sex. I was thinking about having sex.'" Heather laughed again. "What a freak. People were mimicking her all afternoon. I'm surprised you missed it."

Ed waited for her to finish without even a smile. What had happened to the guy's sense of humor?

Heather needed a way in. She needed to make Ed

talk to her. She sat back in her chair and rolled a piece of her hair between her finger and thumb.

"I've heard Gaia's stoking a major crush," she said, tossing a dart into the winds.

Ed remained wary. "Oh, yeah?"

"So says the rumor mill," Heather said provocatively. She took a calculated risk with a second dart. "Word is, the crush is on you. Tannie got a look at her notebook in precal. . . ."

Bull's-eye. Ed's cheeks flushed. He met her eyes with poorly masked excitement and curiosity.

On the one hand, Heather was pleased that her instincts served her so well. On the other hand, it pissed her off that Ed was obviously falling victim to Gaia, too. Had Gaia Moore been put on earth to punish her?

Ed crumpled an empty sugar packet tightly between his fingers. "I don't know about that," he mumbled. Guarded as he was, he did want to talk. "I think it's more about sex."

Heather yawned. Once she got started, it was genuine. "What do you mean?"

"Oh, I don't know." Ed seemed to wave a thought away. "She wants to lose her virginity. I guess if she's telling Ms. Rupert's class about it, it's not a big secret."

Heather looked in her purse, ostensibly for lip balm. "And who's the lucky guy?" she said suggestively.

"She hasn't said. It's a mystery."

"Aha." In near perfect detail, Heather's mind called up the image of Gaia and Sam sitting together on that bench in the park. Heather was starting to get an unpleasant feeling about this.

Heather located the tube of Chap Stick and ran it over her lips. "It's not a mystery to me," she said confidently.

"What do you mean?" Ed asked tentatively, crushing the bit of paper in his palm.

"It's obvious," Heather said, getting up from the table, "that the lucky guy is you."

It was a mean thing to say since Heather didn't believe it, but when she saw the naked hope and pleasure in Ed's eyes, her anger took over and she told herself he deserved it.

Stupid,
moron,
shit-head
CJ **impossible**
was
sticking
his stupid
gun in her
face again.

EVER SINCE SHE'D WOKEN FROM THAT

dream, Gaia was so distracted, she could hardly remember to breathe regularly or feed herself or put one foot in front of the other when walking.

The Vigilante

Ow. She kicked her big toe hard against a ledge in the cracked cement sidewalk and stumbled forward.

She certainly couldn't be bothered to come up with appropriate kiss-ass behavior for the vice principal, which was why she'd sat through detention, which was why she was walking home late.

She arrived at the corner of the park. Cut through or take the long way?

In her state, the right thing to do was go around. How was she going to make the dream happen if she got shot today?

She cut through, anyway. To do anything else was purely against her nature.

Would Sam be at the chess tables today, and if so, what should she say? It was time to get serious about her plan. No more being shy. No more being awkward. Her dream emboldened her.

Oh God, and there he was. She spotted him from the back, playing chess with Zolov. His elbow rested on the edge of the table, and he cradled his head in his hand. The last of the day's sun turned his tousled hair into gold. She could see a bit of his profile, the sensual curve of his mouth.

It was the perfect opportunity to proposition him, but she couldn't seem to make her feet go forward. She called up the dream again, but far from emboldening her, it turned her cheeks red and made her feel very shy. Those were the lips that had made her feel . . .

She heard scrambling behind her and spun around. *Oh, shit.* She took off at a run. CJ was lying in wait, of course, as she certainly knew he would be. Why was she so stupid? Couldn't she give up the death wish for even a day or two? At this rate she *deserved* to die a lonely, bitter, parentless virgin.

She cursed herself as she sprinted through the park and westward toward Sixth Avenue. It would be busy there this hour, hopefully busy enough to lose him.

Gaia raced onto the avenue. *Beeeep! Beeeeeeeeeeeep!*

"Get the *hell* out of the *street!*" somebody screeched.

A maroon commercial van swerved to avoid her and plowed into the back of a taxicab. Gaia heard the crumpling of metal. The taxi rear-ended a black Mercedes-Benz convertible. The Mercedes drove up onto the sidewalk and crushed its headlight against a parking meter.

Oh, Jesus. Gaia ducked behind a stopped garbage truck as the air filled with shouting drivers slamming doors and the excited buzz of pedestrians crowding to watch the show. No one was hurt, Gaia was pretty sure of that, and the chaos gave her a second to collect herself. She spotted CJ on the curb, his eyes wildly scanning the street for her.

Don't move, she told him silently. *I'll be right there.*

This was all she needed—a chance to see him without being seen. She noticed with huge relief that he'd stuffed the gun back in his jacket. The sidewalk where he stood had largely emptied of people, who were drawn to the activity a little ways down the street.

Ducking as she crept along, she used the line of stopped cars to conceal herself. She had him directly in her sights, not ten feet away. *Now go!*

She pounced. In a single graceful move she captured both of his arms and wrenched them behind his back. She dragged him several yards off the busy avenue to the relative backwater of Minetta Lane. CJ growled and twisted his body to free his arms. He succeeded, or at least he thought so. The truth was, she was happy to let him come at her as long as the gun stayed out of his hands.

"Bitch," he hissed at her with a snarl. He took a step back to get some leverage, drew back his right arm, and launched his fist at her face. She dodged it easily. She felt relaxed, even—shamefully—a little excited. For Gaia a fistfight against one other person hardly drew a sweat. And CJ was just the kind of asshole she most enjoyed putting in his place.

He hauled off again, this time aiming the punch at her stomach. She caught it long before it landed. His exertion threw him so far off balance, she used the offending arm to lay him out on the pavement with the smallest effort.

He quickly found his feet and stood up, bellowing a long string of obscenities. He was squaring off, spitting mad, trying to find some way at her.

All right. It was tempting to linger but not a good idea. Time to close this thing out. He leaped at her sloppily, swinging both arms. She ducked and landed a swift, hard jab in his stomach. He doubled over, unable to breathe. She kicked him on the shoulder and sent him sprawling to the pavement. Now she knelt by his head, wrapped her forearm around his neck, and pulled him up onto her lap. She plunged her other hand roughly into his jacket, feeling around for the gun.

CJ gaped at her with surprise and fear, still unable to catch a breath. He probably thought she was going to kill him. And he did deserve it. What a joy it was to reverse their roles, to have him right where she wanted him. He should have known he didn't have a prayer against her one-on-one. Few people did. That wasn't bragging; it was just a fact. The gun was what threw everything.

"Don't you know better than to open fire in a crowded street, you stupid bastard?" she barked at him. Where was the damn gun? She tightened her grasp on his neck and made her way through his pockets. CJ's dark red wool cap got pushed to the side, revealing his stubbly bald head.

Unpleasant as it was, Gaia jammed her hand down his shirt. She saw the ugly black hieroglyphs carved into the skin of his chest and made a mental note to never, ever consider getting a tattoo.

Okay. Now she was getting somewhere. She felt the cold butt of the gun with her fingertips. What a huge relief. In a rush of hopefulness she felt the possibility of this whole insane episode coming to an end and the world stretching out with her alive in it.

Maybe she could calm down about this sex thing and go about a relationship like a normal human being. Maybe she could take on the search for her dad in a thoughtful and intelligent way.

She gripped the gun, which CJ had secured in the tightly belted waistband of his pants.

Maybe she could—

Gaia shouted in surprise as an arm closed around her own neck. Her thoughts scattered, and she lost her hold on the gun as she was wrenched backward.

"Leave the kid alone!" a voice thundered much too close to her ear. She snapped her head around to look over her shoulder. Less than a foot away was the red face of a very large man in a disheveled suit jacket and tie.

What—?

The large man dragged her back another few feet. By now CJ had sprung to his feet and lightly patted the gun still tucked in his pants.

"Did she get your wallet off you?" the man asked CJ, concern clear in his voice. "You go tell the police all about it, son. There's a squad car around the corner."

Unbelievable. Gaia was speechless.

This guy wasn't a friend of CJ's, a fellow thug from the park, as she'd briefly imagined. This was a suit-wearing, forty-something-year-old, white-collar stranger on his way home from work. This was an angry citizen taking justice into his own hands. A vigilante. He believed she was mugging CJ. He was *protecting* CJ!

What an awful joke. CJ, out on bail, concealing an illegal weapon, had every reason not to seek the help of New York's finest. He only stayed long enough to sneer at Gaia, pull his hat back down over his ears, and smile.

"You're dead!" CJ shouted over his shoulder at Gaia as he took off at a run into the bedlam of the Village on a Friday night.

The big guy was practically strangling Gaia, but she was too miserable at the moment to do anything about it.

"I've heard about girl gangs," the man was saying, not to Gaia, but not to anyone else, exactly. "That kid may not want to turn her in, but you can be sure I'm not letting her go."

Obviously the man meant it because he started

yanking Gaia toward Sixth Avenue. Was there any point in telling him the magnitude of his mistake?

"Um, sir?" She loosened his grip around her neck so she could breathe and speak. "You have to let me go now." She locked her feet on the pavement and stood firm.

He stood up tall and puffed out his chest in indignation, even as he attempted to `crush her trachea`. He was at least six feet four and very powerfully built. His hair was dark and thinning on top. He looked like an ex–offensive lineman. Unless he was some kind of wretched, hypocritical wife beater, he probably wasn't used to fighting girls.

"Kids like you gotta be kept off the street," the man told her. "I don't want to hear any sob stories. You can save it for the cops."

Gaia sighed. Things were not going her way. "Look, sir," Gaia said reasonably. "I don't want any more violence tonight, but if you won't let me go, I'm going to have to force you, and it could hurt."

The man looked at her in disbelief. Then he laughed dryly. "You're going to hurt *me?*"

"I don't want to. I realize you're just trying to help out. I appreciate that."

He laughed again.

"I'm serious," Gaia said. "Let me go now."

He stared at her with `undisguised amusement`. "You're scaring me."

"Sorry, then," Gaia said flatly.

She gave him about ten more seconds to withdraw. She actually did feel bad, but what was she supposed to do? She wasn't getting booked and spending several more hours of her life in a police station. It brought back memories of the worst hours of her life. There was just no way.

She placed both of her hands on the man's arm that circled her neck. Without any more force than necessary, she took a deep breath and flipped him over her shoulder onto the ground.

He landed hard, what with being so huge and old. He let out a terrible squawk. As he lay there writhing in discomfort, staring at her as if she'd grown second and third heads, all traces of amusement disappeared from his face. She hoped very genuinely that he would feel better tomorrow.

"Sorry," she said again before she ran off.

"THAT'S HER! THAT BLOND GIRL!"

No More Thinking

Gaia was rounding the corner of Bleecker Street less than sixty seconds later when she heard another commotion behind her. Gaia turned her head partway, and out of the corner of her eye she saw two police-men pointing after her. The big man in the suit had managed to sic the cops on her in record time.

She didn't turn her head any farther or slow her steps. The cops hadn't really seen her face yet, and she meant to keep it that way.

It was wrong and bad to run away from cops, but Gaia was really tired now, and she hadn't done any-thing illegal, except maybe flip the balding guy, but he was strangling her, and he deserved it. Furthermore, she had given him ample warning.

She would just run away from them this one time, she promised herself. In the future she would be extra friendly and helpful to the police.

She was coming up on her favorite deli when she had a brainstorm. The hatch to the basement, a sprawling black hole in the sidewalk in front of the store, was open. She could disappear without having been seen, and the cops would probably be happy to forget about the whole thing. Were they really going to blame a high school kid for roughing up a guy three times her size? She practically dove into its darkness. She pulled the heavy metal doors shut be-hind her and clung to the top of the rickety conveyor belt used to stock the supply rooms. She heard foot-steps banging along overhead. Hopefully they be-longed to the cops.

Ugh. The place was pitch black and smelled awful.

It was unfortunate to be winded and gasping for breath in a place where the air was thick with dust and rotting food. There were certainly rats down below, but she didn't want to think about that too much.

Gaia glanced at the glowing hands of her watch. Five minutes took several hours to pass. At last she opened one of the doors a crack and peered out. Never had New York City air smelled so fresh. No sign of any police.

She opened it another few inches. She was either home free or a very easy target. Still no sign. Time to make her move. She threw open the hatch door and climbed out. Once on the sidewalk, she spun around.

What she saw made her freeze. Her blood seemed to stop in her veins. Black blotches clouded her vision. She put her head down to prevent herself from fainting, and when she looked up again, he was gone.

It wasn't a cop. It wasn't CJ. Who knew where he'd gone? The man she'd thought she'd seen in that split second looked uncannily familiar. He looked, although she was sure she'd imagined it, like her father. It couldn't have been. She was low on oxygen, overtired, overwrought. It couldn't have actually been him. But it shocked her to her core just the same.

On trembling legs she found her way home. She stopped at the bottom of the stoop, trying to regain her breath and her sense of balance. She prayed Ella wouldn't be home yet.

Deep, cleansing breaths. In, one, two, three. Out, one, two, three. She put her hands on her hips and bent her head low to keep the blood flowing into it. She wasn't going crazy. There could be people in the world who looked a little like her dad. Was that so impossible?

It was a crazy night. With all she'd been through, who could blame her for a minor hallucination?

"Say good-bye, bitch."

Gaia choked on her cleansing breath. Stupid, moron, shit head CJ was sticking his stupid gun in her face again. How much more could she take in one night? She was completely beyond reason. She was exhausted and mad and frustrated and totally freaked by the sight of that familiar man.

Without thinking, she shocked both herself and CJ by wrenching the gun right out of his hand and throwing it as hard as she could down Perry Street. She wanted him away from her. Now. That was it.

CJ ran after it.

"Can't you leave me *alone* for a couple of *hours,* you little *shit?*" she screamed after him.

Then she lumbered up the stairs to the front door, carrying with her the discomforting knowledge that in addition to losing her heart and her pride, she had also lost her mind.

The only thing she'd managed to keep was her virginity.

Wearing Patience

"THAT STUPID, STUPID GIRL!" HE paced the floor of the loft, pausing briefly to kick an ottoman out of his way. "Ella, did I not order you to kill that lowlife the same way you killed his friend? What is the problem here?"

Ella glared at the parquet floor. "I said I'm trying, sir."

"Clearly not very hard. You are a trained assassin, need I remind you, and he is a pathetic, imbecilic teenager. Do you honestly need backup?" He beckoned to his two omnipresent bodyguards, who stood at attention several yards away.

"No," Ella said firmly.

He glared irritably at Ella. Was she not adequately frightened of him anymore?

He methodically took a gun out of his drawer, walked over to her, and pressed the barrel to her forehead. "Ella, you know I would as easily kill you as ask you this a third time?"

She didn't meet his gaze. "Yes, sir."

"I've taken some pains placing you with that doormat George Niven, so I'm forced to be patient with you. But know this, Ella. My patience is wearing."

No, she wasn't frightened enough. He fired the gun so that the bullet nearly grazed her nose and ruptured a windowpane with a blast of noise. Ella jumped back in shock. Her eyes were momentarily filled with fear.

There. That was better.

"Trust me, Ella, if something happens to that girl, I will kill you and everyone you have ever cared about. I need Gaia, and I need her alive."

He walked to the wall of windows, watching the dying sun set flame to New Jersey's sky in a lurid show of color.

Perhaps it was time to move forward. Perhaps it was time to bring Gaia in.

HOW LONG HAD HE BEEN SITTING here? Tom wondered, looking up at the ceiling of the diner absently. Cracks riddled the surface of the plaster, buried under multiple coats of high-gloss light orange paint. The color was the same as the bun sandwiching the burger that sat on his plate, which he hadn't found the appetite to eat.

Clinging

He truly hadn't expected to see Gaia. He hadn't prepared himself for it. Now his fragile hold on life's priorities were shattered once more.

His baby. His child. His and Katia's. His throat ached at the memory of her face. He'd known she'd be grown-up now, much like a woman, but he didn't *know*. He hadn't been ready for it.

He'd always imagined she would grow up to be a beautiful woman, being Katia's daughter, but he was surprised by precisely how. She wasn't petite like her mother. She was tall and lanky, like him. Her hair had stayed that glorious pale yellow. He would have guessed it would fade and darken, as most child hair did, but hers hadn't. It had remained straight and soft looking. Her eyes were still deep, challenging blue. Some blue eyes looked pale and watery—more an absence of color than a color itself. But Gaia's were rich with pigment, a dense, tumultuous, changeable blue.

He'd desperately wanted to go to her. To hold her for just a few minutes. To tell her he loved her and thought of her every hour of every day. He needed her to know that she would never be alone; she would never be unloved as long as he was alive.

And if he had, what would she have said to him? Would she have glared at him in anger? In hurt? Could she ever forgive him for abandoning her?

Tom pulled his eyes back down from the ceiling, pinning them to the chipped Formica table on which his hands rested. What was the use of imagining it? He couldn't hold Gaia. He couldn't talk to her. To contact her would be selfish and put her in greater danger than she could ever know. His presence here at all was a terrible, senseless risk.

Five years ago he'd clung to Katia, and in doing so he'd as sure as killed her himself. He couldn't do that to Gaia. He'd already hurt her enough.

His desire
rose to an
unquenchable **from**
thirst as he **the**
burrowed his
lips **waist**
in her soft, **down**
buttery
hair—

"GAIA, IS THAT YOU?" ED FARGO stared at the pretty brunette in the wide-brimmed straw hat, sunglasses, and flowery dress standing in the doorway of his family's apartment.

Condom Shopping

"Yes. Duh," she replied somewhat impatiently.

Ed studied her for another moment in confusion. "Why are you wearing a wig?"

"What wig?" Gaia asked.

"Have you been a brunette all this time and I just didn't notice?" Ed asked, feigning innocent surprise.

Gaia rolled her eyes. "I'm not wearing a wig, smarty-pants. I colored my hair with washable dye," she explained reasonably.

"Oh. Aha. Okay, then."

Ed shut the door behind him and locked it, and he wheeled along next to her down the hallway to the elevator. Gaia, typically, didn't offer any more information.

"Would you mind if I asked why?" Ed asked as the elevator arrived and Gaia pushed him in.

Gaia tapped her foot on the linoleum floor. "What happened to your promise not to ask questions?"

"I meant I wouldn't ask questions about big stuff," Ed said defensively. "Parents, past, unusual abilities. Not hair color. But fine. Don't tell me if you don't want."

132

Gaia sighed huffily. "Fine, I will tell you. But don't chicken out on me, okay?"

Ed put his head in his hand. "I have a feeling I'm not going to like the explanation very much."

"Okay?" Gaia pressed.

"Okay," Ed replied weakly.

The elevator arrived at the lobby, and the doors opened.

"Remember I told you CJ was out to get me?" Gaia asked, following him out of the elevator. "Well, he's still out to get me, and I'm sick of hiding out in my room. I wanted to go on this errand with you, but I don't want him to open fire again, particularly not at you. So that's why I look like this."

Ed swallowed. He let his wheelchair roll to a stop. "CJ is likely to open fire in the middle of the day?"

"Not if he doesn't recognize me," Gaia said breezily.

"But if he does?" Ed demanded.

"Yeah. Probably." Gaia took hold of the back of his chair and rolled him to the entrance of the building.

"Gaia! What do you think you're doing?"

"You said you wouldn't chicken out," Gaia reminded him, `rolling contentedly along.`

"I didn't realize my *life* would be in danger," Ed complained.

"It won't be," Gaia assured him without sounding at all convincing.

"Gaia! Stop pushing me! I'm being hijacked here!"

Gaia stopped. She took a breath. "Sorry," she said, like she meant it. She turned him around. "You're right. I'll take you back."

"No. I'm not saying . . . I'm just—" Ed sputtered. Why was Gaia so frustrating all the time? How did she always manage to stay in control of every situation? "Gaia, stop! Just stop."

Gaia stopped. She let go of the chair.

"Thank you," Ed said. He looked around the dull gray lobby with its drab fifties decor and hoped that no one he or his parents knew was within hearing distance of this conversation. "Now, don't roll me anymore."

"I'm sorry," Gaia said. "I really am. I won't do it again."

He glared at her in silence.

"Do you want to come or not come? It's totally up to you," Gaia said solicitously. "I promise I won't *touch* your chair."

She actually looked sweet as she waited for his response. Man, she made a fine brunette. Errrg. He knocked his knuckles against the armrest. Of course he would go with her, even if he *was* going to get shot at. That was the really pitiful thing.

"All right, Gaia," he said after he'd made her wait long enough. He wheeled into the bright sunshine of First Avenue, and she followed. "But slow down, okay? You're making me nervous."

"I'll try. It's just that I've had a rough couple of days, what with not getting killed and all."

134

"Right," Ed said, wondering how he'd ended up with such a friend.

They walked across the avenue and took East Sixth Street past all the Indian restaurants toward Second Avenue. Ed could smell the curry.

"So where are we going?" Ed asked.

"To buy condoms," Gaia replied.

(Cough.) "To buy"—Ed paused to clear his throat so his voice wouldn't come out squeaky—"condoms?"

"You gotta be safe," Gaia pointed out.

Ed scratched his head behind his ear. "Yes. Yes, you do," he said slowly. "Can I ask who they're for?"

"Me," Gaia said.

"Um . . . Gaia?"

"Yeah?"

"I don't know if you ever got to the unit in health class where they covered this stuff, but . . . uh, condoms are usually intended to be worn by the—"

Gaia punched him on the shoulder playfully but still too hard. "I don't mean I'm going to *wear* one, dummy."

He waited for her to offer some corrected version of her plan, but of course she didn't.

"So you're buying them for a guy?" he tried out.

"Yes," she said.

"And that guy would be . . . ?"

Gaia looked at him over her dark glasses. "Remember how I told you I wanted to have sex?"

"Yeah?" That was a hard conversation to forget.

"Well, obviously I'm going to need some condoms," Gaia explained as if she were speaking to a person with a very low IQ.

"Obviously," Ed said. His heart was racing, and he was feeling a bit queasy. He was miserably uncomfortable both with the remote hope that Gaia intended to have sex with him and the idea that she was planning to have sex with somebody else.

"Can you tell me who the lucky guy is?" His choice of words made him think of the conversation he'd had with Heather the day before. Had Gaia really written something about him in her notebook? As hard as Ed was trying to sound light and carefree, he felt his life's happiness was hanging on her answer.

"Nope," Gaia said.

Ed felt oddly relieved. "Okay. Let me ask you this. Have you told this person you're planning to have sex with him?" He hated himself for fishing, but he couldn't help it.

Gaia suddenly looked ill at ease. "No, not exactly."

"So you're just going to pounce on him in the dead of night?"

Gaia looked offended. "No. I'm not," she replied stiffly.

"Then what?"

"When I'm ready, I'm going to just go to where he

lives and . . . ask him," Gaia explained a little defensively.

"Just ask him."

"Right."

"I see."

"Does that sound so bad?" she asked. Were her eyes searching, or was he imagining it?

She stopped in front of a discount pharmacy on Third Avenue and gallantly held open the door while he passed.

"Kind of unorthodox, I guess, but not . . . *bad*, exactly."

Gaia was already studying the selection hanging on the wall behind the counter. "So what do you think, Ed?" she asked him, squinting at the labels. "Lubricated? Ribbed? Ultrasensitive?"

Ed tried to breathe evenly. For a girl who'd been concerned about awkwardness a couple of days ago, she was really `taking this in the teeth`. "Jeez, I don't know," he said feebly. He scanned the back wall, which was jam packed with every brand of embarrassing merchandise—birth control, tampons, pregnancy tests, laxatives, hemorrhoid medicine. What sick mind decided that all that stuff went behind the counter where you had to ask for it by name? "You pick."

She pointed out the package she wanted to the cashier man, who wore a sweater vest and a name tag that said, "Hi, my name is Omar." Omar, looking curious and somewhat amused, spent an extra-long time locating Gaia's choice. At last he slapped the bright red box on the counter, and Gaia paid up. Ed realized Omar was giving him approving, `go-get-'em` looks.

"Have fun," Omar said as they left the store.

Ed was certain his face was probably the shade of a ripe strawberry. He suddenly wished he weren't wearing a bright orange tie-dyed T-shirt.

"Do you think the guy is going to say no?" Gaia asked as they started back in the direction of his building.

"I'm not saying that."

"But you're thinking that," Gaia accused.

"No, it's just . . . I mean, look, Gaia, it's not your everyday thing to do to a guy."

Gaia nodded thoughtfully. "I realize that. I do. But I'm a little desperate here. I figure I can stay alive till tomorrow, but maybe not after that. If there's any chance of losing my virginity before then, I've just got to do it. Tonight."

"Tonight?" Ed couldn't hide his shock.

"Yeah."

"Tonight," Ed repeated numbly.

"Yes, Ed. Tonight. Saturday night."

`Ed's brain felt like it was shutting down.`

"So I'm just going to go right to his room and ask. Nicely, of course. I won't insist or anything. And if he seems really reluctant or . . ."

"Freaked out," Ed supplied.

138

"Or freaked out," Gaia allowed, "I'll just tell him the truth."

Gaia paused to let him say something, but when he didn't, she surged ahead. When she was with Ed and her mouth got going, there was no stopping her.

"The truth is good. The truth is your friend. Seriously. I'll just say to him, Look, I'm probably going to get shot in the head tomorrow, and I really want to have sex before I go, so would you mind?"

Gaia looked at Ed again for some response. He couldn't even work his mouth anymore.

"And even if he thinks I'm completely repulsive and would rather have sex with his aunt, well, he probably still won't want to refuse a girl's dying request, will he? What do you say?" She turned to Ed with a genuinely hopeful look on her face.

Ed struggled for words. "I—I say. I say . . . have fun."

"PLEASE TABULATE YOUR RESULTS

The Wrong Girl

according to the format Dr. Witchell presented in the lecture on Thursday."

The very droopy-looking kiss-ass teaching assistant droned on as Sam pictured the way Heather would look when she appeared in his room that night.

It was unfortunate that his lab section of biochemistry had to meet on Saturday. It was especially unfortunate on *this* Saturday, when his mind was impossible to contain.

Would she wear that short black skirt that made him drool? Maybe one of those miniature T-shirts she had that showed off her belly button? And what about under it? It probably wasn't a good idea for him to go there right now, but he couldn't help it. He pulled his chair up so his waist pressed against the table and further obscured his lap with his notebook. It was highly embarrassing to get excited in class— something he hadn't done since seventh grade.

He'd made his way into Heather's sexy satin bras before. That was a pleasure he was looking forward to. But it was the new frontier that piqued his interest. Would she wear satin panties to match, like the women in those lingerie ads?

Suddenly he wasn't picturing her clothes anymore; he was picturing himself taking off her clothes. He couldn't help that, either. And as the fantasy evolved he wasn't under the harsh fluorescent lights of a science lab anymore but in his (now almost clean) dorm room in low romantic light (he made a mental note to buy a candle). His body pressed against her soft skin, his hands exploring her luxurious curves. Her soft, dark hair tickled his chest. His lips trailed up her neck and under her chin.

He sighed (almost inaudibly) and kissed the lids of those mysterious eyes, the bridge of her thin, straight nose, the plains of her bewitching face. His desire rose to an unquenchable thirst as he burrowed his lips in her soft, buttery hair—

Sam looked up in alarm. The blissful fantasy screeched to a stop with jarring suddenness. It felt like somebody had ripped the needle off an old vinyl record spinning a Mozart symphony.

He wasn't kissing Heather. Where had this fantasy gone so far awry? Heather didn't have hair or eyes or legs like those. Somehow Gaia had arrived in his reverie uninvited. He should have been jolted, surprised, even repulsed by her sudden presence in his bed, but was he? No. The look and feel of her had sent his desire into some completely new stratosphere.

This was not good. This was very bad. What was he going to do?

"Sam . . . ? Sam, uh . . . Moon, is it?"

Sam blinked several times. It took him a moment to bring the TA's face into focus. When he looked around the lab, he realized that except for the TA, he was all by himself. The class was gone, over. The TA was gazing at him as if he were a particularly puzzling specimen in a petri dish.

"I've kind of got to close up here, if you . . . uh . . . don't mind," the TA pointed out.

"Sure. Sorry," Sam said feebly, trying to coordinate his limbs to lift him out of his chair and walk him out of the classroom. "See you," he said over his shoulder.

Still in a fog, he walked down the corridor of the science building and out into the windy courtyard, where the bright, hopeful afternoon sun was threatened by blotchy gray clouds gathering on the horizon.

Little-Known Facts about me:

The summer before my sophomore year, I fell in love. It was the most idyllic summer you could possibly imagine. My family had rented a house in East Hampton that year. My mom and sisters and I stayed for the whole season, and my dad came out on weekends. Those were the days when my dad's business was doing really well.

Ed Fargo was spending the summer at his aunt and uncle's place just a few blocks away. Ed's folks are teachers, but his aunt is this big-time lawyer with a beautiful house right on the beach.

I was working at the farmers' market in Amagansett, and Ed was working at a surf shop on the Montauk Highway. Ed is a year older. You've met Ed, so you know he's seriously good-looking, funny, charming, self-deprecating, super-sharp, and generally a great guy. He was also an amazing surfer. This all took place before his accident, as I'm sure you've already guessed.

HEATHER

Anyway, our love story would take too long to describe here, but it was the most magical time of my life. Someday I'll turn that story into a romance novel, maybe somebody will even make a movie of it, and I'll earn millions of dollars.

The climax of that summer, so to speak, was a night in August, when Ed and I made love on the beach. The moon was full, and the surf was so gentle, we lay together in it. It was the first time for both of us. It was too perfect ever to be described in words, so I won't try.

One month later Ed was paralyzed from the waist down. He spent the next several months in the hospital and in physical therapy. He lost a year of school. Now he's sentenced to a wheelchair for the rest of his life.

Technically, I didn't break up with him. But I would have. Ed let me off the hook by doing it for me—that's the kind of guy he is. I was under a lot of pressure from my parents and everything. They didn't want me spending my youth taking care of a guy in a wheelchair—a guy they felt no longer had "possibilities."

Ed never acted like he hated me after that. In fact, we're still sort of friends. But in his eyes, when I have the courage to look, I see profound disappointment that can never be repaired or forgotten.

I don't need to tell you my parents love Sam. Gorgeous, brilliant, world-class-chess-playing, premed Sam. I'm only eighteen, but they'd be overjoyed if I married him tomorrow. It would relieve some of their financial pressure, I suppose.

You're probably wondering why I told Sam I'm a virgin. The reason is because Gaia is a virgin. I know it for a fact. I don't want Gaia to be able to give Sam something I can't.

Here's a little-known fact

about Ed Fargo: He has a personal fortune of twenty-six million dollars. Probably more now because the settlement came over a year and a half ago, and money like that earns a lot of interest. His parents, acting on the advice (and guilt, I guess) of his aunt, sued over the accident, even though Ed begged them not to and he refused to testify.

Ed won't let anybody touch the money. He will never tell anyone he has it. I only know because I read about the windfall in the newspaper—no names, of course, but I'm one of the few people who know the strange circumstances of the accident. In fact, I first heard about the case because Ed's parents contacted me about testifying.

Here's another fact about Ed. His reproductive organs, to put it clinically, still work perfectly well. Not that it matters to me anymore.

Heather paused at the door, hesitant **ready.** for some **or** reason to **not.** commit herself to this strange night.

GAIA WAS AS CLOSE TO NERVOUS AS

a girl who lacked the physical ability to feel nervous could be. She had taken a long bath and spent hours picking out a bra and underpants that wouldn't be completely embarrassing if revealed. She'd brushed her teeth twice.

She spent several minutes naked in front of the mirror, worrying that she was too fat. After she talked herself out of that, she worried she was too skinny—bony limbed, underdeveloped, and flat chested.

She couldn't stop herself from making comparisons to Heather. Her body wasn't as feminine as Heather's. Her breasts weren't as big as Heather's. Her feet were definitely much bigger. Her hair wasn't as thick as Heather's.

Gaia had even reverted to the tactics of a seventh grader by calling Sam to make sure he was in his room, then hanging up as soon as he'd answered.

Now, standing in the middle of the floor, wearing the slinky pink dress she'd "borrowed" from Ella and a pair of heels, she felt like a big, oafish fraud. Why was she even putting herself through this? Sam would take one look at her and tell her to get lost. Why did she think he would be attracted to her? Why in the world would he consider going behind Heather's back for *her*? Even if Gaia *was* going to be out of the picture by tomorrow.

She glanced at her watch. Arg. Urmph. It was

almost eight o'clock. If she didn't leave now, Sam would probably head out for the evening, and she'd go to her grave a virgin.

She took one last look at herself. No, this wasn't going to work. She was no seductress. She wasn't going to fool anybody. She pulled the dress over her head and kicked off the heeled sandals. If she was going to go, she'd go as herself. She'd be honest. She pulled on jeans and a T-shirt and dug her bare feet into her running shoes. She thrust the package of condoms into her bag.

As a safety measure she tucked her hair into a wool cap, which she pulled low over her eyes, wrapped a scarf over most of the bottom of her face, and slipped on a pair of glasses with heavy black frames. Not exactly sexy, but neither was a severe head wound.

Thankfully Ella was out, so Gaia could walk down the stairs like a sane human being. She locked the door behind her and struck out into the cool October night, knowing that this was going to be the greatest single night of her life or a complete and total nightmare.

"THE GREEN OR THE BLACK?" HEATHER
asked her sister Phoebe.

Hesitant

Phoebe leaned back on her elbows on Heather's unmade

bed and sized her up. "The green is prettier; the black is sexier."

"Black it is," Heather said, pulling the close-fitting sweater over her head. "Can I borrow that gauzy dark red skirt?" she asked, scanning the many piles of clothing that covered her floor.

"Big night tonight?" Phoebe asked suggestively.

"I hope so," Heather answered in a way that was mysterious but didn't openly invite further questioning.

On the one hand, it was annoying that Phoebe came home from college almost every weekend. She was a sophomore at SUNY Binghamton and hated it there. She referred to it as Boonie U. and was constantly composing the personal essay for her transfer application. Heather reasoned that if Phoebe spent even half that time on her courses, she could actually make the grades to transfer. Heather didn't mention this to Phoebe, of course. Phoebe's old room had been partitioned off and rented out, so Phoebe stayed in Heather's room, and she was quite the slob. On the other hand, Phoebe had managed to accumulate lots of nice clothes—who even knew how—and usually let Heather borrow them.

"Sure," Phoebe said. She got up from the bed and planted herself in a chair at Heather's vanity table. Phoebe leaned close to the mirror and pursed her lips. "Only it's dry-clean only, so don't mess it up."

"Yes, ma'am," Heather said, locating the skirt and pulling it over her hips. Phoebe was taller, but Heather was a little slimmer. "How does it look?"

"Fine," Phoebe said without even giving her a glance. She was rooting through her capacious makeup bag. "Have you seen my brandy wine lip liner? It's Lancôme, and it cost like twenty bucks. I'm sure I had it when I came last weekend."

Heather ignored her. Phoebe was always losing things and subtly blaming other people.

Heather slipped on her black nubuck loafers and checked her hair and makeup one last time. She felt keyed up and a little shaky. She wasn't sure where excitement ended and nervousness began. She checked her purse again to make sure she had the condoms.

"Okay, Phoebe, I'm taking off. See you later."

"See ya," Phoebe said absently, without taking her eyes from her reflection in the mirror.

Heather paused at the door, hesitant for some reason to commit herself to this strange night.

"Wish me luck," she added in a quiet voice, wishing in a way that this were a night from their innocent past in which the two sisters would practice gymnastics in the living room for hours and try to stay up late enough to watch *Saturday Night Live.*

But Phoebe was already too deeply involved in her cosmetics to respond.

"OUCH. SHIT," SAM MUTTERED, putting his index finger in his mouth. He'd tried lighting the candle, but the wick was buried in the wax, and when he'd dug for it in the hot wax, he'd burned himself.

Sincere

He lit the wick again. It took this time, but the flame was sputtering and underconfident.

He sniffed at the air. Crap. The candle was advertised to smell like vanilla, which he'd hoped would cover any residue of dirty-room odor, but instead it smelled like floor cleaner.

He was nervous. He couldn't help himself. He glanced again in the mirror. It seemed stupid to take pains with his clothing when the whole point of this evening was to be taking them off as quickly as possible. He'd actually brought his khakis with him into the bathroom and taken an extra-steamy shower in the hope of getting out some of the wrinkles. He'd put on his softest oxford shirt and carefully rolled up the cuffs. It reminded him of Christmas Eve. All those hours he spent wrapping and tying up presents, when it was all torn up and discarded in a matter of moments.

It was already after eight. His suite mates had gone out. The place was eerily quiet.

He was ready for this. He wanted it. He wanted Heather. As he repeated those words in his head, he felt like a quarterback in the locker room, revving himself up for a big game.

He conjured up an image of Heather's lush body and felt his hormones starting to flow. And it wasn't just sex that he wanted, although face it, what guy could turn that down? He cared about Heather. He really did.

Sam found himself pacing the small (clean) room, reassuring himself. He wanted to do right by Heather. Her honesty and openness were genuinely touching to him. He wouldn't betray that or ever make light of it. Sure, he'd wrapped himself up nicely tonight, but she was the one giving the gift.

When the knock on the door came, the sound seemed to reverberate in his bones. He went to the door slowly, knowing who it was, of course, telling himself he wanted her fervently and yet wishing in a way it were somebody else.

AGAINST HIS BETTER JUDGMENT, TOM

A Failed Experiment

Moore saw Gaia rounding the corner of West Fourth Street and followed at a safe distance. As a father he needed to see her safely to her destination, wherever that was. Then he would get on a plane back to Lebanon and resume his mission, leaving romantic notions and painful memories behind.

Based on her strange outfit, Tom guessed Gaia knew she was in danger. With her remarkable hair stashed away under her hat and a scarf and glasses obscuring her face, she was almost unrecognizable. Gaia was well adapted to taking care of herself, he told himself as he followed her east toward Fifth Avenue. He'd taught her the skills she'd need, and her miraculous gifts more than outstripped his teaching and his own abilities, in truth.

Tom, too, had been a prodigy. He had an extraordinary IQ, almost perfect powers of reasoning, and an intuitive genius for understanding the motivations of the human mind—particularly the criminal mind. He had been virtually fearless until he lost Katia. After that he wore fear like a coat of chain mail every day of his life. Tom sometimes imagined that he represented nature's first—though failed—experiment at an invincible creature. Gaia represented its subsequent and much more perfect attempt.

Gaia paused for a traffic light, and Tom took the opportunity to pull out his cell phone. He pushed two buttons, connecting instantly with his assistant. "We'll fly from the base at nine-thirty," he told him.

It was with some sense of relief that he watched

Gaia approach the door of a large building flanked by stone benches on either side. He could see from the awning that it was an NYU building, a dorm. It seemed a safe and relatively ordinary place for a girl to begin her Saturday night. He chuckled to himself at the pleasure it gave him to think that Gaia had friends and an active social life.

Maybe she would be okay. Maybe she could actually be . . . happy. The thought suffused him with unexpected joy.

Suddenly he was glad he had come. He was reassured. He could imagine his Gaia thriving here in New York. That knowledge would strengthen him for almost any trial.

He was just backing off when a glint of metal caught his eye from across the street. His thoughts and perceptions went into warp speed. It was a young man standing in the shadow of a tree, holding a .44-caliber pistol. The young man brought it up to eye level and trained it directly on Gaia.

Tom was across the street in a fraction of a second, never diverting his gaze from the gun. He was nearing his target, ready to throw his weight into the man, when suddenly the young man withdrew the gun. The young man's gaze was still trained on Gaia, but the hand with the gun hung at his side. Tom pulled up short, backing up against the side of a building to escape the young man's notice. When Tom looked back across the street, he realized that Gaia had already disappeared into the building.

Tom closed his eyes for a moment and caught his breath. Had that gun actually been trained on Gaia? Could he have been imagining the danger to her? With a sense of foreboding, Tom watched the young man conceal the gun under his shirt and stroll across the street, stopping under the well-lit awning. The young man glanced into the building and then took a seat on one of the stone benches. Tom knew he was settling in to wait.

Distress mixed with frustration as Tom took out his phone once again and pushed the same two buttons.

"Make it eleven," he told his assistant in an unhappy voice.

My views on Luck:

Before my accident, I used to think I was the luckiest guy in the world. Then I had my accident, and I sort of believed I deserved it because nobody stays that lucky. I used to think that luck got around to each of us equally. When things went badly, you were sort of saving up for a stretch of good luck. When things went too well . . . You get the idea.

According to this theory, I would be in for some good luck, right? I mean, a guy who's in a wheelchair shouldn't have parents who bicker constantly, for example, or an older sister who's ashamed of him. He shouldn't be abandoned by the girl he believed to be his one true love.

But the theory is wrong. Luck doesn't shine her light on each of us equally. She is arbitrary, irrational, unfair, and sometimes downright cruel. There are people who spend their entire lives basking in her glow, and others never seem to get one goddamned break.

Luck is powerful. Don't mess with her. Accept her for what she is and make the best of it. I can't stand that people are constantly blaming other people when bad stuff happens to them. Somebody trips on a sidewalk, and they sue some innocent bastard for millions of dollars. It's *not* always somebody else's fault. Sometimes it's just luck. Bad luck.

Luck is unpredictable. She's not your friend. She won't stand by you.

Maybe in heaven it's different. I do hope so.

But here on earth, my friend, those are the breaks.

He couldn't
hold back
much longer
without a
really good
reason.

SAM HAD A NEW RESPECT FOR

biology. Although his mind floated somewhere near the acoustical tiles on the ceiling, his body did all the things a body needs to do in order to successfully propagate the species.

The Big Moment

He gently, efficiently removed Heather's sweater and expertly navigated her tricky front-fastening bra. He gazed at her lovely breasts hungrily, `feeling the blood flow to his nether regions quadruple in under two seconds.` He pulled her skirt over her perfectly shaped hips, revealed dark purple satin panties equal to his daydreams, and forced himself not to go further yet.

Biology was exerting so much force, Sam had to battle himself not to remove that last bit of Heather's clothing or to pick her right up off the floor, put her on his bed, and hurtle forward into the main event. But he was a gentleman. He'd toughed it out before, and he could do it again. His older brother once told him that if you found you were undressing the girl *and* yourself, take a break and ask yourself whether you're pushing too hard.

Sam stuck to the advice, although it seemed like hours before Heather got around to removing his shirt. `She seemed a bit tentative to` him. Not scared, but not entirely sure of herself, either.

"We can stop anytime," he murmured against her ear, although biology was begging her not to take him up on the offer.

"No, I'm good," she whispered back.

She punctuated her point by sliding her hands under the waistband of his khakis. From his perch on the ceiling he heard a moan come from deep in his chest.

Now he saw his pants on the floor and only his blue-and-green-plaid boxers standing in the way of nudity. Soft, delicate lips poured kisses over his chest and stomach.

It was weird. His body was fully aroused and responsive, and his mind was remote. Was there a psychological term for this? Was there a treatment for it? Was this at all what death felt like?

He bitterly wished he could get his mind into the action. He'd picked a fine day for a complete out-of-body experience, he mused ironically.

"Ready?" he whispered, taking her hand and leading her to the bed.

Before taking a step, he studied her expression, waiting for her cue. Her face was flushed and intense, but not exactly the picture of lustful ecstasy. Was she holding back? Was she regretting this?

Or was he projecting *his* feelings onto her?

He took his eyes from her body so that biology would ease its choke hold for a moment. "Are you sure, Heather? We don't have to do anything you don't want. We've got plenty of time."

In response she sat down on the bed, placed a hand on either side of his waist, and pulled him down on top of her. She commandeered his mouth with kisses so he couldn't ask any more questions.

"I'm sure. I'm sure I want to do it now," she said against his ear. Why did her tone suggest more grim determination than arousal? Suddenly he felt her hands on the elastic waist of his boxer shorts, pulling them down. Another moan escaped him. He couldn't hold back much longer without a really good reason.

"I love you," she whispered to his chest. He couldn't see her eyes to gauge the depth of her words.

"Mmmm," he said, knowing that wasn't the right answer.

Apparently she didn't need to hear more. She wriggled out of her own panties and pressed the full length of her naked body against his. His body was pounding with pleasure and anticipation. His mind was surprised by her assertiveness and her . . . hurry. It almost seemed like she was in a hurry.

The big moment was upon them, and biology was demanding they surge ahead. Sam felt for the condom on the table by his bed. With her help he put it on. With her guiding, demanding arms he entered her. Again he heard the deep groan thundering from his chest. He heard her breathy sigh. At last his mind was pulled down into the whirlpool. At last the sensations became so fierce and so pervasive, his body and mind joined together. At last he was consumed.

So much so that he didn't notice that a slight breeze from a crack in the door had snuffed the fragile flame of the floor-wax-scented candle.

THE HALLWAY OF SAM'S DORM

Cruel Luck: 1

looked surprisingly like the one in her dream, but Gaia's feelings were different. She didn't feel sexy and bold. She felt insecure and deeply self-conscious.

First she knocked on the outer door that read B4–7. Sam's room was B5, so it had to be through there. While she waited for an answer, she pulled off her wool cap and shook out her hair. She unwound the scarf and stowed the ugly glasses in her bag. Her eyes caught the package of condoms floating at the surface of her bag, and the eager box threw her confidence even more.

Gaia knocked again. She waited for what felt like two weeks, but nobody came. Had Sam managed to slip out between the time she'd called and now? She thought she heard a noise inside. Was it okay to go in? Was it kind of a public room?

The thought of trudging back home to Ella and George's house in defeat, potentially only to be hunted down by CJ, was so unappealing, she turned the doorknob and walked inside.

It was a good-sized room, housing four desks, a minifridge, a hot plate, bookshelves, piles of sports equipment, notebooks, jackets, a couch that looked like it had been retrieved from a dump, and a very large television set. Gaia took a deep breath. No people, though.

Could Sam possibly be in his room? Maybe he was sleeping and he hadn't heard her knock. What if she were to creep in and climb into bed with him? Would he start screaming and call the police? Or would they have a beautiful, semiconscious, dreamlike sexual encounter? Gaia's head began to pound at the thought.

She walked very quietly toward room B5. Her spirits lifted. It was just her luck. The door was open a crack, and she heard a sound from inside. It sounded almost like a sleep sound.

Gaia took another deep, steadying breath. *Do it,* she commanded herself. *You have to try.* She put out her hand and placed it lightly on the knob. The brass sphere was a little wobbly in her palm. She gave it the lightest push and let it swing open.

Physicists were always crowing about the speed of light, but in this case the light from the common room seemed to filter into the small chamber slowly, as though well aware it was not a welcome guest. In this case, light traveled at the speed of dawning horror, of rude awakening, of hopes being dashed—but no faster. Before Gaia's round, naked eyes, the form on the bed was illuminated.

Two forms.

SAM HAD BELIEVED HIS BODY

and mind joined together as he made love to Heather. But in truth, they weren't actually joined until several seconds later, when his senses alerted him, in fast succession, to the subtle creaking of the door, the surprising influx of light, and most importantly, the stunned face of Gaia Moore. That was *actually* the moment when his body and mind snapped back into one piece.

GAIA HAD NEVER SEEN ANYBODY

having sex before, so the image was raw, crude, strange, terrible, and electrifying at the same time.

2 1/2

She should have dashed out of there instantly, but her astonishment seemed to lock her muscles, giving her eyes ample time to torture her with the sight of Sam's naked body, poetic even under these circumstances. His long, lean form was cupped against Heather's, their hips joined, dewy sweat shared between chests and arms, their legs a mutual tangle.

But by far the worst moment came when Sam turned and saw her. Her pain was too big to hide, she knew, and scrawled flagrantly on her face. Sam was baring his body, but she was caught exposing her soul. Her secret pain, her crushed hope, her sickly envy, and her queasy fascination were there for all to see. Worst of all, Sam saw her see him seeing all of this.

At last her muscles freed her, and she ran.

It wasn't until afterward that she realized she hadn't bothered to look at Heather. Heather didn't really matter much.

3

WHEN SAM LOOKED AT GAIA'S

face, he thought his heart broke for her, but he realized later that it broke for himself.

HEATHER WATCHED GAIA'S FACE

Just Cruel

with a disturbing sense of excitement. As full and complex as Gaia's expression was in that surreal moment, Heather knew she wouldn't forget it.

Heather realized later that she hadn't even looked at Sam's face. Somehow she knew his response without needing to look. At the time, it didn't really seem to matter much.

Just when
she'd settled
herself on
that bench
and he'd
gotten her
temple
between the
crosshairs,
she'd taken
off again.

**the
chase**

GAIA STRODE DOWN THE SIDEWALK,
tears dribbling over her cheeks, past
her jawbone, and down her neck,
hair streaming in the breeze. Her hat
and scarf and whatever were someplace. What did it matter? If CJ
wanted to shoot her right now, he
could be her guest. In fact, she
might ask him if she could borrow his gun.

At that moment she would have burned her eyes
out rather than have to see that picture of Sam and
bitch-girl ever again. But now the image was stored in
her brain for good. Or at least until one of CJ's bullets
came to her rescue. "CJ!" she called out semideliriously.

She walked blindly under the miniature Arc de
Triomphe that marked the entrance to the park. She
staggered to a bench and collapsed on it. She hid her
face in her hands and cried. Her shoulders heaved and
shook, but the sobs were noiseless. Why did her life always go this way? Why did it always seem to take the
worst-possible turn?

Whenever she made the mistake of caring, of
wanting something badly, life seemed to take that desire and smack her in the face with it.

What had she done to deserve this? Was it because
she was strange? A scientific anomaly? Just plain made
wrong? If she had fear, like a normal girl, would she also
have been allowed to have a mother and a father and a

boyfriend? And if so, was there any way she could go back and renegotiate the deal? Give me fear! she would say. Give me tons of it. Give me extra; I don't care.

No more caring, that was the golden rule. Forget about "do unto others" and all of that crap. Life's one great lesson was: Do not care. Not caring was a person's only real protection.

In the midst of sobs and tears and internal ranting, something made Gaia look up. Afterward, when she thought back, she couldn't say precisely what it was. But for whatever reason, she turned her tear-stained face up at that moment, and a terrible night became a perfectly mind-shattering one.

There, not fifteen feet away, standing against the trunk of a compact sycamore tree, was her father. In that split second she saw that he was thinner than he was five years before, that his face was more lined and angular, that his reddish blond hair was cut very short now, but he was unmistakably her father.

Gaia didn't jump to her feet as the result of any specific thoughts or decisions. One minute she was collapsed on the bench, and the next minute she was running toward him. He didn't run to her with open arms in slow motion the way long-lost relatives do in old movies. He gave her a look that was both surprised and pained, then he took off in the other direction.

Gaia followed him without thinking. She had to. She couldn't have stopped herself if she'd tried.

EXACTLY ON SCHEDULE, GAIA HAD
seen him standing under the tree.
They had locked eyes, and she had
recognized him. As if on cue, she
ran toward him, and he ran away
from her. It's what her father
would have done.

10th St. & 5th Ave.

Now he would lead her to his
loft on the Hudson River, just as he had planned. He
was about to meet Gaia face-to-face. Excitement, true
excitement, bred in his heart for the first time in many
years.

For this great meeting the playing field wouldn't be
even, of course. But when was it? He would go into it
knowing everything about Gaia Moore, knowing her
present, her past, her mother . . . intimately. She would
go into it believing he was her father.

CJ CURSED IN FRUSTRATION. HE
was so completely consumed by
anger, he couldn't think straight
anymore. Just when she'd settled
herself on that bench and he'd gotten her temple between the
crosshairs, she'd taken off again. He

17th St. & 6th Ave.

stowed his gun before anybody saw him and followed her.

Now he was badly winded, running, walking, dodging throngs of pedestrians, weaving through wide avenues clotted with traffic, staying with her each and every step. Not for a second would he lose sight of her blond hair, which luckily for him practically glowed in the dark.

Tonight was his night. He'd make sure of it. This couldn't go on another day. Tarick and his boys had made it clear. If he didn't kill Gaia tonight, he'd be dead by morning.

TOM KEPT THE YOUNG MAN WITH

17th St. & 7th Ave.

the gun clearly in his sights as he ran. Here was an example of why agents were never allowed near the business of protecting their families. Tom had seen Gaia's face when she'd emerged from the dorm building, tear soaked and racked with misery, and he'd stopped thinking like an agent and started thinking like a father. He'd lost a step, screwed up.

Gaia had narrowly avoided a bullet, and now they were on the run.

SAM HAD NEVER PUT ON CLOTHES

faster. He felt disgusting about leaving Heather at such a moment, but his more urgent feeling was the need to catch up to Gaia and . . . what? He had no idea. Make her feel better? Make himself feel better? Tell her he wanted

Back Up a Minute

her desperately, body and soul, and the fact that he'd just been making love to Heather was an odd, irrelevant coincidence? That would be a complete lie, yet also true at the same time.

"Heather, I'm really, really sorry," he said to her numb-looking face as he raced for the door. He wasn't so sorry, however, that he waited for a response or even looked back at her once. He felt disgusting.

The elevator was many floors away. He ran for the stairs instead. He took them two and three at a time, stumbling at the bottom and practically crashing into the serene lobby like Frankenstein's monster. Gaia was gone, of course.

Sam ran to the door and scanned the sidewalk in either direction. No sign of her. Now what? If Sam hadn't felt the frantic pangs of a drowning man, he would never have involved the security guard in his predicament.

"Uh, Kevin, hey. Did you see a girl, a blond girl around eighteen, rush out of here?" Sam asked.

Kevin paused for an infuriating two and a half seconds to consider. "Tall, pretty, crying?" he asked.

Oh God, she was crying. "Y-Yeah, that's probably her," Sam snapped, feeling an irrational desire to cram his hand down Kevin's throat and pull whatever informative words he had right out of there. And Sam *liked* Kevin. He and Kevin talked about the Knicks five out of seven nights a week.

Kevin paused again, savoring his important role in Sam's drama.

"Did you see which way she went?" Sam prodded, wild-eyed.

Kevin sighed thoughtfully. "Coulda been downtown," he said at last. "I'm pretty sure she walked downtown."

Sam was already at the door and out of it. "Thanks, Kevin. I really appreciate it." Most of his thanks were wasted on passersby on Fifth Avenue.

He ran toward the park. Of course she'd gone to the park. Every major event in his brief life with Gaia (with the notable exception of this evening) had taken place in the park.

Suddenly Sam had it in his mind that this was a good sign. If Gaia had gone to the park—their place, really—she would want him to find her there. If she was in the park, that would mean Sam could somehow repair this disaster.

When he caught a glimpse of yellow hair, sagging shoulders, and a face buried in familiar hands on a bench near the entrance, his heart soared irrationally. He would take her in his arms; he didn't care. He would tell her he loved her. How weird was that? But it was what his heart was telling him to do. He did love her. He loved her in a way he'd never come close to loving anything before. He'd known it for a while, even if he was too cowardly to say it or act on it. Now he would cut through all the chaos and defensiveness and confusion. He would take a risk for once in his life.

I love you. I love you, Gaia. The words were on his tongue, he could practically feel her in his arms, and suddenly, without warning, without even appearing to see him, Gaia leaped off the bench and started running.

Sam was destroyed. But he did find a reserve of insanity that pushed him to follow her.

A Brief Visit with Heather

HEATHER SAT VERY STILL ON SAM'S bed, half dressed, with her chin resting in her hands. The room was dark; the suite was perfectly quiet.

In her mind she knew she felt horribly wronged and betrayed and mistreated by Sam, but her insides felt strangely dry. She felt too dry for tears or any of the really muddy emotions. Why was that, exactly? Why did she feel so oddly calm and lucid?

When she thought of Gaia's ravaged face, she felt a burst of gratification and maybe even joy. They had a word for this in German, her mother's first language. *Schadenfreude*. It meant shameful joy—taking pleasure in somebody else's pain.

Heather knew she should have felt shamed by this, but she didn't. She should have felt shocked and furious at Sam, but she didn't quite. Maybe later.

Maybe she was just numb.

Or maybe in her heart she already knew that Sam had fallen in love with Gaia and that he had never truly been in love with her.

Or maybe it was really all because of Ed. Because of the awful things that happened with Ed, Heather's heart wasn't the soft, supple muscle it had once been.

ED FLICKED OFF THE LIGHT IN THE

And Another with Ed

hallway. He wheeled back into his room and unbuttoned his shirt—his best, softest shirt. On the collar lingered a tiny whiff of the cologne he'd put on after his shower. It brought on a pang of wobbly self-pity, and the self-pity brought on anger and discontent. Self-pity was the single worst feeling there was, particularly if you happened to be in a wheelchair.

He hoisted himself into his bed and struggled to take his pants off his immobile legs. A close second, in the race of worst feelings, was helplessness.

Ed didn't need to brush his teeth. He'd brushed them twice two hours ago.

Why was he so sad? He didn't really think Gaia was going to come, did he? No, not really. Not rationally. But he'd made the mistake of listening, just a little, to the seductive whispers of that rotten, misleading bastard called Hope.

If there was some way Ed could have strangled Hope and put the world out of much of its misery, he would have.

Instead he laid his head down on his pillow and cast a glance at the glowing blue numbers of his clock radio. It was 10:02. Only 10:02. Not so late.

What if Gaia . . . it was still possible. . . . And maybe she . . .

Ed groaned out loud and put the pillow over his head. It did nothing to drown out the whispers.

If her own father was leading her into an ambush, **hell's kitchen** what was there to live for, anyway?

GAIA'S MIND WAS BLANK. HER existence was all and only about keeping the tall man in the gray sweatshirt—her father, she reminded herself—in her vision. At this point Sam, Heather, and CJ were strangers to her, inhabitants of a different planet.

39th St. & 11th Ave.

The fact that her father was running away from her was immaterial. The reasons for his presence here didn't cross her mind. She made no consideration of what she'd do or say when she caught him. Past and future no longer shaded her thoughts.

She wouldn't let him get away. She *would not* let him get away. Her consciousness was only as big as that thought.

Pedestrians, cyclists, cars, trucks, pets passed in an unobserved blur. She didn't pay attention to which streets she took and where they'd lead. Chasing was so much easier than being chased because it required no strategy.

The man—her father—was fast. He was clever. He almost lost her when she collided with the Chinese-food deliveryman someplace on the West Side. Her dad was still pretty nimble for an old guy. But Gaia was unstoppable. She was too focused to feel loss of breath or any ache in her muscles. Her father had trained her too well for him to have any hope of losing her.

Now they were in the West Forties, Hell's Kitchen, she believed it was called, and her father was showing signs of exhaustion. From Eleventh Avenue he peeled off sharply to the left onto a dark side street. Gaia pulled up short and turned to follow. In this creepy neighborhood the streets and sidewalks were virtually deserted. Streetlights were few and far between. She saw that the side street dead-ended into the West Side Highway. Her father had disappeared into a building. Which one, though? A second passed before her fine hearing picked up a thud. The inimitable sound of a closing door. Gaia traced the sound to the door belonging to the last building on the street, one overlooking the Hudson River. Quickly she raced around the corner to determine if the building had a second entrance on the river side. It didn't. She had him.

JESUS, WAS SHE EVER GOING TO

44th St. stop? CJ felt like his lungs were on the verge of collapse. He was in no shape to scramble thirty-some blocks uptown and all the way west to the river, much of it at a dead run.

Gaia was running away from him, but she never

once looked over her shoulder to see him coming. Not even when he'd nearly picked her off on Hudson Street, after she'd collided with the Chinese guy on the bike. He'd locked on her head at point-blank range, and she'd stopped to help the Chinese guy up! The girl had ice in her veins. She wasn't a regular person.

When she turned off on the side street, CJ skidded to a hard stop, almost losing his balance. Gaia slowed down, then walked to the entrance to the building at the very end of the street and stopped. CJ didn't move from the corner. He felt his heart pounding like a jackhammer. But now it wasn't just exhaustion. It was excitement, too.

He secured the gun in both hands. He brought it up almost to eye level. Why wasn't Gaia moving—getting her ass out of there? Didn't she know he was there? She was crazy! She was a dead woman.

He tensed his right index finger on the trigger. "This is for Marco," he whispered. And with a huge, heady surge of accomplishment, he pulled the trigger and blew her away.

TOM MOORE WATCHED THE YOUNG gunman from a distance. With deep concentration he observed the young man aim the pistol, aiming his own weapon almost **Bang** simultaneously. He pulled the trigger and heard two explosions, a fraction of a second apart. With fear spreading through his heart he watched the young man go down. It was a good wound. Enough to scare a guy like that off. For now, he was out of the equation, and all that mattered was Gaia. Tom bolted around the corner in flat-out panic.

Gaia was alive. She was standing at the entrance to a building, looking around to see whence the shots had come. She was unharmed. She didn't even appear particularly concerned. Had she any idea how close that bullet had come to ending her life?

Tom ducked out of sight again. With relief flooding his body, he slid to the pavement and allowed himself a moment of rest to slow his speeding heart. Then he took out his phone and connected with his assistant. "There's a man down. I need you to report it to 911. Make the call untraceable."

SAM WAS WEARY AND CONFUSED and

fast losing his grip on reality. He'd chased Gaia for at least two miles of congested city streets up to this godforsaken neighborhood and onto a side street as dark and empty of people as a New York City street could be. What was she thinking? Did she have some plan in mind? And was he crazy, or was there more than one other guy following her?

What was Gaia into now? What had she really come to tell him when she'd barged into his room tonight? Nothing was clear to him anymore—except that Gaia was a source of astonishing complexity and trouble, and of course he knew that already.

Sam staggered along the street, catching a flitting glance of Gaia's back disappearing into an old loft building that faced the river. Now what the hell was he supposed to do?

He didn't pause to answer his own question. He just followed her, of course. He hoped she wasn't leading them both to their deaths. And at least if she was, he hoped he would get a chance to tell her that he loved her (in addition to finding her stupendously annoying) before he went.

GAIA FOLLOWED HIM UP THE STAIRS

on silent feet. Did he know she was still behind him? Did he know she could hear his footsteps perfectly well in the darkness? She was certain her father could have evaded

Her Father

her more skillfully than this. Was it possible he wanted her to find him after all? What could it mean?

Complicated questions were filling up the purposeful blank that had been her mind. Eleven floors up, he exited the staircase. The heavy cast-iron door banged to a close behind him. She waited a second before following.

This had the feeling of an ambush. Gaia knew she should be cautious and prudent, but on the other hand, if her own father was leading her into an ambush, what was there to live for, anyway?

She walked through the door and found herself suddenly in a vast, well-lit loft. The ceiling soared twenty feet above her, and the floor under her feet was highly polished parquet. Enormous floor-to-ceiling windows spanned the entire wall facing the river. She could see the lights of New Jersey across the way and a garishly lit cruise boat churning up the Hudson.

She blinked in the light, regained her bearings, and turned around. There, standing before her, not ten feet away, was her father. He wasn't running from her any longer. He stood still, gazing into her face.

"Gaia," he said.

The raw pain
that lived
hidden
inside her **not**
every **nothing**
day of her
life had
broken free.

GAIA'S HEART WAS VOLCANIC.

Tears threatened to spill from her eyes.

It was really him. He was here with her. For the first time in almost five years she had before her the thing she'd yearned for most.

In those long, empty years she'd hardened her heart against him with anger and distrust, commanding herself not to care, not allowing herself the hope that he would ever come for her.

But now, in his presence, her heart's protective shell was cracking and threatening to fall away. She'd been so strong, so capable for all that time, and now she felt that the pressure of the misery and frailty and helplessness built up over those lonely years could flatten her in a torrent of sorrow and self-pity.

She was like the toddler who'd lost her mother in the grocery store, facing miles of grim, dizzying aisles and shelves with numb courage, not allowing herself the luxury of tears until she was back in her mother's arms.

Now Gaia's tears distorted her father's familiar features, the blue eyes so much like her own. It brought upon her wave after wave of memories that she hadn't allowed herself since he'd disappeared.

188

Her father scrupulously drawing castles when she loved castles, horses when she loved horses, boats when she loved boats. Making her waffles every Saturday morning through her entire childhood as she sat on the counter and told him stories. Teaching her algebra, basic chemistry, martial arts, gardening, marksmanship.

He was teaching, always teaching her, but he made it fun. On Mondays he would speak to her only in Russian, and she and her mother would make blintzes and potato latkes for dinner. On Tuesdays they'd speak only in Arabic, and she and her mother would make kibbe and hummus and stuffed grape leaves. He and her mother took her on hikes in famously beautiful places all over the country to teach her about the natural world.

Most other fathers Gaia knew were good for one game of catch on Sunday after the NFL games had ended. Gaia's was different.

Now Gaia's father took a step closer. She didn't move.

That blissful childhood was what made it almost impossible to survive the night her mother was murdered and her father disappeared. She needed him and missed him so desperately, crying for him every single night, not understanding at first that he was really gone. And it wasn't beyond his control, the way it was for her mother. He was still alive. He chose something else in his life over her, and even when she became so

189

severely depressed that she could barely eat or sleep or talk for weeks and then months at a time, still he stayed away. He never once called her or wrote. She wanted to die then just so her father would know that he had broken her heart.

Could she ever forgive him for that?

He took another step closer. And another.

His face was close and vivid now. A question hovered in his eyes.

Gaia's heart was a war zone. On the one side was the happiness and devotion her father gave her for her first twelve years. On the other was the brutal neglect for the past five. Which side was more powerful? Would Gaia's love or the anger win out?

She was watching his face very closely.

"Gaia," he said again, tentatively. He reached out to her.

Suddenly the battle shifted. Gaia wasn't sure exactly why. It was something in the way his mouth moved, something indescribably subtle, that made her know that this man was different than the one she'd adored above everything else for twelve years. Something fundamental had changed between the way he was then and now. She couldn't put her finger on it.

The anger surged forward in a fierce offensive, beating back the love with ruthless energy. The victory in battle was so quick and so decisive that when her father came another step closer and reached out his arms to embrace her, Gaia recoiled. Feeling the brief touch of his hands on her shoulders, she experienced no warmth, no affection. Nothing.

Well, not nothing. Anger.

She experienced such powerful anger that she shoved him away from her. "I don't want to see you," she told him.

The anger was building. It was terrifying. The raw pain that lived hidden inside her every day of her life had broken free, and she couldn't control it. She shoved him again, harder this time.

There was sadness and confusion in his face as he stumbled backward, or some semblance of it. She couldn't tell. She didn't know this man. His expressions weren't familiar to her.

She drew back her arm and connected her fist with his jaw. It made a satisfying crack. It was horrible, unspeakable of her to do this, to treat her own father this way.

And yet his expression conveyed no pain. He never took his eyes from her.

She was hauling off for another blow when her arm caught behind her. She spun around and realized for the first time that there was another person in the room. Over her shoulder she saw a tall, very broad man with dark clothing, short dark hair, and a completely blank expression.

Who was this? she wondered distantly, from beyond her rage.

The man held Gaia's arm tightly and twisted it behind her back.

What could her father have meant by this? Gaia wondered, staring at him in indignant disbelief. Was this some kind of ambush after all?

It didn't matter. The oversized man provided an opportune release for Gaia's exploding rage. With some zeal she broke his grasp. Instantly she grabbed a fistful of his hair in one hand and shoved her other hand under his armpit. She positioned her legs for the greatest leverage and swung the son of a bitch over her shoulder, laying him flat out on the wood floor.

She waited for him to scramble back up to his feet before she buried another jab in his stomach and kicked him brutally in the chest.

She was dangerous now. She wasn't in control. She had to put him away before she really did harm. She calculated the exact spot on his neck and struck fiercely with the heel of her hand. The man crumpled to the floor without a glimmer of consciousness, just as she'd expected. He'd wake up in a while. He'd be fine. It was her own wildfire temper that caused her concern.

Her father watched her intently. Beseeching her. She couldn't look at him anymore. If she didn't get out of there, she would do something she would truly regret.

"It's too late. You stayed away too long," she muttered to him as she turned and walked away. He was no longer her handsome, magical father; now only a pale reminder of sickening betrayal and loss, she needed him out of her sight.

She wished he were dead. That way she could treasure the time she had with him. She could carry on in life with the belief that love was real and happiness could be trusted. Now that cherished time, the foundation of her existence, was fatally poisoned by the knowledge that her beloved father had been a soulless viper all along.

TOM MOORE STOOD SWEATING IN

The Dark Half

the dark stairwell on the eleventh floor of the largely abandoned loft building. He had a terrible feeling about this. Why had Gaia come to this place? He felt certain there was grave danger here. He sensed it so strongly, his brain clouded with dark, impenetrable fear. He hadn't had this feeling in a long time.

He was preparing to follow her when he heard the

metal door creaking open just a few feet away. He hurled himself backward, concealing at least most of his body behind dusty boxes in the corner of the landing. He crouched there silently.

Gaia staggered through the door and into the stairwell. Her face displayed pure psychic pain. He stopped breathing as she walked within inches of him. Clearly she didn't see him because she continued down the stairs.

Tom felt as if his heart were being ripped from his chest. This was too hard, being near Gaia, seeing her pain, and not being able to help. But he was involved now, and how was he ever going to pull away again?

He knew he would follow her, but before he did, he needed to see what was beyond that stairwell door. Gaia had emerged physically unharmed, but nonetheless something had destroyed her in there.

He had a bad feeling about it. A black curiosity. Even as he crept to the door, he advised himself against it.

He opened the door with ultimate gentleness, wincing in anticipation of the slightest creak. He pulled it open about a foot and took a deep breath. Slowly, silently he peered into the giant loft, his hand poised on the trigger of his gun.

Tom's glance lighted ever so briefly on a man of his own age and build sitting in the middle of the floor, elbows resting on knees, chin resting in hands, silently contemplating.

194

That man sitting on the floor was exactly Tom's build and exactly his age—to the hour. His face was more familiar to Tom's than any other, and yet Tom flew from the scene with the singular horror of a man who has seen the dead rise and walk.

Tom knew it was the man referred to, in his short, explosive life among the terrorist underground, as Loki, after the Norse god of the netherworld. But he also knew that the man's given name was Oliver Moore and that he was supposed to have died five years ago.

It was Tom's alter ego, his dark half, his brother.

"YOU LET HER GO?" ELLA ASKED IN

disbelief, returning to the loft from the floor below.

Loki said nothing. He sat there, meditative.

"After all that, you let her go?"

If You Love Something . . .

It was a great failing of Ella's that she couldn't keep her temper under control. She was self-destructively trying to get a rise out of him, and he wasn't in the

195

mood to play. Ella made a grave error in allowing her dislike of Gaia to get the best of her.

For a man who had risen above (or perhaps fallen below?) his emotional impulses long ago, it was rather confounding to feel the sting of Gaia's rejection. He should have been delighted to see the rage and hatred she held for her father—or a man she believed to be her father, at any rate. Instead, in some primal way, he longed to see love in her eyes, no matter who she believed him to be. She was his daughter after all, genetically if not actually. She was the child of the woman he'd loved. In all of the sordid, black history between him and Katia and his brother, Gaia was the prize, and he meant to win her.

"You've lost her now," Ella prodded sullenly.

Loki stood and stretched. He walked toward the windows, admiring the sparkling panorama with fresh eyes. Suddenly he felt enormously hungry, like he'd woken from a very long sleep.

"Until Monday, perhaps," Loki informed her with a careless yawn.

"And why will she be back then?" Ella demanded snappishly.

Loki stood inches from the window, staring out, his hands pressed against the cold glass. He was in no particular hurry to answer Ella. He studied the dark precarious cliffs of New Jersey's Palisades for a long time.

"Because I've detained a certain friend of hers. We'll keep him. Weaken him for a day or so. On Monday morning Gaia will learn that if she doesn't come for him when I wish, I will murder him."

Bad Choice

SAM LAY ON THE CONCRETE FLOOR, feeling the thumping ache in his shoulder and ribs, dully considering the pale shaft of light that crept into the far side of an otherwise black space. Where was he? Where was the light coming from? Why had he come here, and who wanted to imprison him?

He hadn't caught up to Gaia. He had no idea where she'd gone. But the insidious suspicion had taken root in his mind that she had led him here just to be beaten up and held captive by two large men in ski masks. Blind, lovesick moron that he was, he'd chased her right into a trap.

Why, though? What had he done? Who were these people, and what could they possibly want from him?

He heard the wail of sirens coming close and wished without much real hope that maybe they were coming for him.

197

This was a truly depressing twist. It was so awful that a part of Sam—not a part relating to his shoulder or ribs—almost wanted to laugh.

He'd had a choice between a safe, loving girlfriend and a seamy, mysterious troublemaker, and whom had he chosen? He had abandoned the culmination of a long-desired sexual encounter for a mad dash through city streets and the privilege of getting beaten up and locked up in a deserted building on the far West Side.

`He had a choice, and he'd chosen wrong.`

GAIA'S LIFE FELT BLEAKER AND

more desolate than the trash-strewn street where she walked. In one night the few joys she'd had or hoped for were obliterated. Her father—the idea of her father—was `irretrievable`. She had no choice but to accept now that Sam would never be hers. In her misery she allowed herself to imagine the scene between him and Heather after she'd run off. Sure, they were embarrassed, but once they got over it, they probably had a good laugh at her expense and got back to business—Sam more passionately than before in his joy

Being Brave

and relief to have Heather in his bed and not a psychotic miscreant like Gaia.

She walked slowly down the forsaken street, wondering in the back of her mind where CJ was with his gun. She was ready for him now. Plans 1 and 2 had crashed and burned with equal horror. Not a single hope had survived the collisions. She officially had nothing to live for.

Chill winds blew off the Hudson. She was probably cold, she realized, but she was too numb to register it.

She looked around. Wasn't it just her luck that even CJ disappointed her when she wanted him?

Well, she reasoned, she could always load up her pockets with rocks and wade into the Hudson. She could always walk into the screaming traffic of the West Side Highway. She could find her way to the roof of any one of these buildings and leap off. It's not like her demise was dependent on CJ. *Suicide is the most cowardly act,* a voice inside Gaia's head reminded her. Where had she heard that?

For some reason, the smell in the air reminded her of the smell off the lake at her parents' old cabin in the Berkshires. Who knew why. This was gritty urban water, and that was pure mountain runoff.

For some reason, the smell reminded her of her mom, and the memory of her mom magically brought an image into her mind. It was her mom's face, clear and sharp—shaded by Gaia's raw feelings, maybe, but

199

otherwise accurate. It was the way her mom looked dangling her bare feet off the dock, watching Gaia's attempts to fish for dinner, although she knew perfectly well that Gaia would end up throwing every single fish back into the lake.

It made Gaia's heart come back to life a little because this was something approaching a miracle. Gaia could never remember her mother's face clearly. It drove her crazy that she couldn't. And yet here, in the midst of Hell's Kitchen, was Katia's beautiful and beloved face.

And for some reason, seeing her mother clearly right now reminded Gaia of something else.

Although she had lost the two things she longed for, it somehow opened up the opportunity for something she wanted even more. She had the chance to keep on living, even though she didn't think she could.

At the moment it felt to Gaia like a chance to be brave.

here is a
sneak peek of
Fearless™ #3:
RUN

The dream is thick in my eyes, and I want to wake up but I can't. The dream holds me in, grasping me with its sweaty hands.

I am alone, walking through darkness on a sidewalk that wavers in and out of being. When it is solid beneath my feet, I can walk quickly, and I am elated and excited to reach my destination. But then the darkness swirls, eating the sidewalk, and I drop, spiraling downward, until the ground returns. Objects begin to appear in my peripheral vision—street signs, mailboxes, a flight of stairs. I know them. They remind me that I am on my way to Sam.

His dorm is in sight now—tall, much taller than any other building anywhere ever, and all the windows are dark but his. His glows with the faintest pearl-pink light. I don't know how I know it's his room, but I do. So I jump.

And I'm rising, up, up into the night sky. A huge wind meets me, carries me toward the building. I am being placed down gently inside the dorm, at Sam's door. In the dream, I step away from myself, just to get a look at my face, to see what real happiness looks like when I'm wearing it.

Then I hear the noises. Noises coming from behind the door— sounds like soft growling, and deep sighs, sounds which seem to caress each other. I open the door and whisper, "Sam?" and the whisper echoes like an explosion, and there they are.

They. Them. Him. Her. (Not me. I'm just looking.)

The wind returns, fiercely, pummeling me. Funny, it only flutters Heather's hair a little, making her look like some super-model in a fashion photo.

And Sam, he's all tangled up under her, or around her, or . . . well, they are entwined. And even though I don't have a whole hell of a lot of experience in this area, I know what they've been doing to get into that position,

and believe me, it wasn't a game
of Twister.

So I scream. It's a gargley
noise, a deep, disgusting bellow.
I look down at the floor, and
scattered around my feet are all
these broken shards of something
brilliant red, glassy, shiny.
Looking at them makes me feel
strangely empty. It takes me a
moment to realize that these are
the pieces of my broken heart.
(One corny, cliché image per
dream is allowed.)

Then I look back up at
Heather; needless to say, I
really want to kick her ass. But
suddenly, she's no longer the
willowy supermodel she was a moment ago. She's changing before
my eyes, morphing into a hideous
creature, some kind of huge, mutant insect, with a bulging skull
and spiney legs, and curved
fangs, which are about to puncture Sam's throat.

My first thought: Serves him
right.

My second thought: You can't
lose your virginity to the guy if
the Heather Bug eats him whole. So
I reach out to take his hand . . .

And he reaches out for mine . . .

And our eyes meet. It's like
heat lightning, I swear. Things
are looking up.

So I tell the Heather Bug to
disappear, and since it's my
dream, she does.

And I make my way across the
room to Sam. He's telling me I'm
beautiful, and I'm a killer chess
player, and that he wants me.

Wants me. I close my eyes, and
I'm thinking, the feeling's mutual.
And then it's me, tangled up with
Sam, and we're kissing, and somewhere in the dream, my nerve center
registers a feeling it doesn't recognize in real life.

Fear.

Fear that he might be disappointed. Fear that when all is said
and done, he'll choose Heather anyway, even if she is a bug.

But the fear melts away, because

in the dream, Sam whispers, "I
love you, Gaia."

Then—BAM—back to nightmare
mode. Because I've just opened my
eyes, and I'm back out in the dark
on the sidewalk and I'm running.

Running after someone who
looks just a little too damn
familiar.

My father.

And since it's me in my dream,
I do the one thing in this world
I know I'm really good at.

I throw a punch that knocks
the breath out of him, and sends
him stumbling backward for miles,
and miles, and miles . . .

And I wake up.

Crying.

One of his
eyes was
black-and-
blue,
swollen
shut, and he
looked
frighteningly
pale. Weak.

save

sam

GAIA HAD JUST STEPPED OUT OF

the shower, when she heard his
voice floating up the stairs to
greet her. She wrapped a towel
around herself, went to the landing, and leaned into the stairwell.

You've Got Mail

"Ed?"

"Yeah."

"What the hell are you doing here?"

She heard him chuckle. "Fine, thanks, and you?"

Gaia smiled in spite of herself. "Sorry. I had sort of
a rough night."

"What else is new?"

She imagined him shaking his head at her.

"You can tell me all about it over breakfast," he
called. "I brought bagels."

"Really?" Her stomach grumbled loudly. One thing
this city had going for it—the authentic, fresh-out-of-
the-oven bagels. They almost made up for the high
price of Apple Jacks.

"Yeah. So c'mon down."

"I'm totally naked, and I'm dripping wet!" Gaia yelled,
wishing Ella hadn't left ridiculously early this morning so
she could be shocked by this exchange. At least she'd
taken George with her. The last thing Gaia would want to
do was give her sweet old guardian a heart attack.

"I repeat," said Ed, chuckling again, "c'mon down!"

Gaia rolled her eyes, trying to ignore the flirtatious

1

undertones of the remark. Five minutes later, she'd slipped into her most worn cargo pants and a gray T-shirt and was on her way downstairs, her hair spraying drops of water all over her shoulders. On the landing, she paused to study the familiar snapshot that hung in a frame there on the wall—the shot George had taken so long ago of Gaia and her parents. Gaia had tried to get rid of it, but Ella had insisted it remain. Gaia squinted at the photo, looking hard at her father.

Her father. She'd seen him two nights ago. Two nights.

And he'd disappeared—again.

Her stomach churned, both with confusion and sadness. Why had he run from her? Why had he shown up in the first place?

Was it some paternal sixth sense that dragged him back into her life? Did he somehow know she'd been on the verge of losing her virginity, and he'd crawled out from whatever rock he'd been hiding under all these years to give her a good, old-fashioned, heart-to-heart talk on morality, safe-sex, and self-control?

Or was it just one more whacked-out coincidence in her life?

She leaned closer to the photo and stared into his eyes.

They were soft, kind, intelligent eyes—and the smile was genuine. The man she'd met on Saturday night had not seemed genuine at all. The warmth and gentleness she saw in the picture had been missing from the man who'd approached her that night. He was different, somehow. Lesser.

"I guess abandoning your kid and living on the run takes a lot out of you," she muttered, heading down the hall.

In the kitchen, Gaia was met by the heavenly aroma of fresh bagels and hot coffee. Ed, who had positioned his chair close to the table, looked up from spreading cream cheese on a poppy seed bagel. "You didn't have to get dressed on my account."

She was annoyed at the blush his grin brought to her face. "Shut up."

"Do you think it's kismet that this place is handicap accessible?"

Gaia raised an eyebrow. "It's either kismet . . . or the building code."

"I'm serious," said Ed. "Do you have any idea how many places in this damn city aren't?"

She felt a pang of pity, but squashed it fast. "So what's kismet got to do with it?"

"You happen to live in wheelchair-friendly digs. I happen to be in a wheelchair." Ed shrugged. "It's like the universe is arranging it so that we can hang out."

"The universe clearly has too much time on its hands." She sat down and pulled her knees up, leaning them against the edge of the table.

"Like lox?"

"Not especially."

"Then I'm glad I didn't buy any." Ed pushed a steaming cup of coffee across the table toward her. "Three sugars, no cream, right?"

Gaia nodded, refusing to be charmed by the fact that he remembered, and took a careful sip. She could feel him staring at her.

"You look like hell," he said, shaking a lock of brown hair back off his forehead. "I mean, in a gorgeous, sexy, fresh-out-of-bed sort of way. But still, pretty hellish."

"Thank you, I try." She took another, bolder sip of the hot coffee. "I told you, I had a rough night." Gaia paused, letting the steamy liquid warm her from the inside. "Make that a rough weekend."

"Now we're getting to it," Ed said, rubbing his hands together. "You were unsurprisingly un-findable yesterday, Gaia. So let's hear it." He broke off a piece of bagel and popped it into his mouth. "Who was the lucky guy and how did the ceremonial shedding of the chastity belt go?"

Gaia ignored the bile rising in her throat, picked up a marble bagel, and took a gigantic bite. There was a reason she'd avoided Ed all day yesterday—the need to avoid forced emotional spillage. "Subtlety isn't exactly a talent of yours, is it, Ed?" she said with her mouth full.

"Look who's talking."

He had a point there. She studied Ed for a moment—the just-this-side-of-scruffy hair, the eager-yet-wary brown eyes, the dot of dried blood on his chin where he'd cut himself shaving. Gaia hated that she had to talk about this, but she did. She'd sucked Ed into the whole sorry situation when she'd confessed her virginity. He might as well know the truth.

Gaia closed her eyes. Shook her head. Sighed.

"It didn't happen," she said.

Ed dropped a knife onto the floor with a clatter. "It didn't?"

"Ed!" She opened her eyes and glared at him. "Think you can sound just a little more amused by that?"

"Sorry it didn't work out for you." Ed cleared his throat and she could swear he was stifling a grin behind his steaming coffee. "So what happened?"

Gaia took another aggressive bite of bagel. "Let's just say somebody beat me to it."

"Shut up!" Ed's eyes opened wide. "Gaia, you have to tell me who we're talking about here. You can't keep me in this kind of suspense. I have a weak heart."

"You do?" Gaia asked, reaching for her coffee.

"No," Ed admitted.

"It was Sam Moon."

A sudden shower of chewed bagel bits pelted Gaia's arms. "God, Ed! Food is to go in the mouth. *In*," Gaia said, brushing off her arms.

"You walked in on Sam and . . . Heather?" Ed choked out while simultaneously attempting to wipe his mouth.

"Ironic, isn't it?" Gaia asked, flicking one last bagel wad off her elbow.

Ed looked as if he were watching his life flash before his eyes—backward and in 3D stereo surround sound. Gaia had never seen skin so pale before in her life. She'd forgotten for the moment that Heather meant something to Ed as well. A big something.

"Man." Ed let out a long rush of breath. His eyes were completely unfocused. "That had to suck."

"Could've been worse," Gaia said with a half-hearted shrug. It had been worse. The night had been full of mind-bending surprises. But she wasn't about to tell him that. No need to burden Ed with her highly dysfunctional family matters over breakfast.

"Worse than walking in on the object of your seduction in bed with your mortal enemy?"

Gaia nodded, but she was saved from expanding on her comment by the sound of the phone ringing.

Ed reached behind him, snatched the cordless from the counter, then slid it across the table to Gaia. She hit the button and held the receiver to her ear. "Hello?"

At first, nothing.

"Hello?"

"Gaia Moore?"

Her eyes narrowed. "Yeah? Who is this?"

The voice was distorted, like something from a horror movie. "Check your e-mail." It was a command. Maybe even a threat.

She felt as if ice were forming in her veins. "Who the hell is this?"

"Check your e-mail," the voice growled.

The line went dead.

Gaia was on her feet, running for George's computer, which, luckily, he always left on. When she reached the den, she flung herself into the chair and punched at the keyboard. Ed, maneuvering his chair through the rooms, appeared soon after.

"What's going on?"

Gaia was too morbidly curious to bother answering Ed's as yet unanswerable question. She clicked the "Read Mail" icon and stared at the screen as it choked out the early cryptic shadows of a video image, tapping her fingers impatiently on the mouse as the picture emerged . . . slowly . . . slowly . . .

It was someone with his back to her, hunched forward. His surroundings were vague, too much light. Gaia reached for the speaker, in case there was audio. There was. Static, at first. Distant, fuzzy, then clearing.

"Maybe it's Heather, playing a joke," offered Ed. "To get even."

"I don't think so," said Gaia, her voice tight.

And then she heard his voice . . .

"Gaia . . . ?"

Her heart seemed to freeze solid in her chest. No, no, no, no.

But the voice through the speaker repeated itself. "Gaia." *No!* "Sam?"

As if he'd heard her, he turned to the camera, and

suddenly there was Sam's face on the computer screen. One of his eyes was black and blue, swollen shut, and he looked frighteningly pale. Weak.

Ed angled his chair close to the desk. "Oh, shit."

Sam's face vanished, replaced by a blank screen, and then there was a blast of static from the speakers, as the same distorted voice addressed her. "Gaia Moore. You can see from this footage that we have a mutual friend. Sadly, he's not feeling well at the moment. Did you know Sam is a diabetic? No, I would imagine you didn't . . ."

Ed stared at the blank screen. "Who the hell is it?"

Gaia shushed him with a sharp hiss, as a graphic began to appear on the screen—a message, snaking its way from the right side, one letter at a time: C . . . A . . . N Y . . . O . . . U

The voice continued as the letters slid into view. "He's well enough for the moment but around, oh, say, ten o'clock this evening, he'll be needing his insulin, quite desperately. And that, my darling Gaia, is where you come in. You must pass a series of tests. If you do so by ten o'clock tonight, we will free Sam. If you do not . . ."

The graphic slithered by: S . . . A . . . V . . . E

". . . He will die!"

S . . . A . . . M . . . ?

For a moment, the question trembled there on the dark screen. CAN YOU SAVE SAM? Then the letters went spinning off into the infinite background, and another message appeared in an eye-searing flash of brightness. It read:

> You will find on your front step a
> videotape. You will play it during your
> first-period class. DO NOT view the
> tape prior to showing it in school.

Without warning, the e-mail broadcast returned, showing a close-up of Sam's beaten face, frightened eyes, his mouth forming a word, and the word came screaming through the speaker in Sam's voice.

"Gaia!"

Then, nothing. The image and the audio were gone, and the computer whirred softly, until George's sickening screen saver—a scanned-in photo of Ella—returned to the screen.

Gaia sprung up from the chair, and flew to the front door, which she flung open. The early-morning October air sparkled and the neighborhood was just coming alive with people on their way to work and school. Gaia paid no attention. Her eyes searched the front stoop until they found the package.

She lunged for it.

Gaia had no idea who had done this. She had no idea why. But she wasn't about to ask questions.

Not with Sam's life on the line.

Some secrets are too dangerous to know . . .

ROSWELL
HIGH

In the tiny town of Roswell, New Mexico, teenagers Liz Parker and Max Evans forged an otherworldly connection after Max recklessly threw aside his pact of secrecy and healed a life-threatening wound of Liz's with the touch of his hand. It turns out that Max, his sister Isabel, and their friend Michael are surviving descendants from beings on board an alien spacecraft which crash-landed in Roswell in 1947.

Max loves Liz. He couldn't let her die. But this is a dangerous secret he swore never to divulge - and now it's out. The trio must learn to trust Liz and her best friend Maria in order to stay one step ahead of the sheriff and the FBI who will stop at nothing in hunting out an alien…

Available NOW from Pocket Books

She clicked the mail icon and stared at the screen as it choked out the early, cryptic shadows of a video image, and she tapped her fingers impatiently on the mouse as the picture emerged . . . slowly . . . slowly . . .

It was someone with his back to her, hunched forward. His surroundings were vague, too much light. Gaia reached for the speaker, in case there was audio. There was. Staticky at first. Distant, fuzzy, then clearing.

Clearing . . .

"Maybe it's Heather, playing a joke," offered Ed. "To get even."

"I don't think so," said Gaia, her voice tight.

And then she heard his voice. . . .

"Gaia . . . ?"

Her heart seemed to freeze solid in her chest. No, no, no, no.

But the voice through the speaker repeated itself. "Gaia."

No! "Sam?"

As if he'd heard her, he turned to the camera, and suddenly there was Sam's face on the computer screen. One of his eyes was black-and-blue, swollen shut, and he looked frighteningly pale. Weak.

Ed angled his chair close to the desk. "Oh, shit."

Don't miss any books in this thrilling new series
from Pocket Books:

FEARLESS™

All Pocket Book titles are available by post from:
**Simon & Schuster Cash Sales, P.O. Box 29,
Douglas, Isle of Man IM99 1BQ**
Credit cards accepted. Please telephone 01624 675137,
Fax 01624 670923, Internet http://www.bookpost.co.uk
or email: bookshop@enterprise.net for details

FEARLESS™

FRANCINE PASCAL

RUN

POCKET
BOOKS

An imprint of Simon & Schuster UK Ltd
A Viacom Company
Africa House, 64-78 Kingsway, London WC2B 6AH

Produced by 17th Street Productions,
an Alloy Online, Inc. company
33 West 17th Street, New York, NY 10011

A CIP catalogue record for this book is
available from the British Library

ISBN 0671 03748 X

3 5 7 9 10 8 6 4

Printed by Cox & Wyman Ltd, Reading, Berkshire

RUN

Do you know what hell is?

I do.

It's not fire and brimstone. Not for me, anyway.

It's watching your hopes die.

It's watching the guy you love—the guy who makes you understand why that poor sucker built the Taj Mahal, why Juliet buried a dagger in her chest, why that Trojan king destroyed his entire fleet—making love to another girl. A girl you despise.

It's seeing your father—a man you believed was a superhero—for the first time after five long years only to discover he was a dishonorable creep show all along.

Hell is experiencing both of those things in one night. Hell is the way the ceiling looks above your bed when you open your eyes the next morning. Hell is the morning after that, when the ceiling looks just as hopeless, and you realize the pain

GAIA

hasn't begun to fade and that
maybe it never will.

That is hell.

What is heaven?

I don't know.

I had an idea about it a couple of days ago, but that was before hope died.

If you happen to find out,
will you let me know?

One of his
eyes was
black-and-
blue,
swollen

save

shut, and he

sam

looked
frighteningly
pale. Weak.

"HELLO? ANYBODY UP THERE?"

Gaia had just stepped out of the shower when she heard the voice floating up the stairs to greet her. She wrapped a too-small towel around herself, went to the landing, and leaned into the stairwell. It was a familiar voice, but not one she expected to hear before eight o'clock in the morning.

You've Got Mail

"Ed?"

"Yeah."

"Um . . . what the hell are you doing here?"

She heard him laugh under his breath. "Just fine, thanks, and you?"

At the sound of his voice, a minute ray of happiness filtered down into the blackness of her mood. She hadn't spoken a word out loud since Saturday night, since everything . . . happened. Now it was Monday morning, and her words were so far back in her brain she had to hunt around for them. "N-Not that fine," she responded hoarsely. "I had . . ." How could she begin to convey the true horror that was her life? "Sort of a rough weekend."

"What else is new?"

She heard both affection and wariness in Ed's voice. He knew a "rough weekend" for Gaia meant more than teenage angst—that it would involve things like firearms and kickboxing.

4

"Tell me about it over breakfast," he called. "I brought bagels."

Her stomach grumbled loudly. One thing this city had going for it—authentic, fresh-out-of-the-oven bagels. They almost made up for the high price of Apple Jacks. She glanced down at herself and the small puddle forming under her feet. "I'm wearing a hand towel and a few cups of water," Gaia said, wishing Ella hadn't left early this morning, so that she could be disturbed by this exchange. At least Ella had taken George with her wherever she'd gone. Gaia disliked offending George as much as she enjoyed offending Ella.

"I repeat," said Ed, laughing again. **"C'mon down!"**

Gaia rolled her eyes, trying to ignore the undertones of the remark. Two minutes later, she'd slipped into her most-worn cargo pants and a gray T-shirt and was on her way downstairs, her hair dripping water over her shoulders. On the landing, she paused to study the familiar snapshot that hung in a frame there on the wall—the photograph George had taken so long ago of Gaia and her parents. Gaia had tried to get rid of it, but Ella insisted it remain. She squinted at it, looking hard at her father.

Her father. She'd seen him two nights ago. Actually seen him and spoken to him. *And decked him,* she reminded herself bitterly.

After that he'd disappeared—again.

Her stomach churned, both with confusion and

5

with sadness. Why had he shown up here after all this time? What could it mean?

Was it some paternal sixth sense that had dragged him back into her life? Did he somehow know she'd been on the verge of ditching her virginity, and he'd crawled out from whatever rock he'd been hiding under all these years to give her an old-fashioned heart-to-heart talk on morality, safe sex, and self-control?

Or was it just one more whacked-out coincidence in her life?

She leaned closer to the photo and stared into his eyes.

They appeared to be soft, kind, intelligent eyes—and the smile looked genuine. The man she'd met on Saturday night had not seemed genuine at all. The warmth and gentleness she saw in the picture had been missing from that man. He was different, some-how. Lesser.

Apparently abandoning your kid and living on the run could take a lot out of a person. In the kitchen, Gaia was met by the aroma of fresh bagels and hot coffee. Ed, who had positioned his chair close to the table, looked up from spreading cream cheese on a poppy seed bagel. "You didn't have to get dressed on my account."

She was annoyed at the blush his grin brought to her face. "Shut up." Her eyes narrowed. "How did you get in here, anyway?"

"Door was unlocked," Ed said. "You should really talk to your roomies about that. I mean this is a nice neighborhood, but why court robbery, or worse?"

Gaia collapsed into a chair. That was weird. George never left the door unlocked. Must've been another brilliant Ella maneuver.

"Do you think it's kismet that this place is handicap accessible?" Ed asked suddenly.

Gaia raised an eyebrow. "It's either kismet . . . or the building code."

"I'm serious," said Ed. "Do you have any idea how many places in this city aren't?"

She felt a pang of pity but squashed it fast. "So what's kismet got to do with it?"

"You happen to live in wheelchair-friendly digs. I happen to be in a wheelchair." Ed shrugged. "It's like the universe is arranging it so that we can hang out."

"The universe clearly has too much time on its hands." She sat down and pulled her knees up, leaning them against the edge of the table.

"Like lox?"

"Hate them."

"Then I'm glad I didn't buy any." Ed pushed a steaming cup of coffee across the table toward her. "Three sugars, no cream, right?"

Gaia nodded, refusing to be charmed by the fact that he remembered, and took a careful sip. She could feel him staring at her.

"You look like hell," he said, shaking a lock of brown hair back off his forehead. Suddenly he appeared to realize this was not a smart thing to say to a girl—any girl. "I mean . . . in a good way," he added lamely.

Gaia gave him a sidelong glance. "That's funny. I feel like hell." She took another, bolder sip of the hot coffee, letting the steamy liquid warm her from the inside.

"Now we're getting to it," Ed said, clasping his hands together and then cracking his knuckles. "You were unsurprisingly unfindable yesterday, Gaia. So let's hear it." He broke off a piece of bagel and pointed it at her. "Who was the lucky guy and how did the ceremonial shedding of the chastity belt go?"

Gaia ignored the bile rising in her throat, picked up a marble bagel, and took a gigantic bite. There was a reason she'd avoided Ed all day yesterday—the need to avoid forced emotional spillage. "Subtlety isn't exactly a talent of yours, is it, Ed?" she said with her mouth full.

"Look who's talking."

He had a point there. She studied Ed for a moment—the just-this-side-of-scruffy hair, the eager yet wary brown eyes, the dot of dried blood on his chin where he'd cut himself shaving. Gaia hated that she had to talk about this, but she did. She'd sucked Ed into the whole sorry situation when she confessed her virginity. Like it or not, over the past few weeks she had made Ed a friend, or something very close. He might as well know the truth.

Gaia closed her eyes. Shook her head. Sighed.

"It didn't happen," she said. And her whole body felt empty.

Ed dropped the knife onto the floor with a clatter. "It didn't?"

"Ed!" She opened her eyes and glared at him. "Think you can sound just a little more amused by that?"

"Sorry it didn't work out for you." Ed cleared his throat, and she could swear he was hiding a grin behind his steaming coffee. Some friend. "So what happened?" he asked.

Gaia took another aggressive bite of bagel. She chewed and swallowed before answering. "Let's just say I was witness to somebody beating me to it."

"Shut up!" Ed's eyes opened wide. "Gaia, tell me who we're talking about here. You can't keep me in this kind of suspense."

Say it, she commanded herself. Just say it. "It was Sam Moon."

A sudden shower of chewed bagel bits pelted Gaia's arms. "God, Ed! Food is to go in the mouth. *In*," Gaia said, brushing off her arms irritably.

"Do you mean you walked in on Sam and . . .

9

Heather?" Ed choked out while simultaneously attempting to wipe his mouth.

Somehow, saying it out loud gave Gaia a bit of distance. The words were vibrating in the fragrant air of the kitchen. Outside of her instead of inside. "Ironic, isn't it?" Gaia asked, flicking one last bagel wad off her elbow.

Ed looked as if he were watching his life flash before his eyes—backward and in 3-D with surround sound. Gaia had never seen his skin so pale. She'd forgotten for the moment that Heather meant something to Ed as well. A big something.

"Man." Ed let out a long rush of breath. His eyes were unfocused. "That had to suck."

It didn't suck. Sucking was getting busted for going seventy in a thirty-five-mile-an-hour zone. Sucking was losing a dollar in a Coke machine. Sucking didn't *hurt*.

"Could've been worse," she mumbled with a shrug. She wouldn't have believed it, except that it had actually gotten worse. The night had been full of mind-bending surprises. But she didn't need to share them now, if ever. They were highly dysfunctional family matters to be discussing over breakfast.

"What could be worse than walking in on the object of your seduction in bed with your mortal enemy?"

It was a decent question. Gaia was saved from needing to explain by the sound of the phone ringing.

Ed reached behind him, snatched the cordless from

the counter, then slid it across the table to Gaia. She hit the button and held the receiver to her ear. "Hello?"

At first, nothing.

"Hello?"

"Gaia Moore?"

Her eyes narrowed. "Yeah? Who is this?"

The voice was distorted, like something from a horror movie. "Check your e-mail." It was a command. Maybe even a threat.

She felt as if ice were forming in her veins. "Who is this?"

"Check your e-mail," the voice growled.

The line went dead.

Gaia was on her feet, running for George's computer, which, luckily, he always left on. When she reached the den, she flung herself into the chair and punched at the keyboard. Ed, maneuvering his chair through the rooms, appeared soon after.

"What's going on?"

Gaia was too morbidly curious to answer. She clicked the mail icon and stared at the screen as it choked out the early, cryptic shadows of a video image, and she tapped her fingers impatiently on the mouse as the picture emerged . . . slowly . . . slowly . . .

It was someone with his back to her, hunched forward. His surroundings were vague, too much light. Gaia reached for the speaker, in case there was audio. There was. Staticky at first. Distant, fuzzy, then clearing.

Clearing . . .

"Maybe it's Heather, playing a joke," offered Ed. "To get even."

Gaia was so intent on the image she barely heard him. "I don't think so."

Over the computer speakers she heard his voice. . . .

"Gaia . . . ?"

Her heart seemed to freeze solid in her chest. No, no, no, no.

But the voice through the speaker repeated itself. "Gaia."

No! "Sam?"

As if he'd heard her, he turned to the camera, and suddenly there was Sam's face on the computer screen. One of his eyes was black-and-blue, swollen shut, and he looked frighteningly pale. Weak.

Ed angled his chair close to the desk. "Oh, shit."

Sam's face vanished, replaced by a blank screen, and then there was a blast of static from the speakers as the same distorted voice addressed her. "Gaia Moore. You can see from this footage that we have a mutual friend. Sadly, he's not feeling well at the moment. Did you know Sam is a diabetic? No, I would imagine you didn't. . . ."

Ed stared at the blank screen. "Who the hell is it?"

Gaia shushed him with a sharp hiss as a graphic began to appear on the screen—a message snaking its way from the right side, one letter at a time:

C . . . A . . . N . . . Y . . . O . . . U . . .

The voice continued as the letters slid into view. "He's well enough for the moment, but around, oh, say, ten o'clock this evening he'll be needing his insulin, quite desperately. And that, my darling Gaia, is where you come in. You must pass a series of tests. You must pass these tests by ten o'clock tonight. If you do not, we will not wait for the diabetes to take over. If you do not pass these tests in the allotted time . . ."

The graphic slithered by: S . . . A . . . V . . . E . . .

". . . we will kill him."

S . . . A . . . M . . . ?

For a moment the question trembled there on the dark screen. CAN YOU SAVE SAM? Then the letters went spinning off into the infinite background, and another message appeared in an eye-searing flash of brightness. It read:

You will find on your front step a videotape.
You will play it during your first-period class.
DO NOT view the tape prior to showing it in school.

Without warning, the e-mail broadcast returned, showing a close-up of Sam's beaten face, his frightened eyes, his mouth forming a word, and the word came screaming through the speaker in Sam's voice.

"Gaia!"

Then nothing. The image and the audio were gone,

13

and the computer whirred softly until George's sickening screen saver—a scanned-in photo of Ella—returned to the screen.

Gaia sprang up from the chair and flew to the front door, which she flung open. The early October air sparkled, and the neighborhood was just coming alive with people on their way to work and school. Gaia paid no attention. Her eyes searched the front stoop until they found the package.

She lunged for it.

Gaia had no idea who had done this. She had no idea why. But she wasn't about to ask questions.

In that instant, it didn't matter that Sam had had sex with Heather or that he didn't return Gaia's overwhelming love for him and probably never would.

Sam life was in danger. For now, that was all that mattered.

"WHAT ARE YOU DOING?" ED demanded, wheeling himself out from the exit under the stoop, afraid for a moment that the package might explode in her hands.

But Gaia had grabbed her everpresent messenger bag and was down

The Knight

the steps. Ed aimed his chair to the left, toward the sidewalk. He could barely see Gaia over the row of potted shrubs as she sprinted away.

He caught up to her three corners later. One good thing about being in a wheelchair—even New York drivers slowed to let you cross the street.

She was bouncing on the balls of her feet, waiting for the light to change.

"Gaia, hold on. You can't just go to school and put that thing in the VCR!"

She didn't turn to face him. "Watch me."

"What if it . . . I don't know . . . what if it starts spewing out poisonous gas or something?" Ed offered.

"This isn't a *Batman* episode, Ed!" Gaia spat out, glancing over her shoulder. "What do you think, the Penguin sent that e-mail?"

"No, but somebody just as wacko did!"

"Somebody who's got Sam." Her voice was grim. Determined.

"Yeah, I get that. But we need to think about this. You don't know what's on that tape." He shook his head. "Okay, I admit, toxic vapor is a little extreme. But this whole thing is freaky, and I'm just saying we should be careful."

"You be careful," she snapped. "I'll be quick."

"Do you *never* think before you act?"

"Ed! Listen!" She grabbed the armrests of his

15

wheelchair and leaned over to look him directly in the eyes. She was so close he could see the pores in the perfect skin around her nose. Her hair was still wet against her cheeks. "I don't know who is doing this or why," she said. "But I have to help Sam."

In the next second he watched, helpless, as she flung herself out into the middle of traffic. A cab swerved. A UPS truck hit the brakes. A bike messenger careened off a mailbox.

But she made it.

He expected her to go right on running, but when she hit the opposite sidewalk, she turned and looked at him.

It was probably the fastest look in the history of eye contact, but that look was loaded. It was part defiance, part desperation, and part apology.

"Go!" he shouted, his voice raw. "I'll see you there."

She nodded almost imperceptibly, then took off down the street.

He followed as fast as his confinement allowed. Thinking.

She wanted to sleep with Sam. Sam Moon. But she hadn't. It had taken complete self-control to keep from popping a wheelie in his chair when she'd confessed that. Saturday night had been torture—the thought of her in someone else's arms, of someone else kissing her, had kept him awake all night. Awake and angry and sick to his stomach.

Because he loved her desperately. In mind, in spirit, in body. He wanted her.

So what if she wanted Sam? Seeing him with Heather must have cured that, right? The fact that she was rushing off to his rescue, no questions asked, just meant she was noble. One more thing to love about her.

Ed's remark about the universe setting them up came back to him, and he cringed. Stupid. Childish. Pathetic.

Yet on some level he'd meant it. He'd found her, that first day in the hall at school. She'd been so lost, and so not wanting to be lost. Ed knew how lost felt. He'd felt it every day since he'd first sat in this chair. Every day he was set apart.

He approached school and entered the crush of people. He imagined Gaia in her first-period classroom, slamming the mysterious video into the VCR. What the hell is on the tape? he wondered, feeling panic press into him.

And if he had to, could he rescue her from it?

He smiled bitterly at the ridiculous image. Sir Edward of Useless Limbs, the knight in not-so-shining armor, rushing in to rescue the fair Gaia, Lady of Brutal Ass Kickings.

Remember that, pal? Three punks in one shot. And

17

without even having to touch up her lip gloss afterward. His lady had no need for a knight. And, anyway, knights rode horses, not chairs.

He broke from the pack of students and rolled toward the handicapped entrance.

As he did on every other day of the school year, Ed entered the building alone.

To: ELJ
From: L
Date: October 11
File: 776244
Subject: Gaia Moore

   She is even more beautiful up close. And far
more dangerous. For now, we proceed as planned.
The trials have begun. We will test her limits. I
want to see how far she will go for this boy.
What she will risk. How much she is willing to
lose.

   The boy suffers, but it is all in the name of
authenticity.

   I have no doubt she will succeed on her own;
however, if any complications should arise to
impede her various quests, I will arrange for
assistance. Her safety, as ever, is of utmost
importance. She must not fail—for all roads lead
to me. Tonight I will secure my position in her
life. There is much to alter. Much to gain.

To: L
From: ELJ
Date: October 11
File: 776244
Subject: Gaia Moore

  I understand what is expected of me. The note is already written and waiting to be planted. Other objects with regard to this aspect of the plan are also in place.

  GN and I will leave the city early. He will not be there to help her or to interfere in any way. He will not suspect a thing.

  Tonight I will meet the pawn and see that he is where we need him to be, and when.

Sam's face. Sam's bruised face. It came out of that computer at me like a kick to the teeth. And then he had to go and call my name like that.

I wonder if fear feels anything like desperation. Because that's what I felt when his voice came reverberating out of those speakers.

He called *my* name.

This probably sounds totally inappropriate, but there was a moment there . . . There was a moment there when I was glad he was calling *me*. And I can think of only two possible reasons why.

Reason #1. The kidnapper told Sam he was zapping his image to *my* computer, so who else's name *would* he say?

But I doubt the kidnapper is giving him any information pertaining to his rescue, so the chances of his knowing he was even being filmed are pretty

slim. Besides, he doesn't know
about my . . . talents, or my
weird life, so why would he be
calling out to me for help? It's
not like he'd expect me to be
able to come crashing in and
kick his captor's ass—which I
would do in a heartbeat, if only
I knew where he was. So that
brings me to:

Reason #2. He's thinking of
me. (Could it be?)
   Thinking of me insofar as a
guy in hypoglycemic shock (or
whatever it's called when dia-
betics need insulin) who may
also be suffering a concussion
can think.
   Like maybe he screamed "Gaia"
because Gaia was the first thing
that came to his mind.
   Gaia. *Me.* Gaia.
   I don't know.
   What I do know, though, is
this: As long as there's an
ounce of strength in my body, I
am going to do everything I

possibly can to do what that
son-of-a-bitch kidnapper challenged me to do.

I'm going to save Sam.

And when I find out who did
this to him, I'm going to take
the guy down.

She told
herself the
only thing

independent

that

film

mattered was

that she'd

passed the

first test.

"NO, MAN! NO, MAN, *PLEASE!* DON'T!"

CJ closed his eyes as Tarick lifted one rock-solid fist and slammed it against CJ's skull. His eye felt as if it had been dislodged from its socket, and his mouth instantly filled with blood.

Weird Shit

"You let her go?" Tarick shouted, coming at CJ again. This time he wrenched CJ's arm—the one in the sling. The one with the bullet hole in it. The pain shot through his entire body like an explosion, and everything went blurry. CJ sank to the grimy concrete floor on his knees and then fell forward, savoring the feel of the cold, grainy surface against his cheek. It smelled like burnt cigarettes and blood. CJ knew it was the last smell he'd ever experience if he didn't do something.

"Kill him." Tarick's voice.

"Now."

"No! No! Wait!"

He heard them loading the gun.

"I can still do it!" CJ shouted through the pain.

Suddenly he was being wrenched to his feet, and Tarick used one beefy hand to push CJ up against the wall by his neck. "We should have let you bleed to death in the first place, you useless piece of shit." Tarick spat in CJ's face, but CJ couldn't move a muscle. He just let the gob slide down the side of his nose and onto his chin.

"I can still do it," he repeated pathetically, choking on the words. Joey was hovering behind Tarick, gun clenched in his hand. He didn't even look sad or scared. He just looked ready.

Tarick released him and he fell to the ground, sputtering for breath. He bent over at the waist, thought better of taking his eyes off Joey, and forced himself to straighten up.

"Please, Tarick," CJ said, his eyes stinging. "Weird shit is always happening around this bitch. Guys with guns, like she's got a protector or something."

Tarick laughed, showing his yellowed teeth and flashing the stud that pierced his tongue. "This isn't a storybook, CJ," Tarick said. "She don't have a fairy godmother."

Joey cocked the gun.

"Please, man," CJ said, trying hard not to whimper. "Just give me one more chance. I won't let you down again."

Tarick's eyes roamed over CJ's broken and battered body. He sucked at his teeth, ran a hand over his shaved and tattooed head. He glanced at Joey, then looked back at CJ.

"All right, man," Tarick said with a quick nod. "You get one more chance."

27

CJ let out a sigh of relief and closed his eyes. Then Tarick's voice cut through the darkness, his breath impossibly close to CJ's ear.

"Screw it up again, and I kill you myself."

HEATHER GANNIS DID NOT WALK SO

much as float. With her delicate chin tipped upward slightly, she moved purposefully but gracefully through the posthomeroom

Floating

throng. The look of disdain on her pretty face was to remind the Gap-clad masses that she was, and would always be, their superior. Even if she didn't necessarily feel like it. They were the ones who'd elevated her to that status. She was the one who had to struggle daily to perpetuate the illusion.

She floated, seemingly high on her own significance, weightless in the knowledge that she, and she alone, had the best hair, the best blouse, the best ass.

She was Heather Gannis, too ethereal to simply walk.

That was how they saw her, anyway, and that was what they expected, maybe even needed. And she was the one they'd elected to provide it for them.

Sometimes she thought she'd be willing to chuck the whole popularity thing in a heartbeat. Other times, having swarms of admirers had its perks.

And so she'd float.

Today, though, she had to work harder than usual to pull it off. Today she was dealing with stuff. Big-time confusion. Insecurity—not about her beauty or her position at school, of course. Insecurity beyond the ordinary is-there-lipstick-on-my-teeth variety.

And Heather's self-doubt came in the form of the same pitiful little mutant who'd put her in the hospital. Gaia Moore.

What kind of name was that, anyway? Guy-uh. Sounded like a Cro-Magnon grunt rather than a name.

And Cro-Magnon girl had ruined everything. Shocker.

Saturday night had started out perfect. Then it had gotten even better.

She'd been in Sam's arms—securing what was hers, giving him what he wanted before Gaia had the chance to make an offer of her own.

Heather's motives for Saturday night had been part romance, part strategy. Sleeping with Sam would cement their relationship—take it to the next

29

level. She was reasonably certain that Sam would forget Gaia completely if he believed Heather was committed enough to make him her first.

Sam wouldn't really be her first, of course—she'd lost her virginity to Ed long ago—but he'd *believe* that he was. She'd (briefly) considered telling him the truth, but decided "first" sounded so much more devoted than "next." Ed was her secret, and she was going to keep it that way.

But Gaia had her grubby little hooks in Ed, too. It made Heather's skin crawl to think about that. Ed followed Gaia around like a damn puppy dog.

She realized she was aching to see Gaia, maybe right now, in the hallway, where she could create some big, ugly scene that would make her look great and Gaia look even more pathetic than before.

She remembered with the small section of her brain in which she stored information about school that Gaia was in her first-period class. Fine. She could destroy her there just as easily. Smaller audience, but better acoustics.

Heather's mind spun (but she kept floating) and images of Sam, catapulting off the bed to chase after Gaia, burned in her mind. The Slim-Fast bar she'd eaten for breakfast threatened to come up. What had he been thinking? What was wrong with him, leaving her for Gaia, and just on the brink of . . . well, of everything?

But that bitch—that disgusting, creepy little bitch had shown up, and Sam had freaked.

On the upside, Gaia had looked absolutely miserable upon catching them in the act. Maybe now she'd get the message and back off. The girl had proof now, proof that Sam and Heather were the real deal. Of course, Sam's running after her might have given Gaia cause to wonder. . . .

Damn him! Why had he left? And why hadn't he called? That had been Saturday. This was Monday! No call, no personal appearance. She could have been home crying all weekend and he didn't even care.

A chill shot through her. What the hell had taken place when Sam caught up to Gaia Saturday? Had she said something, done something, to override Heather's sexual surrender?

Was there anything that *could* override sex for a guy? She doubted it, but still. Evidently Gaia had some weird power over Sam. Had she been able to use that power on Saturday, even as his hair was still tousled from Heather's own fingers?

Heather mentally checked her expression. No creases. No frowning. She had to look distant, aloof, as calm as always or else they might suspect. She lowered her eyelids slightly, pushed out her lower lip—sexy, sullen, unconcerned, and floating. Christ, this was getting old.

31

They called out to her, waved. Occasionally she'd reply, but not often enough to give them any substantial hope. And tomorrow she'd do it again.

And tomorrow. And tomorrow.

Shit! That reminded her. She had a Shakespeare quiz later this morning, and she hadn't even opened her notebook. What was it old Willie had said about the moon? The inconstant moon. Sam Moon. Inconstant, big time. Changeable. Fickle. And in love with Gaia Moore?

Maybe.

Heather entered her first-period class and immediately scanned the room to see if Gaia was there. To her amazement, the loser was actually present, actually had the nerve to show her face! Heather prepared herself to deploy her patented secret weapon—a look of death that could make even the thumb-heads on the wrestling team shiver in their sneakers—but Gaia seemed to be looking right through her.

Oh, this one was good. Most girls who found themselves on Heather's shit list would be groveling already. But this freak of nature had the audacity to diss her. On some level Heather was actually impressed. It was almost a relief to know there was someone who didn't shed all self-respect the minute Heather threw her a look.

Okay, so it was impressive. But it still pissed her off.

Heather slammed her books onto her desk, accepted some hellos from neighboring students, then noticed that the classroom television was on. The screen was blank—the same bright blue Tommy Hilfiger used last spring—and the VCR light was blinking.

Thank God! Heather thought. A video was about all she could handle this morning. Probably something about the Civil War. Wait. This was economics, not history. Okay, something boring about supply and demand, then. Perfect.

She wouldn't even have to watch. She could study for Shakespeare and write vicious things about Gaia on the desktop. And wonder if Sam was out of her life for good now.

And if he was, was he in Gaia's life instead? Losing him would be bad. Losing him to her would be unbearable.

God, did that little witch actually believe she could do battle with her? Did she think she was better than Heather Gannis? And if she thought she was, how long would it be before the rest of the people in this school—flock of sheep that they were—began thinking it, too?

She didn't want to think about this. Not now. She wanted to get her mind off Gaia and Sam. She'd allow herself one nasty piece of desktop graffiti, then maybe she'd watch the stupid video after all.

33

SITTING THROUGH HOMEROOM WAS

torture. What could the cassette possibly contain? Wicked neo-Nazi propaganda? Gang recruitment information? Or maybe something closer to home—a biographical account of her messed-up life, edited for the sole purpose of humiliating her in public? But since Gaia had no idea who'd kidnapped Sam, she couldn't even begin to pinpoint a motive, and therefore could not even venture a guess as to what purpose this video, this "test," might serve.

She was about to find out. First period. The moment of truth.

If anyone was surprised that the video was starting before the teacher was present, they didn't mention it. Someone at the back of the room hit the lights. Gaia glanced over her shoulder and saw it was Ed, who'd just arrived. He was supposed to be in English now, wasn't he? But here he was, for moral support.

First bagels, now this. She felt a small cyclone of warmth in her stomach. So this was what friends did for you, huh? Gaia squelched the warmth. She couldn't risk getting used to it.

Ed shot her a look that was part encouragement, part panic. She turned away fast.

34

The blue screen gave way to a sudden blast of snowy static, then the scene focused.

It appeared to be a wide-angle shot of the upper half of a bedroom. The room was dimly lit, but Gaia could make out posters on the walls, an NYU pennant, a wide window with the blinds pulled.

And there were noises.

The usual New York background noises, of course—distant sirens, car horns, blaring radios. But over those came the more interesting noises.

Sounds like soft growling and deep sighs, sounds that seemed to caress each other.

Now where had she heard that before?

And then the camera panned down, pulling a form into focus.

It was an odd angle from which to film. Even Gaia, with her lack of experience in both filmmaking and lovemaking, knew that. The subjects were unidentifiable. There was a broad back, encircled from below by svelte, ribbonlike arms that tapered into delicate hands and graceful fingers. But the camera angle was designed to provide no clear view of either face.

The noises deepened, grew urgent, began to resemble words.

"Oh. Oh my—"

All the air seemed to flee Gaia's lungs at once. She knew that voice. And now that she looked closer, the blanket covering the bottom half of the couple looked pretty familiar as well.

They, them, him, her.

Gaia gripped the edges of her desk. Shit! What should she do? Let it run? Or jump up (assuming she could actually get her body to jump, since she seemed to be paralyzed) and turn the thing off? After all, sooner or later she'd be making her own cameo in this film.

The class was catching on now, and the howling began. As far as Gaia could tell, they hadn't recognized the female lead just yet. The star herself, in response to the provocative remarks of her classmates, had only just looked up from something she was scribbling on her desktop.

The graceful fingers were now clawing at the broad back.

Out of the corner of her eye, Gaia could see Heather studying the screen. Heather's first instinct, it appeared, was to smile. Hell, it was funny! Funny, as long as it wasn't your inaugural sexual liaison being screened in first-period advanced-placement economics.

Gaia kept her eyes slanted in Heather's direction and watched as the perfect smile flickered once, then vanished. Realization flared in Heather's eyes just as her video incarnation was uttering her first line of dialogue.

"Oh my God . . . Sam!"

To which oh-my-God-Sam replied, *"Heather!"*

Busted!

Gaia snapped her attention back to the screen. Sundance, eat your heart out. Whoever this independent-film director was, he certainly had a flair for timing, because it was at this point that AP econ was allowed to enjoy the first close-up shot of the movie.

And it featured none other than Heather Gannis, perspiring elegantly, eyelids fluttering, flawless teeth clamped down on her lower lip.

The class exploded in reaction. Some of them shrieked in disbelief. Some laughed, some applauded wildly. Most just gasped. Heather, in a surprising gesture that made Gaia feel almost sorry for her, covered her face with one trembling hand and began to sob.

Gaia wondered absently if anyone had seen her stick the tape in the VCR. If they had, this could get really ugly really fast. As if it weren't ugly enough already.

Two of Heather's girlfriends sprang to her side, ostensibly trying to comfort her.

"Somebody eject it!" one of them demanded.

"No pun intended!" replied someone on a choke of laughter.

Another of Heather's sidekicks—a girl named Megan—got up and moved toward the front of the room to turn off the television. Was it just Gaia's imagination, or did Megan seem to be taking her sweet time getting there?

AP econ was treated to a few additional renditions of "Oh my God, Sam!" before the electric-green-painted acrylic nail of Megan's index finger connected with the off button.

Instantly the class shut up, as if some cosmic off button had been punched as well.

The room went completely silent. Silent, except for the muffled gulping of Heather's crying.

Shame washed over Gaia.

Worse than fear, she guessed. It had to be.

Suddenly Gaia found herself silently pleading with Heather to go: Run. Get out. The silence pulsed as she kept her eyes glued to her desktop, willing her sworn enemy to escape. The girl was a bitch, sure, and a monster. But nobody, not even Heather, deserved this.

And then, as if she had sensed Gaia's unspoken plea, Heather catapulted out of her seat and stumbled toward the door. Megan and the other two handmaidens went running after Heather, looking appropriately concerned. But just before Megan disappeared through the door, she turned and fixed Gaia with a glare that Megan probably thought was menacing.

She knew. Which meant that in about 1.5 seconds Heather would know, too.

Ed made his exit as well, and the teacher picked that moment to arrive, stepping through the door but looking over her shoulder into the corridor.

"What's happened to Miss Gannis?" she asked.

"I think she lost something," one of the boys answered, biting back laughter. A giggle rippled through the room.

The shame swelled. Who was the monster now?

"Turn to page thirty-four," the teacher said.

In the wake of the X-rated video they'd just seen, the teacher's lecture on inflation and upward trends incited a few scattered chuckles and snorts. But Gaia was barely aware of them.

Numbly she wondered what Ed would say. He might be furious with her. After all, he and Heather had a history. Or maybe he'd just say, "I told you so," which, of course, would be even worse.

She told herself the only thing that mattered to her was that she'd passed the first test, and that Sam was one step closer to safety.

She hoped.

GAIA HUNG BACK AFTER THE BELL,

High School Drama

until the classroom had emptied. Then she snatched the video and stuffed it into her beat-up messenger bag. She'd destroy it later. Crush it, or burn it, or something equally absolute. The last thing she needed was for it to wind up playing 24/7 on the Internet—the scene of her nightmares playing out for the global community's entertainment.

Ed was waiting for her in the hall.

So were Heather and a sea of salivating spectators.

Gaia took one look into Heather's very wet, very red, very livid eyes and considered walking right past her, rather than enduring the obligatory scene of high school drama that everyone was expecting. But Gaia stayed rooted in place. She'd done what she was about to be accused of. Some remote part of her was eager to clothe herself in blame. Maybe even needed to.

"Where did you get it?" Heather asked, her voice surprisingly even. "Where did you get that tape?"

"I found it," Gaia answered. True. There was the requisite murmur from the crowd at this stunning tidbit of noninformation.

Heather's perfectly lined eyes narrowed. "You're not even going to deny it was you?"

"No." Another murmur, this one louder.

"Are you going to explain?" Heather took a step closer. Megan and the other sidekicks exchanged a look that said things were about to get interesting.

"I didn't know what was on the tape," Gaia said with a shrug. Also true.

Heather let out a noise that was somewhere between a shriek and asphyxiation. "Tell me where you got it," she said. She was right in Gaia's face. The tangy sweetness of her perfume made Gaia's nose itch. The girl was brave. But then, she did have the entire school behind her. And she didn't know what Gaia was capable of. Not that Gaia had any intention of letting Heather find out—let alone the ever-growing crowd.

"I already told you," Gaia said.

And then Heather pushed her. It was the kind of push that normally wouldn't have affected Gaia in the slightest—had she been expecting it. But Heather had caught her off guard, and Gaia stumbled backward until her shoulders pressed into the wall.

The crowd let out a little "ooh." Gaia righted herself, standing up straight for the first time in recent memory.

Heather took the slightest step back, betrayed herself with the smallest flinch. Gaia was sure she was the only one who saw it.

"What kind of psychotic freak are you?" Heather said loudly, shoving Gaia again.

This time Gaia didn't budge. "The kind of psychotic freak you don't want to push again," she said under her breath.

There were a few things Heather could do at this point, and Gaia watched her face with interest as

Heather ran through the possibilities in a fraction of a second. Where would the roulette ball land?

Would Heather:

A) call Gaia's bluff and push her again?

B) lose her shit and run?

Or

C) back off with some catty remark, thereby making herself look like the bigger person and the victor?

"You're not worth it," Heather said.

So it was going to be C.

Good choice.

There was a disappointed muttering from the male contingent, a sigh of relief from the females. Heather backed up, fixing a wry smile on her face. "You do realize that your life at this school is beyond over," she said, then snorted a bitter laugh. "Not that it ever started."

The masses laughed and scoffed and made general noises of agreement.

Gaia said nothing. Moved not an inch.

Heather took this as cause to smile even wider, and turned to her friends. "Show's over."

And with that the crowd dispersed, punctuating Heather's threat with their own disgusted looks and comments.

Gaia didn't bother to look like she cared. She didn't care. Heather's idea of hell was social failure, but Gaia knew better. For Gaia, the ridicule of her fellow high school students was about as distressing as a hair in her spaghetti. Gaia took a deep breath. She'd let Heather have her moment. That was the best she could do in the way of an apology.

Now she could get back to what really mattered. Sam.

ED WAS THE ONLY ONE LEFT. ED

Close to Home

and the few hallway stragglers who'd unluckily been too late to catch the action.

"You were right," Gaia said sharply before he could open his mouth. "I shouldn't have shown it without a preview."

Ed shrugged. "You didn't know. You couldn't have known."

Gaia's shoulders slumped. "Heather . . ."

"Good call not pummeling her, by the way," Ed said matter-of-factly.

"Yeah, well, she had enough for one morning."

Ed reached up, took Gaia's hand, and squeezed it. Gaia pulled away instantly, but Ed didn't even blink. "I wouldn't feel too bad about putting Heather in a compromising position if I were you," he said. "I think that was more Sam's responsibility, anyway, if you know what I mean."

"Ed!" Gaia said tersely.

"Sorry." He raised his hands in surrender.

Gaia adjusted her bag on her shoulder. "Forget Heather. Here's what I don't get—the e-mail said that showing the video was a test. So what did it prove? I mean, what could humiliating Heather have possibly gained for the kidnapper? If the video made some kind of demand or threat, that would make sense. But this was just . . . humiliating. And cruel."

Ed nodded. "I know what you mean. It was more like a practical joke. A demonic one."

"Maybe the kidnapper just wanted to see if I'd follow directions," Gaia said, glancing over her shoulder at the rapidly emptying hallway. "Which brings me to—"

"To how the kidnapper is going to know what you do and don't do," said Ed, finishing the thought for her.

Gaia sighed. "I guess we can safely figure that I am under constant surveillance."

"Guess so."

Gaia sighed. "Creepy."

"Very."

"So where's the next test?" Gaia said, glaring at the grate-covered hallway clock. "If I have to jump

44

through a bunch of hoops before ten o'clock tonight, why didn't they just give them all to me at once?" She was bouncing up and down again, raring to go. She didn't like this feeling of being watched, of being manipulated, of being out of control.

Sam was out there somewhere, suffering, and there was nothing she could do about it until these assholes decided to contact her. How was she supposed to handle this?

"I could be *done* by now," she said, watching the seconds tick by.

"You know what worries me?" Ed asked, his forehead creased. "Whoever this guy is, he seems to be striking very close to home."

"What do you mean?" Gaia wrapped her arms around herself. The anticipation was making her feel like she was going to explode through her skin.

"I mean you got lucky," Ed said, maneuvering his chair around a line of people waiting for the water fountain. "You went to Sam's room with a mission, remember? It could just as easily have been you on that tape, Gaia."

Gaia tightened her grip on herself. She hadn't thought of that.

"Who knows? Maybe it was *supposed* to be you." Ed lowered his voice as a group of teachers passed. "And that would mean that whoever planted the camera in Sam's room has a serious inside line on you. I mean, even beyond constant surveillance. It's almost like he can read your mind. This can't be just about Sam."

Gaia checked the clock again. "It's not like I know anything about Sam." *Except that I love him . . . and I hate him,* she added silently as the contents of the video burned in her mind.

"But if the kidnapper wanted money or attention or something, why would they contact you?" Ed asked. "Wouldn't they send a ransom note to his parents or something? This whole thing is pretty random."

Gaia stopped walking and stared at a crack in the cinder block wall just above Ed's head. "So you think it's about me." Not a question.

"You're the one with all the secrets, Gaia," Ed said, lifting his chin in an obvious attempt to arrest her line of vision. "Whatever they are."

Gaia scanned the hallway again. No one suspicious. Nothing out of place. "Aren't you glad I won't let you ask questions? You're safer not knowing."

"Somehow I don't feel all that safe." Ed started moving again, narrowly missing the open-toed sandal of an oblivious freshman.

"God! Where are they?" Gaia blurted, covering her watch with her hand as if she could make time stop. "What if they sent another e-mail?" She started bouncing again, as if she were a boxer psyching herself up for a fight. "I can't just stand around like this. I have to find him."

They continued down the hall in silence, Gaia staring every passerby in the eye, glancing over her shoulder every third of a second. When she reached her second-period class, which she had no intention of sitting still through, the teacher met her in the doorway.

"Ms. Moore, I just received a note asking me to send you to the main office to pick up a package," Mrs. Reingold said with a vapid smile.

Gaia's heart gave a leap of actual joy. *Good. Let's get on with it.*

"Receiving gifts at school, are we?" Mrs. Reingold continued. "Do we find this appropriate?"

Gaia was about to tell the teacher exactly what *we* could do with *our* idea of appropriate when Ed pinched her leg.

"You must have left your lunch at home this morning," Ed said.

"Yeah," Gaia snapped, glancing at the withered old teacher. "My parents don't like me to go through the day without three squares."

When Mrs. Reingold closed the classroom door, Gaia spun on her heel and practically flew to the main office. Ed was right behind her.

She burst into the office, told the principal's secretary who she was, and was handed a sealed envelope.

Ed was waiting for her back in the hall. For a moment she just stared at the envelope.

"Please tell me you're about to read the nominees for Best Picture," said Ed, his face a little pale.

"I wish." Gaia leaned against the water fountain. She slid her finger beneath the flap and tugged, then pulled out a sheet of paper and began to read it aloud: "'Kudos on the successful completion of Test One.'" She looked up from the paper and frowned at Ed. "Kudos? Oh, great. So the guy's not only a maniac, he's a dork."

"A dangerous dork, Gaia. Keep reading."

Wrrrzzzzzzzz.

I am Sam Moon.

They said my name. I heard them. Good, because maybe I forgot it. Sam Moon, Sam Moon, Sam Moon, Sam Moon.

Wrrrzzzzzzzz. Clank. Wrrrzzzzzzzz.

They grabbed me. That much I know. But who? Why?

Wrrrzzzzzzzz. Clank.

If that damned noise would just . . . stop. It comes in through a window I can't see. That . . . noise. That . . . grinding, scraping, scratching, humming, rumbling.

WrrrzzzzzzClankWrrrzzzzzz.

NearFarAlwaysLouderSofter . . .

Wrrrzzzzzzzz. God! Numbing my brain.

Not just the noise the ques-tions my own questions I have never wondered so hard it's making me queasy all this not knowing my blood is screaming it's pounding in my temples I can taste my own bile I keep

shaking and I want to peel my
skin off—

And I want to kiss Gaia.

Did I? Once? I did, I think.
She was soft. Her eyes took me.
Took me right in. Nothing bluer,
ever. Nothing so generous, or
alone and . . .

Wrrrzzzzzzzz clank wrrzz.

Shit, what the hell happened
to my face? Oh Yeah, Guy With A
Fist With A Ring. And the voice.
Not the Fist's voice, somebody
else's.

Pokey? Smokey? Low Key? Loki.

His voice, then the fist.
Damnthathurt.

Then how come they haven't
killed me yet? Or have they?
Maybe I'm supposed to be heading-
forthelight already.

Jesus, I'm losing it. I'm not
dead. Okay? *I'mnotdead.* Just . . .
focus. Right, that's right. Focus.

I amSam MoonI am Sam . . . Sam
I am.

Remember? Yes. I remember. I
am sitting on my mother's lap

yesterday last week now later.
Athousandyearsago. Letters are
new, words are strange. I am
small—

And safeAnd she is reading to
me. Something about . . . what?

Eggs? Yes. And Ham. Green Eggs
and Ham. Yes! And Sam I am.

I said,

Sam *I* am

and we laughed and laughed and
laughed.

God I want to laugh again.
Now. Right now.

*Wrrrzzzzzzzz clank
wrrrzzzzzzzz.* Laugh!

Do I remember how? Try. You
can't laugh if you're dead. Be
alive. Laugh.

Try. I must be laughing, because look how they're looking at
me.

Uhhg. Something burns my
throat then my tongue then my
lips. Laughing hurts.

And I'm vomiting. I'm puking.

That happens. Diabetic. Me.

It's warm on my chin slick

smearing down onto my shirt. It
reeks. Bad.

Someone comes, cleans me up.
Not gentle. Not like Mom did.

Mom?

Wrrrzzzzzzzzzclankwrrrzzzzzzzz.

The noise, damn it! It's mess-
ing up the story. Inahousewitha
mouseinaboxwithafox.

Wrrrzzzzzzzzz. Clank. Wrrzz.

Focus. Remember . . . how did
it start? Where was I before I was
here? What was I thinking before I
couldn't think? Focus . . .

Heat. And shoulders. And a
silky throat.

Heather. Me. Together. So together. Mmmmmm . . . almost good.
But I'm wishing beyond it. I'm
wishing for Gaia.

Wrrrzzzzzzzzz clank wrrzz.

And then . . . Gaia.

Gaia. Jesus. Gaia. No, don't go
. . . I'm sorry. And then . . .
running. Darkness and streetlights and . . . where? Where did
she go? And then the arm across
my chest, the hands around my

throat.

And *wrrrzzzzzzzz* I'm here
again, over the noise again.
Still.

Oh, God. What the hell is happening? I don't know. I can't
know. Knowing is somewhere else.
And it all fades into the noise.

Wrrrzzzzzzzz clank.

Gaia?

Wrrrzzzzzzzz . . .

. . . zzzzzzzz . . .

His weird talent had been the cause of his wife's death. Would it now take his daughter's life as well?

daddy's home

TOM MOORE STARED AT HIS DESK,

which was piled high with top secret government files, profiles of the world's most threatening terrorist groups, and all other manner of classified information. At this moment, though, the most important document on it was the unfinished letter to his daughter.

Father Knows Best

> *Dearest Gaia,*
>
> *I was closer to you Saturday night than I've been in years. Close enough to be reminded that you have my eyes, your mother's nose, and our combined determination.*
>
> *Close enough to see you nearly shot.*
> *Close enough to save your life.*

The pen trembled in his hand. Thank God he'd been there. His bullet had only hit the punk's shoulder, but it had been enough. For the moment, at least. Gaia had gotten away. Maybe the bullet had sent a message: Back off. Stand down. Give up. Tom could only hope. And anyway, there were other dangers stalking Gaia—ones far more grave, far less predictable.

One, he knew, was a sick son of a bitch with

whom, forty-some-odd years ago, Tom had shared a womb.

The thought made him physically ill. His brother. His twin brother. A deadly psychopath with a vendetta against Tom. Loki. Tom knew the name from the research his outfit provided. But he would have known it, anyway.

When they were children, his brother had fixated on the idea of Loki, the Norse god. A Satan-like hero, consumed by darkness and evil. It was no wonder that as an adult, he would adopt this moniker, under which to pursue his hateful purpose.

Tom said the word out loud. "Loki." It literally stung his vocal cords.

But what about his own name, his undercover name? Enigma, they called him. Definition: anything that arouses curiosity or perplexes because it is unexplained, inexplicable, or secret.

He gave a humorless laugh. Yes. That I am, he thought. I am a secret to my own child.

The name was dead-on. Tom Moore was an enigma, even to himself. He had been from childhood, when his remarkable talent had begun to make itself known. Why was he able to think the way he did? Why was he capable of solving the unsolvable? Why could his brain take in seemingly random patterns of words and numbers and make sense of them?

He could decode, decipher, predict, and presume with terrifying accuracy.

In high school he'd discovered, much to his amusement, that he could open any combination lock in the building. Handy for dropping little love notes into the lockers of cute girls (his buddy Steve's idea, and favorite pastime). But even now, so many years later, he still wanted to know why he could work codes and riddles so easily. Not *how*. He didn't care how, but how *come*? Why should this responsibility have fallen to him?

And it was such an awesome responsibility. He had no formal, written job description. In fact, as far as he knew, there was not a shred of printed information on him anywhere. But in his own mind he'd boiled his job description down to one sentence: Save the world.

Perhaps it was better that this ability had wound itself into the double helix of his DNA instead of his twin brother's. At least, Tom told himself, he used his skill for good. If Loki had been born with such a knack . . . Tom shuddered to think about it. Genetic predisposition was a freaky thing.

Gaia, for example. Her body chemistry was a source of even greater astonishment. It was as if the gods had said, "Let's give her brains, and beauty, and charm, and grace, and physical strength, but hold the fear. No use mucking up the gene pool with that useful emotion."

Again, why?

Tom let out a long rush of breath, expelling the question with the air in his lungs. He'd wondered too hard, too long on that one. Ironic: The only other conundrum besides himself that he couldn't solve was his own daughter.

So instead, he hid from her. And hid her, too.

Apparently not so well.

Because now Loki had her in his sights. And that filthy little street punk, whose ignorance was surpassed only by his willingness to hate, was stalking her.

Tom looked down at the unfinished letter, ran his finger over the greeting.

Dearest Gaia,

His talent had been the cause of his wife's death. Would it now take his daughter's life as well?

Not while there was breath left in his body, he vowed to himself.

He picked up his pen, hesitated, then added another line to the letter.

Daddy's home.

Then, as he did with every other note, letter, and card he'd written to Gaia over the last five years, he stuffed it into a file drawer and locked it away.

Not sending it was hard.

But sending it would make things so much harder.

KUDOS ON THE SUCCESSFUL COMPLE- *tion of Test One. You are now to commit an act of theft—a very specific act. George Niven has a computer disk that is of interest to us. You will find this disk and drop it off in Washington Square Park. There will be a man there to receive it. He will be disguised as a homeless man and he will have a cart. Bring the disk to him, Gaia, and do it fast. Time, after all, stops for no man. Not even for Sam . . .*

"They want me to steal from George," Gaia said, tearing her eyes from the note.

"Huh?" Ed blurted, following along as Gaia hurried down the hall, second period completely forgotten.

"What do they want one of George's disks for?" Gaia wondered aloud. She'd practically forgotten Ed was there. George used to be a Green Beret with her dad, and they'd been in the CIA together. Were the kidnappers somehow connected to the government?

Oh, shit. Maybe George still had connections. Maybe he had nude photos on someone in the Pentagon. Or maybe the disk simply contained his recipe for barbecue sauce, and this was just another sham test, to get her to prove she was in this 100 percent.

But what if it wasn't barbecue sauce? It was

possible. After all, she'd sensed that George had always known where her father was. He never said anything; it was just this gut feeling she had. And now that her dad was back in town . . .

Could something terrorist-related be going down in Washington Square Park? Something involving CJ and the late Marco, and all those other small-time white-supremacist swine?

And what did any of this have to do with Sam? Why hadn't they just taken her?

If only they had just taken her.

"Gaia, have you heard a word I said?" Ed's voice suddenly broke through her stream of consciousness.

"No," she answered, unfazed.

"Well, I was just wondering if we're forgetting about school for the day, since you seem to be heading for the exit," Ed said.

Gaia stopped as the automatic door swung open with a loud buzz. "I think you should stay here," she said, glancing briefly at Ed's wide brown eyes.

"No way," Ed said determinedly. "This is no time to become Independent Girl." He pushed his way through the door and out onto the street. Fortunately, the school administration was a tad lax about keeping an eye on the handicap exits.

"Ed, I'm not *becoming* anything," Gaia said, stomping after him. A brisk October wind caught her hair and whipped it back from her face. "I just don't want you involved."

"I'm already involved," Ed said, staring straight ahead.

"Ed—"

"Gaia."

The tone of his voice made her pause. She might as well let him come home with her. She'd derail his efforts then. Somehow. She couldn't have him out on the street with her, where he was an easy target.

"Fine," she said, unwilling to let him get the last word. "But stay out of my way." She sidestepped past him and walked a few feet ahead, making sure to keep up a fast pace.

Gaia and Ed were halfway to George and Ella's house before either one of them spoke. Actually, she would have liked his advice, but how could she ask for it?

A) That would make her look needy, and she'd rather be dead than needy.

And

B) He didn't have all the facts.

As far as Ed could assume, George's computer files were most likely limited to bank statements and hints on preparing tangy marinades. He didn't know about George's past, which might in fact turn out to be continuing on into his present.

The question: Was Gaia willing to turn over one computer disk, which might, perhaps (and that was one gigantic perhaps there), contain a bunch of classified government crap that could help some terrorist destroy the world?

Or could she just let Sam die?

"So . . . does this disk or file or whatever have a name?" Ed asked finally. "Maybe it'll give you some clue about what it is."

Loyal *and* smart, that was Ed. Gaia scanned the remainder of the note and found the name.

And stopped in her tracks.

The file was called Scaredy Cat.

ELLA HAD LEFT A NOTE. OBVIOUSLY

No Warrant

Gaia had overlooked it in the commotion of the morning.

She found it on the hall table when she barreled in.

Surprised George with a day trip to the country. We won't be home until late. Ella.

"Finally," said Ed. "Something goes your way."

63

"Lucky me," Gaia responded, crumpling the note and tossing it over her shoulder as she tore through the house toward George's office. The stupid note reeked of Ella's perfume—some one-of-a-kind, New Age concoction she paid an arm and a leg for. Some freaky witchlike person in Soho produced it exclusively for her. It smelled like dead roses on fire and it made Gaia gag.

Gaia headed straight for the disk organizer on George's desk and quickly flipped through the contents. Nothing promising.

Like there was really going to be a disk marked Scaredy Cat in big red letters. Like anything could be that easy. Gaia pulled out a drawer and dumped the contents on the desk. Papers flew everywhere, and pencils, paper clips, and tacks scattered across the smooth wooden surface. A pair of worry beads hit the floor and rolled noisily into the corner.

"George is gonna love that," Ed said, wheeling into the room.

"Somehow neatness isn't my number one priority at the moment," Gaia said, rooting around in the mess. Again, nothing. Gaia groaned in frustration and went for the file cabinet.

Ed hit a key on the computer keyboard, reviving the machine from sleep mode. "Listen," he said, not taking his eyes off the screen, "I've become pretty proficient on this little modern convenience lately. I mean, until Arthur Murray comes up with swing lessons for paraplegics, there aren't a whole hell of a lot of ways for me to kill time."

Gaia didn't want to laugh, but for his sake she forced a smile.

"So I'm gonna hack around for a while and see if I can figure out who sent that e-mail," Ed said as the computer whirred to life.

"That's great," Gaia said absently. Great was an overstatement, but Ed locked up in George's office was a lot safer than Ed out on the street with some psycho kidnapper running around.

Gaia quickly leafed through files with yuppie titles like "IRS 1994" and "Appliance Warranties." She slammed the drawer so hard a framed certificate fell off the wall and clattered to the floor.

"Gaia, you're scaring me," Ed said.

"This is taking too long," she said, bringing her hand to her forehead and scanning the room for possible hiding places.

How many tests had the kidnappers set up? What if she didn't have time to complete them all? That disk could be anywhere. His briefcase. His underwear drawer. A safe-deposit box at some random bank. It could be with George in the country, for all she knew.

She glanced at the captain's clock on the wall. There was no time.

Gaia slammed her fist into the file cabinet. It didn't hurt nearly enough. But it did knock down a picture of Ella.

The picture clattered facedown on the desk. Gaia studied it for a moment. Pay dirt.

The front part of the frame wasn't sitting flush against the backing. It was bulging slightly, and there was a gap between the two parts. Gaia turned it sideways, gave one good shake, and the next thing she knew, she was holding several floppies, one of which was labeled Scaredy Cat. God, what a lucky break.

"I'm outta here," she said, grabbing her bag.

"Wait!"

But she couldn't wait. If she waited, she might have time to think about the fact that someone out there wanted information on her. Her. Not some secret government stash of anthrax or the plans to the Pentagon.

Her.

Gaia Moore.

And Sam might die because of it.

She wasn't waiting around to think about that.

You've got a
nice ass,
for an angel.

not
a
perfect
world

CJ LEANED AGAINST THE OUTER

wall of the arch that led into the park. He liked that arch. It was this big, beautiful thing— a knockoff of some bigger one from . . . where? France, maybe. He'd probably know if he hadn't quit going to school.

Who cared what it was called, anyway? He just liked it. He liked to look at beautiful things.

Like her.

Weird. He hated her. But man, he had some pretty crazy fantasies about her. She pulled him. All that strength and power wrapped up in all that soft sexiness. It gnawed at something in him.

Sometimes he thought about killing her.

Sometimes he just thought about her.

There was one daydream in particular he returned to over and over. In it, he'd be chasing her through the park, and she'd be totally freaked-out scared, and he'd grab her from behind—rough, but not enough to do any real damage. Maybe just a small bruise. A lasting ache.

And he'd spin her around and her hair would get all tangled up in his fingers.

Then she'd look up at him with those intense eyes, those sky-colored eyes, and she'd start begging.

First just begging him not to kill her, but then it would change.

She'd be begging him to kiss her.

And damn, he'd kiss her right. And then . . . then she'd love him. And he'd have the power. All of it.

But CJ knew better. He knew to put hate in front of love every time. That was the way it was with him and his boys. Hate put you in control, but love controlled you. So he let his mind slither back to hating her.

And then, as if he'd conjured her, she was there.

Sun in her hair. And that body. Those lips . . . on his lips.

Shit! Enough of this bullshit. He had to breathe deep. Once. Twice. Steady. He had to remind himself that the one thing he wanted to do more than kiss her was kill her. He *needed* to kill her if he wanted to stay alive himself.

He adjusted the sling on his arm. The other asshole he wanted to kill was whoever the hell had shot at him Saturday night.

The bullet had punctured his biceps, and damn, it had hurt. Still hurt. One of his boys had cleaned it out and given CJ the sling. Can't go to the hospital with a gunshot wound. They report it to the cops.

But CJ was sure it had hurt even more when Tarick had twisted it that morning. That wasn't a pain CJ was going to forget anytime soon. And it was all because of the bitch.

CJ focused on Gaia.

She paused, tilting her chin in his direction, like maybe she could hear him thinking about her. His heart thunked in his chest. His hand clenched into a fist. But she didn't see him. She kept walking.

Why wasn't she in school? This chick was damned unpredictable.

He watched her walk for a moment, liking the way her hips moved, imagining kicking her hard in the stomach. In some remote recess of his mind, he knew this made him a damn sick dude. In the one remaining brain cell that could still tell good from bad, he understood his thinking was damaged.

But he'd turned on the world, and right now she was his closest target.

OKAY, NOW *THIS* WAS A PROBLEM.

There were, on this crisp October morning, eight—count 'em, eight—homeless people by the fountain in Washington Square Park. And five of them were the proud owners of shopping carts.

70

Why hadn't the kidnapper foreseen this possibility?

Maybe he had. Maybe he just needed a little comic relief, and watching Gaia try to find the correct one was it. Will the real undercover operative for Sam's crazed kidnapper please stand up?

Well, at least she was able to eliminate the three cartless ones right off the bat. That left only five derelicts from which to choose.

The note had said a homeless *man*, hadn't it? Yes, it had. So the two bag ladies were out of the running.

Three remaining contestants. Gaia would need a closer look.

She clutched the disk in her pocket. She should have copied it. But Ed was at the computer, and if the files really were about her, there was no way she could let him see the contents. It would have taken too long to get him out of there, get everything copied, and clear off the hard drive.

Too much time away from the task at hand. Saving Sam.

She approached the first homeless man—a guy who appeared disconcertingly young to her. Thirty-eight, thirty-nine years old at the most. In a perfect world, he'd be walking his kid to kindergarten right now, grabbing a cab to his corner office on Wall Street, making the upright decision not to sleep with his secretary.

71

But this was not a perfect world, this was New York. And the guy was rooting through a trash can in search of his breakfast.

"Excuse me . . ."

He kept digging.

Gaia stepped forward. She could smell him now, ripe with his own humanity.

"Excuse me."

The guy whirled. "Get the hell away from me, bitch!"

Well, that was uncalled-for. So much for charity. She frowned at him. "I'm supposed to—"

"This is *my* trash can," he thundered, shaking a half-eaten apple at her. "Mine! So go 'way. Go on! Get out! Mine!" He bit the apple, then placed it inside a filthy old tennis shoe in his shopping cart (presumably to snack on later).

Yummy. Next?

Gaia made her way toward a slumped figure sitting on the ground. A crudely printed cardboard sign propped up in his lap read Desert Storm Veteran.

Well, that didn't take long, Gaia mused grimly. The Gulf War took place—what? Seven, eight years ago? She would have imagined it took at least a whole decade for one's life to fall apart so completely.

Gaia approached him, then bent forward and whispered, "Are you . . . looking for me?"

The guy looked up at her. "Yes," he said.

Thank God. Gaia reached into the pocket of her jacket for the disk. She drew it out, then hesitated. How could she be sure this was the guy?

"Yes," the man said again. "I am looking for you!" He reached out and grabbed Gaia's hand, wrenching the disk from her grasp with his grimy fingers.

Please tell me this is the right guy, she pleaded to herself silently. He grabbed the disk for a reason, right?

"I've been looking for you for a long time," the guy said. "You're the angel of the Lord, ain'tcha?"

And the reason was . . . he was totally insane.

Oh, shit.

"You've come to take me on to the Promised Land. I knew it the minute I saw that hair. That's the hair of an angel, all right. Only the Almighty Himself makes that color hair."

"Yeah. The Almighty and L'Oréal," Gaia snapped. She leaned down toward him. "Give me back the disk."

"No!" he shouted, clutching the floppy. "You've come to save me!"

"No. I've come to save Sam."

"So call me Sam." He was full of logic. "Just bring me on to heaven. Lead me there, angel. Take me."

"Believe me, mister, if *I* brought you to heaven, we'd most likely get jumped on the way." Gaia made a grab for the disk, but the guy was quick. He stuffed it into his grubby shirt.

"Give it to me," she demanded evenly.

"No! Not until you bring me to meet my Maker."

Gaia was starting to see red. Oh, he was going to meet his Maker, all right. He just wasn't going to like the method by which Gaia would send him there.

She pressed her fingers to her temples in frustration, demanding some patience from herself. She didn't want to have to pound the guy. He was already so pathetic as it was. She glanced around the park, hoping for inspiration, and found it.

"Okay," she said at last. "I'll bring you to meet your Maker. But if I do, you have to give me back my disk. Deal?"

The man nodded.

Gaia helped him up and started walking. He followed.

"Hey. You've got a nice ass for an angel."

Gaia almost laughed in disbelief. How could she have come to this? If her situation hadn't been so totally dire, she would have allowed herself a long, cathartic laugh. "The Lord's a real stickler for fitness," she muttered.

Gaia led him straight to one of the homeless people she'd eliminated in the first round. He was taller than her Desert Storm vet, with long, flowing gray hair and mismatched sneakers. "There he is," she said, pointing.

"That guy? In the ripped-up overcoat? That's God?"

Gaia nodded, hating to lie even under these circumstances. Hadn't somebody once said there's a little bit of God in every one of us?

"He don't even have a cart!" Gaia's companion was incredulous.

"Go figure."

The man scowled at her. "Listen, angel, you better not be shittin' me."

"Angels don't shit people." That much had to be true.

"He's drinkin' whiskey."

"Yeah, well . . ." Gaia shrugged. "He's been under a lot of pressure lately."

The homeless man hesitated, then reached into his shirt and withdrew the disk. Gaia snatched it before he could change his mind. She was about to run, but he spoke, and the emotion in his voice pinned her to her place. "Thank you, angel."

Gaia swallowed hard. "No sweat."

She took off for the fountain, putting her conscience on ice.

Her real contact was seated on a bench near it. She was beyond irritated at herself for not noticing the obvious signs before. So much for maintaining her wits.

The guy was straight from central casting, with his dirt-streaked face half hidden beneath a tattered hat, the shabby clothes, the wire shopping cart filled with trash bags and empty cans. What differentiated him from the others was that, unlike "God" with his mismatched sneakers, this guy was wearing a brand-spanking-new pair of expensive lug-soled boots.

Gaia approached him, feeling hollow. This man was one of the kidnappers. This man was in some way responsible for what was happening to Sam. He or someone he knew had inflicted pain on the person she loved.

She could have killed him, but that might get Sam killed.

There was no choice. For now she would do as they said. She wouldn't ask questions.

She reached into her pocket and withdrew the floppy disk, keeping her eyes firmly fixed on the visible lower half of the man's face. There was nothing recognizable. She memorized every detail in case she needed it later.

Cleft in the chin. Small scar on the jaw. Patchy stubble. Dark complexion.

Gaia moved closer, ready for even the slightest movement on his part. But he remained motionless, seemingly unaware of her.

She stepped up to the cart, dropped the disk into it, then turned to walk away.

"Tkduhplstkbg," the guy mumbled.

She stopped. "What?"

"Plastic bag. Take it."

Gaia squinted against the bright sunshine. On the handle of the shopping cart hung a small plastic bag from a Duane Reade drugstore. She reached for it cautiously. It was heavy.

She recognized the weight, and a surge of disgust filled her.

"No," she said.

The man lifted his eyes to her and glared. "Take it."

Gaia felt her free hand clench into a tight fist. One nice solid jab to the bridge of his nose and this guy would wake up in the next zip code.

But she couldn't. She had to think of Sam.

So she took the bag with the gun in it.

STREET SONG
for Her

Sidewalk sweet, she stands alone
In night and streetlamp
While the world sweats summer and
sirens sing
And hate pours down from the city sky
like a wicked rain,
it wets us all
until we're soaked with anger,
and fear enough
to make friends of enemies
and choices that burn like the heat
like the blades, like the bullets
like the broken promise
that I make
Even as I watch her where she stands
two steps from evil
one step from me
But in this world
You walk with danger
or you walk
alone.

He could see
the slim
silhouette
of a
switchblade
in the
punk's back
pocket.

what
the
hell
is
this?

GAIA SAT ON THE EDGE OF THE
fountain and placed the bag between her knees. She stuck one
hand in, letting her fingers
brush the butt of the gun for a
moment before fitting her palm
around it. It felt dead and
weighty.

Partners in Crime

And familiar.

Gaia hated guns. But she knew how to use them.

Her father had taught her marksmanship. While
other daddies were taking their nine-year-old
daughters to toy stores and ice cream parlors, Tom
Moore was bringing Gaia to the firing range, or far
into the woods with a rifle and a rusty tin can for a
target.

And she'd been a natural. From the start, she'd
rarely missed, and by the time her father had finished
training her, she didn't miss at all. Even
now, years away from the experience, she could still
hear the report of her last shot in the forest behind
their home. The deafening explosion of the shotgun,
the distant screaming *ping* of the bullet hitting the
can.

It blended in her memory with another explosion
and another scream.

Instinctively she let go of the gun. She pressed her
fingers against her eyes to make the memory go away.

Think of Sam. Think of him.

She fished around inside the bag, in case there was something else. There was.

A note.

"Of course." Gaia withdrew the note and read it.

Within the next twenty minutes, you will commit a crime. You may choose your victim, but you are to limit your territory to this park.

"My territory?" Gaia snarled.

You are not to go easy on this victim. The enclosed is to assist you in this task. You will also be required to enlist the assistance of a young man named . . .

Gaia felt the presence beside her at the exact second she read the name.

Renny.

She looked up and blinked. Renny was standing there, staring at her. This kidnapper had some major timing going on.

"Did I scare you?" he asked, taking a small step back.

"Not quite," she said.

He swallowed, gulped.

"Please tell me you're done with those skinhead assholes," Gaia said, looking Renny hard in the eyes, her mind leaping from one suspicion to the next.

"I am." Renny looked down at his sneakers. "But it's not that easy," he murmured. "You try living on the streets without anybody to watch your back."

"You don't live on the streets," Gaia said.

He met her gaze, his eyes almost black. "I don't *sleep* on the streets, Gaia. But I live here."

She considered his reasoning. It was true. Renny had nowhere else to go. From the sorry state of his clothes and the random bruises he was always sporting, home seemed less than appealing. So he lived for this park, those chess tables. And in how many places would a thirteen-year-old Hispanic poet be accepted? She sighed, remembering some of the verses he'd recited to her. That edgy, soulful poetry of his made her feel as though he'd scraped the words up off the sidewalk and strung them together into something that sang.

He straightened his shirt with his still small, wiry hands. Sometimes his obvious frailty pained Gaia—especially when he was trying to act tough.

She put her thumb beneath his chin and nudged it upward, so that he was looking her in the eyes. "Who sent you here?"

He shrugged.

"Don't bullshit me, Renny. This is important. Whoever sent me this . . ." She held up the bag, noting the sincerely puzzled expression in his eyes. "You really don't know?"

He shook his head hard—a childlike gesture. It made her heart feel empty.

"Tell me what happened."

He sat down on the rim of the fountain and leaned forward to rest his elbows on his knees. "I got a phone call at home."

"What were you doing at home on a Monday morning?" Gaia asked, trying to sound stern. She could barely pull it off.

"I go home for lunch sometimes," he said, shrugging. She narrowed her eyes at him. "Hey, you're not in school, either."

The boy had a point.

"Go on," Gaia said.

Renny took a deep breath. "Guy says, 'Go to the fountain in the park.' So I go."

"Did he threaten you?"

Renny gave her a lopsided grin. "Not really. 'Cept his voice sounded like he ate nails for breakfast, so I figure it's better if I do what he says."

Gaia was about to ask if the nail-eating voice had mentioned Sam, then thought better of it. The less Renny knew, the less danger he'd be in—relatively speaking, anyway. If the kidnapper knew his name, not to mention his phone number, he was already in this up to his eyeballs, based merely on the fact that he was associated with her.

"We have to pass a test," she said softly.

"A test?" He whistled low. "That doesn't sound good. That's what the guys told me just before they handed me that pistol to point in your face."

Gaia considered inquiring as to what sort of punishment Renny had faced in the wake of failing that test, but decided against it. She didn't think she could handle that at the moment.

"We have to, uh, commit a crime."

His big eyes got bigger. He said nothing.

"Something random. Something sort of rough." She held up the bag. "There's a gun in here."

"Damn."

"Yeah, damn," she said, staring across the park at a couple of fighting pigeons. "We've got to do it here. Now."

Renny mulled this over for a minute or so. "Why?"

"I don't want to tell you. Just trust me. If we don't . . ." She finished with a shrug.

"I'm in," he said.

Gaia nodded. She wasn't sure if that was good news or bad news. She had to think, to figure out the best way to go about this. Maybe there was a way to make the crime look real without actually harming anyone. She did know there was no way in hell she was going to fire that gun. She'd wield it, swing it around at whomever she ultimately chose to hassle, but she would not pull the trigger. The kidnapper would just have to settle for that.

Her eyes roamed the park, landing finally on the chess tables.

And there he was.

She recognized him immediately. The sleazebag. The well-dressed, self-important slimeball she'd played once—and only once, because he kept grabbing her thigh under the chess table. His name was Frank, she believed. He was about forty-seven, forty-eight years old but looked at least sixty with all his wrinkles. Tanning-salon regular, diamond pinky ring, woven loafers, even in October.

Jerk.

Gaia despised him. He'd hustled Zolov once, taking advantage of one of the sweet old guy's less lucid moments. Gaia figured Frank had walked away with Zolov's entire Social Security check that day, then used it to pay Lianne.

Lianne. Another pathetic story. Lianne was fourteen and a prostitute. Gaia was repulsed by her, but somewhere in her heart she felt sorry for her, too. The girl must have had one horrifying life to resort to turning tricks. And Frank was her best customer. Illegal, and disgusting.

The more Gaia thought about it, the more she decided she wouldn't entirely loathe roughing up Frank.

All she could hope was that wherever the kidnapper was watching from was far away enough to make Frank look like an innocent citizen, undeserving of Gaia's attack.

Without a word, she stood and made her way toward the chess tables.

Without a word, Renny got up and followed her.

TOM WIPED HIS GLASSES ON THE

inside of his shirt, then replaced them on the bridge of his nose. He was dressed blandly, in khakis and a denim shirt. Over his reddish blond curls he wore a suede baseball cap in dusty **Downright Nervous**

blue. The brim was tugged low on his brow.

He was invisible, leaning there against the tree. Watching.

Watching as his daughter strode purposefully away from the fountain. There was a scrawny kid with dark hair and golden skin tagging along with her.

But what was in the bag?

He lifted the brim of his cap a fraction of an inch and squinted at the plastic bag she was clutching. His heart took a nosedive when he realized what was in it. The outline of the object bulged unmistakably against the red-and-blue lettering of the pharmacy's logo.

Unmistakable to him, at least. Tom sent up a silent prayer thanking the gods for the indifference of New Yorkers. They would probably not even notice the girl, let alone the bag, let alone its contents.

She leaned down and whispered something to the kid. Pointed to the bushes. The kid nodded and they kept walking.

He kept his eyes trained on her as she crossed to the chess tables. A small, sad smile kicked up the edges of his mouth. Chess. His favorite game. And Gaia's. `The first time she'd beaten him, she'd been only eight.`

Tom stepped away from the tree for a better view, looking utterly preoccupied with nothing in particular, but seeing, feeling, every step she took.

She was approaching a middle-aged guy in an ugly designer suit who was seated on the losing side of a chessboard.

The kid looked a little jumpy. This bothered Tom. Street kids didn't get jumpy without a good reason. And this kid looked downright nervous. Maybe even scared.

Gaia didn't look scared. Gaia never looked scared.

What she looked, lifting the bag and pressing it to the shoulder of the ugly suit, was `determined`. Tom moved away from the tree.

Why was she doing this? Had his leaving poisoned her so badly that she'd taken up petty crime? Or was there more to it?

Of course there was. He knew that was the real burden of the life he'd given her: For Gaia, nothing would ever be exactly as it appeared. Nothing would ever be simple. There would always be layers, dimensions, motives, and questions. And horrible choices.

But why was she choosing this? What had brought her here? Had her confusion and loneliness made her an easy mark for a gang? Had his absence led her to join one? Had she, in search of something resembling a "family," been sucked into their evil world?

No. Not Gaia. The girl was smart and, he knew, good. Good at her core, good in her very essence.

This was something bigger. More dangerous. Something enormous must have been at stake. And clearly her sense of urgency was overshadowing her good judgment.

This was not robbery for robbery's sake.

But it was still robbery.

Tom had to stop her, but how? Could he create some kind of distraction—knock over a homeless guy's cart, perhaps? Draw her attention away from what she was about to do, long enough to bring her back to her senses?

He took two long strides in her direction, then stopped cold.

The punk. The punk he'd shot at the other night. His arm was in a sling, and he was running toward Gaia.

Tom shuddered. He could see the slim silhouette of a switchblade in the punk's back pocket.

He meant business.

Tom should have rid the world of this menace Saturday night, when he'd had the chance. But Tom had let his emotions affect his accuracy. He'd missed his opportunity.

And now his hands were tied. This was a crowded park, in broad daylight. So for the moment, much to Tom's revulsion, CJ would have to be allowed to live.

Tom wondered what Gaia had done to piss CJ off. Maybe the kid had come on to Gaia once, and she'd blown him off. With a creep like CJ, a broken heart could easily become a fatal attraction.

There were only two things Tom knew for sure. One was that for the second time in less than forty-eight hours, he was going to have to put himself between Gaia and death. The other was that he was willing to do it.

FRANK LOOKED UP FROM HIS NEAR-

Your Money or Your Life

defeat on the chessboard and raised one bushy eyebrow at Gaia. "What the hell is this?"

Gaia, her hand on the gun inside the bag, pushed the barrel harder into his shoulder. "*This* is a gun," she told him in a matter-of-fact voice. "Let's go somewhere a little more private."

"Oh, for Christ's sake."

Renny took off for the bushes that lined the east side of the park. "Follow the kid," Gaia said. Frank just stared at her, wide-eyed.

"Let's go," said Gaia, cocking the hammer.

"Jeez! Hey. Jeez!" Frank wriggled up from his seat and slowly followed Renny. His opponent, for obvious reasons, got up and fled. Two people at a table nearby scooted farther away. Gaia didn't have much time.

She shoved Frank in the back so he would hurry up, and he ducked behind the bushes. Gaia could only hope that the all-knowing kidnapper could see them back here and wouldn't miss her command performance.

Renny went to the edge of the bushes to keep watch, and Gaia grabbed Frank by the back of his collar, jerking him around to face her. He swore, swatting at her like a `cartoon boxer,` managing to clip her on the chin. She released him, used the hand that wasn't holding the gun to slap his face, then grabbed a handful of his greasy hair and pulled him to her.

"Didn't your mother ever teach you not to hit girls?" she asked, her nose practically touching his. He smelled like bourbon and chewing tobacco. Gaia had to struggle to keep from hurling.

Renny turned from his post. "Give us your wallet," he demanded in a forceful voice that sounded like it came from someone much bigger and older.

"You're supposed to be keeping watch," Gaia spat out. Renny turned around again.

"Give us your wallet," Gaia echoed.

"Yeah. Yeah, sure." Frank shoved a trembling hand into his breast pocket, withdrew a fat billfold, and slowly offered it to Gaia. For a moment it just sort of hung there between them, off the tips of his fingers.

It was almost too easy. Gaia had a feeling the kidnapper had been hoping for a bit more drama. The asshole had thought this out well. Do this too quickly and easily, and the kidnapper probably wouldn't be satisfied.

Take too long and she'd end up stuck in jail.

And Sam would die.

Gaia swallowed hard and narrowed her eyes at Frank. "Look petrified," she ordered. "Cry."

Sweat poured from his temples down his cheeks. "What, are you kiddin' me?"

"Does it look like I'm kidding?"

He gave a nervous laugh. "No, sweetheart. It don't."

His use of the word *sweetheart* nearly caused her to

slap him again. "Cry," she repeated dryly, casually lifting her knee into his groin.

"Uhhnnfff!" Frank doubled over. "You little . . ."

"I don't see any tears," Gaia hissed, taking hold of his fleshy neck and applying a firm grip to the pressure point.

"Ahhh . . ." Frank's face contorted in pain, then he let out a satisfactory sob.

Gaia didn't let go. "No more sharking Zolov or anybody else," she commanded fiercely from above.

"Yeah," moaned Frank. "Yeah. Okay."

"Gaia?" Renny said tentatively. "I think we have to go."

She let go of Frank's neck and took a small step backward. He straightened up cautiously and handed over his wallet.

"This never happened," she hissed.

To her surprise, Frank gave her a cold smile. "Aye, yo. You think I'm gonna tell anybody I got held up by two little shits like youse? A freakin' Rican who ain't got hair on his chest, and his partner, the prom queen?"

At that Gaia shoved the bagged pistol right under his chin. "You *ever* insult me like that again, and I'll kill you!"

Then she grabbed Renny and ran.

Prom queen, my ass.

CJ WAS HEADING TOWARD HER LIKE

Meanwhile, Back at the Arch . . .

a tiger running down a wounded gazelle.

Gaia had no idea, focused as she was on committing her felony. The guy in the ugly suit was doubled over.

But Tom's eyes were trained on the tiger. The tiger had his hand on the knife.

Tom sprang into action. He hurdled a park bench, dodged someone on skates, and connected with the tiger in a check that would have done Lawrence Taylor more than proud.

CJ hit the pavement.

Tom kept running.

And Gaia was gone.

THE COP SKIDDED UP TO THE CURB

Two Blocks Later . . .

and got out of the car as though he were auditioning for a walk-on in *NYPD Blue.*

"Hey! You two."

Damn.

Gaia could feel the change in Renny as he walked alongside her. He tensed, and his body temperature climbed at a rate that was actually detectable.

Fear, she thought. So those are the symptoms, huh? Her own body was cool, her heartbeat slow and steady. Even when faced with losing Sam, the guy who made the future seem worth living, still she didn't feel fear. She felt anger, determination, frustration. But no fear. If she couldn't feel fear for Sam, couldn't feel the heartrending, temperature-raising emotion that every other human being felt, could she really love him?

She was drifting. She had to focus. She had to make use of the capabilities she had, not mourn the one that was missing.

"Don't panic," she whispered to Renny. "They can smell it." Or so she'd heard.

"Young lady . . ."

Gaia turned and graced the cop with an innocent smile. "Were you talking to me, Officer?"

"Yes."

He was really young. It could have been his first day on the job. He had one of those square chins that was pretty much a prerequisite for joining the police force.

"Is something wrong?" Gaia asked. She made no

attempt to hide the plastic bag. Both the gun and Frank's wallet were still in it.

"I've just come from the park."

She looked suitably blank, patient. Renny, however, was bouncing, shifting his weight, preparing to split. She wished he'd just stand still.

"There was a mugging," the cop continued.

Gaia gasped. Nice touch. "Oh my God."

"Nothing too serious. Guy's wallet was stolen. Couple of eyewitnesses said it was two kids. Boy and a girl." He cleared his throat, an unspoken apology.

He hated this. Gaia could tell. A serious young law enforcement officer like him should have better things to do than hassle a couple of kids. Gaia could actually see him thinking this. She wasn't sure whether to be thankful for or repulsed by his obvious attraction to her. It might just get them out of this.

"Well, we didn't see anything," she said with a dainty shrug. "We weren't even in the park."

The cop nodded. "Why aren't you two in school?" he asked, as if it had just occurred to him.

"We're home-schooled." Gaia fired this out so quickly that even she believed it. "My mom teaches us." She put an arm around Renny's shoulder, pressing down ever so slightly, to get him to quit fidgeting. "This is my stepbrother."

Another nod from Glamour Cop. He hesitated, as if he might ask for their names, but didn't. He turned to get back in the car, then turned back.

"By the way, what's in the bag?"

"The bag? What's in the bag?" Gaia knew she sounded like an idiot, but the question had caught her off guard. She'd thought they were home free.

"What's in the bag?"

Nothing. Just a gun and a stolen wallet.

Then she heard Renny say, "Tampons."

It was all Gaia could do to keep from laughing out loud.

"Tampons," Renny repeated, snatching the bag from Gaia. He held it out to the cop, but his eyes were on Gaia. "I hope I got the right kind," he said in the most disarmingly innocent tone Gaia had ever heard from him—maybe from anyone. "Superabsorbent, you said, right? The deodorant kind?"

He turned his doe eyes back to the cop. "She gets embarrassed, see, so I go into the pharmacy and get 'em for her." He gave the bag a little shake. "Wanna check?"

The cop, looking embarrassed himself, shook his head. "No," he said with a slight croak. "Not necessary."

He ducked back into his car and drove off.

Gaia was gaping at Renny in disbelief. "Where'd you learn to lie like that?"

"I dunno." He threw her a crooked grin. "Home school, maybe?"

Gaia wanted to hug him, but of course she didn't. Instead she pressed her index finger forcefully into his chest. "Lying. Bad. Stealing. Worse. I only did this because somebody's life is in danger, and I had no other choice."

Renny opened his mouth, probably to ask whose life, but Gaia barreled right along.

"From now on, I want you to stay the hell away from that stupid gang. You don't need them to watch your back." She paused, hoping she could pull off the next sentence without sounding like a total Hallmark card. "You've got me, all right? I'll . . . watch your back."

She didn't wait around to see the expression on his face.

Media people who have a
problem with rap music, contro-
versial movies, or premarital sex
like to throw around the term
"family values."

I don't mind saying I don't
even know what the hell they're
talking about.

I mean, okay, I'm not an
idiot. I *know* what they're talking about—two parents with college degrees, kids in clean
sneakers, mass or service or temple (whichever is applicable)
every weekend, meat loaf on
Monday night, freshly cut grass,
and a minivan. Yeah, I know what
they mean.

I just don't know it from
firsthand, personal experience.
Anymore.

Consider my family, for example. My current one, that is.
Absentee (big time) father, well-
meaning concerned guardian,
bitchy wife of guardian, chess
geeks whose last names I don't
even know. That, at present, is

as close as I come to having a family.

Can you imagine this crowd sitting down to meat loaf and mashed potatoes some evening?

And what about Renny? He's been so brain-poisoned he actually thought he could purchase himself a family (of violent, hate-obsessed misfits) with a bullet to my face. What makes me ill is wondering how majorly screwed up the kid's real family must be in order for violent misfits to constitute an upgrade.

But the only family I can seem to think about right now is Sam's.

They've got to be somewhere in the realm of decent, don't they? Or else how could they have produced such a perfect human being as Sam?

All right, so he's not *perfect*—there's that 108-pound wart on his ass (you know her as Heather), and the guy's a master of the mixed signal. But if he's

not Mr. Perfect, he's certainly
Mr. Pretty Damn Close.

The thing that's turning me
inside out now is the fact that,
for all I know, his parents are
sending him a package of homemade
peanut butter cookies baked by
his little sister (for some reason, I imagine he has one), with
a note saying that Uncle Mort
says hi and they'll see him on
parents' weekend. Maybe they are
at this very second dialing his
number, calling him up just to
say hi, and since he's not answering, they'll simply assume
he's at the library, studying for
some huge exam.

Maybe they're eating meat loaf
and mashed potatoes, and complaining that he only calls home
when he needs money.

But the point is, their son's
life is in danger and they have
absolutely no idea.

That's killing me.

I mean, okay, *my* life is in
danger and *my* father has

absolutely no idea. But somehow
that doesn't bother me as much as
Sam's family not knowing.

I guess maybe because I'm figuring if they knew, they'd actually care.

Whereas if my father knew,
he'd have to stop and think to
remember who I was before he
could go back to whatever it is
that he's been doing all these
years and continue to not give a
shit.

It wasn't that she didn't want to pray for Sam. She just wasn't sure how.

she's no angel

IT DIDN'T MAKE SENSE.

Ella had dragged him all the way up to Greenwich, cooing and purring about some private time together, enjoying the romance of the countryside on an autumn morning.

Cozy in Connecticut

So what did she do the moment they arrived?

She dropped herself into a chair at the most Manhattan-like cafe she could find and ordered a double martini. At ten forty-five in the morning.

George ordered coffee for himself, then reached across the table and took her hand.

"This was a great idea," he said, hoping to divert her attention away from her drink. "You and me, the country..."

Ella nodded, glancing around the cafe.

"So what's on the agenda? Picnic on the Sound? A little sailing, perhaps?"

Ella sighed. "Oh, I don't know. Shopping, maybe."

"Shopping?" George raised an eyebrow. "Honey, you can shop anytime in New York. I thought the idea was to come up here and do something that involved grass and trees and quiet country lanes." He'd known when he married her that she wasn't exactly an outdoorswoman, but surely even the most pampered Manhattanite would be enchanted by the old-time New England charm of this town.

Ella wrinkled her nose. "Country lanes, George? Really."

"Sure. Me and you, the breeze, the sunshine. Some cozy little grotto somewhere . . ."

She looked as if she was considering it. "Well . . ." She sighed, lifting her dazzling eyes to his.

A wave of pure attraction washed over him. The truth of it was that he didn't really much care what they did, as long as they were together. He would try to talk her into doing something slightly more romantic than signing credit card receipts, but he wouldn't push. Whatever she wanted was, in all sincerity, fine with him.

So he was smitten with his own wife. So sue him.

The beverages came, and George let go of Ella's hand to allow the waiter to deliver her martini. When he reached for it again, she made a quick grab for the drink.

George sat back in his chair, telling himself she was just thirsty.

"What time is it?" she asked.

He checked his watch. "Close to eleven. Why?"

Ella lifted one shoulder in a shrug. "We'll take the two-thirty train back to Grand Central."

"Back?" George tore open a sugar packet and poured it into his coffee. "We just got here. Listen, there's supposed to be a beautiful little horse farm just a few towns away. I read about it in the travel section of the *Times*." He gave his wife what he hoped was an irresistible grin. "How about we shop this morning, then we can spend the afternoon cantering through some of those sprawling open fields we passed on the way into town?"

"Those weren't open fields. Those were people's yards."

He laughed. She didn't.

"C'mon. What do you say to a little horseback riding?"

She sighed again, causing her ample chest to swell against the satin of her blouse. "I'm not exactly dressed for riding," she said, then gently, seductively caught her lower lip between her teeth. "But if you really want to . . ."

She had him. And they both knew it.

"Shopping it is." George lifted the cup to his lips, tramping down the prickle of disappointment. A moment or two passed before he spoke again. "Have you noticed that Gaia's been acting a little distracted lately?"

"Distracted?" repeated Ella, as if she herself hadn't been paying attention. She looked over her husband's shoulder and out the window.

"I'm worried about her."

"Don't be." Ella traced the rim of her martini glass with one slender finger. "She's a teenager. They're a species unto themselves. What looks peculiar to us is perfectly normal for them."

"Normal, huh? Saturday night she came home sweating, panting, all out of breath—"

"Oh?" Ella pursed her lips in disdain. "Were you waiting up, George?"

"No. Well, not exactly. I just happened to be awake."

This time she did laugh. "And did you go to her? Ask her if all was well? Tuck her in?"

George shook his head. "Maybe I should have."

"She's seventeen!" Ella exclaimed in a patronizing tone. "And as far as the sweating and panting goes, well, that's exactly the kind of reaction a teenage girl would experience after spending hours teasing some poor boy in the backseat of his car!"

"C'mon, Ella," said George, his face flushing at her inference. "I don't think Gaia —"

"Oh, please! She's no angel, George, as much as you'd like to believe she is." Was it his imagination, or was there bitterness behind her voice?

"She's been through a lot," George said, eyeing his wife warily.

Ella rolled her eyes. "So you've said—often."

"I still think I should have talked to her the other night," George said, turning his profile to her and staring out the window. "She's lost so much." George had no idea what it was like to be a teenage girl. He could barely recall what it was like to be a teenage boy. But he knew what it was like to have someone he loved snatched away. He remembered that vividly.

"We're all she has," George said, finally turning back to Ella. "Maybe she's lonely—"

"Fine, George," said Ella, sighing. "Gaia's lonely. Not horny—just lonely. The point is, she probably would have told you to mind your own business, anyway." She paused, then said pointedly, "She's not our child."

At this George felt a familiar jolt—a longing. *Our child.* His, theirs, hers. His eyes searched Ella's questioningly.

"Oh, no." She held up her hand like a traffic cop and laughed again. "Don't even go there, George Niven. We've discussed it." Her other hand went to her `firm, flat tummy`. "This figure is not to be tampered with." She cleared her throat, then added, "Yet."

It was the most unconvincing "yet" he'd ever heard in his life. The waiter returned with more coffee for him and a fresh martini for Ella. Three olives this time, instead of two. Clearly he hadn't heard her remark about flat-tummy maintenance. Or maybe he just liked her.

They sipped their drinks without further conversation until the silence was interrupted by the bleating of her cell phone.

She flipped it open. "Yes?"

George watched her near-expressionless face as she listened. After almost two full minutes, she said, "Fine." Then she hung up.

"Who was that?"

"No one important," she said, plucking a plump olive from the toothpick in her glass.

George smiled teasingly. "No one important who?"

She looked at him. "If you must know, it was Toshi. My feng shui appointment has been canceled for tonight."

"Oh." George lowered his gaze to the table.

Toshi, huh? He wanted to believe her, but at the same time he had a very strong hunch that the call had had nothing to do with feng shui.

If Ella had any hunches regarding his hunch, she didn't show it.

She went right on drinking her martini.

And, he imagined, waiting impatiently for five fifteen.

GAIA STUFFED FRANK'S TACKY EEL-

Another West Side Story

skin wallet into the pocket of her faded sweatshirt jacket and shoved the gun into the bottom of the messenger bag. She took a deep breath and let it out slowly.

So she'd just conducted her first mugging.

It was not a good feeling. Gaia kicked at a crumpled-up McDonald's bag as she walked along the cracked sidewalk. She didn't like playing the part of a lowlife, even if the joke was on Frank.

But it was all about saving Sam. Gaia booted the bag into the sewer. The end justifying the means, and all that. Very Machiavellian.

So where was the next test? Once again she was left with downtime while Sam was sitting alone somewhere, suffering. Gaia felt her heart squeeze painfully as she remembered Sam's swollen face. She pressed her eyes closed, as if she could block out the image. Could she find fear—even a tiny shred of it—if she kept that image in her mind's eye?

This was torture. Maybe that was the point.

Trying to distract herself, she pulled out Frank's wallet again and flipped it open. There was a stack of bills inside, and Gaia pulled them out, counting quickly so that no street thugs would spot her and get any ideas. Three hundred and fifty bucks. Not bad. What the hell was she going to do with it?

When she looked up, Gaia noticed she had stopped right in front of St. Joseph's Church. That couldn't be a coincidence. She stuffed the money and wallet back into her pocket and ducked inside the church.

The place was perfectly quiet. There was no one in sight, and the sunlight streaming through the stained-glass windows revealed dancing particles of dust. Gaia

110

found herself thinking how weird it was that all churches always smelled the same. Not that she'd been to very many—just enough to know they all had that same damp, smoky smell.

As Gaia wandered down the carpeted center aisle, she wondered how many times "Amen" and "Please, God" had been whispered in there. She got the feeling that if she listened carefully enough, she might hear the echoes.

It occurred to Gaia that if the kidnappers were still watching her closely, a deserted church would be the perfect place for them to attack. Gaia wished they would. It would be nice to get this over with. Kick some ass, find out where Sam was, get him, and then go the hell home. She was tired of this already.

There was an alcove toward the front of the church with a brass stand in it. On the stand were rows upon rows of stubby white candles in little glass holders, some red, some blue. Gaia smirked. Religious *and* patriotic.

Gaia knew what the candles were for. One night when she'd first moved in with George and Ella, she'd stayed up late, unable to sleep, and watched a rerun of *West Side Story* on TV. Natalie Wood, as Maria, had a little setup like this one with the candles and everything, right in her apartment. She was lighting candles and saying prayers.

Gaia went to the alcove and found what she was looking for—a worn wooden box with Donations painted painstakingly across the front. Gaia was pretty sure she was supposed to make a contribution before lighting a prayer candle. Someone had to pay for all that wax. Fine with her. She stuffed Frank's money into the box. She figured that $350 bought her the right to start a bonfire. But she wasn't exactly good with prayers. She wasn't even entirely sure of what religion she was supposed to practice. Her family was one big melting pot.

Next to the candles there were a bunch of skinny sticks, like extralong toothpicks, sticking out of a little pot of sand. The ends on some of them were charred.

Okay, I get it, she thought. You use a lit candle to light the stick, then use the stick to light your own candle.

She picked up one of the long, fragile sticks. Should she or shouldn't she?

Part of her felt like a serious hypocrite. But a bigger part of her felt she needed help from wherever she could get it.

She breathed in the church smell and thought about Sam. He didn't deserve this. No one deserved this. It was all her fault.

Then she poked the stick into the flame of one of the burning candles. What prayer went with that one?

112

she wondered. Had it been bigger than hers? Had it been answered?

She held the stick over an unlit candle and for a moment just watched the flame dance. Then, in spite of her $350 donation, she slammed the burning end of the stick into the sand and got out of there.

It wasn't that she didn't want to pray for Sam. She just wasn't sure how.

GAIA RAN ALL THE WAY HOME,

A New Video Release

hoping at every turn that she'd be stopped by another crazed fake homeless man with a note. No such luck.

She was ready to scream with frustration when she rounded the corner onto Perry Street and caught a glimpse of George and Ella's front stoop. There was a package. Time for a sprint. It seemed like forever before the box was in her hands, but the card had her name on it. And since she didn't belong to the Jam of the Month club or anything, she was pretty sure it was from her friendly neighborhood kidnapper.

She let herself inside (still no Ella, thank God) and took the stairs to her room in threes. After slamming her bedroom door and locking it behind her, Gaia pulled the Duane Reade bag out of her messenger bag and shoved it, gun and all, under her bed.

Then she tossed her messenger bag on her mattress, sat down at her desk, and opened the box. Wonderful. There was another video inside. And, of course, another note. This was getting old.

"Wonder what this movie's rated," Gaia muttered.

Gaia gathered up her stuff again and jogged back downstairs to the living room. She shoved the tape into the VCR and hit play.

Gaia's eyes narrowed as an image of her own face—so close up she could count her own pores—flickered onto the screen. The camera panned back to reveal her and Renny sitting by the fountain. She felt the blood start to rush through her veins, bringing an angry flush to her face.

Whoever had filmed this had been so close. How could she have missed him? How stupid was she?

Lowering herself onto the plush couch, Gaia watched as she and Renny crossed the park. It was like some kind of morbid home movie.

Isn't Gaia adorable, sticking that pistol into Frankie's shoulder, stealing his wallet, kneeing him in the groin?

She hit the off button, pulled the cassette out of

the slot, and proceeded to `tear its celluloid guts out`. After that, she did the same to the tape of Sam and Heather, which was still in her messenger bag. Then she unfolded the note that had come with the new tape, and read it.

Then she read it again.

Suddenly Gaia really wished she'd lit that candle.

You are doing surprisingly well. Your next test may not be so easy. Your friend in the wheelchair is to be your next victim. No violence is necessary. What we want is for you to HUMILIATE him. In public.

This humiliation, Gaia, is to be thorough. Uncompromised. You will emotionally destroy this young man.

And if you are wondering why . . . don't. You need no reason other than that I require you to do it.

IF YOU FAIL, SAM MOON WILL DIE.

TOP TEN WAYS TO EMBARRASS A
KID IN A WHEELCHAIR

10. Buy him a pogo stick.

9. Ask him how often he has to
   have his tires rotated.

8. Tell him you'd like to borrow
   his chair to guarantee yourself a good seat for *Cats*.

7. Attach a bumper sticker that
   reads Warning: I Break for
   Orthopedic Surgeons.

6. Totally fawn over him, and tell
   him how sorry you feel for him.

5. Totally ignore him and pretend
   he doesn't exist, like everybody else does.

4. One good shove down the handicap ramp.

3. Invite him to visit the top of
   the Statue of Liberty.

2. Ask him, "You must really feel
   like a loser during the
   national anthem, huh?"

1. Say something—anything—of a
   sexual nature, implying that
   it's not just his legs that
   are permanently limp.

   I can't believe I am even capable of coming up with these
things. It makes me sick. I make
me sick.
   How am I going to do this?
   Why are they making me do
this?

And then the
world went
surreal on
him. Because
Gaia was not
Gaia.

like

lox?

ED ROLLED HIS CHAIR OUT OF HIS

eighth-period class and into the crowded hallway. He'd made it back to school in time for the chem exam, which, unfortunately, had been even more difficult than he'd expected. With all of the in-

Seduction 101

sanity running through his head, he'd be lucky to pull a C plus. Of course, in light of what was happening to Gaia and Heather, not to mention Sam, a C plus didn't sound too terrible.

The good news was that the morning's searching had yielded major information.

It was the noise. A noise he knew. Or used to know.

He'd sat there in George's study for over an hour, viewing the video e-mail of Sam over and over. Just as he was about to pack it in Ed had noticed a noise in the background. It had been there all along. He couldn't imagine how he'd missed it, unless his eyesight was shutting down from all the staring and his ears were taking over. But as soon as he detected it, he recognized it.

Wrrrzzzzzzzz. Clank. Wrrzz.

It was a noise he himself had made for years. A noise he'd never make again.

And he knew there was only one place in New York

City where that noise could occur precisely the way it sounded in the background of the e-mail.

Wrrrzzzzzzzz. Clank. Wrrrzzzzzzzzz . . .

"Ed, man! Totally nice ride. You got serious air on that one, dude. Is this the most bodacious ramp in the city or what? Let's see it again. Go for it!"

Wrrzz. Clank.

Yeah, Ed knew the noise.

He pushed aside the memory and gritted his teeth at the way the crowd in the hallway parted for him.

At least it meant getting to a private place to use his phone faster, although the chances of Gaia being home were slim to none. If the girl was going to insist on being the reluctant superhero, the least she could do was invest in a cell phone.

Ed rounded a corner, and there she was. Right in the middle of the jostling, locker-slamming crowd. No dialing necessary.

His smile was automatic. (Not to mention the reaction from a more southern portion of his anatomy.) He waved, relishing the way he could see her eyes burning like blue flames, even from this distance.

"Good news," he began, but the rest of his greeting caught in his windpipe. She was striding—no, more like stomping—in his direction. Panic engulfed him. What had happened? Had Sam been hurt? Worse thought: Had she?

She stopped about a foot in front of him.

And then the world went surreal on him. Because Gaia was not Gaia. Everything about her said hatred—the rigidity of her shoulders, the tightness of her face.

"Hey," she barked. Yes, barked. It was a horrible sound, one he couldn't reconcile with the sexy, slightly raspy voice he loved hearing over the phone every night.

He stared at her, peripherally aware that people were slowing down, glancing their way. They were curious, but not committed just yet. School was over, after all. There were soccer balls to dribble, lattes to drink, boyfriends to kiss.

"Hey . . . freak."

Okay, now she had their attention. Ed opened his mouth to say something but hadn't the slightest idea what that something should be. His eyes slid over her carefully. Was she bruised? No. Drugged? Didn't seem to be. Brainwashed? Not likely.

What was going on?

She said it again. "Hey, freak."

Ed wished he could make himself meet her gaze. "Something I can do for you?"

A strangled sound came out of her mouth. It took him a second to understand it was supposed to be laughter.

"I doubt it," she said. "In fact . . ."

He noted that her fists were clenching and unclenching.

"In fact, I doubt there's anything you can do for any girl in this school."

This earned her an "ooh" from the onlookers, and she let her eyes fall purposely to his midsection. Ed felt scalded by the heat of them. His heart hit the badly scuffed floor. She couldn't possibly have just said that.

"So am I right, Ed?" she prodded. "I mean, we all know you're paralyzed from the waist down, but I'm curious. Does *anything* still work?"

Horror filled him as she came closer. She placed one hand on each of his chair's armrests and smiled wickedly. "Aren't you going to tell me?" she asked in a seductive tone he might have liked under different circumstances. "Or am I going to have to find out for myself?"

This piece of cruelty was rewarded with another "ooh."

Ed's brain vaguely registered that not one single son of a bitch in the crowd was making an attempt to defend him. But he didn't actually care about them. He cared about her. Too much.

And she was destroying him. Why?

His voice decided to work without his permission, and he heard himself say, a bit pathetically, "You're enjoying this, aren't you?"

"Yes," she assured him, still smiling. "I like torturing you. About as much as I like lox."

Lox.

"Like lox?"

"Hate them."

His heart surged. This wasn't real. She was faking. He pulled his eyes to hers at last. And she answered him. It wasn't a word, or an action, or even an expression. It was something deeply unnameable in her eyes.

This was her next test. For some inexplicable purpose, the kidnapper wanted her to hurt him. So be it. He'd play along.

Unfortunately, one of the male spectators chose that moment to get righteous. He stepped forward and said, "Leave him alone."

Ed wouldn't have believed it, but in that second he could actually *see* her resolve falter. One word from a pseudo-Samaritan and she was ready to crumble—her belief in this heinous charade was that fragile.

He felt her begin to back away, and he knew he couldn't let her. Too much was riding on it. Sam's life. More important, possibly her safety.

So Ed lifted his chin. "You wanna know if it still works?"

She blinked, clearly taken aback by this reaction. He kept his eyes glued to hers. *Don't quit, Gaia. I understand. Don't back down.*

One corner of her mouth twitched.

"Yeah," she said, her reluctance audible only to him. "I wanna know if you're still man enough to do it."

"Well, that depends." Ed reached forward, catching

her around the waist and pulling her onto his lap. "Are you woman enough to make me want it?"

The crowd's "oohs" rose to a crescendo now, and the applause that erupted froze her.

"C'mon, Gaia," he urged, knowing she had to bring this full circle to satisfy the kidnappers. "Make me."

"Fine, I will."

"Fine. So do it."

"Fine."

She leaned toward him—somehow the movement was at once gentle and violent—until her mouth was dangerously close to his.

"Principal!"

Suddenly the crowd scattered like rats, leaving Ed unkissed and alone in the hall with Gaia, who was sitting sidesaddle across his thighs. Now that they were alone, she made a move to exit his lap, but didn't get far.

"I think maybe you should get off me now," Ed suggested calmly.

"I'm trying!" Gaia snapped in reply. The zipper on the outer pocket of her cargo pants was caught on his sweater, and she was struggling to disengage herself. "I promise you this is not what I want to be doing right now."

He chuckled. "Yeah, you just keep telling yourself that, Gaia."

Ed could hear the principal's footsteps approaching the corner of the deserted hallway. Gaia let out a little yelp of frustration.

"Scared?" he baited.

"Annoyed," she said. She let go of the zipper and met his eyes for a second. "And very sorry," she added under her breath. "Not scared."

She tried jerking her leg sideways, and wound up straddling him.

"We might want to wait until *after* the principal's come and gone," he said.

The sound of the principal's whistling floated toward them. "I really think you should get off me, Gaia."

"Hey, nobody told you to put me on your lap," Gaia said calmly. She stopped struggling. Was she just going to let them get caught like this?

"Well, nobody told you to seduce me in the middle of the hall!" Ed said, trying to push her off him. She really was stuck.

"As a matter of fact," she hissed, lowering her face to his until their noses were touching, "you're wrong. Somebody did."

Then came the principal's booming voice. "Mr. Fargo! What is the meaning of this?"

Suddenly his head contained more than its allotted share of blood. Ed toyed with the idea of making a joke—something about extra credit for biology class—but decided against it.

"Miss Moore, kindly remove yourself from Mr. Fargo's . . . er . . . lap."

126

"If you get me a scissors, that just might be possible," Gaia said.

Sarcasm. Ed closed his eyes. Good strategy, Gaia.

Principal Reegan gave them his patented I've-seen-it-all-already-so-don't-even-bother stare. "I'll inform Ms. Strahan that she can expect you both in the detention hall," he said. He turned on his heel and walked off.

"Good one, Gaia," Ed said with a sigh.

Gaia stared after Reegan. "Do you think that means he's not going to get me a scissors?"

Heather
Gannis was
nothing if
not brave. **armor**
She proved
that every
day, didn't
she?

BY THE TIME GAIA AND ED ARRIVED

at the detention hall, Ed had a hole in his sweater, and Gaia had a chunk of blue cotton sticking out of a zipper on her

Detention

thigh. Apparently it was a slow day for the school rebels. The place was practically deserted. Of course, Robbie Canetti was there because Robbie Canetti was always there.

He looked up from his notebook when Ed and Gaia entered. "Hi," he said.

Ed said hi. Gaia didn't bother. Ms. Strahan glanced at them, then went back to correcting papers.

Ed wheeled himself to the back corner of the room, and Gaia flung herself into a chair, letting it scrape against the floor loudly. Her leg immediately started to bounce up and down. There was no way she was staying trapped in this box for the next hour.

She leaned forward, pressing her elbows into her knees to stop her legs from spasming. "I have two things to say," she said, looking Ed in the eye. "One, I didn't want to do what I did out there. I really am sorry."

"I know," Ed answered seriously. "What's the second thing?"

"The second thing is that I'm outta here." She stood up and started past him, but Ed grabbed her wrist.

"I know where Sam is," he said.

Gaia froze. Relief, confusion, and disbelief rushed through her, clouding her vision. She fell back into her chair. "What?"

Ed shot his eyes toward Ms. Strahan, then Robbie. When he was sure neither was listening, he whispered, "I know where they're holding him."

It was all Gaia could do to keep from screaming. She wasn't sure if she should hug him or kill him. "Why didn't you tell me this before?"

Ed actually blushed. "You didn't exactly give me a chance back there, G."

"Where is he?" Gaia demanded, feeling a strong urge to hold him upside down and shake the words right out of him.

Clearing his throat, Ed pushed his hands against his armrests and shifted in his chair. The gesture took forever. "He's in Tribeca. I actually pinpointed the street." Ed's expression was all self-satisfaction. Gaia was leaning away from hug and toward kill, but she kept her cool.

"How did you figure it out?" she asked in a whisper.

Ed leaned forward. "I just kept replaying the e-mail," he said excitedly. "By, like, the nine billionth time, I started to register this sound in the background. Over and over, this sound. And I recognized it. It's skateboarders."

"Skateboarders?" Gaia hissed, her shoulders so

131

tense they were practically touching her ears. "Ed, skateboarders can be anywhere."

"No." Ed shook his head. "This noise was distinct. It was boards on a ramp—an extreme ramp, with a major slope. And I know for a fact there's only one ramp like that in this whole city. I practically used to live there."

His eyes were glassy, and she could tell he really missed this home away from home.

Gaia would have loved to let him slip into a fit of nostalgia, but this wasn't the place, and it definitely wasn't the time.

"Ed."

He rubbed his hand over his face. "Anyway, I heard that sound in the background, and I realized that Sam's got to be somewhere in the vicinity of that ramp. He's gotta be in one of those buildings."

Gaia stood up. "So let's go."

"Go? Gaia, we can't go."

"Ms. Moore?" Ms. Strahan warned. Gaia didn't care.

"Why not?" she asked Ed. "Because we've got detention?" She looked around the room, holding her palms out like a balance, pretending to weigh the options. "Let's see. Sam's life, detention. Detention, Sam's life." She frowned at him. "I'm going."

She started for the door, but Ed reached out and grabbed her wrist.

"Ms. Moore," came another warning.

Ed actually yanked on her arm, tugging her backward and forcing her into her seat. She looked at him for a moment, stunned.

"No, Gaia. Not because we have detention," Ed hissed, his eyes flashing. "Think about it. You know the kidnapper's watching every move you make. You're at his mercy. If he figures out you're planning a search-and-rescue operation, he might just kill Sam on the spot."

"Yeah, but . . ."

"I know you want to swoop in there and rescue Sam," Ed said. "But you have to make sure you're thinking straight."

Gaia sighed in exasperation.

"Even if you could get to Sam without having the lunatic kidnapper catch on, how are you going to get him out?" Ed asked. "The guy's a mess, Gaia. He's weak, remember?"

Gaia felt as if her head were being pumped full of molten lava. She pressed the heels of her hands to her temples and squeezed her eyes shut.

"So why'd you even bother to tell me where he was?"

"Because I knew you'd want to know," Ed whispered, shaking his head. "Look, Gaia, I'm aware you're not going to let me tell you what to do. I'm just telling you what I think."

She gave the desktop a good slap. Everyone in the room jumped but her.

"Okay, I've had about enough of this, Ms. Moore," Ms. Strahan said in what Gaia assumed was supposed to be a threatening tone.

"You got something against hearing what I think?" Ed whispered with a grin.

"I've got something against being trapped in a classroom when I should be out doing something constructive," Gaia answered, standing again. "And don't ask me what, because I don't know, but I have to get the hell out of here!"

"Gaia—"

"That's it, Ms. Moore."

But Gaia barely registered the warnings. She was already halfway down the hall.

HEATHER DID NOT LEAVE SCHOOL

immediately following first period.

That would have been the cowardly thing to do, and Heather Gannis was nothing if not brave. She proved that every day, didn't she? Swimming with the sharks (as she secretly referred to her friends) with only her Almay pressed powder for armor.

So she'd stayed at school and toughed it out. She'd handled all those pitiful looks they threw at her, the feigned sympathy, the understanding hand pats. It was so patronizing. Didn't they know she knew? Didn't they realize she could see through them like a Victoria's Secret peignoir? They loved that she'd been humiliated. They got off on it.

As soon as the final bell sounded, Heather escaped them all.

And now she was on her way to Sam's dorm.

She walked—all right, so it was more like a subdued run—toward Washington Square Park, taking the opportunity to think. There hadn't been a clear thought in her head all day. The rigors of maintaining a stiff upper lip, seeming to be grateful, and acting suitably flustered had taken all her energy. She had also been forced to accept hug after hug after hug from all those guys who said they only wanted to comfort her, but really just saw her grief as perhaps their only chance to press their deprived bodies against her legendary one.

Pigs. Idiot pigs. But, she reminded herself for the twelve zillionth time, she'd invited popularity, worked for it, and now had to live with the consequences. What was that old saying? Live by the sword, die by the sword. Yep. Same went for popularity.

By the time she reached Fifth Avenue, Heather was convinced she had it all figured out. Sam had secretly filmed them, and then somehow had carelessly allowed the tape to fall into the wrong hands. The hands of Gaia Moore.

Or maybe it hadn't been carelessness on Sam's part. Maybe it had been part of a horrific conspiracy. Maybe—for some reason she could not even begin to imagine—Sam had taped their encounter, then *given* the tape to Gaia to screen in econ.

That would explain why Gaia had shown up that night. That would explain why Sam had run after her. They were working together to ruin Heather's life.

Why? She had no idea. But she was definitely going to find out.

Heather reached Sam's dorm, stomped into the lobby, and was met by the security guard.

Right. She'd forgotten about that little roadblock.

"Can I help you?" he asked.

Heather smiled automatically. The guy was beefy, maybe in his late twenties. She could tell this rent-a-cop position was probably a dream job for him—second only to his lifelong fantasy of changing his name to the Raunchy Raider and becoming the darling of the professional wrestling circuit.

"Hi," she said. "I'm just going up to visit my boyfriend."

He drew himself up tall. He was obviously very important. "I'll need to see your university ID."

Lucky for Heather she could blush on command. "You think I'm in college?"

The guy smiled. "Aren't you?"

Heather shook her head coyly. "I'm only in high school. But he's expecting me...."

"Sorry, sweetheart."

Don't *sweetheart* me, you pumped-up piece of shit. "Please?" She smiled and gave him her best little head tilt. "Look. He gave me a key."

She produced Sam's dorm key from the back pocket of her jeans. Okay, so he hadn't actually given it to her. She'd stolen his spare copy in a fit of immaturity back when they'd first started getting serious. It had made her feel special to have it—her boyfriend's college dorm room key. And her friends had thought she was beyond lucky. Now her petty crime was about to come in handy.

"Look, honey," meat-for-brains said, "I don't care if the guy gave you his key. I don't care if he gave you his tuition money, all right? The bottom line is, you're not getting in here without a valid New York University ID."

Heather ground her teeth. "Can't you call him? He'll come down and get me."

137

The guard's eyes slid over her body like maple syrup on a stack of pancakes. "I'm sure he will." He picked up the phone. "What's his number?"

She gave it to him. He dialed.

"Busy."

"What?"

"The line's busy."

This threw her. Sam's line was never busy. A black hole formed in her stomach. Maybe he had it off the hook.

Maybe he was so desperate to avoid her that he'd instructed this steroid-shooting side of beef who used too much hair gel not to let anyone fitting her description anywhere near the elevator.

Disgusted, Heather turned on her heel and stalked out onto the cold street.

"SO NOW WHAT?"

Gaia shrugged. "I don't know." Ed had followed her out of detention, and now she was following Ed down the handicap ramp. A late afternoon chill crept into the neck of her sweatshirt, causing goose bumps to break out on her skin. "Maybe they're gonna have me

The Works

scale the Empire State Building in my underwear."

"I'd like to see that," Ed joked.

"Seriously. There's got to be another test, doesn't there?" Her eyes made a wide sweep of the area. "But what? When?"

Bring it on, she willed silently. Come on! It was like waiting to throw a punch, or waiting to have one thrown at you. Come and get me. Come and get me.

When they reached the sidewalk, Ed angled his chair to allow a food vendor to pass by with his stout, steaming cart.

"Y'know what's weird?" Ed asked. "The last tests came at you like rapid fire, so where the hell are they?"

"Maybe the guy's taking a coffee break," Gaia dead-panned. "Maybe he's a union kidnapper."

Ed's face became tentatively hopeful. "Or maybe you're done."

"Done?"

"Yeah. Maybe they're satisfied," Ed said with a shrug. "Maybe the next message is gonna be, 'You may reclaim your diabetic boyfriend at your earliest convenience.'"

"Don't call him my boyfriend," Gaia said.

"Yes, ma'am."

Absently Gaia watched the hot dog vendor drag his moving eatery to a halt. When he banged open a metal compartment, the uniquely New York aroma of frankfurters and sauerkraut reached her. Her stomach growled fiercely, and she realized she hadn't eaten a thing since the three bites of bagel she'd had at breakfast.

"Hungry?" she asked Ed.

"Sure."

Gaia approached the vendor. "Two. With the works."

"The works," the guy mumbled, grabbing two empty rolls and placing the hot dogs into them.

Gaia watched as he clumsily spooned relish and onions onto them. More of the condiments wound up in his hand than on the dogs. Well, maybe if the jerk took off those dark glasses and pulled his hat up from over his eyes, he'd be able to see what he was doing and—

"Sam says hi."

Gaia's eyes snapped up to the vendor's face.

He thrust the hot dogs into her hand. Her first instinct was to shove them both up his nose. The guy pulled off his sunglasses and gave her the hands-down wickedest stare she'd ever seen. Anyone else would have passed out from the ferocity of it, but Gaia met his gaze. And, since she *had* been born with whichever chemical component created hunger, took a sloppy bite of the hot dog.

The sham vendor was obviously thrown by her calm.

"Sam says hi," he repeated, less icily. He reached into his apron, removed a piece of paper, and held it out to her.

She glanced over her shoulder at Ed. "He's out of hot pretzels," she said sarcastically. "Will you settle for a ransom note?"

Ed was wide-eyed. "God. Are they everywhere?"

Gaia took the note, and seconds later the phony hot dog guy was gone.

She handed Ed his hot dog, which he just sort of stared at, as if he'd never seen one before. Gaia decided to read to herself and give Ed a couple of seconds to recover.

> Clearly you did not understand what I meant by HUMILIATION, as you and your friend in the wheelchair are still on speaking terms. Momentary embarrassment in the school corridor was not what I had in mind, Gaia. I wanted him out of your life, but I see this has not happened. For this reason, you will perform another test, the most difficult thus far. Before I return Sam to you this evening, you will be required to . . .

Gaia looked up from the note and blinked at Ed. "What? What does it say?"

"Uh . . . it says I'm doing really well. Listen." She skipped to the final paragraph, cleared her throat, and read aloud. "'Sam will be turned over to you this evening at 10 P.M. in Washington Square Park. Choose

141

any pathway. I will find you. FYI—Mr. Moon's health is failing, so I suggest you be prompt.'"

"Is that all it says?"

She swallowed hard and nodded. No reason to tell him how personal the kidnapper was getting with his notes. No reason to tell him—

"Man. He must be pretty sick." Ed was looking pale.

"It says I have to get his insulin from his dorm room," Gaia murmured. His room. Like she wanted to revisit that memory anytime in the next century.

Ed nodded. "Hope we can get into his room."

"You'd be surprised how easy it can be," said Gaia, frowning.

"That's if it's unlocked," Ed reminded her.

"True." Her eyes dropped unwillingly to the note, that one sentence . . .

Ed lowered an eyebrow at her. "You okay?"

Gaia nodded.

"Well, you might not be after I make this next suggestion." He took a deep breath. "I think we're going to need Heather."

"Need Heather? For *what?*" Gaia asked. "Fashion advice on what to wear to a hostage rescue?"

Ed tossed his untouched hot dog into a nearby trash container. "For the key to Sam's room. I'm guessing she's the only person we know who might have one."

Gaia felt her muscles tighten with anger. He was

probably right. And the last thing she needed was to get nabbed for breaking and entering. She wouldn't be helping anyone from jail. Having Sam's room key was crucial.

She ate the rest of her hot dog in two angry bites, then glared at him. "Heather it is," she said with her mouth full.

Ed watched her swallow with a look of near disgust. He'd never looked at her like that. But then, she figured she was doing a pretty good impression of a boa constrictor.

"Are you sure you're all right?"

"I'm fine," she lied, glancing at the note again—at another part she hadn't read out loud. At the part that said, *"Kill CJ."*

Loki hovered there another moment, allowing his icy laughter to rain down on Sam.

a little buzz

"HI."

CJ turned. The woman was talking to him. The beautiful woman in the tight blouse.

He did his little shoulder thing—loosened himself up. Slouched. "Wus'up?"

She smiled. "I've seen you around, you know."

It's a Date

"Yeah? Well, I ain't seen you." At least not in a while. She used to walk through the park every day, but not lately. It was hard to forget a body like that. She smelled great. Expensive. And her legs went on till Tuesday.

"What's your name?"

"CJ."

"Nice to meet you, CJ."

She reached for his hand and shook it. Talk about silky skin.

"Listen, CJ, I don't usually do this sort of thing, but I was hoping you might like to go out with me. Tonight." The way she fixed her eyes on him made things inside his body stir. Things he didn't even know were there.

Brain cramp! This gorgeous, uptown piece of ass was asking him out? Sure as hell sounded like it. For a moment there was no Gaia.

"Uh ... uh ..." Damn, he had to get it together.

"Well?"

Shit, this one was friendly. She was pressing her palms against his chest now.

"You don't have plans, do you?" she asked in a husky voice.

Well, as a matter of fact, he did. He was going to kill Gaia tonight. But then again, maybe he could do both.

The woman was giving him this very seductive little pout. "Please say you'll meet me tonight. There's a band playing in the park. And I love to dance. . . ." She pushed her hips against his and swayed. "Do you like to dance?"

CJ nodded. He liked her perfume. It was giving him a little buzz. Smelled like burning flowers or something.

"Good. So it's a date, then?" She tossed her hair back and looked up at him through her thick lashes. "We'll meet tonight, in the park."

"Yeah. Yeah." He backed up from her slightly, trying to play off the fact that every inch of his body wanted to pounce on her right now. No use letting the lady know she had the power. "That'd be cool. In the park."

"I'll meet you at the fountain," she said, making even the word *fountain* sound dirty. "Say . . . nine-thirty?"

"Yeah. sounds good."

"Till then . . ."

"Yeah."

She turned to walk away, and he remembered that walk. He and Marco used to study it. When she'd gone half a block, he called out to her. "Yo, girl. What's your name?"

She didn't bother to answer.

TO: L
FROM: E
RE: CJ

Arrived in NYC early and met with pawn. He'll
meet me in the park at nine-thirty.

If all goes as well as this, he should be dead
before the band plays its first set.

LOKI CRUMPLED THE FAXED MEMO AND
dropped it into the wastebasket.

"Dead before the first set?"
He smiled sardonically. "That's
what I like to hear." His laughter
was an ugly, guttural rumble in
his throat. He turned to Sam.

Poor, poor Sam.

Dying, really, right before
his eyes. A shame.

What the Kidnapper Said

Loki walked toward his
hostage, who was huddled in a shivering heap on the
floor, and studied him in silence for a long moment.

Well, he could understand what his niece saw in

the boy. He was certainly nice-looking. At least, he had been, before that unfortunate incident in which his face collided with that fist. Tsk, tsk. And, of course, his medical condition was really `taking its toll`.

"Sam?" Again, louder. "Sam!"

The boy lifted his head slightly and let out a ragged breath.

"Sam Moon," said Loki thoughtfully, rolling the name over his taste buds as though it were a new wine he was tasting. "Tell me about yourself, Sam."

The only reply was `the shuddering of Sam's body`.

"Cat got your tongue, boy?" Loki sneered. "Ah, yes. Just as well. I generally prefer to do the talking in situations such as these. I do so enjoy being in control."

He was circling Sam now, like `the predator he was`. "You're aware, I imagine, that my niece is quite taken with you?" His eyes turned hard as he stared at the prone form before him.

Loki stopped walking, folded his arms across his chest, and glared down at Sam. "That, as you must understand, is not an easy thing for an uncle to accept. I wonder, would you be worthy of her? Because an uncle has certain expectations for his only niece, Sam. He wants the best for her, wants only her happiness. I know it may not seem that way, given current circumstances, but it is true. Gaia, you might say, `has become my whole world`."

Loki lifted his foot and used the toe of one of his three-hundred-dollar wing tips to give Sam's languid body a hard nudge. "So tell me, Sam Moon," he demanded. "Are you the boy who will make Gaia's dreams come true?"

Loki hovered there another moment, allowing his icy laughter to rain down on Sam.

Then in a voice so slick and close to silence that Loki barely heard it himself, he asked Sam Moon one last question.

After that he walked away, the heels of his expensive shoes drumming the highly polished floor of the loft.

He didn't turn around.

He should have.

HE FELT THE LAUGHTER BEFORE HE

heard it. An ugly rumble from across the room. Guttural, like an animal choking.

The first footsteps—approaching. A presence, near. Then, words:

Sam Moon.

I enjoy . . . control.

What the Hostage Heard

Gaia . . . taken with you . . . my whole
world.

A kick to his rib cage. A shouted question:

. . . dreams come true?

And then, in the slightest whisper:

Do you love her, Sam?

Sam's bruised eye throbbed as he lifted his head.
He had not attempted to use his voice in nineteen
hours, but with what he sincerely believed might be
the very last breath in his body, over the sound of fad-
ing footsteps, Sam answered.

"Yes."

Gaia and Heather.

When you look at them and take them at face value, one might wonder how one person (namely, me . . . and possibly Sam) could love them both in one lifetime.

Gaia is tall, blond, powerful, and favors brown clothing.

Heather is shortish, brunette, a slave to the masses, and never wears brown unless a respected fashion writer tells her it's the "new black."

But Gaia and Heather are more alike than the general public might think.

The first similarity? They'd both kill me if they heard me say that.

The list goes on.

Neither one of them is as brave as she thinks she is. They both have a lot of secrets. (Heather's I pretty much know, Gaia's I'm not sure I want to know.) They both have trust is-sues. I've never known two peo-ple with such a gift for

sarcasm. They are both extremely
beautiful.

And they both have a thing for
college guys.

So it's not hard to see why
one guy could love them both in
the same lifetime.

The real question is, why do I
bother?

"Heather? It's Jeff Landon.... So, uh, are you busy Saturday night?"

phone tag

RRRING. CLICK. BEEP.

"You've reached the Gannis residence. Please leave a message at the beep. Thank you."

Sex in School

"Heather! It's Megan. Oh my God! I am still so totally freaked out by what happened at school today! I cannot believe Sam, like, actually taped you guys doing it. And gave it to *Gaia*? That's like—ugh—*so* unbelievably tasteless. It's like, okay, why don't we all just go on *Jerry Springer*? I mean, like, what if you were wearing weird underwear or something, y'know? Okay, so, like, call me as soon as you get in. Bye."

Click. Beep.

What kind of idiot was Megan? She knew Heather didn't have her own phone line. She knew Heather's answering machine was in the family room, where anyone could overhear a message coming in. Heather's parents were actually really good about not snooping, and they would never purposely listen to an incoming call. But what if they happened to be passing through the family room while Megan was ranting about she and Sam "doing it"? Idiot.

Rrring. Click. Beep.

"Hi, it's Ashley. I skipped school today to get my hair highlighted, but I just heard the best dirt! This morning somebody actually showed a video of people having, like, *sex*—in school! Well, no, I mean, they weren't having sex in school, they showed the video in school. The sex was, like, someplace else. I don't know who was on the tape, though, 'cuz I heard it from Jen, who heard it from Mallory, who heard it from . . . I dunno, like, somebody. But now I'm, like, so bummed that I dropped AP econ! Oh! Hey! You're still in that class, aren't you? So *you* must have seen it. Cool. All right, so call me with the info!"

Click. Beep.

It had been going on all day. She'd already erased at least twenty messages on this very topic. But she refused to take the phone off the hook, in case Sam tried to call.

To explain himself.

To apologize.

To tell her he'd had nothing to do with that damn video.

She'd come home from the disaster at the dorm and spent the last hour lying on the family room sofa, screening calls.

Rrring. Click. Beep.

"Heather! It's Jeff Landon. Heard about your film debut. Whoa. Didn't know you were into that kind of thing. So, uh, are you busy Saturday night?"

Beep.

Heather chucked a throw pillow at the answering

machine. It missed by about three feet and bounced off the top of the television. She sighed, then rolled over onto her stomach. Sam's dorm room key bit into her hip. It was still in the front pocket of her pants. She pulled it out and stared at it for a second before flinging it, too, across the room, where it knocked over a framed photo of her and Sam at a Yankees game.

Rrring. Click. Beep.

"Heather, it's Megan again! Are you there? Pick up! I just heard that band Fearless is playing in the park tonight. The drummer's a total hottie! Wanna go? Maybe it'll, you know, cheer you up or whatever. Call me."

That was it! Heather had officially had it. She was taking the phone off the hook, and for all she cared, Sam could go to hell. Let him call. Let him get a busy signal. Let him come over with a dozen long-stemmed roses and apologize in person, like a normal boyfriend!

She was just reaching for the handset when the phone rang again. She jerked her fingers away as though she'd been shocked, then listened.

Click. Beep.

"Hi, Heather. It's Ed. Fargo. Listen, I realize this call must come as a shock, but I have something really serious I need to talk to you about. It's important. It's . . . uh . . . about Sam. He's in trouble. Well, actually, not

158

trouble. More like danger. There's something we have to get out of his room. We're talking life and death here. Sam's life and death. So we were thinking, since you probably have a key to his room, you would bring it to us. Heather, you've got to help us. . . ."

Heather picked up the handset. The machine shut off, routing Ed's voice directly through the phone as she pressed it to her ear.

"Heather? Are you there?"

She had two words for him: "Who's us?"

The Key

"WHAT DO YOU MEAN, SHE DOESN'T

want me involved?"

"I mean," said Ed, wheeling fast to keep up with Gaia's furious pace, "she's all for helping Sam, but she doesn't want you to be a part of it."

"*Part* of it? Part of *it*?" Gaia punched her right fist repeatedly against her thigh as she walked. "Doesn't the airhead realize that I *am* it? Didn't you explain that to her?" Gaia slammed directly into a man in a business suit, sending him sprawling. "Sorry," she mumbled over her shoulder. The guy swore after her but was too busy restuffing his briefcase to give chase.

"No, I didn't. I'm guessing it would have done more harm than good." Ed stopped at the corner, waiting for the light. He glanced warily over his shoulder. Gaia half hoped the suit would come yell at her. She needed a good excuse to hit something.

When Ed had explained that Gaia was involved, the news had, naturally, sent Her Royal Heatherness into convulsions. After some careful negotiations, Ed had managed to get her to agree to discuss it in person—without Gaia.

"So she's not expecting me?" Gaia asked, holding her hair back from her face to keep it from whipping into her eyes.

"No," Ed answered, staring at the rushing traffic.

"Great."

Gaia stopped fuming long enough to check out the neighborhood. It was a little to the east of the area that was really upscale. It wasn't bad. But there was nothing much to recommend it, either. The streets were lined with smallish apartment buildings that were falling into disrepair—chipping paint, cracked moldings, windows scratched with graffiti. Plus it seemed like the garbage hadn't been hauled off in weeks.

"Where are we going?" Gaia asked.

"Heather's."

Gaia lifted an eyebrow in the direction of the

nearest worse-for-wear apartment building. "You mean she doesn't live in some yuppie co-op somewhere in the eighties?"

"Not anymore," Ed said flatly.

They continued in silence for two blocks, then turned a corner and found Heather waiting for them on the sidewalk in front of a nondescript, graying apartment building.

Ed waved.

Heather fired Gaia a hateful look from thirty paces off.

"I told you not to bring her," Heather said, crossing her arms over the front of her suede jacket.

"This is important," Ed told her. "Gaia's involved, whether you like it or not."

Heather looked like a rabid alley cat. She ignored Ed, focusing all her attention on glaring at Gaia. "Are you sleeping with Sam?"

Gaia rolled her eyes. "Oh, give me a break—"

"Are you?" Heather's mouth contorted with fury.

"Heather!" Ed blurted. He wheeled his chair between the two girls. "This isn't about you," he said firmly, leveling her with a stare. "This is about Sam."

Heather glanced at him, a flicker of interest in her eyes. "Right, so what's going on? How do you even know him?"

Gaia let out an exasperated sigh. The girl had a talent for pointless questions.

"It doesn't matter how I know him," Ed said. "What matters is he's been kidnapped."

"Kidnapped?"

The color drained from Heather's face, and Gaia felt her stomach flop.

That was what fear looked like. Gaia found herself fighting back a wave of what could only be called jealousy. She cared for Sam more than anyone would ever know. Yet again she felt deep discomfort at the knowledge that when his life was threatened, she couldn't feel this most basic emotion. But a `conscience-free zone` like Heather Gannis could. Heather could have natural feelings when the guy they both loved was in danger.

Gaia felt like a voyeur as she watched the tears forming in Heather's eyes. She made herself look away.

"By who? Why?" Heather asked.

"We're not sure," Ed said. "Somebody's holding him hostage."

"Oh my God!"

"We think we can rescue him, but we're running out of time."

"Rescue him? When?"

Probably needs to check her Week-at-a-Glance, Gaia thought cynically. *"Sure, I can pencil in Sam's rescue for tonight—unless there's a sale at Abercrombie."*

"Tonight," said Ed.

Morbidly curious, Gaia watched Heather closely, feeling an inexplicable loneliness. Heather's eyes were so huge, so filled with terror, they threatened to overtake her whole face. She was actually quaking. Gaia couldn't pull her eyes away. She knew what fear looked like. But what did it *feel* like? *What?* And would she ever know the extent of what she was missing?

"Oh my God," Heather said, her voice quivering. "Oh my God, oh my God!"

"Calm down," said Gaia. "Freaking out isn't going to help anything."

"Shut up!" Heather glared at her. "Just shut up and go away."

"She's not going anywhere," said Ed.

"I don't even want to look at her!" Heather sputtered.

"Then don't," snapped Gaia. "Just give us the key so we can—"

"You're not going without me!" Heather exploded. "Sam is still *my* boyfriend. And besides, it's not the key that's the problem. It's the pit bull of a security guard."

Gaia remembered the guard. She'd slipped by him without much trouble on her own, but all three of them? A towhead, a homecoming queen, and a Boy Scout on wheels. They weren't exactly an inconspicuous bunch.

163

Heather turned to Ed, and her voice ironed itself into a reasonable tone. "I have to do *something*. I want to help him."

"You'll be helping him by giving us the key," said Ed. "That way, we can get his insulin and bring it to him tonight when they release him in the park—"

Gaia brought her hand down hard on Ed's shoulder, effectively shutting him up, but not soon enough. She watched Heather's face as the information was sent to her mental mainframe.

Damn.

"I'm coming with you. I have to be the one to bring it to him." Suddenly she was overcome with either real emotion or really good acting technique. Her eyes filled with tears again, and her breathing was fast and shallow. "He'll need me," she cried. "He'll need me to take care of him. I'm going with you."

"Oh, no!" Gaia exploded. "No way."

"Heather," Ed said calmly, "it's too dangerous."

She glared in Gaia's direction. "Why is it too dangerous for me and not her?"

Gaia wouldn't have minded showing her. Instead she said, "It's dangerous for everyone. Especially Sam. But I'm going because the kidnapper contacted me in the first place."

Something shifted in Heather's eyes as she digested

this information. She seemed to suddenly grow smaller. "Why you?"

"I don't know," Gaia said honestly.

Heather crossed her arms over her chest. "Who do you think you—"

"Yo! Enough." They both snapped their heads around to face Ed. "This isn't helping Sam."

Gaia swore under her breath. Sam's life was in jeopardy, and here she was arguing with Bad-Attitude Barbie. She had to let Ed work on Heather alone for a minute. She turned and headed back toward a small convenience store she'd noticed near the corner.

If all else failed, she could knock Heather's lights out and just take the key.

But something told her that wasn't going to be necessary. Ed would be able to convince her. Maybe it was the residual tenderness she heard in his voice every time he talked to her or about her. Maybe it was the way Heather changed—almost indiscernibly, but still, *changed*—when Ed looked at her, as though something were happening inside her that she didn't want or expect. It was as if Heather were locked out of her own soul and somehow Ed still had the key.

For the life of her, Gaia could not figure out why that annoyed her so much.

But it did.

GAIA WAS COMING OUT OF THE
store, finishing up her Mars
bar, when Ed appeared.

"I've got good news and
bad news," he said.

"Is the bad news that
you couldn't think of anything more original to say
than that?" Gaia asked through a mouthful of nuts
and chocolate. She crumpled the wrapper and shoved
it into her sweatshirt pocket with the two other
chocolate bars she'd bought. Gaia didn't know much
about diabetes, but she thought Sam might need
them.

"So where is she?" Gaia asked, glancing past Ed.

"She'll meet us here in a few minutes," Ed said, stu-
diously avoiding eye contact. "She went inside to get
the key."

Gaia's body rippled with relief. "She's
going to give it up?"

"More or less," Ed answered, picking at the hole in
his sweater.

"I'm not sure that's possible, Ed," Gaia said impatiently.

"She's coming with us to the dorm," Ed said, pushing his shoulders back, trying to look defiant.
"There's no way around it."

Gaia tilted her head back, staring up at the rapidly

166

darkening sky. "Do you think she's gonna be able to keep her head when she sees Sam in the park, all beaten and bloody, being shoved around by some guy in commando gear who's holding `a sawed-off shotgun to his head,` and who knows what else?"

Ed looked a little white. "She'll be long gone before we get to the park."

Gaia had to bite her lip to keep herself from commenting on his use of the word *we*. He didn't know it yet, but *he* was going to be long gone, too. There was no way she was going to drag Ed into that little scenario. But perhaps it was best not to mention that just yet.

"What makes you so sure she'll be gone?" Gaia asked, leaning back against the brick wall of the convenience store.

Ed smiled and his eyes filled with mischief. `Gaia knew what was coming` before he said it.

"Because I have a plan."

He didn't
think he
could handle
the humilia-
tion if his

brainless

first-ever
covert-
action plan
crashed and
burned.

ED WHEELED HIS WAY INTO THE

dorm and took a look around. The lobby smelled of beer-dampened carpet and the bottle's worth of CK One with which the guard had obviously drenched himself.

Mission: Not-So-Impossible

Hmm. Ed would have pegged this one for a Brut by Fabergé type. Go figure.

"Hi."

Behind his desk, the guard averted his eyes and gave him a nod.

Typical. Can't look the cripple in the eye.

Ed aimed for the elevator.

Waiting . . . waiting . . .

Okay, so gimme the ID speech already. He checked his watch. Seven twenty-eight. C'mon, buddy. Ask for the card.

Nothing.

Ed hit the elevator button hard. The Neanderthal glanced in his direction and dredged up an awkward grin.

Damn! Don't tell me the quasi-cop is too soft-hearted to hassle a guy in a wheelchair.

Above the elevator, the number 3 lit up. It would

reach ground level any second, and Ed would be able to roll right on. No distraction, no clear avenue for Gaia and Heather.

Over his head, the number 2 blinked orange.

"Excuse me," he said. "I'm heading up to see a friend, but I'm not sure I'll be able to find his room. Those letters and numbers are kinda confusing. Can ya help me out?"

Not until you see my ID, right? Go ahead, say it!

"The letter stands for the wing," the guard explained. "A is to the right, B to the left. There are four rooms to a suite and they're all clearly marked."

"Thanks," Ed muttered. He was starting to sweat. He didn't think he could handle the humiliation if his first-ever covert-action plan `crashed and burned`.

For a second the guy just looked at Ed and seemed to be trying to decide what to do.

C'mon, brainless. Card me, already. Then the elevator announced itself with a loud *ding,* and the door opened.

"I've never been in any of these dorms before," Ed said. He raised his voice a few decibels louder than necessary. `"I don't go here."`

There! Now he's got no choice.

The Neanderthal cleared his throat. "Listen, pal," he said in a regretful tone. "I really can't let you up if you don't have an ID."

171

Finally! Ed narrowed his eyes as the elevator door slid closed. "What do you mean?"

"University policy. Sorry." The guard shoved his beefy hands into his pockets. Damn, he was uncomfortable. "Nonstudents can't—"

"Nonstudents?" Ed challenged, spinning his chair toward the guard. "You sure you don't mean people in `wheelchairs?`"

The guy looked at him, waylaid. "Huh?"

"C'mon, man. You know the real reason you're not letting me get on this elevator is because I can't walk into it on my own two feet," Ed said, his face growing red. He should get an Oscar for this one.

"No. That ain't it." Now the Neanderthal was sweating, too. "It's just—"

"Yeah, right! I've seen this crap before," Ed shouted, gripping the armrests on his chair. "It's always the chair. It's `discrimination.`"

Now the guy was getting pissed. "It has nothin' to do with the chair. It's the rule. No ID, no admittance."

Ed gave him a disgusted look, then turned his chair again and reached for the elevator button.

"Hey!" barked the guard, hurrying out from behind the desk. "I told you—"

"What are ya gonna do?" Ed chuckled wickedly. "Hit me?"

With that, they began to argue in earnest.

"ALL RIGHT, WE'RE GOING IN," GAIA

7:31 said from her position outside Sam's dorm.

Heather rolled her eyes, but when Gaia pushed through the lobby door, Heather followed. Ed had managed to lure the guard out from behind his station, so Gaia and Heather tiptoed behind the guard's back and slipped into the stairwell.

All politeness, Gaia held the door open, allowing Heather to go through first. No idiot, Heather shot Gaia a suspicious look, but Gaia could practically see her train of thought. Heather didn't want Gaia behind her, but the thought of getting to Sam's room first was tempting.

Heather sneered at Gaia and brushed past her.

"You're welcome," Gaia snapped in a whisper.

Heather started to jog, and Gaia followed close behind. It was torture having Heather's scrawny ass in her face, but it was going to be worth the sacrifice in about five seconds. Gaia let Heather get up three half flights of stairs before she made her move.

Gaia reached up and grabbed Heather's ankle, sending the girl sprawling on the concrete landing between the first and second floors.

"Get off me!" Heather yelled.

Holding Heather down with one hand, Gaia seized the key from Heather's grasp with a mercury-fast action that would have done even the most seasoned New York purse snatcher proud.

Gaia pulled Heather to her feet. "Sorry, but it was necessary," Gaia muttered.

"I-I'm going to-to *kill* you," Heather shrieked, struggling to no avail.

"Me first," Gaia said, trying not to enjoy the terror in Heather's eyes. She wasn't going to kill her, of course, though it was tempting. She did, however, need to shove Heather down a few steps, both so she could get to Sam's room without further interference, and so the overweight guard could catch Heather.

Gaia gave Heather one hard push, and Heather yelped. She stumbled down the half flight and landed at the bottom with a thud. It looked like it hurt at least a little.

At that moment Gaia heard Ed yelling at the guard. Right on cue.

"Some chick just snuck into the stairs! Yeah! Yes! I swear! Brown hair! Pink shirt!"

Heather was struggling to her feet as Gaia heard the sound of the lobby door to the stairs banging open.

It was time to get out of there.

"Later, Heather!"

Gaia took off up the stairs. She heard Heather start after her, but the guard had already caught up.

"Where do you think you're going?" he asked, panting.

"Get *off* me!" Heather screamed. "Gaia! *Gaia!*"

Gaia smiled as she sprinted down the fourth-floor hallway.

GAIA STOOD OUTSIDE THE DOOR OF

Dorm Room Revisited

room B4 and held her breath. The last time she'd been here Sam had been making love to Heather.

How could she bring herself to go in there?

"Don't be such a sentimental idiot," Gaia told herself, shaking off the self-inflicted melodrama. "This is a college dorm room. I should have a nickel for every sexual encounter that's taken place in here."

She slid the key into the lock.

The doorknob fell off in her hand.

For a moment she just stared at it.

Son of a bitch!

The damn thing had been broken all along! Not even lockable. So they hadn't needed the key after all.

And, by association, they hadn't needed Heather. What a waste of time!

Then again, it had provided the opportunity for Gaia to give Heather a good hard shove. Truth be told, that had actually been kind of cathartic.

She opened the door. And there it was. Sam's bed.

Gaia stepped into the room, keeping her mind on her task. Insulin. Must find insulin. Don't even look at that framed photograph of Heather over there on the dresser. Could she possibly be wearing any more lip gloss?

Insulin, damn it! What was the matter with her?

Gaia seemed to remember the stuff had to be refrigerated. Her eyes swept the room and found a minifridge in the corner. She opened the door. Two bottles of mineral water, a small mountain of those plastic packets of duck sauce that come with Chinese takeout, and a small zippered nylon case.

She opened the case. Pamphlet of instructions. Vials. Syringe.

A wave of emotion washed over her. It was like holding the definition of *vulnerable* in her hands. Sam—perfect, brilliant, gorgeous Sam—had this to contend with. This frailty. This tiny physiological flaw, this infinitesimal defect in body chemistry. This burden. This disadvantage.

Tell me about it.

She stuffed the case into the oversized pocket of her cargo pants, then got up to leave. But there was that damn bed again.

Gaia hesitated perhaps a fraction of a millisecond. Then she threw herself onto the bed. Don't think about the fact that the last time you saw it, Heather was between the sheets. Think about Sam.

Sam's bed.

Sam's sheets. Sam's pillow. Gaia buried her face in it, breathing deeply. Maybe there was something of him still clinging to the pillowcase—an eyelash, maybe, or an echo of a dream.

"Oh, God, Sam . . . I'm so sorry."

She clutched the pillow to her body.

I don't want to kill anybody, her brain said for the hundredth time since she'd read the last directive. *I don't want to kill. I don't want to kill.*

Images flooded her mind, drowning her brain: Sam at the chessboard. Sam coming to see her in the hospital. Sam on the park bench.

And then it was CJ. CJ chasing her down Broome Street. CJ in the police lineup. CJ holding a gun to her head. And firing. And . . .

Gaia sat bolt upright.

She knew what to do.

Rook to knight four.

Queen's knight. Castle. Pawn.

Wrrrzzzzzzzzz. Clank.

I see Gaia's fingers on a chess piece. She pushes the smooth, angular knight with her index finger. And Zolov clicks his false teeth in appreciation of her genius.

The sound bullies me.

Wrrrzzzzzzzzz, clank, wrrzz. I only want to sleep. Sleep. But my levels are off, and my own blood poisons me.

Time is running—check.

Checkmate.

Blackness surrounds me, cold, flat, then it erupts into a pattern of squares. Clean, sharp-cornered red bruises interrupt my blackout. The board spins in its own dimension until I am above it, leaning, knowing, playing. I hear the sound of the plastic piece scraping the cardboard squares.

Wrrrzzzzzzzzz.

The hunger is huge. The blackness quivers. I place my hand around Gaia's on her knight.

And sleep.

Oh, God. Is this what forgiveness feels like?

bring it on

GAIA FOUND ED WAITING AT THE

southwest corner of Fifth Avenue and Tenth Street—the designated meeting spot. It was dark out, and he sat in a square of light pouring out of the lobby of the building behind him.

"Get it?" he asked.

"Got it." She nodded, patting the nylon case inside her pocket. "C'mon, let's go. There's somewhere I have to be."

Gaia started walking toward the park, and Ed quickly caught up with her.

"How'd it work out with Heather and the guard?" Gaia asked, hoping to keep him from asking where exactly she had to be.

A shadow of guilt crossed his face. "It got pretty hairy. She was ballistic when they tossed her out."

"Tossed her out, huh?" asked Gaia, savoring the image. "You mean that literally, right?"

"Pretty much," Ed said. "From what I overheard, it seems our little Heather tried to get in to Sam's room earlier today. The guard recognized her and thought she was some crazed stalker, so he totally ignored her when she was shouting about you getting away. They took her to the main security office. She fought him like you wouldn't even believe, kicking, swearing, snorting. . . ."

"So she didn't get around to implicating you?" Gaia asked, glancing up at the arch at the north end of Washington Square Park. It was illuminated at night, and Gaia couldn't help thinking it was beautiful. It was kind of like a beacon.

"I'm sure she tried," Ed said, following her gaze. "But no way were they gonna believe her." He shook his head. "Man, I feel sorry for the guy who had to interrogate her."

"What time is it?" she asked. If he noticed she wasn't really paying attention to the conversation, he didn't say anything.

He checked his watch. "Only eight ten. We've got plenty of time before we have to go to the park."

"Excuse me?" Gaia said. "*We've* got plenty of time?"

"What is it with you women and pronouns today, huh?" Ed asked.

Gaia shoved her hands into her pockets. Her fingers automatically closed around the candy bars. "I'm serious, Ed. I'm going to do this alone."

Ed scoffed. "No, you're not."

"Yes, I am."

"No, you're not."

"Yes, I . . ." Gaia threw up her hands. "Ed, this isn't open to debate. You said it yourself, to Heather—it'll be dangerous."

He had no idea how dangerous, of course, because

181

he was unaware of the last note's final directive. But she wasn't about to tell him she'd be murdering a gang member in cold blood this evening, which wasn't exactly the sort of thing that required an escort.

He stopped wheeling. "And you think just because I'm in this chair . . ."

"Oh, please! Save the politically correct guilt trip for somebody who gives a shit, okay?" Gaia spat out. "Yes, you're in a wheelchair. Yes, in this case it's a liability. It makes you slow, and obvious, and a real easy target."

Ed looked at her a moment, then turned away.

Damn. She hadn't meant that the way it sounded. Well, no, actually she'd meant it exactly the way it sounded. It was the truth, for God's sake. Of course, she'd neglected to mention her most important reason for not wanting him there.

"Listen," she said, not quite gently, but as close to it as she could stand to get. "I'm not saying this stuff to hurt your feelings—if I wanted to do that, I'd tell you what I really think of your taste in clothes." He didn't face her, but she could feel him smiling. "I've got to do this myself, Ed. Because . . ."

At last he turned. "Because?"

"Because if anything happened to you . . ." Gaia pulled her jacket close to her as the wind picked up, and sighed. "If anything happened to you, the world would be a much sadder place," she finished so quietly she wasn't certain the breeze had left any of her words for Ed to hear.

A few hundred years went by before Ed finally spoke. "Thanks, Gaia."

"Yeah, whatever." Gaia picked at a hangnail. "Let's not make this a mush fest, okay? You know you're, like, my only friend on the planet. So what good would it do me to let you take a bullet to the skull?"

She handed him Heather's key, careful not to let her hand touch his.

"Get this back to her," she said.

"Don't you want to keep it?"

Gaia shook her head. "He gave it to her, not to me."

"Yeah," Ed replied softly, lowering his eyes. "I know exactly what you mean."

She figured he was thinking back on his bygone relationship with Heather, because his tone was tender in the extreme. She sighed again.

"I gotta go," she said, looking off toward the center of the park.

He raised his eyes, surprised. "Now?"

"Yeah, well . . . I have to stop back at my place. I've gotta get something." Something she really didn't want to get. Something that should just have been left in its uninspired hiding place forever.

"What?"

Gaia hesitated, waiting for an appropriate lie to shove its way to the front of her brain. Then her mind zoomed back to the Duane Reade bag, the cop, Renny.

"Tampons."

"Oh." Ed's face flushed faster than Gaia had ever thought possible. "Well, uh . . . be careful."

She grinned. "With the tampons?"

"Gaia!"

"I'll be okay." Her brows knitted together, and she stared at Ed seriously. "I'll be okay as long as you stay far, far away from the park tonight."

Ed sighed and shook his head. "Fine."

She was three steps away when she turned around again. "Promise me, Ed. Promise me you will *not* come to the park."

He nodded. "I promise."

If she hadn't been thinking so hard about killing CJ, she might have recognized that Ed was as good a liar as she was.

ELLA WOULD NEVER GET TIRED OF
doing Loki's dirty work.

Especially when it in-
volved her running her hands
over the bare chests of
well-built young men like CJ.
Okay, so they were rolling in

Seduction 201 (AP)

the dirt behind a bush off some pathway in the park—
not exactly a classy setting. But she knew how to make
the best of any situation.

This one was as sexy as he was mean. She'd always
liked that combination.

Marco was good. CJ was much, much better.

And he was amazed by her. Well, of course. He was
probably used to teenage sluts with grungy hair and
too much black eyeliner. He'd never seen actual silk
this close before, let alone touched it.

*Now, here's where I sigh for him, nice and deep—
make him think I've never had anything this good before.*

CJ smiled hungrily.

He's so proud of himself. Look at him showing off! It
was almost cute.

That's right. One more button.

He breathed her name. Or what he thought was her
name. So amazed. So grateful. He had no idea there was
a blond assassin on her way there to murder him.

*Well . . . if you've gotta go, this is definitely the way to
spend your final hour.*

He asked why she was laughing.

"I always laugh when I'm ready," she said seductively. "Are you ready?"

Over his shoulder, she checked her watch. Ten till
ten. Then there was a sound from a nearby tree. It was a
miracle she even heard it over CJ's moaning and heavy
breathing. It was a signal: She's here.

Okay, you darling, dangerous boy . . . let's make this quick.

"Yes, CJ! Yes . . . *Yes!*" Perfect timing! And then . . .

"CJ, I hear someone. . . ."

He rose to his knees with a nice lazy smile, tugged up his jeans, and peered through the leaves.

"Shit!"

"What is it?" He was looking for his shirt. No luck.

"Shit. It's her. I gotta go. Sorry."

The "sorry" threw her a bit. I suppose I have to act like I care. "Don't go, CJ! Wait!"

He didn't even realize she'd taken his gun.

He leaned down and gave her a hard kiss on her mouth and told her he'd see her again; he *promised*—in this rough, almost heartbreaking voice—that he'd see her again. Then he took off. She sat up, buttoning her blouse, surveying the damage to her skirt.

Gaia, he's all yours.

GAIA ENTERED WASHINGTON SQUARE
Park.

It was nine forty.

The concert was supposed to start at ten. The band was already doing sound checks. The squeal of feedback from

Parks and Wreck

the microphones echoed above the gathering crowd. Gaia watched the arriving fans with a combination of interest and longing.

What must it be like, she wondered, to have nothing else to do on a Monday night besides go to a concert in the park? No gangbangers to ice, no hostages to free . . .

What's it like just to be normal?

Well, she decided, looking around at the crowd, *normal* was a relative term—this was the West Village, after all. Tattoos and navel rings required.

So where the hell was CJ?

It was almost funny that she was looking for him for a change. The problem was, she hadn't expected to actually have to look. He'd been like clockwork in the past, always just sort of there—lurking, looming, stalking. Tonight, though, when it was absolutely imperative that their paths cross, he was a no-show.

How nauseatingly ironic was that?

Reasoning that even a brainless wonder like CJ might find the band concert too public a place to hunt his prey, Gaia plunged into the semidarkness of the pathway that led to Washington Square West.

She'd noticed that morning that a few leaves had begun to change. Change. Die. It was all in how you looked at it, but where just weeks ago there had been nothing but thriving greenery, there were now little glimpses of color. Throughout the expanse of billowing green, the brown-red leaves clung like scabs. They drew the eye automatically, as though to remind you that death refused to go unnoticed.

The shadows engulfed her, and the trees muffled the sound of the band and the band watchers. It was odd—even after all the horrific stuff that had happened to her in this park, she still liked it, liked the way it smelled, liked the way it rustled. She marveled at the weird, restless peacefulness of the place.

Even tonight. Even with a .38 in her waistband and CJ on the prowl.

And Sam . . .

Was he here somewhere? What if the kidnapper wasn't really going to release him? What if . . .

No. She couldn't dwell on that possibility. Sam was here. He had to be.

Did the kidnapper have him in a half nelson behind some tree, a rag stuffed in his mouth to keep him quiet? Then again, if Sam was in as bad shape as the last note had indicated, none of that would be necessary, would it?

So maybe he was writhing in the dirt in unbearable agony, clinging to his gorgeous existence by a mere thread, closer—like the drying leaves—to death than to life.

Gaia's skin prickled; her heart was practically doing the lambada in her chest. She wouldn't have

Sam back until she dealt with CJ. So where was he?

"C'mon, you dirtbag. Show your ugly face."

Even as she whispered it, she heard him. He was maybe fifteen feet behind her but approaching fast. And then he was on her, his hand slamming down on her shoulder, jerking her around to face him.

She reached out with both hands, grabbed him around the neck, and yanked his face down to connect with her head.

Nose—busted. No question. Good. It would go nicely with the sling on his arm. He staggered backward, groaning. "You bitch!"

"Whatever." Gaia nailed him with a series of front kicks to his gut, then spun around, swinging her left leg in a high arc that landed like a wrecking ball against the side of his jaw.

He fell sideways, hitting the pavement with a rib-bashing thud. Gaia pressed her foot between his shoulder blades, pinning him to the ground while she reached into the waist of her pants for the gun.

"You know," she said through clenched teeth, pressing the gun into the flesh behind his right ear, "as much as you really do deserve to die a very painful death . . ."

He flinched as the sole of her sneaker dug deeper into his back.

"As much as you deserve it . . ."

She sighed and lifted her foot. It took him a second to recognize he was free. As soon as he did, he leaped to his feet, and Gaia found herself making the very incongruous observation that this idiot was running around the park at night in October without a shirt on.

He stood very still, staring at her. She held the gun about an inch from his chest.

She had to make it look real without actually killing him. Had to make it look as though she'd tried and failed.

She cocked the hammer. "Hit me," she said, slicing her voice down to a whisper.

"Huh?" He was looking at her as though she were nuts. Maybe she was.

"Hit me," she snarled again, waving the gun.

CJ, obviously, was not very good at following directions.

She leaned closer to him. And wanted to gag. *Smoked rose petals.* Another divergent thought: The freaky witch in Soho is scamming Ella good. Unless . . .

Gaia ducked. CJ's heavy fist caught her in the cheekbone, throwing her slightly off balance. Good enough. She aimed the gun into a tree and fired.

Apparently CJ was only just realizing he'd left his own firearm elsewhere. He froze.

Gaia stumbled a little for dramatic effect, then pointed the gun at him. "Look out, asshole. This one's gonna be closer."

She aimed and fired. The bullet passed so close to CJ's face he could have kissed it.

"That's two," she whispered, watching as CJ fell to his knees and covered his head with his arms. He was begging her not to shoot.

`Again she pulled the trigger.`

CJ winced.

And Gaia whispered, "Bang!"

She had to. Because the bullet that should have been loaded in the third chamber of the gun's barrel was safely hidden in a Duane Reade bag under Gaia's bed.

It was as if eternity made itself visible, swelling around her, slowing the spin of the earth. Gaia swore she saw leaves changing in the chasm of time that elapsed between the steely click of the trigger and CJ's moment of recognition.

`No bullet.`

She gave him a wicked smile. "Déjà vu, huh?"

That's when he ran.

Gaia let out a huge rush of breath, then swung her gaze across the shadows that shrouded the path. She knew the kidnapper was out there somewhere, watching. "Hope you fellas got all that," she muttered. "Hope you bought it."

Her answer was two heavy hands coming down on her shoulders. `Hard.`

Evidently they hadn't bought it at all.

She could
fight like a
machine,
full force,
pumped on
fury and
desire.

eyes

like

hers

OKAY, SO MAYBE LYING RIGHT TO

her face wasn't exactly the best way to make her fall in love with him. But what choice did he have?

911

"Promise me you will *not* come to the park tonight."

Yeah. Right.

Sure, she was gutsy. Sure, she was powerful, and capable, and—all right, he'd even give her deadly. But she was his. At least in his heart she was his, and even a—what was it she'd called him? A `liability`? Yeah. Even a liability like him knew that you absolutely, positively did not let the love of your life do something like this alone.

So he followed her.

The band crowd was a good cover. He had to keep his distance on the path, though.

`She still hadn't spotted him.` He was at least twenty yards behind and to her left, in the shadow of a rest room building. He didn't have a weapon; he didn't even have the use of his legs. He did, however, have a cell phone, which he would use to dial 911 the minute it looked like Gaia was in trouble.

What was he thinking? It always looked like Gaia was in trouble. What he meant was, the minute it looked like Gaia was out of her league. That's when he'd call for help.

Ed watched as a figure emerged from the bushes, and when he recognized it, he felt fear more intense than he could ever have imagined. It was that gang punk CJ. The one who'd tried to kill her.

"Shit!" Keeping his eyes glued to Gaia, he flipped the phone open. (Power ... 9 ... 1 ...) "Whoa! Nice head butt!" (End) Man, could she kick! Bam, bam, bam!

She had the looks of a supermodel and the speed of Jean Claude Van Damme. Ooh! Right in the jaw. Nice. CJ went down.

Another cramp of fear gripped Ed when he saw Gaia reach into the waistband of her pants. What the hell was she doing with a gun? And what the hell was she standing there *talking* to CJ for?

Ed's heart jerked in his chest, and then he was watching CJ hit her! The bastard!

(9 ... 1 ...)

Holy shit! She fired, missed, but ha! The sound had sent CJ to his knees. Okay, she was back in control. (End)

The next shot was close! And then she was pulling the trigger again. And ...

No bullet?

(9 ... 1 ... 1 ... Send)

"Ed?"

He looked up. "Heather?"

GAIA'S ARMS WERE PINNED BEHIND

her back when the man appeared
from out of the bushes. He was
dressed—appropriately enough, Gaia
supposed—in black. Black slacks, very
expensive black sweater, and black
shoes, also pricey. She immediately
discarded any assumptions that the
kidnapper was somehow connected with CJ's scrubby
little street gang. These guys were big-time crime.
Money. Maybe even brains.

Men in Black

"You failed!" growled Mr. Monochromatic.

Gaia shrugged as best she could with the compromised use of her arms. "I tried."

"Not good enough!"

"It's not my fault you boneheads loaded the gun
wrong!" Gaia reasoned.

"Shut up!"

She rolled her eyes. "Fine, I will."

Gaia struck like lightning. She shoved her elbow
upward, a nice crack to the underside of her captor's chin, freeing her arms. Before the man in black
even had time to advance, she'd delivered one
powerful jab to the back of guy number one's
neck, knocking him out. He hit the ground like a
rag doll.

Then, in one graceful sweep, Gaia turned and
wrapped the man in black up in a headlock, pressing

the gun—the fourth chamber of which did contain a bullet—to his temple. "I'd prefer to let this do my talking for me, anyway."

The guy grunted.

"I want Sam!" she called to the darkness. "Now. Or this guy's dry cleaner is gonna be looking for a way to get brains out of cashmere!"

Somehow, impossibly, this little corner of the park seemed to be deserted. Had they cleared the area or something?

The guy laughed.

Gaia made herself ignore it. "A trade!" she shouted. "Sam for this guy. Right now. Or I blow his freakin' head off."

The guy laughed again. Gaia arched an eyebrow. He wasn't supposed to be laughing. He should have been begging his buddies to make the trade, save his life.

"What's so funny?" she demanded.

"Shoot me," the guy said. "He won't care."

"What's that supposed to mean?" Gaia asked. "Who won't care?"

"I mean," gurgled the man in black (because Gaia's forearm was still crushing his esophagus), "my employer won't give a damn." The mirth had vanished from his voice now. "He'll probably kill me himself for this."

Damn it! Gaia loosened her grip but didn't release him. She had to think. She had to . . .

Sam!

He was there. Being pushed out from behind a stand of broad oaks by another black-clad villain.

Gaia's heart lurched. Oh, God, Sam! He looked half dead. Gaia had never seen skin so pale before in her life. His face was covered with a sheen of sweat that matted his dirty, greasy brown hair to his forehead. One of his eyes was swollen shut, and the other twitched like a dying bee's wing. There was a spot of blood beneath his right nostril. The jerk in the suit was dragging him like a sack of flour.

Gaia was so overwhelmed with grief that she almost let go of her own charge. She caught herself in time, though, gave him a nice whack with the butt of the gun, then let him crumple to the ground, unconscious.

"Sam!" she screamed.

Did he flinch? Had he heard? Hard to tell. She made a move to go to him, but his captor had suddenly produced an automatic weapon.

And he was aiming it directly at her heart.

"JESUS!" IF ED WEREN'T ALREADY sitting down, he might have passed out. "Heather!"

She was standing there, holding

Hysteria

the cell phone she'd just snatched out of his hand. He could hear the operator's voice coming through the mouthpiece.

"Hello? Nine-one-one emergency? Hello?"

Apparently Heather was oblivious. She punched the end button.

"How dare you feed me to the wolves like that!" Heather fumed, hands on hips.

He quite seriously wished he could strangle her. "Heather, listen. I'm not kidding around. You have got to get out of here!"

"You can't tell me what to do, Ed," she spat out, her eyes wild. "It's not like we're going out anymore."

Like he'd ever told her what to do when they were together. He decided to chalk that inane remark up to hysteria, which she was clearly on the verge of.

"Heather . . ."

"Where the hell is that little bitch?" she demanded. "And where is Sam? He'd better be all right, or I swear I'm holding you and Gaia responsible. Now, where are they?"

Ed clenched his teeth and jabbed his finger in the direction of a spot on the pathway, roughly twenty yards ahead. "There they are."

Heather looked.

Fortunately, he was able to reach up and flatten his hand over her mouth in time, or her shriek would have certainly given them away.

HE SLAMMED THE SILENCER ONTO

his .44, then stepped out onto the path in front of CJ, who skidded to a flailing halt. The kid had his gun now. He must have found it and grabbed it so that he could go back and finish Gaia off.

Father/ Hood

That wasn't going to happen.

Blood still gushed from his nose, and his bare chest was scraped raw. When he saw the gun, his dark eyes got huge. He lifted his hand and aimed at the gunman's chest. That was all that was needed.

Perhaps the last thought ever to register in CJ's brain was something along the lines of He's got eyes like her.

The bullet hit him just above the bridge of his ruined nose, right in the place where all thoughts began.

And ended.

He remained on his feet a good five seconds, a tiny rivulet of crimson trickling from the corner of his mouth, his eyes bulging with what looked more like surprise than anything else.

Then his knees buckled.

And he began to fall.

And with the soundless echo of the boy's last, unspoken plea raging in his mind, Tom Moore disappeared into the darkness before CJ even hit the ground.

GAIA HEARD IT, LIKE SOMETHING OUT

of a dream.

Boogie Knights

A song. What was it? She knew it. Her father used to like it. An oldie. The lead singer's intro over the sound system came floating through the cool night to reach Gaia.

"A classic from the seventies . . . 'Rescue Me,' by Aretha Franklin . . . so let's boogie!"

Boogie? Oh, please.

And then the bouncy tune, and in the singer's gravelly West Village voice, the lyrics: "Rescue me, I want your tender charms, 'cause I'm lonely . . ."

Great. So now the hostage rescue had a sound track.

A surge of memory nearly blinded Gaia as the familiar song wrapped itself around her. Her mother and father, one night in the cozy family room of their house. The radio blaring. It was a classic even then. "Rescue Me." She was six. Laughing. So were they. Dancing. All of them. They were dancing.

Rescue me. Rescue me.

The scream ripped itself from her throat, drowning out the distant melody. Gaia threw herself at the man with the gun, slapping his arm out of the way, sending the gun spiraling into the night sky. He lunged for her, and Sam, unsupported, slipped to the ground.

Her fist plowed into the guy's abdomen, lifting him off his feet. Her foot slammed into his rib cage. She heard him grunt. "Ugh!"

Ugh. We have an ugh. Do I hear an ummphff? She grabbed a handful of his hair and shoved his face down hard against her knee.

"Ummphff!"

We have an ummphff, ladies and gentlemen!

The guy dropped forward, landing on his hands.

Gaia closed by giving him a good old-fashioned kick in the ass. His chin hit the pavement with a sound like breaking glass.

And then her own breaking began—the breaking down, the shutting off, the surrender of all strength. She was familiar with the experience; it happened every time. She could fight like a machine, full force, pumped on fury and desire. Her might was boundless, but only as long as that fuel was in supply. This fight had sucked up every ounce of energy she possessed.

And now she was spent. Her knees softened. Her limbs tingled. Breathing took on an entirely new caliber of effort.

And the lead singer of the band sang, "Rescue me."

It wasn't just in her head, as it seemed. It was blasting through most of the park. She staggered toward Sam, fumbling in her pocket for his insulin, and went down on her knees beside him.

"Hang on," she whispered. At least she thought she whispered it. Maybe she just thought it. He opened his good eye—just a slit, but still, it opened. "Hang on."

She prepared the syringe according to the directions she'd forced herself to memorize on her way from her house to the park. In her weakened state, the needle seemed to weigh a thousand pounds, and then it was entering Sam's flesh. Swift, smooth. Strangely intimate. She was injecting life back into him.

She withdrew the needle. The night spun in slow circles. The singer sang, "Rescue me." Gaia told herself to get up. Stand. Run. For help. But she couldn't seem to lift herself from the pavement.

As it turned out, she didn't have to. The guy in the black sweater was on his feet again. He grabbed Gaia and hauled her up. Her legs buckled. He was crushing her against him, her back to his chest.

Oh. A knife. At her throat. How inconvenient.

And Sam. On the ground, stirring now.

The shot came from behind her. An excellent shot, piercing her captor's shoulder but leaving her untouched. He went down, screaming.

She staggered forward a few steps and landed in the grass.

A man—a golden-haired man—thundered onto the scene. A police officer? No. The Incredible Hulk?

A knight. Yes. A valiant knight.

To rescue me.

Gaia wanted to smile but couldn't seem to send the message to her face.

The knight was standing over her now. His face was so concerned, so familiar. *Dancing in the living room, and laughing with Mom. Rescue me.*

The knight was her father.

He crouched beside her, lifted her head, stroked her hair.

Oh, God. Is this what forgiveness feels like?

"Gaia?" he whispered. "Gaia, I don't want you to misunderstand. I'm not who you think I am."

She squeezed her eyes shut. *Please don't say that.*

"I'm not Tom. But I'm your family. I'm . . . your father's brother. His twin."

She finally made her mouth work. "His . . . brother?"

The knight nodded. "I've wanted to find you, and take care of you. But I wasn't sure how you'd react. So I waited. Tonight I had no choice but to show myself. I'm sorry if this is painful, Gaia. I'm so sorry. But I'm here now. I'm with you. You're my brother's child. And I love you."

Gaia drank in his words. An elixir. A potion.

She had a family. She could feel the strength returning to her body, with the hope. With the love.

"There's a lot to explain," he whispered, "but I can't now. I have to go. As long as you're safe . . ."

Gaia opened her eyes and looked at him. "No . . ."

He nodded, stroking her hair. "It's all right. You'll understand soon. I promise, I won't be far. I'll come back for you. I swear it."

Gaia struggled to sit up. It was as though her nerves had turned into live electrical wires.

Then her uncle placed one `gentle kiss` on her forehead, and he was gone.

Don't cry, she told herself, greedily pulling air into her lungs in quick, sharp breaths. Don't.

Her uncle had saved her. Her family.

"Gaia!"

She turned. "Ed?" But before she could ream him for following her, she spotted a figure flinging itself toward Sam.

Her eyes widened. "Don't . . . even . . . tell me."

"She saw the whole thing," Ed said.

Gaia watched Heather pick up the nylon case from where it lay on the ground beside Sam. She watched her place her perfectly manicured hand on his forehead, `her perfectly glossed lips on his cheek.`

And she watched Sam open his eyes.

She was a good twenty feet away, but even from that distance, Gaia heard his whisper. It seemed to explode in the deepness of the night. `"Heather?"`

"Yes," sobbed Heather. "I'm here, Sam. I'm here."

Gaia saw him try to smile and she saw his grateful

eyes move from Heather's face to the nylon bag and then back to her face. His voice was trembling with exhaustion and emotion when he asked, "Did you . . . save me?"

Gaia closed her eyes. This wasn't happening.

To her credit, Heather didn't say yes. But she didn't say no, either.

Sam is okay.

He thinks Heather saved him, but he's okay.

CJ's dead.

I didn't kill him, but I saw them zipping up the body bag and hoisting him into the ambulance, so he's dead.

I have an uncle.

I'd never heard of him before today and he's been absent for my entire life—even longer than my dad—but I have an uncle.

Before today I hadn't thought it was possible for life to get any more surreal.

Today proved me very, very wrong.

here is a
sneak peek of
Fearless™ #4:
TWISTED

Sometimes I wonder what I would say if I were ever asked out on a date.

You'd think that since it's never happened to me, I might have had some time in the past seventeen years to formulate the perfect response. You'd think that with all the movies I'd seen, I would have at least picked up some cheesy line. Some doe-eyed, swooning acceptance.

But I pretty much stay away from romantic comedies. There's no relationship advice to be had from an Arnold Swarzenegger film.

Besides, you can't formulate the perfect response for a situation you can't remotely imagine.

I figure that if it ever does happen (not probable) I'll end up saying something along the lines of, "Uh," or slight variations thereof.

"Uh . . . unh," if the guy's a freak.

"Uh . . . huh," if the guy's a non-freak.

I wonder what Heather said to Sam when he first asked her out.

Probably something disgustingly
perfect. Something right out of a
movie. Something like, "I was
wondering when you'd ask." Or
maybe Heather asked Sam out. And
he said something like, "It would
be my honor."

Okay. Stomach now reacting badly.
Must think about something else.

What did Heather say when Ed
asked her out?

Okay. Stomach now severely
cramping.

So what happens after the "Uh . . .
huh"? Awkward pauses, I assume. Idiot
small talk, sweaty palms (his), dry
mouth (also his), bad food. (I imagine
dates don't happen at places where
they have good food—like Gray's Papaya
or Dojo's.)

And I won't even get into what
happens after the most-likely
difficult digestion. What does
the nonfreak expect at that
point? Hand holding? Kissing?
Groping? Heavy groping? Sex?

Stomach no longer wishes to be
a component of my body.

Must stop here.

Luckily, I won't ever have to
deal with any of this. Because no
nonfreak will ever ask me out.
And no freak will ever get more
than the initial grunt.

He was going
to tell **risking**
Gaia Moore
that he **it**
loved her.

EVEN BACK WHEN HIS LEGS WORKED,
Ed had never been fearless.

People who had seen him on
a skateboard or a pair of in-lines
might have been surprised to
hear it. There had been no stairs
too steep to slalom, no handrail
he wasn't willing to challenge, no
traffic too thick to dare. Anyone would tell you, Ed
Fargo was a wild man. He took more risks, and
took them faster, than any other boarder in the city.

The Decision

The dark secret was that all through those days, almost
every second, Ed had been terrified. Every time his wheels
had sent sparks lancing from a metal rail, every time he
had gone over a jump and felt gravity tugging down at his
stomach, Ed had been sure he was about to die.

And when it didn't happen, when he landed, and
lived, and rolled on to skate another day, it had been a
thousand times sweeter just because he had
been so scared. It seemed to Ed that there was nothing
better than that moment after the terror had passed.

Then he lost the use of his legs and grew a wheelchair
on his butt, and everything changed. A wheelchair did
not give the sort of thrills you got from a skateboard.
There had been a few times, especially right after he realized he was never, ever going to get out of
the chair, that Ed had thought about taking the contraption out into traffic—just to see how well it played

1

with the taxis and delivery vans. That kind of thinking was scary in a whole different, definitely less fun way.

Legs or no legs, Ed wasn't sure that any stunt he had pulled in the past had terrified him as much as the one he was about to attempt.

He was going to tell Gaia Moore that he loved her.

Ed had been infatuated with Gaia since he first saw her in the school hallway. He was half smitten as soon as they spoke, and all the way gone within a couple of days.

Since then, Ed and Gaia had become friends—or at least they had come as close to being friends as Gaia's don't-get-close-to-me force fields would allow. To tell Gaia how he really felt would mean risking the relationship they already shared. Ed was horrified by the thought of losing contact with Gaia, but he was determined to take that chance.

For once, he was going to see what it was like to be fearless.

Sour Seventeen

ONE IDIOT AN HOUR. GAIA FIGURED that if they would let her beat up a butt-head per class, it would make the whole day go oh-so-smoothly. She would get nervous energy out of her system, add a few high points to her dull-as-a-bowling-ball day, and by the time the final bell rang the world would have eight fewer losers. All good things.

It might also help her keep her mind off Sam Moon. Sam whose life she had saved more than once. Sam who was oblivious to her existence. Sam who had the biggest bitch this side of Fifth Avenue for a girlfriend, but didn't seem to notice.

And still, Gaia couldn't stop thinking about him. Apparently, somewhere along the line, she had also been taught self-torture.

Gaia trudged out of her third-period class and shouldered her way though the clogged hallway with her cruise control completely engaged. Every conscious brain cell was dedicated to the ongoing task of what to do about her irritating and somewhat embarrassing Sam Problem.

It was like a drug problem, only slightly less messy.

Gaia tried to sidetrack her consciousness with a number of past favorites:

- How much she hated school
- How much she hated Ella
- How much she hated her father

And the newest:

- How much she hated Heather Gannis

And the fact that Heather had had sex with Sam. And the fact that Heather had taken the credit for saving Sam. And the fact that Heather got to hold hands with Sam and kiss Sam and talk to Sam and—

Gaia came to a stop in front of her locker and kicked it hard, denting the bottom of the door. A couple of Gap girls turned to stare, so Gaia kicked it again. The Gap girls scurried away.

She glared at her vague reflection in the battered door. In the dull metal, she was only an outline. That's all she was to Sam. A vague shadow of nothing much. A joke.

For a few delusional days, Gaia had thought Sam might be the one. The one to break her embarrassing record as the only unkissed seventeen-year-old on planet Earth. Maybe even the one to turn sex from something as hypothetical as the equations in calculus class into a good, solid, warm reality. But it wasn't going to happen.

There was not going to be any sex. There was never going to be any kissing. Not with Sam. Not ever.

Gaia popped the door of her locker open, tossed in the books she was carrying and took out another at random without bothering to look at it. Then she slammed the door just as hard as she had kicked it.

The poor locker door looked like someone had used it as a trampoline.

This was it.

Gaia had to get her shit together before more helpless inanimate objects suffered the same fate.

She squeezed her eyes shut for a moment, squeezed hard, as if she could squeeze out her unwanted thoughts.

Even though Gaia knew zilch about love, knew less about relationships, and knew even less about psychology, she knew exactly what her girlfriends, if she had any, would tell her.

Find a new guy. Someone to distract you. Someone who cares about you.

Right. No problem.

Unfortunately it had taken her seventeen years to find a guy who didn't care about her.

NAVIGATION OF HIGH SCHOOL HALL-

ways takes on a whole new meaning when you're three feet wide and mounted on wheels.

The Attempt

Ed Fargo skidded around a corner, narrowly avoided a collision with a janitor, then spun right past a knot of students laughing at some private joke. He threw the chair into hard reverse and did a quick 180 to dodge a stream of band students lugging instruments out a doorway, then he powered through a gap, coasted down a ramp, and took the next corner so hard he went around on one wheel.

Fifty feet away, Gaia Moore was just shutting the door of her locker. Ed let the chair coast to a halt as he watched her. Gaia's football shirt was wrinkled and her socks didn't match. Most of her pale hair had slipped free of whatever she had been using to hold it into a ponytail. Loose strands hovered around the sculpted planes of her face and the remaining hair gathered at the back of her head in a heavy, tangled, tumbled mass.

She was the most beautiful thing that Ed had ever seen.

He gave the wheels of his chair a sharp push and darted ahead of some slow walkers. Before Gaia could take two steps, Ed was at her side.

"Looking for your next victim?" he asked.

Gaia glanced down, and for a moment the characteristic frown on her insanely perfect lips was replaced by a smile. "Hey, Ed. What's up?"

Ed almost turned around and left. Why should he push it? He could live on that smile for at least a month.

Fearless, he told himself. Be fearless.

"I guess you don't want us to win at basketball this year," he started, trying to keep the tone light.

Gaia looked puzzled. "What?"

"The guy you went after this morning, Brad Reston," Ed continued. "He's a starting forward."

"How did you hear about it?" The frown was back full force.

"From Darla Rigazzim," Ed answered. "She's talked you up in every class this morning."

"Yeah, well. I wish she wouldn't." She looked away and started up the hallway again, the smooth muscles of her legs stretching under faded jeans.

Ed kept pace for fifty feet. Twice he opened his mouth to say something, but he shut it again before a word escaped. There was a distant, distracted look on Gaia's face now. The moment had passed. He would have to wait.

No, a voice said from the back of his mind. Don't wait. Tell her now. Tell her everything.

"Gaia . . . ," he started.

Something in his tone must have caught Gaia's attention. She stopped in the middle of one long stride and turned to him. Her right eyebrow was raised and her changing eyes were as blue-gray as the Atlantic fifty miles off the coast. "What's wrong, Ed?"

Ed swallowed. Suddenly he felt as if he were back on his skateboard, ready to challenge the bumpy ride down another flight of steps—only the steps in front of him went down, and down, and down forever.

Ed shook his head. "It's not important."

I love you.

"Nothing at all, really."

I want to be with you.

"Just . . . nothing in particular."

I want you to be with me.

"I'll talk to you after class."

Gaia stared at him for a moment longer, then nodded. "All right. I'll see you later." She turned around and walked off quickly, her long legs eating up the distance.

"Perfect," Ed whispered to her retreating back. A perfect pair, he thought. She's brave to the point of almost being dangerous, and I'm gutless to the point of almost being depressing.

And with
those words,
Gaia's
painfully
seventeen-
beautiful
year streak
officially
came to an
end.

THE SCHEDULE WAS A XEROX.

The Offer

Maybe a Xerox of a Xerox. Whatever it was, the print was so faint and muddy that David Twain had to squint hard and hold the sheet of paper up to the light just to make out a few words.

He lowered the folded page and looked around him. People were streaming past on all sides. The students at this school were visibly different. They moved faster. Talked faster. Dressed like they expected a society photographer to show up at any minute. They were, David thought, probably all brain-dead.

Still, nobody else seemed to be having a hard time finding the right room. Of course, the rest of them had probably spent more than eight minutes in the building.

A bell rang right over his head. The sound was so loud that it seemed to jar the fillings in his teeth. David winced and glanced up at the clanging bell. That was when he noticed that the number above the door and the room number on the schedule were the same.

A half dozen students slipped past David as he stood, stunned, in the doorway. He turned to follow, caught a bare glimpse of movement from the corner of his eye, and the next thing he knew he was flying through the air.

He landed hard on his butt. All at once he bit his tongue, dropped his books, and let out a sound that reminded him of a small dog that's been kicked. The books skidded twenty feet, letting out a spray of loose papers as they went.

The bell stopped ringing. In the space of seconds, the remaining students in the hallway dived into classrooms. David found himself alone.

`Almost.`

"Sorry."

It was a mumbled apology. Not much conviction there.

David looked up to see a tall girl with loose, thick blond hair staring down at him. "Yeah," he said. There was a warm, salty taste in his mouth. Blood. And his butt ached from the fall. At the moment those things `didn't matter.`

"You okay?" the girl asked, shoving her hand in her pocket and looking as if she'd rather be anywhere but here.

"Yeah," he said again, reaching back to touch his spine. "I'm fine. Great."

The girl shook her head. "If you say so." Her tousled hair spilled down across her shoulders as she reached down to him.

"Thanks." David let her help him to his feet. The girl's palm was warm. Her fingers surprisingly strong. "What did I run into?"

"Me."

David blinked. "You knocked me down?"

The blond girl shrugged and released his hand. "I didn't do it on purpose."

"You must have been moving pretty fast to hit that hard." David resisted an urge to rub his aches. Instead, he offered the hand the girl had just released. "Hi, I'm David Twain."

The girl glanced over her shoulder at the classroom, then stared at David's fingers as if she'd never experienced a handshake before.

"Gaia," she said. "Gaia Moore." She took his hand in hers and gave it a single quick shake.

David was the one who had fallen, but for some reason the simple introduction was enough to make this girl, this painfully beautiful girl, seem awkward.

"Great name," he said. "Like the earth goddess."

"Yeah, well." The girl looked down at the floor and shrugged before glancing back at David. "If you're okay, I need to get to class."

David shook his head. "No," he said.

Gaia blinked. "What?"

"No," David repeated. "I'm not okay." He leaned toward her and lowered his voice to his best thick whisper. "I won't be okay until you agree to go to dinner with me tomorrow night."

13

"UH . . . HUH."

The Response

"What?" David asked, his very clear blue eyes narrowing.

He was a male. He was, apparently, a nonfreak. He was not Sam. He got the affirmative grunt before Gaia could even remind herself of the ramifications.

"I said, uh-huh," Gaia said evenly, lifting her chin.

"Good," he said. "There's this place called Cookies & Couscous. It's more like a bakery than a restaurant. You know it?"

Of course she knew it. Any place that had cookies in its name and was located within twenty miles of George and Ella's automatically went on Gaia's mental map. "On Thompson."

"Right." He nodded and a piece of black hair fell over his forehead. "We can eat baklava, wash it down with espresso, and worry about having a main course after we're full of dessert."

"When?" she said. Oh, good, Gaia. Look eager. Look eager when you're anything but.

He smiled. "Tomorrow? Eight o'clock."

Gaia nodded almost imperceptibly.

His smile widened. "It's a date."

And with those words, Gaia's seventeen-year streak officially came to an end.

14

I AM AN IDIOT.

Gaia stared down at the toes of her battered sneakers and wondered how long it would be before she threw up. Or ran out of the room. Or exploded.

Maybe Connecticut

Taking a date from a guy you had known all of ten seconds seemed like such a desperate thing. A total loser move. Like something a girl who was seventeen and had never been kissed might do. The whole thing was starting to make her more than a little nauseated.

Who knew what this David guy expected out of her? Gaia the undated. Gaia the unkissed. Gaia the ultimate virgin.

Maybe it was a setup. Maybe Heather and some of the certified Popular Crowd (also known as The Association of People Who Really Hate Gaia Moore) had put this guy in her way just so they could pop up at her so-called date and pull a *Carrie*.

Gaia closed her eyes. Stupid. Definitely stupid.

"Uh, you're Gaia Moore, right?"

Gaia looked up from her desk and found a tall blond girl standing in front of her. From the way people were up and moving around the room, class had to be over. Gaia had successfully managed to nondaydream away the entire period.

15

"Are you Gaia?"

"Uh, yeah." Gaia was surprised on two counts. First was that the girl knew her name at all, the second was that she actually pronounced it right on the first try. "Yeah, that's right."

"I'm Cassie," said the girl. "Cassie Greenman."

How wonderful for you, thought Gaia. She had noticed the girl in class before. Though she hadn't seen her running with the core Popular People crowd, Gaia assumed that Cassie was in on the Anti-Gaia Coalition.

"Aren't you worried?" asked Cassie.

"What am I supposed to be worried about?" asked Gaia. She wondered if she had missed the announcement of a history exam or some similar nonevent. Or maybe this girl was talking about Gaia's upcoming date. Maybe Heather and her pals really were planning some horrible heap of humiliation. Maybe they were all standing outside the door right now, ready to mock Gaia for thinking someone would actually ask her out. Not that Gaia cared.

The girl rolled her eyes. "About being next."

"The next what?" Gaia asked.

"You know." Cassie raised a hand to her throat and drew one silver-blue-painted fingernail across the pale skin of her throat. "Being the next one killed."

Killed. That was a word that definitely drew Gaia's attention. She sat up straighter in her desk. "What do you mean, killed?"

"Killed. Like in dead."

"Killed by who?"

The blond girl rolled her eyes. "By the Gentleman."

Gaia began to wonder if everyone had just gone nuts while she wasn't paying attention. "Why would a gentleman want to kill me?"

"Not *a* gentleman," Cassie said. "*The* Gentleman. You know—the serial killer." She didn't add, "Duh," but it was clear enough in her voice.

Now Gaia was definitely interested. "Tell me about it."

"Haven't you heard? Everyone's been talking about it all morning."

"They haven't been talking to me."

Cassie shrugged. "There's this guy killing girls. He killed two over in New Jersey and three more somewhere in . . . I don't know, maybe Connecticut."

"So?" said Gaia. "Why should I be worried about what happens in Connecticut?"

That drew another roll of the eyes from the blond girl. "Don't you ever listen to the news? Last night he killed a girl from the university right over on the MacDougal side of the park."

Now Gaia wasn't just interested, she was offended. The park in question was Washington Square Park, and that was Gaia's territory. Her home court. Since coming to New York, she had been living in an old brownstone with George and Ella Niven. But the room at the top of the brownstone was not home. Washington Square Park was home.

From the chessboards to the playground, all of it was hers. She used it as a place to relax, and as a place to hunt city vermin. Gaia had been in the park herself the night before, just hoping for muggers and dealers to give her trouble. She had found nothing. The idea that someone had been killed just a block away made the muscles at the back of her jaw draw tight.

"How do they know it was the same guy?" she asked.

"Because of what he . . . does to them," her informant replied with an overdone shiver. "I don't know about you, but I'm dyeing my hair jet black till this guy is caught."

"Why?"

Cassie was starting to look a little exasperated. She pulled out a lock of her wavy hair and held it in front of her face. "Hello? Because all the victims had the same color hair, that's why. You need to be careful, too."

"I'm not that blond," said Gaia.

"Are you nuts? Your hair's even lighter than mine." The girl gave her a little smile. "It's not too different, though. In fact, ever since you started here, people have been telling me how much we look alike. Like you could be my sister or something."

Gaia stared at the girl. Whoever had said she looked like Gaia needed to get their eyes checked. Cassie Greenman was patently pretty. Very pretty. There was no way Gaia looked anything like her.

"You're nothing like me."

18

Cassie frowned. "You don't think . . ."

"No."

"I think we would look a lot alike," insisted Cassie. "If you would . . . you know . . . like, clean up . . . and dress better and—" She shrugged. "You know."

All Gaia knew was that all the cleaning up and good clothes in the world wouldn't stop her from looking like an overmuscled freak. She wished she was beautiful like her mother had been, but she would settle for being pretty like Cassie. She would settle for being normal. "Thanks for giving me the heads up on this killer."

Cassie wrinkled her nose. "Isn't it creepy? Do you think he's still around here?"

"I wouldn't worry too much." Gaia stood up and grabbed for her books. "If he's still here, he won't be for long."

Not in my park, she thought. If the killer was still there, Gaia intended to find him and stop him.

Suddenly she felt pinpricks of excitement moving over her skin. For the first time all day, she felt fully awake. Fully engaged. Fully there. She needed to make a plan. She needed to make sure that if this guy attacked anyone else in the park, it was Gaia.

As terrible as it was, in a weird sort of way the news about the serial killer actually made Gaia feel better. At least she had stopped thinking about her date.

Some secrets are too dangerous to know . . .

ROSWELL
HIGH

In the tiny town of Roswell, New Mexico, teenagers Liz Parker and Max Evans forged an otherworldly connection after Max recklessly threw aside his pact of secrecy and healed a life-threatening wound of Liz's with the touch of his hand. It turns out that Max, his sister Isabel, and their friend Michael are surviving descendants from beings on board an alien spacecraft which crash-landed in Roswell in 1947.

Max loves Liz. He couldn't let her die. But this is a dangerous secret he swore never to divulge - and now it's out. The trio must learn to trust Liz and her best friend Maria in order to stay one step ahead of the sheriff and the FBI who will stop at nothing in hunting out an alien...

"Are you Gaia?"

"Uh, yeah." Gaia was surprised on two counts. The first was that the girl knew her name at all; the second was that she `actually pronounced it right` on the first try.

"I'm Cassie," said the girl. "Cassie Greenman."

How wonderful for you, thought Gaia. She had noticed the girl in class before. Although she hadn't seen her running with the core popular-people crowd, Gaia assumed that Cassie was in on the anti-Gaia coalition.

"Aren't you worried?" Cassie asked.

"What am I supposed to be worried about?" Gaia wondered if she had missed the announcement of a history exam or some similar `nonevent`. Or maybe this girl was talking about Gaia's upcoming date. Maybe Heather and pals really were planning some horrible heap of humiliation.

Not that Gaia cared.

The girl rolled her eyes. "About being next."

"The next what?" Gaia asked.

"You know." Cassie raised a hand to her throat and drew one silver-blue-painted fingernail across the pale skin of her throat. `"Being the next one killed."`

Don't miss any books in this thrilling new series
from Pocket Books:

FEARLESS™

All Pocket Book titles are available by post from:
**Simon & Schuster Cash Sales, P.O. Box 29,
Douglas, Isle of Man IM99 1BQ**
Credit cards accepted. Please telephone 01624 836000,
Fax 01624 670923, Internet http://www.bookpost.co.uk
or email: bookshop@enterprise.net for details

F E A R L E S S ™

FRANCINE PASCAL

TWISTED

POCKET
BOOKS

An imprint of Simon & Schuster UK Ltd
A Viacom Company
Africa House, 64-78 Kingsway, London WC2B 6AH

Produced by 17th Street Productions, Inc.
A division of Daniel Weiss Associates, Inc.
33 West 17th Street, New York, NY 10011

A CIP catalogue record for this book is
available from the British Library

ISBN 0671 77345 3

1 3 5 7 9 10 8 6 4 2

Printed by Cox & Wyman Ltd, Reading, Berkshire

TWISTED

There are circles in Hell.

My father—back when he still cared that I was alive and breathing—used to make me read. Not easy stuff. Even when I was a kid, there was no *Winnie-the-Pooh*, no *Little House on the Prairie*. Not for me.

It was all about the classics. *Hard* classics.

One of the moldy oldies he put under my nose was *The Inferno*, by Dante. This book was seriously tough sledding. The whole thing was written in verse, and it was full of political stuff that didn't always make a lot of sense, and the language was creaky to say the least. But there were good parts.

In this story a guy gets led all around Hell to see how everybody is punished. A lot of it is kind of like you would expect. Lots of demons with whips. Fire. Snakes. That kind of thing.

But the idea that stuck with me was the way Hell was divided

up in circles. The dead guys up
in the first circle don't have it
so bad. It's just kind of rainy
and dull up there. But the really
bad people, like murderers (or
members of a political party
Dante didn't like), they get
shoved way down to a circle where
they have to run around without
feet or burst into flame or get
eaten by big lizards or melt like
candles.

I remembered this book the
other day and started thinking
that my life could be sliced up
in the same way as hell.

There are the little things.
Finding out the deli is out of
Krispy Kreme. Losing a chess game
against some moron I should have
schooled. That's the gloomy,
first-circle sort of hell.

Then there's having to live
with George and Ella. George knew
my father, but I don't really
know him. Ella didn't know my
father, doesn't know me, and I
don't even *want* to know Ella.

She's definitely a deeper level of hell.

The next level down is high school. It gets a level of hell all to itself.

Below that comes Sam and Heather. I wouldn't throw Sam in a pit by himself. I mean, Sam's the guy I want to be with. The only guy I've ever wanted to be with. But Sam is with Heather, and together they deserve pitchforks and brimstone.

Then there's my father. My father disappears, doesn't write, doesn't call, and doesn't give me a clue about what's going on. Now we're getting really deep. Snakes and fire. Demons with weird Latin names.

And my mom. The way I feel when I think about her. When I think about her death. Well, that brings us right down to the bottom.

The way Dante tells it, the very bottom layer of hell isn't hot. Instead it's a big lake of ice with people frozen inside.

They're stuck forever with only
their faces sticking out, and
every time they cry, it just adds
another layer of frost covering
their eyes.

   Put my whole life together,
and that's where I am. Down on
the ice. Some days I feel like I
have a pair of skates. Other days
I wonder if Dante didn't get it
wrong. Maybe the ice isn't the
lowest level after all.

Her big pal
gave her a
little love
pat—enough
to bounce
her from
the wall
and back to
his beefy
hand.

**the
high
school
circle**

PRETTY PEOPLE DO UGLY THINGS.

It was one of those laws of nature that Gaia had understood for years. If she ever started to forget that rule for a second, there always seemed to be some good-looking asshole ready to remind her.

Jerkus High-schoolensis

She stumbled up the steps and pushed her way inside The Village School with five minutes to spare before her first class. Actually early. Of course, her hair was still wet from the shower and her homework wasn't done, but being there—actually physically inside the building before the bell rang—was a new experience. For twelve whole seconds after that, she thought she might have an all right day.

Then she caught a glimpse of one of those things that absolutely defines the high school circle of hell.

Down at the end of the row of lockers, a tall, broad-shouldered guy was smiling a very confident smile, wearing very popular-crowd clothes, and using a very big hand to pin a very much smaller girl up against the wall. There was an amused expression on Mr. Handsome's face.

Only the girl who was stuck between his hand and fifty years' worth of ugly green paint didn't look like she thought it was funny.

Gaia had noticed the big boy in a couple of her classes but hadn't bothered to file away his name. Tad, she thought, or maybe it was Chip. She knew it was something like that.

From the way girls in class talked, he was supposed to be cute. Gaia could sort of see it. Big blue eyes. Good skin. Six-five even without the air soles in his two-hundred-dollar sneakers. His lips were a little puffy, but then, some people liked that. It was the hair that really eliminated him from Gaia's list of guys worth looking at.

He wore that stuff in his hair. The stuff that looked like a combination of motor oil and maple syrup. The stuff that made it look like he hadn't washed his hair this side of tenth grade. "What's the rush, Darla?" the Chipster said. "I just want to know what he said to you."

The girl, Darla, shook her head. "He didn't . . ."

Her big pal gave her a little love pat—enough to bounce her from the wall and back to his beefy hand.

"Don't give me that," he said, still all smiles. "I saw you two together."

Gaia did a quick survey of the hall. There was a trio of khaki-crowd girls fifty yards down and two leather dudes hanging near the front door. A skinny guy stuck his head out of a classroom, saw who was doing the shoving, and quickly ducked back in. Gaia had to give him some credit. At least he looked. Everybody else in the hallway was Not Noticing so hard, it hurt.

Gaia really didn't need this. She didn't know the girl against the wall. Sure, the guy with the big hands was a prime example of Jerkus highschoolensis, but it was absolutely none of Gaia's business. She turned away and headed for class, wondering if she might avoid a tardy slip for the first time in a week.

"Just let me . . . ," the girl begged from behind her.

"In a minute, babe," replied the guy with the hands. "I just need to talk to you a little." There was a thump and a short whimper from the girl.

Gaia stopped. She really, really didn't need this.

She took a deep breath, turned, and headed back toward the couple.

The easiest thing would be to grab the guy by the face and teach him how soft a skull was compared to a concrete wall. But then, smashing someone's head would probably not help Gaia's reputation.

Words were an option. She hadn't used that method much, but there was a first time for everything, right?

She could try talking to the guy or even threatening to tell a teacher. Gaia didn't care if anyone at the school thought she was a wimp or a narc, or whatever they called it in New York City. That was the least of her problems. Besides, they already thought she was a bitch for not warning Heather about the park slasher.

Before long, Gaia was so close that both partners in the ugly little dance turned to look at her. Tough Guy's smile didn't budge an inch.

"What?" he said.

Gaia struggled for something to say. Something smooth. Something that would defuse this whole thing. She paused for a second, cleared her throat, and said . . .

"Is there . . . uh, some kind of a problem?"

Brilliant.

The guy who might be named Chip took a two-second look at her face, then spent twice as long trying to size up the breasts under Gaia's rumpled football shirt.

"Nothing you gotta worry about," he said, still staring at her chest. He waved the hand that wasn't busy holding a person. "This is a private conversation."

The girl against the wall looked at Gaia with a big-eyed, round-mouthed expression that could have been fear or hope or stupidity. Gaia's instant impression was that it was a little bit of all three. The girl had straight black hair that was turned up in a little flip, tanned-to-a-golden-brown skin, an excess of eye shadow, and a cheerleading uniform. She didn't exactly strike Gaia as a brain trust.

9

Not that being a cheerleader automatically made somebody stupid. Gaia was certain there were smart cheerleaders. Somewhere there had to be cheerleaders who were working on physics theories every time they put down their pom-poms. She hadn't met any, but they were out there. Probably living in the same city with all the nice guys who don't mind if a girl has thunder thighs and doesn't know how to dress.

"Well?" demanded Puffy Lips. "What's wrong with you? Are you deaf or just stupid?"

Gaia tensed. Anger left an acid taste in her throat. Suddenly her fist was crying out for his face. She opened her mouth to say something just as the bell for first period rang. So much for being on time.

She took a step closer to the pair. "Why don't you let her go?"

Chip made a little grunting laugh and shook his head. "Look, babe. Get out of here," he said to Gaia.

Babe. It wasn't necessarily an insult—unless the person saying it added that perfect tone of voice. The tone that says being a babe is on the same evolutionary rung as being a brain-damaged hamster.

Gaia glanced up the hallway. Only a few students were still in the hall, and none were close. If she planned to do anything without everyone in school seeing it, this was the time.

She leaned toward him. "Maybe *you'd* better get out of here," she said in a low voice. She could feel the

10

cheerleader's short breaths on the back of her neck. "You don't want to be late for class."

The sunny smile slipped from Chip's face, replaced by a go-away-you're-bothering-me frown. "Did you hear me tell you to go?"

Gaia shrugged. It was coming. That weird rush she sometimes felt.

"I heard you. I just didn't listen."

Now the expression on Chip's face was more like an I-guess-I'm-going-to-have-to-teach-you-how-the-world-works sneer. "Get the hell out of my way," he snapped.

"Make me."

He took his hand off Darla and grabbed Gaia by the arm.

Gaia was glad. If she touched him first, there was always the chance he would actually admit he got beat up by a girl and charge her with assault. But since Chip made the first move, all bets were off. Everything that happened from that first touch was self-defense.

Gaia was an expert in just about every martial art with a name. Jujitsu. Tai kwon do. Judo. Kung fu. If it involved hitting, kicking, or tossing people through the air, Gaia knew it. Standing six inches from Mr. Good Skin Bad Attitude, she could have managed a kick that would have taken his oily head right off his thick neck. She could have put a stiff hand through his rib cage or delivered a punch that drove his heart up against his spine.

But she didn't do any of that. She wanted to, but she didn't.

Moving quickly, she turned her arms and twisted out of his grip. Before Chip could react, she reached across with her left hand, took hold of the guy's right thumb, and gave it just a little . . . push.

For a moment Puffy Lips Chip looked surprised. Then Gaia pushed a little harder on his captive digit, and the look of surprise instantly turned to pain.

He tried to pull away, but Gaia held tight. She was working hard to keep from actually breaking his thumb. She could have broken his whole oversized hand like a bundle of big dry sticks. The real trick was hurting someone without really hurting someone. Don't break any bones. Don't leave any scars. Don't do anything permanent. Leave a memory.

"What do you think, Chip?" Gaia asked, still pushing his thumb toward the back of his hand. "Should you be shoving girls around?"

"Let go of me, you little—" He reached for her with his free hand.

Gaia leaned back out of his range and gave an extra shove. Chip wailed.

"Here's the deal," Gaia said quietly. "You keep your hands to yourself, I let you keep your hands. What do you think?"

Chip's knees were starting to shake, and there were beads of sweat breaking out on his forehead. "Who are—"

12

"Like I really want you to know my name." She pushed harder, and now Gaia could feel the bones in his thumb pulling loose from his hand. Another few seconds and one was sure to snap. "Do we have a deal?"

"Okay," he squeaked in a voice two octaves higher than it had been a few seconds before. "Sure."

Gaia let go. "That's good, Chip." The moment the physical conflict ended, Gaia felt all her uncertainty come rushing back. She glanced up the hallway and was relieved to see that there was no crowd of gawkers. That didn't stop her from feeling dizzy. She was acting like muscle-bound freak girl right in the main hallway at school. This was definitely not the way to remain invisible.

Puffy Lips stepped back and gripped his bruised thumb in his left hand. "Brad."

"What?"

"Brad," he said. "My name isn't Chip. It's Brad."

Gaia rolled her eyes. "Whatever." She lowered her head and shoved past him just as the late bell rang.

Another day, another fight, another tardy.

Things Gaia Knows
School sucks.

Ella sucks.

Her father sucks.

Heather Gannis sucks big time.

Things Gaia Wants to Know
Who kidnapped Sam?

Why did they contact her?

What was with all those stupid tests?

How could she have let the kidnappers get away after everything they'd done to her and Sam?

Why did Mr. Rupert use the words "all right" more often than most people used the word "the"?

Who killed CJ?

Why did she never know she had an uncle who looked exactly like her father?

Was said uncle going to contact her again?

Did she even want him to after he'd been nonexistent for her entire life?

Why did anyone in their right mind choose to drink skim milk?

Was she really expected to pay attention in class when there were things going on that actually mattered?

The Decision

EVEN BACK WHEN HIS LEGS WORKED, Ed had never been fearless.

He sat in his first-period class and stared at the door. Any moment, the bell would ring. Then he would go out into the hallway and Gaia would appear. Any moment, he would have his chance. In the meantime he was terrified.

People who had seen him on a skateboard or a pair of in-lines might have been surprised to hear it. There had been no stairs too steep to slalom, no handrail Ed wasn't willing to challenge, no traffic too thick to dare. Anyone would tell you, Ed Fargo was a wild man. He took more risks, and took them faster, than any other boarder in the city.

The dark secret was that all through those days, almost every second, Ed had been terrified. Every time his wheels had sent sparks lancing from a metal rail, every time he had gone over a jump and felt gravity tugging down at his stomach, Ed had been sure he was about to die.

And when it didn't happen, when he landed, and lived, and rolled on to skate another day, it had been a thousand times sweeter just because he had been so scared. It seemed to Ed that there was nothing better than that moment after the terror had passed.

Then he lost the use of his legs and grew a wheelchair

on his butt, and everything changed. A wheelchair didn't give the sort of thrills you got from a skateboard. There were a few times, especially right after he realized he was never, ever going to get out of the chair, that Ed had thought about taking the contraption out into traffic—just to see how well it played with the taxis and delivery vans. That kind of thinking was scary in a whole different, definitely less fun way.

Legs or no legs, Ed wasn't sure that any stunt he had pulled in the past had terrified him as much as the one he was about to attempt.

He stared at the classroom door, and the blood rushing through his brain sounded as loud as a subway train pulling up to the platform.

He was going to tell Gaia Moore that he loved her.

He was really going to do it. If he didn't faint first.

Ed had been infatuated with Gaia since he first saw her in the school hallway. He was half smitten as soon as they spoke and all the way gone within a couple of days.

Since then, Ed and Gaia had become friends—or at least they had come as close to being friends as Gaia's don't-get-close-to-me forcefield would allow. To tell Gaia how he really felt would mean risking the relationship they already shared. Ed was horrified by the thought of losing contact with Gaia, but he was determined to take that chance.

16

For once, he was going to see what it was like to be fearless.

Sour Seventeen

ONE IDIOT AN HOUR. GAIA FIGURED that if they would let her beat up one butthead per class, it would make the day go oh-so-smoothly. She would get the nervous energy out of her system, add a few high points to her dull-as-a-bowling-ball day, and by the time the final bell rang, the world would have eight fewer losers. All good things.

It might also help her keep her mind off Sam Moon. Sam, whose life she had saved more than once. Sam, who was oblivious to her existence. Sam, who had the biggest bitch this side of Fifth Avenue for a girlfriend but didn't seem to notice.

And still Gaia couldn't stop thinking about him. Daydreaming her way through each and every class. If her teachers had tested her on self-torture, she would have gotten an A.

Gaia trudged out of her third-period classroom and shouldered her way through the clogged hallway,

17

her cruise control engaged. Every conscious brain cell was dedicated to the ongoing problem of what to do about her irritating and somewhat embarrassing Sam problem.

It was like a drug problem, only slightly less messy.

It was bad enough that Sam was with Heather. Even worse was Heather getting credit for everything Gaia did. Gaia had nearly lost her life saving Sam from a kidnapper. She had gone crazy looking for him. And then Heather had stepped in at the last second and looked like the big hero when her total expended effort was equal to drying her fingernails.

Not to mention the fact that the kidnappers had gotten away after they spent an entire day ordering her around as if she were a toy poodle.

Gaia suddenly realized she was biting her lip so badly that it was about to bleed. Whenever she thought about how the nameless, faceless men in black had used her, she got the uncontrollable urge to do serious violence to something. Then, of course, her thoughts turned directly to Heather.

And the fact that Heather had sex with Sam. And the fact that Heather had taken credit for saving Sam. And the fact that Heather got to hold hands with Sam and kiss Sam and talk to Sam and—

Gaia came to a stop in front of her locker and kicked it hard, denting the bottom of the door. A couple of Gap girls turned to stare, so Gaia kicked it again. The Gap girls scurried away.

She snarled at her vague reflection in the battered door. In the dull metal she was only an outline. That's all she was to Sam, too. A vague shadow of nothing much.

For a few delusional days Gaia had thought Sam might be the one. The one to break her embarrassing record as the only unkissed seventeen-year-old on planet Earth. Maybe even the one to turn sex from hypothesis into reality. But it wasn't going to happen.

There wasn't going to be any sex. There was never going to be any kissing. Not with Sam. Not ever.

Gaia yanked open the door of her locker, tossed in the book she was carrying, and randomly took out another without bothering to look at it. Then she slammed the door just as hard as she had kicked it.

She squeezed her eyes shut for a moment, squeezed hard, as if she could squeeze out her unwanted thoughts.

Even though Gaia knew zilch about love, knew less about relationships, and knew even less about psychology, she knew exactly what her girlfriends, if she had any, would tell her.

Find a new guy. Someone to distract you. Someone who cares about you.

Right. No problem.

19

Unfortunately, it had only taken her seventeen years to find a guy who didn't care about her.

NAVIGATION OF HIGH SCHOOL HALL-

ways takes on a whole new meaning when you're three feet wide and mounted on wheels.

The Attempt

Ed Fargo skidded around a corner, narrowly avoided a collision with a janitor, then spun right past a knot of students laughing at some private joke. He threw the chair into hard reverse and did a quick 180 to dodge a stream of band students lugging instruments out a doorway, then he powered through a gap, coasted down a ramp, and took the next corner so hard, he went around on one wheel.

Fifty feet away, Gaia Moore was just shutting the door of her locker. Ed let the chair coast to a halt as he watched her. Gaia's football shirt was wrinkled, and her socks didn't match. Most of her yellow hair had slipped free of whatever she had been using to hold it in a ponytail. Loose strands hovered around the sculpted planes of her face, and the remaining hair gathered at the back of her head in a heavy, tumbled mass.

She was the most beautiful thing that Ed had ever seen.

He gave the wheels of his chair a sharp push and darted ahead of some slow walkers. Before Gaia could take two steps, Ed was at her side.

"Looking for your next victim?" he asked.

Gaia glanced down, and for a moment the characteristic frown on her insanely kissable lips was replaced by a smile. "Hey, Ed. What's up?"

Ed almost turned around and left. Why should he push it? He could live on that smile for at least a month.

Fearless, he told himself. Be fearless.

"I guess you don't want us to win at basketball this year," he started, trying to keep the tone light.

Gaia looked puzzled. "What?"

"The guy you went after this morning, Brad Reston," Ed continued. "He's a starting forward."

"How did you hear about it?" The frown was back full force.

"From Darla Rigazzi," Ed answered. "She's talked you up in every class this morning."

"Yeah, well, I wish she wouldn't." She looked away and started up the hallway again, the smooth muscles of her legs stretching under faded jeans.

Ed kept pace for fifty feet. Twice he opened his mouth to say something, but he shut it again before a word escaped. There was a distant, distracted look on Gaia's face now. The moment had passed. He would have to wait.

No, a voice said from the back of his mind. Don't wait. Tell her now. Tell her everything.

"Gaia . . . ," he started.

Something in his tone must have caught Gaia's attention. She stopped in the middle of one long stride and turned to him. Her right eyebrow was raised, and her changing eyes were the blue-gray of the Atlantic fifty miles off the coast. "What's wrong, Ed?"

Ed swallowed. Suddenly he felt like he was back on his skateboard, ready to challenge the bumpy ride down another flight of steps—only the steps in front of him went down, and down, and down forever.

He swallowed hard and shook his head. "It's not important."

I love you.

"Nothing at all, really."

I want to be with you.

"Just . . . nothing in particular."

I want you to be with me.

"I'll talk to you after class."

Gaia stared at him for a moment longer, then nodded. "All right. I'll see you later." She turned around and walked off quickly, her long legs eating up the distance.

"Perfect," Ed whispered to her retreating back.

A perfect pair. She was brave to the point of almost being dangerous, and he was gutless to the point of almost being depressing.

Sometimes I wonder what I would say if I were ever asked out on a date.

You'd think that since it's never happened to me, I might have had some time in the past seventeen years to formulate the perfect response. You'd think that with all the movies I've seen, I would have at least picked up some cheesy line. Some doe-eyed, swooning acceptance.

But I pretty much stay away from romantic comedies. There's no relationship advice to be had from a Neil LaBute film.

Besides, you can't formulate the perfect response for a situation you can't remotely imagine.

I figure that if it ever does happen (not probable), I'll end up saying something along the lines of "uh" or slight variations thereof.

"Uh . . . uh," if the guy's a freak.

"Uh . . . huh," if the guy's a nonfreak.

I wonder what Heather said to Sam when he first asked her out. Probably something disgustingly perfect. Something right out of a movie. Something like, "I was wondering when you'd ask." Or maybe Heather asked Sam out. And he said something like, "It would be my honor."

Okay. Stomach now reacting badly. Must think about something else.

What did Heather say when *Ed* asked her out?

Okay. Stomach now severely cramping.

So what happens after the "Uh . . . huh"?

Awkward pauses, I assume. Idiot small talk, sweaty palms (his), dry mouth (also his), bad food. (I imagine dates don't happen at places where they have good food—like Gray's Papaya or Dojo's.)

And I won't even get into what happens after the most likely difficult digestion. What does

the nonfreak expect at that
point? Hand holding? Kissing?
Groping? Heavy groping? Sex?

Stomach no longer wishes to be
a component of body.

Must stop here.

Luckily I won't ever have to
deal with any of this. Because no
nonfreak will ever ask me out.
And no freak will ever get more
than the initial grunt.

And with
those words,
Gaia's

painfully
seventeen-
beautiful

year streak

officially

came to an

end.

THE SCHEDULE WAS A XEROX.

The Offer

Maybe a Xerox of a Xerox. Whatever it was, the print was so faint and muddy that David Twain had to squint hard and hold the sheet of paper up to the light just to make out a few words.

He lowered the folded page and looked around him. People were streaming past on all sides. The students at this school were visibly different. They moved faster. Talked faster. Dressed like they expected a society photographer to show up at any minute. They were, David thought, probably all brain-dead.

Still, nobody else seemed to be having a hard time finding the right room. Of course, the rest of them had spent more than eight minutes in the building.

A bell rang right over his head. The sound of it was so loud that it seemed to jar the fillings in his teeth. David winced and looked up at the clanging bell. That was when he noticed that the number above the door and the room number on the schedule were the same.

A half-dozen students slipped past David as he stood in the doorway. He turned to follow, caught a bare glimpse of movement from the corner of his eye, and the next thing he knew, he was flying through the air.

He landed hard on his butt. All at once he bit his tongue, dropped his brand-new books, and let out a sound that reminded him of a small dog that had been kicked. The books skidded twenty feet, letting out a spray of loose papers as they went.

The bell stopped ringing. In the space of seconds the remaining students in the hallway dived into classrooms. David found himself alone.

Almost.

"Sorry."

It was a mumbled apology. Not much conviction there.

David looked up to see a tall girl with loose, tangled blond hair standing over him.

"Yeah," he said. There was a warm, salty taste in his mouth. Blood. And his butt ached from the fall. At the moment those things didn't matter.

"You okay?" the girl asked, shoving her hand in her pocket and looking like she'd rather be anywhere but there.

"Yeah," he said again, reaching back to touch his spine. "I'm fine. Great."

The girl shook her head. "If you say so." She offered her hand, even as her face took on an even more sour expression.

Her tousled hair spilled down across her shoulders as she reached to him.

"Thanks." David took her hand and let her help

him to his feet. The girl's palm was warm. Her fingers were surprisingly strong. "What did I run into?"

"Me."

David blinked. "You knocked me down?"

The blond girl shrugged and released his hand. "I didn't do it on purpose."

"You must have been moving pretty fast to hit that hard." David resisted an urge to rub his aches. Instead he offered the hand the girl had just released. "Hi, I'm David Twain."

The girl glanced over her shoulder at the classroom, then stared at David's fingers as if she'd never experienced a handshake before.

"Gaia," she said. "Gaia Moore." She took his hand in hers and gave it a single quick shake.

David was the one who had fallen, but for some reason the simple introduction was enough to make this girl, this painfully beautiful girl, seem awkward.

"Great name," he said. "Like the Earth goddess."

"Yeah, well, if you're okay—"

David shook his head. "No," he said.

Gaia blinked. "What?"

"No," David repeated. "I'm not okay." He leaned toward her and lowered his voice to his best thick whisper. "I won't be okay until you agree to go to dinner with me tomorrow night."

"UH . . . HUH."

The Response

"What?" David asked, his very clear blue eyes narrowing.

He was a male. He was, apparently, a nonfreak. He was not Sam. He got the `affirmative grunt` before Gaia could remind herself of the ramifications.

"I said, uh-huh," Gaia said evenly, lifting her chin.

"Good," he said. "There's this place called Cookies & Couscous. It's more like a bakery than a restaurant. You know it?"

Of course she knew it. Any place that had *cookies* in its name and was located within twenty miles of her room automatically went on Gaia's `mental map`.

"On Thompson," she said.

"Right." He nodded, and a piece of black hair fell over his forehead. "We can eat some baklava, wash it down with espresso, and worry about having a main course after we're full of dessert."

For a moment Gaia just looked at him. He was tall. Gangly. Almost sweet looking. `Very not Sam`.

"Baklava," David repeated with a smirk. "Buttery. Flaky. Honey and nuts."

Gaia nearly smiled. Almost.

This could take her mind off Sam. The kidnappers. The uncle. Heather.

"When?" she said.

He smiled. "Tomorrow? Eight o'clock."

Gaia nodded almost imperceptibly.

His smile widened. "It's a date."

And with those words, Gaia's seventeen-year streak officially came to an end.

HEATHER GANNIS COULDN'T BELIEVE

The Unsaid

what she was about to do, but there was no getting around it. There were too many things that had to be said. Things that couldn't go unsaid much longer. Not without Heather going into a paranoid frenzy. And frenzy was not something Heather did well. She liked to be in control. Always.

She looked at her reflection in the scratched bathroom mirror, tossed her glossy brown hair behind her shoulders, took a deep breath, and plunged into the melee that was the post-lunch hall crowd.

Even in the crush of people it only took Heather about five seconds to spot Gaia Moore. And her perfectly tousled blond hair. And her supermodel-tall body. Before she could remind herself of how stupid it was to do this in public, Heather

31

walked right up to Gaia and grabbed her arm.

Gaia looked completely surprised.

"We have to talk," Heather said.

Even more surprised. Gaia yanked her arm away. "Doubtful," she said.

Heather fixed her with a leveling glare as she noticed a few curious bystanders pausing to check out the latest Gaia-Heather confrontation. "Bio lab," Heather said. Then she turned on her heel and made her way to the designated room.

She almost couldn't believe it when Gaia walked in moments later.

Gaia raised her eyebrows and shrugged, tucking her hands into the front pockets of her pants. "Call me curious," she said.

Wanting to remain in charge, Heather slapped her books down on top of one of the big, black tables and rested one hand on her hip. "Who kidnapped Sam?" she asked evenly.

"I don't know," Gaia said, suddenly standing up straight.

"Right," Heather said, her ire already rising. "Then why did they contact you?"

"I don't know," Gaia repeated.

Heather scoffed and looked up at the ceiling, concentrating on trying to keep the blood from rising to her face. "Is that all you're going to say?" she spat. "You asked for my help, then you tripped me on the stairs, and I spent two hours stuck with the idiot police at NYU trying to convince them I wasn't some crazed stalker, and all you can say is, 'I don't know?'" She was sounding hysterical. She had to stop.

Gaia shrugged. It was all Heather could do to keep from clocking the girl in the head with her physics book. She took a long, deep breath through her nose, and let it out slowly—audibly. Then she picked up her books, hugging them to her chest, and walked right up to Gaia, the toe of her suede boot just touching the battered rubber of Gaia's sneaker. The girl didn't move.

"Stay away from Sam," Heather said, trying to muster a threatening tone. It wasn't the easiest thing in the world. Gaia had threatened her. Gaia had hurt her. Gaia had almost gotten her killed.

The girl was like a statue.

Heather stepped around Gaia and headed for the door. She stopped to look behind her and Gaia was frozen in place, as if someone were still standing before her speaking.

"Freak," Heather muttered. And with that, she was out the door.

Before Gaia could snap out of it and come after her.

THE PENCIL SNAPPED. IN THE

silent lecture hall the noise seemed as loud as a gunshot.

Thirty pairs of eyes turned toward Sam Moon, and from the back of the hall came a muffled snicker. Sam closed his eyes for a moment, then slowly raised his hand.

"Yes, Mr. Moon," the physics professor said with a tone of tired amusement. "You can get another."

Sam closed his blue test folder and searched quickly through his book bag for a replacement pencil. All around him he could hear the quiet scratching of lead on paper as the rest of the class hurried to complete the exam. Sam's progress on the test couldn't exactly be called hurrying. There were one hundred and twenty questions on the test and exactly fifty-seven minutes to answer them all. With forty-five of those minutes gone, Sam was on number twelve.

He finally located another pencil and put the bag back on the floor. He looked down at the next question, touched the pencil to the paper. The pencil snapped into four pieces.

This time there was nothing muffled about the laughter.

The physics professor, an older man with a comb-over so complex, it was a science in itself, let loose a heavy sigh.

"Mr. Moon, if this test is causing you so much stress, might I suggest you try a pen?" he said with a sneer. "I would not want to be responsible for chopping down whole forests of precious trees just to keep you supplied with pencils."

Sam would have liked to smack the guy. He would have liked to ask him if he'd ever taken a physics midterm two days after being released by a group of as yet unidentified kidnapping psychos. He would have liked to get up and leave the room.

He didn't. Sam Moon did not shirk responsibility. It wasn't in his blood.

Ignoring the remnants of the last wave of laughter, Sam dug through his book bag a second time, extracted a ballpoint, and went back to work. Even the pen gave out a little squeak in his hand, as if the plastic was that close to breaking.

It wasn't just his recent trauma that was causing his tension, although it had less than nothing to do with the exam—less than nothing to do with frequencies and waveforms and photon behavior.

The real tension came from the tug-of-war that was going on in his brain. On one end of the rope was Heather Gannis. The lovely, the popular, the much-sought-after Heather. The Heather that Sam was dating. Assisting on her end of the rope was a whole army of good reasons for Sam to stay in his current relationship. There was beauty—which Heather certainly had. And there was sex, which Heather was willing to provide. And there was a certain reliability. Sam knew Heather. He could count on Heather. He might not always like everything about Heather, but he knew her. There were no surprises on that side.

And of course, she had saved his life.

Dragging the rope in the other direction was Gaia Moore. There was no army on Gaia's side. The girl brought nothing but frustration, confusion, mystery, and imminent danger. Technically she was a mess. And from the moment Sam met her, Gaia had seemed to stumble from one disaster to the next. But at least Gaia wasn't boring. She was anything but.

If Sam's head had staged a fair fight, Team Heather would have dragged Gaia right off the field so fast, she would have had grass burns on her face. But something inside Sam wouldn't let that happen. Something in him kept holding on to Gaia's end of the rope, keeping her in the game.

He closed his eyes for a moment and put his hands against his temples. He had to stop thinking about Gaia. Thinking about Gaia when he was already committed to Heather was wrong. More than that, the way he thought about Gaia all the time was getting to be more than a little like an obsession.

"Ten minutes, people," said the professor. "You should be getting near the end."

Sam shook his head, flinging away the rope and all

its hangers-on. He studied the next question on the test and scribbled out an answer. Then he tackled the next. And the next. When he managed to concentrate, Sam found that the answers came easily. Sometimes it was nice to have the powers of a good geek brain. He sped through a series of equations without faltering, flew past some short answers, and was within five questions of the end when the professor called, "Time."

Sam gathered up his things and carried his paper to the front of the room, relieved. At least he had cleared the Gaia fog from his brain long enough to get some work done. He hadn't embarrassed himself. Not this time, anyway.

But he wasn't sure how long that would last. The battle in his head was still picking up steam. Soon it was going to be a full-blown war.

Maybe Connecticut

GAIA STARED DOWN AT THE TOES OF her battered sneakers and wondered how long it would be before she threw up. Or ran out of the room. Or exploded.

Accepting a date with a guy she had known all of ten seconds seemed like such a desperate thing. A total loser move. Like something a girl who was seventeen and had never been kissed might do.

The whole thing was starting to make her nauseated.

At least it had already served its purpose. She wasn't thinking about . . . all those things she didn't want to think about.

Who knew what this David guy expected out of her? Gaia the undated. Gaia the untouched. Gaia the ultimate virgin.

Maybe knocking David down had spun his brain around backward. Left him with a concussion that led to his asking out the first girl he saw.

Or maybe it was a setup. Maybe Heather and some of the certified Popular Crowd (also known as The Association of People Who Really Hate Gaia Moore) had put this guy in her way just so they could pop up at her so-called date and pull a *Carrie*.

Gaia closed her eyes and moaned. "Stupid. Definitely stupid."

"Uh, you're Gaia Moore, right?"

Gaia looked up from her desk and found a tall blond girl standing in front of her. From the way people were up and moving around the room, class had to be over. Gaia had successfully managed to obsess away the entire period.

"Are you Gaia?"

"Uh, yeah." Gaia was surprised on two counts. The first was that the girl knew her name at all; the second was that she `actually pronounced it right` on the first try. "Yeah, that's right."

"I'm Cassie," said the girl. "Cassie Greenman."

How wonderful for you, thought Gaia. She had noticed the girl in class before. Although she hadn't seen her running with the core popular-people crowd, Gaia assumed that Cassie was in on the anti-Gaia coalition.

"Aren't you worried?" Cassie asked.

"What am I supposed to be worried about?" Gaia wondered if she had missed the announcement of a history exam or some similar `nonevent`. Or maybe this girl was talking about Gaia's upcoming date. Maybe Heather and pals really were planning some horrible heap of humiliation. Maybe they were all standing outside the door right now, ready to mock Gaia for thinking someone would actually ask her out.

Not that Gaia cared.

The girl rolled her eyes. "About being next."

"The next what?" Gaia asked.

"You know." Cassie raised a hand to her throat and drew one silver-blue-painted fingernail across the pale skin of her throat. `"Being the next one killed."`

Killed. That was a word that definitely drew Gaia's attention. She sat up straighter at her desk. "What do you mean, killed?"

"Killed. Like in dead."

"Killed by who?"

The blond girl shook her head. "By the Gentleman."

Gaia began to wonder if everyone had just gone nuts while she wasn't paying attention. "Why would a gentleman want to kill me?"

"Not *a* gentleman," said Cassie, "*the* Gentleman. You know—the serial killer." She didn't add "duh," but it was clear enough in her voice.

Now Gaia was definitely interested. "Tell me about it."

"Haven't you heard?" Cassie pulled her books a little closer to her chest. "Everyone's been talking about it all morning."

"They haven't been talking to me."

Cassie shrugged. "There's this guy killing girls. He killed two over in New Jersey and three more somewhere in ... I don't know, maybe Connecticut."

"So?" said Gaia. "Why should I be worried about what happens in Connecticut?"

That drew another roll of the eyes from the blond girl. "Don't you ever listen to the news? Last night he killed a girl from NYU right over on the MacDougal side of the park."

Now Gaia wasn't just interested, she was offended. The park in question was Washington Square Park, and that was Gaia's territory. Her home court.

From the chessboards to the playground, all of

40

it was hers. She used it as a place to relax and as a place to hunt city vermin. Gaia had been in the park herself the night before, just hoping for muggers and dealers to give her trouble. The idea that someone had been killed just a block away. . . .

"How do they know it was the same guy?" she asked.

"Because of what he . . . does to them," her informant replied with an overdone shiver. "I don't know about you, but I'm dying my hair jet black till this guy is caught."

"Why?"

Cassie was starting to look a little exasperated. She pulled out a lock of her wavy hair and held it in front of her face. "Hello? Because all the victims had the same color hair, that's why. You need to be careful, too."

"I'm not that blond," said Gaia.

"Are you nuts? Your hair's even lighter than mine." The girl gave a little smile. "It's not too different, though. In fact, ever since you started here, people have been telling me how much we look alike. Like you could be my sister or something."

Gaia stared at the girl. Whoever had said she looked like Gaia needed to get their eyes checked. Cassie Greenman was patently pretty. Very pretty. There was no way Gaia looked anything like her.

"You're nothing like me."

Cassie frowned. "You don't think . . ."

"No."

"I think we would look a lot alike," insisted Cassie, "if you would . . . you know . . . like, clean up . . . and dress better. . . ." She shrugged. "You know."

All Gaia knew was that all the cleaning up and good clothes in the world wouldn't stop her from looking like an overmuscled freak. She wished she was beautiful like her mother had been, but she would settle for being pretty like Cassie. She would settle for being normal. "Thanks for giving me the heads up on this killer."

Cassie wrinkled her nose. "Isn't it creepy? Do you think he's still around here?"

"I wouldn't worry too much." Gaia stood up and grabbed for her books. "If he's still here, he won't be for long."

Not in my park, she thought. If the killer was still there, Gaia intended to find him and stop him.

Suddenly she felt pinpricks of excitement moving over her skin. For the first time all day she felt fully awake. Fully engaged. Fully there. She needed to make a plan. She needed to make sure that if this guy attacked anyone else in the park, it was Gaia.

As terrible as it was, in a weird sort of way the news about the serial killer actually made Gaia feel better. At least she had stopped thinking about her date.

"A SERIAL KILLER," ED SAID SLOWLY.

Dead Already

Words he never expected to say unless he was talking about some movie staring Morgan Freeman or Tommy Lee Jones.

Gaia nodded. "That's right."

"And you're excited about this?"

Why was he not surprised?

"Not excited. It's more . . ." She tipped back her head and looked up at the bright blue sky, her breath visible for one split second each time she exhaled. "Yeah, well. Kind of."

Ed stopped talking as they moved around a line of people waiting for a hot dog vendor, then took up the conversation again once he was sure no one was close enough to hear. "Don't you think that's a little—"

"Crazy?" finished Gaia.

"That wasn't what I was going to say." Ed stopped in his tracks and looked up into her eyes, rubbing his gloved hands together. Early November in New York City. Almost time to put away the cotton gloves and whip out the leather. "But since you said it—yeah, it seems more than a little Looney Tunes."

Gaia was silent for a moment. She walked a few steps away and stood next to the fence that bordered the playground. Ed followed.

As usual, the equipment was overrun with bundled-up kids. Anytime between dawn and sunset the playground was packed with screaming children. A little thing like someone getting killed in the park wasn't enough to empty any New York jungle gym. They were too few and far between. The sound of laughter and shouting mixed together with traffic around the park until it was only another kind of white noise – the city version of waves and seagulls at the beach.

"This is important," Gaia said at last. "I have to get this guy."

Ed stared at her, trying to read the expression on her beautiful face. Usually that was easy enough. On an average day Gaia's emotions ran from mildly disturbed to insanely angry. But this expression was something new. Something Ed didn't know how to read. "Does this have something to do with Sam's kidnapping?" he asked. "Why exactly do you have to ... get him?"

Why and you being the operative words.

Gaia pushed at her tangled hair to get it out of her face but only succeeded in tangling it further. "Because I do," she said, looking down at him. "And I don't think this has anything to do with Sam. This guy is killing blond girls, not college guys. But this also isn't just some loser snatching purses or some asshole junkie waving a knife to feed a crack habit. This is serious."

"Some of those assholes kill people," Ed pointed

out, tucking his hands under his arms. "Stopping them is important, too."

"Yeah, but not like this. This guy, this *Gentleman,* he's killing people because he wants to do it." She stared out at the kids on the swing sets, and Ed saw that her ever-changing eyes had turned a shade of blue that was almost electric. `"This guy likes what he's doing."`

Ed was chilled to the bone. He blamed it on the sudden, stiff breeze that picked up dead leaves and general city debris all around them. But he knew it was more about Gaia's words.

"What do you know about this guy?" he asked.

Gaia shrugged, hooking her bare fingers around the metal links of the fence. "Nothing, really. He kills blond girls. I'm not sure how many."

"Why is he called the Gentleman?" Ed asked.

"I don't know that, either. I don't really know anything about him . . . yet."

There was one `particularly loud playground scream,` and Gaia's eyes darted left, searching for possible trouble.

Ed ignored the kids and stared at Gaia's profile. Looking at her was something he always enjoyed, but this time he was looking with a purpose. He hadn't known Gaia for that long, but he had never seen her back away from anything she set out to do. From what he could read of the expression on her face, Gaia was

determined to stop this killer. Ed could either get behind her or get out of the way.

"Maybe I could help you," he said.

Gaia shook her head. She didn't even look at him.
"I don't want you getting hurt."

Ed tried hard not to be insulted. "Hey, we've been
through this before. I'm not going to be out here playing Jackie Chan. That's your job. I just thought I could
help you fill in the holes."

"Holes?"

"Holes." He tilted his head in an attempt to catch
her eyes. "Like I did with Sam."

She blinked, and her grip on the fence tightened.
There. She couldn't deny he'd been indispensable
when Sam was kidnapped. He'd figured out where
they were holding Sam—not that the information had
played a role in rescuing him. But he'd helped Gaia get
the key to Sam's room from Heather—not that they'd
needed it. But he *had* caused a distraction so that Gaia
could sneak into the dorm. Of course, if he hadn't
been there, she probably wouldn't have needed a distraction in the first place, but—

"Ed—"

"Let me at least read up on the guy," Ed interrupted before she could shoot him down. "Maybe I
can figure out what he's about. What he's got against
girls with pigment-challenged hair."

Gaia turned away from the kids and knelt down

next to the chair. It was a move that usually made Ed angry—he didn't want people bending down beside him like he was a three-year-old—but anything that brought Gaia Moore's face closer to his own was an okay move in Ed's book.

"Okay," she said. "But you do research. *Only* research. I do the . . . other. Maybe together we can exterminate this guy."

We. Together. Ed liked the sound of that. It wasn't just Gaia going after a killer. It was Gaia and Ed. Batman and Robin. Partners.

"All right," he agreed. "I'll dig into the Net. Maybe stop by the library."

"Good," Gaia said. She smiled. In a strained way.

Forced or not, two smiles in one day from Gaia Moore had to be a record. Still, something about this whole thing had Ed moderately wiggy.

"Want me to call you tonight?" he asked.

"I'll call you," Gaia said. She started walking again, and Ed hurried to keep up. "If you can get some info in the next couple of hours, maybe I can bag this loser before he moves on to a different neighborhood."

She made a sound that might almost have been a laugh and ran the long fingers of her right hand through the heavy mass of her tangled hair. "Besides, I'm busy tomorrow night."

"What's tomorrow?" Ed asked.

47

"I've got a date." Gaia glanced over at Ed. For a split second she looked small, vulnerable. Like what he was about to say mattered. Unfortunately, Ed's heart was in his mouth, temporarily making speech impossible.

"A date," Ed replied finally. "Wow." Articulate, it was not, but he was pleased to hear that his voice sounded normal. He even managed to keep a smile on his face.

But if the serial killer came for him, Ed wouldn't have to be afraid. He felt dead already.

Girls I have liked:
Jenn Challener
Aimee Eastwood
Raina Korman
Ms. Reidy
Jennifer Love Hewitt (Okay, I was fourteen)
Storm, Rogue, Jubilee, Jean Grey
The lady behind the counter at Balducci's

Girls I have loved:
Heather Gannis
Gaia Moore

Girls who have ripped out my cardiovascular muscle and squashed it under their feet:
Heather Gannis
Gaia Moore

Anyone besides me sensing a pattern around here?

One glance
from afar
was all he
needed. But
he needed it
like he
needed
oxygen.

the
gaia
flu

THE PARK WAS JUST A SHORTCUT.

Give in to Insanity

The fastest way from point A to point B.

Besides, cutting through the park would take Sam past the chess tables. Not that he had time for a game, but it never hurt to see who was playing. He had to keep up on the competition. See who was new. Check out who was winning, who was losing. It wasn't like he was looking for anyone in particular. Nope. Not at all.

Except that he was.

Truth? Sam was sneaking through the park, looking for Gaia. Not to meet her, not to talk to her, just to *see* her. One glance from afar was all he needed. But he needed it like he needed oxygen.

Before Sam met Gaia, the park had seemed like the one safe place in his life. Sure, it was a hangout for muggers and junkies, scam artists, aging hippies, and gang members. If you wandered off the path on the wrong day or stayed too long on the wrong night, you could be beat up, maimed, or even killed. Every place had dangerous people, but Washington Square Park had more than its share.

Sam knew about that firsthand.

But none of that stopped him from loving the place. When he was hanging out in the park, he could relax. Nobody at the chess tables cared if he wore the right things, said the right things, or hung with the right people. Playing chess in the park was one situation where Sam could lean back and let his inner geek rise to the surface.

Gaia had ruined that.

From the first time they played, Sam had developed this weird kind of spastic tick. No matter who he was playing, every ten seconds Sam had to look up from the board to see if he might catch a glimpse of blond hair flying loose in the wind or a beautiful face centered around a scowl.

Sam had seen plenty of stories about obsessive-compulsive people. People who can't leave the house without locking the door ten times or who wash their hands a hundred times a day. He just hadn't expected to become one of those people. Glance at the chessboard, look around for Gaia. Move a piece. Check for Gaia. It was more than sick. It was pathetic.

What was worse was that he had no idea how he really felt about Gaia. Sam had good reasons to hate her—had once even told her he hated her—and the kidnapping should have only made him hate her more.

The kidnapping. Something Sam was trying so hard not to think about even though the questions kept flashing through his mind at warp speed.

Why me?

What did they want?

Did they get it?

Who were they?

Why did they let me go?

And, of course, what did Gaia have to do with the whole thing?

He'd been chasing Gaia when it happened. And he had the vague, possibly imagined memory of Gaia's named being mentioned by one of the kidnappers while he was semiconscious and half dead on a concrete floor. That was the thought that always gave him pause.

Kidnappers mentioning Gaia = kidnappers knowing Gaia = Gaia having something to do with the torture he was put through = Sam should hate Gaia.

But Sam was pretty sure that wasn't how he felt. If it was hate, it was a weird kind. Still, this obsession couldn't be love. It was more like an illness. The Gaia flu. Gaia-itis.

If she had anything to do with what happened to him, she must have been just as much a victim as he was. That had to be it.

Suddenly Sam found himself carefully scanning the park.

He was looking for her now—going out of his way and looking. This wasn't just the possibility of a random encounter anymore. And he was supposed to be on his way to meet his girlfriend.

53

Sam tucked his chin and kept walking. Eyes down. Hands in pockets. Too bad he didn't have side blinders like the horses that drew carriages through Central Park.

He needed a cure for this disease. Brain surgery. Strong anti-Gaiotics. At the very least, a good psychiatrist.

When he got to the chess tables, Sam found them almost deserted. Only a handful of regulars were playing, taking money from the usual mix of naive college students and overconfident businessmen who strolled through the park. A couple of would-be players were sitting across from empty seats, hoping for fresh victims.

No Gaia.

Sam felt a swirling mixture of disappointment and relief. It was kind of like the feeling he got when someone else took the last scoop of Ben & Jerry's. It was probably good for him to skip that ten zillion additional calories; it just didn't feel good at all.

Zolov was at his table, of course. He was in the middle of a game, so Sam didn't stop to talk. Not that talking would have bothered Zolov. Zolov might be a little crazy, but he knew how to concentrate on chess.

A middle-aged Pakistani looked at Sam with a hopeful expression. "You want a game, Sam?"

He shook his head. "Not today, Mr. Haq. Sorry."

"Oh, sit down and play," the part-time taxi driver, full-time chess hustler said. "It won't take long."

When Sam considered the way he'd been playing lately, that part was probably true. "Sorry, I really don't have time."

Since Sam had become Gaia infected, he had become Mr. Popularity at the chess tables. Everyone wanted to play him. He had lost money to people he used to put down in ten minutes.

Past the chess tables, Sam picked up the pace. Heather wasn't the kind of girl who took well to waiting.

Sam slipped through the not-so-miniature marble Arc de Triomphe at the center of the park and was almost out of the park. Then he saw her.

Gaia was thirty feet away, talking to a guy in a wheelchair. He recognized the guy. It was Ed Fargo, Heather's ex. But Sam didn't spend any time looking at Ed. That would be a waste of Gaia time.

Her hair was light and golden in the sunlight. Sam couldn't tell what Gaia was saying, but her face was incredibly animated. Even from where he was standing, Sam imagined he could see the deep, shifting blue of Gaia's eyes. A little gray in the center. Streaks that were almost turquoise. It was only imagination, but he had a very good imagination when it came to Gaia.

For just a moment another image of Gaia started to seep into Sam's mind. An image of Gaia in the dark, leaning over him, urgently whispering to him. Sam's heart froze in his chest.

The kidnapping.

He knew that couldn't be right. It was Heather who had come in at the last second to save Sam and give him the insulin he so desperately needed. Not Gaia. Still, there was something about the events that scratched at the insides of his skull.

The path Gaia was walking angled away from Sam. If he stood there for another ten seconds, she would be out of sight. To keep up with her, all he had to do was take ten fast steps. Another ten steps and he would catch her.

All he had to do was forget Heather, forget everything, and follow Gaia. All he had to do was give in to insanity.

Sam took the first step.

HEATHER LOOKED AGAIN AT THE watch on her wrist. Time.
Time and then some.

Times Ten

She stretched her neck, looking around for Sam.
Heather wished he hadn't asked her to meet him at the entrance of the park. She didn't have to go inside, but even the sidewalk was still way too close.

Heather didn't like the park. She had been cut

there, almost killed by some maniac. Since then she had looked at the clumps of trees and clutter of equipment as hiding places for thieves, murderers, and worse. It didn't surprise Heather that some brainless girl had gotten herself killed there. She was only surprised that it didn't happen more often.

The park held monsters. She was sure of it.

Heather checked her watch again. Ten minutes late. If it had been anyone but Sam, she would have left. She was beginning to wonder if she had the place or time wrong when Sam suddenly stepped into view. Heather put on her best smile and raised her hand in a little wave.

Sam didn't respond. He was walking right toward Heather, but he didn't even seem to see her. There was a distant, distracted look on his face. His curly, ginger-colored hair seemed a little more mussed than usual. Even his normally crisp tweed jacket looked wrinkled. Heather didn't appreciate the change.

Sam had been ill, and of course, there was the whole kidnapping thing, but still. He needed to take better care of himself. After all, appearance was very important. Sam knew that.

Sam took two more steps, stopped, and looked into the park.

For a moment Heather worried that Sam might really be sick again. Or maybe he had been attacked. There was a confused, stunned expression on his face.

Maybe some lunatic in the park had hit him on the head. Maybe he was hurt.

Heather started walking toward him quickly. She was almost close enough to touch him when Sam moved again. But he didn't come toward Heather. He stepped off the path and into the grass.

Heather frowned. "Sam?"

Sam jumped. He whipped around and stared at Heather with wide eyes.

"Um. Uh." He stopped and cleared his throat. "Heather."

The way he said it made it seem like he was surprised to see her. Heather couldn't put her finger on it, but something about his expression irritated her. A slight blush tinted her cheeks. She crossed her arms over her chest.

"What's wrong, Sam? Are you okay?" She tried to sound concerned and earnest. It came out as defensive and accusatory. Luckily, Mr. Oblivious didn't seem to notice.

Sam nodded quickly. "Yeah, sure. I just . . ." His face suddenly flushed an incredible bright red. "I just got lost in thought."

Heather's eyebrows scrunched together. She tried to smile again, but it was more difficult this time. "Oookay," she said. "C'mon. Let's get out of here."

Lacing her fingers with Sam's, Heather started to lead him out of the park. He was coming out of the bizarre stupor—walking like a normal person instead of shuffling like he had moments before. In fact, within seconds he was practically pulling her arm out of its socket.

What was with him? He was acting like something had him spooked. Heather glanced back in the direction Sam had been looking when he'd stopped in place. For a fraction of a second, a moment so short it might have been imagination, Heather thought she saw someone stepping behind a group of trees—someone with pale blond hair.

Heather's blood went cold and hot at the same time. It had only been the barest glimpse, but she knew who that blond hair belonged to. Gaia Moore. And Sam didn't want Heather to see her.

"Sam? What's the rush?" Heather said, just to see if he would tell her the truth.

"Nothing," he said, still pulling.

Heather felt a familiar feeling of humiliation, mixed with anger and tinged with fear, slip through her veins. God, she hated Gaia. Heather hated Gaia more than she had ever hated anyone in her whole life. More than everyone she had ever hated in her life put together. Times ten.

Sam stopped pulling when they reached the far corner, but Heather kept her hand locked together with his as they strolled down the sidewalk. Sam was saying something to her, making suggestions about where they might go, what they might do. Heather gave vague, one-word answers to his questions without really hearing them. It was her turn to be distracted.

Since her first encounter with Gaia, Heather had been burned, humiliated, stabbed, hospitalized, ego bruised, deprived of her boyfriend on various occasions, and detained by the NYU security force.

None of that came close to the reason Heather hated Gaia. It was the way Sam acted around Gaia. Like he couldn't think or breathe. Like he'd never seen anything like her.

And then there was the fact that Gaia was beautiful. She was beautiful without even trying. And that brought Heather to the real heart of it. Not the beauty. Heather hated Gaia because she didn't seem to try, didn't seem to care what others thought of her. Gaia dressed like a refugee. She said whatever she wanted. She never even seemed to notice how guys turned around to watch her when she went by. Gaia acted like she didn't think she was pretty, but Heather knew better than that. Gaia had to know. She just didn't care.

It was driving Heather mad—in every sense of the word.

Sam suddenly stopped walking. His grip on Heather's hand tightened to painful intensity.

Heather came out of her daze and struggled against his tight grip. "Sam? Sam, what's wrong?"

"Nothing," he replied in a harsh whisper. He

stopped again and shook his head. "Nothing. Don't worry about it."

Heather stared at him. For a moment she had a terrible premonition that everything between them was over. Ice went down her spine, trickling slowly over every lump in her backbone. *He's going to tell me he's dumping me. Dumping me for Gaia Moore.*

But Sam wasn't even looking at Heather. She followed the direction of his gaze and saw a newspaper stand. Right away Heather spotted the thing that had captured Sam's attention.

Splashed across the front page of the *Post* was a color photo of a young blond girl. Under the picture was the caption KILLER TAKES 6TH VICTIM.

Heather untangled her fingers from Sam's and went in for a closer look. From a distance, the girl in the picture looked a lot like Gaia. A tabloid twin. This had to be the girl that the serial killer had murdered the night before, the one that everyone had been talking about at school.

It wasn't Gaia. Still, Heather felt a little thrill go through her. As sick as she knew the thought was, the idea of Gaia and murder just seemed so right.

ANOTHER BLOND BEAUTY DEAD

GENTLEMAN KILLER PLANTS BLOODY KNIFE IN HEART OF NYC

After a killing spree that has left victims scattered from Connecticut to New Jersey, the serial killer known only as the "Gentleman" has taken his act off Broadway—slicing up an NYU coed just a block from the school's campus.

Carolyn Mosley, 20, a freshman at NYU, was found dead this morning by maintenance workers at Washington Square Park, say city officials. The manner of death points to a connection with the string of killings committed by the infamous serial killer, the Gentleman, according to officials.

Police have been reluctant to share details of the killer's technique, but sources have confirmed that this Gentleman is no gentleman. Death in the Gentleman's victims has been brought about by numerous knife wounds, according to information released by New Jersey police. Victims have received multiple stab wounds and have suffered "extreme violence and extensive damage," according to reports on the previous victims.

"Their throats were cut so badly, they were nearly decapitated," said Stanley G. Norster, a detective who investigated the Gentleman's killings in Connecticut. "There's an incredible amount of anger in these killings. A rage."

Police have admitted to withholding some details of the Gentleman's actions in previous crimes. The FBI has been involved in this investigation for several weeks, and a psychological profile of the killer has been prepared, but this profile has not been made available to the public. Sources inside the coroner's office indicate that the bodies show evidence of torture. The killer apparently administered dozens of cuts and other injuries before the killing blow. The killer didn't stop with death. Other signs

Continued on page 12

NYU Student Killed in Washington Square Park

NYU—A New York University student was found dead early this morning only two blocks from the university campus, according to police. Carolyn Mosley, 20, a freshman at NYU, died as a direct result of blunt trauma and numerous stab wounds, officials say.

The body was discovered in the southwestern part of Washington Square Park by maintenance workers responding to a report of a gas leak. No leak was found, but Ms. Moser's body was found at the location of the alleged leak. Police spokesmen refused comment when asked about the possibility that the gas leak was reported by someone involved in the murder.

Mosley was last seen leaving a restaurant on MacDougal Street around 11 P.M., according to officials. The student worked part-time at the restaurant and worked her regular shift there the evening of her death.

No suspects have been named; however, the condition of the body has led to speculation that the case may be related to a series of killings in Connecticut.

Police have scheduled a press conference for 3 P.M. to discuss the case. Case files from the possibly related murders in other states have been requested, according to police.

From: E.
To: L.

    Last night's events confirm Delta presence.
High probability of encounter with primary subject and subsequent risk. Advise.

From: L.
To: E.

Continue to monitor activity. Do not intercede at this time. Will personally visit site within twenty-four hours.

I want to see what happens.

They had nothing
in common at
all—nothing

numbering

except a general **the**
similarity
of features **dead**
and the fact
that they were
all dead.

ONE AFTER ANOTHER, THE FACES

Pretty Girls

and names of the Gentleman's victims appeared on the computer monitor.

Debra Lemasters—more cute than beautiful, with her hair pulled back in a ponytail and wide blue eyes that stared out from a yearbook photo.

Amanda Loring—older, taller. Holding a track trophy aloft while teammates cheered.

Susan Creek—eyes more gray than blue, thinner than the rest. She looked so sad, it was almost as if she knew what was coming.

Clarissa Richardson—very pretty but looking awfully uncomfortable in a tight, off-the-shoulder formal gown and a paper crown that proclaimed her queen of the junior prom.

Paulina Dree—sitting on horseback, her father standing beside her, both smiling. She had a great smile.

And finally, poor Carolyn Mosley, posing in cap and gown, a high school diploma rolled in her hand. Valedictorian of her class. Her family's pride and joy.

The youngest of them was fifteen, the oldest, twenty. They were six young women from three different states. None of them had known one another. Most but not all were good students. Most but not all had participated in some sort of organized athletics. They shared no common hobbies. They didn't read the same books, or like the same music, or share the same dreams.

They had nothing in common at all—nothing except a general similarity of features and the fact that they were all dead. And blond hair.

Gaia's hair, thought Tom Moore. He scrolled through the pictures again.

If he looked closely, he could see a little of Gaia in each of the dead girls. It was far more than the hair. The dead girls weren't identical, but they shared a similar bone structure—wide eyes, strong cheekbones, high forehead. Pretty girls, all of them. Of course, Tom was sure that none of them was as pretty as Gaia. But then again, Tom might be more than a little prejudiced—he thought his daughter was the most beautiful young woman in the world.

Six dead girls who all looked a little like Gaia Moore.

"What have they done?" Tom whispered to the empty room. He leaned back from the monitor and stared into the shadows. "What have *we* done?"

IT NEVER GOT DARK IN THE CITY.

Not really dark the way it had in other places. Like Connecticut.

He strolled down the sidewalk, careful never to touch

anyone he passed. He didn't like to touch people. He didn't like to be touched.

The sun was already going down, but the sky overhead only shifted from blue to a kind of dingy yellow as the lights came on. It wasn't anything close to real darkness. After only three days in the city, he still thought the dirty, nearly starless sky seemed terribly odd.

He craved the darkness.

He moved off the sidewalk and headed down the curving path that led out under the trees. A handful of children were still indulging in a few last minutes of play, but there were parents on hand to watch and a policeman standing at the edge of the playground. A pair of street musicians were putting away their instruments and counting up handfuls of change and folded bills.

They were scared. All of them were scared of the coming night.

He could feel it, almost taste it. For a moment he had a desire to rush into the center of them, screaming and waving his arms, just so he could watch them scatter. He fought down that desire.

No matter how fun it might be to see them run, it wasn't his reason for being in the park. There was important work to be done—a higher purpose. Nothing could be allowed to get in the way of that purpose.

He walked on, passing two more policemen on his way to the chess tables. Like the playground, the boards were almost deserted. Two men still squinted at a game in the failing light. At another table an old man slowly packed away his chess pieces.

The old man looked up as he passed. "You wanting game?" he said. "I will play you."

"No, thanks, Gramps." The idea of playing this guy actually made him smile. The man was ridiculously ancient, with sun-spotted skin and flyaway tufts of white hair. Beating him at chess couldn't possibly be a challenge.

Killing him would be even easier.

It would be a mercy, really. Put the old fool out of his misery. Maybe he would do it. Not as a main course for the evening, but just as a warm-up exercise. Something to keep his fingers busy.

The old man shuffled away, and the moment passed. Pointless, anyway. It was no fun without a real struggle.

He moved away from the tables and down the tree-lined paths. Even in the middle of the park there was nothing that approached true darkness.

But under the trees and in the shaded places, it was dark enough for his purposes.

The form on
the ground
didn't even
look like a
girl. It **chalk**
barely
looked like
a person.

DEATH DIDN'T LEAVE MUCH OF A

permanent stain. Not on the park, at least.

Stalking a Stalker

Gaia reached out and caught a strip of the yellow tape in her hand. Crime Scene—Do Not Cross.

As if yellow tape created some magical force field that could keep everyone away. Gaia wondered if police tape had ever stopped anybody in the history of the world from jumping into the middle of a crime site. The temptation was just too much. Even when you weren't stalking a stalker.

Considering how everyone had been talking up the murder at school and in the papers, Gaia had expected to find the park swarming with cop types. She had thought there would be uniforms keeping back the crowds. Whole squadrons of trench-coat-wearing detectives combing the ground, examining every blade of grass for a clue like a flock of investigating sheep. There should have been technicians spreading fingerprint powder. Flashing lights. Enough doughnuts to soak up a swimming pool of coffee.

Instead there was only this dark patch of grass. If there had been detectives, they were long gone. There wasn't a single cop left to keep people from ignoring the warning on the flimsy yellow tape. No one had even left behind a doughnut.

Losers.

Still, Gaia had a hard time stepping over the line. It wasn't like she was afraid of getting caught. Gaia didn't do afraid.

Maybe it was some new desire to be a law-abiding citizen. She wasn't sure. But the idea of going across the tape, going to the place where the body had been, made Gaia feel weird. Like something way down inside her wasn't quite as solid as it should be. Squishy.

She stood there and took a few deep breaths of evening air before the squishiness started to fade. After all, there was nothing out there but grass.

Gaia ducked under the tape. Inside the magic line the ground was all dented and bumpy—like it had been walked on by a herd of elephants. Maybe there really had been hundreds of detecto-sheep here after all.

The grass in the field was soaked with dew. By the time she'd taken a dozen steps, Gaia's sneakers were soaked through and cold water was making little burping noises between her toes. A lovely way to start a long evening.

Almost dead center in the field she saw the rough outline of a body marked in white. Just like in the movies. Only this line wasn't made from tape. It was powdered, chalky stuff, like they use to mark the base-lines at a ball game.

75

Somewhere in the back of Gaia's head, random associations started to fire.

Strike three. You're out. Game over.

When she considered where she was standing, this seemed more than a little sick. But Gaia had never claimed to be in complete control of what went on in her head.

She stood with the toes of her wet sneaks almost touching the crumbling chalk line. The form on the ground didn't even look like a girl. It barely looked like a person. It was just a rough outline with something like a hand pointing one way and two blocky leg things shooting off the other end.

Despite all the violence Gaia had seen in her life—despite all the violence she had caused—there was something about this scene that gave her pause. She wasn't scared; she just felt ill. Ill and numb and . . . responsible. And sad. Where there had been a girl with warmth and memories and a smile, there was now just chalk and dew. It was almost too much for her.

Gaia turned away, wanting to block out the images of premature dying, but her eyes were drawn back as if some unseen thing were pulling her.

Gaia was no big believer. She didn't go in for ghosts, or voodoo, or little leprechauns with colored marshmallow cereal. If people wanted to call themselves witches, that was cool with Gaia as long as they didn't expect her to believe in witchcraft. She might be an overmuscled, fear-deprived, jump-kicking freak girl, but Gaia didn't skim the tabloids for predictions or use a Ouija board to communicate with the dead. For all the weirdness in her life, she knew where to draw the line between what was real and what was not. Or at least, she thought she did.

But the area inside the police tape gave Gaia a bad feeling. Something worse than a mugging or robbery had happened there. And Gaia could still feel it.

She looked up from the line on the ground and did a quick check of the trees around her—just in case any werewolves or zombies were approaching. Then she laughed at herself.

Still, he could be out there. Right there.

There was that whole bad film noir/cheesy paperback theory that criminals return to the scene of the crime.

It sounded like an idea dreamed up by a lazy detective or by some writer who didn't know where to go with the plot. Just sit on your ass, and the killer will come to you. In Gaia's book that was way too easy to be true.

There was no real reason to think the killer might come back to this place. None at all. Gaia had the whole park to patrol. She couldn't stand here all night, staring at an empty field. Glaring at the trees made about as much sense as her Sam obsession.

But when she looked again, something was out there. Right at the bottom of a bunch of little ash trees, stuck in a chunk of shadow was—something. Maybe someone.

The all-over sickness she had been feeling started to turn into the more familiar `let's-go-kick-some-ass buzz`. Gaia took a slow step toward the shape in the shadows. She squinted until her eyes watered. Was someone really there? She couldn't be sure. She took another step. It was so hard to see. The shape in the shadows could be a crouching person, or it could be a shrub or a trash can.

Then the shape moved.

HE WAS UP AND RUNNING BEFORE

she had a chance to blink. There was no reason to run, really. He could just kill her now.

`He wasn't afraid of her.`

No Killing Tonight

But he was in the mood for a challenge. He wanted to run. Run until it hurt. Until the air coming in and out of his lungs burned the delicate flesh of his throat.

He wanted her to feel the same thing.

And so he ran. There was no way she would catch up to him. Which meant no killing tonight. But that was okay.

He wanted to see what she could do.

GAIA'S LEGS WERE PUMPING EVEN

Gaia vs. Bad Guy

before her brain had finished realizing that it really was a person out there. Someone had been there in the shadows, watching her. Now the person was running. So was Gaia.

She made it out of the chewed-up field and jumped the police tape on the far side. For a moment she stood there, frustration tightening her throat. It was a terrible thing to be ready for a fight and not find anyone to punch.

Then she saw the shadow guy again. He was a hundred feet away, cutting across the grass by the side of the path. Gaia started after him.

Then something strange happened.

The average Gaia-versus-bad-guy race lasted all of five seconds. It wasn't that she was Ms. Olympic Runner, but the same thing that made Gaia strong also made her pretty damn fast in a sprint. Her father said it was part of being fearless. That little regulator that keeps people from pushing their muscles to the absolute limit was absent without leave in Gaia. She could push her legs a hundred percent. Maybe further. Gaia could even push her muscles so hard that she broke her own bones.

Disgusting but true.

There was a price to pay for beating herself up like that, but the upside was irresistible—before Gaia began to fade, most losers were on the pavement.

Not this guy. Shadow Man was fast. More than fast. A real speed demon.

Gaia and the shadow whipped along the path through the heart of the park, jumped a hedge, and skirted a gnarled old oak. Gaia didn't gain a step. She could never get close enough to see more than a hazy form in the distance. Several times she almost convinced herself that nothing was out there but shadows—no man at all. But she didn't stop.

By now Gaia was solidly in the zone. Nothing mattered in the world but catching the guy in the shadows. The chessboards came and went in a blur. The playground. The sprinklers. Then they were out of the park, powering north on Fifth Avenue.

In the back of her mind nagged the vague thought that she had no clear reason to pursue him except for the fact that he was running away from her. But the chase was on, and her instincts pushed her hard to catch him.

She zipped past knots of people and saw startled faces turning her way. A woman jumped back as Gaia thundered past. A guy dropped a bag of groceries, and apples went bouncing along the sidewalk.

Gaia didn't slow. They had been running now for a solid minute at a speed that would have been impressive for a ten-second sprint. Her chest heaved in and out as she tried to draw in all the air in New York.

Then she realized she was gaining on the shadow. Not much, but the gap was definitely closing.

Another hundred yards and she had gotten close enough to see that he was wearing some kind of long, floppy black coat. Not a trench coat, but something from a cowboy movie. A duster.

How could he run this fast in that thing?

Gaia followed as the duster flapped past the trendy crowd waiting outside Clementine's, past the glowing signs at Starbuck's, and on across fourteenth Street without even looking at the streams of passing traffic. Her heartbeat seemed to move up through her body with every step. One moment it was pounding against Gaia's ribs. The next it was beating in her throat. The next it was throbbing in her skull.

Shadow Man took a hard right onto a side street, then ducked down an alley. Gaia was right behind him. The gap between the two runners had closed to no more than fifty feet. Forty.

A mesh fence blocked one end of the alley. Gaia slowed a step, getting ready to fight, but the guy in the black coat didn't hesitate. He jumped up, landed one foot on a Dumpster, and sprang from there to the top of the fence. Two steps and he was over the ten-foot barrier. He hit the other side running.

"*What?*" Gaia gasped.

She might not get scared, but she was still quite capable of being amazed.

Gaia ran up to the fence, looped her hands in the mesh, and flung herself upward. She flipped head over heels and her feet came down on the top of the gate. A very slick move.

Then the top of the gate sagged, and she fell.

The pavement wasn't friendly to Gaia's knee. She hit with a force that sent jolts of fire running up her thigh and set off flares of white light in her head.

Gaia stayed there for the space of two breaths. Then she got on her feet and ran again.

Black Coat had widened his lead on Gaia to a good hundred feet, but she soon had it back to fifty. He cut right again, this time along University Place. Gaia followed.

The pair sprinted past a series of nightclubs. The door of each one spilled out different music, but Gaia went past them so fast, they blended like notes in some insane song. Disco high C. Jazz G. Bass blues.

Thirty feet.

Shadow Man was wearing running shoes. Gaia could see them now. The off-white soles flashed at her under the flapping hem of his long coat. She found something comforting about the shoes. At least it was nice to know he wasn't running so fast in penny loafers.

Twenty feet.

A policewoman shouted at Gaia as she dashed across Fourteenth Street and headed south. She didn't bother to stop. If the policewoman wanted Gaia, she had better start running.

Now Gaia realized the man had brought her right back to Washington Square Park, and they ran through shadows cast by huge oaks and ghost white birch.

Ten feet.

Gaia could almost reach out and touch the flapping coat. Almost. The air in her throat tasted like fire, and there were little sparks of white light dancing in her eyes. In another ten seconds this psycho was hers.

Then somebody screamed.

Gaia thought for a second it was her. She was hurting badly enough to scream.

Then the sound came again from somewhere off to her right.

Five feet.

All Gaia had to do was keep running and she could catch the black coat. But what if she caught him and he turned out to be innocent? Really fast, but innocent.

What if the Gentleman was killing someone else in the park right that second? Gaia tried to get her oxygen-starved brain to make a decision. Another scream.

"Oh, shit," she wheezed through her breathing.

Gaia turned right, leaving Black Coat to run on into the night, and dashed toward the commotion.

It didn't take her ten seconds to find who was doing the screaming. Standing under a pool of light was a young girl in blue jeans and a black sweater. Tugging on her purse strap was a potbellied, long-haired guy with a tangled brown-and-gray beard that went halfway down his chest. The girl had both hands clamped to her purse and her feet well planted. She was putting everything she had into it. The guy might outweigh her by a good fifty pounds, but she was giving him a fight.

"Let go!" the girl cried.

The guy laughed. "Come on, baby. I need it worse than you."

Gaia didn't think either one of them saw her coming. By then she was running at roughly the speed of a 747 pulling out of JFK. Gaia didn't slow a bit as she tucked in her head, lowered a shoulder, and smashed into Brown Beard.

The impact was enough to make Gaia fall to her bruised knee and send fresh neon bolts of pain ripping through her body. The bearded guy was knocked at least ten feet. He lay facedown on the grass with one hand stretched out over his head and the other trapped under his body. For just a second Gaia flashed back to the chalk outline on the ground. Hand up, legs spread.

She shook her aching head to clear away some of the fog and climbed to her feet. It seemed like a long way up.

"Y-You . . . ," Gaia started, then took a breath and tried again. "You okay?" she asked the girl.

The girl nodded. Gaia couldn't see her clearly, but she was very tall and very slim. Delicate looking. And she was definitely young. Way too young to be walking around the park alone at night. Of course, who was Gaia to talk?

"Who are you?" the girl asked.

"I—" Gaia couldn't think of a good answer. If she even had a name, she had misplaced it somewhere.

Somewhere back along the long minutes and longer miles of her run. Gaia turned around and staggered back the way she had come.

"Where are you going?" the girl called.

Gaia didn't bother to answer. There wasn't enough air to talk and run.

She put up her arms, drew in a deep breath, and started back to the spot where she had last seen the shadow man.

Gaia made maybe three whole steps before the ground jumped up and gave her a hard slap in the face.

You'd think that I wouldn't have a very vivid imagination. I'm a science geek, right? I play chess. It's all analytical. It's all about numbers, proofs, strategies.

Solid definitions.

There's no room for imagination.

But sometimes I don't even believe what my mind can come up with. There are things living in my head I'm sure any shrink worth his cheap spiral notepad would kill to delve into.

My imagination is especially vivid when it comes to Gaia Moore.

And not in the way you think. I'm not a total pervert. Although . . . Well, yes, the brain does travel in those circles, but I'm a guy. You have to forgive it.

I'm talking about the sick side of my mind. The dark side. The side a lot of people probably have but don't talk about. And

ever since this afternoon, that
side has been transmitting Gaia
pictures. Not pleasant Gaia pictures.

Pictures of Gaia dead. Pictures
of Gaia cut. Pictures of Gaia
bleeding and crying and gasping
and sputtering. They only last
for seconds at a time before I
drive them away. But in those
seconds they scare me to death.
They arrest every functioning
part of my body and take the
breath out of me.

Why?

Because they could become reality.

Ed stared at
the handset in
confusion.
"Who is this?"

the
connection

"Sam Moon,"
said the voice.
"I'm trying to
reach Ed."

ED HIT THE KEYS ON HIS COMPUTER

so hard, the whole desk started shaking. The words on the word processor screen glowed back at him.

Serial Killer Junkie

```
    LOSER. LOSER.
LOSER. BIG LOSER. ALL THOUGHT AND NO ACTION MAKES
ED ONE GIANT LOSER. LOSER. LOSER.
```

Somewhere, three screens' worth of LOSERs away, there was a letter that started with "Dear Gaia." It was a letter that explained everything. It was a letter that put into words all the things Ed wished he could have said that morning.

LOSER, Ed typed one last time, moving his fingers slowly across the keys and striking each one as if he meant to knock a letter from the keyboard.

```
    L. O. S. E. R.
```

He closed his eyes for a moment and rubbed at his temples. It turned out that losing, or at least not getting the woman you loved, caused a massive headache. Three aspirins had gone down his throat and Ed still felt like his skull was going to bust wide open. He almost wished it would.

With a sigh he moved the mouse up to the corner of his document and clicked the close button.

Save changes? the machine asked.

Ed clicked on the No button and watched as both his letter to Gaia and his three-page tribute to self-pity blinked into nothing.

He took in a deep breath, turned his back to the computer, and rolled over to the heap of books lying on his bed.

He had braved the snarling stone lions and endless wheelchair ramps at the main public library to come up with this stack. Six books, all of them about serial killers and murderers. Ed wondered if the librarians would add his name to some list they kept behind the counter. Serial killer junkies. Murder geeks. Or maybe Hannibal Lecter wanna-bes.

It was possible they even suspected that he was the Gentleman. But Ed doubted that. Sometimes being in a wheelchair was a weird kind of being invisible—no one ever looked at the wheelchair guy as a threat.

Ed grabbed the first book off the stack and flipped open the pages to the introduction. Staring back at him was a wild face framed by wilder hair. It was a woodcut picture of a killer from the Middle Ages—a man who had killed dozens of children near a small village in France. In the picture the man held a child

91

in one hand. Not all of a child. Part of the body had already been eaten.

A quick flip of the page and Ed was facing newspaper sketches of a shadowy Jack the Ripper stalking the streets of Whitechapel in a cape and top hat. Across from the sketch was a diagram of a woman who had been dissected more completely than Ed's frog in freshman biology.

Another page and there was a black-and-white photo from the 1930s. This time the killer was a calm-looking man from Germany who had ground some of his neighbors into sausages. Flip.

He was looking into the fantastically mad eyes of Charles Manson.

On the next was the dumpy face of John Wayne Gacey.

Flip. Jeffrey Dahmer.

Flip. A middle-aged Russian guy with thick-framed glasses. Maybe he had killed fifty. Maybe it was a hundred. No one knew for sure.

Ed tried to read more of the text around the pictures, but he was having a hard time concentrating. And for an admittedly frivolous reason, when he considered the subject matter in front of him.

Gaia had a date. Ed's chance had been there. All he'd had to do was roll up to Gaia, open his mouth, and tell her how he felt. She had been right there. Right there.

Of course, she could have shot him down. Absolutely *would* have shot him down in flames. A girl like Gaia. Ed had to be crazy to think he could ever be more than friends with Gaia. He should be glad she even noticed him.

Ed looked down at his book and stared into the face of the Russian killer. A world that could put Ed in a wheelchair and have Gaia making a date exactly at the wrong moment seemed like just the kind of world that could produce a serial killer. They were probably as common as cockroaches.

The phone rang.

Ed stared at it with mixed emotions. It was a little early, but he had no doubt that it was Gaia on the other end. Usually, he called her, but since she was going to be out patrolling, and he was going to be fact-finding, she'd said she'd call him when she got in.

On most nights Ed looked forward to the late-night Gaia call. She was never exactly a blabbermouth, but compared to the way she was at school, Gaia was far more open on the phone. The phone calls were the only times when she really spilled her thoughts. Ed loved it. He just wasn't sure he could take it right now. Not after everything that had happened. He didn't think he could sit there and make happy noises while Gaia talked about her upcoming date. The thought made his blood curdle.

Who was this date-worthy guy, anyway? Where had he come from? And what gave him the right to ask out Perfection Personified?

The phone rang again. If Ed didn't answer, he wouldn't have to hear about the mystery guy. He wouldn't have to kick himself for being such a gutless wonder.

Of course, if he stopped answering, Gaia might never call again.

Ed scrambled for the phone.

"Hey," he said as he lifted the receiver, "I know why they call him the Gentleman."

"Is this Ed Fargo?" said a voice on the other end of the line. A guy's voice.

Ed stared at the handset in confusion. "Who is this?"

"Sam Moon," said the voice. "I'm trying to reach Ed."

Sam Moon.

Ed knew who Sam was. They had even spoken a time or two, but that certainly didn't make them friends. Back in the days when Ed had traveled sans wheelchair, Heather had been his girlfriend. Now she was Sam's.

"What do you want?" Ed's voice came out a little rougher than he had intended.

"It's about Gaia Moore," said Sam.

Wonderful. Did Sam have a date with her, too? Maybe she'd lined up the football team for the weekend. Open wound. Salt at the ready. "What about Gaia?"

"It's just that . . . well—"

Ed wasn't breathing. "Well, what?"

"You're her friend, right? I've seen you together."

"I'm her friend," Ed agreed. And that was probably all he was ever going to be. Once again tiredness and anger got the better of him. Still, it was nice that Sam had noticed. Maybe he was even **jealous**. "If you're looking for tips on asking her out, you better talk to someone else because—"

"I'm not calling about anything like that," Sam said quickly.

"Then what do you want?"

Sam took a deep breath.

"I want you to help me save Gaia's life."

"ARE YOU AWAKE?"

Quite Contrary

Gaia looked up. Or tried to look up. All she could see was dark and slightly less dark. Neither one of them seemed to form any shape that made sense.

"Don't worry," said a voice from the not so dark. A girl's voice. "I'm going to go call an ambulance."

95

"Uhh," Gaia grunted. She struggled to move her rigid jaw muscles. "Nuhhh."

No. Don't do that.

"Do you want me to stay with you?"

What Gaia wanted was for this disembodied voice to go away and leave her alone so that she could recover.

It was the most irritating thing—the real price of stressing her body in ways that no human being was built to take. For a few seconds, at most a few minutes, Gaia could push herself way past the limits of normal human strength and endurance, but when that time limit was up, Gaia's body went on strike. Her muscles stopped talking to her brain, and her body stopped moving. It would pass soon enough, but until it did, Gaia was absolutely helpless.

It was a feeling she didn't cherish.

"Look," said the voice. "I don't know what's wrong with you, but I don't think you're dying."

Great diagnosis, Doc.

"So I'm going to sit here with you and make sure you're okay." Gaia felt a warm body next to her arm. It didn't feel all bad, but she didn't want it there. "If you're not, I guess I better call an ambulance."

"Gooo way," Gaia managed to whisper. Gradually her muscles were waking up again, but she was still embarrassingly weak. She could probably get up; she just didn't want to try it in front of this girl.

Just how long had she chased the man in the black coat? Had they run two miles? Three miles? More than that? Every second of the run had been at a dead sprint. Add in a badly bruised knee and a shoulder that just might be dislocated, and Gaia felt like crap. Tired, abused crap.

Finally Gaia pushed her scraped hands onto the pavement and stood up shakily. She'd only been out for seconds, but it felt like an eternity to her.

"I think you really are going to live," said the girl.

Gaia licked her lips. "You sound surprised," she said in a harsh voice.

The girl shrugged. "Well, I've seen a lot of things, but I've never seen anybody kick ass one second and go into a coma the next. What are you on, anyway?"

Gaia started to laugh at the absurdity of the question, but it turned into a cough. A harsh, racking cough.

"You sure you don't want to go to the hospital?" the girl asked, reaching for Gaia's arm. "St. Vincent's is right down the street."

"No." Gaia shook her head. "I'll be all right. Really."

"Whatever you say," the girl said, eyeing her with disbelief.

Gaia turned her head and had to fight down a fresh wave of dizziness. "Where is he?"

"The guy who was after my purse?"

Gaia nodded.

"Don't know," said the girl. "He ran off. The way you hit him, I'd be surprised if he's not on his way to the nearest emergency room with a half-dozen cracked ribs."

All the systems in Gaia's body were coming back into action like a computer being booted up after a long sleep. Unfortunately, her nerves were waking up along with her muscles. There was pain everywhere.

Gaia thought she heard something behind her and turned quickly. Nothing was there, but the head rush that overtook her was so overpowering, she momentarily stumbled. The red-haired girl reached out for her.

"I've got . . . oof!" The slim girl stood in close and held Gaia with both arms. "Damn, girl. You're solid."

Solid. That was a nice way to say she weighed as much as a water buffalo.

"I'll be okay," she said. "Just go on. Let me sit here a little longer, and I'll be fine."

"Nope. If you're not going to let me take you to the hospital, you at least have to let me buy you a cup of coffee," the girl said. "Not that you need to add caffeine to whatever weird substance you've got running through your veins."

Gaia closed her eyes. "I don't think—"

The girl shook her head. "Come on. A double latte is the next best thing to surgery."

Gaia started to laugh, but it was still a bad idea. It made too many things hurt too much. Maybe sitting and sipping would be the best things for her right now. Besides, if Shadow Man came back, she couldn't be sure she could defend herself.

"All right," Gaia agreed. "Coffee."

Perfectly Pathetic

HE WATCHED FROM THE BEST darkness he could find. Sweat poured down from his temples. His back. His underarms. His lungs felt like they'd been roasted over an open flame. Bent at the waist, holding his hands above his knees, he fought for breath. She was good. He had to give her that. But the scene in front of him made his pulse race faster than any sprint ever could.

She was also down. And she wasn't getting up. Couldn't, apparently. Not without help.

It was all he could do to keep from laughing through his gasps. How pathetic. How perfectly pathetic.

A skinny girl with tangly red hair was aiding the one. The target. The ultimate trophy.

His eyes narrowed into slits as his breath started to slow. He could take them both. Two for the price of one. He could practically smell them from here. The fear would smell even better. He licked his lips. He could almost taste it.

As the girls shuffled off, he straightened his back. There would be no satisfaction in taking her now. Not when she couldn't even walk on her own. The side dish wasn't enough to sweeten the deal.

He wanted a fight.

He would have what he wanted.

But there were too many cops around. Too many pissants. There would be no more girls in the park tonight.

Unless, of course, he dragged one there.

Once, when Gaia was a baby, she was playing in a sandbox in Central Park. It was a sunny day in early spring. I remember because Katia was picking buttercups and tickling Gaia's chin with them.

We turned our backs on Gaia for one moment. Just to clean up our picnic before retrieving her and heading for home.

Suddenly, out of nowhere, a crazed pit bull came charging at Gaia. She was two. Only two. Sweet. Small. Seemingly helpless.

Before I could blink, the pit bull was bearing down on Gaia and her playmate. With the attack instinct of an animal, my lovely daughter leaped at the wild dog and sank her baby teeth into the dog's hind leg.

That was when we knew we had a very special girl on our hands.

There was a
distinct
possibility **mary**
she could
like this
girl.

Sharing Stories

GAIA'S ARM WAS FLUNG AROUND THE red-haired girl's shoulders as they stumbled their way across the winding pathways. The muscles in Gaia's knee felt like they had been stomped flat, `stripped raw,` and rubbed in coarse salt.

They neared the entrance of the park and found a young policeman with an unlikely handlebar mustache standing guard over the end of the pathway. Gaia made an effort to stand up straighter, putting less of her weight on her smaller companion. The last thing she wanted was for the cop to think she was drunk or on some kind of drugs.

"`What do you two think you're doing in there?`" the policeman called as they approached.

"Just taking a walk," the red-haired girl said.

The cop gave a snort. "You picked a bad place for a walk. Didn't you hear what happened in the park last night?"

"They're only slicing up blonds," the girl replied. "It's in all the papers."

"I wouldn't be too sure about that." He paused and looked them over. "Besides, your . . . *friend* is about as blond as they come."

There was something about the way he said *friend* that caught Gaia's ear. Maybe it was because she was so tired, but it took her a moment to put the idea together.

Two girls. Walking alone. Arms around each other.

This guy thought they were lesbians.

Gaia leaned harder on her companion and smiled. Might as well give him a show. His already ruddy face darkened, and there was a spark of interest in his eyes.

Men. So predictable. He quickly glanced away.

"We're leaving the park now," Gaia said. "So we'll be okay."

When the policeman looked at them again, he seemed a little irritated. "Be careful," he said. "If you have to come back this way, go around the outside of the park."

"Sure," said the girl. "Thanks for the profound advice."

They moved away and turned down Sullivan Street toward a row of cafes. Tired as she was, Gaia watched the stream of people moving in and out of the buildings with interest. Living in the city that never slept certainly had its high points. Getting coffee and doughnuts at any hour of the day or night was civilization at its peak.

Now that there were other people around, Gaia thought again about her weakness. She pulled her arm away from the red-haired girl's shoulders. "I can make it on my own now."

"You sure?" The girl kept her arm at Gaia's waist for a few steps, as if measuring her steadiness, then let her go. "For someone who was unconscious five minutes ago, you've made a miraculous recovery."

"I heal fast," said Gaia.

"Let's hope so." The girl stopped by a narrow building with a red door and a long list of coffees displayed in the window. "Come on—I'm buying."

Inside, the place showed signs of being in the middle of a theme change. There was a blackboard over the counter that read Coffee Cannes and a big-screen TV stood in a corner playing some film with subtitles, but the framed movie posters had all been taken down and stacked in a corner. In the front half of the shop the tables had been removed along both walls, and even though it was after eleven at night, workmen were busily installing computers and workstations in their place.

The red-haired girl found a table as far from the chaos as possible—which wasn't very far—and dropped her slim body into a cane-bottomed chair.

"I'm going to stop coming to this place when they're finished with the remodeling," she said. "It was cool to get my coffee with a Bergman flick. Caffeine and data is not my mix."

Gaia carefully bent her swollen, tender knee and eased herself into a chair across from the girl. "You don't have to buy," she said. "I've got cash."

"Save it." The girl slid her purse from her shoulder and dropped it in the center of the table. "If it weren't for you, I wouldn't have any money to pay for this, anyway. The least I can do is buy you a cup."

Gaia looked up at the board above the counter. Coffee and milk appeared in every possible combination. "Coffee," she said. "Just coffee. Nothing fancy."

The red-haired girl grinned. "I know exactly what you need." She twisted in her seat and shouted to the man behind the counter. "Hey, Bill, bring two cups over here. And none of that weak-assed Colombian. Bring the *stuff*."

The man behind the counter gave a tired nod and turned to a row of gleaming steel machines. A few moments later he dropped two huge mugs on the table, then turned without a word and went back to his post.

The coffee in the mugs produced tall plumes of steam, but that didn't stop the red-haired girl from lifting her mug and taking a long gulp. She shivered as she lowered her coffee. "Ahhh, as long as there's coffee, life goes on."

Gaia took a tentative sip. It was strong, bitter, and blazingly hot. It also seemed to carry a caffeine kick that rivaled espresso. Gaia could almost feel the coffee circulating in her veins. Perfect.

The girl reached a small hand across the table. "I'm Mary," she said.

Gaia took the hand. "Gaia."

"Gaia." The girl squeezed her fingers for a moment before releasing them. "Cool. Like the goddess."

Gaia blinked. Was it just her, or were people around here getting smarter? "Hardly a goddess."

"Well, you were certainly a powerful force of nature tonight," said Mary. She lifted her cup and took another slug of hot coffee, then she planted her elbows on the table and looked at Gaia. "Wait a minute—I know you."

Gaia's shoulders tensed.

"You do?"

Mary nodded. "I saw you at a party. You were there with Ed Fargo." She stopped and grinned. "Heather Gannis went nuclear on your ass."

Gaia rolled her eyes. It figured. "Yeah, that was me."

"Cool," said Mary. "So, you know Ed?"

Gaia nodded. She suddenly felt even more self-conscious. Ed was one of the few people who had seen her in the middle of a postfight collapse. Pretty soon the two of them would be sharing stories.

"Uh," Gaia mumbled. "Can I ask a favor?"

"You don't have to ask," said Mary. She made a dramatic sweep of her hand. "As an ass-kicking goddess, anything you want is yours."

"Cool. I mean, okay." She took a breath. "Could you please not talk about what happened tonight?"

"Not even with Ed?"

"Especially not with Ed," said Gaia.

Mary looked disappointed. "Well, all right." A mischievous smile crossed her face. "It would make a hell of a good story, though. The way you hit that guy, I thought—" She shook her head. "I don't know what I thought."

Gaia took another careful sip of the hot brew and studied the girl across the table. She was tall, at least as tall as Gaia, ridiculously thin. But her features weren't "elegant." Mary had a short, narrow nose set above full lips. Her eyes seemed almost too large for her head and were colored an intense green, with hardly any traces or flecks of other colors. Her skin was pale and freckled, yet there was something exotic about the angle of her big eyes. But the feature that really caught the attention was the hair. Surrounding Mary's face and tumbling down her back was a tangled mass of curls, curls, and more curls. She kept pushing them out of her face, and they would bounce right back.

She was oddly beautiful.

"Where did you come from, anyway?" Mary asked. "What were you doing in the park?"

Chasing a supersonic serial killer.

"I was just out for a run," Gaia lied. "I heard you yell and thought maybe I could help."

Mary nodded, a smile on her lips. "You definitely helped. You probably saved my life."

"I didn't save your life."

"How do you know?"

Gaia shook her head. "That guy you were fighting was just an ancient hippie. He probably wanted some money for drugs."

"That guy was an ancient hippie with a *gun,*" Mary said.

"Gun?" Gaia frowned and tried to think back. "I didn't see any gun."

"It was there," said Mary. "He had it in one hand and pulled on my purse with the other. I thought he was going to kill me."

"Why didn't you let go of the purse?" asked Gaia. She hated the question as soon as it was out of her mouth. People were always saying that. Sit still. Don't fight. Give the bad man your purse like a good victim.

"No one gets my purse," said Mary. "All my shit's in there." She stopped for a second, then lowered her voice. "Actually, I guess there's nothing in there that's worth dying for, but I was just pissed off. I hate not being able to walk across the park without someone bothering me."

Now that was a sentiment Gaia could fully agree with. "You really think that guy had broken ribs?"

Mary grinned broadly. "I sure hope so."

Gaia half smiled. There was a distinct possibility she could like this girl.

But she wasn't making any promises.

THE BLACK MERCEDES PULLED UP

behind a long line of police cars, the early morning sunlight glinting against their windshields. A few of the officers standing by gave it a glance, but no one moved to order the car away. Slowly the rear window rolled down.

Loki looked out. It was ridiculous. Absolutely ridiculous. There had to be at least fifty policemen in the park. They were everywhere, from uniforms standing guard by the gate to technicians literally up in the trees.

Loki couldn't stop himself from laughing. It was all so silly. If there ever had been any clues in this place, this herd of cattle had destroyed them. Not that he expected the police to catch the killer. Not this killer.

Loki raised his window and pushed open the door. "I'm going to go over and take a closer look."

"Do you want me to come with you?" asked the woman in the front seat.

"No. Wait here. This shouldn't take long."

"Yes, sir," said the woman.

Loki climbed out and started toward the park.

A tall, African American officer blocked his way. "I'm sorry, sir. No one is admitted to the park this morning."

"Official business." Loki reached into the pocket of his overcoat and pulled out a badge case. He flipped open the case and held an FBI identification card up for the policeman to see. It was a fake, of course, but it was a very good fake. It came from the same machines that produced badges for actual FBI agents.

The officer looked from the card to Loki and back again. "Maybe I should get my lieutenant," he said uncertainly.

"There's no reason to do that," said Loki. "Just move out of my way."

The policeman stepped aside.

Loki moved on up the path. The day had started out overcast, and low clouds still blocked the rising sun, but as he approached the actual crime scene, Loki put on a pair of dark sunglasses. There were still a few men left in the NYPD who had once worked with him as a young government agent. It was many years in the past, and even that identity had been false, but in case any of those men happened to be on the murder investigation team, Loki didn't want to be part of an uncomfortable reunion.

The crime scene was in a grassy field near the corner of the park. A pleasant enough place, with benches, trees, and gray squirrels that dodged around the policemen's feet. Pleasant, but utterly boring.

Loki ignored several other policemen who tried to talk to him and walked straight to where the body lay crumpled on the ground. It was a young girl, as expected, with long blond hair splayed out in a fan around her head. There was blood matted into the hair. More blood on the ground.

"Can I help you?"

Loki looked around and saw a plainclothes officer. From the man's cheap coat and old-fashioned hat, he had to be a homicide detective.

"I'm Frank Lancino, Connecticut state police," Loki said. He reached into his coat and produced another identification card. Just as fake. Just as good. "I've been called in to consult on this one."

The detective nodded. "I heard they were talking to your guys." He jerked his head toward the body. "What do you think? Same asshole you had up your way?"

Loki knelt next to the body. The girl had been killed with a knife, but not with a single wound. There were cuts on the arms. Cuts on the legs. Puncture wounds that went all the way through the body and a long slice that cut halfway around her neck. "Yes," he said. "Yes, this certainly looks like the work of our boy."

The detective sighed. He jammed his hands into his tweed overcoat. "What are we going to do about this? Any ideas?"

Loki straightened. "First you need to talk to your

technicians." He pointed at the ground. "If they can't do a better job outlining a body than that, who knows what else they missed."

"That outline's not from this body."

"It's not?" Loki looked at the detective curiously.

"That's from the previous victim," said the detective. "It looks like the killer did this one on the same spot as the one from the night before."

Loki had to fight back a smile. It was a nice touch. A very nice touch. He squinted at the trees around them. What were the odds that the subject of this investigation was out there right now, watching them? Loki thought it was very likely. Every artist wants to see the reaction to his work.

"Can I ask you some questions about the cases you've seen?" asked the detective.

"Later," said Loki. "I need to get to the station house. I'm sure I'll see you there."

Loki quickly retraced his steps and retreated to the car. The woman hustled around to open his door for him, then jumped back behind the wheel to steer the big sedan away from the curb.

"It's going to be interesting," said Loki.

The woman's green eyes were reflected as she glanced at him in the rearview mirror. "When do you think they'll meet?"

"Soon." He glanced out the window at the passing scenery. Rushing pedestrians. Colorful awnings. A man hosing down the sidewalk. It was another world. "Even now they could be moving toward a meeting."

"And when they meet?"

Loki gave a quiet laugh. "It will be one unbelievable fight."

"What if she dies?" the woman asked, her voice tight.

"Well, then, she's failed," Loki said. If she couldn't handle this, she was of no use to him, anyway.

"She has more training," the woman said. "You've seen how she can fight."

"Yes," Loki agreed. "But he has another advantage. He knows what he is. He knows what he's capable of."

"What is he capable of?" asked the woman.

"Anything."

GAIA WOKE UP, THEN WISHED SHE hadn't.

She rolled over and sat up in the bed with a groan. Even before she peeled back the covers, she had a good idea of what she was going to find, and the real thing didn't disappoint.

Dress for Distress

Her right leg was bruised from thigh to ankle. Her knee was one big scab, and every color of the bruised-and-abused rainbow decorated her leg—all the way from battered purple-blue to super-sickening yellow-green.

There was still a lingering whole-body soreness from her adventures the night before, but it wasn't as bad as she had predicted. Gaia was relieved to find that despite how awful her leg might look, it wasn't too stiff. She could walk without a problem, but it was going to be a while before she was up for another run like last night's.

She grabbed a pair of scuffed jeans from the back of a chair and carefully worked them up her injured leg. Then she pulled a hooded sweatshirt out of the closet and slipped it on. One glance in the mirror told the story. Gaia Moore, girl geek.

Why should today be any different from every other day?

She started toward the bedroom door, then had a startling thought. Today was different from every other day. Today she had a date.

Gaia groaned, limped back to the mirror, and took a longer look. She wasn't encouraged by what she saw.

Would there be time to change after school? Maybe. But what if David saw her in school? If he saw her like this, he would want to cancel.

Which would probably be a good thing. She

shouldn't have said she'd go out with him in the first place.

But that thought hadn't even made it across her brain before another one chased it.

What was wrong with going out with a guy? Couldn't she just allow herself to be normal for five seconds?

Gaia shook her head. It was too early in the morning to start arguing with herself. It was *always* too early to argue with herself. She half expected a little devil and angel to pop up on her arms and start debating.

"I'm going," she said aloud. "I'm going, and that's it."

"If you're talking about school," said a voice in the doorway, "then it's about time."

Gaia spun around and saw Ella standing in the doorway. As usual, Ella looked like she was dressed for an evening at the clubs. Even at eight in the morning the *über*-bitch looked ready for dancing. Or an affair. Probably whichever option presented itself first.

This morning her ensemble was a short, glossy leather skirt topped off by a green blouse with a neckline that showed the top of her breasts. Her scarlet hair was swept back from her face, worked into an elaborate coif that Gaia couldn't have reproduced given an entire week.

"Ever heard of knocking?" Gaia asked.

Ella arched one perfectly plucked eyebrow. "Not in my own house, I haven't." She waved a lacquered nail at Gaia. "What are you doing up here talking to yourself? School starts in ten minutes."

"Then I'm not late yet."

Ella gave a sigh that held all the exasperation in the world. "Just don't expect me to give you a ride. I have a business appointment this morning."

Gaia nodded. "Getting started a little early today, aren't we?"

The comment brought a frown to Ella's cherry red lips. "And what is that supposed to mean?"

"Nothing," said Gaia. "It's only that I noticed that you had a . . . business appointment last night, too. One that kept you out pretty late. Seems like you've had one every night since George went out of town."

Now Ella's lips pressed together so hard that Gaia was sure she'd have to reapply her lipstick. "Careful, Gaia." For a moment Ella looked almost dangerous. "George has done a lot for you. Your father meant the world to him. It would be ungrateful to insult his wife."

Gaia was about to make a reply to that when she noticed something odd about Ella's choice of words. "'Meant'?"

"Pardon?" Ella replied.

Gaia took a step toward her. "You said my father

117

meant something to George." Did Ella know something about him? Had something happened?

"Did I?" The sarcasm in Ella's voice was so acid, it could have eaten through steel.

Gaia was amazed to find that her throat was getting tight. She had trouble speaking. "Yes, you did." She was angry at herself. She'd shown Ella too much vulnerability.

Ella gave a sly smile that would do any cat proud. "Just a slip of the tongue, I'm sure." She turned away. A few seconds later, Gaia could hear the tapping of Ella's pointed heels down the stairway.

For several long moments after that, Gaia could only stand there, trying to catch her breath and get her thoughts under control. Her father had left her. He didn't care anything about her, so why should she care about him? Still, the tightness in her throat didn't want to leave.

"He's not dead," she told herself.

Ella was just trying to screw with her. That was all. Superbitch in action.

Gaia looked again at the girl in the mirror. Now she saw not only a beast with tree trunk legs and lumberjack shoulders, with tangled hair, dressed in tasteless clothes. Now the beast had bloodshot eyes, too.

There wasn't much Gaia could do about the legs or shoulders, at least not in ten minutes, but she could try to do something about the clothes. She stripped off the worn jeans as fast as she could without descabbing her knee and tossed them on the bed. The sweatshirt followed. Then she confronted the dreaded closet.

The trouble with Gaia's wardrobe was that nothing inside the closet looked much better than the things she'd been wearing. Gaia had a pair of capri pants, but they did nothing but accentuate her she-hulk hips and legs. There were a few dresses wrapped up in dry-cleaner plastic. Gaia hadn't worn them in years.

Besides, any sort of skirt was out. Unless she wore it with jet black hose, the Technicolor glory of Gaia's bruised leg was bound to show. Even with black tights there was the possibility of blood and ooze and . . . nope. No skirt.

Gaia finally settled on a pair of drab olive drawstring pants. They weren't too attractive, but at least they were clean—and they hid her legs. Gaia fumbled through crumpled sweaters and sweatshirts before settling on a slightly less baggy black sweater.

She studied the results in the mirror. Lumberjack shoulders. Tree trunk legs. Tangled hair.

Unless the grunge look came back before first period, Gaia was as fashion-free as ever.

119

But serial killers were different. They weren't run-of-the-mill **genuine** killers **monsters** who happened to get away with it more than once.

ED HAD DONE STUPIDER THINGS

Odd Couple

in his life—most of them on a skateboard, surfboard, or other so-called extreme-sport implement, but this was high on his list of "I can't believe I'm doing this" moments.

He was skipping first period—cutting school—to see a guy who had stolen his old girlfriend. Worse than that, he was cooperating with a guy who obviously loved Gaia. Ed wasn't an idiot. Sam could spout that "oh I only want to help her" bullshit all day and into the next, but the truth was that Sam was seriously into Gaia. Worst of all, Ed knew that Gaia was seriously into Sam. The whole situation tied his intestines in knots. Big ones.

The assigned meeting place for their little get-together was the chess tables in the park—neutral ground. But the police still had the park closed off, so that spot was out. Instead Ed was patrolling the sidewalk along the north border, hoping to intercept Sam. And if he missed him, that was just too bad.

"Ed?"

Ed turned and saw Sam walking toward him. "What's wrong? Don't they have clocks in college? I was about to give up on you."

Instead of answering the question, Sam hooked his

thumb toward the park. "What's going on? Why the big crowd this morning?"

"Haven't you heard?" Ed asked, glancing at the organized mayhem. "The Gentleman made another call last night."

Sam's eyes flicked toward the trees at the edge of the park, and the tan went out of his square-jawed face. "You don't think . . . I mean, it couldn't have been . . ."

Ed seriously considered letting him stew for a moment, but his conscience got the better of him. "It wasn't Gaia."

"You're sure?"

"Yep," Ed said with a nod. "The TV guys say this one happened before eleven last night. I talked to Gaia after that."

Sam still looked concerned, but the concern was tainted by obvious envy. Score one for the Ed-man.

"Was she okay?" Sam asked.

"She was fine." Actually, the conversation had been disappointingly short. Gaia had said she was tired, and she hadn't wanted to talk about the murders. But Ed liked the idea that he knew more about Gaia than Sam did. Sam might be on Gaia's short list for sex, but Ed was the one Gaia talked to every night.

Sam fiddled with the collar of his oxford shirt. "Are the police any closer to catching this guy?"

Ed shrugged. "If they have any suspects, the papers aren't mentioning it. Except the *Post*—I think they've pinned it on Elvis, or aliens, or a coalition of brunettes jealous of all that fun blonds are supposed to have."

Sam only nodded. "I'm worried about Gaia."

That was the heart of the matter. That was what had convinced Ed to cut school and meet with a guy who he barely knew—but who he hated on general principle.

Sam was afraid because of how closely Gaia resembled the first girl killed in the park. For Sam it was about protecting a girl he feared was in danger.

For Ed it was a different story. Ed knew the big secret, and from the way Sam talked, he was pretty sure that Sam didn't. Sam apparently loved Gaia, but he didn't know that Gaia was Wonder Girl. He didn't know she could slice and dice Bruce Lee without breaking a sweat.

Ed was proud to be in on it. But it gave him more reason to be scared for her. Gaia wasn't just the killer's ideal victim; she was actively seeking the killer's attention. She was all set to find this demon, shove his teeth down his throat and his arms up his nether regions, then put in a call to the police. Case over. City saved.

It had seemed like a good idea. There wasn't much Gaia couldn't handle.

But Ed was no longer so sure. Between the phone call from Sam and his stack of serial killer bios, Ed worried that maybe Gaia was in over her head. Sure, she could land a roundhouse kick with the best of them. He had seen her take out three thugs in one go. But serial killers were different. They weren't run-of-the-mill killers who happened to get away with it more than once. These guys were strange, creepy. They were genuine monsters.

Ed was pretty sure that Gaia wasn't experienced in taking on monsters. When it came to these guys, she needed just as much help as the next person. Problem was, Gaia would never recognize the fact that she might need help—let alone admit it.

"What have you found out?" asked Sam.

Ed nodded toward a bench along the perimeter of the park. "Let's go over there where you can sit down," he said. "I'm tired of looking up at you."

Sam followed instructions. He went to the bench, sat, and waited for the Ed report.

"You know the basics, right?" Ed asked.

"Six victims," Sam started, then he turned his head and looked over his shoulder. "Seven now, I guess. Connecticut, New Jersey, and here. All of them stabbed, all of them blond, all of them around Gaia's age and size." He stopped and ran one hand through his ginger-colored hair. "That's about all I know. I don't even know why they call him the Gentleman."

"I do," said Ed. "It's from an old movie, *Gentlemen Prefer Blondes.*"

Sam nodded slowly. "I've seen it. Marilyn Monroe, right?"

"Bingo."

Sam looked down at the ground and shook his head. "That's not much help. How are we going to catch this guy before he has a chance at Gaia?"

"We're not," Ed replied.

Sam's head jerked up sharply. "What do you mean?"

Ed rolled slowly back and forth in front of the bench. Wheelchair pacing. "You're the college guy. Isn't it obvious that if three states' worth of cops can't catch this guy, we're not going to do it?"

Sam's frown grew deeper. "Then why are we even talking?"

"Because," said Ed. "We don't have to find the killer." He raised one hand and pointed in the direction of the school. "We only have to stick to Gaia."

GAIA WAS THIRTY MINUTES LATE

to first period. Even compared to some of her previous arrival times, it was a new achievement in nonpunctuality. Even so, her teacher decided to ignore her.

Gaia had barely started at this school, and already she had been the butt of so many jokes, people were getting tired of it.

It was a good plan. Give them so much to laugh about that it wears them out. Too bad she hadn't actually *planned* to do it.

Gaia settled into her seat and the public address speakers crackled to life.

"May I have your attention, please?" said the voice of an unseen school office worker. "This is a school-wide announcement."

The last event deemed worthy of a schoolwide announcement had turned out to be a pep rally. Earth-shattering stuff.

"Due to recent events, the school will be closing early today. The last period will end at one P.M. Additional counselors will be on hand in the lunchroom for any students who feel they would benefit from a counseling session. School hours will return to normal tomorrow. Thank you." The voice ended with another squirt of static.

The announcement of an early end to the school day drew a few muted cheers but didn't get nearly the reaction that Gaia had expected. She leaned toward a skinny, red-haired guy at a nearby desk.

"What events are they talking about?" she asked. "Why let us out early?"

The redhead nodded his pointy chin toward a desk at the front of the room. An empty desk.

Gaia stared at the desk, trying to remember whose body normally filled it. It wasn't Hateful Heather. Heather was in her usual place of power at the center of the room. It wasn't Ed. Ed wasn't in this class. Gaia frowned as she tried to remember. It was . . . It was . . .

Cassie Greenman. The girl who had told Gaia about the killing the day before. The girl who had said they looked alike.

Gaia turned to the red-haired guy again. "What happened to Cassie?"

Redhead moved his lips to form a single word. Gaia didn't have to be much of a lip-reader to make it out. Gentleman.

The headache that had only threatened in Gaia's bedroom suddenly came on with full force. "Where?" she asked.

The guy looked toward the teacher and tried to avoid Gaia's attention.

"Where?" she said again, more than a little louder. "Where did it happen?"

"In the park at eleven o'clock," the redhead shot back. He picked up his book and opened it, angling the pages so they formed a screen to ward off Gaia.

It didn't matter. Gaia had asked all the questions that mattered. She closed her eyes and tried to fight back waves of nausea and confusion. It was too coincidental, too weird. Cassie knew about the murderer. Why in the world would she be any-where near the park at eleven o'clock at night?

How could Gaia have failed a second time? It almost felt like this killer was taunting her. Once again he had struck right under her nose. And this time it had been someone Gaia knew.

Gaia had thought she could catch this guy before he did any more damage. She had maybe hoped there was something good in being fearless. Maybe even something good in being a muscle-bound freak. Something that made her life worthwhile.

Obviously she was wrong.

I make friends pretty easily. I'm fun, I'm loud. I know how to have a good time.

People are drawn to me.

But I'm not always drawn to them.

But this Gaia person? I genuinely like her. She intrigues me. That's why I gave her my number and told her to call if she ever felt like hanging out.

It's obvious she never will, but it's a gesture. And when you make a gesture, sometimes people feel they owe you something. And when people feel they owe you something . . . Well, that can come in handy from time to time.

MARY

The sooner
the informa-
tion reached
Sam, the **a simple**
better the **job**
chance of
saving Gaia.

Murphy's Law

TOM MOORE TUGGED DOWN ON his brown cap and did his best to shade his face. He had no reason to suspect that anyone would recognize him on the campus of NYU, especially dressed as he was in the brown uniform of a package delivery-man, but it didn't pay to take chances.

Years of experience had taught Tom that Murphy's Law was always in full operation when you were un-dercover. If anything could go wrong, it would. Even when nothing could go wrong, it went wrong, anyway.

Today's expedition into the city seemed like a sim-ple thing—drop off a package, run, and hope that the person getting the package knew what to do with the information it contained. That only made Tom more cautious. It was the simple jobs that turned into nightmares.

He felt a little odd, walking between the square buildings along Washington Place. Part of it was the feeling that any older person gets visiting a college or high school. An out-of-place feeling. Only Tom didn't need to be surrounded by kids to feel out of place. He was out of place just being alive.

He reached the gray concrete steps of the dorm and hurried inside. Put on the right uniform, and you can get anywhere. Show a little paperwork, and people will even point out the right door.

Three minutes later, Tom had walked through a disheveled common room and was rapping his knuckles against a dented oak panel marked B4. He'd hand the boy the box and go.

A feeling of guilt added to Tom's uneasiness. This boy's relationship to Gaia had already led him into serious trouble. Involving him further might well get the boy killed.

Tom shoved away the guilt. He had to do what he could to protect Gaia. It would be impossible to get the information directly to her—Gaia was under almost constant observation. If Tom tried to get close, he would only get himself killed. And more to the point, Gaia as well.

There was no response to his knock. He tried again, rapping a little harder this time.

"Package," he called through the closed door. "Package for Sam Moon."

One of the doors on the other side of the common room opened, and an overweight young man, his hair shaved down to a dark stubble, stuck out his head.

"He's not here," he said, a strong southern accent in his voice. "I saw him leave about half an hour ago."

Tom frowned. "Do you know where he could be?"

The stubble-haired neighbor shook his head. "He

usually comes back here between classes. You want me to hold on to that for him?"

Tom's fingers instinctively tightened around the package. He ran through the possibilities. He could try to find Sam elsewhere. He had pulled the boy's class schedule off the Internet, and he could always wait for Sam outside a classroom. Unfortunately package delivery companies didn't usually ambush people in hallways.

He could try coming back later, but that had its own set of risks. The sooner the information reached Sam, the better the chance of saving Gaia.

Tom looked at the boy with the shaved head. There was no reason to think he couldn't be trusted. No reason except that he appeared to have about as many brain cells as a ceiling beam.

"If I give it to you, will you be able to give it to him today?" Tom asked.

"As soon as he shows up," the boy promised.

Tom hesitated a moment longer, then nodded. "Sign here," he said. He passed a clipboard over, watched the boy sign it, and then—reluctantly—handed him the box.

The boy stepped back and started to close the door.

Tom grabbed the edge of the door and held it open. "This is an important package," he said. "You need to see that he gets it right away."

"Yeah," the boy replied, obviously perplexed. "Sure." He pulled on the door, and Tom let it go.

"Tell him it's from Gaia," Tom said to the closing door. "An important package from Gaia."

The door closed with a click, and a moment after, Tom heard the sound of one, two, three locks being set. He stared at the old, scratched wood door for a moment, then turned and started out of the building.

He was aware that he hadn't acted like a deliveryman. It didn't matter. Sam's neighbor could think anything he liked.

As long as he delivered the package.

GAIA NEVER KNEW A PIECE OF furniture could scream.

It was there in every class she had shared with Cassie Greenman. A desk. An empty desk.

It was just a plain desk, scratched up and written on by so many students, it was hard to even make out where one set of initials stopped and the next one started. A couple of pieces of plastic, some plywood, and twisted-up metal. But every time Gaia looked at it, she heard this weird kind of wailing down deep in her brain.

She wondered if she was going crazy—even more crazy than usual. But Gaia didn't think she was the only one who heard the screaming.

All day, other people kept glancing over at the desk. The Empty Desk. And every time they looked that way, they'd get this expression on their faces. Instantly zoned. Even the teachers seemed to be looking at it as if they expected the desk to answer a question or make a comment on the class.

It was profoundly weird.

Gaia knew they cut a couple of hours off the day, but by the time the last bell rang, she would have sworn that she had been in school for at least three weeks.

If anybody had asked her what had been covered in her classes that day, Gaia couldn't have repeated a word. Not that she was ever Ms. Perfect Attention. But ever since the morning announcement the only sound track in Gaia's head was the screaming desk and a running loop of her conversation with Cassie.

As far as Gaia knew, it was the first time she had ever talked to Cassie. And the last.

The thing that really bugged Gaia, the thing she just could not get around, was this:

What in hell was Cassie Greenman doing in Washington Square Park at night? It didn't make any sense. Cassie had seemed genuinely scared of the killer. She had even talked about dyeing her hair to take her off the victim list. Cassie Greenman might not have been a rocket scientist, but anyone smart enough not to play on subway tracks would have known better than to go into the park.

Except Gaia, of course, but that was different.

Gaia took a last took at the screaming desk as she staggered out of class. It had eyeball magnetism, that desk. It was like a tooth missing right in the middle of someone's smile. You couldn't stop looking at it. Gaia wondered how long it would be before someone else sat there and filled in the gap. She was willing to bet that desk was going to be empty for a long time.

Gaia made it down the hall, pounded her locker into submission, and shoved her stuff inside.

Why hadn't she seen Cassie in the park? It wasn't exactly teeming with people. How could Gaia have missed her?

Thoughts of Cassie grew so thick, it was like walking around in a literal fog. Gaia trudged slowly along the hallway, lost to the world. Then she started around the corner by the school office and ran smack into what felt like a concrete wall.

She gave a mumbled "sorry" and started to move on.

"It's all right. At least this time you didn't knock me down."

Gaia looked up at the voice. "Huh?"

"Hi," said David. "Remember me? David Twain, boy obstacle."

Gaia blinked away the tangle of twisted thoughts. David hadn't felt like a wall yesterday. Last night must have taken more out of her than she thought. "What are you doing here?" she asked.

David grinned. "It's school. They make you go."

"I mean . . ." Except Gaia didn't know what she meant. Her brain was still deep in the Cassie zone, and she was having a hard time getting it back in the real-world dimension.

"I'm going to have to start wearing football pads," David said, rubbing at the back of his neck. Gaia watched his forearm where he'd rolled up his sleeve. He was better looking today. Somehow the thought pissed her off.

"Sorry," Gaia said again, stepping around him. "I'm not all here at the moment."

"Yeah, I've seen the studies," David said, shoving his hands in his pockets. His binder was tucked under his arm with one book. There was no backpack. Gaia brought her hand to her forehead, confused by her inadvertent observations. Since when was she interested in this kind of thing?

"What studies?" she asked, focusing in on the little space of skin between his dark eyebrows.

"About you," David replied. "Four out of five

137

doctors warn that you're a major source of bruises."

Gaia shook away the last of the Cassie fog and tried to concentrate on what David was saying. Some part of her brain told her that she had just missed a joke, but she was in no mood to go back and figure it out.

"Whatever." Another brilliant response from Ms. Gaia Moore, ladies and gentlemen.

David smiled. Dimples. Annoying.

"Well, *whatever* you are or aren't, I *was* looking for you," he said. "In fact, looking for you was my number-one objective for the afternoon."

"Why?" The fog was rolling back in.

"The date, remember?"

Gaia blinked. Date. For a moment the words belonged to a foreign language. Something they might say in the jungles of Borneo or maybe on the far side of the moon. Then she remembered. Coffee. Baklava. Her first ever genuine date. It was amazing what a little thing like murder could make you forget.

"Look, David," she said. "Maybe we shouldn't. You know, because of . . . Cassie and all."

His face was quickly overtaken by an expression of concern. "I'm sorry. Were you two close?"

"No. It's not that. It's . . ." Gaia wondered how David would react if she explained to him that she was the ugly sister of Xena, Warrior Princess, and

Cassie was one of the helpless peasants Gaia was supposed to protect from the rampaging hordes. "It bothers me."

David nodded. "It bothers me, too." He gave a quick look around the hallway. "I just moved here last week. Everybody keeps saying that New York is this really safe place, that there's not nearly as much crime as people say. They act like it's all in the movies. But I get here and there's this big murder thing going on."

Gaia shrugged. "They're only killing blond girls. You shouldn't have to worry."

That off-center smile crept back onto his face. "Yeah, but I kind of like blond girls," he said in a low voice. "I want to keep them around."

It wasn't the smoothest response in the world. On the Skippy scale, Gaia marked it closer to regular than extra creamy. But he was trying.

"Okay," she said. "Maybe we could go somewhere. Just for a little while."

"Anywhere you want," he replied. "If you don't feel like dessert, maybe we could just go over to Googie's and grab a burger."

Googie's. Yet another spot on Gaia's Guide to the Village. It was a place so tacky, it was . . . really tacky. "For a guy who's only been here a couple of days, you sure have homed in on prime sources of empty calories."

David patted his disgustingly flat stomach. "I have

a list of priorities whenever I move." He raised his hand and started ticking off the points. "First, locate an immediate source of sugar. Two, find a good greasy burger. Three, pin down a decent pizza." He lowered his hand. "Once all that's done, you're ready to move on to number four."

Gaia raised an eyebrow. "What's number four?"

The dimples retreated, and David looked at her for the first time with a completely serious expression. "Find the right girl to share it with."

Gaia had to give him credit. He was Not Sam, but he was good. She did a quick top-to-bottom survey. Chinos: pressed, but not too neat. Khaki shirt over black T-shirt: again, looking a little less than perfect. Just an average guy. And average was okay with her.

Gaia did a little mental arithmetic. If what she had heard was right, then both victims had died in the park in the middle part of the evening, somewhere before midnight. If Gaia was in place by nine-thirty, ten at the latest, she should be ready to tackle the killer if he came back for thirds—not that she would be the only person looking for him there tonight. She'd still have time for a quick dinner, a change of clothes, and working her way past Ella.

Not that the last part was hard. Ella had been off doing Ella things every night for a week.

"You're sure you want to go out with me?" Gaia

asked. She knew it was tempting fate, but she felt like she had to give him a final chance to back out.

David nodded. "Absolutely."

"Then here's the deal. Meet me at Third and Thompson at six, and we'll eat."

"What's at Third and Thompson?"

"Jimmy's Burrito." Gaia gave him her best excuse for a smile. "Even greasier than Googie's."

SAM LEANED AGAINST THE COOL STONE

A Simple Plan

of the Washington Square Park arch. He looked around to make sure that no one was watching, then pulled a small yellow radio from his pocket and squeezed the trigger on its side. Even alone, he still felt like an idiot.

"Do you see her?" he asked. He let go of the trigger, then quickly pressed it again. "Over."

There was a moment of silence before Ed's voice came back. "Yes, I see her. I'm in a wheelchair. I'm not blind. Over."

"Which way is she going? Is she heading toward the park?"

Static.

"Ed? Is she going toward the park?"

Static.

"Ed?"

"You're supposed to say 'over' when you're done."

"Over, for God's sake. Is she going toward the park? Over," Sam snapped.

Static.

"Ed? I said over."

"I heard you. I was just moving to keep up with Gaia. Have you ever tried to roll and use a walkie-talkie at the same time?" he hissed. "Next time you decide to steal radios, I suggest you get one with a headset. Over."

Sam pushed the trigger again. "I didn't steal these. I paid for them."

It was at least temporarily true. They were good radios, guaranteed to have at least a two-mile range and fourteen channels, and they had fancy built-in scrambling so no one else could listen in on the conversation. Very nice radios. Also very expensive.

There was no way Sam could afford to keep them. So he had paid for them at an electronics store with a thirty-day return policy. As soon as Operation Protect Gaia was over, the radios were going back. At the moment they were paid for.

"Which way is Gaia going?" Sam asked again. "Over," he added quickly.

"It looks like she's going home," Ed's voice replied. "Probably to get ready for her date. Over."

Sam stared at the radio in his hand. He had to have heard that wrong. "Say again."

Static.

"Ed?"

"You didn't say 'over.' Over."

Sam squeezed the radio, envisioning Ed's neck between his fingers. "Can you forget the stupid 'over' and just repeat whatever it was you said?"

"I said, she's going home." There was a hint of laughter in Ed's radio voice.

Sam gripped the radio. "Not that part."

"Then what . . ." Static. "Oh, you mean the date."

"What date are you talking about?" It took all his effort to release the talk button so he could listen for a response he was sure he didn't really want to hear.

"Don't you know about the date?" More glee. Obvious this time.

Sam was glad there was at least a mile of space between them. If Ed had been close enough to reach, the Gentleman wouldn't be the only one in the park committing murder.

"Obviously I don't know about the date," Sam said slowly. "If I knew about the date, would I be asking about the date?"

"Gaia has a date tonight," Ed's voice replied. His

voice had changed. There was resignation in it now. "She warned me about it yesterday."

No one had warned Sam. Of course, Gaia and Sam weren't on the best of terms. They had basically no reason to speak at all. But Sam still felt blindsided by the enormity of Ed's announcement.

Gaia had a date. *She's not yours,* he reminded himself. *She was never yours.* Somehow he still felt betrayed.

"Who is she going out with?" Sam asked.

"A new guy," Ed replied flatly. "David something." Sam was about to ask another question, but before he could, Ed's voice came again. "I need to move again if I'm going to keep her in sight."

Sam pushed himself away from the cold marble of the arch. "All right. Call me if she comes back out. We'll work out positions."

"Roger," said Ed. "Over and out. Ten-four. Copy tha—"

Sam switched off the radio. He flicked a switch that would make it ring like a telephone if Ed called, then dropped it into his jacket pocket.

Sam went through a mental list of questions about the date, but he couldn't think of how to ask them without sounding jealous. Was he jealous? He thought about it for a moment and decided the answer was yes. He might not be able to define his own feelings about Gaia, but he was sure about one thing—he didn't want her going out with anyone else.

With Gaia gone back to her brownstone to prepare for the unthinkable date, Sam wasn't sure what to do. He could hang around the park for the afternoon, maybe get in a game. But losing a game of chess didn't seem very appealing without at least the chance of seeing Gaia.

After a few moments of indecision he turned to go back to his dorm. This was probably the only chance he was going to get to shower, eat something, maybe even grab a quick catnap. He would be back on duty soon enough.

Sam strolled across Washington Square North and headed uptown. The plan he and Ed had worked out was a simple one—until the Gentleman was caught, killed, or had moved on to another state, they would keep Gaia under close observation. Close observation defined as spying on her night and day.

There were two upsides to this plan. First, it would keep Sam occupied, thus keeping his mind off the obsessive kidnapping questions. Second, the plan involved seeing Gaia. A lot.

For today both Sam and Ed would both be on duty. If Gaia appeared, they would stay close. If Gaia got in trouble, they would help her. If they made it through the first day, they would switch over to working in shifts. Ed would watch Gaia during the school day; Sam would take over in the afternoons. It seemed like a simple plan.

Sam only hoped the killer was caught before Sam died from exhaustion.

A group of skateboarders went past, headed for the park, followed closely by a knot of laughing kids. The police had kept Washington Square locked up for most of the morning, but now that the barriers were down, the usual park population was rushing in to fill the void.

Sam cast a sideways glance as a barrel-chested man in a Greek fisherman's hat strolled past, a newspaper tucked under his arm. The man didn't seem familiar. He definitely wasn't a regular. Maybe he was the killer.

Another man went past. This one had a narrow, hatchet-shaped face and wild, bushy eyebrows. Killer material for sure.

There was a middle-aged Asian woman wearing a long, dark coat—an awfully heavy coat for a day that was pretty warm. She could have hidden anything under that coat. After all, even if the press called the killer the Gentleman, there had been no witnesses to the killings. Who was to say this Gentleman wasn't a Gentlewoman?

Sam was looking at another man when he realized how crazy this was. Of course these pedestrians didn't look familiar. Fifty thousand people must walk down Fifth Avenue to Washington Square on any day of the week. Maybe more like a hundred thousand. Sam couldn't possibly recognize them all.

It was time for Sam Moon to stop playing Sam Spade. A blast of sugar laced with caffeine, some sack time, and an icy shower were all required. Any order would do.

He managed to make it back to his dorm without spotting any more serial killer wanna-bes on the streets. But that didn't mean there wasn't still one out there. Maybe Sam could just have the caffeine and the shower. The nap would take too long. He couldn't leave Gaia out there alone while he snoozed. So no nap.

That decision made, Sam actually felt a tiny bit better. He walked through the common room and was about to open the door to his bedroom when he heard another door open.

"Hey, Sam," said a voice at his elbow. "Think fast."

Someone who had gone through high school playing basketball would have had an instant response to those words. Sam played chess. He turned around just in time to take a cardboard box between the eyes.

"Ouch," he said as the small package bounced off his forehead and thumped to the floor.

"You got bad hands, Moon." Sam's suite mate,

147

Mike Suarez, leaned back against his door frame, grinning.

Sam reached for the package. "My hands are okay; it's my head that's slow." He picked up the box and turned it over in his hands. "What's this?"

"Delivery guy brought it for you this morning," Mike replied. "That's all I know." He shrugged and winked. "You better work on those hands."

"Right." Sam returned the smile, although he felt more like smacking Mike's head right back.

Sam turned to the door and pushed it open, reminding himself for the umpteenth time that he really had to get that lock fixed. As soon as he was inside, he looked at the package again, wondering who might have sent it. It was a small box, little bigger than a stack of index cards, and the label had no return address.

There was only one way to find out. He grabbed the paper at the edge of the box and started to tug.

"Sam?"

This time the voice came from inside his room. Sam looked up in surprise and saw `Heather sitting on the edge of his bed.` "Heather! Jesus, you scared me."

Heather smiled at him. "We didn't have the best night last night," she said. "I thought I would try to make it up to you."

Sam opened his mouth to say something else, but

the subject slipped away before it could get to his tongue. Heather's long, rich brown hair had been set loose to spill around her shoulders. She was wearing a short, black skirt that ended well above her knees and a white shirt. A big white shirt.

"That's my shirt," he said.

Heather nodded. "I borrowed it." Her lips pursed into a pout. "I'm sorry. You want me to take it off?"

"No, I—"

The pout on Heather's lips was replaced by a sly smile. "I was hoping you would say yes." She raised her fingers to the top button and slowly slipped it open. Then she moved down to the next. "I think we should try again, Sam," she said. "The last time didn't end so well, did it?"

Her tone was inviting, but her eyes conveyed a whole other message. She was giving him a chance to make it up to her. Make up for chasing after Gaia and leaving her naked. Alone. Unsatisfied. One chance.

There was no way Sam was stupid enough to disappoint her. He didn't want to.

He quickly shoved the little package into his coat pocket next to the yellow plastic radio and closed the door.

Apparently there would be no nap, no shower, and no caffeine.

"Soon I'll be through the main course." He looked at Loki **stranger** over his shoulder. "I think I'll take up brunettes for dessert."

"YOU MIGHT AS WELL COME OUT,"

The Thing

Loki said calmly. "I know that you're following me."

The boy stepped out from the trees and stood in the dry grass at the edge of the sidewalk. "Well, if it isn't my dear uncle Loki," he said in a cheerful tone. "Whatever brings you here?"

Loki kept his hand in his pocket and closed his fingers around the comforting bulk of his 9-mm pistol. "You couldn't resist, could you?" he said. "You had to come and watch."

The boy shrugged. "I admit, there is a certain pleasure in watching all the little bugs scurry around." He waved his hands extravagantly. "The police run here. The FBI runs there. And you run in between."

"Do you think this is funny?"

"Oh, very," the boy said. "But that's not why I'm here."

"Then why are you here?" Loki took a half step back. He tried to judge the odds. His skills with a firearm weren't as polished as they had been ten years before, but he was still quite fast. He could pull his semiautomatic pistol and get off ten rounds before most men even realized he had moved. But against this boy . . . Loki thought his chances of surviving were no better than fifty-fifty.

The boy turned and looked back through the

screen of trees at the people passing through the park.

"Actually," he said, "I was only taking in the menu. Picking out a little something for tonight." He gestured at a group of girls laughing near the fountain. "There are so many possibilities here."

Loki studied the boy as if he were a stranger. It was almost true. A year before, the boy had been just that—a boy. A boy with an unusual predilection. Then he'd been unsure of himself. Awkward. Looking to Loki and others for guidance.

A year could change everything. The man—the thing—that Loki faced had as little relation to that uncertain boy as a kitten did to a tiger. In every way that counted, he was a stranger.

"I didn't think any of that group would be to your taste," Loki replied, glancing at the gaggle of young women.

"No?"

"I thought you were only after blonds."

The stranger with a familiar face laughed. "So true," he said. "But that was only the appetizer. Soon I'll be through the main course." He looked at Loki over his shoulder. "I think I'll take up brunettes for dessert."

Loki frowned. He wasn't squeamish. He never had been. One life lost, a hundred lives lost, what did it matter? But there were things he cared about: years of work, research, effort. Those things should never be wasted.

Against his better judgment he took a step forward. "Come back," he said. He thought about touching the stranger's shoulder but decided against it. "Come home."

"Home?" The boy made a noise that might have been the start of laughter but quickly turned into something more like a growl. "Home," he said again. His face twisted into a sudden sneer, and he began to pace back and forth between the trees and the edge of the concrete path, his black coat billowing in the wind. "Couldn't you find a better word than *home?*"

"It was your home," Loki said in his most reassuring tone. "For most of your life you were—"

The boy whirled. His eyes were sharp. "Oh, don't say happy," he snapped. "It was an experiment. A rat cage. A prison. Not a home. And I was never, ever happy in that box." He raised his arm and pointed an accusing finger at Loki. "That place is the reason I'm here. The reason for everything."

Loki sighed. It was a sad, tired sound, the sound of an old man who was past his prime and weary of the world. It was a sound Loki had practiced.

"All right," he said. "I don't suppose there's anything I can say to make it better now." Hidden in the pocket of his coat, his hand tightened on the grip of the pistol. He began to raise the barrel.

The boy blinked, and as quickly as it had come, his

rage seemed to evaporate. A broad smile returned to his face.

"Don't tell me you're going to shoot me," he said. "Not after you've come so far to ask your poor prodigal son to come back to the farm."

For ten seconds they stood in silence. Loki had no idea what the boy was thinking, but his own mind was playing over scenarios as fast as a chess computer trying out moves. In this game there were only two opening moves: Leave the boy alone or kill him. Each of those moves had its possibilities and its dangers. Loki made a quick glance around and judged his distance from the other people in the park. There were no police nearby, and the risk of auxiliary damage was low. Now was the time.

"I was wrong to let you out," said Loki. "You're undisciplined. Unready. You have to come back with me."

"Or you'll kill me," said the boy.

Loki nodded. "Yes."

The boy was fast. Incredibly fast. One moment he was ten feet away. The next Loki's hand was hit by a rock-hard blow that sent the automatic pistol spinning away. Before he could react to that first attack, a fist cracked against his chin. He reeled backward, red fog swirling in his brain.

Strong hands caught Loki by the shoulders and spun him around.

"You made me the way I am for a purpose," the boy hissed in a low whisper, "but I've got my own objectives now. The first one is to kill your golden child." The fingers tightened. "And then I'm coming for you."

The boy released his grip, stepped back, and smiled. It was almost serene. He touched one finger to his forehead in a mock salute, then turned and strolled casually across the park.

Loki watched him go. In a way, he was greatly relieved that he hadn't managed to kill the boy. He couldn't be certain if it was the right decision.

But he would know soon enough.

THE BEST THING ABOUT HAVING A

A Happy Gaia

date at Jimmy's was that it had all the ambiance of a shoe box. Maybe less.

That didn't mean Gaia didn't like it. Ambiance came way, way down on the list of her requirements in a restaurant. Way below sour cream and globs of melty cheese.

Besides, no ambiance equaled no need to dress up. No need to dress up equaled no need to worry about changing clothes. No need to worry about changing clothes equaled a happy Gaia.

That was the theory. In the real world she decided to make a change.

What she really needed was something dark. Something nice. Cool. Something sort of *Matrix-like*. Something that would hide stains.

Fat chance of finding it in her closet. This was depressing. For a split second Gaia thought of the red-haired girl. Mary. The smudged number on the crumpled coffeehouse napkin in the pocket of last night's jeans. Had Mary meant it when she said to call her? Was that what girls did? Call for advice before dates?

Right. Like that was going to happen.

Gaia went back to the black jeans she had looked at in the morning and decided to give them another try. They fit a little snug—snugger than she would have liked across her bulging butt. Still, they didn't look too bad.

She stared a few minutes longer, then closed her eyes, reached in, and selected a hanger at random. Gaia opened her eyes to peek. A big denim shirt. Not an inspired choice, but at least a choice.

She gave her hair a few strokes, pulled it back, and slipped it through her one and only scrunchie. There. She was dressed, and the whole thing had taken less than half an hour. It had to be a new record.

Gaia checked the clock. Plenty of time to cruise by the park, lose a game to Zolov, and still be early for her date.

Date.

Gaia felt a shimmery feeling in her legs. Not a major quake, but at least a 3.5 on the do-I-really-want-to-go-through-with-this scale. The date was only a couple of hours away, and she still couldn't get a good handle on the idea. Gaia was going to a restaurant. With a guy.

It wasn't a completely unknown situation. She had been out on social occasions before. Of course, the last time was probably when she was twelve. It wasn't completely unheard of. Except this time the guy was actually coming because of Gaia. He would look at Gaia. And talk to Gaia. Worse, he would expect Gaia to talk back and be interesting for minutes on end.

She wondered if she could just keep her mouth full of burrito and let him talk. Guys liked to talk. That's what she had heard, anyway.

With this stellar plan in place Gaia started downstairs, sure that she was on her way to end her status as the world's oldest undated girl. It was possible that she would even break the great kiss curse.

But a new obstacle was waiting for Gaia before she reached the ground floor. She closed her eyes and sighed.

157

She'd forgotten about the Wicked Witch of the Wonderbra.

Ella looked at Gaia over the rims of her purple-tinted sunglasses. "Where are you going?"

"Nowhere," Gaia replied.

Ella smirked. "Then maybe you shouldn't go. It's getting late."

"Late?" Gaia pointed at the window beside the staircase. "It's barely after four. It's broad daylight out there."

Ella pursed her glossy lips. "I know, but with all those murders going on, I really think you need to stay in. It's just too dangerous."

The person on the stairs looked like Ella. The perfume drifting toward Gaia in invisible clouds certainly smelled like Ella. But her mind had clearly been replaced by the mind of someone else—someone who cared if Gaia kept breathing.

Or at least bothered to pretend to care.

What the hell was she supposed to say? Part of her just wanted to walk out like she normally would, but some morbid part of her was tempted to play along.

"I . . . uh . . . won't stay late." That was at least partially true. Gaia could circle back by the brownstone after her early date with David. Then she could slip out again as soon as Ella got over this caring fit.

Ella waited a few seconds, then nodded. "All right," she said, "but whatever you do, stay out of the park.

And try to get home before eight. It's a school night."

Gaia stared. Body snatchers were definitely at work. This whole conversation could not be occurring. Not with Ella.

She tried to answer but could only manage a nod. Ella's behavior had baffled Gaia beyond the ability for rational speech.

SAM WONDERED IF YOU COULD

Timing Is Everything

drown in hair. Heather's hair was long and lush and altogether beautiful to look at. Breathing through it was a different story. No matter how Sam turned in the narrow bed, he seemed to end up with a suffocating curtain of brown spilling over his face.

Heather murmured something and snuggled against him. Her soft skin felt extraordinarily warm against his legs and chest.

Like Heather, Sam was nearly unconscious in a postsex daze. It was amazing. Sex was like the greatest sleeping aid in history. One minute he was more charged up than he had ever been in his life, the next minute his arms and legs seemed to weigh a thousand tons. Each.

Sam pushed open a gap in Heather's hair wide enough to permit a breath of air. He couldn't allow himself to actually sleep. With the serial killer working the neighborhood, Heather's parents would panic if she was out late. And Sam had something to do. Something important. But for the moment he couldn't remember exactly what it was. He settled himself against Heather's warm softness and began to slide toward sleep.

This wasn't so bad. He could live with this. Having a beautiful girl naked in your bed was about as close to perfect as life could get.

For the moment, at least, Sam's obsession with Gaia seemed distant. Silly. There was nothing wrong with Heather. So what if she didn't know what a rook was? So what if she had a small cruel streak? It would be okay. It would work out. He was sure that he could love Heather.

Except, as his drowsiness pulled him down the slope toward true sleep, he brushed his lips against Heather's brown hair and imagined it was gold.

A buzzing alarm began to sound. Sam groaned and flapped his arm at the clock on the bedside table. He smacked the button over and over, but the noise kept coming.

"Mmmm." Heather rolled over and brushed her

lips against his face. "Turn that off," she whispered.

"I'm trying." Sam propped himself up on one elbow and picked up the clock. He pressed the button again. He slid the alarm switch to off, but the noise didn't stop. He stared at the clock blankly for a few seconds longer, then realized what was wrong.

The sound wasn't coming from the clock.

Sam scanned the room, searching for the source of the noise. It wasn't the phone. It wasn't the stereo. It was . . . a coat.

Across the room Sam's jacket was lying folded across the back of a chair—not the neatest fold in the world, but then, he had been in sort of a hurry to get undressed. For some reason, the coat was buzzing.

"Sam," Heather called. "Please. That's so annoying."

"Sure. Right." Still more than half asleep, Sam carefully eased himself away from Heather and rolled off the side of the bed. He stumbled over discarded clothing, banged his knee against his desk, knocked over a stack of books, and made it to the coat without generating any more noise than a rogue elephant in a bell factory. He fumbled in the pocket of the coat and grabbed something. What he pulled out was a bright yellow plastic radio.

Sam's heartbeat slammed to a stop.

Oh, yeah. The radio.

Free of the coat, the buzzing noise was louder than ever. Sam flipped the radio over and over in his hands, searching for the switch. At last he located the trigger on the side and pressed it. The buzzing stopped.

Sam breathed a low sigh of relief. He would call Ed back as soon as he could, but in the meantime at least the radio was quiet. The last thing he wanted to do was explain to Heather what he—

"Sam?" said a loud voice from the radio. "Sam, are you there?"

Panic shot through Sam. All remains of the after-sex sleepiness were blown away in an instant. He looked at the bed, trying to ascertain whether Heather was waking up, then he squeezed the trigger on the radio.

"I'm here," he said as softly as he could.

"Took you long enough," Ed's voice replied. "I've been sitting here buzzing you for the last five minutes. I was about to give up."

Sam wished he had.

Heather rolled over on the bed and stretched her hands above her head. "Sam," she said in a voice that was half a yawn. "Who's on the phone?"

"Nobody important," Sam replied with forced cheerfulness. "Go back to sleep." He lowered his voice and spoke into the radio. "Look, can you call me back later?"

"Hey, this thing was your idea." The quality of the radio was plenty good enough to pick up the irritation in Ed's voice. "Are you going to help me or not?"

"What's happening?"

"She's in the park," Ed answered. "She's been playing chess against that old guy. The Russian."

"Zolov," said Sam. "He's Ukrainian."

"Whatever. The game's over, and she's leaving."

Heather raised her head and rubbed at her eyes. "Sam . . ."

"Just a minute." Sam walked across the small room and stood as far from Heather as he could. "Look, can't you follow her?" he whispered to the radio.

"I'm too obvious," Ed replied through a crackle of static. "If I leave the park, she's going to see me."

Sam sighed and closed his eyes. They should just let her go. This whole business was seriously screwed up.

Sam squeezed the trigger, ready to tell Ed to pack it in.

For a full five seconds Sam held down the little button, but the words wouldn't come. If he gave up and something happened to Gaia, Sam would never be able to live with himself. That much he knew.

"All right," he said in a low tone. "Watch her as long as you can. I'll be right there."

"Hurry."

Suddenly Sam noticed a small plastic switch at the top of the radio. He flicked it, and the speaker inside went dead.

He'd found the off switch. Great timing.

Heather sat up and held the white sheets against her chest. "What's wrong?" she asked.

"Um, nothing," Sam said. He moved across the darkened room and found his clothes lying on the floor. Still trying to be as quiet as he could, he picked up his pants and began to slide them on.

"Where are you going?" asked Heather. There was a lingering fog of sleep in her voice, but it didn't hide an edge of irritation. "Aren't you going to stay with me?"

Sam ran a hundred excuses through his mind, but all of them seemed too lame to speak.

He could always tell her the truth. On the other hand, he wasn't ready to die.

"I have a class," he said.

"Now?" Heather pushed her hair back from her face and frowned at him. "I thought you had a short day on Tuesdays."

"It's a lab," Sam replied. He dragged out his shirt and began to put it on as fast as he could. "A . . . um, makeup lab from one I missed earlier."

"How long will it take?"

That depends on Gaia.

"A couple of hours," he said. "Three at the most." He finished with his shirt, dropped into a chair, and started putting on his shoes.

Heather stretched her long, bare legs but didn't get up. "Then I guess I better get dressed, too. I have to get home."

"Okay," said Sam. He stood up. "I've got to run, or I'll be late."

Heather pulled the pillows together and leaned back against them. "All right," she said. "Mind if I use your shower before I go?"

Sam smiled. "No problem. I wish I could stay."

He did wish he could stay. Although the decision to watch over Gaia was already made, Sam felt a fresh wave of indecision.

After all, the last time he'd left Heather to chase Gaia, he'd ended up kidnapped and half dead.

It would be nice if he could stay here. It would be nice if he could think of nothing but Heather.

It would probably be a lot safer, too.

But the undefined feelings he had for Gaia Moore were too hard to ignore.

Sam picked up his jacket and put it on. As he did, he noticed the small package still nestled in the right-hand pocket. He took out the box and held it up to the light. Small box. Brown paper. Nothing special. He started to leave the package behind, then he changed his mind and dropped it back into the

165

pocket. If he ended up on a nightlong Gaia stakeout, he would at least have something to look at.

"Well, I guess I'm going," he said as he moved toward the door. "Are you going to be all right going home by yourself?"

"I'll be fine."

There was a new tension in Heather's voice that caught Sam's attention. He turned back to her and looked at her lovely face. "Are you sure?"

"I'm sure," said Heather.

Sam wanted to ask her more, but Ed was waiting and Gaia was moving. If he was going to catch up to them, he needed to get outside. "Okay, then, bye."

He turned and grabbed the doorknob. He was halfway into the hall when Heather called again.

"Sam?"

"Yes?" he replied without turning.

"Does this have anything to do with her?"

Heather named no names, but Sam didn't bother to ask for a definition of "her."

"No," he said in a hoarse voice. He cleared his throat and tried again. "No, it's just class."

He waited a few seconds more, but Heather said nothing else. Sam stepped through the open door and left.

"I fear nothing," David said. "That's another of my special powers."

david

AT FIRST GAIA WAS FEELING FAIRLY

pleased with herself. She was
handling this date thing okay.
No pressure. She had even kept
it together in her game against
Zolov. She'd lost, of course, but
she always lost to Zolov. At least
this time she had come close.

The Wild Burrito

She tugged at the scrunchie in her hair as she
walked. There was absolutely no reason to get tense
about this dinner. They were only going to grab fast
food from a cheap restaurant. Nothing fancy.

She was fine—right up until she turned the corner
onto Thompson. The closer Gaia got to Jimmy's, the
more she could feel a pressure pushing her backward.
It was as if there were this weird wind coming from
the restaurant. It blew harder as Gaia got closer until
every step toward the restaurant was like pushing into
a gale. Other people walked down the sidewalk with
no trouble, but Gaia felt like any moment the wind
might grab her and send her flying back across the
park.

Gaia slowed. Jimmy's Burrito was only a dozen
steps away, but they were hard steps to take. She
steeled herself, squared her shoulders, and walked to
the door.

Lightning didn't strike. No earth-
quakes shook the ground.

Gaia took a deep breath. She glanced inside, scanned the tables and booths. No sign of David.

Maybe he wasn't coming.

David had probably wised up at the last moment. Maybe he had talked to someone else at school. Maybe he had finally come to his senses. Whatever the case, it was clear he had realized that dating Gaia was a big mistake.

Disappointment settled into Gaia's empty stomach like lead, but there was an equal amount of relief. No David. No date. There was still some chance of potential irritation if the story "How Gaia Got Stood Up" became part of the next day's grind of boring school gossip. But Gaia doubted that would happen. The story was too dull, considering what was going on.

"So what do you recommend?" a voice asked.

Gaia turned to find herself face-to-face with David. She struggled for something witty to say, but her well of wit was experiencing a drought. "I, um . . . I see you found the place."

David tapped a finger against the tip of his nose. "Able to detect taco sauce at a hundred paces." He held up his arms and pretended to flex huge muscles. "It's one of my secret powers."

Gaia forced a smile. She actually *wanted* to smile, but her face wasn't responding to her brain, so she had to force it. "You have others?"

"Too many to number," David said. He crowded in close to Gaia and leaned forward to look at the menu taped up against the window. "What's good here?"

"Depends on what you think is good." He was very much in her personal space. Gaia stepped aside, hoping it wasn't the wrong thing to do. He didn't even blink.

"Anything," he said. "As long as it's hot."

"They have plenty of hot," Gaia said. Another smile. This one didn't take as much effort.

"I am the terror of hot peppers everywhere." David stepped past Gaia and pulled open the front door. "Jalapeño parents tell stories of me to frighten their children."

This time Gaia actually laughed. Suddenly all the tension she had felt about this date seemed completely stupid. David was just a person. A funny person who, for some reason, seemed to like her. None of those things was bad. Not everything she did had to turn into a disaster movie. Did it?

She stepped through the open door and waited for David to follow. "I'm not talking about wimpy peppers like a jalapeño," she said as he entered.

"Jalapeños are wimpy?"

"Extremely," she said. She was bantering. This was banter. Who knew?

They walked past the newsstands inside the door. Gaia picked out a booth off to the side of the

170

restaurant and slid her butt across the red vinyl seat.

"They serve serious peppers here," she said. "They don't mess around."

David dropped into the seat across from her and pulled a plastic-coated menu from between two bottles of hot sauce.

"So what makes a serious pepper?" he asked. "I'm ready to do battle with any vegetable in the place."

"Good." Gaia reached across the table and plucked the menu from his hand. "Then I'll order for us."

"Go ahead," said David. "I'm not afraid."

Gaia looked at his blue eyes. Something weird was going on. She actually felt, well, almost comfortable. This was not her. This was some other girl who actually knew how to talk to other human beings.

A waitress approached, and Gaia delivered the order. David picked up the menu again after the waitress left. "What's the special burrito?" he asked.

Gaia snatched the menu a second time. "Just a burrito."

David's eyes sparkled. "But what's so special about it?"

"You'll see," said Gaia.

Much to her own surprise, Gaia was actually enjoying herself. So far, at least, she hadn't suffered from a brain fart causing her to say something inexcusably stupid. It was only a matter of time, of course, before she was revealed as a hopeless social outcast, but at least she was enjoying a few moments of normal life.

"So . . . ," David said.

Gaia stared at him. "So . . ."

They lapsed into silence. Uh-oh. This was getting less good. Gaia pressed her hands against the sticky vinyl. Was she supposed to say something? Was *he* supposed to say something?

That was when the emergency cop-out system flipped into action. Gaia stood up, nicking the edge of the table with her bad knee.

Ow.

"Where are you going?" David asked.

Gaia took a deep breath. "Bathroom."

"SO YOU'VE PROVED YOU'RE AN IDIOT

with nothing to say," Gaia told her dripping reflection. The cold-water-in-the-face splash had done nothing for her spirits. It had only served to form huge blotches on her shirt and soak the hair around her face. Lovely.

Not Quite Normal

She might as well go back out there and seal the deal. Send him running for the hills. If the city had any.

Gaia opened the door and was headed back down the dark, grimy hall past the kitchen when she heard a huge crash, followed by a bloodcurdling scream. She stopped in front of the open kitchen door.

There was a fire. A big one.

This could really put a damper on her already dampered date.

Without hesitation Gaia strolled into the kitchen, took the phone out of the hand of a trembling fry cook, and hung it up before he could dial 911. She grabbed the fire extinguisher and yanked it off the wall, walked over to the searing, leaping flames, and doused them with one good squirt.

The sprinkler system didn't even have time to kick in.

Gaia turned and looked at the three white-clad, grease-stained kitchen workers who were huddled in the corner, looking like they'd fallen there out of shock. From the way they were gaping at her, she could have been an angel plunked in the middle of their crusty linoleum floor directly by the hand of God.

Gaia flushed. Sometimes she forgot her reactions to danger weren't quite normal.

She took a deep breath and tried to smile. "Uh . . . you can still make the burritos, right?"

"EVERYTHING OKAY BACK THERE?"

David's face wore a worried expression as Gaia returned to her seat.

Family Stuff

"Fine," she said, averting her eyes. She cleared her throat noisily. "And dinner is on the house."

He glanced past her toward the kitchen, a question obviously forming. "Why did they—"

"So how do you like New York?" she interrupted, placing her hands flat on the table. Lame question. Better than trying to deal with his.

He narrowed his eyes at her, obviously mulling his options. Which line of questioning was better/safer/more intriguing? Finally he leaned back into his bench, resting one arm across the top.

"I'm not sure yet if I like it," he said.

Gaia smiled, glad he'd made the right choice.

He looked toward the windows at the front of the restaurant. "It's great to get a burger anytime you want," he continued, "and to find an open bookstore at three A.M., but I think it's just too crowded for me."

"I like crowds," Gaia said, watching a group of people standing in line to pay their bill. "It's easy to get lost in them. Go unnoticed."

She felt her skin flush. She stared at the chipped tabletop. She hadn't just said that, had she?

174

"I can't imagine you'd go unnoticed anywhere," David said.

Gaia blushed more deeply. He hadn't just said that, had he?

"Anyway, I don't know if I'll be here long enough to adapt," David said.

Gaia glanced up. "You just got here. Why would you be moving?" Why wouldn't he be moving? She'd waited seventeen years for a first date. She'd probably be waiting another seventeen for a second.

"You know." David shrugged. "Family stuff." For the first time he looked a little uncomfortable.

"Following your parents' jobs?"

Now David looked down at the table. "My parents are . . . I'm not with my parents."

Gaia felt a nearly irresistible urge to touch him. "That's something we have in common," she said. "My parents are gone, too."

David raised his head. "That's weird, isn't it?"

For a moment they just looked at each other. This silence wasn't nearly as uncomfortable as the first.

"What is this?" David asked.

"What?" Gaia asked back.

David pointed up. "This music," he said.

A song played from invisible speakers. Gaia hadn't noticed it until that moment. She strained to hear.

Her waiting dark heart,
The violence in her eyes,
The hunger in my body,
The things she denies.

"It's this band called Fearless," Gaia replied, shaking her head slightly. "They play around here."

"Fearless?" David repeated, raising his eyebrows.

Gaia confirmed with a nod. At one point when she'd first moved to New York, it had seemed like this random band with this ironically appropriate name was following her around. It was almost too bizarre. But now it didn't even affect her. She was used to it.

The waitress came back with two oval platters loaded with burritos, corn flour tacos, and heaps of seasoned rice and beans. Gaia took her plate and dug in quickly, sweeping together a blob of sour cream, rice, and a chunk of steaming burritos. The combination of flavors was almost too good.

David eyed his plate. "What are all these little brown peppers?"

"Ever heard of *habañeros?*" Gaia asked through a mouthful of food.

His eyebrows scrunched together. "I don't think so."

Gaia grinned at him. "Good luck."

David picked up one of the peppers between his fingers, examined it for a moment, then tossed it into his mouth. Gaia heard it crunch between his teeth. A moment later David's blue eyes opened so wide, they looked like they might fall out of their sockets.

"Wow," he whispered.

"Pretty hot?" asked Gaia.

He nodded. "I don't think I'm really tasting it. It sort of made my ears ring."

Gaia took another bite of her own meal and watched as David chewed his way through a second pepper. "Most people are scared to death of those things."

David took a third pepper and crunched it. A red flush spread over his face, and he trembled.

"I fear nothing," David said. "That's another of my special powers."

Gaia looked at him. Maybe they had more in common than she thought.

SAM MOON WAS AN IDIOT.

Nope. Even *idiot* didn't sound bad enough. It was an insult to idiots everywhere.

The Other Guy

He had started out in situation A. In situation A he was lying in bed with a beautiful girl. A beautiful naked girl. A beautiful **naked** girl who wanted nothing more than to be with him. A girl with whom he had just had sex.

But from there Sam had proceeded straight to situation B. In this case he was up, out of bed, and running off to chase a different girl. Only this girl didn't want him. Probably hated him. Definitely didn't want to have sex with him.

Oh, yeah, and she was on a date with someone else.

As Sam crossed the street and stopped in the middle of the crowded sidewalk, he hoped his parents would someday have another son. He would be wrong ever to pass these pitiful genes along to the next generation.

Sam stood across from Jimmy's Burrito and watched Gaia eat her dinner with the guy she was dating. The back of the guy's head was nothing special. From what Sam could see, the pair were eating, talking, and even laughing.

Gaia was laughing.

Sam's heart squeezed. He tried to think of all the times he had been with her—which weren't many. Now that he thought about it, Sam wasn't sure he had ever gotten her to smile, much less laugh.

Gaia was having a good time. Meanwhile Sam was miserable in every way possible. He felt guilty. Tired. Jealous. Foolish. You name it. If it was bad, he felt it.

Sam leaned back against a brick wall and tried to

keep his head down. He didn't have a hat, or a big trench coat, or even sunglasses to make him harder to recognize. If Gaia looked out the window and saw Sam looking back, it would be the perfect end to a perfect day.

The radio buzzed in his pocket. Sam hated the sound. First thing in the morning these suckers were going back to the store. He dragged out the radio and squeezed the trigger.

"What do you want? *Over*."

"A report," Ed replied. "You haven't even told me if you found her."

Sam said nothing.

"Sam?"

He smirked. "You didn't say '*over*.'" He sounded like a child. He didn't care.

"Over," Ed said.

"I found her," Sam replied. "She's okay. They're eating."

"Where?"

"Jimmy's Burrito."

Gaia laughed again. Another slice to the heart.

"Jimmy's?" Ed laughed. "Man, he got off cheap."

Sam glanced across the street and saw that Gaia was washing down a bite of something with her drink. He also saw that at least two people were giving him odd looks.

Sam turned his back to them. "Ed, I have to get off," he said.

"I need more details," Ed replied. "Booth or table?"

"Booth," Sam said through clenched teeth. He braced his free hand against the wall. "I'll talk to you later."

"Same side or across from each other?"

Sam rolled his eyes. "Across from each other."

"What are they eating?"

"Ed!" Sam shouted into the radio. "I can't tell what they're eating, and I don't read lips, so don't bother to ask what they're talking about. I'll call you if anything happens."

He snapped off the radio before Ed had a chance to reply and shoved it back into his coat pocket. His fingers brushed against the little box. Sam took it out. It didn't look like much.

Sam took a glance at Gaia, then tore at the paper on the outside of the box. Whoever had wrapped it had used plenty of tape. It took him a lot of tugging and tearing to get the paper unraveled. Once the paper was crumpled in his pocket, he was left with a featureless box of gray cardboard. He snapped a couple more pieces of tape and lifted off the lid.

The first thing Sam saw inside was a piece of folded paper. At the top of it was written *Sam Moon*. He picked it up, unfolded it, and started to read.

Sam—

I know that you have some connection with Gaia Moore. I hope that you continue to feel affection for her and that you will take the concerns expressed in this letter seriously.

Gaia is in danger. If I could take direct action to save her, I would, but circumstances prevent my appearance.

Instead I am passing this information along to you in hopes that you will know what to do with it. Watch out for Gaia. She is stronger than she appears to be, but she is not as strong as she believes. She can be hurt.

She needs you, Sam. Don't let her down.

Don't reveal the existence of this package or note to Gaia. For her own safety there are things she cannot know.

By the time he was done reading, Sam's heart was pounding in his ears. He read through the note again, clutching the page. There was no signature, no clue as to who had sent the package.

This little scrap of typing paper was about the weirdest thing Sam had ever run into in his life. Sure, he had been standing on the street playing undercover cop, but this note was straight out of some spy novel.

His immediate suspicion was that Ed had sent the package. Who else could have known that he was involved in any way with Gaia? It had to be a joke. If he called Ed on the radio, Sam could probably get Ed to confess.

But the longer he stood there, the less Sam believed in his own theory. Certain words in the note kept drumming against his brain.

Gaia is in danger.
She can be hurt.
She needs you, Sam.

He folded the note and shoved it back into his jacket pocket. Then Sam looked inside the little box again. There was another folded sheet of paper. With shaking hands Sam pulled it out and found that it was some kind of information form. Name. Age. That sort of thing.

Only this form had been attacked by someone with a big, fat black marker. Whole lines of the form were completely blacked out, but Sam could still read a few things.

Eyes: Blue

Several lines below that was another clear line.

IQ: 146

So whoever this sheet belonged to, they had blue eyes and they were smart. Sam wondered for a second if the sheet was about Gaia, but then he spotted another piece of uncovered info.

Height: 6' 2"

Gaia was tall for a girl, but not anywhere close to that tall.

The biggest area of readable type was a box of text marked Evaluation.

Subject demonstrates almost complete lack of empathetic response. Does not act under social

constraints. Does not operate in a frame of be-
havioral mores. It is our opinion that this subject should be considered deeply sociopathic.
Extreme caution is recommended.

Sam glanced back up at the glowing windows of
the restaurant. What did any of this have to do with
Gaia?

Sam put away the sheet. All that remained in the
box was a small black-and-white photo. Sam pulled it
out and raised it closer to his eyes.

Sunset was coming on fast, and the streetlights were just beginning to flicker. In the gloom Sam
had to squint to make out the grainy, low-quality photo.

The guy in the photo was young. He had short, wavy
black hair and a squared-off chin. There was a flat, angry
expression on his face. He seemed a little familiar. Sam
knew that he had seen the guy in the photo before.

Then he remembered where.

Sam let the box fall out of his fingers and ran right
through the traffic on Thompson. He drew a chorus
of horn blasts as he darted between the cars, and a
couple of people had to slam on their brakes. Sam
didn't care. He charged up the steps into Jimmy's,
shoving people out of the way as he went.

But when Sam got inside, the booth at the side of
the restaurant was empty. Gaia was gone.

His eyes
narrowed, and
his teeth
clenched **double**
together so
hard, Gaia **dare**
could see the
muscles bulge
at the corner
of his jaw.

"WHAT TIME ARE THEY CLOSING

David

the park?" David asked.

"I heard they were closing it at seven," Gaia responded. "Both the killings happened sometime around eleven or twelve. They probably want to make sure they get everybody out well ahead of that."

She took a deep breath and watched the fog it caused disappear into the night sky.

"Let's go," David said.

Gaia looked at him. There was no way to know what he was thinking. His expression conveyed nothing.

"It's almost seven," Gaia said. "The police probably won't let us in." Not that that mattered to her.

"Are you scared?" David asked.

A challenge. Interesting. Gaia felt the skin around her eyes draw tight.

"I'm not scared," she said.

"Then let's go." David pointed. "If they have the gates blocked, we can always sneak over the fence."

Gaia stopped, hands in pockets. She looked him directly in the eyes, giving him a chance to back out. "If we go into the park, we'll probably get caught."

"So?" He kept walking. She followed.

"So, they'll put us in jail," she said. "Aren't you scared of that?"

"No." He turned to look at her, walking backward. "I guess I'm just naturally fearless."

"WHAT DID YOU SAY?"

Gaia stumbled to a stop on the sidewalk and leaned against the iron fence that guarded the park's south side.

David shrugged. "I said I was naturally fearless." He struck a dramatic pose, chin lifted, chest out, eyebrows lowered. "Intrepid explorer David Twain, ready and able to penetrate the deepest mysteries of unexplored regions."

Two Davids

Coincidence. That's all it was. It wasn't like *fearless* was a word reserved just for her. "You really aren't scared to go in the park?"

"Not me," he said. He folded his arms over his still puffed-out chest and raised an eyebrow. "What about you, little lady?" he said with a Hollywood cowboy accent. "You a-feared to go in that thar patch of woods?"

There was something odd going on here. Something had shifted.

This seemed like the same funny, talkative guy Gaia had shared burritos with back at Jimmy's. Obviously it was the same David. Only now it seemed like there was somebody else there, too. Like there were two completely different people looking at her with those dark blue eyes.

"All right," Gaia said, refusing to tear her gaze from his. "Let's go."

"Cool," David said. He stood up on the tips of his toes and looked over her head. "But there's already a cop down by the entrance. You're probably right that they won't let us by."

Gaia looked up at the fence. "So I guess we'll have to go in this way."

She braced herself, bent low, and jumped. Gaia's beat-up right knee protested, but she still managed to grab the top of the fence. A few seconds later she was over and in the bushes on the other side.

David clapped in rapid applause. "I think you're doing the wrong thing by staying in school," he said through the fence. "You should definitely run off and join the circus."

"I'll think about it," Gaia replied. "Are you coming over here, or are you too much of a chicken?"

There was nothing funny about David's reply this time. His eyes narrowed, and his teeth clenched together so hard, Gaia could see the muscles bulge at the corner of his jaw. He wasn't happy.

He jumped for the fence. With his longer arms he had no trouble grabbing the iron crossbar at the top. It took him a little longer to pull himself up, and he wasn't nearly as smooth working his way over the top, but less than thirty seconds later he dropped to the ground beside Gaia.

"I told you," he said. "I'm fearless."

Gaia started to wonder if maybe he was telling the truth.

"WHERE'S THE SPOT?"

"This way," Gaia replied. She circled a small fountain and pushed south past the makeshift stage where bands sometimes played on the weekends. She was moving fast. She wanted to get there and get it over with. "Why do you want to see it, anyway? You're not some kind of murder groupie, are you?"

David laughed. A normal laugh. "No. Absolutely not. I just wanted you to know I wasn't afraid."

"You keep saying that." She looked toward him, then back at the path, her ponytail of golden hair flipping back and forth as she moved. "Why are you so worried about not being afraid?"

David took a couple of quick steps and moved up to walk beside her. "I just think it would be cool, that's all. Not to be afraid of anything."

"Why?"

"Because then you'd really be free, wouldn't you?"

Gaia blinked. Interesting theory.

They passed under a group of oaks, and the shadows thickened around them. "Being fearless wouldn't make a person happy."

David reached up and snapped off a small dead limb. "Why not?" he said. "It's being afraid of things that makes people sad."

Gaia shook her head. "That's not true. Even without fear you still get lonely, or angry, or depressed."

"There's nothing wrong with angry," David said. "Sometimes you have to be angry. Sometimes it's what you need."

Gaia couldn't argue with that. "And what about the others?"

"What? Sad and lonely?" David shrugged. "I don't really feel those things."

Gaia reached the edge of a concrete path and stopped. "It doesn't sound like you feel much."

"All I need."

For a moment the two of them stood in silence, then Gaia turned her back on him, raised a hand, and pointed at the open space on the other side of the path.

"This is it," she said. "This is where they found the bodies." She turned back to look at David. She met his gaze dead-on. "But I think you already knew that."

DAVID REACHED BEHIND HIS BACK

and pulled out a long knife. The blue-steel blade was almost black in the dim light, but the sharp edge caught the glow from distant streetlamps and threw off glittering sparks.

Painless

Damn, he loved that.

"You're smarter than I anticipated," he said. "I like it." He stretched out a hand to Gaia. "Come on, I'll make it painless."

"No, you won't," Gaia said.

David grinned. "You're right. This is going to hurt like hell."

There was a
wildness in
his eyes. **the**
gentleman
How had she
not noticed
it before?

"I'M NOT THE ONE WHO LET HER
get away," Ed's voice
crackled through the
radio.

The Rescue Party

Sam glared at the lit-
tle yellow transistor. "I
was distracted," he said.
"Besides, it doesn't mat-
ter now. We've got to find a way into the park."

"I'm with you on that," Ed replied. "So, what's the
plan?"

Sam looked across the street. There were now
two policemen standing by the nearest entrance to
the park, and he didn't think for a moment that the
officers were just going to step aside and let
them in.

"I'm going to have to go over the fence," Sam said
after a few seconds' thought. "I don't see any other
way."

"What about me?" asked Ed. "I don't know if
you've noticed, but I'm not very good at going
over things."

The thought had already occurred to Sam, but
he didn't have a solution. "I need your help so I
can get in. You come down here and distract the
police."

Ed sighed. "That's me. Ed Fargo, distraction
specialist."

"What?" Sam asked, confused.

"Forget it," Ed answered. "Distract them how?"

Sam glanced around and winced. Every second counted. There was no time to argue. "I don't know. Ask directions. Fake a heart attack. Just get them looking the wrong way long enough for me to climb the fence."

He didn't wait for Ed's reply. Instead he switched off the radio and dropped it into his pocket. He darted across the intersection, took a last longing look at the gate, then walked quickly toward the corner where the police would be far away and nearly out of sight.

Sam was only halfway to the corner when he got a break. The sounds of yelling and of running feet came from the direction of the entrance. Sam turned and saw the policemen wrestling a man with a potbelly and a stiff, graying beard.

It was the best chance Sam was going to get. There was no point in waiting for Ed when there was already a perfect distraction. He hurried across the sidewalk, bent low, then jumped for the top of the fence. His fingers managed to catch the square bar at the top, but the metal bit painfully into his palms. He started to bleed. Gritting his teeth, he slowly pulled, kicked, and scrambled his way to the top.

He stopped there for a second to catch his

breath. Down at the entrance the police were busy putting handcuffs on the bearded man. No one was looking.

Sam smiled. He had made it. Now he only had to find Gaia before it was too late.

He started to jump, but his foot slipped and his jump turned into a fall. The cuff of his pants caught on one of the points at the top of the fence. Sam pendulumed back and smashed against the fence with bone-jarring force. He kicked his feet, but the thin strip of fabric held him in place as firmly as a rope. He grabbed at the bars and tried to pull himself back up.

A hand grabbed Sam by the collar and jerked him away from the fence. Upside down, he found himself staring into a stern face topped with iron gray hair and an NYPD cap.

"What do you think you're doing, son?"

"I've got to get into the park," said Sam. "There's this girl, and she's in danger."

"Really?" The policeman grabbed Sam's arms and pulled them roughly behind his back. A moment later Sam felt hard, cold steel close around his wrists.

"What are you doing?" Sam shouted.

"My job," said the policeman. "What's your name?"

"Sam . . . Sam Moon."

"Well, Sam Moon, you're under arrest."

GAIA ALMOST LAUGHED.

You Die

She'd always thought she had perfect bad-guy radar. How wrong she was.

"What are we going to do now?" she said. There was a wildness in his eyes. How had she not noticed it before?

He looked at Gaia as if she were completely brain-dead. "Oh, please!" He pointed his nose up in the air and put on a thick British accent. "That should be immediately obvious to the most casual observer." Then he looked her directly in the eyes. "You die."

He was about to lunge. But Gaia wasn't going to take on a knife. "What's the matter? Scared to fight me hand to hand?"

David paused. He looked at the knife. His knuckles turned white. "I fear nothing from you," he said. He placed his weapon on the ground.

Gaia had to struggle to watch him and not look at the knife. Watch the opponent's every move. Every twitch. It was a basic rule of fighting, something her father had told her a thousand times.

But she couldn't stop herself. She checked the position of the knife. And that's when David hit her.

Gaia had been hit before. You didn't make it through the belts in any martial art without having your ass handed to you a hundred times. Gaia's nose

195

had been bloodied by the best. But she was sure she had never been hit harder than that first blow from David.

He hit her with a `straight left` that knocked Gaia all the way across the path. She snapped through the stupid plastic police tape at the edge of the field, slipped on the grass, and fell.

Judo saved her life. To the naked eye, judo seems to be all about grabbing people by the arm and flipping them in the air. That wasn't it at all. `Judo was about falling.`

Gaia was falling backward. If she fought against that kind of fall, she would only spin her arms in the air and still end up sitting on the grass. Instead Gaia went with it. She pushed off hard, threw back her hands, and took the fall, using her arms as `shock absorbers`. Another quick push and Gaia was back on her feet.

David was almost on top of her. He swung again, but this time Gaia caught his wrist and pulled it past her.

For a moment they were almost face-to-face—so close, all Gaia had to do was move her lips to end her long kissing drought. The thought turned her stomach.

David pulled left, then quickly back to the right. It was an elementary move, and Gaia was braced for it, but David was very strong. Gaia was great at keeping her balance, but not even she could keep her balance when both of her feet were off the ground. That wasn't a rule of judo—that was a rule of gravity.

She didn't go down, but it was close. Before Gaia could recover, David drove a pile-driver fist into her side so hard, Gaia imagined she could hear her ribs crack. Maybe it wasn't imagination.

David grabbed at Gaia. He took her arm, jerked her back toward him, and threw another punch. Gaia blocked with a forearm and drove a knee into his gut at the same time.

David released his grip on her and fell back a step. Gaia didn't let him.

She took a quick step forward and delivered a kick that took David across the hip. Another that struck him in the thigh. He staggered and stepped back again.

This was more like it. Gaia spun, trying to deliver a solid kick to the body.

David blocked it easily. He took the blow against the flat of one palm, pushed sharply to throw Gaia off balance, then followed the push with a straight left that took her right between the eyes.

This punch was even harder than the first. The sound of his knuckles hitting her skull was amazing. It was like somebody had broken a rock with a sledgehammer. Like an ax biting into a tree.

Sparks of red light swarmed through Gaia's eyes. Her ears started to ring. All at once her arms and legs gained fifty pounds each.

She tried to get her hands up to block, but they didn't listen to orders. Another punch whistled in and hit her on the temple. This one was a right hook. That was another thing Gaia had learned early about fighting: If you're going to get hit in the face, get hit by a straight punch. Straight punches hurt, but if you get hit from the side, `hurt doesn't even come close.`

The night flashed into bright shades of yellow and blue. There was a sound in Gaia's ears like the roar from a hundred seashells.

She backpedaled fast and managed to avoid the next shot. Another punch came. Blocked. Another. Dodged. Another. It glanced off the top of her head without shooting any fireworks through her skull, but this time she felt `the warm flow of blood` across her forehead.

Gaia kicked out wildly and was lucky to hit David in the side. She didn't think it really hurt him, but at least it made him back off.

"Getting scared yet?" David taunted.

Somehow David knew about her, but this wasn't the time to figure out how.

Gaia didn't waste breath on talking. Her head was starting to clear, but the blood from her forehead was dripping into her eyes. Gaia's ribs ached, and the knee she had messed up the night before was starting to get in on the complaints. If she was going to end this on her feet, Gaia had to end it soon.

David launched another punch, but it was a long overhand right, and Gaia had time to get out of the way. She feinted a punch with her left, ducked his response, and stepped back. Did the same thing with the right and took another backward step.

There was a rhythm to David's fighting. If Gaia could work it out, she could time her shots and plaster him without taking blows of her own. All she needed was time.

Suddenly David lunged forward and grabbed Gaia with both his arms. Grabbing like that was a really stupid move—unless you were as strong as a gorilla. David could have made gorillas beg for mercy.

He squeezed the breath out of Gaia in a painful rush, and this time she knew the cracking sound had to be at least one of her ribs turning into a two-piece. She kicked her feet along David's shins, but he didn't let her free. So Gaia lowered her head and butted him in the face.

David howled. His nose exploded in blood. He lost his hold on Gaia and clamped a hand over his face.

Gaia drew a painful breath and jumped forward. She got off a kick to the chest, and David was staggering.

Then a kick to his side, and he groaned. His hand came away from his face. Blood spilled over his lips and dripped from the point of his chin. In seconds his shirt was stained by a spreading pool of darkness.

He punched. Gaia blocked and counterpunched. It wasn't a perfect hit on his solar plexus, but it was good enough to make David gasp for air. She hit him again, driving her fist into his gut so deep, Gaia wouldn't have been surprised to feel his backbone.

David made a wild, flailing punch. Gaia blocked it easily. He threw another, and she turned it aside. He stepped back. He was breathing hard, and Gaia could hear air whistling through his smashed nose.

"What about you?" she said. "Still fearless?"

"I . . . don't . . . have . . . anything to fear from you," he said.

It was time to end this thing. Gaia started forward, planning to put her foot where David's face was, but something grabbed her by the ankles. She glanced down. Tape. Stupid yellow police tape. Somehow yards of it had become tangled around her legs. It snapped easily enough, but it distracted Gaia for a second.

A second was too much to give up in the middle of a fight.

When she looked up, David's fist was six inches from her face and coming in fast. Gaia tried to dodge, but the blow still caught her on her right jawbone.

This time Gaia didn't just see sparks. This time she went someplace. Someplace where squirrels played banjos and the trees were cotton-candy pink. The seashells were roaring again, and this time they were joined by a brass band. Gaia tried to put out her hands and catch herself, but for a second there she couldn't even tell if she had hands. Gaia didn't know if she was standing or lying on the ground.

She wasn't even sure if she was still alive.

It took a few seconds for the furry-tailed rats to put away their instruments and the night to go back to something like normal. When it did, Gaia figured out that she was on the ground. There was something under her hands. Grass, but something else, too. Something gritty and crumbly. It took her a moment to realize that it was chalk—the chalk that had marked the body lines of the dead girls.

From somewhere behind her Gaia heard David laugh. "That's great," he said. "That's perfect. I'll go get the knife. You just stay put." His smashed nose turned "that's" into "dat's" and "great" into "gweat." It would have been funny if he wasn't about to kill her.

Gaia struggled to sit up, but the best she could manage was to roll onto one knee. The banjos might be packed away, but her head was still spinning. Everything hurt.

David didn't seem to be in much better shape. He limped as he crossed the field and stopped near the path for a moment to lean against a tree. He was banged up pretty good, but he was still going to kill Gaia. He knelt down beside the path and reached for the knife.

Gaia saw salvation coming from twenty feet away. David saw it, too, but he was slow. He barely managed to turn his head before Ed Fargo hit him like a freight train.

David was coming. He was climbing along Gaia's body, and he still had his knife.

a time to die

GAIA WOULD HAVE SCREAMED FOR

Ground Rule Double

Ed to stop if she'd had the time. The collision happened with such speed that it looked more like a car accident than a wheelchair ramming.

One of David's hands, the one reaching for the knife, was trapped under a wheel. Instantly every finger on that hand had snapped, one after another, like twigs. The metal frame of the chair caught him under the arm, rolled him over, and left him sprawling on the ground. His head hit the asphalt with a sickening crack, and Gaia saw every limb of his body go slack.

David was down for the count.

At the moment of impact Ed was thrown up and out. He flew almost twenty feet in a low arc before he thumped to the ground between a pair of pines. Freed of his weight, the chair rolled on another few paces, curved, then toppled on its side.

That was when Gaia hit the ground. The paralyzation had set in.

For the space of five seconds everything was still and quiet. Then the broken bodies started to move.

David was up first. Gaia couldn't believe her eyes.

She'd thought he was done. Unconscious. Useless. Yet he climbed to his feet, clutching his broken, bleeding hand against his chest. Who *was* this guy?

"Gonna . . . kill . . . you both," he grunted. He looked in the grass, located the knife, and lifted it in his good hand.

Gaia struggled to rise. She had to stop him.

She couldn't move. Gaia's muscles twitched and squirmed like bags full of snakes, and she was barely able to raise her head from the ground.

David looked at her, then looked at Ed. Slowly his split lips widened into a horrible, bloody grin.

"Which one first?" he said.

Me, thought Gaia. Come for me. But even her mouth had shut down. She could do nothing but watch as David decided who would die.

EVERY BRANCH GRABBED AT HIS

A Hundred Feet Away

coat. Every stone seemed to be out to trip his feet.

Tom Moore ran desperately through the woods. Loki wasn't the only one with fake identification, but it had taken Tom much longer than he expected to convince the police guarding the park that he should be allowed inside.

He pulled the gun from his coat pocket as he ran and thumbed off the safety. He only hoped it wasn't too late.

GAIA OPENED HER HAND AND CLOSED

it again. It wasn't much, but it was something. Her body was returning to her.

A dozen yards away, David limped toward the pilot of the overturned wheelchair. Ed had his hands under him and was dragging himself back as fast as he could. It wasn't fast enough. David would be on him in seconds.

The Last Reserves

Ed was about to die.

Gaia reached down and pulled at her reserves of strength. The tank was almost empty. She absently thought of what her father used to say when he had driven the family car long past the point the needle dropped to *E*.

Vapors. I'm running on vapors.

Slowly she rolled over onto her trembling arms.

Painfully she pushed her aching legs under her and climbed to her feet.

David glanced at her, then continued after Ed.

Gaia tried to go toward them, but she could barely manage a step. Her head swam, and her knees were weak. She wasn't going to be fast enough. There was only ten feet between David and Ed. There was at least thirty feet between Gaia and David. There was no way for Gaia to get to Ed in time.

"Hey," she called in a hoarse whisper.

David kept after Ed.

"Wasn't I the one you wanted?" Gaia's voice was a little stronger this time.

The gap between David and Ed was down to five feet. David raised his knife to strike.

"Hey, chicken!" Gaia screamed.

David froze.

"Are you afraid to fight me?"

David pivoted like a rusty screen door and looked at Gaia. "I'm not afraid of you."

"Then show me."

Gaia had trained herself to hold back. Even when she was fighting a mugger or a thief, she was careful to stop, not injure. She threw those rules away.

David staggered toward her with the knife held high. He pointed the glittering blade toward Gaia's face and swung the edge from side to side.

David was strong. David was fast. But by now Gaia

knew one thing for sure—David wasn't well trained. She leaned back her arm as if she were going to throw a punch.

That was all it took to draw David's attention. He leaped at her with surprising speed.

Gaia fell back. Her balance was gone. She was going to hit the ground—there was no stopping that—but there was enough strength in her legs for one last good kick. She pivoted on her left foot, kicking and falling at the same time.

David's right leg broke with a noise like a gunshot. A thin, high whine escaped his blood-smeared mouth as both he and Gaia toppled to the ground.

Seeing Stars

GAIA LAY ON HER BACK IN THE grass, biding her time. She knew David thought she was spent. Done. Gone. But she was just waiting. Overhead, the gloomy clouds that had covered the sky all day finally parted. Stars peeked through.

She'd never seen stars in the city. But they were up there now, sparkling down at Gaia as if they had come out just to watch the bitter end.

From somewhere nearby she could hear sounds of breathing. They weren't pleasant sounds. The breathing was kind of wet, as if the person making the noise was pulling as much blood as air into his lungs with every breath.

A hand grasped Gaia's ankle. Another closed on her knee. Something hard and cold pressed against the skin of her leg.

David was coming. He was climbing along Gaia's body, and he still had his knife.

Patience. Patience.

One of David's hands came down in the middle of Gaia's stomach with painful force. The other hand, the hand with the knife, slid along her arm.

It was strange. After a lifetime of feeling alone, or embarrassed, or just plain angry, what Gaia felt now was calm. She had done everything she could. Somewhere, way down in her brain, a voice was calling for her to get up. Get up and fight. But that voice was faint and far away.

Gaia was tired. Very, very tired. But maybe, just maybe, if she waited until just the right moment, she could finish this thing. And maybe she could live through it.

Tangled black hair came into view. Even from this close, Gaia could barely recognize the face as David's. His nose flattened like a pancake. His face painted over in blood. His lips pulled back in a snarl of rage.

Slowly David dragged himself beside Gaia. Then he raised the knife and held it above her chest.

"See?" he croaked through bloody lips. "See, I'm the best after all. I can beat you. I'm the best."

Gaia had no idea what he was talking about. David sat up straighter, raised the knife high, and plunged it down at Gaia. She raised her arms. Watched his eyes widen in surprise. And then it happened.

THE SOUND CAME THREE TIMES, all very close together. Hiss. Hiss. Hiss. It was like the noise of air being let out of a bicycle tire. Like water falling on a hot skillet.

Popped

DAVID'S SHOULDER ERUPTED. HIS body twitched around to the left, and blood poured out across his chest. There was a cracking, and for a moment Gaia saw something white exposed in the core of his wounds.

Splatter

Bone.

"I . . . ," said David. "You . . ." A bloody foam spilled from his lips. It hit her face with a sickening splatter. David toppled off of Gaia and fell still at her side.

For several seconds Gaia lay there, trying to understand what had happened. Something had hurt David. Something had stopped him.

She wasn't going to die. Not now. It seemed like an impossible thought.

Someone stepped into view at the edge of the clearing. Gaia turned her head for a better look.

She saw a tall figure in a trench coat. She saw the gun in his hand. She knew the face. Her uncle. Apparently he couldn't call or write, but he had an uncanny ability to materialize when she was in danger.

The figure at the edge of the clearing only stood there for a few moments. Then he turned and stepped back into the shadows of the trees.

Gaia closed her eyes.

IT TOOK ED NEARLY TEN MINUTES TO

Exit, Stage Left

get his wheelchair upright, get his battered self into it, and roll across the damp ground to Gaia's side. For every one of

those ten minutes he harbored the unthinkable thought that she was dead.

And yet when he actually reached the center of the
clearing, he was amazed to see Gaia sit up and push
her ratty hair away from her face.

Total, utter, complete, euphoric relief.

Ed calmed his heaving chest before he let himself
open his mouth. "Hey, Gaia," he called. "Your new
boyfriend's the killer."

Gaia made a tired, gasping noise that might have
been laughter on the planet Exhaustion. She
stood slowly, swayed on her feet for a few seconds,
then staggered over to lean against Ed's chair.

"Thanks for the update," she said. "How did you
get in here?"

"Easy." Ed rapped his knuckles against the armrest
of the wheelchair. "I got in while Sam was getting arrested."

Gaia blinked. "Sam got arrested?"

"Worked out great as a distraction," Ed
said with a grin.

"Okay," said Gaia. She shook her head and swayed
so badly that she almost lost her grip on the chair.

"What happened?" asked Ed. "I couldn't see what
was going on. I was so afraid. . . . I mean, I was afraid
he was going to . . ."

"Kill me?" Gaia nodded slowly. "He almost did.
We'll leave him for the police."

David suddenly moaned. His broken, bleeding hand scrabbled at the grass.

Gaia pulled back her foot and kicked him again. The moaning stopped.

Ed looked at her and shook his head. "You know, sometimes I can't tell if you're really brave or just perpetually pissed off."

TOM KNEW HE HAD TO GET MOVING.

Broken Once Loki and his operatives had figured out that Tom Moore was here, they wouldn't pass up the chance to bag him when they had it.

He turned to leave and heard movement behind him. Quickly he pressed himself against the dark trunk of an elm and waited.

A man was coming across the field. It was a tall man, a man Tom had no trouble recognizing.

Loki walked straight across the trampled field. He paused a moment beside the broken form on the ground. Then he knelt, grabbed the boy by the hair, and delivered a sharp slap across the face.

David groaned.

"Wake up," said Loki. Another slap. "Open your eyes."

The eyelids fluttered.

"She shot you?" Loki said. "She used a gun?"

The boy on the ground said something. From his place by the trees, Tom couldn't hear the words, but he could hear Loki's reply.

"Home?" Loki shook his head. "I'm afraid that boat has already sailed. You're worthless to me now."

The boy spoke again, and this time Tom could make out his words.

"I'll tell," he said. His voice was high and raw, like a child who had been crying. "I'll tell them everything."

"Yes." Loki released his grip on the boy's blood-soaked hair and stood. "Yes, I'm sure you would."

Tom knew what was coming next. He turned away from the scene and started to make his way through the woods. He had gone no more than a dozen steps before he heard the gunshot.

There have always been horror stories about first dates, blind dates, setups, hookups, and probably a bunch of scenarios I've never even heard of.

But this has to be one for the record books.

This is the type of thing that could only happen to someone as undateable as me.

At least I didn't kiss him.

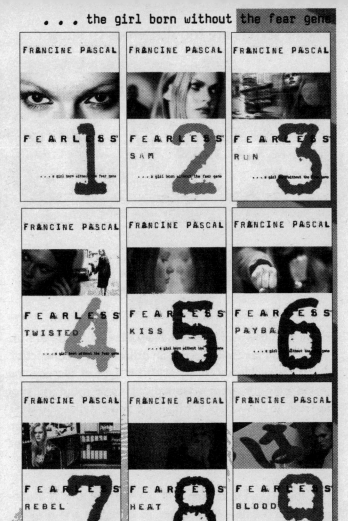

. . . the girl born without the fear gene

FRANCINE PASCAL
FEARLESS 1
. . . a girl born without the fear gene

FRANCINE PASCAL
FEARLESS 2
SAM
. . . a girl born without the fear gene

FRANCINE PASCAL
FEARLESS 3
RUN
. . . a girl born without the fear gene

FRANCINE PASCAL
FEARLESS 4
TWISTED
. . . a girl born without the fear gene

FRANCINE PASCAL
FEARLESS 5
KISS
. . . a girl born without the fear gene

FRANCINE PASCAL
FEARLESS 6
PAYBA
. . . a girl without the fear gene

FRANCINE PASCAL
FEARLESS 7
REBEL
. . . a girl born without the fear gene

FRANCINE PASCAL
FEARLESS 8
HEAT
. . . a girl without the fear gene

FRANCINE PASCAL
FEARLESS 9
BLOOD
. . . a girl born without the fear gene

Some secrets are too dangerous to know . . .

R O S W E L L
H I G H

In the tiny town of Roswell, New Mexico, teenagers Liz
Parker and Max Evans forged an otherworldly connection
after Max recklessly threw aside his pact of secrecy and
healed a life-threatening wound of Liz's with the touch of
his hand. It turns out that Max, his sister Isabel, and their
friend Michael are surviving descendants from beings on
board an alien spacecraft which crash-landed in Roswell
in 1947.

Max loves Liz. He couldn't let her die. But this is a dangerous secret he swore never to divulge - and now it's
out. The trio must learn to trust Liz and her best friend
Maria in order to stay one step ahead of the sheriff and
the FBI who will stop at nothing in hunting out an alien…

Available NOW from Pocket Books

The cut felt deep.

The little bitch had punched her.

Despite the pain Ella bit down harder now, feeling oddly energized as more blood welled into her mouth. It tasted sharp and bitter, like acid.

Gaia had punched her. Her.

It *was* acid, she decided, stepping swiftly onto the third floor. Acid, pumping through her heart, coursing through her veins. She could feel it—couldn't she?—burning in her cheeks, raging in her ears. It would dissolve her. It *was* dissolving her. Eating her from the inside out. She had to hurry. There was no time to lose.

Ten feet down the hall to her dressing room.

Her gun was in the dressing room.

Don't miss any books in this thrilling new series
from Pocket Books:

FEARLESS™

All Pocket Book titles are available by post from:
**Simon & Schuster Cash Sales, P.O. Box 29,
Douglas, Isle of Man IM99 1BQ**
Credit cards accepted. Please telephone 01624 836000,
Fax 01624 670923, Internet http://www.bookpost.co.uk
or email: bookshop@enterprise.net for details

FEARLESS™

FRANCINE PASCAL

KISS

POCKET
BOOKS

An imprint of Simon & Schuster UK Ltd
A Viacom Company
Africa House, 64-78 Kingsway, London WC2B 6AH

 Produced by 17th Street Productions, Inc.
33 West 17th Street, New York, NY 10011

A CIP catalogue record for this book is
available from the British Library

ISBN 0671 77344 5

3 5 7 9 10 8 6 4

Printed by Cox & Wyman Ltd, Reading, Berkshire

KISS

I'll probably never have kids. I'm not just saying that. There are a few really good reasons to think so:

1. I can't even manage to get a guy to kiss me, let alone . . . all that;

2. I seem to have very, very bad family karma (if you believe in karma, which I don't, but it's kind of a fun word to say);

3. Somebody tries to kill me at least once a week.

If you knew me at all, you'd know I'm not being a wiseass when I say that. Let me give you a quick example: I went on the first real date of my life recently, and the guy tried to murder me—literally—before the night was over. So, really, what are the chances I'm going to stick around on this earth long enough to find a guy to love me so much that I'd actually want to have kids with him in the far distant future?

But if by some miracle I ever

did have kids, I would never, never, never have just one.

I remember this old neighbor of mine telling me how great it was to be an only child, how you got so much more support, love, attention, blah, blah, blah, blah. How you didn't have to share your clothes or fight over the bathroom.

I would die to have a sister or brother to share my clothes with. (Although to be honest, what self-respecting sibling would want any of my junk?) I fight over the bathroom with *my-self* when I'm feeling really lonely.

The summer I was thirteen, the year after my mom . . . and everything, it was over a hundred degrees practically the entire month of August, so I used to go to this public swimming pool. All the lifeguards, and lifeguards-in-training, and life-guards-in-training-in-training, and swim team members chattered and gossiped and giggled while I sat on the other side of the pool. I never made a single friend. One day I overheard my foster creature at the time say, "Doesn't it seem like all the other kids at this pool arrived in the same car?"

That, right there, is the story of my life. I feel like the whole rest of the world, with all their brothers and sisters and parents and grandparents and uncles and aunts, arrived in one big car.

I walked.

The neighbor I mentioned earlier, the one who was so psyched about only children? I think he neglected to consider how the whole scenario would look if you didn't have parents.

Gaia sucked in a few shallow gasps of air, raised a pair of wide, haunted eyes to his, and whispered, "I see dead people. . . ."

the color of fear

"MRS. TRAVESURA?"

At first Ella Niven didn't realize the voice was speaking to her. Then she remembered. *Travesura* was the Spanish word for "mischief." It was the name she'd given when she'd first made the appointment.

Flesh Crawler

She looked up from her magazine. The stunning Asian receptionist was smiling down at her. "The doctor will see you now."

Ella nodded. Setting down the magazine, she grabbed her purse and the shopping bag resting beside her chair and followed the woman.

There were several other women in the posh waiting room. All were reading magazines. All were the indeterminate age of the extremely wealthy—somewhere between thirty-five and death. Clearly most of them had consulted the plastic surgeon many times before this.

Ella noticed that most of the women also had shopping bags with them. She recognized the familiar logos of Chanel, Saks Fifth Avenue, Bergdorf Goodman, and a couple of other Fifth Avenue boutiques, all glimmering like badges of honor.

Ella's own shopping bag was from Tiffany. As she crossed the room, she was acutely aware of each of the other women taking note of the robin's egg blue bag in her hand.

The receptionist led her out of the waiting room and into a long, gray corridor. At first Ella thought the walls were made of slabs of marble—but was shocked to realize they were actually enlarged, black-and-white close-ups of human flesh. A gigantic palm here. A colossal kneecap there. She'd never considered how the wrinkles and creases of one's skin could look like striations in rock.

Up ahead, the corridor ended in a pair of brushed-aluminum doors. The receptionist indicated that Ella could continue on alone. When Ella was within a yard of the metal doors, they glided open soundlessly.

The office was large and spare. Floor-to-ceiling windows wrapped around two sides of the square chamber, giving a panoramic, sixty-story view stretching from Central Park to the East River.

As Ella entered, the doctor was standing behind a large, black desk that gleamed like highly polished onyx. Oddly, it was bare except for a light blue folder that seemed to float—weightlessly—above the slick surface. It must have been an optical trick.

The doctor was tall, and pale, and bald. He wasn't dressed in a physician's white coat, as Ella had expected. He wore a black suit over a black turtleneck.

Drawing closer, Ella discovered that her initial impression was wrong again. The man *wasn't* bald. His hair was white, but cropped exceptionally close to his skull. His skin was the same ghostly color. That's what had created the illusion of baldness.

Still, the doctor's eyes were his most remarkable feature. They were deep set and a light shade of yellowish green. They gleamed like cat's eyes beneath his brow. In all her life she had never seen eyes that color.

Not on a human, anyway.

"'Mrs. Travesura,' I presume?"

His tone of voice made it clear he knew it wasn't her real name.

She nodded cordially. "How do you do."

The doctor didn't answer but gestured to the chair opposite him—an artsy contrivance of chrome bars and black leather straps.

The doctor sat down. "I understand, from our initial conversation, that there is a certain . . . procedure . . . that you wish me to perform."

"That is correct."

"Now. If I am not mistaken, you are . . . shall we say, *employed* by a certain L—"

"Exactly," Ella interrupted. She needed to shut off this particular line of inquiry as quickly as possible. "I am. He, however, is not to be contacted under any circumstances. I must shield him from this undertaking. It is of utmost importance."

The doctor nodded, but he looked skeptical.

Ella knew he had past connections to Loki. That's

how she had found him. But if he were to contact Loki directly, Ella knew her plan would be derailed instantly. Loki would accuse her of deep, twisted jealousy. But the fact was, when Ella succeeded with this plan, and Tom Moore arrived at the bedside of his poor, disfigured, comatose daughter, Loki would be forced to give Ella the credit she was due.

For now, she needed to change the course of the conversation. She cast her gaze at the mysterious blue folder and gestured toward it.

It worked. "Ah . . . the portfolio," he explained, placing his hand lightly on the folder. "It represents my . . . *side business,* if you will. 'Before' and 'after' photographs of some of my more *interesting* accomplishments." He slid it across the desk toward her. "Care to take a look?"

Ella stared down at the ice blue folder in front of her, but she didn't touch it. She didn't need to see what was inside.

"Oh, c'mon . . . go ahead." He pushed the folder a few inches closer to her. "Aren't you in the least bit curious?" His tone was friendly. Flippant, almost. But— glancing back up at him—she saw that the man's eyes had locked on her with the cold, intense scrutiny of a snake. It was as if he were mentally willing her to look at the pictures. Daring her, even.

When she didn't respond, he reached forward and started lifting the cover. "Just take one little—"

"I'm familiar with your work," she interrupted.

The doctor instantly snapped his hand away. The folder whispered shut.

He shrugged. "Suit yourself."

Ella had the feeling she'd just failed some kind of test. She tried to regain ground.

Sitting up taller, she leaned forward slightly, bowing her shoulders so that her cleavage was displayed at its most alluring angle. "Believe me, Doctor," she began in a persuasive voice, "I wouldn't be here if I weren't already *highly* confident about your . . . skills."

If the doctor noticed her breasts, he made no show of it. His eyes remained locked on her own.

"And yet," she went on—leaning forward a little more—"regardless of your expertise, I think you may find this particular . . . patient . . . to be an *extremely* unwilling subject."

"Many such patients *are* reluctant," the doctor agreed. "At first." His eyes seemed to sparkle at some dark, private memories.

"This one is different," Ella stated firmly. She was growing annoyed. Why wasn't he looking at her chest? She leaned forward even more. "You might as well know, Doctor: You're not the first . . . professional . . . I've contacted in this matter. Others have tried to treat this patient. They failed."

"My success rate is impeccable," the doctor assured her. "And as I informed you at the outset, Mrs.

10

Travesura, one gets what one pays for." He stressed this last phrase meaningfully.

Ella took the hint. Reaching down, she picked up the Tiffany shopping bag that was lying at her feet. She placed it on the desktop, sliding it toward the doctor across the slick surface. As she did so, her hand accidentally brushed up against the folder.

Despite herself, she flinched.

The doctor noticed this, and his lips curled in mild amusement. He took the Tiffany bag, glancing inside.

Ella watched him and waited. She didn't expect him to react at the sight of the money; he was no doubt used to seeing such large sums of cash. She was waiting for him to notice what *else* was in the light blue bag.

The doctor's smile faded. Reaching into the bag, he removed a small, rectangular device. It might have been a cellular phone, except that it had a tiny LCD monitor where the earpiece should be. He held it up, a question forming in his bile-green eyes.

"It's a tracking device," she explained before he could ask. "Satellite technology. Effective within a fifty-mile radius. It allows you to pinpoint the precise location of a radio transmitter." Opening her purse, she withdrew a tiny metallic chip about the size of an aspirin. "*This* transmitter, which will be planted on the subject tonight."

She paused to gauge the doctor's reaction. It was crucial that he go along with the plan.

"Interesting," was all he said. He placed the tracking device down on his desk and sat back in his chair, steepling his fingers together on his chest.

Keeping her voice steady, Ella continued: "You will use the device to track the subject. There is a telephone number on the back. Once you have completed the job, you are to go to the nearest pay phone and call this number. Is that understood?"

The doctor stared at her over his fingertips. "Perfectly."

Was he mocking her? She couldn't tell. But she didn't care now. This transaction was drawing to a close.

"Good," she said. "Well—uh, *Doctor*—I believe that about covers it."

She stood up. So did he. She would not let him try to shake her hand. The thought of being touched by those long, bloodless fingers made her flesh crawl.

There was only one more matter to square away before she could leave.

She placed her hands on his desk. "I have to make sure we're perfectly clear on one point," she informed him, trying to make her voice as threatening as possible. "You may be as . . . *thorough* . . . as you desire. In fact, I encourage you. But it is of the *utmost importance* that the subject makes it through the procedure. *Alive.*"

The doctor stepped around his desk, smiling widely and warmly. "Your concern, Mrs. Travesura, is quite touching," he said, his voice dripping with sarcasm. "But it's unnecessary."

He suddenly dropped his smile—and with it, his act. "The subject will live. I can assure you of that." His voice was much colder now. `Deader. As devoid of life as his skin.` "There's no challenge in it for me otherwise."

He nodded at the folder, still sitting on his desk. "*They* all lived," he informed her, his voice ringing with chilling pride.

GAIA MOORE MOVED QUICKLY ALONG

Shortcomings

West Fourth Street in the direction of Washington Square Park, not bothering to slow her pace for her friend, Ed Fargo, who wheeled along a yard or two behind her.

As she walked, Gaia switched the strap of her beat-up canvas messenger bag from her left shoulder to the right. It was a smooth, fluid movement—one she made often over the course of her day. If she was doomed to have the overdeveloped deltoids of a Russian gymnast, at least she'd make sure they were *equally* overdeveloped. Being a supermuscular freak was bad enough. Being a lopsided one was too much to bear.

Gaia was painfully self-conscious about her body. Even now she was aware of her muscular arms and shoulders, although they were safely camouflaged beneath the bulky yellow-green Polartec parka she'd started wearing since the weather turned cold.

Long ago she'd given up trying to fight it. No amount of doughnut scarfing could erase the six-pack definition of her abdominals. Her genetics were simply stacked against her. Her muscles were as much a part of her as her blue eyes and her light hair and her extreme devotion to chocolate.

"Jesus, Gaia, could you slow down? The speed limit is thirty miles an hour, last I checked."

Gaia cast a glance back at Ed. "Why don't you speed up? You've got *wheels,* for God's sake."

It was a game they played. If she'd actually slowed down for his benefit, Ed probably would have clocked her. He appreciated pity exactly as much as she did.

The chess tables were coming into view. Gaia hoped there would be a new face today so she could earn some money for lunch.

Over the past three months she'd developed a reputation among the chess players. When she'd first arrived on the scene, it had been fairly easy to score a twenty-dollar game. That was in late August. Now the only regular who would play her for cash was old man Zolov, an international master. Since Gaia had helped save Zolov's life back in September, the "undefeated chess champ" of Washington Square suddenly began losing to her at regular intervals. A little *too* regular. It seemed as if they'd traded the same twenty dollars back and forth ten times in the past week.

And then there was Sam Moon. Sam could also get a game off her, but he was a different story entirely. They had played only once. They played to a deadlock until she'd freaked out and forfeited her king. Sam wouldn't take her money, but he had walked off with her heart that day.

Impatiently Gaia gathered her long hair from where it blew in her eyes and mouth and threw it behind her back. She'd forgotten to bring a hair band.

Maybe if she were lucky, Zolov would let her win today.

If she were really lucky, Sam Moon wouldn't show up at all.

Ed had caught up and started badgering her the way he'd been doing all day. "Gaia. Do the line from the movie. *Pleeeease?*"

And maybe—if she were really, *really* lucky—a certain someone would get his wheelchair caught in a sewer grate any moment now.

She glanced in annoyance at her self-appointed best friend. What had she done to deserve him?

"I'm not going to do it, Ed. So you can stop asking."

"Please, Gaia? I'm going to Pennsylvania tonight, so I won't get to see you for a whole four days. Besides, I promise I won't laugh this time. I promise."

"That's what you said the last time. *And* the time before that." God, why had she ever attempted that stupid imitation? She was just fooling around in the cafeteria at school, and Ed acted like it was the most hilarious thing he'd ever seen in his life. He wouldn't shut up about it.

"That was the old me. I've changed since then. I swear."

"The only thing you've changed is your underwear—and that's debatable."

"*Guy-uhhhhhhhhh . . .*"

"Oh, sure, whine my name. That'll convince me."

"I'll pay you."

"You don't have enough money."

"Oh, you might be surprised."

"I doubt it. Seeing as you can't even afford socks that match." She gestured at his feet.

Ed shot her a confused look. "What are you talking about?"

"Your socks. Are you celebrating Christmas a month early? Or did you get dressed in the dark this morning?"

Gaia had walked a good ten paces before she realized Ed was no longer at her side. She spun around.

He'd stopped in the middle of the sidewalk and was bent over in his seat, staring down at his feet with a strange, aggravated expression on his face. "Aw, man. You're kidding me, right?"

Gaia put her hands on her hips. "Kidding you? You put them on, elf boy, not me."

Ed squinted up at her. "Great. Thanks. Make fun of the color-blind guy. Go ahead."

Gaia cocked her head. "You're not color-blind," she pronounced.

Ed frowned, crossing his arms. "I think I would be the one to know."

Gaia stared at him. Her hands slipped from her waist, flopping at her sides. "Seriously? You're color-blind?"

"Hey—don't worry. You can't catch it." Ed slapped his wheels, gliding toward her once more.

"It's just that you never told me."

"Hmmm, that's funny. It's usually one of the first things I say to people: 'Hi, I'm Ed. I'm color-blind.' I think it's good to get one's physical shortcomings out of the way, y'know, *up front.*" He rolled to a stop in front of her feet, then peered furtively around the park. "Now, uh, Gaia, don't let this next bit of info freak you out, *but . . .*" He leaned in toward her, shielding his mouth with one hand conspiratorially. ". . . I'm *also* in a wheelchair."

Gaia was too busy looking at Ed's feet to think of a

good comeback. One green sock, one red. Could he really not tell them apart? Not at all? She raised her gaze to his eyes, studying them, not sure what she was looking for. They were a dark brown with gold lights. Eyes the color of a double espresso, she found herself thinking. Inwardly she groaned. *Guess you don't need those refrigerator magnets to write crappy poetry.* The point was, Ed's eyes didn't *look* color-blind. They looked . . . well . . . like regular, everyday eyes.

Regular, everyday, *annoyed* eyes.

"Please, by all means, Gaia. Keep staring at me like that. It does wonders for my self-esteem."

"Sorry—" Gaia barely had time to scoot out of the way as Ed blew past her. "It's just that you're the first . . . I mean, I never knew a person who was color-blind. What's it like for you?"

God, I must sound ridiculous, Gaia thought, stepping after him. Why don't I just say, Hey, Ed, you can't see colors, and I can't feel fear. Let's start a club!

Once she was beside him again, Ed looked up at her, amused. "Are you feeling okay, Gai?"

"Yeah. Why?"

"Because you asked me a question."

"And?"

"*And* . . . didn't you sort of stipulate way back when that we wouldn't ask each other questions because if *you* ask *me* something, that would mean *I* get to ask *you* something in return?"

This time it was Gaia who stopped in her tracks. "Right. You're right, Ed. Forget that I asked."

"No, no, no, no, no," Ed said, swiveling around to face her with a mischievous grin. "Not so fast. You can't back out now. A deal's a deal." He rubbed his hands together gleefully. "So—I believe the category is color blindness. What's the question gonna be?"

"*Does it make you jealous?*" She was startled to hear her own voice saying those words. She hadn't meant to say them out loud.

Ed blinked a couple of times. "Jealous?" he repeated, sounding confused. "What do you mean?"

Gaia chose her next words carefully. "Do you ever feel . . . upset . . . that other people can . . . experience something that you . . . can't?"

"Upset? Not really." He shrugged. "After all, it's not like being color-blind means everything looks black and white to me. I mean, I still see things in color. For example, I can tell that jacket of yours is the color of mucus. It's just that certain colors look alike to me. Mostly I have difficulty telling reds from greens." He pointed down at his feet. "Obviously."

Gaia self-consciously eyed her jacket. "Do you ever wish you *could* tell the difference?"

Ed nodded. "Well, sure. There was a pretty ugly incident involving hot sauce a few years back." He grimaced at the memory. "But most of those taste buds grew back. Eventually." He scratched the back of his neck. "Traffic lights pose a theoretical problem, but I figured out at a young age that red is on top, and green is on the bottom. Aside from that, I don't really think about it too much . . . except when I commit the very occasional fashion faux pas and some heartless person goes and points it out to me." He shot her a fake-hostile glance but quickly leavened it with another shrug. "But—honestly?—I can't say I'm jealous of people who aren't color-blind."

"Why's that?" Gaia prompted.

Ed bit his lip, thinking. "Hmmm . . . I can't explain it all that well, but it's sorta like this: I can't imagine a world with more colors than I see it in already. I just can't. And . . . well . . . I don't think you can truly be jealous of something if you can't imagine having it in the first place. Besides"—he ran a finger across the arm of his wheelchair, adding casually, almost to himself—"there are better things to be jealous of."

Gaia gave him a rare smile. What *had* she done to deserve him?

After a moment he looked away self-consciously. "Uh . . . did any of that make sense?"

She nodded. "Yeah. It did."

"Good." Ed sat up a little taller in his seat. "So, I believe now it's *my* turn to ask *you* something."

Gaia took a deep breath, then let it out slowly. "Shoot away." Part of her almost wished he *would* ask her one of her secrets. Considering all he'd witnessed over the past three months, she supposed it was a wonder he hadn't guessed them all already.

Ed stroked his chin thoughtfully, gazing skyward. "Let's see now. . . . I get to ask the mysterious Gaia Moore a question." He was clearly savoring the moment. "Anything I want. . . . Anything at—"

"You got five seconds, Ed."

"Okay, okay!" Ed scowled at her. Then he snapped his fingers. "Here's one: Where'd you learn how to—no, no, scratch that." He waved his hand in the air as if erasing an imaginary chalk mark. "I got a better one: Why don't you ever talk about your—" He stopped himself short again, reconsidering. "No, not that one, either. How about—"

Gaia let out a low grumble.

Ed looked up at her, as if he were just struck by an idea. "Say. Can I ask you to *do* something instead?"

Gaia cocked a wary eyebrow. This actually represented an easy way out, but she didn't want him to know it. "I suppose. . . ."

Ed grinned evilly. "Do the line from the movie."

"Except that."

Ed pointed at her with both hands. "Oh, no! You can't back out of it now. A deal's a deal."

Gaia glanced at her watch. "Wow, what do you know? It's already the end of lunch period."

"Gaia!"

She sighed, resigned. "Fine. But you better not laugh this time."

Ed pantomimed zippering his lip.

Gaia held up a warning finger. "I'm not kidding, Ed."

Now he crossed his heart, holding up three fingers in the Scout salute.

"All right." She moved a couple of steps to a nearby bench, plopping down on the hard, cold slats. Clearing her throat, she cast a wary eye around the immediate area. Aside from a cluster of sooty-looking pigeons pecking at the ground nearby, this particular section of the park was empty. Thank God.

Ed repositioned his wheelchair in front of her for a better view.

Gaia sucked in a few shallow gasps of air, gripped the neckline of her coat with two white-knuckled fists, raised a pair of wide, haunted eyes to his, and whispered, over a trembling lower lip: *"I see dead people. . . ."*

Ed the Expressionless Eagle Scout managed to maintain his deadpan for an entire second and a half. Then he let out a guffaw so loud, it echoed clear across the park, sending the pigeons exploding skyward in a frenzied, flapping cloud. It was a wonder he didn't flip himself over backward.

Gaia slapped her hands down on the bench, standing up in annoyance. "What's so funny? I thought I was pretty good that time."

"Good?" Ed was doubled over now, his face bright pink. "*Good?*" He could barely choke out the word through his laughter.

"Okay, that's it." Gaia kicked the side of his wheel with her boot and huffed off. "I'm outta here."

A few seconds later she could hear him behind her, struggling to catch her. "Gaia—wait—please—" All the laughing had left him panting for air. Good. She purposely picked up her pace. "Please—Gaia—wait up—I'm sorry—I'm sorry, but—it's just that—if you could *see* what you—"

She turned around. "Spit it out, Ed."

Ed placed a hand on his chest, taking a moment to catch his breath. "You have got to do the most terrible impression of being scared I have ever seen in my life."

He cracked up again.

Gaia hoped the sudden flush in her cheeks appeared to be a reaction to the cold.

Ed, my color-blind friend, you have no idea. . . .

I used to think you could pretty much divide people into two categories: those who believe in love at first sight and those who don't.

I was a proud member of the second category. I used to think you fell in love with your brain. . . . Um, that came out wrong. Let me rephrase. I used to think your brain was in use when you fell in love. You sort of decided it over time, like I did with Heather. I saw her, I thought, man, that girl is beautiful. I talked to her, I thought, yeah, and she's smart and funny, too. I spent some time with her and thought, hey, we actually like a lot of the same stuff. I kissed her and thought, yo, this is fun. After that, as far as my brain and I were concerned, we were in love.

Then I met Gaia Moore. Every time I've ever had anything to do with Gaia, my brain has said, shit, this girl is nothing but pain, misery, and trouble. And in this case my brain was totally right. But in spite of my brain's lack of cooperation, I've fallen in love with her. It happened the first time I ever saw her. It was like a clap of thunder, a bolt of lightning, a monsoon, all those cheesy metaphors I never believed before (although there actually was a monsoon going on at the time). There is no good reason for me to love Gaia. There are only good reasons against it. Every day I struggle to release myself from it. Every day I try to convince myself that it will go away.

So anyway, I guess you could say my brain is sticking with the second category, claiming that no, there is no such thing as love at first sight. My heart has betrayed it in favor of the first category, arguing, yes, absolutely, it's the only kind of love there is. And now my brain and my heart aren't even on speaking terms anymore. When I said "divide people," that wasn't exactly what I had in mind.

I told my friend Danny about this theory, and he told me he also had a theory for how to divide people: those who divide people into two and those who don't.

Her arms were
around him,
her
heartbreaking **hell**
scar pressed **hath**
against his
chest, her **no**
lips
against **fury . . .**
his ear . . .

". . . AND MEDEA, SO CONSUMED

was she by her bitter jealousy, so desperate was she to take vengeance on her unfaithful husband, Jason, that she murdered her rival with a gift of a poisoned cloak and then went on to kill her own children. . . ."

A Good Idea

Heather Gannis glanced up at the animated face of her literature teacher, Mr. MacGregor, who was talking much louder than necessary and brandishing a paperback edition of Euripides. Jesus, why were parents so up in arms about violence on television? The seriously grisly stuff was happening in these Greek plays.

She heard a snort of laughter from the back of the room. She turned quickly, recognizing the laugh before seeing its owner. Ed Fargo, her former true love, was laughing at something Gaia Moore had written on the corner of his notebook. The sound of it was corrosive in her ears.

Gaia could make Ed laugh. It was a rare ability and another affront to add to the long list.

Heather wasn't superstitious. Unlike the ancient Greeks, she didn't believe in fate. She wasn't religious and had little tolerance for the wu-wu astrology and Ouija board crap many of her friends were into.

But for Gaia, she made an exception. Gaia, with her fairy-tale yellow hair and her long, graceful limbs, was too terrible to accept at face value. How could one girl captivate Heather's boyfriend, enslave her ex-boyfriend, humiliate her, nearly get her killed, and completely destroy her self-confidence in less than three months? Gaia was a clear message from Somebody Up There that Heather deserved punishment.

Since Gaia had arrived in September, her evil had radiated. First there were the slashings, culminating in Heather's own near death. Then there was the stuff that happened to Sam. Then Cassie Greenman. Heather, like the rest of the school, was haunted by her murder.

All these tragedies weren't a coincidence. They just weren't.

". . . So for Monday, I'd like you all to read *Oedipus Rex*." Mr. MacGregor wrapped up his lecture just as the bell rang, signaling the end of a very long day at Central Village High. "Have a great Thanksgiving holiday, folks."

The classroom burst into cusp-of-vacation activity. Heather sighed as she jotted the assignment in her notebook. She had a feeling that play was going to be another doozy.

"Hey, chick."

Heather glanced up as two of her friends, Carrie Longman and Melanie Young, materialized at her desk. "Hey," she said, digging around to find a smile. "Whatsup?"

"You feel like Ozzie's?" Melanie asked.

Heather carefully piled her books and zipped them into her backpack. Her eyes landed momentarily on her empty wallet. A large mochaccino at Ozzie's cost over three bucks. Her friends thought nothing of buying two of them a day. Heather couldn't keep up, and she refused to let anybody else buy one for her. The old Gannis pride kicked in triple strength when it came to shallow displays of fortune. Or lack thereof.

Besides, she had something important to do this afternoon. Something she'd put off for too long.

Heather stood and smoothed her long, slim, blood-colored skirt. She strode out of the classroom, and her friends followed close behind. "Can't make it. Sorry," she said breezily.

"Oh." Carrie hovered at Heather's locker, taking a moment to regroup. "How about Dean & Deluca? They have those excellent caramel brownies. We can go to Tower Records after and get started on Christmas shopping."

"You all go. Maybe I'll catch up later," Heather said noncommittally. "I've got something I need to take care of this afternoon."

Melanie and Carrie stared at her in silence, obviously hoping she would elaborate. She didn't feel like it. She slammed her locker shut. She pulled on her black nylon jacket and slung her backpack over her shoulder. "See ya. Leave your cell on, Carrie."

Once Heather was rid of them, she slipped into the

bathroom. She got weirdly obsessive about her appearance every time she was about to see Sam, although she knew her boyfriend was even more oblivious to her subtle efforts than most guys.

She studied her face and her hair. She applied a coat of lip gloss and ran a brush through her long, smooth hair. No perceivable difference. Staring at the high neck of her white T-shirt under her soft, black V-necked sweater, she suddenly had an idea. Ever since "the incident"—the slashing that had put her in the hospital late in September—she'd worn a scarf or a shirt or sweater with a high neck every time she left her apartment. Now she discarded her jacket, dropped her backpack on the floor, and pulled both the sweater and the T-shirt over her head at the same time. She pulled the two garments apart, folded the T-shirt neatly into her backpack, and put the sweater back on.

She spent another minute gazing at her reflection. Yes, that was a good idea.

SAM TIPPED BACK HIS HEAD AND

Choose rested it on the top of the park bench. He closed his eyes and soaked up the low, late autumn sun. For the end of November, the air was sweet and warm. Probably almost sixty degrees.

Wednesdays were his favorite days. His classes ended early, so he allowed himself to hang out at the chess tables. That was one of the great things about college— those one or two class days that left you lots of time to waste . He'd already hustled twenty bucks off an unwitting stranger, then given it right back to Zolov in a rout. It was a weird form of charity, but whatever. Hustle from the stupid and lose to the smart. 'Twas the season.

"Hey, handsome."

He lifted his head and blinked open his eyes. Heather was bearing down at twenty feet, beautiful as ever in her red skirt and whispery black jacket. He heard the dry acorns cracking under the heels of her boots.

"Hi," he said, rubbing his eyes. "How's your day?"

"Okay," she said. "The usual high school plundering of spirits. How 'bout you?"

He laughed. Heather was so cool, so together. Never awkward or at a loss for words. "Oh, you know. Wasting some more of my youth at the chess tables." He paused. "Looking forward to tomorrow."

Instantly he felt annoyed at himself for having gilded the truth like that. He was looking forward to the gauntlet of the Gannis family Thanksgiving in the very plain sense of the phrase—observing that it would take place in the near future. He wasn't looking forward as in eagerly anticipating it.

"Oh, yeah?" She angled her head coyly, causing a curtain of shiny chestnut hair to fall forward over her shoulder. It reminded him of sex, which started that tingly feeling spreading through his body, which in turn made him feel guilty about what had happened the last time they had sex. And the first time they had sex.

"Looking forward to my dad's dry, stringy turkey? My mom's sickly turnip-brown sugar thing?" she challenged. "Looking forward to Phoebe eating nothing and complaining about Binghamton? Lauren talking on her cell phone straight through dinner? Hmmm." She appraised him with one lifted eyebrow. "Are you telling me the truth?"

Sam laughed again, wishing his heart would listen to reason once in a while. "Well. *You'll* be there."

Heather awarded him a little smile. She pointed to the spot on the bench next to him. "Is this seat taken? Do you mind if I sit?" Her tone was light, but he registered that her eyes were serious.

He scooted over fast, feeling ungentlemanly. "Of course. Definitely. Sit."

She sat and dropped her backpack on the other side of her. She wasn't so close that any part of her was touching him, but neither was she so far that he couldn't feel her warmth. "Listen. There's something I need to talk to you about." She turned to face him, nailing him with her odd-colored eyes. They weren't blue, but they weren't not blue, either.

"Sure, of course." He was getting nervous now. He was saying "of course" too much. "Talk away."

"It's kind of serious. Just to give you fair warning. It's something we've been needing to talk about for a while now."

"Of c—" He clamped his mouth shut. He felt like strangling himself. "Okay. I'm warned."

Heather took a deep breath. "I know that you have some kind of . . . *relationship* with Gaia Moore."

Sam could tell it was painful to her to say the name, and he felt awful.

"I know that you know her somehow, and I need you to tell me what's going on between you."

Sam swallowed. Jesus, Heather had a knack for getting right to the point. He hoped his face didn't betray his dire discomfort. He needed to choose his words carefully. He cleared his throat. "There's nothing going on."

Liar. You think about her every hour of every day.

"I barely know her. I've hardly ever spoken with her. There's never been anything . . . romantic between us."

But you wish there were. You dream about her at night.

Sam glanced up, reminding himself that he was

having a conversation with Heather and not with himself.

"So what *is* there between you?" Heather pressed. "Why was she there the night we . . ." She trailed off and then started again. "How did she know you'd been kidnapped? Why did you need to leave in such a hurry the last time we were together in your room?"

All the saliva in Sam's mouth had dried up, and from what he could tell, it was never coming back. He tried swallowing again. "Honestly, Heather, I don't know. The last couple of months have been so strange. I really don't know anything about her." That last bit, finally, was a sincere answer.

"Have you ever . . . *been* with her?" Heather stopped and tried again. Here was a girl who accepted no cowardice, particularly not in herself. "Have you kissed her? Hooked up with her? Had sex with her?"

"No," Sam answered firmly. *But God, how I've wanted to.*

Heather looked relieved but no less serious. "Okay, here's the really important thing I need to say to you." She pulled one sleeve of her sweater up over the palm of her hand. "I don't like Gaia Moore. I hate her. I think she's dangerous, and I wish she'd stay away from you." Heather caught her breath for a second before she rushed on. She was nervous, but admirably determined. "I need you to tell me now that whatever there is between you is over. That you won't have anything

35

to do with her anymore." She fixed him with her eyes again. "Because if you can't, it's got to be over between you and me. You have to choose."

Whoa. Sam looked down at his jeans, pressing his hands into his thighs, raising his shoulders up around his ears. This was hard-core. This was much more than he'd ever expected. He had to think.

Heather was not only offering him a choice; she was offering him a way out. He could be free of the guilt and the craziness. He could be free to figure out what the hell *was* going on between him and Gaia.

"So is it over?" Heather asked, her voice quiet and wobbly.

Sam turned to her. The answer he'd been contemplating withered in his throat. Her eyes were round and glazed with tears. Her jacket had fallen open, and the low V neck of her sweater revealed a long, jagged rent in the delicate white skin along her collarbone. The cut through which she'd lost so much blood and nearly her life. It was still angry red in color. Still unhealed.

His mind flashed back to that night. Finding Heather in the park, lying in a puddle of her own blood. The strange, dissonant whirlpool of hospital sounds and smells and colors, then the unsettling piece of information that a girl from Heather's class, a girl named Gaia Moore, had seen the gang member with the knife in the park and she'd passed up an easy opportunity to warn Heather.

Sam's gaze was riveted on the wound. He couldn't seem to look away. All the while Heather kept her head up, seemingly unaware of what he was seeing and feeling.

"Sam?"

He dragged his eyes back up to her face. He was miserable. He was filled with shame. He was torn in two. "Heather, it's not only over. It never began."

Her arms were around him, her heartbreaking scar pressed against his chest, her lips against his ear by the time he realized that he hadn't said which girl he was talking about.

"Why are you like this?"

That is a question I've heard from a lot of adults in my life. Some of them related to me, some not. If they don't ask it outright, I see the question in their eyes. And I'm not being paranoid. Trust me.

"Like this" in my case means loud, impulsive, messed up, combative, undisciplined, annoying. Other stuff, too.

The reason the question gets asked so often, with such impatience, is because there's no easy explaining when it comes to me.

I come from a nice family. Two parents, not one. We're rich, not poor. We're well educated. Or I should say, they're well educated. They pay lots of attention to me. They read me books when I was little. They made me drink my milk. It's really not their fault.

I have two nice brothers. They both go to good colleges now.

MARY MOSS

Growing up, they only teased me
and beat me up the normal amount.

Why am I like this?

I don't know. Some people have
a lot of space between thinking
and saying or thinking and doing.
I don't have any. Some people
look at themselves from the outside and try really hard to make
what they see look good. I stay
on the inside. I'd rather feel
good than seem it.

Sometimes I love that about
myself. Sometimes I hate it.

Why am I like this?

I don't know. I have a couple
of theories, though.

It was not
of "utmost
importance"
that the . . . **like**
"subject" be
a
kept alive.
That had **woman**
been
scorned
their
mistake from
day one.

GAIA RESTED HER HEAD IN HER

hand, staring at what remained of her frozen pizza, trying to fight off a terrible wave of loneliness. It seemed mean-spirited of biology to have left fear out of her

Worse Than Stupid

DNA but to have made her feel loneliness so acutely.

The Nivens' brownstone was empty and quiet except for the odd siren or car alarm blasting from Bleecker Street. Those were sounds you stopped hearing when you lived in New York City. Like a buzzing refrigerator or the hum of an air conditioner. You incorporated them into your ears.

The kitchen was sparse and orderly as usual. There was no sign, other than her plate on the faux-country wooden table, that a seventeen-year-old girl had just prepared and eaten her dinner there. Gaia was camping at the Nivens' more than actually *living* there. Low-impact camping. After five years in foster homes she'd learned never to settle in too much, never to get comfortable.

George had been called away on business just before the Thanksgiving holiday. She liked George. He was awkward with her, but sweet and well meaning. He had known her father. She would even feel disappointed by his absence, but like the sirens on Bleecker

Street, disappointment was something so customary, Gaia hardly felt it anymore.

On the plus side, when George was gone, Ella was usually gone, too. And Ella was most nearly likable when she was gone.

Gaia washed her plate, dried it, and returned it to the cabinet. `No trace.`

Thanksgiving wasn't Gaia's favorite holiday. The day was designed around warm family get-togethers, parents, grandparents, uncles, aunts, cousins. Blitzing yourself on great food. Thinking about all the wonderful things your life had brought you and feeling grateful for it.

Gaia had no family anymore (save one recently discovered man claiming to be her uncle, whose name she didn't even know). On account of that, she had trouble feeling grateful. Instead it brought to mind the wonderful things that life had taken away from her, which sent her down the spiral of thanklessness. And that didn't require a special day. That was every day.

Gaia peered into the fridge. She was still hungry, craving something sweet.

Apparently George had done the shopping for Thanksgiving before he'd been called away. The refrigerator was crammed with food, including a massive raw turkey on the bottom shelf.

It was a little depressing, seeing all the food that George had bought and now wouldn't get to cook.

Depressing but not exactly tragic. Although George could find his way through a tuna casserole, Gaia suspected his culinary talents `fell a few drumsticks short of turkey with all the trimmings.`

Ella certainly wasn't going to do it. Gaia doubted George's dumb wife could figure out the recipe for ice. The only way Ella would put her hands in a turkey was if her `Celine Dion CD` had been shoved inside.

It was revolting how tightly Ella had George wrapped around her finger. For a person who made a living in the intelligence community, George Niven was pretty moronic when it came to matters in his own home. You didn't have to be in the CIA to see that Ella was playing him.

No, the only way that bird was getting cooked was if Gaia did it herself.

Without warning, Gaia's mind was flooded with a rush of overlapping images. Memories of another time, another place.

Chestnut stuffing . . . cranberry relish . . . a fire in a stone hearth . . . an ivory chess set, the pieces carved to look like Norse gods: Odin, Frigg, Thor, Loki . . . a man's sudden, shocked laughter: "My God, she just beat me, Kat!" . . . a gravy boat shaped like a swan and a woman's accented voice, saying: "It's lovely, isn't it? It was my grandmother's. Her name was Gaia, too. . . ."

The mental pictures evaporated at the sound of the

front door being unlocked, followed by the sharp, staccato click of high heels on the marble entranceway. The hall light snapped on.

Gaia glanced over at the wall clock. 9:51.

Great. Apparently Ella's coven decided to wrap things up early tonight.

Quickly Gaia reached across the counter and flicked off the light. She closed the refrigerator, not hungry anymore.

It was uncanny: No matter how hungry Gaia was, whenever Ella approached, appetite retreated. Maybe it was an allergic reaction to Ella's unique combination of silicone, hair spray, suffocating perfume, and spandex microminis.

With the refrigerator door closed, the kitchen was swallowed up in shadow. The only light now came from the hallway and the faint red glow cast by the microwave's digital display.

Gaia stood silently in the reddish gloom, mentally urging Ella to stay away from the kitchen. She was hoping to hit the park this evening, maybe see if she could lure a mugger or two. A run-in with Ella would put a damper on that plan. Ella would pull the Carol Brady routine, and Gaia was in no mood to answer stupid, pointless questions at ten o'clock at night. "How was school?" "Great! I purposely blew my history exam and scammed sixty bucks at the chess tables before dinner, and now I'm gonna go to the park to

45

kick some punk ass clear into tomorrow. Thanks for asking!"

She had the sneaking feeling Ella would *not* be amused.

Gaia listened closely for signs of life, but all she could hear was the loud ticking of the grandfather clock in the hall. When Ella still hadn't appeared after sixty more ticks, Gaia stepped cautiously into the corridor.

Maybe this was her lucky night. Maybe Ella had gone upstairs already, sparing Gaia the scary sight of a grown woman who still looked to Barbie for fashion cues.

No such luck.

Ella was standing smack-dab in the middle of the foyer. True to form, she was sporting a metallic turquoise miniskirt with matching pumps, topped off with a fuzzy pink angora sweater that had probably been too tight on the baby she stole it off of.

Gaia's luck hadn't completely abandoned her: Ella was faced away from her and hadn't heard her approaching. Gaia could still avoid detection. In fact, she was all set to scurry back into the kitchen—until she saw what Ella was holding.

Avoiding detection suddenly stopped being important.

"What do you think you're doing?"

Ella spun around, one hand still buried deep in the pocket of Gaia's electric yellow-green Polartec coat. For a second she just stood there—frozen, guilty—then she narrowed her eyes, jutting out her chin in defiance. "What does it look like? I'm searching for drugs." She started rifling through the pockets once again, as if daring Gaia to stop her.

Gaia was across the foyer in three swift strides. "Let me save you some trouble, Ella. There aren't any." Grabbing hold of her coat, she yanked it hard out of Ella's manicured clutches.

Ella reacted as if she'd been slapped, her hands recoiling like two wounded pink spiders.

Gaia stared her flatly in the eyes. "And for future reference? I don't do drugs." Then, just in case Ella still didn't understand, she added: "Leave my stuff alone."

Ella's nostrils flared. "You think I don't know what you do?" she accused. "You think I don't see you sneaking out of here at night, heading to the park? I know what goes on out there." She jabbed her finger at the front door, tossing her copper-colored hair indignantly.

Gaia rolled her eyes. "*Please.*" To Ella's blow-dried mind, the only reason Gaia might possibly want to go to Washington Square Park was to do drugs. Well, if that's what she wanted to believe, let her. There was no way Ella would buy the truth, even if Gaia had the patience to tell it to her. Which she didn't.

Besides, how did you explain that your hobbies

47

included luring out and beating up would-be felons for sport?

Hell, even someone with a measurable IQ would have a hard time believing that one.

Gaia turned to leave, but Ella suddenly seized her sharply by the arm, spinning her around.

"I know what you are."

Ella's press-on nails felt like five plastic knives gouging through the flannel of Gaia's sleeve.

Gaia jerked out of the woman's grasp. "Trust me, Ella. You don't know the first thing about me."

Ella was physically shorter than Gaia, but her stiletto pumps put them at roughly the same eye level. Idly Gaia found herself wondering just what color Ella's eyes would appear to the color-blind Ed Fargo. To her they were the ugly, radioactive green of mint jelly. Did that mean they would look *red* to him? Or would Ella's *hair* look *green?* Somehow the mental image of a red-eyed, green-haired Ella wasn't too hard to conjure.

Ella's lips curled into a sneer. "I knew you'd be trouble the minute you set foot in this house. George wouldn't listen to me, of course. 'Poor little Gaia, she's had such a hard life. She needs our help.'"

Gaia was impressed. For a bimbo with no discernable skill as a photographer, Ella could do a pretty mean impression of her husband's voice. She'd obviously missed her calling in life.

Ella continued tauntingly: "Well, I got news for you. Maybe that wounded-bird routine works on George, but it never fooled me. Not for *one minute*." She punctuated the last two words with two sharp pokes to Gaia's shoulder.

Gaia glanced down at the spot where Ella had touched her. "Are you through?"

"Not quite. I also know you're doing everything in your power to flunk out of school."

Gaia raised an eyebrow. "Really?" *And what was your first clue, Nancy Drew? The string of* F*'s, maybe?*

"That's right. Your principal called to say that you're officially on academic probation." Ella smiled smugly. "Congratulations, Gaia. And after only three months. I hear at your last school, it took you a whole semester."

Whoa. This was definitely *not* the Carol Brady moment Gaia had anticipated five minutes ago. Gaia didn't know *what* role Ella thought she was playing tonight, but if the woman was hoping to get some kind of reaction from her, she'd have to keep on hoping. Gaia wasn't going to give her any satisfaction.

Ella crossed her arms and shook her head in mock pity. "Poor George. He still has some misguided notion that you're intelligent—that we'll actually get rid of you in a couple of years when you go to college. Ha!" She made an ugly snorting sound. "*That's* a joke. Do you think colleges would even *touch* a person with

49

your grades? Do you?" Ella leaned forward, lowering her voice to a whisper. "Or do you think colleges simply let in little blond girls who can beat old drunks at chess and are friends with cripples?"

Gaia's hands involuntarily curled into fists. Her heartbeat accelerated. But she kept her voice remarkably cool and collected as she warned: "You should watch what you're saying, Ella."

"*This is my house!*"

Ella's voice exploded with such raw, unbridled rage that Gaia found herself backing away defensively. "In *my* house I say what *I* want *and you listen!*" Her breath was hot on Gaia's face.

My God, Gaia thought, who *is* this person? This wasn't the old Ella who Gaia knew and disliked. She had seen that Ella angry before, and it had never been anything even remotely close to this. *This* person . . . this was someone different. Someone wholly unfamiliar.

The woman's face was contorted in a mask of fury. Her pupils were mere pinpricks in two poisonous green irises. Her lips were curled away from her teeth.

"Things are going to change around here, *starting now!* From now on, you come straight home from school. No stops in the park, no chess games. *Understand?* You're going to go to your room and you're going to do your homework. No phone, no TV.

And at night you're going to stay in this house if I have to nail every damn window shut myself. You're going to stay in this house if I have to nail your *goddamn feet to the floor!*"

Whoever this person was—Ella or her more evil twin—Gaia had finally had enough.

"I don't have to take this from you," she informed the crazy woman standing before her. "You're not my mother."

"I'm *not?*" Ella reared back, slapping her left breast in a truly third-rate imitation of shocked dismay. "No, I suppose I'm not," she continued, leaning forward again, green eyes narrowing into slits. "*My* heart's still *beating.*"

Gaia watched her fist smash into Ella's face before her brain even knew she was throwing the punch. It was that automatic. That impulsive. As uncontrollable as a sneeze and (good thing for Ella) about as sloppy as one, too. Unlike her more thought-out punches, this one barely connected with its mark, catching the underside of the woman's jaw.

Not that it made a big difference.

Ella spun, crumpling to the marble floor like a sack of bricks, landing on her hands and knees.

Everything was suddenly deathly quiet.

For the next fifteen seconds there was nothing but the sound of Ella's steady, heavy breathing and the slow, rhythmic ticking of the grandfather clock in the hall: *Ticktock. Ticktock. Ticktock.*

Gaia felt like she should do something—*say* something—but she didn't know what. "Sorry" didn't seem right. For one thing, she wasn't sorry. Not yet, anyway. Maybe later she would be.

Instead she just stood there, frozen in place, absently rubbing the knuckles of her right hand, watching Ella's shoulders rise and fall, rise and fall, inside the tight angora sweater.

Ticktock. Ticktock. Ticktock.

After another fifteen seconds Ella slowly crawled away from Gaia toward the foot of the stairs. Once there, she reached up and grabbed hold of the banister, then hoisted herself to her feet. Her spandex skirt had bunched up around her waist, and she took a moment to pull it back down. She smoothed down her sweater. Then, squaring her shoulders, she started slowly up the stairs.

She was halfway to the second floor when Gaia found her voice.

"Ella . . ."

Above her, Ella paused but didn't turn around. Tilting her head slightly, like a sleepwalker hearing her name being called, she said softly: "Wait there." Her voice sounded strange. Thick.

She continued up the stairs.

Gaia watched as Ella's legs disappeared from view.

Listened as the click of Ella's heels faded away, drowned out by the clock in the hall.

Ticktock. Ticktock. Ticktock.

It sounded remarkably like a time bomb.

BLOOD. SHE WAS TASTING HER OWN

Dissolving

goddamn blood.

Once she was out of Gaia's sight, Ella moved more quickly. Around to the next flight of stairs. Eighteen steps to the third floor. Right foot, left foot, right foot. Up, up, up.

Her tongue felt too large for her mouth. It was too wide, too thick. As she mounted the stairs, she explored her tongue's surface with her teeth, wincing as her incisors sank into the gash she'd bitten into it when the little bitch had punched her.

When the little bitch had punched her.

The cut felt deep.

The little bitch had punched her.

Despite the pain she bit down harder now, feeling oddly energized as more blood welled into her mouth. It tasted sharp and bitter, like acid.

Punched her. Her.

It *was* acid, she decided, stepping swiftly onto the

53

third floor. Acid, pumping through her heart, coursing through her veins. She could feel it—couldn't she?—burning in her cheeks, raging in her ears. It would dissolve her. It *was* dissolving her. Eating her from the inside out. She had to hurry. There was no time to lose.

Ten feet down the hall to her dressing room.

Her gun was in the dressing room.

She didn't care what Loki would say. Didn't care what he would do.

She was tasting her own goddamn blood!

Besides, she knew what had to be done now. It was obvious.

Loki had been wrong. Loki *was* wrong.

It was *not* of "utmost importance" that the "subject" be kept alive. That had been their mistake from day one.

As long as his daughter was alive, Tom Moore wasn't going to risk her life by showing his face anywhere near her.

But the bastard *might* come to her funeral.

TICKTOCK. TICKTOCK. TICKTOCK.

Gaia stood in the foyer. Watching the stairs. Waiting for Ella to return.

Should she stay? Try to fix this gaping **GO**

rupture? Was there any point? Could she make herself apologize for George's sake?

Stay or go?

Ella was insane. This night was insane.

Stay or go?

She could hear Ella's footsteps again. She was coming back down the stairs now, rounding the landing one floor above.

Without realizing she'd made a decision, Gaia let her long strides carry her down the hallway. Numbly she pulled on her coat and threw her bag over her shoulder. The cold doorknob filled her hand, and she turned it with a click.

"Good-bye, house. Good-bye, George," she whispered. "Sorry about this."

She had a feeling as she stepped out the door that she wouldn't be coming back.

I remember the summer I started carrying pennies.

I was five years old, and we were living in our Manhattan apartment. My mom's dad got sick late that spring. He was dying, it turns out. Every weekend when we'd drive my mother to visit him in his hospital in New Jersey, my dad would take me to the Jersey shore.

You see, when you're driving back into Manhattan from the Jersey side, you have to go through a tollbooth. Nowadays things are pretty high-tech, with laser scanners and special stickers you can get for your car, but back then my dad would pay using tokens.

Of course, to a five-year-old, a coin's a coin. And to me, those tokens looked just like pennies.

Somehow, in my little-kid brain, I concluded that in order to get back home, you needed pennies for the tolls. From that moment on, I started carrying extra pennies with me. Just in case.

For some reason, I had this silly notion that my parents could somehow lose me. You know—just take their eyes off me around a corner or something and not be able to find me again. Maybe all kids think like that when they're small. Anyway, I wanted to make sure that if I ever got separated from my folks, I'd have enough money to pay the toll and get back home on my own.

Later on, when I was older and knew better, I still carried pennies. By then it had just become this sort of superstitious habit of mine. My talisman. My good luck charm.

It wasn't until I was in sixth grade that my father finally noticed and asked me about it. When I explained the whole tollbooth story to him, he laughed. Told me I always worried about the wrong things.

A year later my mother was
killed and my father took off,
leaving me behind.

So I guess it wasn't such a
silly notion after all.

I don't carry pennies for good
luck anymore. They don't work all
that well, as it turns out.

Mary attached
herself to Gaia
by the hand,
and Gaia let **a**
herself
be pulled **reason**
toward a wait-   **to**
ing group that,
for the moment **stay**
at least, could
pass as friends.

THERE WERE TIMES WHEN A
four-dollar vanilla latte
with an extra dollop of
foam seemed like the
answer to every single
one of life's problems.

Red Light, Green Light

Tonight it just seemed
like an overpriced cup of
coffee.

Sitting at one of the window seats at the Starbucks
on Astor Place, Gaia forced herself to take another slug
of the sickly sweet concoction. It wasn't easy. Ten minutes ago it had been lukewarm. Now it was closer to
cold. It reminded her of the milk left over from a bowl
of sugar cereal.

Outside, across Fourth Avenue, the giant clock face
on the side of the Carl Fischer building showed that it
was almost eleven.

God, what a night. Living with George and Ella
had never been great, but it was a place to be. A place
to keep what little stuff she had. And her tenuous toehold in their house had made her a New Yorker. She
liked that.

Now it was gone, and she had that slightly
metallic, nauseating taste in her throat
that came with running away. Or drinking
syrup-sweet coffee soup. Or the combination.

She knew the taste because she'd run away before.

Never successfully, though. She always ended up back where she started or in a different foster home, facing even greater doubt and suspicion from her newest "family."

This time would be different. Packed into the various zippered compartments of her messenger bag and parka were bills totaling over eight hundred dollars—three months of chess winnings. She carried it on her all the time. It was ironic. She used to carry pennies for luck. Now she kept twenties for when her luck turned sour.

It was a lot of money, but it wouldn't last long in New York City. She would be smart to leave town.

With that thought, a picture bloomed in her mind. The face of Sam Moon, sitting across the chess table from her, drenched by rain, staring directly into her heart as no one, man or woman, ever had.

It would be hard to leave him. It would be crazy to stay for him.

Then there was Ed. Her first real friend since . . . forever. She was addicted to Ed.

And to the park. And the action. The density of criminals. The number of places where you could buy doughnuts at 2 A.M. The sirens.

But tonight Ed had taken off with his family to drive to Pennsylvania for a classic Thanksgiving with bickering parents and adoring grandparents. He wouldn't be back until Sunday. It just pointed out how different they really were. How different they would always be.

Sam belonged to somebody else (whom she incidentally hated). Ed was a decent, good person with a family who loved him. Far too decent for her.

There was nothing for her here.

She tipped her head and rested it against the cold glass window. The pale, late November color of her hands picked up a green glow from the traffic light at the intersection just beyond the window. Go.

Predictably, a minute later, her hands were bathed in red. Stop.

For minutes at a time she watched hypnotically as her hands changed from green to red.

Go. Stop.

Walk. Don't walk.

She'd let the traffic light decide her fate.

Behind her, there was a complaint of hinges and an inrush of street noise as someone pushed into the Starbucks through the side entrance. A second later Gaia was assaulted by a blast of arctic air. She felt its icy fingers snake around her neck and trickle down her spine and watched in morbid fascination as the skin of her arms pebbled into gooseflesh.

The sight transfixed her. It always did.

She traced a fingertip along the surface of her forearm—slowly, exploringly—from the crook of her elbow to her wrist. Every tiny, raised bump gave her a tiny, perverse thrill.

Gooseflesh. A symptom of fear.

Of course, in Gaia's case, it was just hair follicles reacting to an extreme change of temperature. That's all it would *ever* be with her. Still, she liked to believe that in some small, weird way, getting goose bumps was like getting a tiny glimpse into what fear felt like. The simple fact that she could experience one of fear's physical manifestations made her feel less . . . different, somehow. Less freakish. More . . . human.

The goose bumps were beginning to fade.

Gaia sighed. Who was she trying to kid? She would *never* know what fear was like. No more than Ed could know what it was like to tell red from green.

Red and green. Gaia suddenly remembered her appointment with Destiny. Would she stay or would she go? Taking a breath, she raised her eyes and looked out the window.

The light was yellow.

Gee, thanks, Destiny. You sure know how to toy with a girl's emo—

Gaia's thoughts were interrupted by something reflected in the plate glass window. Someone was rushing up behind her. Someone with red hair.

Before she could turn around, something cold and metallic was pressed against the back of her neck. "Don't make a move," a female voice warned.

Gaia didn't move. She just sat there, staring down at her arms.

There wasn't a single damn goose bump in sight.

MARY MOSS WAS EXPECTING THE

girl's shoulders to jump or at least her muscles to tense. They didn't, although Gaia did turn her head quickly. "Your money or your life," Mary growled, pressing the metal tube of lipstick into Gaia's back.

Mary snarled menacingly, waiting for a reaction.

Gaia didn't look scared, but she didn't look quite tuned in, either. She was glowing red from a traffic light outside, and her eyes were wide and confused.

Mary softened her expression and produced the tube of lipstick for Gaia to see. "Gaia, it's me. Mary. Are you okay?"

Gaia seemed to pull her eyes into focus. She took the lipstick and examined it.

"It's called Bruise," Mary offered. "Great color, poor firearm."

Now Gaia was green. She handed the lipstick back.

"How's it going?" Mary asked, taking the seat across the little table from Gaia and tucking the lipstick tube in the outside pocket of her backpack.

Gaia looked pretty out of it. Her light hair was gathered in a messy wad at the back of her head. Her acid green jacket was half inside out, hanging untidily over the back of the chair, and her messenger bag was clamped between her feet on the floor. On the table before her was the better part of a once frothy coffee substance.

Gaia rubbed her eyes. "Sorry. You surprised me. I'm—I'm . . . all right. How 'bout you?" she answered vaguely.

Mary studied the girl's face, wondering what was really up, knowing she'd probably never know. That was part of what made Gaia fascinating to her.

"Great. I'm not going to sleep tonight," Mary announced.

Gaia was paying attention now. "Oh, yeah?"

"Yeah. The night before Thanksgiving is one of the great nights in New York. It's a night for locals."

Gaia looked puzzled. "As opposed to . . ."

"Tourists. Gawkers. The bridge-and-tunnel crowd. Hardly anything that New York is famous for is actually happening for the locals. Broadway shows. Carriage rides through Central Park. Those dumb theme restaurants. The stores on Columbus Avenue."

"Um. Okay," Gaia said, not caring enough to argue if she did happen to disagree.

"Obviously the parade tomorrow is a major gawk

fest. But tonight, right outside the park, they blow up the floats for the parade. That part is still fun. It doesn't really get good until after midnight, so I'm going to a club first to hear this very cool neighborhood band. You want to go?"

Gaia just looked at her, waiting for her to finish, clearly not feeling a big need to act friendly. That was another thing Mary liked about her. "Well. Thanks and all," Gaia said distractedly, tapping her fingers against the table. "But—"

"You have other plans," Mary finished for her.

Gaia cocked her head. "It's not that. It's—"

"So come," Mary said.

Still there was hesitation in Gaia's face.

"You've got a curfew?" Mary tried.

Gaia shook her head.

"Your folks wouldn't be into it?" Mary suggested.

Gaia shook her head. "No folks."

"No folks?"

"I don't have any," Gaia said. Just a statement of fact.

"Jesus. I wasn't expecting that answer. God. Sorry."

Gaia's eyebrows collided over her nose. She was angry. "Sorry for asking me a perfectly normal question? Why do people say that? Why do they always flip out and apologize for no reason?" Her eyes were intense, challenging.

Mary's own anger reared up instantly. "I'm not

sorry I asked you the question, you idiot," she snapped. "I'm sorry your parents are dead."

Gaia's eyes widened, then her face got calm. "Oh."

"Fine," Mary said. She got up to order a triple espresso from the lone counter person. Starbucks sucked, but her favorite café had just changed management and installed computers every five feet. She turned back to Gaia, pleased to see the girl had gotten over her anger just as quickly as Mary had. "So, you coming?"

Gaia looked somewhat bamboozled. "I guess. Sure."

". . . I'M BLIND. I'M EMPTY. I'M

Just Like

Sam

stupid. I'm wrong. . . ."

Gaia wasn't quite sure how this had happened.

She'd gone from being a bleak New York casualty, a teenage runaway, to being a frivolous club kid. Here she was, sitting in a round, red velvet booth at a downtown club surrounded by New York's young indulgents, listening to a band, Fearless, whose name and lyrics dogged her life in the creepiest way.

". . . I need you to tell me I'm not what I am. . . ."

The singer was ranting. Gaia stared into her vodka and tonic and tried not to think about it too much.

Most of the people at the table, including Mary, were on their third drinks before Gaia had drunk a third of her first. She didn't like alcohol very much. For one thing, it didn't taste good. Maybe that was babyish of her, but it was true. Besides, from what she could tell, the real reason people drank was to dull their fear. Not what Gaia needed. What if alcohol consumption pushed her from zero fear into negative fear? Gaia slid the sweaty glass a few inches toward the center of the table. That didn't seem like a good idea.

She turned her head as Mary tugged on a piece of her hair and then glided toward the dance floor. "You're having fun," Mary shouted over the din. It was more command than question. "Want to dance with us?"

"No," Gaia mouthed. It did actually look like fun, but somehow it didn't seem right, punching Ella out cold and hitting the dance floor in the same two-hour period. She felt obligated to remain dysfunctional and sullen for at least another hour.

Still, she couldn't help smiling at Mary, who was whirling like a dervish through the crowds. Mary was a wild dancer, not surprisingly, and her hair paid no attention to gravity. Gaia couldn't help admiring her. Mary had none of the self-consciousness that sometimes made it embarrassing to watch a person dance.

Gaia glanced at her watch. If she was leaving town, she needed to get going. Traveling on Thanksgiving was notoriously bad. It would be smarter to catch a train or a bus tonight. That way she could sleep in transit and not have to pay for a place to stay.

All of Mary's friends were dancing now. Gaia was alone in the booth. The place was packed, and she felt a bit self-conscious taking up this seating area for eight. She realized a guy standing by the bar was looking at her. No, make that staring. He appeared to be at least thirty. Ick.

Oh, shit, he was coming toward her. She directed an intensely unfriendly expression at him. *Go away now. I do not like you.*

He turned back to the bar. Ahhh. Good. Gaia had to hand it to herself. She could give a mean look like nobody.

Gaia gazed around the club. She'd never been to a place like this before. It was loud. It was dark. People were having fun. It seemed like a great place to go if you were a bored New York City kid looking to hook up. It was a weird place to go shortly after you'd decked your so-called foster mother, on a night you were running away for good.

But what if she *were* just a regular kid, stressed out

and angst ridden in a contained, urbane, happy kind of way, looking to hook up? It was a fun game to play sometimes.

She scanned the bar. There was a guy near the front windows who was sort of cute. He had hair the same color as Sam's. His nose and chin couldn't compare, though. And he appeared to be at least five inches shorter than Sam.

Another guy in a booth two away from hers had a good smile. Nice teeth. A little crooked. His eyes were nice, too. Not like Sam's, of course. Not turn-your-world-over nice. Besides, he was wearing one of those big, fancy metal watches. She hated those.

She slid her drink around in its little puddle on the glass table. The volume in the place notched up even higher. She turned to the entrance and saw another cluster of people packing themselves in. Her eyes froze. Oh, wow. There. That guy was beautiful, Gaia thought distantly. Tall, perfectly built. He had gorgeous red-brown-blond hair, neither wavy nor curly but somewhere in between. Just like Sam, her mind informed her dreamily.

Holy shit. Gaia sat up very straight. He wasn't *like* Sam. He *was* Sam. Her mind raced. Her heartbeat quickened. Goose bumps sprouted on her arms. *Almost like fear.* But not fear. Something else.

Gaia's eyes darted to the faces of Sam's nearest companions.

Clunk. Down slid her hopes.

Yes, indeed. The good-news, bad-news duo. Hateful Heather was in her usual spot right there beside him. Why *shouldn't* Sam and Heather make an appearance on this night from hell? How could it be otherwise?

Gaia averted her gaze. She pointed her face at the tabletop. She really didn't want them to see her. A word from Heather might just throw her over the edge.

Suddenly she felt terribly conspicuous in the booth by herself. Where were Mary and all her friends? Why couldn't they park their damn butts in the booth for five minutes and stop having so much fun? Grrrr.

Gaia rested her face in her hand, using her fingers to cover up almost the entire part of her face that Sam and Heather could feasibly see from their angle. She would just stay like that until they got busy dancing or went to the back, and then she'd leave. She'd head for the bus station. Fine.

Oh, no. She couldn't actually look up to confirm her suspicion, but she had a terrible feeling that the group, which included her favorite couple, was heading straight toward her booth. There was definitely a shadow moving in. No. Go! Go!

"Excuse me? Would you mind if we shared your booth?" It wasn't a voice she recognized. Could she get away with not looking up?

"Excuse me!"

Go away, she urged silently.

"*Excuse me!*"

All right, that was annoying. She snapped her head up just as Heather and Sam registered the reality of whom they were about to share a booth with.

Who looked least happy? Sam? Heather? Gaia?

Hard to say.

Gaia thought she gave a mean look, but Heather's was better.

Gaia shot to her feet. "All yours. I was just going."

Six pairs of eyes stuck on Gaia as she fumbled to put on her parka. It seemed to take two hours. First it was inside out. Then she couldn't get her hand through the sleeve. As she grabbed for her bag, she knocked over her drink and spritzed the group with watery vodka and dead tonic. Why couldn't she keep her beverages to herself?

She couldn't bring herself to look at Sam. This wasn't happening.

"Gaia, wait." It was Mary, suddenly positioning herself as a bulwark between Gaia and the booth stealers. "Where are you going?"

"I—I gotta go. Now."

Mary looked around. She took in the presence of Heather. A light dawned in her eyes. "Hey, if it isn't the charming Ms. Gannis. Gosh, I remember the last time we were all at a party together. You were riding quite the welcome wagon that night."

Heather was silent.

Mary gave Gaia a confident smile and spoke loudly enough for Heather's benefit. "Don't worry, Gaia. If Heather treats you like that again, I'll smack her."

Heather looked stunned. A couple of Heather's friends seemed to think Mary was kidding around. Gaia didn't look at Sam to gauge his reaction.

Mary attached herself to Gaia by the hand, and Gaia let herself be pulled toward a waiting group that, for the moment at least, could pass as friends.

"Bitch," Mary mumbled to Gaia, not letting go of her hand. "Let's get out of here."

Gaia felt like crying as she bobbed along after Mary. Nobody ever took care of her like that. Gaia was so taken aback, she didn't know how to feel.

Following the electrified red hair, she experienced a rush of real warmth in spite of the stiff, late-autumn breeze.

Maybe there *was* a reason to stay in New York for a while longer.

HEATHER FELT LIKE SHE WAS CHEWING

Poison

on a lemon. She couldn't seem to get the sour taste out of her mouth or remove the pinched expression from her face.

Sam sat down next to her, stiff as a two-by-four, saying nothing.

That was the best strategy. They would just let this pass and get on with their night. No need to talk about it.

"Who is that girl?" Sam's friend Christian Pavel wanted to know.

"You mean Mary Moss? The redhead?" Heather heard her friend Jonathan Singer respond.

"No, the blond one."

Heather waited numbly for the conversation to be over. She tried to think of some effective way to change tracks.

"That's Gaia Moore," Jonathan said flatly.

"She's unbelievable," Christian said.

Every person at the table waited in uncomfortable suspense to hear the precise way in which Christian Pavel found Gaia Moore unbelievable.

"She's gorgeous. A total goddess. Do you know her? Can you introduce me?"

No one said a word. Heather's mouth was drawn up like a twist tie. She felt like crushing all ten of Christian's toes under the table.

Sam cleared his throat. "H-H-Have you all seen this band before?" he asked the group gallantly, putting a wooden arm around Heather's shoulders.

Conversation resumed. Heather watched Gaia's back disappear through the door. She wished she could give Gaia a poisonous cloak.

74

Then again, Gaia's phlegm-colored jacket was pretty poisonous as it was.

Lustful Looks

SAM SAT IN THE BOOTH, AS CROSS and sullen as a sleep-deprived toddler. Too sullen to drink. Or dance. Or make small talk.

He was annoyed at Heather for being his girlfriend. He was annoyed at Christian for looking lustfully at Gaia. (That was *his* department.) He was annoyed at Gaia for a whole list of things:

1. Not being his girlfriend;
2. Looking so spectacularly beautiful;
3. Ruining his life;
4. Ruining his relationship;
5. Not meeting his eyes for a single second tonight;
6. Not being his girlfriend.

Mostly he was annoyed at himself. For blundering deeper into the thing with Heather. For being so goddamned stiff and awkward tonight. For not talking honestly with Heather about what was really going on. For having blown a perfectly good chance to do so.

For still staring at the door fully forty-five minutes after Gaia had walked through it.

My Dear Gaia,

Having seen you so recently (though you did not see me), my pain at being apart from you is only stronger. You have grown into a formidable woman, Gaia, as your mother and I knew you would. Your strength and intensity still astound me. I see now that you have the spirit to fight fiercely for your life, and that is a great comfort to me.

My other comfort is the knowledge that at last you have a good home with my kind old friend George. It's a safe place. I trust George will do his very best by you. I'm glad to know you'll have Thanksgiving there, with someone who truly cares for you.

Each year at Thanksgiving, I write to tell you that you are my reason for thanks, my reason for living. Each year, with my heart full of hope, I pray that next year we'll spend this holiday together. And though realism chips away at my hope, I'm still praying.

Know that I love you, Gaia. That you are always in my heart.

Tom Moore signed the letter and thought about Katia. Twice a year he allowed himself to cry for her, and this was one of those times.

When he was done, he walked to the file cabinet.

The top drawer was stuffed full of letters like this one. He found the manila folder labeled Thanksgiving Letters and dropped it in.

He dug his hand in the pocket of his corduroy trousers and felt the penny that lay in the bottom. Perhaps, with luck, this would be the last time he would need to write to Gaia on Thanksgiving.

Gaia clutched the stretchy plastic in her fist as they rose under a cloud of helium, higher and higher.

fun, for a change

"WHAT *THE DEVIL* WENT ON THERE
tonight?" Loki's voice thundered.

Ella stood before him, heavy with a strange mixture of shame, pride, and frustration. Her jaw throbbed, and her tongue felt like it belonged to somebody else. "We fought.

The Good Uncle

She punched me. She left." Ella didn't bother to mention the part where she got out her gun and went after Gaia, fully intending to blow her brains out. Luckily that part didn't appear on the surveillance tape.

"Stupid woman, have you lost your mind?"

Ella cupped her jaw tenderly. There would be no sympathy from him. That was certain. "The girl hit me."

"I would have hit you, too, the way you carried on," Loki said sharply.

Ella held her painful tongue. It was as expected.

"Absurd self-indulgence," he spat, pacing across the soft, honey-colored herringbone floorboards. Last month he had a vast loft above the Hudson River. Tonight she'd been ordered to meet him in a starkly modern apartment building on Central Park South. He'd only be there so long as he kept perfect anonymity. Then he'd relocate again. "Why I put up with you, I do not know."

Ella remained quiet. He'd get bored of the tirade eventually. The greatest mistake would be to attempt to defend herself. That would only inject a surge of energy into the project. Where Loki was concerned, what the world gained in a terrorist, it had lost in a lawyer.

His angry voice faded into a dull roar. Ella stared out the large picture windows, waiting for him to be done. Three-quarters of a mile uptown, the enormous helium balloons for the Thanksgiving Day parade were rising to life from the lawns of the Museum of Natural History on Seventy-seventh Street. Long ago, in her other life, she'd gone with friends to watch.

That was before Ella had been "discovered." Well before Gaia had come into their lives, a much more perfect fulfillment of Ella's early promise. Ella felt a wave of nausea climbing her chest.

"Ella!"

She turned to him. Oh. He was finished, then. He'd asked her a question of the nonrhetorical variety. "I'm sorry?"

"You are sorry. A truly sorry creature. I asked you why you were caught with your arm in Gaia's coat."

"I was planting the tracking device," Ella replied.

"And were you able to complete that *onerous* task?" His voice was laced with sarcasm.

"I was."

"Fine. And I gather you've chosen someone to perform the job?"

"Yes." Ella fiercely hoped he would not ask who that was.

"Well, then. With any luck we'll be done with Tom shortly." He smiled the least cheerful smile Ella had ever witnessed. "That should be fun. And then the real plans begin."

"SO WHO DO YOU LIKE?" MARY

asked. "Clifford, the big red dog? Random Rugrat? Snoopy?"

The night was misty. The octagonal stones around the beautiful, castlelike Museum of Natural History were slick with yellow and brown leaves. Gaia and Mary were still clutching hands like kindergarten best friends, running through the crowds, watching the enormous balloons come to life.

"Spiderman is cool," Gaia observed, gazing at the balloon reaching four stories into the sky. A net above them kept the balloons on good behavior until the parade began in the morning.

"Spiderman is already up, up, and away," Mary said somewhat breathlessly, pulling Gaia along. "We need to pick one that's only partway blown up."

"We do?" Gaia asked.

Mary raised her eyebrows mischievously. "We do."

Gaia caught up even with her. "What exactly are you planning?"

"Something fun. You'll see." She glanced over at Gaia. "You scared?"

"Uh-uh," Gaia replied.

"Here." Mary yanked her to a stop. "These ones are good. Shhh. Stay still a minute."

The ones Mary was referring to were huge ponds of half-inflated plastic, one red, the other green. Gaia couldn't tell what they were.

Mary looked around. "Okay, follow me. Move quickly, before anybody sees us."

Gaia nodded, intensely curious.

Mary paused in thought. "Hang on. Which one? Red or green?"

"I don't care," Gaia said.

"Pick!" Mary ordered.

Gaia rolled her eyes. "They're the same. It doesn't matter. I don't even know what we're doing."

Mary was still glaring at her expectantly.

"All right, fine. Red," Gaia said.

"Go," Mary hissed.

She darted around the growing balloon to the side

that was closest to the museum fence and used the fence for a boost. She transferred her weight from the fence to the balloon, clamored up the `soft, loose plastic`, then rolled down into the sagging middle. Gaia followed close behind. When they settled in the middle, they had to cling to the plastic to keep from rolling on top of each other.

"This is cozy," Mary said, laughter in her voice.

"I still don't know what we're doing," Gaia said.

"Shhh. Stay still. We have to keep quiet."

Mary's excitement was contagious. "Why?" Gaia asked.

"'Cause the last time I did this, I got arrested," Mary explained happily.

"Oh," Gaia said.

"Scared yet?" Mary asked.

"Not yet," Gaia replied.

`Gaia heard the rush of helium into the balloon get louder.`

"Cool," Mary whispered. "They're turning it up."

"They?"

"The inflators," Mary said.

"Is that a word?" Gaia asked.

Mary's giggle came out like a snort. "I think so."

Gaia felt the helium filling the space under them. They were rising appreciably. "Now what?" she whispered.

"We wait," Mary said. `She reached for Gaia's hand and held it again.` Gaia was so unaccustomed to physical contact (apart from punching people) that it felt weird to her. Weird, but nice, too.

As the minutes passed, the plastic began to fill and grow around them. Soon the thin, rubbery plastic was puffing up all around them, becoming more and more taut.

"What is this balloon, anyway?" Gaia asked.

Mary lifted her head and looked behind her. "Judging from the green one next door, I think it's an M&M."

"An M&M?"

"Yeah, look." Mary rolled partly onto her side and pointed at the green twin.

"We're on a giant red M&M?" Gaia realized she was getting punchy because for some reason, this seemed hilarious.

"Okay. This is where it starts to get fun." Mary's face was flushed with anticipation. "Hold on tight, okay? I think we've got a facial feature of some kind here."

It was thrilling. Gaia clutched the stretchy plastic in her fist as they rose under a cloud of helium, higher and higher. She was amazed nobody had seen them yet. She twisted her head and saw the buildings above. The ritzy apartment buildings on one side, the museum on the other. They were rising faster now, above the streetlights, nearing the tops of the trees.

Closer and closer to the gauzy, dark purple night sky. She looked ahead to the ever improving view of Central Park with its dark carpet of trees and the twinkly lights along Fifth Avenue.

Gaia felt her own breath swelling inside her chest. It was magical. "Beautiful," she whispered to Mary.

Mary squeezed her hand.

Gaia tried to stamp this feeling, these sights, into her brain so she could remember them later, when she needed to convince herself there was happiness in the world.

"Oh, shit!" Mary suddenly cried, puncturing Gaia's reverie. Mary yanked her hand from Gaia's, pinching wildly at the plastic of the balloon to steady herself. "I'm losing it, Gaia!"

The plastic had grown so taut under their hands, it was hard to keep holding. Mary's grip was slipping fast.

Gaia turned to her new friend, expecting to see fear in the girl's eyes. Instead she saw wide-eyed thrill.

"Gaiaaaa!" Mary was yelling. "Eeeeeee! This is where it gets *really* fun! When I say go, let go!"

A laugh erupted from Gaia's throat. This was crazy. It *was* fun.

"Go!" Mary screamed.

"Ahhhhhhhhh!" The two girls' voices mingled in a

scream as they slid on their stomachs all the way down the growing mountain of balloon and landed hard on the ground.

They lay there for a moment in a tangled clump.

"Are you okay?" Mary asked, pushing her hair out of her face, trying to organize her limbs.

"Okay? That was awesome!" Gaia jumped to her feet and pulled her friend beside her. "Let's do it again."

Mary laughed and swatted Gaia on the shoulder. "I *knew* we were gonna get along."

TWO HOURS LATER GAIA LAY BESIDE

Extra Love

Mary on the grassy part of Strawberry Fields and watched the first light of sun spread across the sky. The air felt damp and surprisingly mild.

Gaia fell in love with the place on first sight. She loved the curving pathways and the odd accumulation of humanity gathered on the handsome benches. She loved the white-and-black mosaic that said "Imagine" in the middle.

"This is my favorite place," Mary said, grabbing the sentiment right from Gaia's mind.

"I see why." Gaia turned her head to see Mary's face.

Mary yawned and raised her arms, stretching long fingers toward the sky. Gaia caught the yawn from her.

"Hey, Mary?"

"Yeah."

"Thanks for inviting me along on this night. It's been great."

Mary turned to her and smiled. "It wouldn't have been great without you."

Gaia must have been very tired because she was saying things she would never normally say. She was forgetting to censor her feelings and words, forgetting what the consequences could be. "And thanks a lot for looking after me at that bar."

"No prob," Mary said to the sky. "I always take care of my friends."

Gaia thought for a few moments. "Why is that?" she asked. Her voice was so quiet, she wasn't sure it would carry to Mary, two feet away.

Mary yawned again. She put her fingers into her fiery hair. "Because I can afford to."

Gaia squinted at her. "What do you mean?"

"I get a lot of love. From my folks, my brothers. I have extra."

In the pale morning light, that seemed to Gaia both a totally unexpected and beautiful thing to say. She tried to imagine what kind of parents would love Mary so well *and* let her stay out all night, doing whatever she pleased. "Why not keep it for yourself?" Gaia heard herself asking. It was unusual for her brain to connect to her mouth so directly. "That's what most people would do."

Mary considered this. "I have trouble holding on to it."

Silence enveloped them again.

After a long time Mary turned on her side and propped herself up on her elbow. "So, what are you doing for Thanksgiving dinner?"

Gaia hesitated. She couldn't say she was doing nothing. It was too pathetic. It was begging for sympathy and an invitation. But she couldn't lie, either. She had a feeling Mary wouldn't buy a lie very easily. "Oh. Well. I was thinking I might—"

"Wait a minute," Mary broke in. "Why am I asking? I know what you're doing."

Gaia furrowed her brow. "You do?"

"Yeah."

"Okay. So?"

"You're eating with my family."

"I am?"

"You are. You definitely are."

"Are you sure?"

"Completely, one hundred percent sure."

Gaia couldn't help but let a smile out. "Great. I'll let myself know."

THE DOCTOR TIED THE BELT OF

his nondescript and greatly
despised tan trench coat. In
recent years he'd become attached to very fine clothes.
But this coat continued to
be useful to him when he
was conducting his "side

A Crowded Thursday

business." It was not only too boring to warrant notice, but of such an inferior material that it was machine washable. That part was important.

Pausing briefly at the corner of Fifty-fifth Street
and Fifth Avenue, he studied the information stored in
the tracking device. Now, this was a very busy
girl. First the West Village, then Astor Place. Then
the remote East Village, then West Seventy-seventh
Street, Central Park, and what appeared to be a high
floor of an apartment building on Central Park West
and Sixty-fifth Street. Did teenagers no longer find
sleep necessary at all?

He would need to follow her carefully. He wanted
this job done by midnight, and her current location—
no doubt in a private home—was far less than ideal.
That whorish woman—what was her less than amusing alias? Travesura?—had assured him this girl spent
a lot of time on the streets and in public places. It had
better be so.

He touched his trusted knives, tied up in

felt casing in his roomy pocket. This girl was reported to be quite beautiful and exceptionally strong. That was enticing to him. That's why he'd taken on the job.

"Excuse me!" he snapped, nearly colliding with a shabby-looking woman pushing a stroller containing a shabby-looking infant.

He tried to remember why there were so many people—so many children—milling around the streets of New York City on a Thursday morning at nine o'clock.

For me, Thanksgiving is a mixed bag. On the one hand, there's turkey with stuffing and my grandfather's apple pie. I love that. On the other hand, there are turnips and pumpkin pie. I'd like to know: Who really likes pumpkin pie? Let's all be honest.

On the one hand, there are people like me, hanging out with my grandparents. I love them. On the other hand, there are people like Gaia, who have nobody. That's heartbreaking.

If you think about it, even the first Thanksgiving was in no way a cause for bilateral cheer. I mean, sure, the Native Americans had shown the Pilgrims how to farm the land, and they were psyched about their first harvest. But what did the Native Americans have to celebrate? Alcoholism, VD, and blankets infected with smallpox.

One arm. Two arms. The fab- ric settled with unexpected ease over her stomach and butt, the skirt grazing a few inches above her knees.

too nice

"THIS IS TOO NICE." GAIA SAID

The Red Dress

it out loud to the Victorian-colored glass chandelier that hung over the vast, pillow-laden guest bed in Mary's family's apartment.

Being friends with Mary was too nice. Mary's unbelievably huge and fantastic apartment on Central Park West was way too nice. The smell of roasting turkey and buttery stuffing was too nice. The thought of spending Thanksgiving with a real family for the first time in five years . . . too nice to think about.

Gaia tried to remind herself to keep her suspicions close around her, but Mary, this place . . . it was dazzling. Can't you just enjoy something? she asked herself impatiently. Accept that some places, some people are purely nice?

She didn't have time to answer herself. There was a knock on the door, and seconds later, Mary opened it partially and poked her head in. "Hi."

"Hi."

"Did you sleep?"

"Like a vegetable."

"Me too. Guess what time it is?"

Gaia shrugged. She wasn't used to having someone talk to her while she was lying in bed. She wasn't a slumber-party kind of girl. She sat up and hugged a pillow on her lap.

"One o'clock. P.M. Big meal is in one hour."

Gaia cleared her throat. What exactly had she'd gotten herself into here? "Is it a dressed-up sort of thing?" Her voice came out squeaky. She didn't want to bring up the fact that she had no home, no possessions, and certainly no Central Park West party clothes at the moment.

Mary had a knack for coming to Gaia's rescue without Gaia even having to ask. "Just a little. I've been laying out stuff in my room. I have the most fabulous dress for you. Come on."

Gaia sat on the edge of the bed. She was wearing a big gray T-shirt she'd worn under her flannel shirt last night. Her legs were bare, her feet covered by white cotton socks. "Like this?" she asked.

"Sure," Mary said. "It's just down the hall. No brothers in sight. I mean, in case you care."

Mary was under the mistaken impression that Gaia was a normal human being who did things like this. The easiest thing would be to play along, to pretend she had comfy pals whose clothes she borrowed, in whose homes she felt perfectly fine wandering around in a T-shirt and socks.

Gaia was a terrible actress. She skulked down the hall and darted into Mary's room like an escapee from Attica.

Once the door was shut, she made herself relax. Mary wasn't kidding about laying out clothes. If there was a carpet in the spacious room, it would have taken an archaeologist to find it. Only the rough shapes of the various pieces of furniture were apparent under thick piles of clothes.

Mary was unapologetic about her colossal slobbiness. Gaia liked that in a person.

"Okay, you ready for the perfect dress?" Mary asked.

Gaia nodded.

"Tra la." Mary held up a tiny, red, crushed velvet dress with a plunging neckline.

Gaia stared. "Are you kidding? I couldn't fit my left foot into that dress."

Mary frowned. "Have you tried it? No. Shut up until you try it."

Gaia held out her hand for it. It weighed about three ounces. "Yes, ma'am. I've never been dressed by a fascist before." Feeling large and self-conscious, Gaia pulled the T-shirt over her head and quickly yanked the dress over her head and shoulders. One arm. Two arms. The fabric settled with unexpected ease over her stomach and butt, the skirt grazing a few inches above her knees.

Mary was surveying the progress with her hands on her hips. When Gaia turned around, her frown blossomed into a smile. "Wow! See?" She took Gaia's hand and pulled her in front of the full-length mirror on the back of her closet.

Gaia gazed at herself in genuine surprise. The dress actually fit. Granted, it was made of stretchy stuff. And it did cling to her gigantic muscles in an unforgiving manner.

"I look like Arnold Schwarzenegger in a dress," Gaia mumbled.

"*What?*" Mary demanded. "I'm going to smack you, girl. You look incredible."

Gaia turned around to examine her backside. "I have incredibly huge muscles."

Mary blew out her breath in frustration. "Guy-aaaaa," she scolded. "You have the body every woman would die to have. You have the long, defined muscles that keep the rest of us slogging it out in overpriced gyms around the country. You have to see that."

"I see Mr. Universe."

"Shut *up!*" Mary roared. Now she was mad. She held out her hand. "So give it back. Seriously. I mean it. If you can't appreciate that it looks beautiful, you don't deserve to borrow my goddamned dress."

Gaia cast her a pleading gaze. "Look, I'm trying. I really am." She studied herself in the mirror for another minute, trying to see herself through other eyes.

The dress really was extraordinary. Gaia loved the too long sleeves and the way they flared at the wrist. "Please let me borrow it?" Gaia asked, weirded out by hearing those words in her voice. "I'll say anything, true or untrue. I am Kate Moss. I am a waif. I can't do a single push-up."

Mary laughed. "Fine. It's yours. In fact, you can have it for keeps. After seeing you in it, I won't be able to stand the sight of me."

Now it was Gaia's turn to glare. "Hang on. *You're* allowed the exaggeratedly negative body image, but not me? Who made these rules?"

Mary waved a hand in the air. "Point taken. Never mind. But keep the stupid dress." She gestured at the snowstorm of clothes. "I have others, as you may have noticed." She rooted around the bottom of her closet and threw Gaia a pair of black cotton tights.

"Thanks," Gaia said.

"Oh, and here."

"Ouch." A dark red, forties-style pump flew out of the closet and hit Gaia on the shin. Thankfully, she dodged its mate.

"Sorry," Mary murmured. Now she was gathering jewelry for Gaia.

"What size are your feet?" Gaia asked, staring suspiciously at the shoe.

"Eight."

"I wear eight and a half," Gaia said.

Mary was busy untangling a clump of necklaces. "So? Close enough."

Apparently Mary didn't get hung up on little matters like housing all five toes.

Again, though, Mary was right. The shoe was close enough to fitting. Gaia put on the second one and stomped around the room, trying to get used to the heels.

Mary spent the next twenty minutes coaxing Gaia into the makeup chair, and the twenty minutes after that brushing Gaia's hair, spangling her with jewelry, and hunting down the exact right shade of lip gloss. At last she was done. "Oh my God, my brothers are going to be drooling," she announced, nodding at her finished work.

Gaia did feel prettier, but she also felt like someone else.

"Are you ready to meet the clan?"

If Gaia had the potential to feel nervous, now would have been an obvious time. "I guess so." She looked at Mary. Mary was still wearing blue nylon warm-up pants and a wife-beater tank top. Light freckles stood out on her thin shoulders and arms. Her hair was possibly the craziest mess Gaia had ever seen.

"Oh, I'm fine," Mary claimed. Her eyes darted around the room, and she picked up the first thing in her path, a blue chenille sweater, and stuck her head through. "All set," she confirmed.

Gaia was speechless as she followed Mary out of

the room. She remembered what Mary had said about not holding on to love very well.

"HOW ARE THE POTATOES COMING, Sam?" Mrs. Gannis's voice floated into the kitchen.

Sam looked up from the huge aluminum pot. He felt like a wolf with its leg caught in a trap. He finally understood the wolf's perverse temptation to chew off its own leg.

Why had he insisted, in that breezy, thoughtless way, that he would take care of the mashed potatoes? At the time, mashed potatoes seemed like the simplest thing on earth. You get potatoes; you mash them.

Besides, he'd figured this important job in the kitchen would keep him out of the fray of tense Gannis-family relations. It would give him a little breathing room from Heather, too, which they both needed. It had gotten to the point where every single thing brought them right back into the danger zone. A casual question from Heather's mother about what they'd done the previous night, an innocent reference to chess, a song on the radio about a girl with blond hair. Not being in the same room with Heather or talking about anything at all seemed the safest bet.

But Sam now understood that making mashed potatoes belonged in a category with particle physics, only harder. Before you mashed them, you had to cook them to make them soft, it turned out. How were you supposed to do that? First he'd thrown the whole pile in the oven, but what was the right temperature, and how long would it take? Then he took a cue from the one meal he'd ever made successfully—spaghetti. You made hard noodles soft by boiling them. So he boiled up the potatoes. It seemed to take hours before they were soft.

Now he was beating the crap out of those poor, boiled potatoes, working up a sweat. On the table was a whole tool kit of discarded instruments. The dinner fork was too small, obviously. The plastic whisk was wimpy. The metal slotted spoon made a tremendous racket. At last Mr. Gannis had acquainted him with a tool called a masher. A masher! A holiday miracle. Who could have guessed there'd be an implement built for this exact purpose?

Now he was madly mashing. Only the potatoes still didn't look right. Mashed potatoes were supposed to be smooth and pale yellow in color. These were lumpy and riddled with brown skin. Oh. Something occurred to him. You were supposed to take the skin off first, weren't you? He tried to fish out the bigger pieces of skin. It was hopeless.

Well, maybe they tasted good. He took a taste.

They tasted slightly more flavorful than air. All right, well, that's what salt was for. He shook in a small blizzard of salt.

He cast an eye at the fridge. Hmmm. He took out a box of butter. He remembered his mom once saying that her motto for cooking was, When in doubt, add butter. He threw in a stick. He threw in another stick. He was still in doubt. He threw in a third.

He stirred, hoping his mother hadn't just been being witty.

"SO, GAIA, HOW LONG HAVE YOU lived in New York?"

Now Gaia remembered

Disappointment

the problem with meeting strangers, particularly the parents-of-friends variety of strangers. They asked you things.

Gaia chewed a piece of turkey breast and tried to look agreeably at Mary's mother. She swallowed it with effort. "Well, I guess I—"

"No questions," Mary interrupted, coming to Gaia's rescue yet again. "No interrogating Mary's new friend, Mom."

Mary's mom laughed, which Gaia thought was pretty sporting of her. She gave Gaia a conspiratorial look. "My daughter is very bossy. You may have noticed this."

Gaia liked Mary's mom so far. She had dark red hair, sort of like Mary's but far better behaved. She wore cropped black wool pants and a bright orange velvet button-down shirt that clashed mightily with her hair. It wasn't standard middle-aged mom apparel, but it wasn't a grown-up person trying too hard to be cool, either.

The family's cook, Olga, appeared at Gaia's elbow with a steaming silver serving dish of baby vegetables. They were tidy and beautiful, not the creamed vegetable slop that usually showed up on Thanksgiving. Gaia guessed from Olga's accent that she was Russian and that she hadn't been speaking English for long. "Thank you," she murmured, trying to serve herself without bouncing baby potatoes into her lap. Or Mary's dress's lap.

"The food's fantastic," Mary's brother said to Olga.

Was he Paul or Brendan? Gaia couldn't remember. He was the cuter one, though, with light blue eyes and a quarter-inch of stubble on his chin.

"Absolutely," Mary's father agreed. He raised his glass for at least the fourth time in the meal. "Let's give thanks for Olga, a godsend." They all clinked glasses and agreed yet again. Gaia noted that there was sparkling water in his glass and not wine.

Olga seemed pleased with the attention. "Stop eet, Meester Moss," she ordered coyly.

Out of the corner of her eye, Gaia saw Mary stand up.

"I gotta pee. I'll be back in a minute," Mary announced to the table at large.

Mary's mom smiled in her forbearing way, and Gaia saw an emotion she wasn't sure how to analyze. There was something in the woman's face that struck Gaia as both worried and apologetic at the same time.

Suddenly Olga was back at Gaia's elbow, this time holding a basket of corn bread. It smelled like happiness. "Would you like some?" Olga asked.

Remotely, without really thinking about it, Gaia registered that Olga's words came out clear and crisp, without an accent.

"Of course. It smells delicious. Did you make this, too?" Gaia asked politely.

She served herself a fat piece of corn bread, and when she looked up, the entire Moss family, minus Mary, was staring at her. Olga was staring, too.

Gaia glanced from face to face. Oh, shit. What had she done now? These stares were too extreme to signify she'd used the wrong fork. She felt her mouth to see if she was wearing a mustache of cranberry sauce or anything.

"You speak Russian," Mr. Moss declared.

"I do?" Gaia found herself asking dumbly. She looked back at Olga and realized what must have happened. Olga must have murmured to her in Russian, and she must have answered in Russian without thinking. "I—I guess I do. Some, anyway," Gaia said, her fingers pinching and pulling at the napkin under the table.

Gaia felt badly thrown by this. Her mother spoke Russian to her from the time she was a baby, and Gaia grew accustomed to switching back and forth between languages hundreds of times a day. But those words gave her a feeling on her tongue that she associated purely with her mother. She hadn't spoken Russian in five years.

The table was still silent. Gaia felt her vision blurring. She stood up, keeping her gaze down. "Excuse me for just a moment," she mumbled.

"Of course," Mrs. Moss said.

Gaia walked blindly from the dining room and down the hallway. She hadn't meant to go to Mary's room, exactly. She just wasn't thinking.

The moment she opened the door to Mary's room, Mary froze. Gaia took two steps forward and froze, too.

Mary was bent far over her dressing table. Her eyes, turned now to Gaia, were large. In her hand was a rolled-up tube of paper. On the tabletop was a mirror, and on the mirror were several skinny rows of white powder cut from a tiny white hill. A razor blade winked at her in the light.

Gaia was naive and inexperienced, but she wasn't stupid. She knew what Mary was doing, and it made her feel sick.

She stared at Mary for another moment before she turned and left the room. She strode to the guest room and gathered her bag and coat.

She forced herself to take a detour on the way to the elevator.

"Mr. and Mrs. Moss," she announced from the entrance to the dining room. "I'm so sorry, but I have to go. Thank you very sincerely for letting me come."

She made her way to the elevator vestibule without a backward glance. She shrugged on her coat as the car descended. Yellow-green jacket. Red dress. She thought of Ed.

Outside on the street a siren blared, surprising her with its jarring unpleasantness.

"MY GOD, SAM, THESE ARE THE best potatoes I've ever eaten," Mr. Gannis said heartily, serving up his fourth helping. Sam hoped he wasn't going to be responsible for putting the man in the hospital with a heart attack.

He looked at the other plates around the table.

Each of the four underfed Gannis women still had on her plate an untouched pile of potatoes so calorie packed, they were bleeding butter. Heather met his eyes apologetically. "They're awfully, um . . . rich."

Dear Ed,

I'm sorry not to be saying this to you in person, but good-bye. I have to leave New York for a while. Things got out of hand with Ella, and, well . . . hopefully I'll get the chance to tell you about it someday.

It's time for me to set up a new life. I'm almost of legal age to be on my own now. And with all of my useful skills and abilities—not to mention my sunny temperament—I should have all kinds of great job possibilities:

> *Waitress*
> *Counter-person at 7-Eleven*
> *Tollbooth attendant*
> *Dishwasher*

So before I go, I just wanted to tell you this one thing, and I hope you'll forgive me for being sappy. But as I wracked my brains to think of stuff to be thankful for, the only thing I felt sure of is you. You are a much better friend than I've ever deserved.

I will never ever forget you for as long (or short) as I live.

> *Gaia*

He wheeled back
and opened the
door just wide
enough so that

pennsylvania

station

he could

toss the
bloody scalpel
into the trash
can.

GAIA LOOKED UP AT THE BIG

destination board that hung above the expansive waiting area of Penn Station. The board operated like the tote board on *Family Feud*—its tiles turning to reveal all the destinations. "Survey says . . . Trenton—Northeast Corridor—track 12—5:09." "Survey says . . . Boston—New England Express—track 9—5:42."

The place was ugly and crowded, and it smelled bad. And by the way, she wondered sourly, whose brilliant idea was it to call the train station smack-dab in the middle of New York City Pennsylvania Station? Hello? Ever take a geography class?

She felt tired and sad and cranky, no longer riding the powerful surge of anger and indignation that made it much more satisfying to run away.

She eyed the different cities, having absolutely no idea where she wanted to go. If she could go anywhere, she'd choose Paris. The Latin Quarter. She'd sit at the terrace of a quaint café across from the Notre Dame cathedral. Sip a double espresso as she read some poems from Baudelaire's *Fleurs du mal*. But that wasn't going to happen. Not today, anyway. She didn't have a passport, let alone money for the flight.

Hmmm. Maybe Chicago. She'd always wanted to visit the museum there. If she couldn't go to Paris, she could at least sit for an hour in front of Gustave

Caillebotte's wall-sized painting, *Paris Street, Rainy Day*. She first saw it in an art magazine she was flipping through while waiting to have a wisdom tooth pulled. The dreary scene spoke to her. Ambling along a cobblestone street on a gray, rainy day. That was her.

Engine, engine, number 9, going down the Chicago line. If the train falls off the track, do you want your money back? Yes. Y-e-s *spells yes, you dirty, dirty dishrag—you.*

She waited in the Amtrak ticket line behind a twenty-something couple from Jersey who—Gaia gathered from overhearing—had met the night before in an East Village club. They couldn't keep their hands off each other. Pinching, groping, giggling. It took everything Gaia had not to gag before she finally reached the window, where she came face-to-face with Ned, the ticket vendor.

She leaned forward to speak into the round voice amplifier.

"Chicago. One way."

He visibly perked up at the sight of her. His eyes leered at her from behind the thick Plexiglas.

"Going all by yourself?"

"Yeah. Is that a problem?"

"No . . . I just thought . . ." He raised his eyebrows suggestively.

"Thought what?"

"I don't know, a girl as pretty as yourself. Just seems like you'd have a . . . companion."

She sighed. "Well, I'm alone. Is there a sleeping car on that train going to Chicago?"

He swiveled on his seat and clacked a succession of keys at his computer. "Not until nine-thirty tonight."

"How about another train, then? Is there any train with a sleeping car leaving soon? Doesn't matter where it's going."

He looked at her. Then back at his screen. Ten more seconds of clacking. "There's a train to Orlando leaving in about an hour."

Gaia took a moment to ponder Orlando. It was a light-year away from this rainy day. It was an artificial city populated by tourists and the people who served the tourists. It was the land of water slides and theme parks, of Mickey Mouse and Jaws: The Ride.

"There's definitely a sleeper car?" Gaia wanted to confirm.

"There is a sleeping compartment, yes," Ned replied.

"I'll take it."

What the hell. She needed a vacation. And a little sun never hurt anybody. If it was warm enough, maybe she'd even buy a bikini. Hit the beach.

But she still had a whole hour to kill. After Ned slid her ticket under the window, she leaned a final time into the voice amplifier.

"Is there someplace that sells stamps around here?"

THE DOCTOR QUICKENED HIS STEPS

Getting Acquainted

as he approached the escalator that would carry him down into the bowels of Penn Station, unquestionably the most hideous train station in the country. But he was pleased to be here. He was downright overjoyed that his target had abandoned her safe perch up on Central Park West and come down here.

The ugly, subterranean corridors of this station were hardly fit for any human pursuit, but the place fit his needs quite perfectly.

According to his device, she was less than two hundred feet away. He began scanning the crowds in the hope of identifying her, acquainting himself a little with her face before he went to work.

GAIA REREAD HER LETTER TO Ed.

Out of Order

She was seated at the counter of a small coffee-and-muffin place in the train station's row of shops and eateries. What a stupid letter.

113

She went to crumple the letter, then stopped herself. She needed to say something to him. She thought of him calling her on Friday night at eleven o'clock, expecting another of their ricocheting, sleepy, oddly intimate conversations. He'd call her and find out she wasn't there. Really, really wasn't there.

Gaia sighed. She propped her chin in her hand. This was harder than leaving had ever been before. None of the other places had Ed.

Or Sam.

She folded her letter carefully and put it in the envelope. She wrote out Ed's address and placed the stamp in the corner so it wasn't crooked.

She felt the eyes of a man slumped at the next table over, hovering on her legs. She turned to him.

"Letter to Mom and Dad, sweetheart?" he asked. The smell of stale alcohol on his breath made Gaia wince.

Okay, she thought. That's it. She was sick of being leered at. Time to lose the dress. First the smarmy ticket vendor, now this loser.

"That's right. *Honey*," she said. Turning her attention back to the envelope, she licked the inside edge of the flap and sealed it.

"I like to watch you do that."

Gaia narrowed her eyes at the old pervert. Blech. As she got up, she knocked over her half-filled paper cup of coffee so that it spilled into the man's lap.

114

"Oh, I'm sorry," she lied. Then she swung her bag over her shoulder and took off.

A minute later she arrived at the women's rest room. A hand-scrawled sign taped to the door read Out of Order.

Perfect. She didn't need to pee. She could change her clothes in peace. But pushing open the door, she was immediately struck by the most powerful stench this side of the Hudson. She wanted to bolt, get out of there, but the room was empty—it would take her only a minute. Slip off the dress; pull on the jeans and sweatshirt. Off. On. Go. Like a pit stop at the Indy 500.

Just as long as no one lit a match.

She hurried to a stall. Holding her breath, she quickly slipped off Mary's shoes. She was peeling off the tights when all of a sudden she heard the door fly open.

"Let go of me!" a young female voice demanded.

Gaia looked through the crack of her stall: Two thugs had just entered, dragging behind them a teenage girl, dressed in a Nike sports bra, a leopard-print skirt, and just one stiletto heel. The other one must've been out there somewhere, floating among the sea of arrivals and departures. Quickly Gaia pulled the tights back up over her waist.

"Let's have it, bitch," ordered the shorter of the two, the one with the New Jersey Devils baseball cap.

115

"I don't got it. I swear," the girl cried.

The girl's hair was blond and tangled. She looked no older than Gaia—maybe sixteen or seventeen. Like Gaia, she'd probably done the rounds in foster care. Like Gaia, she'd probably run away at least once. Gaia suspected she was a prostitute and that the bigger guy was her pimp.

Each of the men grabbed one of the girl's pale arms, and together they shoved her into the dirty, white-tiled wall. She cried out in pain but managed to protect her head.

Gaia watched from the stall, letting her anger grow inside her chest. She hadn't had any real release in days. The anger was right there, so easy to call upon. There was her rage at Ella. Her fury at crazy, misguided Mary who had everything in the world and chose to screw it up.

"We're not playing games this time, sunshine," said the big, bearlike thug, whose belly hung out from a black T-shirt that asked, Got Milk?

Gaia saw his big, paw hands fumbling, then heard a noise. Flick. The Bear underlined his threat by holding up a fierce-looking switchblade that gleamed under the fluorescent light. "Now, let's see it, or you'll have a brand-new face to look at in the mirror." He held the knife against her cheek.

Gaia threw open the door of her stall.

The two men turned to stare at her.

Gaia forgot until she read the particular looks in their eyes that she was still wearing Mary's clingy, short red dress.

"Check you out," the man in the Devils hat said, studying her appreciatively. "We've got a regular party happening in here."

"Get off her," Gaia said.

"Pardon?" the big one asked, curiosity and amusement flashing in his eyes.

Gaia came closer. She spoke loudly and enunciated her words clearly. "Get off the girl. Let her go."

The Bear shook his head. "Is this your business? I don't think so. Why don't you stand aside, sweetheart? It'll be your turn next."

Gaia liked to protect her conscience by being absolutely clear about her intentions before she did harm. "I'm warning you. I'll kick your ass if you don't lay off her."

They both guffawed at her. "Len, grab her," the big one instructed the smaller guy. "This is gonna be fun."

Len did as he was told. When he reached for Gaia's arm, she backhanded him hard against the side of his neck. She caught him by surprise. He staggered sideways. Gaia kicked him hard in the chest and watched him slam into the hand-drying machine and slide to the floor. Len was disappointingly easy.

"Holy shit."

Gaia turned her head to see the Bear staring at her

117

with astonishment. She'd talked enough. She went after him.

The Bear was holding that blade, which made her approach trickier. She didn't hesitate, though. He stood to confront her, as she gambled he would, and she grabbed the knife-wielding arm by the wrist and bent it sharply behind him. She wrenched the other arm back to join the first and pulled him down so she could lodge her knee in his back.

The Bear groaned in pain. `The blade clattered to the ground.` The girl backed off into the corner, shivering.

Gaia let his arms go. Now that the blade was out of the way, she could give him some room.

He literally growled as he turned on her. He raised his arm to punch her in the jaw, but she caught it long before it landed and took the force of his own sloppy effort to flip him onto the linoleum. It was kind of a trademark move of hers. Effortless. Fairly graceful. Totally satisfying.

She backed up a few steps and let him get up. She hated herself for enjoying it, but she did. The Bear deserved anything she gave him and much more. He'd obviously spent too long believing that women could be intimidated. Let him remember this.

It was all he could do to get himself back on his feet. He staggered toward Gaia, swinging at her. His lack of skill was pitiful. There wasn't much point in trying to make it a real contest. She clipped his jaw with her right fist. She very likely broke his nose with her left. She wanted to leave him a memento.

His eyes displayed real fear now. Although Gaia couldn't feel fear, she was astute at recognizing its signs. Wild, darting eyes, rapid, shallow breaths. Gaia took that as her cue to finish him. She landed a hard, fast blow to a calculated spot under his ear. As expected, he crumpled to the floor, unconscious. Gaia knew he'd feel like shit when he came to. But he *would* come to and not much worse for the wear, either.

Suddenly the girl was shrieking. Gaia heard movement behind her. Much closer than she was expecting. Before she could regroup, the smaller guy appeared in the corner of her eye and shoved her hard in the back, sending her sprawling across the floor. Gaia got up fast, but he was barreling toward her.

Gaia turned, smashing his face with a roundhouse kick so powerful, she was sure she'd knocked him out. But she rushed the kick and threw herself badly off balance. She lost her footing, and her head came down hard against the corner of the porcelain sink.

Gaia groaned, holding the side of her head. She put both of her hands on the side of the sink for support and swayed back up to her feet.

At last the wretched-smelling room was quiet. The girl was backed against the tiled wall, gazing at Gaia with a stunned expression. "Are you okay?"

Gaia nodded. "I think so."

The girl put her hands up to her cheeks. "God, I

don't know what to say. Thank you. I never had any-one stick up for me before. Is there anything I can do for you? Buy you a coffee?

Gaia shook her head, then leaned herself up against the wall for support. Her eyes closed. Her head was pounding ferociously. She'd hit it hard.

"Hey," the girl said, reaching out to her.

"I'll be fine," Gaia tried to assure her. "Just give me a minute." She shielded her eyes with her hand. Her pupils were reacting sluggishly to the bright, fluores-cent light above.

Gaia started to slide down along the wall until she ended sitting up on the floor. Right next to the girl.

"I'm gonna call 911."

"No!" Gaia ordered. "I just need to rest." She started to drift, to give in. "Rest," she murmured again. And then she blacked out.

"ALL ABOARD FOR THE SOUTHERN Star, now boarding on track 12. All aboard!"

A large segment of the Penn Station crowd shuffled in unison toward the steps that led down to the waiting train.

120

He shuffled right along with them, his yellow-green eyes darting wildly. Searching for his target. His tracking device told him he was at point-blank range.

He reached the platform and caught a glimpse of her—a blond in a yellow-green Polartec jacket, carrying a black messenger bag. She was just stepping into one of the train's sleeper cars. He calmly made his way through the frantic human herd and boarded the same car, but at the other end. He walked with haste and purpose through the car, noticing the blond up ahead. She was scanning the compartment numbers as she advanced, finally entering one near the middle—on his left. Number 33A.

He arrived there not more than ten seconds later, pausing a moment to close his trench coat over his tie—a Salvatore Ferragamo yellow silk, dotted with little teddy bears. A client had given it to him a few years back to thank him for the perfect cheekbones he had given her. And they were perfect. He had truly outdone himself. So in the name of mastery and precision, he always wore the tie for these unholy moments. It had become part of the ceremony. Priests wear their robes; he wore his Ferragamo teddy bear tie under his cheap, washable trench coat.

He slowly, silently turned the brass handle of the compartment door and entered.

"Hey!" the blond snarled. "This one's taken."

"Is that right?" he replied with `zero inflection` in his voice. Then he grinned like a used car salesman as he stepped inside.

"Hey!" she repeated. "What do you think you're doing?"

He just kept smiling and closed the door behind him, pulling down the shade to cover the small window.

FIVE MINUTES LATER, HE STEPPED off the train. One of the conductors, doing some final work on the platform, gave him a curious look.

"Wrong train." The doctor tossed him a shrug, pretending to be embarrassed. "I must be blind."

He made his way back up the steps, back to the vast waiting room with the giant destination board. On the way he couldn't help thinking that the redheaded woman was a little off in her assessment. The girl was hardly "tough." Annoying, maybe, but tough? And her face wasn't so pretty, either. He imagined a little sculpting work on that nose would make for a significant improvement. . . . Perhaps a little Gore-Tex in those thin lips. An injection for those premature lines in her forehead. Under different circumstances he would have certainly left his card.

Oh, well . . .

He stopped at the rest room, whose door had a crude Out of Order sign taped to it. A perfect place to get rid of the instrument. But when he opened the door, the stench that hit him was so overwhelming, he had to quickly close it. He started off, then changed his mind. He wheeled back and opened the door just wide enough so that he could toss the bloody scalpel into the trash can.

A few feet to the left of the trash can he saw the prostrate body of a teenage girl. She was graceful, blond, quite pretty, in fact. Probably strung out on drugs. From the bruise on her face it looked like somebody had beaten her up. Her pimp, no doubt. It was pitiful, really.

He tossed the scalpel and watched it sink cleanly to the bottom of the trash can.

Too bad, he thought as he was making his exit. It had been such a trusty tool. Why, he had used it just that morning on Mrs. Gardner. Carved her the best-looking chin money could buy.

After I hit my head in the train station, I saw red and green sparklers bursting in front of my eyes. I must have passed out after that because I had this weird, dreamlike reverie about Ed and his being color-blind. Don't ask me why.

In my dream I was color-blind, too. I couldn't see green, which my whacked-out mind was convinced was the color of fear. Green looked the same as red, but red wasn't the color of fear, according to my dream self. What was red the color of?

It became this desperate, urgent thing I needed to figure out. What was red the color of? Green was fear; what was red?

What was red?

Well, red is the color of tomatoes, you might say sensibly, and shut up already. But you know how dreams are.

Anyway, I guess it was around then that I came to.

GAIA

Heather was too hurt to feel it. Her heart was on autopilot once more. "You've fallen for her, haven't you?"

not a penny

HER VISION AND AWARENESS CAME

back slowly. She blinked open her eyes and then closed them again. Then came the smell.

A Freaking Mess

What the hell was that? Where was she?

Gaia forced open her eyes. Oh God. The bathroom. The awful bathroom in the train station.

She sat up and looked around her. The thugs she'd fought were still passed out on the other side of the room. One of them was breathing loudly, fitfully. The other was clutching his jaw and moaning. They'd be up and at it soon enough.

And the girl. Where had the girl gone? Suddenly Gaia froze. She clambered to her feet, ignoring the searing pain in her temple. She checked the floor around her. She checked the stall where she'd begun to change. Mary's shoes were just where she'd kicked them off, but her bag was gone. Her bag with her wallet and her money and her clothes and shoes. Oh Christ, and where was her coat? Her coat with the train ticket to Orlando inside the pocket.

It was gone. All of it. Shit.

Well, that was gratitude for you. Save somebody's ass, and they'll rob you blind. Give a lot, and they'll take a lot more.

Shit!

She moved to the sink, splashed cold water on her badly bruised face. When she looked in the mirror, she got a shock. The left side of her face, her cheekbone all the way up to her temple, was already covered by an ugly purple bruise. The corner of her lip was bleeding, not to mention her mascara. Mary's velvet dress was ripped in two places. She was a freaking mess.

She retrieved the shoes and squeezed them on her sore feet, trying not to let herself cry. Now what? She'd arrived at the station full of cash and ready to start a new life.

She'd be leaving it broke and broken.

"WHERE IS GAIA? I THOUGHT SHE'D be joining us."

Hunted Prey

Ella took a protracted sip of her third glass of merlot, letting the velvety nectar wash over her tongue. Then she made a whole show of sliding back the sleeve of her blouse to glance at her watch.

"Oh, my, it is getting late, isn't it?" she said, wondering just how Gaia was doing. Although the obnoxious girl had run, she had certainly not gotten away. It was helpful that Gaia had taken off *after* Ella had slipped the tracking device into her coat pocket.

Ella sat with two of George's old agency friends and their wives. They were gathered at a table for six in the opulent dining room of La Bijou, an haute-cuisine restaurant on West Sixty-fourth Street, off Broadway. Most of the patrons here were silver-haired, silver-spooned socialites who just an hour earlier had been watching the new opera across the street at Lincoln Center. The waiters were French to a fault.

And then there was the menu. A menagerie of hunted prey, ranging from roasted duck to wild Scottish hare to rock Cornish hen with the word of caution to be careful of possible bird shot.

This was George's consolation prize to Ella for his being called away on Thanksgiving. The restaurant was fine with her; the company, a bore.

"I would so like to see Gaia, that poor thing," Mrs. Bessemer agreed. "Her parents were such lovely people."

Ella stifled a yawn. She shrugged daintily. "Gaia is a teenager, as you know. Her appearances are difficult to predict. I told her of course how much you'd all like to see her, but . . . Gaia has a mind and a schedule of her own." Ella lied effortlessly, without even needing to listen to herself.

Besides, she has an appointment with a doctor, Ella added silently. She tapped her menu. "Listen, why don't we just go ahead and order? I'll order a little something extra for Gaia so when—if—she comes, she can join right in. I'm sure she won't mind."

That said, her beeper went off. She opened her purse, extracted the beeper, and looked at the number. "That's probably her now. If you'll excuse me, I'll be back in a moment."

THE DOCTOR STOOD INSIDE THE

Insult and Injury

phone booth just outside Penn Station's southwest entrance, annoyed at this particular aspect of his written instructions. Who used a phone booth anymore? It was rather galling. He'd punched in the beeper number as instructed, and now he waited for the ring. There it was.

"Mrs. Travesura, I presume?"

"Yes, Doctor. Is it done?"

"Of course."

"Excellent. And in what condition is our patient?"

The woman could barely contain the pleasure in her voice.

"Alive, as promised," the doctor responded. "Though not likely to recount her experiences anytime soon." He wouldn't reward her with the graphic details.

"No one saw you?"

The doctor sighed impatiently. "Absolutely not."

"I'm sure. Now, did you remove the bug from the pocket of her coat?"

This had grown annoying, verging on insulting. "Mrs. Travesura. I am a professional. You need not grill me on these absurd details."

"I apologize . . . *Doctor*. If you'll permit me one last question?"

He sighed again. "Yes."

"Are you holding the tracking device in your hand?"

"I am."

"Good. Good-bye, then, you disgusting, evil bastard."

The doctor was blinking in fury, barely able to process the childish affront, when the device began beeping in his hand. He held the readout close to his face, trying to discern the message in the darkness of the booth.

He could make out numbers scrolling across the screen. 5 . . . 4 . . . 3 . . . 2 . . . 1 . . .

The explosion ripped the tiny booth apart.

GAIA TURNED AT THE SOUND OF

No Refunds

the explosion. Virtually everyone in the station jumped at the noise. Within a minute she heard a symphony of sirens.

She glanced ahead of her in frustration at the single open ticket booth. She glanced behind her at the ten or so people who continued the line, all of whom looked as cranky as she felt. She didn't care if her own feet exploded. There was no way she was losing her place in this line.

Scores of policemen were zipping in and out the south doors of the station. Many civilians were running around, too, wanting a piece of the action.

"There was a bomb!" she heard somebody shouting. "Right out front. Blew up a phone booth!"

There were lots of oohs and ahs and murmurs throughout the station, but Gaia was morbidly amused to see that not a single person left her line.

Just wait until the camera crews from the local news get here—then it will really be a circus, Gaia found herself thinking.

Another ticket salesperson opened a second window. That would speed things up. Minutes later, Gaia was waved forward. Before she reached the window, she realized she was being reunited with her old friend Ned.

"How can I help you?" His eyes showed not a flicker of recognition. Apparently she was a lot less attractive battered and bruised.

"Remember me? I bought a ticket to Orlando from you about an hour and a half ago. The sleeper car?"

His face was blank.

"Well, listen, my ticket got stolen. I need to get a refund."

Ned shrugged. "Sorry. Train 404 to Orlando is long gone. Unless you can produce the ticket, I can't give you a refund."

Gaia rolled her eyes. "How can I produce a ticket if it got stolen?"

Ned's face was devoid of interest or sympathy. "No ticket, no refund."

Gaia was starting to feel desperate. If she couldn't get a refund, she'd have no money. Not a cent. Nothing. How long could she last on the streets of New York flat broke? Even the flophouses cost a few dollars. "Ned, please. We're . . . *friends,* practically. Can't you help me out here? I really, really need the cash."

Ned shook his head. He wouldn't look anywhere near her eyes. A pretty, confident, sexily clad girl with a wallet full of cash was interesting to Ned. A bruised, desperate, penniless girl was not. He focused his gaze over her head. "Next?" he called to the person at the front of the line.

Suddenly Gaia felt overcome by a wave of dizziness so powerful, it almost made her sick to her stomach. She grabbed the edge of the high counter to steady herself. "Ned! Ned. Please. Don't be an asshole. Just listen to me for a minute, okay?" Gaia could hear her voice rising in her ears. "Ned! *Ned!*" God, if he weren't enclosed in the bullet-proof booth, she'd love to belt him. "Ned!"

The next thing Gaia knew, there was a police officer, a young Hispanic man with a crew cut, grabbing her by the arm. "Come on, miss," he said. "There's a long line here, okay? Gotta keep it moving."

"But I—" Gaia grabbed her arm back. "My ticket got stolen. And all my money. And I really need—"

Gaia stopped. He wasn't listening. It was hopeless. She could tell the policeman was looking her over, and she could tell exactly what he was thinking, too. Gaia was wearing a shredded, clingy minidress, high heels, and a big bruise on her head.

"Come on, miss," he said again. His voice was patient, tired, pitying. "Do you want to step out of the way, or do you want me to arrest you? I'd think a girl like you would have good reason to stay out of the way if you can help it."

A girl like you. It was obvious he thought she was a hooker. A hooker addicted to drugs who'd just been shaken up by her pimp. It was ironic, but that was exactly what she looked like. While the *actual* drug-addicted hooker who'd been shaken up by her pimp was zipping off to Orlando in a pair of jeans and a fluorescent yellow-green Polartec jacket, carrying almost 450 bucks in her pockets.

Gaia wondered if her luck could be any worse.

HEATHER LAY BACK ON THE COUCH

The (Other) Magic Word

and rested her head on Sam's lap as he flipped channels with the remote control. Without looking at her, he rested his hand on her stomach. She felt her iridescent pink silk blouse riding up over her belly button. She studied his face above her. It was so unbelievably handsome. His strong jaw was smooth and clean shaven for this event. His brownish gold hair had gotten long and was curling around the collar of his cobalt blue oxford shirt. His complicated hazel eyes were framed by long black lashes. She wanted those eyes on her. On her face, her hair, her breasts, the bare swath of skin above her skirt.

But at the moment his eyes were riveted on the television screen as he burned through almost a hundred channels' worth of programming. It was hopeless sitting in a room with a boy, a television, and a remote control. You never got any attention or even the pleasure of watching any one show for longer than three minutes.

She smiled up at him. She didn't mind. This was the kind of relationship problem she enjoyed having.

She heard clinking sounds from the kitchen. Her parents cleaning up the last of the dishes. She heard the faint sound of laughter—Lauren talking on the phone. From her and Phoebe's room she heard the inevitable hum of the stair-climbing machine, Phoebe's most prized possession. God forbid an ounce of turkey should stick to her hips.

"Having a nice Thanksgiving?" she asked Sam.

"Hmmm," he said, his eyes not flickering from the screen.

"My dad loved your potatoes."

"Mmmm."

Sam wasn't going to talk, obviously. But he did move the remote control to the hand that rested on her stomach. He used his free hand to caress her forehead, softly pushing her hair back from her face. She breathed in deeply and let out a sigh of pleasure. It felt so nice, she wished they could just stay like that forever.

For the first time in weeks she felt truly relaxed. The dinner had gone fairly well. No hysterics or anything.

She was relieved to have finally confronted Sam with the Gaia issue and gotten the answer she wanted.

"Hey, wait, hold it there a minute," she ordered. The local news was showing footage of the Thanksgiving parade. She used to love that when she was a kid. The camera zoomed in on one enormous balloon after another: `Barney, some pig or other, a Rugrat,` two gigantic M&M's. She remembered sitting on her dad's shoulders for hours—so long that both her feet would fall asleep—and watching the floats and marching bands go by.

The report on the parade ended abruptly, and the picture changed to show a gloomy-looking Penn Station lit up by dozens of red flashing lights.

"God, what happened there?" Heather mumbled.

"Shhh," Sam ordered, leaning in to listen.

". . . Two mysterious tragedies here in one evening," the telegenic special reporter was saying into the camera. "Are they related, and if so, how? That is what detectives are asking tonight as they start a two-pronged investigation here in Penn Station."

The camera moved to show a phone booth that had been blown to bits. Twisted metal and glass were everywhere. "A bomb was detonated here, outside of New York City's busy Penn Station, less than an hour ago. . . . One person dead, not yet identified . . ."

The camera moved to show a stretcher carrying a

girl. ". . . And in a second calamity, a young girl, not yet identified, was brutally slashed and disfigured in her sleeping compartment in a train pulling out of Penn Station at 6:47 P.M. She remains in a coma at Roosevelt Hospital . . ."

Beneath her, Heather felt Sam's legs go rigid. "Oh my God," he whispered. "Jesus."

Suddenly Sam was on his feet, dumping Heather's head rudely onto the couch. She sat herself upright quickly. "Sam, what's your problem?"

Sam was stammering, pointing at the TV. "Th-That's—could that be? I think that might be Gaia's coat! That green coat? Oh my God."

Sam was pacing, holding his head, unable to watch the screen and then watching it again. "Her hair. Do you see her hair? It's blond. Is that Gaia? Could that be her?"

Heather glared at him in disbelief. He was *freaking*. Absolutely freaking. She'd never seen him anything like this. She wanted to slap him.

She went closer to the TV and studied the picture. Yes, she recognized that hideous jacket. She squinted and tried to get a look at the face, a crazy mixture of emotions swarming around her heart.

Just before the camera switched back to a shot of the shattered phone booth, Heather caught a glimpse of the girl's face. It was heavily bandaged, but she could see enough to know it wasn't Gaia.

137

Sam paced. His face was the color of skim milk.

Heather angrily snatched the remote control from his hand and used it to switch off the TV.

"What are you doing?" Sam demanded fiercely. He tried to take the remote back. His eyes were wild.

"Calm down!" she shouted at him.

"Heather! Please!" He made another grab.

"Calm down, you idiot! It *wasn't her!*" she screamed at him.

Those were the magic words. Sam stopped moving finally. In his beautiful hazel eyes Heather saw so much hope and relief, she thought she might throw up.

Sam took a breath. "What did you say?"

Heather didn't try to hide the disgust in her face. And Sam was so far away, he didn't seem to see it or care. "I said, it wasn't her. It wasn't Gaia," Heather repeated flatly.

"Are you sure?" Sam asked, his eyes too vulnerable for words.

Heather couldn't help wondering, in a profoundly awful way, whether anybody, *anybody* would ever care about her as much as Sam seemed to care for Gaia right now.

Real rage began smoldering in her stomach. Couldn't he at least *pretend* he didn't adore Gaia so deeply? Couldn't he consider

Heather for *one single second* and attempt to spare her feelings? "I'm sure," she spat out bitterly.

"Oh," he said.

Finally he brought his eyes back to Heather. He seemed to remember she was in the room with him. He took another few breaths. He looked tentative. He was ashamed. But more than that, more than anything, he was relieved that cut-up girl wasn't his beloved Gaia.

In one quiet moment everything was clear. They'd both known the truth long before this. Sam was obsessed with Gaia.

Heather was too hurt to feel it. Her heart was on autopilot once more. "You've fallen for her, haven't you?" Her voice was empty.

Sam ran a hand through his hair, leaving most of it standing straight up. He looked down at the floor, then back to Heather's eyes. "I guess I have." His voice was so quiet, he mouthed the words as much as said them.

At least he didn't lie or try to bullshit her, she told herself. His honesty made for cold comfort, though.

"I don't know why. I'm so sorry," he finished earnestly.

She hated him.

"Don't apologize," she snapped icily. "Just . . . get out of here. I don't want to see you right now. We'll talk about it some other time." Anger was accessible to her right now. Pain was not.

Numbly she strode to the coat closet and grabbed his corduroy jacket. She practically threw it at him. "Please go!"

He looked sorry, all right. Sorry and regretful, but also relieved. So relieved, he was ashamed of himself. He was happy to be getting out of there and away from her.

She hated him.

"I'm sorry, Heather," he said again as he walked out of the apartment. "I'm really sorry."

She hardly waited until he was clear of the door before she slammed it with all her might.

She wheeled around. "I hate you!" she shouted at the empty living room.

For some reason the story of Medea invaded her head again. The bitter, scorned, miserable woman.

Heather went back to the couch and threw all the pillows on the floor. It was lucky for Sam that they didn't have any children.

GRANDPA FARGO'S FAMOUS APPLE PIE

Ingredients:

8 red Rome apples
1 recipe pie crust
$1/2$ cup sugar
$1/2$ teaspoon cinnamon
2 tablespoons flour
pinch of nutmeg
pinch of salt
1 tablespoon butter
1 well-beaten egg

Filling:

Peel and core apples and slice into $1/2$"
wedges. Place in large mixing bowl. Add
sugar, cinnamon, flour, nutmeg, and salt.
Toss until thoroughly blended.

Roll $1/2$ pie crust dough to $1/8$-inch thickness.
Line 9-inch pie plate with dough, allowing $1/2$
inch to extend over edge. Add filling. Dot
with 1 tablespoon butter. Roll out rest of
dough and lay over pie plate, tucking excess
dough along pie-plate edge. Crimp along edge
with knife handle to create a wavy pattern.
Use fork to puncture a few holes into top of
crust in pattern of your choice. Brush top of
pie with 1 well-beaten egg.

Bake at 425 degrees for 15 minutes. Turn
down heat to 350 degrees and bake for $1/2$
hour.

Without
thinking,
she threw
herself on
his **freedom/**
nothingness
bed. It was
sick, but so
delicious.

GREEN. RED. GREEN. RED. OUT the front window of the diner on University Place, Gaia watched the traffic light run its cycle again and again. She thought of Ed.

She'd meant to go, she really had. But here she was again.

She realized she was still shivering. She put her hand to her throbbing head. God, what she would do for a dollar to buy a hot cup of coffee.

"Excuse me, sweetheart, but if you're not going to order anything, I'm going to have to ask you to leave." The waitress wasn't mean. She was old and tired. She had turned a blind eye to Gaia for the last forty-five minutes. Now she was doing her job.

"But it's so cold out," Gaia said, mostly to herself.

"What's that, hon?" The waitress leaned in.

"Nothing, I'm going." It took all of Gaia's strength to climb out of the booth and balance herself on her feet. The room spun around her. She closed her eyes, trying not to be sick.

"Are you okay?" the woman asked.

Gaia opened her eyes. She steadied herself against the top of the vinyl seats. "Yes, I'll be fine," she said. She walked as steadily as she could to the door and steeled herself for the cold blast of wind.

Back out on the street she hugged herself for warmth. She wished she had her coat. She wished she had a blanket. She wished she had anything heavier than this skimpy red dress. And Mary was wrong. These shoes *were* too small. Her feet ached.

She made herself walk. What now? Where could she go? The light to cross Thirteenth Street was red. To cross to the west side of University was green. She crossed.

She kept walking west. Her teeth chattered uncontrollably. When she got to Fifth Avenue, the light to cross was red. The light to cross Thirteenth to the south was green. She crossed.

The wind that whipped up Fifth Avenue seemed to find its way into her skin—into every muscle and nerve and tendon. It chilled her blood in her veins, and her veins circulated that chilled blood all through her body and into her heart.

The light to cross Twelfth Street was red. The light to cross to the west side of Fifth was green. She crossed. Without instructions her feet were taking her to her home in New York City—Washington Square Park. She crossed Twelfth Street and got another green signal to cross Eleventh. The miniature Arc de Triomphe that marked the northern entrance to the park was in full view now.

She glanced up and stopped. The building to her right was familiar. Familiar mostly in a painful way. It was Sam's dormitory, the place where she'd walked in on Sam and Heather having sex.

She started walking and stopped again. Another image appeared in her mind. The broken doorknob. Too well she remembered the wobbly brass sphere almost falling off in her hand, giving her access to one of the worst sights a person could see. But right now, from where she stood, the broken doorknob held a certain appeal.

SAM FELT DISGUSTINGLY LIGHT ON

his feet as he walked down Third Avenue. He should have been miserable or at least heavyhearted. But he wasn't. His muscles were buzzing with life. The world looked new to him. Clean and fresh and in excellent focus.

He looked at the shops on either side of the avenue, closed up for the holiday, with their iron safety gates pulled down and locked. It was the kind of sight that had depressed him when he'd first moved to New York. Tonight he liked it.

He was sorry about Heather. He was sorry *for* Heather. He genuinely was. She didn't deserve to be treated the way she'd been treated. But nor did she deserve to have a boyfriend who thought so constantly of someone else.

And now, for the first time in months, he felt free. Free for the moment, anyway.

Free to be with Gaia, a voice in his mind added.

Hold up, he ordered that voice. He wasn't sure about anything yet. He wasn't sure what the real status was between him and Heather. He wasn't sure whether Gaia had ever looked at him the way he looked at her.

Most importantly, Gaia was a major proposition. For him, he knew, she represented a love-of-his-life possibility. He had to be slow. He had to be careful. He had to make sure he didn't somehow get killed in the process.

He stopped at a red light. His happy legs had covered a lot of ground without him even knowing it. Now where?

He imagined his dorm room. It would be so lonely tonight. The place would be absolutely deserted. But where else could he go? All his friends were back home or visiting relatives. He imagined his family back in Maryland. His older brother was bringing his new girlfriend home to meet the folks. His parents were sorry that he wasn't there, and now, the way things had turned out, so was he.

His mind turned to Gaia, as it often did. Where was she spending Thanksgiving? She didn't have parents; that was one of the few things he knew about her. A very sad circumstance on a day like this. Did she like the Nivens, those people she lived with? Was she in their house on Perry Street right now? Was she happy? On some level he knew she wasn't, and that gave him a deep, achy feeling he didn't often feel for another person.

Why did he care for her like this? How had it happened?

He saw the lights of an all-night diner burning up ahead. It was one of the few establishments open along the whole avenue. Maybe he'd duck in there. Find himself a copy of *The New York Times* and while away the evening with a couple of cups of coffee.

THERE IS NO WAY SAM COULD BE here, Gaia told herself for the tenth time. She was certain of it. Sam was the kind of guy who had a loving family and scores of other good backup options for Thanksgiving in case the family thing wasn't happening. In fact, he was probably sharing warm food and feelings with the she-wolf.

Still, Gaia felt self-conscious as she stepped into the

entrance of the NYU dorm. She was tired of looking like a prostitute in this awful dress. The place was nearly deserted but for the omnipresent security guard at a table a few yards into the lobby. Shit, she'd forgotten about him. He was absorbed in a noisy hockey game playing on the tiny TV perched on the table less than a foot from his eyes.

The warm air felt so good. If she could just manage to stay in here for a few minutes, maybe she'd be okay. Now that she'd finally slowed her pace, the dizziness was coming back.

The guard and his TV were in their own little world. Maybe she could just . . .

"Excuse me? Uh, miss? Can I help you?" Damn. There must have been a time-out in the game or something. The security guard was now staring at her with his full attention.

"H-Hi. I j-just. Um. My f-f-friend lives here, and he inv-v-vited me over," Gaia said. She was shivering so hard, it was difficult to talk.

The security guard got a knowing look in his eyes. "Hey, I'm sorry, sweetheart, but we can't have none of that here." He took in her slinky, ripped dress, her heels, what was left of her makeup. "This is a college building, you know? You oughtta get out of here." He kept jingling his keys in one hand. It seemed like a nervous habit. She noticed that the key ring said Mustang and showed the black

149

silhouette of a horse bucking against a blue background.

"B-B-But I—" Gaia knew there was really no point in arguing. There was no way he was letting her past his table unless she clobbered him, and she simply didn't have the strength. She just wanted to use up a little more time inside. She couldn't face the cold again. What could she talk about with him? The New York Rangers? Cars? Guns?

"Look, kid, I'm sorry. I really am. You look like hell"—he shook his head with a mix of sympathy and disgust—"but you can't stay here."

SAM TOOK OUT HIS WALLET SOON

after he'd sat down at a table to see how much cash he had. He rifled through every compartment. Unfortunately, he had none. He checked the pockets of his jacket.

Moving Right Along

He had no money. Not one red cent.

He remembered now that he'd given Heather two twenties to buy pies for dessert from an overpriced Upper East Side gourmet shop.

He flagged down a waiter. "Excuse me, do you take credit cards?"

The surly waiter fixed him with a look that clearly meant no.

"Do you know if there's a bank or an ATM around here?" he asked.

The waiter looked like Sam had burned his house down. "Twenty-theerd," the man replied in a clipped, Eastern European accent.

"But this is Thirty-first Street," Sam said, wondering why he bothered.

"Twenty-theerd," the waiter said, louder.

Sam blew out his breath. "Okay, thanks." He headed toward the door. It looked like he was going to end up in his dorm room after all.

AS SHE LEFT THE DORMITORY, THE

Moony cold practically knocked Gaia senseless. She was covered head to toe in goose bumps, only they didn't seem the least bit compelling.

Suddenly, a few yards from the building, she stopped. Her eye caught on a logo on the hood of a car parked directly outside the dorm's entrance.

So she wasn't totally senseless. She walked slowly

around the car, studying it for another moment. Then she saw the vanity license plate. RANGER-FAN, it read. Oh God. Could it be? Could there actually be a small piece of good luck in all of this blackness?

Gaia put her hands to her head. She needed to expel the dizziness, to gather her wits and her physical capabilities if she had any left.

Okay, now. She raised her foot to the side of the hood and shoved it hard. The car rocked violently, and a car alarm blasted through the silent night air. Perfect.

She ran to the side of the building and backed herself up against the wall, a few feet beyond the front awning.

Exactly as she'd hoped, the security guard dashed out of the building to check on his precious vehicle. Thank God.

Gaia found enough speed left in her legs to carry her into the building, undetected. With excitement fizzing in her veins she sprinted into the stairwell and up four flights to the door of Sam's suite.

She slowed down. Okay, this was starting to bring back some bad memories. Still, it was warm. There was a bed. She had to put her emotions on ice for a while.

Slowly she opened the door to the common room of the suite, blanking out her mind. Good, it was empty. The door to room B5, with its infamous doorknob, was just ahead.

Please be broken still, she begged of the doorknob. She closed her eyes and closed her hand around it at the same time.

Yes. She let out a breath. It jiggled brokenly in its socket, and she was able to push open the door.

Icy as her emotions—and the rest of her—were, she wasn't prepared for the effect of the smell. The tiny dorm room smelled like Sam. In a good way. In an aching, moony, grab-you-by-the-heart way. The smell intoxicated her. It gave her shivers. Why was it that a smell could evoke a person more powerfully than a million pictures could?

This, she realized, was what people meant when they talked about chemistry.

Without thinking, she threw herself on his bed. It was sick, but so delicious. His bed. Where he slept. She imagined him in his boxers, tangled in the sheets. His shoulders, his torso, his stomach, his . . . God, what heady torture.

She sat up. She had to pull herself together. She was semidemented from bashing her head and from cold and exhaustion. Time to act like a sane person.

First thing was to get out of this dress. She pulled it over her head in one swift move. She pulled the shoes off her miserable feet and stripped off the tights. She wound up the dress, the shoes, and the tights in a ball and sank them into the wastebasket next to Sam's nightstand.

Shower. She needed a shower. She wanted a boiling hot shower so bad, she could feel it.

Aha. There was a towel hanging over the door of Sam's closet. On his bureau were a bar of soap and a bottle of shampoo. Eureka. She had to hope that this dorm really was as empty as it appeared.

She cast off her bra and panties, feeling an unfamiliar and lustful pleasure at seeing them strewn about on Sam's bed. She wrapped herself in the towel and set off in search of the bathroom.

She listened for the sound of the germs, and they led her to a totally filthy and wonderful bathroom off the common room. What could you ask from a bathroom shared by four college students? She didn't care. She loved every microbe.

She blasted the shower as hot and strong as it would go and climbed in.

She gathered sex felt pretty good, but she couldn't imagine it felt much better than hot jets of water pounding against her frozen flesh. Ahhhhhhh.

Suddenly the tiles were starting a slow spin around her. She pressed her palms into her eyeballs. It didn't help. She sat right down on the floor of the shower and let the water beat down on her head. She would wait for the dizziness to pass.

When her body finally felt warm from the outside in, she got back to her feet and scrubbed her hair and face and body and rinsed for ages. She had to force herself to turn off the water.

She wrapped herself in Sam's towel and crept back into his room. Now what? Should she sleep naked or should she . . . hmmm. She went over to Sam's bureau and opened the top drawer. Waiting for her there were a soft, clean, ribbed white tank top undershirt and a pair of well-worn cotton boxers in a faded plaid of blues and greens. Yum.

This night had turned from sheer torment to the most sensual and thrilling experience of her life. She felt a bit like a stalker, but she wasn't doing any harm, was she? She'd put everything back in order before Sam returned. He'd never even guess she was there.

On the floor at the foot of his bed she suddenly spied his shoes, the scuffed leather, lace-up shoes he'd been wearing the day they played chess. For some reason, the sight of them stole her breath. Though empty, the shoes sat in a pose that was strongly suggestive of Sam—of exactly how he stood and walked. It was crazy that a pair of uninhabited shoes could carry so much subtle information about him. But they did. They brought him right into the room with her.

The aching feeling was back in force. She shivered again. An army of goose bumps invaded her arms and legs and back. *Almost like fear.*

It was like fear, but it wasn't fear.

Maybe it was . . . love.

Dear Gaia,

I made a decision today, a few hours after you left. I'm going straight—I'm giving up drugs. Not "one day at a time" or any of that crap. I'm giving it up for good. Right now. When you saw me snorting coke today, I saw myself through your eyes, and I hated what I saw. If I keep going like this, I'm going to die. Yeah, it's that bad. And I don't want to die yet.

You probably wish I'd just leave you alone. You're wondering why I'm dragging you into my problems. I'm not sure, exactly. I'm not a very reflective person. But for some reason, I really do want to be friends with you. I want to be close. (Don't worry. Not in that way. I'm not a lesbian.) I've made a specialty out of not caring what other people think. But I do care what you think. I want you to think I'm a good person.

I have this idea about you and me. I have everything—parents, money, friends, a lot of love. You have nothing. I get so much, and the thing that sucks is, my heart is like a sieve. I want you to have some of what I have. You deserve it, not me.

That's weird, right? Sorry, it's just how I am.

So, anyway, I'm kicking the drugs whether I ever see you again or not.

But I just wanted you to know that wherever you are,

however you feel, you always have a friend out there in the world. Not a perfect friend or anything, but one who's trying to do better.

                    Mary

Mary finished the letter and stuck it in an envelope. She'd get a stamp from her mom later. Then she got an idea. She went to her desk drawer, where she'd had a one-pound bag of M&M's ever since Halloween. She dumped the entire contents on her floor and picked out every last one of `the red ones.` She transferred the letter into a bigger, sturdier envelope and threw in all of the red M&M's to keep it company. She threw in a few green ones, too.

Now she'd need a whole bunch of stamps.

He was
leaning
forward,
leaning
over her. So
close now.
So real.
"Can I?" he
whispered.

**the
color
of
love**

"HEY, BAUMAN, WHAT'S UP?" SAM said to the security guard. "How're the Rangers?"

Something Sublime

Bauman grimaced. "Down by two in the third. How's your holiday, Moon?"

Sam actually thought about his answer. "Good," he said. "Surprisingly good." Except for the fact that all twenty digits had lost feeling about a mile ago. He rubbed his hands together. "Quiet here tonight, huh?"

"Yes, it is," Bauman answered vaguely, his attention back on the game.

"Later. Happy Thanksgiving," Sam called over his shoulder as he entered the stairwell. Not that he expected his bland sign-off to compete with the Rangers. He was pathologically polite. He couldn't help himself.

He took the stairs slowly. Was he the only student in the entire building? It felt almost eerie.

None of his suite mates were around, that much he knew. He swung open the door of the common room. The place was exactly the pigsty he'd left it. He didn't even bother to turn on a light. He'd so completely frozen himself, walking almost seventy blocks, he was eager to strip down and climb under his down comforter.

He took out his key and had started to fit it in the

lock when the doorknob fell off in his hand. "Shit. Gotta get that fixed," he cursed under his breath, as he did two out of three times he entered his room.

A warm, reddish light from the street was filtering through the small window, lighting the bed. . . .

Oh. Jesus. Sam stepped backward. He was suddenly transported to a Three Little Bears moment. There was someone sleeping in his bed.

He stepped forward and froze. His heart stopped beating. He stopped breathing. Brain function shut down.

Could that someone be . . . ?

He turned his eyes to the door and then back to the bed again, sure that the mirage would be gone. It wasn't. There was still a sublimely beautiful blond girl in his bed who looked very much like Gaia.

He'd heard that people hallucinated in the happiest way just before they died of exposure. He hadn't chilled himself that badly, had he?

Now. Time to breathe, lungs. Time to beat, heart. His vital organs appeared to need a little coaching. There. Better. Okay, deep breaths. Yes.

He would just calm down, slow down, and think a minute.

He crept a little closer, terrified that this magnificent vision would disappear if he disturbed the air the slightest bit.

Still there. Please stay, he begged it. If this was a

161

figment of his imagination, then he prayed his imagination would keep it up.

He would just look at her. That would be okay, wouldn't it? Even if it was an imagined version of her, he still wanted to look. The few interactions he and Gaia'd had were so charged or awkward or plain antagonistic that he never got to study her, to see how her face looked in repose.

Her head was turned to the side, and her silken yellow hair—hair he'd fantasized about more times than was good for him—was splayed out on the pillow, leaving a shadow of dampness on the white cotton. Her bewitching eyes were closed in sleep. Her face was serene and lovely beyond description—light freckles over her cheeks. He drew closer. Palest, finest down along her jawline. Her eyelids flickered. He drew back.

She was still again. He came closer. His eyes moved down her neck.

Oh Christ! She was wearing his T-shirt. He felt the blood churning in his ears, gathering in other parts of his body. His T-shirt, which had spent its long, dutiful life covering large, rough stretches of masculine skin, now had the exquisite experience of gracing skin so delicate and fine, it was almost transparent. He envied it.

He saw that the too large shirt had gotten pulled around under her, revealing the sloping side and top of her breast.

He had to look away. Partly because it was too much to take and partly because he felt wrong seeing her like this, without her knowing he was seeing her. Without her wanting him to.

He made himself take a few steps backward and put his hands over his face to regain his composure.

He knew now, more than ever before, that he loved her. He loved her deeply and urgently, with a fierceness that made him know he'd never grasped, even grazed, the concept of love before. But he couldn't go on like this, without knowing how she really felt.

And what if she wasn't real at all but a figment of his fevered, lustful mind?

Well, then she'd be more likely to tell him what he dreamed of hearing.

A Real Kiss

GAIA WAS DREAMING A BLISSFUL dream. Surrounded as she was by the smell and feel of Sam, by his place and his things, it was natural that she should dream of him vividly.

In the dream he was there beside her, sitting on the edge of the bed. He was so close, she could feel his warmth and smell his smell more intensely. An alive smell now.

He took her hand so gently and held it. Just held it. Making her safe.

Consciousness was tickling her eyelids, summoning her. *Please, sleep, stay with me. Don't make me go back yet.*

But it was happening. She couldn't help it. She was waking up in spite of every effort to fight it. She flicked open her eyes.

No.

She closed them again.

How could it be?

She opened them again. Was the dream still with her? . . . Or was it . . .

"Sam?" she whispered, her heart filled with awe.

He was still holding her hand. In the dream and . . . here. He was still holding it, one of his hands cupping her fingers, the other holding her wrist. His beautiful hands with the wide nails and fraying cuticles. The ones he'd used to stomp all over her chess pieces that day in the park when this had started.

"Gaia," he said. She'd never heard her name sound just that way before.

He was leaning forward, leaning over her. So close now. So real. "Can I?" he whispered.

"Please," she said.

He took his hand from her wrist and touched his first two fingers to her elbow, then drew them in an air-light caress up to her shoulder. "Mmmm," she sighed.

As his head hovered over her she looked up at his neck and chin, touching her finger to the place where his whiskers started, moving them up over his jaw, feeling the slight hollow of his cheek, the strong bones that came together at the corner of his eye. He gazed down at her, his eyes voracious and questioning. She turned her head to face him straight on.

"Oh," he said, drawing in his breath. He touched his fingers to the ugly bruise along the side of her cheek and forehead. His face showed real worry. "Are you okay?"

She felt like crying just then. She'd forgotten about everything that had happened. Now she remembered, and she felt ashamed of it and of all the ugliness and violence she represented in Sam's good, peaceful life. "I'm sorry," she said randomly, her eyes filling with tears.

"No, Gaia," he whispered. "Don't. Just . . . be with me."

The feelings inside her were too round and full. She couldn't hold them. Her chest was bursting, and her head was spinning.

He pulled her up so she was sitting beside him and gently held her face in her hands. He put his lips, gentle as sunlight, to the wound on her forehead, then dotted her cheekbone with kisses.

Please, please, please, she begged silently. Wishing.

Oh God. And then he found it, and her wish happened. His lips found her mouth, and the gentleness gave way to intensity. A kiss. A real kiss more perfect than any imagined. She was kissing him back, hungrily, pressing herself against him.

A thought came to her as his lips melted into hers. *This,* she thought, *is the mouth that I was meant to kiss. This is the mouth I will always kiss, and no other.* And blending into that thought was another thought. More a feeling than a thought, because there were no words to it at all. But the feeling was that her lips and her hands had found a home. The one safe, healing place on earth. And that maybe, maybe . . . who could ever say? But maybe she really would have kids someday. (Not just one.) Because there was somebody in the world for her. She knew that now, from this kiss, and nobody could take that away.

His hands held the back of her head now; they were buried in her hair. His lips explored hers. She tasted him and felt him and smelled him all at once. Her senses mixed and blurred. Her blood roared in her ears.

He stood up and pulled her with him. He pressed the entire length of his body against her. She tilted back her head, not wanting to break the kiss. She let her hands explore his graceful, muscular back, his wide, sturdy shoulders. She touched his neck and felt the way his hair curled sweetly around his ears. Digging her fingers into his hair, she pushed him deeper, harder into the kiss.

He moaned. His arms were around her now, gathering her up, holding her as tight and close against him as she could be and still remain a separate person. His lips left hers, landing under her jaw, down her neck, her collarbone.

"Aaaaaah." A breathy sound escaped her lips. The dizziness was overpowering; it was shutting her in. These feelings were too fragile and beautiful to be held, the love too big to fit into her scarred, shrunken heart.

"I love you." Did she think it, or did she say it? Or did he say it? Or did she imagine he said it? Were the words in the air or just in her mind?

Before she could be sure, the darkness engulfed her, and she released herself to the sureness of Sam's arms.

"I LOVE YOU," SAM WHISPERED

Siren Song

against her neck. "I love you."

He'd always wondered what it would take to say those words, how much he'd have to push and prompt and coach himself to utter them. He didn't realize it wouldn't require any intention at all—that the words could come without thought or plan, as naturally and passionately and irreversibly as a kiss, without waiting for his consent.

Suddenly he felt her weight sink into his arms.

"Gaia." He pulled her up to him, finding her face with his lips, kissing her eyelids. They were closed. "Gaia?"

Her eyes didn't open. She breathed a sigh. Her head fell forward, resting against his chest. "Gaia?"

He cradled her head in the crook of his elbow and tipped her back gently. "Gaia? Are you all right? Gaia?"

She had fainted. She was motionless in his arms. All the feelings whirring in his chest changed directions, from pure exultation to surprise and fear.

He picked her up in his arms, cradling her against him. "Gaia. Gaia!" He jostled her, hoping to rouse her. Her head fell back, `exposing her delicate throat.`

"Gaia, please? What happened? Are you okay?" Panic was building. His eyes found the terrible bruise on the side of her head. Could it be . . . ? What if . . . ?

"Gaia, come on. Stay with me here, would you? Please, Gaia." The fear was talking. He was listening only distractedly.

He managed to support her weight with one arm and with the other plucked the phone from his nightstand. He dialed 911.

"Thirty-two Fifth!" he blared into the phone as soon as he heard a voice pick up. "Fourth floor. Send an ambulance."

"Sir, can you tell me what has happened?" the voice urged calmly.

"M-My . . . girlfriend." (Girlfriend?) "She's fainted. I can't rouse her. She hurt her head. Maybe—"

"All right, sir, we'll send the ambulance immediately."

Sam's heart was slamming in his rib cage. Thoughts were careening around his brain like a million errant Ping-Pong balls. "Oh, Gaia, please be okay," he begged her still body.

He laid her down as gingerly as he could on his bed. It was cold out. He needed to cover her. Did she have clothes or . . . ? No time.

He grabbed his thick, terry cloth robe from his closet and wrapped her in it. It was a strange set of circumstances that would force him to willingly cover her magnificent body, not to let his eyes linger over her exquisite stomach and hips and legs.

He found a wool blanket on the shelf and bundled her in that, too. Then he scooped her lifeless body up and strode out into the hallway. He punched the button for the elevator, his ears pricked for the sound of a siren. It was the one time he invited that sound, desperately wanted to hear it.

The elevator came. Sam stabbed at the lobby button.

There it was! The siren! Thank the Lord for a quick response. He raced past a stunned-looking Bauman and met the ambulance just as it was pulling up outside.

Fear blended with appreciation as Sam watched

the emergency medical team burst into action, their limbs and instruments a blur of confidence and precision. He loved them in that moment as much as he loved his parents and friends.

Before a minute had passed, Gaia was bound in a stretcher, hooked up to various medical gadgets, tucked into the back of the vehicle with Sam beside her. The engine roared, the siren kicked in again, and they were off to St. Vincent's, just a few blocks away.

Sam held her hand tight, never wanting to let it go.

"I love you," he whispered to her again, pleading with his crazed heart to stay in his chest for a while longer.

He considered it for a moment, his newly awakened heart. He remembered the puzzling conflict between heart and mind. Well, it was settled now.

In case there was any mystery, he now knew who was in charge.

GAIA WAS FLOATING. SAM WAS there, holding her hand. There were unfamiliar people, sounds, words, things she couldn't make sense of, but there was always Sam. He held her. He gave her his warmth.

Heaven

"I love you." The words came to her in Sam's voice. She wanted very much to open her eyes and see if it really was Sam, and if so, to see if he was talking to her when he said them, as she fervently hoped he was. And if he was saying those words to her, and maybe even if he wasn't, she wanted to say the same words to him.

But she couldn't. She couldn't open her eyes or make words.

Was she alive anymore? Was Sam real? Was he really there with her?

Maybe it was him. More likely it was heaven.

But if this was heaven, if this was what death felt like, then it was okay with her.

I've been trying to figure out why I don't have any tears for Sam tonight.

I do hate him at the moment; that's true.

But I thought I loved him.

All this time I figured I haven't been able to cry over him because I'm too numb. I'm too bottled up and confused to feel things very well.

I never imagined the possibility that I didn't love him.

Because I do love him. I mean, I'm pretty sure I do.

I mean, I do. Don't I?

You know what's really retarded? An hour after Sam left, I called Ed Fargo.

Then I remembered he was in Pennsylvania. He was there for Thanksgiving with his weird, obese grandmother who called me Feather.

Then the
memories
fell into
fragments
and shards
that **hunger**
didn't make
any sense at
all.

ELLA ROLLED HER EYES AT THE

emergency-room doctor in St. Vincent's Hospital. This was a night of highs and lows, currently stuck on low.

More Disappointment

The doctor was talking about Gaia, bleating words like *concussion* and *subdural* something and *hematoma* something else. But he wasn't saying anything about "slashed to ribbons," which was what Ella really wanted to hear.

She was jubilant when she'd first gotten the call from the hospital, sure that her plans had gone off without a hitch. Then she entered a period of confusion after she arrived at the hospital, during which it appeared that Gaia *hadn't* been slashed at Penn Station. Gaia, she was told, had spent several semidelirious hours before a doting Sam Moon brought her to the hospital, unconscious, from his NYU dormitory. The girl who'd been slashed (Ella had followed the story excitedly on the eleven o'clock news) was *not* Gaia, and yet Gaia had found her way to the hospital with some grave problem nonetheless.

Ella perked up when she heard the doctor use the

word *coma,* hoping that her goal might be achieved even without the extra bonus of disfigurement. But wretched, impossible Gaia had miraculously managed to sidestep the coma, in spite of a serious head injury.

"Mrs. Niven, I'm sorry to bother you with all of this information. I'm sure you'd like to see her," Dr. Somethingorother was saying. He was Indian or maybe Pakistani and spoke precise, melodious English.

Ella sighed. She couldn't very well say no, could she? "Of course," she said.

"You'll be pleased to know she's already been moved out of ICU. Her condition is stable."

Whoopee.

Ella followed the white coat up an elevator and down a hallway, through a set of swinging doors, past a waiting room and a nurses' station.

Dr. Whatever turned around to talk some more. "She's not yet fully conscious. Still a bit bleary. Try not to be alarmed. We do expect her to make a quick recovery, but it's never as quick as all of us would like."

If Gaia woke up before she was thirty, it would be too quick. Ella nodded blandly. She hated doctors. Particularly the one she'd blown up earlier in the evening.

The doctor stopped in front of room 448. The

door was partially open. He gestured for her to enter first. She started into the room and quickly stepped backward. She backed out into the hallway.

"Excuse me, Doctor," she said. "But there's somebody else in the room."

The doctor's eyes lit up. "Yes, that's her friend who brought her here. His name is Sam, I think? He hasn't left her side in hours. He is quite devoted to her, no? He is the one who gave us the information to find you."

"Fine," she said. "Very nice. But would you mind asking him to leave? I really need some time alone with my . . . foster daughter." Sob, sob. "Besides," she added in a confidential tone, "if I can speak frankly, I don't like that young man. I wouldn't be surprised if he were part of the reason that Gaia is here in the first place. . . ." She let her voice float off enigmatically.

The doctor hesitated. Clearly he didn't know what to think, and yet he was too polite to question her. "Yes. As you wish," he said.

"I'll just use the bathroom and collect myself for a moment," Ella said, stepping down the hall. "I'll come back when I can see Gaia alone."

A strong instinct was telling Ella she didn't want to be introduced to Sam Moon. A somewhat twisted instinct, but those were the ones she'd learned to listen to.

One Witness

SAM WATCHED GAIA'S EYELIDS for signs of her waking. Just in the last five minutes she'd opened and closed her eyes three times, once almost focusing on his face. His heart soared. Dr. Sengupta said she was going to be okay, and he was starting to believe it.

Sam ran his thumb from the tip of her index finger up her hand and wrist to the soft underside of her forearm. Her eyes flickered.

He leaned over her and buried a gentle kiss on her neck. That was more for him than her. He hoped she didn't mind. The hint of a smile seemed to pull at the side of her mouth. Or did he just imagine that?

What he really wanted to do was to climb into the narrow bed and press her close to him, to hold her with his whole body until she woke up. And after she woke up, too. But you weren't really supposed to do that in a hospital, were you?

Most people hated hospitals, and in theory, Sam did, too. But this hospital, on two separate occasions, had brought him closer to Gaia. It was the site of some of his worst experiences and yet some of the happiest feelings he'd ever had.

"Sam?"

He glanced up. He saw Gaia's doctor and felt slightly abashed. "Yes?"

"I'm sorry to ask you because I can see how much you wish to stay with Gaia, but her guardian, Mrs. Niven, has asked for time alone with her."

Sam knew it was a reasonable request, but his heart was breaking nonetheless. "Maybe I'll just wait in the waiting room for a few minutes till she's done."

Dr. Sengupta took in the state of Sam's hair and clothing with kind eyes. "Why don't you get yourself home and have a rest? Perhaps you could come again tomorrow? Visiting hours, as you might imagine, are long over."

Visiting hours? Sam was no visitor! He was . . . what? Nothing. He was nothing. But `Gaia was his life`. Did that count for anything?

"But I—" He really, really didn't want to go yet. He wanted to help usher Gaia back into the land of consciousness, to be with her when she crossed over. He needed to make sure they both knew that what happened between them was real. "Please, could I just—"

"I'm sorry. I have to respect Mrs. Niven's request." The doctor did look truly sorry.

Sam turned back to Gaia. He took both of her hands and brought them to his heart. He leaned over and pressed his cheek against her good one. "I love you, Gaia," he whispered in her ear. "I can't help it anymore." It might not have been a classically romantic thing to say, but it was true. She'd understand, he knew. He kissed her ear, then straightened up.

Her eyelids were fluttering again. He saw her hands moving against the sheet as soon as he'd released them. Were her hands looking for his? Did he just hope so?

"Thank you, Doctor, for everything," he said, trying not to look as unhappy as he felt. "She's really going to be okay, right?"

"Yes, I believe she is."

Sam trudged out of the room and down the hallway.

"Good luck to you, Sam," the doctor called after him, and the words somehow sounded ominous.

Every cell in Sam's heart was telling him not to leave her now. He was afraid that once he was gone, their magical, frightening night together would be gone, too, with him left as its only witness.

And not the most reliable witness, either.

IT WAS HARD AND CRUEL. IT

Disappointment x 1,000,000,000

downright sucked. In her dream, hovering someplace beyond the living, Gaia had Sam. He held her and told her he loved her.

Here, in reality, she had Ella.

She wished she could go back to being dead.

". . . You have quite a track record, Gaia. Twice in the hospital in two months," Ella was blathering. "You're going to send George's insurance premiums into the stratosphere."

Gaia exerted all her strength propping herself up in the hospital bed. It made her uncomfortable for Ella to see her lying down.

". . . And insurance only covers eighty percent of the bill, you know," Ella continued pettily.

Gaia looked down at her hands. They felt cold and lonely. "Thanks a lot, Ella," she said numbly. "That makes me feel a lot better. If the photography thing doesn't work out, maybe you could get a job with Hallmark in the get-well-card department."

Ella exhaled in annoyance. "And you're a rude ingrate as well."

Gaia closed her eyes, wrapping her misery around her like a blanket. She was right back where she started. She'd thought she'd made a new friend. She hadn't. She'd thought she'd run away. She hadn't.

She'd gotten nowhere, changed nothing.

Her mind summoned an image of Sam. She was kissing him, touching him, wrapping her body around his in his bed. The image brought a deep flush to her cheeks. But that hadn't really . . . They hadn't actually . . . had they?

She glanced at Ella.

What exactly *had* happened to her? How had she gotten here? She tried to piece together the endless, surreal day. She remembered being at Mary's house, of course. She remembered hitting her head on the sink in the bathroom at Penn Station. She remembered passing out—if you could call that remembering.

Things got fuzzier after that. She didn't remember coming to, but she did remember trying to get a refund for her stolen ticket. She vaguely remembered an explosion. She remembered walking outside and being cold.

Then the memories fell into fragments and shards that didn't make any sense at all.

She glanced at Ella again. She could hardly stomach the notion of needing information from the bitch goddess, but how else was she going to know?

Gaia took a breath. She needed to sound as disinterested as possible. "So, anyway, Ella. What happened to me? How did I get here? How did you get here?"

Ella opened her eyes wide in fake surprise. "Wait a minute. You are asking *me* questions about *your* life?"

Gaia shrugged. "You know, severe head wound and all." She touched her hand to her bruise. "I just wondered if the doctors told you anything about how I ended up here."

Ella studied her for a moment. "Actually, yes. Do you really not remember anything at all?"

Gaia shook her head. "Not much."

Ella nodded slowly. "Well, you made quite a little scene. The cops found you outside an NYU dormitory. You were delirious, totally out of it, raving endlessly about somebody named Sam."

Gaia felt her heart clench. The flush returned to her cheeks and deepened by one hundred times. If she'd really believed she'd made her heart tough enough to withstand disappointment, she'd been badly, profoundly mistaken.

"I was alone?" Gaia asked in a small voice, even though she knew she'd regret it. "I came here alone?" She was so far gone, she was giving evil Ella a straight shot at her vulnerability.

"Except for some freaked-out cops, yeah," Ella informed her.

So Gaia's fragments of memory weren't memory at all. They were fantasy. Sam hadn't kissed her, held her, told her he loved her. Those were the crazed delusions of her bashed-in head and her `pitiful, hungry heart.`

She was tempted to bash her head again, to return to the place where she'd had those feelings. Of course they didn't happen in reality. Not in her reality, anyway. It was too nice, too purely good to have happened in her life.

Gaia lay back again. Ella didn't matter. Nothing mattered.

Her misery wasn't a blanket. It was a `strait-jacket` fastened way too tight, threatening to squeeze out her last bit of hope.

I had a terrible thought when I woke up this morning in the bed that Gaia and I had shared, briefly, last night.

I had the thought that I dreamed the whole thing.

I would have stuck with the thought, but I smelled Gaia's faint, sweet smell in my bed. I found more than one long blond hair on my pillow. I found a somewhat tattered red dress and shoes balled up in my garbage can. I confirmed that my under-shirt and boxers were, in fact, missing.

Then I had a fear that was worse than the thought. I was afraid that it had actually hap-pened, but that Gaia wasn't there. I mean, her body was there. But she was so badly hurt and delirious, and practically comatose, that everything I imag-ined between us happened to me. Only to me.

This fear makes me physically sick because I hate the thought

S A M

of having taken advantage of her in some way.

Selfishly, that's not even the very worst part. Even worse, I fear I've opened my stubborn, tyrannical heart to an event—a girl—so stunning and miraculous, I've even gotten my brain to join in on the thrill of it. Only to discover that it never actually happened.

Which could make a man feel like a creep and a big, pathetic fool.

My brain, not surprisingly, is threatening a very sour "I told you so."

That's the fear, anyway. I'm not sure it's the truth.

But I can say this. I never understood loneliness until I woke up in my bed without her this morning.

Maybe Ella was telling me
the truth. Maybe I was discovered
by the cops, raving outside of
Sam's dormitory, and taken to the
hospital alone.

But when I stepped out of the
hospital bed after my night of
observation and walked my bleary
self into the bathroom, I discovered something peculiar. Under my
hospital robe, I was wearing a
man's undershirt and a man's boxers. These are things I know I do
not own. I don't care how hard I
banged my head.

At the back of the boxers,
just under the waistband,
scrawled in permanent black
marker are two wonderful words.
Can you guess them?

1. Sam
2. Moon

These pieces of physical evidence happen to fit with some
memory shards I have—fuzzy, I'll
admit. I have bits of memories of
being in Sam's dorm room, and
putting those things on.

I'm not saying Sam definitely kissed me. I'm not saying he told me he loved me or anything like that.

I'm just saying, maybe Ella was wrong. Maybe she lied. Maybe.

In all honesty, I don't even want to find out for sure. I want to hold onto these pieces of memory—hopes, if you want to be a killjoy. I can't bear to discover these things didn't happen. I need to cling to the possibility that they did.

Because even the *possibility* of something so beautiful could sustain a heart as desolate as mine for a long, long time.

here is a
sneak peek of
Fearless™ #6:
PAYBACK

There was something very satisfying about hearing them scream. He usually let them get out one, good, loud one before he covered their mouths. No one ever responded to one quick scream. They wrote it off as playing. Or a spider sighting. Or crying wolf.

And he so loved the scream.

It made him feel alive. It pumped him up.

It made the sex so much better.

He sat down on his floor and pulled out his black lock box from beneath his bed, flying through the combination with a quick three flicks of the wrist. Inside was his prized possession. The only thing he'd ever had worth locking up.

His journal. His list. His conquests.

He pulled out the tattered book with its dog-eared pages and cloth cover that was just starting to pull away from the

cardboard beneath. Soon it would
be time for a new book. But it
would be so hard to let this one
go. It was like an old friend. It
knew all his secrets. All his
successes. All his triumphs.

Turning to the first blank
page, he rolled the end of his
pen around inside his mouth,
carefully composing his opening.
This wasn't just a place to brag.
It was literature. One day, when
he was long gone, people would
read these pages and know him.
Know everything he was.

They would be awed.

He uncapped the pen and
started his entry.

*Thursday, November 25th.
Thanksgiving.*

*It certainly was a day for giv-
ing thanks. And Regina Farrell will
thank me one day. When she finally
admits to herself that she'll never
have anyone better. . . .*

Spiky, messy
hair. Sideburns.
Expensive
flannel.

sideburns

Not threatening.**tim**
Definitely not
asking for a
beating.

GAIA STOOD ON LINE IN THE cafeteria on Monday afternoon between two groups of people she couldn't possibly have detested more. The F.O.H.'s (Friends Of Heather) or "foes" as she liked to call them, and the turtleneck-wearing jockboys. If there was ever a time to cave in to modern

Basic get–away–from– me signals

technology and use a walkman, this was it. Words were being wasted all around her and she would have given anything for a nice pair of headphones and a lot of guitar-type noise.

"Omigod!" one foe squealed. "You totally should have been at CBGB's last night. The hottest guy opened for Fearless. He was like a Lenny-Rob hybrid."

"Not possible," foe number two said, sniffing a bowl of Jell-O in a perfect imitation of a rabbit, and replacing the bowl on the counter. "God couldn't possibly have blessed anyone with genes like that."

"He's playing again in two weeks," said foe number three, the one with the biggest hair ever to spring from a scalp. "Come and see for yourself."

"I am so there," foe number two promised, placing her nearly-empty tray in front of the register. "*I was at* the Melody last night and you . . ."

Foe number one trailed off as she glanced in Gaia's direction and noticed her not staring. Her top lip actually curled up and she huffed as she turned her back on Gaia, adjusting her tight leather jacket.

"Do you *see* what she's eating?" foe number one sneered. All three foes turned to glare at Gaia's tray. Meatballs. Mashed potatolike substance. Bowl of Jell-O not sniffed by foe number two. Roll with tons of butter patties.

"Do you want some creamed corn, hon?" the lunch lady asked with a pleasant voice.

"Yeah," Gaia answered, mostly to disgust the foes. It worked. They all exchanged a very unoriginal look of grossed-outedness, paid for their food and scurried away.

"There you go, hon," the big lady behind the counter said, heaping on the corn. She smiled at Gaia like she always did and Gaia attempted smiling back. It didn't work, of course, but it was worth the try. Every student in this school might hate her, but at least she was universally loved by the lunch ladies. Gaia was pretty sure she was the only one who actually ate their food.

Gaia handed the woman at the register a crumpled ball of cash and automatically headed for the table she and Ed usually shared. Back corner, underneath the graph that broke down the four food groups as if they were all still in grade school and needed it color-coded for them. She was about to cut left when someone blocked her path.

This was so not the time for anyone to be starting up with her. Not on a Monday when she hadn't eaten and she'd woken up with a sinus headache along with the knowledge that Sam hadn't contacted her once all weekend.

Actually, maybe someone should start with her. She could go for a little punishment-doling.

"You're a brave girl," a slow, drawly voice said.

Gaia looked up into the deepest pair of brown eyes she'd ever seen. Spiky, messy hair. Sideburns. Expensive flannel. Not threatening. Definitely not asking for a beating.

"Are you going to move?" Gaia asked, shifting her tray slightly. Bad idea. Her plate of meatballs slid precariously close to the edge, taking everything with it. It was going over and there was nothing she could do. More public spillage for the Spillage Queen.

"Careful," Sideburns said, righting the tray with lightning-quick reflexes. The kid in the chair next to them pulled himself a little closer to his table. Gaia attempted to move again, beyond ready to end this little encounter, but Sideburns was still holding onto her tray. "Aren't you going to ask me why I think you're so brave?" he asked, ducking his chin in an attempt to make eye contact. What was this guy's deal? Was he immune to basic get-away-from-me signals?

3

"No," Gaia said. Exasperation. There. He had to get that.

He released her tray, crossing his arms over his rather broad chest, but not moving out of the way. Gaia turned around to head back in the other direction, but a complicated melange of backpacks, chairs, and legs blocked her path.

When she turned around again, Sideburns was grinning. "It's just that in the three and a third years I've been here I've never seen anyone eat Greta's meatballs."

Oh, how very original. "There's a first time for everything," Gaia said. She took a step toward him, hoping he wasn't going to force her to take him down with a quick flick of her foot to his shin. He seemed harmless enough, but if she didn't eat soon, this Monday was going to go from suckfest to hell pit in a matter of seconds.

Sideburns flicked a little pink piece of paper out of his pocket and dropped it on Gaia's tray. It had black writing on it and the only word she could make out without actually appearing to be interested was "music."

"Having a little party tonight," he said, turning sideways to let her pass. He held up his hands to give her more room. "You should show."

The irrational part of Gaia's brain couldn't believe that someone had just asked her to a party. Her.

Public enemy number one. The rational part of her brain formulated a sentence and sent it to her voice box.

"I'd rather sing a Barry Manilow song in front of the entire school," she said, moving past him.

Sideburns laughed. "I'll rent a karaoke machine!" he called after her.

Gaia never smiled on Mondays. But if she did, that exchange might have been worthy of one.

AS GAIA LOWERED HERSELF INTO

the chair across from Ed, he plucked a little piece of bright pink paper from her overloaded tray.

"Come one. Come all," Ed read aloud. "Free beer. Free music. Free love." He chuckled and placed the tiny flyer on the table between them. "Going hippy on me, Gaia?"

Screw Him

She lifted one shoulder as she took a swig of her soda. "Some guy gave it to me," she said, jabbing a meatball with her fork. Ed's stomach turned over, and not just because she was actually consuming a cafeteria-made meat substance.

Another guy?

5

More guys?

Didn't he have enough to deal with?

"Who?" Ed asked, trying to keep the psychotic jealousy out of his voice. It was still there, but if she noticed, she didn't show a sign. She just chomped on another meatball as her eyes scanned the room.

"Him," she said finally, pointing with her fork across the large cafeteria at Tim Racenello. Abercrombie boy. Skier. Former friend. Definitely charming. Damn.

"Are you going to go?" Ed asked, pushing his chicken noodle soup sans chicken—a cafeteria specialty—around with his spoon. *Please say you're not going to go. Please say you're not going to go.*

"Ed. Come on. No," she said.

Cool.

"I was kind of thinking about going to see Sam tonight," she said, actually sounding tentative. "You know, find out . . . if there's anything to find out."

Not cool.

"Well, I'll go if you'll go," Ed offered, putting his spoon down and laying his hands flat on the table. The action helped to keep him from sinking into the bottomless black pit that had opened beneath his chair at the sound of Sam's name. Amazing. It was just one little syllable. Sam. More like a grunt than a name.

Yet it held so much power.

"Go where?" Gaia asked, confused. Ed felt his

6

delirious mind step off its rambling path and snap into the now. He wondered if she thought he was offering to go to Sam's with her. Not likely.

"The party," Ed said, forcing a smirk. "Focus, G."

Gaia froze with a forkful of mashed potatoes halfway into her mouth. It took her a couple of seconds to decide whether to eat or talk. She did both.

"You want to go to this thing," she said as soon as she'd swallowed. Statement. Disbelieving statement. When had he lost the moniker of Ed "Shred" Fargo, party animal? As if he really had to ask that question.

"Tim's pretty cool," Ed told her. He hoped against hope she would go against every fiber of her being and agree to go with him. "We used to hang out before my hanging involved the chair."

Gaia's gaze flicked in Tim's direction. "He stopped hanging out with you after . . ." She let the sentence trail off, probably because she still didn't know how Ed had ended up without leg power.

"No," Ed answered the unfinished question. "I stopped hanging out with him. I stopped hanging out with a lot of people." He immediately felt his spirits start to wane. He was coming dangerously close to losing the nonchalant thing he'd gone to great lengths to develop. Clearing his throat, Ed pushed all melancholy thoughts aside. He'd rejoined the social world a long time ago. There was no need to dwell on the dark past. The now demanded his full attention.

"So are you going to go with me or not?" Ed asked, downing a spoonful of his now cold soup. Somehow it tasted better cold. Took the edge off.

"I don't know, Ed. . . ."

She was thinking of Sam. He knew it. He could tell by the regretful little cloud in her eyes. Like she was thinking of him and ashamed of herself for thinking of him. There was only one way to make Gaia agree to party with him. The one way he could get Gaia to do almost anything. Get her angry. Or at least righteously indignant.

"Sam hasn't called, has he?" Ed asked, feeling like the soap scum wad in the corner of his shower. The one with the black mildew gathering on it.

Her eyes flashed. `Score one for the soap scum.` "No," she said flatly.

"Then why are you planning on going over there?" Ed asked casually, pushing his tray away. It hit Gaia's and moved it an inch over the lip of the table toward her.

"I'm not," she said, pushing her own tray back. Ed's went two and a half inches off the end. At least. It was almost too easy. And it made him feel almost too guilty. Almost.

"Then go to the party," Ed said, pushing their trays back so that they were centered evenly on the table. He laced his fingers together and rested his elbows on the arms of his wheelchair. "Screw him."

Gaia blinked. Ed could practically see the little consonants and vowels that made up his words sinking into her brain.

"Fine," she said. "Let's go."

HE WAS IN HER ENGLISH CLASS.

How convenient. She'd never noticed him before, but there he was. Front row, window seat. Good view and a fast escape route. And he was eating a Hostess cupcake. That was comforting. At least he had good taste in food.

First ever Monday smile

Gaia made her way across the room, her battered sneakers squeaking loudly on the linoleum floor. He didn't see her and she didn't exactly have an opening line, so she dropped the bag she was carrying on his desk with a half flop, half clatter.

If he was startled, he hid it well. He chewed, swallowed, and looked up. His eyebrows arched when he saw her, but he recovered quickly and leaned back in his chair, smiling up at her. He had chocolate stuck to his two front teeth.

"If it isn't Gaia the Brave," he said, running his tongue quickly along his bottom teeth to clear the sugary goo. It didn't help the top portion of his mouth, but Gaia wasn't about to point that out.

"Got another one?" she asked, pushing a strand of hair behind her ear. It fell right back into place and she didn't touch it again. Pointless. As were all attempts at grooming in Gaia's book.

Sideburns Tim experienced momentary confusion marked by a quick squint of the eyes. "Another what?"

"Cupcake," Gaia said, shifting her feet. That was when she noticed that Heather Gannis was sitting two rows behind Sideburns Tim, shooting Gaia a glare that was now so familiar to her, Gaia could probably have mimicked it in her sleep. She looked Heather directly in the eye and spoke to Tim. "If you give me a cupcake, I'll come to your little party."

Heather visibly paled. Even her normally lined lips were white. It was all Gaia could do to keep from breaking the no smiling on Mondays rule. It was an odd Monday when that almost happened twice.

Sideburns Tim pulled a single wrapped cupcake out of his bag and tossed it at Gaia. She caught it in one hand without even flinching.

"I don't know if it's your lucky day or mine," he said with a smirk that displayed a small dimple just behind a very light layer of stubble. Probably sexy in some circles. In Heather's circle, from the look of pure horror on the girl's face.

"It's yours," Gaia said. His smirk deepened. She pocketed her cupcake, and walked to the back of the room, allowing herself a brief moment of pride. It had been a long time since she'd come out with a comeback line she liked on the spot, and not approximately three and a half hours later when it was useless.

The fury was coming off Heather in waves. As Gaia took her seat, she wondered if Heather had spoken to Sam this weekend. If she knew what had happened between Gaia and her beloved boyfriend. If she did know, Gaia really wished the girl would clue her in. But somehow Gaia doubted that was going to happen.

In fact, since she hadn't received any idle death threats, Gaia figured Heather was thus far clueless. Maybe even more clueless than Gaia was. Gaia, at least, knew she'd been in Sam's room. Worn Sam's clothes. Even if there had been no touching of the lips, she was sure Heather would throw a Springer-worthy psycho tantrum if she knew what Gaia knew.

Leaning back in her chair, Gaia tore open her package of chocolatey goodness and propped her knees up on the desk in front of her. Sure, Sam hadn't called. Yes, she'd just committed herself to an actual social function. Yes, she was living with a heinous shrew with

11

a special place in her heart for slut clothes and bad perfume. Misery abounded.

But the thought that she actually knew something about Sam that Heather didn't know, was the thing that brought the first ever Monday smile to Gaia Moore's lips.

HEATHER GANNIS WAS HAVING

Sick of Everything

a very bad day, and trying to keep herself from screaming in the middle of English class wasn't making it any easier. Sam was avoiding her, her best friends had all gone out the night before without her and couldn't shut up about it, and the only reason she hadn't gone was because she had fully expected Sam to call her, which he, of course, hadn't.

She traced the pink line down the side of her paper with her pen, pushing so hard she tore a hole in the page. She was getting so sick of everything. Sick of Sam's avoidance of conflict policy. Sick of her friends who dropped money on cab rides and bars like they were a necessity. Sick, most of all, of Gaia Moore.

12

Mr. MacGregor sauntered into the room and immediately started passing out pop quiz papers. Lovely. What kind of person gave a quiz the day after Thanksgiving weekend? It was like the man lived to see students suffer. What next? Was her hair going to start falling out in clumps?

Heather adjusted the collar on her itchy wool sweater and pushed her thick brown mane back behind her shoulders. Whatever she did, she couldn't let her misery show. She needed to constantly keep the three C's in high gear. Cool, calm, collected. Otherwise there would be questions from her legion of followers. And questions, at this point, were something she couldn't handle.

Missy Ryan handed the quiz papers back and Heather took one and passed the stack along. Nothing on the page looked remotely familiar. Her body temperature skyrocketed. Heather turned the paper over with a slap and took a long breath. She had to chill. Now.

She hazarded a glance over her shoulder at Gaia. She, of course, was busily scratching away at her paper, oblivious to the world around her. The girl practically looked happy. That never happened. Something in the cosmic balance of Heather's universe had shifted, and she didn't like it.

Tim asking Gaia to tonight's party was the last straw. Heather faced forward again and twisted a lock of hair around her finger violently, yanking at her scalp. The only thing that had kept Heather going this weekend was looking forward to tonight's little shindig. She'd talked it up to all her friends, making sure they would all be there. There was nothing better than a free party with free dancing and free alcohol, even when her boyfriend was `freakishly AWOL`.

But a party with Gaia Moore present was another story.

A party with Gaia Moore present was something to avoid at all costs. Unless it was a wake and Gaia was the guest of honor.

From: smoon@alloymail.com
To: gaia13@alloymail.com
Time: 2:48 P.M.
Re: Thanksgiving

Gaia,

Thanks for an . . . interesting Thanksgiving.
I'll never forget it. I want to see you, but I
have finals right now and I really have to concentrate on that. Can I call you when I'm done?

—Sam

<<SEND>>

Normally, I don't go in with a plan. I never know who I'm going to want until I'm in the moment. I do have a special place in my heart for brunettes, though. They often think they're ordinary. Plain. Not sexy. They act like they have something to prove. And that always makes things more interesting.

But I'm not averse to the occasional blonde. Redhead. Asian, African-American, Indian, Latina, etc., etc. I'm not averse to anything. Like I said, it depends how I feel in the moment.

Tonight, however, I have a plan. Two, actually. One brunette. One blonde. Maybe neither will resist. But hopefully at least one of them will.

It's the breaking-down process that makes for riveting reading.

"Come on, Gaia," Ella said, placing her napkin on the table. **ready** She was all glee. "Tell **and** George **willing** about your little Sam."

EVEN AFTER HEATHER. EVEN

Ella's Salvation

after Marco. After David. After her father. After every deranged, psychotic, evil, slimy, grime-covered, bad-cologne-wearing, midnight assailant. Even after dealing with each and every one of these hateful beings, Gaia could quite honestly say she had never felt so much rage before in her life.

And from the look on Ella Niven's face, the woman was just smart enough to know that this rage was directed at her.

"You lied to me," Gaia said. There was no surprise in her voice. Only the rage. Ella's face went white for a moment underneath her layers of foundation and powder. She backed away from the foul-smelling sludge she was frying into a black pulp on the stove, and crossed her arms over her chest. Gaia wondered if Ella was remembering when Gaia punched her. Remembering and fearing.

God, she hoped she was.

"I don't appreciate your tone, Gaia," Ella said, wiping her hands on her ruffled apron. Gaia was surprised the woman even knew what an apron was. Or a kitchen for that matter.

"I was with someone on Thanksgiving," Gaia said, trying desperately to ignore the burning, acrid stench that was assailing her nostrils and choking her airways. Her eyes were watering, and she suddenly registered the fact that Ella was actually cooking—or attempting an unreasonable facsimile thereof. She never cooked. Was this just another facet of the torture she had to endure?

Ella took a deep breath—how she managed it Gaia had no idea—and smoothed her blazing red hair behind her shoulders. "And how, exactly, does that make me a liar?"

The disturbing image of Gaia grabbing Ella by the back of the head, slamming her face into the frying pan and holding it there flashed through Gaia's mind. Tempting, but not an option. For the moment anyway.

"You told me there was no one there, at the hospital," Gaia said, leaning into the counter in front of her, her veins throbbing in her forehead. To think there was a time when she'd felt badly for laying Ella out. When she'd regretted punching the woman so hard her knuckles hurt. She only wished she'd done more.

Ella's amphibian green eyes narrowed into angry slits. "That's right," she said calmly. "There was no one with you at the hospital. God only knows what you did before then. I did tell you they found you outside some dorm babbling about someone named Sam." She ran her fingernail along the side of her mouth, reminding Gaia of a cat who'd just finished off the forbidden goldfish. "Is that who you're talking about?" she said with a light laugh. "Maybe he'd just kicked you out of his room."

There was a moment without air. No intake whatsoever. A moment when Gaia's heart felt as if it was about to burst open from the pressure.

Her first inclination was to launch herself at Ella and make her take it back.

Her second inclination was to entertain the idea that she might be right.

That was the standard Gaia-as-masochist inclination.

But no. It wasn't possible. Sam had said thanks. He'd said he wanted to see her again. She was no relationship expert, but if he'd booted her, he wouldn't be saying that. Right?

And he wouldn't have left her outside in the cold, bruised and woozy and half comatose.

Not Sam.

Gaia rounded the counter and in one long stride, got within centimeters of Ella's pointy little face. She was quite satisfied by the rather large jump on Ella's part.

"I swear to you Ella, if you don't tell me the truth right now—"

There was a door slam, and two pairs of eyes darted to the kitchen entry.

"George," Ella whispered, sounding as if she was uttering the name of salvation.

21

"I'm home!" George shouted from the foyer. "What smells so interesting?"

Gaia felt her muscles untighten and she pulled away reluctantly. The threats were going to have to wait for another day, unless she wanted to explain to George why she'd kicked his wife's scrawny ass as his homecoming present.

F E A R L E S S ™

. . . a girl born without the fear gene

What do you fear the most –
Truth or Dare?

Me?

Neither.

So I choose Dare everytime.

What's the point of being fearless . . .

if you can't have fun with it once in a while?

Some secrets are too dangerous to know . . .

ROSWELL
HIGH

In the tiny town of Roswell, New Mexico, teenagers Liz Parker and Max Evans forged an otherworldly connection after Max recklessly threw aside his pact of secrecy and healed a life-threatening wound of Liz's with the touch of his hand. It turns out that Max, his sister Isabel, and their friend Michael are surviving descendants from beings on board an alien spacecraft which crash-landed in Roswell in 1947.

Max loves Liz. He couldn't let her die. But this is a dangerous secret he swore never to divulge - and now it's out. The trio must learn to trust Liz and her best friend Maria in order to stay one step ahead of the sheriff and the FBI who will stop at nothing in hunting out an alien...

Available NOW from Pocket Books